JOHN DEVIL

also translated, annotated and introduced
by Brian Stableford

by Paul Féval

Knightshade
Vampire City
The Vampire Countess

forthcoming:
The Wandering Jew's Daughter
The Black Coats: 'Salem Street

by Villiers de l'Isle-Adam

The Scaffold and Other Cruel Tales
The Vampire Soul and Other Sardonic Tales

JOHN DEVIL

(*Jean Diable*)
by
Paul Féval

translated, annotated and introduced by
Brian Stableford

A Black Coat Press Book

Acknowledgements: I am grateful to the staff of the Bibliothèque Nationale in Paris which provided a photocopy of the text of the original edition of *Jean Diable* (Dentu, 1863) and to Professor Henri Rossi and Jean-Marc Lofficier for commissioning the photocopy. Jean-Marc also supplied several other documents that proved invaluable in researching the introduction and afterword and offered numerous useful suggestions for placing the novel in its context within Féval's career. My good friend Bill Russell provided invaluable assistance in proof-reading the typescript, translating Latin phrases and supplying a good deal of information for the notes that I had been unable to discover for myself. I should also like to thank David McDonnell for proofreading the typescript.

Visit our website at www.blackcoatpress.com

Table of Contents

Introduction

Paul Féval's *Jean Diable*–which really ought to be called *John Devil* even in the original, given that the eponymous character is supposed to be a legendary English bandit–was originally published in serial form in *Le Siècle* from August 1-November 20, 1862. It was Féval's second *roman feuilleton* in that newspaper, which had a larger circulation than the others for which he wrote on a more regular basis; his classic *Le Bossu* (*The Hunchback*) had appeared there from May 7-August 15, 1857.

Le Bossu, the definitive *roman de cape et d'épée*–what would now be called a "swashbuckler"–had been a light-hearted pastiche of the novels of Alexandre Dumas, the most popular of all the writers of *feuilleton*-type fiction. It had gone on to become Féval's most successful book–a position it retains today, having been filmed several times, last in 1997 with Daniel Auteuil in the title role. A theatrical version of *Le Bossu* opened at the Théâtre de la Porte-Saint-Martin while *Jean Diable* was being serialized, on September 8, 1862, and clocked up 254 performances before closing in May 1863. Féval presumably had similarly high hopes of *Jean Diable* and may well have entertained even greater ambitions for it. It was a more ambitious novel, which broke new ground in the field of popular fiction, and its author must have been aware that there was considerable potential in the as-yet-uncultivated literary territory of crime fiction.

Jean Diable was not the first "crime novel" Féval had written; indeed, it carried forward an eccentric sequence of stories featuring exotic criminal conspiracies. It was, however, the first he–or anyone–had written in which such a criminal conspiracy was matched against a properly armed adversary: an officially-empowered detective equipped with a logically-refined procedural method.[1] In the construction of this character, and the description of his methods, Féval established one of the most powerful precedents in popular fiction, and created an archetypal image that startles the modern eye, both in terms of what it includes and what it does not. In a single creative bound, Féval incorporated into his fictional police detective, Gregory Temple, a whole series of features that would eventually become standardized to the point of cliché, while simultaneously omitting certain other narrative elements that now seem blindlingly obvious as basic components of the "detective story." Indeed, the most remarkable thing about *Jean Diable* is that, although it includes and makes much of the character of the detective, it is not a "detective story" at all, in the sense to which we have become accustomed.

---

[1] (see Notes p. 619.)

Féval's optimism regarding the innovative qualities of *Jean Diable*, and the success it enjoyed as a serial, is reflected in the fact that as soon as it had finished serialization, he founded a periodical with the same title, which published 37 issues between November 27, 1862 and August 8, 1863. Féval wrote abundantly for the magazine, often signing his work with pseudonyms, including "John Devil" and "Hans Teufel" (the latter being the German version of the name). In parallel with this enterprise, he published another crime novel, *Les Habits Noirs* (*The Black Coats*), in *Le Constitutionnel* from March 12-July 19, 1863.[2] *Jean Diable* was issued in book form in two volumes by E. Dentu in 1863 and rapidly went into a second printing.

After that, however, Féval abruptly changed direction. When the periodical *Jean Diable* folded, the character of his work underwent a marked transformation; there was a very obvious shift in his priorities. His next novel, *Annette Laïs* (*L'Opinion Nationale*, August 19-November 19, 1863; book, 1864), appeared in a periodical with a much smaller circulation than *Le Siècle* or *Le Constitutionnel*; it had a contemporary setting and a moralistic tone, attacking Paris as a "modern Babylon." It was followed by the brief *Histoire d'un Notaire et d'une Tonne d'Or* (*The Story of a Solicitor and a Ton of Gold*) (*Le Journal pour tous*, May 4-June 15, 1864; book, 1864 as *Roger Bontemps*), a brief social comedy, and *Les Gens de la Noce* (*The Wedding People*) (*Le Progrès*, September 18, 1864-January 15, 1865; book 1865), a comedy of marital disaster.

Féval had made similarly abrupt changes of direction before, forsaking the melodramatic tales of adventure, revenge and criminal conspiracy that had made his fortune in favor of more respectable subjects and mannerisms. As on the previous occasions, he seems to have been hopeful in 1864 of redeeming–or at least massaging–his reputation in support of a candidacy for one of the 40 precious seats in the Académie Française. In the event, the ploy failed, as it had before; he never did get into the Academy. The following year, therefore–just as he had done before–he performed another abrupt U-turn. In February 1865, he became the president of the *Société des Gens de Lettres* (Society of Authors); for the next three years, he used that position to mount a tireless and assertive campaign to raise the prestige of popular fiction and to rail against the literary snobbery that held such work intrinsically inferior to "literary fiction."

The first new novel Féval produced after reverting to his more usual literary strategy was *Coeur d'Acier* (*Heart of Steel*), a sequel to *Les Habits Noirs*. In 1867, when he made the decision to write a whole series of novels featuring the nefarious Black Coats, beginning with *La Rue de Jerusalem* (*'Salem Street*),[3] he bound these novels into a more elaborate scheme that co-opted *Jean Diable*, as well as three earlier novels, *Les Mystères de Londres* (*The Mysteries of London*) (1844), *Beau Démon* (*Handsome Devil*) (1850) and *Les Compagnons du Silence* (*The Companions of Silence*) (1857), into a vast "secret history" extending from the early 17th century to the mid-19th. This move serves to emphasize the fact that Féval was fully aware of the potential that still remained in the rich vein that

he had tried to tap in *Jean Diable*, and set further important precedents for the subsequent development of series as a key element in the evolution of commercial genre fiction.

The eight novels making up *Les Habits Noirs* were continually reprinted, as befits a pioneering exercise in commercial *genrification*, and are still in print today. *Les Mystères de Londres* and *Les Compagnons du Silence* were frequently reprinted too–but *Jean Diable* and *Beau Démon* fell into neglect in spite of their association with the secret history summarized in *La Rue de Jerusalem*. Dentu did reprint *Jean Diable* once more, in a three-volume version, but it had become a text of almost fabulous rarity by the time the fervent crusade that Féval had begun on behalf of popular fiction finally began to bear critical and academic fruit, more than 100 years after his own Napoleonic campaign.

This omission is unfortunate for several reasons. Within the context of the genre that Féval founded with this eccentric set of 12 novels and 37 periodical issues, *Jean Diable* is the lynchpin text. It marks a crucial transition from historical adventure stories that had elements of crime and mystery in them to novels that attempted to be mystery stories first and foremost, foregrounding the battle between officially empowered criminal justice systems and organized crime. *Jean Diable* is not merely the first novel to feature a character who is explicitly labeled as a detective, or to place him within an institution dedicated to criminal investigation (London's Scotland Yard), equipped with an analytical method of investigation which attempts to be rigorously objective; it also illuminates many of the key problems involved in presenting mysteries to the reader: the problem of providing an appropriate viewpoint; the problem of adopting an appropriate moral standpoint; and the problem of managing the reader's expectations.

Modern readers who are accustomed to reading stories in which these various problems have been solved by conventional methods can easily lose sight of the difficulties that the pioneers of crime fiction had to overcome. If Féval's struggles, as manifest in the pages of *Jean Diable*, sometimes seem frustrating to modern readers who know only too well what mistakes he is making, they are also fascinating in their bold exploration of avenues that later fell into disuse–particularly those few that have been opened up again in recent times by writers seeking relief from the bonds of established convention.

Had it not been for the eclipse of *Jean Diable*, Féval would have received due credit for the more obvious of these innovations. Ironically, the man to whom the credit for pioneering modern detective fiction has usually been given, Emile Gaboriau [4]–the father of the French *roman policier*–was Féval's editorial assistant on the periodical *Jean Diable*; he learned his craft as an apprentice to the master. Although *Jean Diable* has not been reprinted in France for more than 100 years, this omission will surely be repaired in the near future; in the meantime, this English edition will hopefully help to set the record straight, and enable the history of crime fiction to recover one of its most important foundation stones.

Seen from a contemporary viewpoint, *Jean Diable* may seem rather unsatisfactory as a mystery story, in that its ending is hard to reconcile with its opening phases. It does, however, contain all the key elements of the not-yet-nascent genre of detective fiction, and it is possible to regard the seeming incoherence of its later chapters as an extra level of complication in the mystery–a possibility I shall address in some detail in an afterword.

The novel's most significant contribution to the history of crime fiction is, of course, the archetype of the police detective, Gregory Temple. During his long and successful (though blithely anachronistic) career at Scotland Yard, Temple has developed a logical method for the analysis of crimes, which he attempts to apply with strict discipline. He carefully tabulates the names of everyone who benefits financially from the crime, or who might have some other motive for committing it, examines the possible reasons that might lead witnesses to offer false testimony, and carefully weighs these suggestions of guilt against such "counter-proofs" as alibis.

All of this may seem elementary to modern readers, and its methodological component had certainly been anticipated to some extent by Edgar Allan Poe's tales featuring the amateur investigator C. Auguste Dupin, but the acceptance of the institutionally-empowered detective and his methodical procedures into modern routines of criminal investigation–to the extent where it is nowadays taken entirely for granted–is an eloquent testament to the anticipatory power of Féval's imagination. In 1862, it was even less familiar in reality than it was in fiction.

In one magnificently iconic scene–in Chapter IX of Part One–we find Gregory Temple working obsessively in Paris, having been hounded out of his position of authority by an assault launched against him by the ingenious master criminal John Devil. His first step in his fight back is to construct a huge blackboard on which he can set out his evidence in tabular and diagrammatic form–an image familiar to everyone who has seen a televisual depiction of an incident room, but then quite unprecedented. Although every detail of the data set out on Temple's blackboard has been carefully set up or cleverly massaged by his adversary, John Devil–who is intent on framing an innocent man for his latest murder–Temple's ever-suspicious mind leads him to make the first breach in this seemingly-watertight scheme of contrived evidence by noticing a blurred postmark, which he scrutinizes with a magnifying glass in order to ascertain that it is indeed a fake. This vital revelation sets him on the path to a complete reinterpretation of the case.

All of this was to become the substance of formula and cliché: in that narrative moment, Féval set in place the image of the modern detective, whose ingenious thought-processes are directed by *clues* revealed by careful observation, routinely drawing upon such talismanic aids as the magnifying glass. A long and

unbroken chain of influences leads from this scene in *Jean Diable* to the contemporary vogue for forensic science detective dramas.

In the form of its plot, *Jean Diable* does not anticipate the most popular formula of detective fiction, but its early phases do foreshadow the subsidiary formula devised by R. Austin Freeman–whose most familiar modern example is the television series *Columbo*–in which the identity of the murderer is known from the beginning and suspense is maintained by the detective's painstaking step-by-step progress through a labyrinth of disinformation. This is, in a sense, even more remarkable; indeed, had Féval's story continued in the direction in which it seems to be headed for the greater part of its length, it might well have remained sufficiently well-known to be hailed as an innovative masterpiece. It did not; like Féval's subsequent career, it veered away in an unexpected direction–but that was a fate to which *romans feuilletons* were always vulnerable.

In order to assist the modern reader in understanding why *Jean Diable* was so unusual in its day, and why what it attempted to do was so important in the evolution of popular fiction, it might be helpful to draw a distinction between story and plot, after the fashion of E. M. Forster's *Aspects of the Novel*.[5]

A story is a sequence of events in chronological order, whose appeal to its audience is simply that its hearers (storytelling is far older than writing) want to know what happened next. Dramatic tension in a story is manufactured and maintained by presenting characters with a potentially-infinite series of hazards that need to be avoided: various threats of violence, traps and predicaments that put them under pressure. The tension can be heightened by increasing the urgency of the hazards, by making them work to tight deadlines and taking them as close as possible to the brink of disaster before facilitating their escapes, and also by providing them with powerful motives to get through the obstacle course: a goal that must be achieved. The goal that frames and motivates the action may, however, be very simple and constant; stories are, in effect, journeys, which only need the idea of a destination to provide a minimal context for each individual situation and encounter along the way.

Plot, as common parlance has it, *thickens* a story. Plots complicate the meaning of individual segments of a story by setting them in a much more elaborate context. The essence of plotting is mystery: each incident in the story becomes more than a threat to be neutralized or a trap to be escaped; it becomes an item of potential discovery that adds another precious jigsaw-piece to some kind of big picture that is slowly taking shape in the minds of the characters and the audience. The hearers of a story are only concerned with what is happening now and what will happen next, but the readers of a plot (the ability to formulate an intricate plot is a corollary of text) need to remember everything that has happened so far, and their anticipation must extend far beyond the outcome of the present predicament, reaching out for the answers to a host of as-yet-unanswered questions.

Plotting is a matter of degree; even the simplest story has a plot of sorts, in terms of the characters' ultimate objectives, and there is no limit to the extent and ingenuity of the complications that might be introduced to create–and then to solve–elements of mystery. In the last 200 years, the art and craft of plotting has undergone a spectacular evolution, involving a dramatic increase in the craftsmanship of writers and a corresponding increase in the sophistication of readers.

Mystery stories now qualify as a genre, many of whose readers qualify as experts–and the heart of that genre is the murder mystery, whose central character is the mystery-solver: the detective. Before Paul Féval wrote *Jean Diable*, however, mystery fiction was in its infancy and characters featured in such stories as solvers had hardly begun to develop the necessary skills. Féval's earlier crime novels had always foregrounded the criminals; they, after all, were the characters who generated the melodrama.

The fact that *Jean Diable* introduces the first fictional mystery-solver who is formally identified as a *detective* is a corollary of its author's attempts to take significant steps in the refinement of literary *thickening* agents. Although Gregory Temple does not succeed in solving the mystery with which he is confronted, and his creator's attempts at *thickening* do not result in a smooth and coherent texture, their actions are heroic nevertheless.

Progress is made by trial and error, and errors can be as informative in their way as successful trials. Paul Féval learned a lot from *Jean Diable*, and so did some of his peers–but the book is more than a mere failed experiment. Whatever difficulties its lumpy plot runs into, it retains many virtues as a story, and it certainly succeeded in demonstrating that the apparatus of conventional melodrama could be greatly enhanced by complication. Some of its key scenes achieve a remarkable heightening of effect from the affectation that they are contributing to a grand design of awesome scope and intricacy, and the fact that the design in question never does become coherent hardly detracts at all from the impact the individual incidents make while the reader is actually experiencing them. In a sense, the most important revelation of the text is that–at least for the majority of readers who are not experts obsessed with logical coherency–it does not actually matter much whether a plot makes sense in retrospect; what matters is the contribution that the mere existence of a mystery can make to the dramatic tension of particular scenes.

Jean Diable is all the more remarkable as an experiment in mystery because it was written for a medium that was extremely inhospitable to the *thickening* of plots. A newspaper serial running on a daily basis could not put too heavy a burden on the memories of its readers, and it had to be shaped in such a way as to appeal to the widest possible constituency; its author had to try as hard as possible to accommodate all interests and all tastes. The feuilletonist's first priority was always to provide melodrama, but he also had to lay on a measure of comic relief, a dash of sentimentality and everything else that readers were known to like, in due proportion. If successful, a serial would have to run to enormous length, so it had to maintain dramatic tension, but it also had to be forgiving of readers with poor memories and readers who had missed some or all of the earlier chapters. The author of a serial also had to contend with the fact that his story would generate feedback from readers as soon as it began to appear, and that he would therefore be continually subject to editorial pressure to shape his work in response to that feedback–and, of course, to the editor's own perceptions of how it ought to develop. However clear the author's own objectives might be, they always remained vulnerable to external interference.

In order to adapt fiction to these circumstances, a feuilletonist had to use techniques that have more in common with those applicable to modern television soap operas and drama series than those already developed by novelists whose primary objective was book publication. *Romans feuilletons* were, of course, reprinted as books, just as many contemporary novels written with book publication in mind obtained some kind of preliminary serialization, but stories that were designed for serialization had to be far more loosely-organized and loosely-packed than stories specifically designed for book publication. The sensible feuilletonist concentrated his creative efforts on making his stories exciting while keeping his plotting very simple and very flexible; the problem with this strategy–as Féval was keenly aware–was that a gold mine of narrative value that only plotting could excavate was going to waste. *Jean Diable* is one of several attempts Féval made to extract some of that gold, and perhaps the most interesting of them.

In recent years, there has been a considerable revival of interest in French popular fiction of the 19th century, which has brought Féval back into the critical and historical spotlight. A special issue of the journal *Désiré* was devoted to Féval's work in December 1970 and a colloquium was held in his native town of Rennes in 1987, whose proceedings were published under the editorship of Jean Rohou and Jacques Dugast as *Paul Féval: Romancier Populaire (Paul Féval: Popular Novelist)*. Jean-Pierre Galvan's survey of his life and work, *Paul Féval: Parcours d'une Oeuvre (Paul Féval: Survey of his Works)*, followed from Encrage in 2000.

Thus far, Féval's translation into the English language has been limited and patchy; a handful of translations–probably all pirated–were issued in the 19th century, mostly in the U.S.A., and this is the fourth volume I have translated, following *Vampire City, Knightshade* and *The Vampire Countess*.[6] I hope to do several more, including *La Fille du Juif Errant (The Wandering Jew's Daughter)* and at least some volumes of *Les Habits Noirs*, because his work seems to me to be doubly interesting, firstly in the manner in which so many of its themes and motifs are echoed–sometimes eerily–in modern popular fiction, and secondly because the process of their composition was a pioneering exploration of many narrative techniques that now comprise the modern writer's repertoire of methods and effects. Both these observations are particularly pertinent to *Jean Diable*, whose status as the first detective novel is only one of its literary assets.

Gregory Temple's attitudes and methods are recapitulated in virtually every detective story we read or see on television, and his obsessive tendencies are far from uncommon. We are more likely now than ever before to see crime in terms of organization, and history in terms of hidden conspiracies, just as Féval liked to do. We are also more likely now to encounter stubborn ambiguity in texts, and to be presented with unreliable narrators. Perhaps, most of all, we are far more accustomed to the scathing sarcasm and corrosive cynicism with which Féval dresses so many of his incidental observations.

Féval's image of the petty society of Miremont–whose role within the story is purely to supply an assortment of observers who deliver a cacophonous commentary from the edge of the literary stage–must have seemed shocking to many of *Le Siècle*'s readers. They would have understood and admitted that products of a society that had suffered as many spectacular reverses as mid-19th century France could hardly help being fickle, hypocritical and relentlessly self-interested, but they would never have recognized themselves in the caricatures that make up the Miremontese bourgeoisie. Today, on the other hand, we can understand such characters perfectly, because theirs is the way of our whole world; if we too refuse to identify with them it is not because we cannot recognize their character traits in ourselves, but only because we are so much cleverer in their expression.

John Devil's ambiguous crusade, as reported in the following pages, was always bound to fail within the context of the plot, because history had already passed its verdict upon it by the time the novel was written; the problem with secret history, used as melodramatic fuel, is that it is logically condemned to climactic obliteration. In the longer run, however, the chaotic confusion of impulses that John Devil represents–whose archetype he was and is–proved irresistible.

Looking back from 1863 to 1817, as the story does, accomplished history was dead set against John Devil's specific ambitions, but it was subtly hospitable to all that he symbolized. When we look back now, from 2005, we can see how forceful the tide of time really was, in that we know only too well how many real criminal megalomaniacs it threw up to take John Devil's imaginary place. Gregory Temple's descendants are our everyday heroes now, and they win almost all the battles they fight in fiction, but that only serves to emphasize the fact that, in reality, the war was lost. In the real world, John Devil–the spirit of ambition that considers pride in its own destiny as an excuse for any and all nasty actions–reigns supreme.

Brian Stableford

JOHN DEVIL

John Devil

Prologue: One Night in London

I. The Art of Discovering the Guilty
and The Book of the Amazing Adventures of John Devil the Quaker

On March 14, 1817, Gregory Temple, Chief Superintendent at Scotland Yard headquarters,[7] was sitting at his long black oak table, holding his forehead in his hands. He was doubtless immersed, as deeply as possible, in the expert deductive calculations that had made his name legendary in the annals of the Metropolitan Police. At that moment, he was still the most perfect image of the detective, fearless and above reproach.

The table, whose wooden surface was usually hidden beneath a multitude of scattered papers, was almost completely clear today; it was easy to count the objects on it. Directly in front of Gregory Temple was a rather voluminous file, whose cover or envelope bore these words: *Assassination of Constance Bartolozzi, February 3, 1817.* To his left was a handkerchief of fine linen and an open letter. The handkerchief was stained with two or three drops of blood and the embroidered inscription *R.T.*; the letter was signed with the same initials. Finally, to his right, there were half a dozen sprawling sheets of printer's proofs, corrected and ready to be returned.

Gregory Temple was then at the height of his well-earned fame as a sleuth. He might have been 50 or 55 years old. He was a small, slender man, very fit despite his apparent weakness, endowed with an extraordinary physical energy. As for his face, it readily assumed a distant resemblance to a bust of the elder Walpole. His forehead, fringed by fair hair that was beginning to go grey, was very highly-developed; his cheekbones stood out sharply beneath his hollow temples, after the Scottish fashion, and his jaw was rounded.

At that moment, you could have seen the strange sparkle of his wide-open eyes, between his spare, convulsively splayed fingers. The eyeballs' prominence–if one can rely on the theory of Gall [8]–was swollen by the most extensive of all his memories. His eyes were fixed with singular intensity on the coarse grey cardboard on which the name of *Constance Bartolozzi* was traced in large characters; they were exerting a powerful, formidable, desperate will. That name evidently provoked a terrible conflict in the field of his conjectures, for his breath was catching in his throat and beads of sweat were rolling slowly down his pale cheeks.

Night was already falling. The room, low-ceilinged but spacious, had no other illumination than the lamp set on the table. The light, filtered through the resinous fabric of the green lampshade, cast vague reflections on the filing cabinets that covered the four walls from top to bottom and the little panes of greenish glass in the latticed windows, behind which strong iron grilles were visible.

Every compartment in the filing cabinets bore a cardboard label. It was common knowledge that Gregory Temple retained in that somber library the key to every criminal puzzle, past, present and future. The great black book of three Kingdoms was there; more than one member of the House of Lords had a record there, it was said, as had the most profligate thieves in St. Giles's.[9] George, Prince of Wales, Regent and Heir to the Crown, was suspected of having searched that arsenal to the very depths in order to arm the battles he had fought three times over with his wife, Caroline of Brunswick.

The celebrated Police Superintendent had been silent and immobile for more than an hour, his eyes fixed upon the name of the dead woman. His two hands finally slid from his forehead, as if to clear away the heavy cloud that blinded his thoughts, and his dazzled eyes closed.

"Constance Bartolozzi," he murmured, slowly. "Prima donna at the Princess Theater. Forty years old... one might believe such actresses are eternally young. Dead in her bed on the night of the third and fourth of February, struck dead by one of those blows that are becoming less rare with every day that passes... One of those blows that terrorize the least timid and which, from the first, I have called surgical strikes, because they bring certain death rapidly and without leaving any trace... As if science herself, in these accursed times, were beginning to lend her aid to crime!"

His clenched fingers extended, as if in spite of him, to cover the name inscribed on the cover of the file.

"It's the first time," he said, through clenched teeth. "The first time that my method has failed. I have a blindfold over my eyes. Darkness surrounds me. I feel as if it will drive me mad."

He paused, and his hand swept the wayward grey hairs from his temples.

"Is it the first time, though?" he asked himself, in a lower voice, while his gaze roamed the filing cabinets and stopped at a label bearing the inscription: *Assassination of General O'Brien–John Devil–Prague, 1813.*

There was a distinctive knock upon the door of the office.

"Come in, Richard," Temple called, reflexively. Scarcely had he pronounced the name Richard, however, when his forehead was clouded more darkly than before. He caught himself up, and said, dryly: "Come in, James."

The door swung on its hinges. A young man appeared, whose tall and admirably proportioned figure was clearly outlined against the white wall of the corridor. He wore the costume of a true gentleman with strict and modest elegance: coat, waistcoat and black trousers, with a white cravat knotted in the Brummell [10] style, as was then the fashion. His face, shadowed by the lampshade, seemed young, symmetrical and remarkably gentle. Gregory Temple fixed him with his piercing gaze, trying in vain to conceal the fever of his impatience, and said: "What news do you have, James? Is there any trace of Richard Thompson?"

"No, sir," the newcomer replied, in a calm and respectful tone. You may be familiar with one of those harmonious male voices that reproduces, in a lower register, the female contralto; you only have to hear it once never to forget it again. Our young man had such a voice.

"That's quite inexplicable!" Temple cried, agitatedly. "Has the Earth opened up to swallow him? James Davy, I have every confidence in your judgment, despite your youth: doesn't Richard's flight seem to you to cast a terrible suspicion upon him?"

"I'm looking into it, sir," James Davy replied, coolly, only then taking a few steps into the office. "There are difficulties of an unusual kind in this case. So far as I am concerned, Richard Thompson is an honest man, until there is proof to the contrary."

"Until there is proof to the contrary..." the Superintendent repeated.

"I know that he was involved in an affair of the heart," James continued. "With whom, I don't know. He has been your secretary and your friend; he must know a great deal, for no one could be close to you without learning..."

Temple's clenched fist rapped upon the table. "I would rather believe him dead," he thought, aloud.

"Of course, sir," James replied, "but you do not have the choice. I have extended my inquiries as far as the house of his mother, Fanny Thompson, in the county of Surrey. It's a cheerful place, full of actors and actresses; Fanny is thinking of returning to the Princess Theater, where Bartolozzi has left a big gap."

Temple's pencil traced a few words on a slip of paper set beneath his hand, upon which he had already made several notes.

"Fanny Thompson," Davy continued, in the same calm manner, "adored her son Richard. If Richard were dead, I would have found the house in mourning."

"Is it true," asked the Superintendent, consulting his notes, "that a very young child is being brought up in Fanny Thompson's home?"

"That's true, sir–and the infant is named Richard, like your former secretary."

Temple indicated to Davy that he should close the door and come closer.

"Thank you, James," he said. "You've done what you can... Since you've been busy with Richard, you doubtless have nothing to tell me about this girl who served as a companion to Bartolozzi–Sarah O'Neil..."

"Sarah O'Neil will be here in a few minutes, sir," Davy put in.

"Here!" Temple exclaimed, startled. "Where was she found, James?"

"In a Lambeth lodging-house, disguised as a man."

"Who tracked her down for me?"

"Me, sir."

"By what means?"

"By following precisely–slavishly, if I may say so–the sequential calculations of probability set out in your book."

Gregory Temple cast a melancholy glance at the proofs that lay on his desk. He took Davy's hand and shook it.

"You're very pale," the young man said to him, with concern.

"Yesterday evening," Temple replied, "the Lord Chief Justice referred to me in public. His Lordship said: 'The Chief Superintendent at Police headquarters is going under, going under.' This morning, I nearly put a pistol to my head and blew my brains out."

"You! Gregory Temple, the strong man!"

"What stopped me," the Superintendent said, slowly, "was the thought of poor lovely Suzanne. If I didn't have a daughter... An angel, rather..."

"What do the words of an old fool matter?" Davy protested.

"I'm going under," Temple murmured, disconsolately. "Going under!"

"Your mind has never been clearer."

"I'm going under! His Lordship has already decided the name of my eventual successor."

"What name?"

"Richard Thompson."

"That's lunacy, sir!" James Davy said. "There must be some mistake."

The Superintendent shook his head. "From February 3 to March 14," he said, very softly, "is 38 days. That's a long time. Thirty-eight days of futile research for Gregory Temple. His Lordship's right: I *am* going under." He paused, then continued coolly: "James, I have the measure of you. You will be one of the shining lights of the force one day... But you have received my final lessons, my son, and I assure you that my career is over."

The young man sat down beside him, as if their mutual sadness had licensed the familiarity. His face, no longer eclipsed the lampshade, was brightly illuminated–but his features suddenly darkened. Despite the masculine amplitude of his face, he was as beautiful as a woman.

"Sarah O'Neil is downstairs," called a voice from the corridor.

"Bring her in," replied Temple, seemingly awoken from a reverie. He deftly lifted the lampshade and placed the lamp behind him, in order to put his features in darkness while illuminating the face of the person who came in.

It was an Irishwoman of 18 or 20, tall and graceful. Temple was immediately struck by her beauty, which was dazzling in spite of the absurdity of her costume.

The Irishwoman's gaze met that of James Davy, and a brief spark flared in the jet-blackness of her eyes. It might have been resentment. James Davy was as still as a statue. The two policemen who had brought Sarah in saluted the Superintendent and left.

Sarah was bare-headed. Over her masculine attire she wore one of those vast red cloaks that the daughters of Connaught drape so lavishly about their handsome stature. Such cloaks often became dull with wear in the muddy streets of the parish of St. Giles's, the hell of the Irish.

Sarah lowered her eyes now, before the Superintendent's penetrating gaze. Even so, there was no trace of fear or anxiety on her beautiful face crowned with lush black hair. One might almost have said that a smile was trying to form on her full lips.

After two or three minutes of silent examination, Gregory Temple said: "You were in service with Constance Bartolozzi as a chambermaid?"

"I read her parts to her, milord," Sarah replied, "and I slept in her room that night, because she was afraid."

"Of what was she afraid?"

"Of people who came to her home that day."

"The *Companions of the Deliverance*?"

"I think that's what they were called."

"Do you know Richard Thompson?"

"I have seen him at the house with his mother."

"Often?"

"Twice."

"Never alone?"

"Never."

Gregory Temple placed his hands on his knees and resumed his silent consideration of Sarah.

"We know nothing about this girl," he murmured, tiredly, "or where she's been?"

"Sir," James Davy said, in a respectfully moderate tone, "would you permit me to take a turn at interrogating her?"

The young woman lowered her eyes and knitted her brows. The Superintendent made a discouraged gesture.

James took up the thread. "Sarah, why did you go into hiding after the murder of Constance Bartolozzi?"

"I was afraid," the lovely woman replied. "The people of Ireland easily find themselves in jail."

"Nevertheless, you will answer my questions honestly, now?

"One does what one can, milord. Besides, I've no reason to tell lies here; my innocence was easy enough to prove. It wasn't the Law that I was most scared of."

"Who frightened you, then?"

"The Quaker." As she pronounced this word, Sarah's voice became lower, as if in spite of herself.

The Superintendent started.

"Would you like to continue the interrogation, sir?" James Davy asked.

"Go on, James, go on," Gregory Temple replied, his voice slightly emotional. "You're a remarkable chap."

The young man collected himself momentarily before continuing. "Sarah, who do you mean by the Quaker?"

The lovely Irishwoman looked at him in astonishment. "That's what everyone calls him," she said.

"You mean–John Devil?"

"Of course–if John Devil is the man they call the Quaker."

"Why were you afraid of the Quaker?"

Sarah hesitated, then replied, with visible disgust: "Because I saw him kill Constance Bartolozzi."

James Davy stopped and turned towards Temple.

The Superintendent said nothing. He put his elbows on the desk and leaned on them. The lamplight that struck him from behind was like an aureole about his huge forehead, where his grey hairs were quivering. His eyes glinted in the shadows and his gaze enveloped the lovely young woman like a net.

"May God punish you, milords," murmured the Irishwoman, "if I ever have cause to regret having told the truth here."

"You're free to speak, and you'll remain free," the Superintendent said. "I pledge my honor on that." He lifted his hand as he added: "Have no fear, you are under the protection of the Law."

Sarah took some time to collect her thoughts, then said: "The *signora* was sound asleep. It must have been 2 a.m. I was asleep in the window-seat when I was suddenly woken up by a slight noise. By the glimmer of the nightlight, I saw a man coming out of the dressing-room. I recognized him at first glance as Prince Alexis, who had spent the evening at the house, and I thought I was dreaming, for I had shown him out myself."

"Prince Alexis!" echoed Temple. "A member of that company that meets at your mistress' home?"

"No... The evening was spent playing whist."

"A false name, then. John Devil, perhaps?"

"Yes, John Devil, the Quaker... But I didn't know then that he was the Quaker. He went to the *signora*'s bed, without his tread making a sound on the floor. I thought his intention was theft, because the *signora* had a golden casket studded with diamonds on her night-table–a present from the Princess of Wales–and her earrings were also diamond pendants. But the Quaker didn't touch the golden casket or the earrings. He put his left hand under the *signora*'s head and his right at her throat. The *signora* let out a faint sigh but she didn't stir. The Quaker wiped his finger with his handkerchief, because the pin of her nightgown had pricked it. I had lifted myself up on my elbow when I first saw him, but since then I had been unable to move or speak. When the Quaker, on turning around, saw me thus, mouth agape at the sight of him, he put his finger to his lips. Then he raised his hand in salute, as if by force of habit, and went back into the dressing-room. How did he get out of the house? God alone knows, for all the doors were locked.

"I went to the *signora* as soon as I could get up. I still had no suspicion that anything was wrong. I tried to wake her. She was dead–dead in her sleep. On the bedcover there was the handkerchief that you have before you now. I recognized it... The brown droplets are the blood of John Devil."

"And you are perfectly sure," the Superintendent asked, "that the false Prince Alexis bore not the slightest resemblance to the son of the actress Fanny Thompson?"

"Perfectly sure, milord."

"But the handkerchief is marked *R.T.*–Richard Thompson."

"I don't know anything about that."

"There are 10,000 people in London," murmured Davy, "who have the initials *R.T.*–and people like the Quaker use stolen handkerchiefs."

Temple picked up the open letter that was beside the handkerchief. "Do you remember reading this to your mistress?" he asked her.

"Yes," she replied. "The *R.T.* at the end of that note signifies Richard Thompson. The young man announced his intention of visiting her that evening, and he did indeed come, I remember, to ask for the termination of some pay-ments that his mother, Fanny Thompson, was making to the *signora*."

Temple wrote some notes in pencil on his slip of paper.

"And what did you do after the murder, Sarah?" James asked.

"I ran away."

"Why didn't you give your testimony at the inquest?"

"The Quaker had put his finger to his lips."

"But now you're talking..."

"Now I have nothing more to fear."

"Why?"

"Because the Quaker has given me permission to speak."

James Davy opened his mouth to continue the interrogation, but the Su-perintendent silenced him with a gesture and got up.

"Sarah O'Neil," he said, sternly, "we are quite close to Newgate here. In an hour, you could be laid out beneath the Press,[11] crying out for mercy with a weight of 2,000 pounds upon your breast... I forbid you to interrupt me! You ha-ven't been accused, my girl, and no one wishes you any harm, but the interests of Justice must be served. Know that I, to whom you are speaking, would give up the last drop of my blood in an instant to know the truth. You have seen this man you call John Devil again, since he has–according to you–removed the gag from your mouth. If you will tell me where the Quaker is, at this moment, I will give you 100 guineas. If you will not, the torture ordained every year by the

King and his Parliament is not yet abolished in England... God damn me! If you will not, Sarah O'Neil, so much the worse for you!"

His gaze weighed upon the lovely Irishwoman, who became very pale. He sat down, though, and looked away for a second. At that very moment, a swift glance was exchanged between Sarah and James Davy, whose eyelids were then discreetly lowered.

Sarah soon recovered her composure. "Milord," she said, as straightforwardly as could be, "everyone knows that Gregory Temple is a just and clear-sighted man. I'll not go under the Newgate Press, for sure, but I'll not get the 100 pounds either, because the Quaker gave me permission to speak at the very moment that he was boarding a ship beneath London Bridge. The wind was blowing from the northeast, milord, perfect weather for sailing down the Thames, and this was 24 hours ago. The Quaker is far away by now, if the ship has not been wrecked."

The Superintendent remained deep in thought for some time. He put the lamp back in its place, set the shade upon it again and turned his back.

"May I go?" Sarah asked.

"Not before giving us, at the very least, a description of this rogue!" cried James Davy, a soldier intent on firing his final round.

Temple was slumped in his chair. He did not deign to offer any sign of life.

Sarah replied with good grace. "Your honors know very well, and better than me, that the Quaker has a whole shopful of faces. I've seen him twice in my life, and if he hadn't told me on the second occasion that it was him, I could have stood next to him for an age without recognizing him. On the night of the murder, he was a man of 30, fresh-faced and innocent, with blond curly hair fringing his skull. His height was about the same as Mr. Temple's, or perhaps an inch more, his eyes blue, his whiskers chestnut-colored, his nose thin and aquiline, his lips pinker than a lady's. When he stood beside me yesterday at the end of Thames Street, he was a big fellow of 40 with grey hairs in his beard and a figure..."

"Get out," the Superintendent said, tiredly.

He followed her to the door with his eyes; his brow was fiercely knitted. Before she had passed out of the corridor, he touched a brass button which stood out from the wall within arm's reach and a bell tinkled outside. A jaundiced face immediately appeared at a little door that opened in the same corner as the desk.

"A woman is going downstairs, Mr. Forster."

"Sarah O'Neil, sir."

"That's the one. Put two shadows on her, day and night."

The jaundiced face nodded to indicate obedience and disappeared. It is presumably superfluous to explain what the word "shadow" signifies in the vocabulary of the English Police.

Temple pulled the file towards him and turned its pages distractedly.

"I'm going under," he murmured. "His eminence, the Lord Chief Justice, has an eagle's eye!" Then he added, in such a low voice that even Davy could not hear him: "That fine filly is our last chance." The Superintendent paused, pensively, then continued brusquely: "What do you think of all that, James?"

"The testimony of this Sarah O'Neil..." Davy began.

Gregory Temple shrugged his shoulders and his tight lips attempted a smile. "Worthless!" he said. "This Sarah is nothing but a pawn. We have a 100 feet of turbulent water over our heads!" He continued, in a calmer vein: "You know, Davy, I once saw an old woman struck instantly blind. What do you think she said? 'I can't see any more?' No, she merely said: 'God protect us, the Sun's gone out!' It's the same with me, my good friend. I try to pull myself together, but that's the fact. It isn't the Sun that's gone out, it's me that's gone blind."

He pushed the file away with one hand, while his other made a fist to beat his forehead. The soft and intelligent gaze of the young man was still upon him.

"Whether the girl is telling the truth or lying," the Superintendent continued, in a bitterly disdainful tone, "is of little importance to us. Lies can be instructive in a criminal trial, even more so than the truth. You're wise enough already to know that. In the Munro and Tornhill case, I marched, with a sure and rapid tread, through the middle of 60 false witnesses. I've read three descriptions of John Devil in this file, all of which contradict one another and the one given by Sarah. I've gone blind, James, and I deny the Sun's existence: I have the profound, absolute, inflexible conviction that John Devil does *not* exist!"

He lifted his eyes again to look at James Davy, who was listening to him calmly and attentively. When he looked away again, Davy suppressed a sigh, seemingly by means of a tremendous effort, and a slight tremor agitated his lip-muscles.

"Sarah saw nothing," Gregory Temple continued, his tone becoming firmer in proportion to the increase in his mental effort. "I would pledge my eternal salvation that she saw nothing! No matter how low I've fallen, I can still distinguish a pack of lies from sincere testimony. Would we have the assassin if we could set our hands on the man who fed her that pack of lies? Is there an assassin? Let's see... We're not in possession of a single definite fact, except for the sudden death of a woman, in her own room, in her own bed, behind closed doors that show no evidence of a break-in. The dead woman's body shows no sign of violence save for a scarcely-perceptible mark on the Adam's apple, similar to the bruise left by the pressure of a thumb.

"Three doctors from the Royal College came to examine it, with all due ceremony. The first said that it was inflicted by a strip of whalebone, and delivered a long diatribe against corsets. The second retorted that it was the beginning of a cancerous tumor, and that his esteemed colleague was devoid of common sense. The third called his esteemed colleagues a pair of mules and said that it was an accidental strain, of a kind observed many times over in singers of both sexes. The autopsy revealed a ruptured blood-vessel, and when I said–bearing in mind that I'm a surgeon too, because it's necessary to know everything to be a Chief Superintendent of Police—when I said: 'Gentlemen, pressure has been exerted upon that spot, in such and such a fashion, by the hand of a skilled man, in order to bring about instant death,' our three doctors cried: 'What did I tell you?' That was the unanimous opinion of these knowledgeable practitioners, save that they had neglected to express it...

"Then again, I ask you, is the testimony of Constance Bartolozzi's other servants consistent with that of this Sarah? No. And who has thrown into it the name of John Devil, or the Quaker, whatever you want to call him? No one in the world. You see, Davy, there's only one undisputed fact, and that is that I'm going under!"

He continued, with a furious light in his eye: "By God, I've overturned their stupid routines! I was strong enough, it seems, when I stamped under my feet the poor mousetraps that had been rusting since the Deluge in the attics of the Metropolitan Police. I created the machinery of detection! I invented a simple, logical, solid instrument: is that so worthless that I can now be cast aside?"

"I have wondered more than once," the young man said, drawing closer, "whether all of this might be nothing but a conspiracy directed against you."

The fire in the Superintendent's eye was abruptly extinguished, and his features took on an expression of mistrust. "Ah!" he said, with a cold smile. "You've thought of that? Well, sir, you're mistaken. John Devil is a phantom, but there is a murderer, and it's behind the phantom of John Devil that the murderer is hiding. Do you know where I shall find the real name of the murderer who disguises himself as that phantom? I'll tell you, if you can't guess. I'll find it in the long list under the hallway, which contains the names of every employee of the Metropolitan Police."

"What!" cried Davy. "Do you think...?"

Temple looked at him briefly. "Your astonishment is unwarranted," he said.

"And it has already reached its limit," the young man replied, quietly. "I had forgotten Richard Thompson."

Temple lowered his forehead into his hands again. "Richard!" he murmured. "Do you understand the nature and import of my suspicions regarding that unfortunate young man? I liked him, just as I have formed an affection for you, newly arrived as you are—but listening to you defending him... It's 27 years since I first passed over the threshold of this office. I've never known the ground give way beneath my feet in this manner—except once—but the crime was a distant one and I believed that I was blinded by the affection I had for the victim. As in this case, there was a mysterious association: the German Rosicrucians. Like the Knights of the Deliverance in the present instance, it seemed to me that they appeared solely to commit the crime. By a singular coincidence, the same name—the name of John Devil—was also thrown in..."

He paused for a moment, shrugging his shoulders. Then, in a firmer voice, he continued: "Just as I imported a heretofore unknown lever into the investigative process, it was necessary that a new formula should similarly be devised to fight the criminal efforts. When cannons are used to lay siege to citadels, they in turn lower their walls and hide their battlements behind the inclined slope of an embankment, opposing the irresistible force that can shatter granite with immovable earthworks. The world is nothing but a fencing-match, but it is not given to any newcomer to discover the perfect riposte to a clever thrust designed by a master-at-arms. It requires wisdom. That which resists me at this moment in time is the Vauban [12] who toys with my artillery, the Saint-Georges [13] who scoffs at my rapier. Not only does he know my method of attack, but I am ignorant of the sequence of his invisible parries. Henceforth, everything around me is strange, like a fever-dream!

"Thus far, the witnesses seem to have invented an uncertain and pointless crime, and the name of the dead woman pursues me like a curse. There is nothing to which I can direct my forceful hand or my inquiring gaze! At this moment, I am left confounded by the miracle, like Pharaoh's sorcerers astonished by a wand more powerful than their own.[14] Then I pause for reflection, reviewing my own armaments. I have observed that the ramparts of the fortress are dug in behind an embankment and that my cannonballs are not striking home. My method is a key to open locks, but if the lock is hidden, what use is a key? But the very skill of the work betrays the workman, and I cry out, sure of my facts, as if I already had a hand on the assassin's shoulder: 'You have taken your weapon from my armory! You have turned to evil purpose that which I forged for good! I recognize you: *you are my pupil*!' "

He was holding his head high. His sharp, clear eyes seemed to be penetrating the veil. His flared nostrils testified to the passion that was in him and the hollow furrows in the highly-developed forehead were full of menace. There was an incredible power of concentration in the man, combined with that redoubtable analytical mind which overcomes all obstacles slowly but surely, as a file wears away steel.

James Davy's cheeks had turned pale, doubtless by virtue of the emotion he felt in seeing for the first time the full measure of this powerful man's commitment to the game. "Sir," he murmured, "you've had other pupils besides Richard Thompson..."

"I'm no longer speaking of Richard Thompson," Temple replied, brusquely. "All those who have been close to me will be put to the test."

"You have other pupils," Davy continued, softly, "than those who have received your precious lessons directly, at close quarters."

"What are you trying to say, sir?" the Superintendent demanded, impatiently.

The young man's slender white finger touched one of the printer's proof-sheets scattered on the desk. "Your book, sir," he said, "is a dangerous master-piece."

The page proof bore the inscription, in large print: *The Art of Discovering the Guilty* by Gregory Temple - Cheap Edition.

"Believe me," James Davy said, respectfully but distinctly. "To enable crime to change the lock, it's only necessary for the Police to display their key."

Gregory Temple remained silent. A blush showed on his face, but was then replaced by a mortal pallor. His hands trembled with the effort he made to control himself. A tear appeared beneath his lowered eyelid. He took the proofs and tore them up, one after another. It was easy to see that this was a condemnation with no appeal.

At that moment, as the last sheet was ripped apart, a commotion began outside in Scotland Yard, full of hoots and bursts of laughter. One hoarse voice soon rose above the tumult in the middle of the square, in the most recent fashion of the English hawker of ha'penny pamphlets, proclaiming: "Read all about it! Hot off the presses! The ink's still wet! The most distinguished author you can buy for a ha'penny! The book of *The Amazing Adventures of John Devil the Quaker*, with portraits of the author, the famous and unfortunate Constance Bartolozzi, and Gregory Temple, Superintendent of Police..."

The conclusion of this discourse was drowned out by a new broadside of laughter, shouts and whistles.

"My father left me well provided for," Temple pronounced, painfully, between clenched teeth. "I have worked here day and night for 27 years, and I am now poor. I shall suppress my book, which is my daughter's inheritance, permanently–because what you say is true, young man: its publication was a sin of pride and a dangerous breach of trust. I have grown old. The Lord Chief Justice insults me. The people mock me. Tomorrow, the King will dismiss me. It's mob rule, James, I don't complain. On the contrary, I'm glad to drink even the dregs from the chalice... Will you do me the favor of going to buy me a copy of this pamphlet sold beneath my window for a ha'penny?"

"Master..." the young man stammered.

"That's an order, sir!"

Davy nodded, and went out. The Superintendent got up. He waited, on his feet in the middle of the room.

When the young man returned, Gregory Temple, standing straight and stiff, took the pamphlet fresh from the press's embrace from his hands. He opened it. On the front page was one of those huge lugubrious engravings in which English caricature imitates none but the worst aspects of its father, William Hogarth.[15] The engraving depicted a see-saw at the center of which was an open coffin containing a woman's body, labeled *Constance Bartolozzi*. Lolling on the high end of the plank, John Devil the Quaker–a jolly fellow recognizable by his huge hat–was distributing copies of his pamphlet. At the lower end crouched the Superintendent of Police–a striking resemblance, equipped with the hundred eyes of Argus, every one of them covered in sticking-plaster. From each mouth emerged a speech balloon, manifesting the coarse wit compulsory in every caricature intended to delight John Bull. La Bartolozzi's said, "I'm waiting," John Devil's exclaimed, "I'm on top" and Gregory Temple's replied, "I'm going under."

The Superintendent stared at this engraving for several minutes without saying a word. Then he sat down again at his desk, took out a large sheet of paper, and wrote the following with a firm hand:

To the Most Honorable Francis Taylor, Marquis of Headfort, Earl Bective of Bective Castle, Viscount Headfort, Baron Headfort, Baron Kenlis in the Peerage of Ireland, Lord Chief Justice of the United Kingdom, etc, etc.

Milord,
I have the honor to resign to Your Lordship's hands my position as Chief Superintendent of Police at the headquarters of Scotland Yard. God save the King!

Gregory Temple

This letter was folded and addressed, after which the Superintendent put his private papers into his large portfolio and offered his hand to Davy, saying: "James, I shall never return here. You will receive, in a few days' time–perhaps as soon as tomorrow–your promotion to Chief Inspector. You deserve it."

"Thank you, sir," the young man said, embracing him fondly. "You are good and generous to the very end. Distant or near, I shall always be your devoted servant."

Temple paused on the threshold. "I take note of your promise, James," he said, gravely. "My entire life henceforth will be a duel fought against the audacious bandit who hides himself beneath the name of John Devil. Help me to discover three things. What enemies did Constance Bartolozzi have? Which of them put an end to her life? Which of them has profited from her death?"

"I shall do everything in my power to help you, sir," James Davy replied.

Gregory Temple passed over the threshold and the door closed behind him.

James Davy listened to the sound of his footsteps fading in the distance. When the last echo had died away in the corridor, a smile rose to his lips. Without saying a word, he slid the bolt and turned back to the table. He took hold of the lamp; then, he made a tour of the filing cabinets, illuminating the label of each drawer. He took out two files, which he placed under his arm. The first was inscribed: *Assassination of General O'Brien–John Devil–Prague, 1813.* The second carried two names: *Helen Brown–Tom Brown.* The contents of each file were placed on the table, in a single pile.

James Davy rolled Temple's armchair towards the fireplace, and installed himself there, within reach of the table, whence he could reach the pieces of paper by stretching out his arm. To look at him, you would have thought him a methodical man sorting through his papers in a leisurely manner, setting apart those of importance while throwing the useless remainder in the fire.

The pile, which diminished rapidly, presumably did not contain many papers worth keeping. Almost all of them were consigned to the flames; only two went into James Davy's portfolio. The final sheet was soon balancing its white ashes on the ardent coals.

James Davy got up and replaced the two empty files in their compartments. Selecting a cigar from his box, he made a spill to light it from the letter signed *R.T.*, which was on the table with the bloodstained linen handkerchief marked with the same initials—but then he changed his mind, and replaced the letter among the other objects on the desk, thinking aloud: "It might still be useful to me..."

He put on his gloves and cast another appraising glance around the office, as if he were asking himself: "Is that everything?" Apparently, it was. He pressed the brass button that set the jaundiced face in motion.

"Mr. Forster," he said, as soon as the face appeared at its spy-hole. "This letter must go at once to the Lord Chief Justice, please... And have someone bring me a Constable's badge."

Mr. Forster took the Superintendent's resignation in one hand and used the other to offer his own badge to the young man—who placed it around his neck and tucked it under his clothes. Then, whistling a tune from a French opera, he left.

It was a little after 8 p.m. Alastair Grant, proprietor of the Bank Corner oyster-house, as merry as a sepulchre, was sitting before one of those comfortable London fireplaces whose raised tripedal grate burns the face while letting the feet freeze. Master Grant was an honest fellow, built like a bulldog. For the present, he was doing nothing, and not thinking either; he had relieved himself of both these burdens for the evening.

A young gentleman, irreproachably dressed, with a face that was noble, gentle and discreet, was introduced to his presence and addressed him without preamble: "Master Grant, you are free, like all the King's subjects, to receive in your house whomever you please, and to sell your produce for the best price you can get; but the City is free, in its turn, to apply to you the common law that closes all cafes, taverns and liquor-sellers from midnight to 6 a.m."

"That's when I make my money," replied the fishmonger.

Oyster-houses are, in effect, special establishments, quintessentially English. They serve shellfish, lobsters, port and sherry all night long. Master Grant's was fashionable; once the theaters were closed, it did not begin to empty until daybreak. It had excellent regulars, with well-trained stomachs that could keep going for six hours on the trot without getting upset, until the moment when the last mouthful was well-and-truly down the gullet.

The young gentleman opened his elegant dress-coat and displayed a constable's medal suspended from his neck. "I am James Davy, from Scotland Yard," he added.

Master Grant's ruddy face remained impassive. Calmly, he said: "What have the Police got against me?"

"Hiring out your boxes to foreign spies," replied the worthy. "Information has been given against you."

"Damn me!" Grant exclaimed, laughing dully. "I let out my boxes to whoever pays, and I couldn't care less about foreign spies. What do you want me to do?"

"To hire me as a waiter for the night."

"So that you can do your job here?"

"Precisely."

Master Grant looked at him sideways. "If anyone were to be arrested in my place..." he began.

"I give you my word," James put in, "that there will be no arrests."

The fishmonger's face cleared up at once, and he called out: "Saunder!"

A young Scot wearing an unbleached apron and carrying a giant napkin came in response to the command.

"Saunder," said Master Grant, "this gentleman here is taken on as head waiter. Give him the uniform so that he can start right away, if that's what he wants." He turned back to the iron grille, reddened by incandescent coals.

A few moments later, James Davy had his own unbleached apron and a napkin.

The English do not appear to appreciate the delights of complete solitude, but they do not like the gaiety of a communal meal any better. You will search in vain there for our private retreats and great dining-halls where the air circulates freely, diverse sharers rub shoulders fraternally and a convivial spirit passes from table to table, eventually forming a deafening concert of cheerfulness. They have found a middle way. Their dining-rooms are fitted with duplicates of large coffins, rather reminiscent of the confessionals stuck to the walls of churches. The name expresses their value, for the English have the courage of their idiosyncrasies and rarely bother to draw a veil over their sinister ugliness. These places of pleasure are unanimously known as *"boxes."*[17] Let us not be intolerant, and allow the English to amuse themselves in their own fashion.

In one of these boxes reserved for customers, two gentleman of a certain age and perfectly respectable appearance were poring over 12 dozen oysters as round as cannonballs–whose spherical shape, it's rumored, our neighbors go to great trouble to obtain by means of *caponization*. Two jugs of port flanked the great Britannia-metal platter supporting the molluscan mountain. Two compartmentalized cruets, containing four kinds of diabolical sauces based on *curry* [18] and red pepper, accompanied the jugs. There was no tablecloth on the pale wooden table, and there were knives with rectangular tips instead of forks.

The two gentlemen of a certain age were in full mourning-dress, and there was a great deal of melancholy in their appearance, but they were devouring their fat oysters with a hearty appetite. The port, as dark as burnished gold, was diminishing rapidly within their jugs.

One of them was fat, dressed in a powdered wig with a little pigtail wagging between his shoulders, bearing a slight resemblance to portraits of King Louis XVIII. The other, taller and with a more orthodox figure, wore a simple wig whose yellowed and curly earpieces descended to his rosy cheeks like a doll's coiffure. While eating, they smiled at one another with amiable confidence, and every time they drank they exchanged a benevolent salute.

Impossible to imagine two healthier specimens than these honest gentlemen; impossible, too, to encounter two more candid physiognomies–but that only goes to show how dangerous it is to judge people by appearances! These two men of a certain age, seemingly so harmless, were both foreign spies! At any rate, James Davy, the new waiter, stopped beside their box after having swept a glance around all the others. He sent the establishment's serving-staff away and stood sentinel behind the partition, in the manner of a man eavesdropping on imprudent conspirators.

"You see, my esteemed cousin Turner," the fat gentleman with the powdered wig was saying, "as soon I saw the unfortunate story in the newspapers, I took the mail-coach and the ferry."

"I did the same thing, my dear cousin Robinson," replied the thin gentleman with the simple curly wig. "I wanted, at least, to shed a sincere tear upon her tomb, and a modest wreath."

"That was my intention too, Turner. Alas! When I think that this very box we're sitting in... The oysters are always very good at Grant's. Do you remember how much poor Constance loved them!"

A double sigh was heard, then Turner replied: "Poor Constance loved port too, even though she preferred sherry... How can it be that an event so cruel and unexpected has carried off the flower of our era! I drink to your health, Mr. Robinson."

"I have the honor of returning the compliment–to yours with all my heart, Mr. Turner."

All things considered, however, these two gentlemen, so quiet and courteous, had something of the foreigner about their costumes and their manners. The stout Robinson's little pigtail, and the earnest Turner's pigeon-wings smacked of the continent; James Davy had apparently not been mistaken. So far, it is true, their conversation did not seem to pose any considerable threat to peace in Europe, but please be patient and hear it through to the end.

From the pocket of his vast frock-coat, whose color was nut-brown, Mr. Turner took a round snuff-box, decorated with a woman's portrait.

After having seen this miniature–which displayed a beautiful person dressed in Turkish costume, complete with a turban–stout Robinson raised his eyes to Heaven. "I have the original on my cigar-box," he said.

Turner smiled proudly and replied, while tapping the snuff-box: "Here's the original."

"Scratch that from your papers!" Robinson cried, excitedly. But he stopped himself, and his pleading expression froze the riposte on Turner's lips. "Let her image be between us," he said, unctuously, "and soothe any frivolous disagreement. That was her costume in *La Révolte au Sérail* [19]–do you remember?"

"Do I remember? She sang the grand aria, my dear Robinson!"

"And her playful duo, my dear Turner!

"And her arietta!"

"And the recitation with the trio!"

They fell silent, because their hearts were too full. Each of them ate a dozen oysters in silence.

"Did you know, my friend, that she was on the wrong side of 40?" Robinson resumed, drowning the immediate anguish of his soul with a glass of port.

"Ah, yes!" Turner replied. "I had the advantage of making her acquaintance at the theater in Lyon in the autumn of 1799, 18 years ago. She was already at the height of her powers."

"1798, myself, at the theater in Brussels. She was just 19. She was already one of a kind... But she would never have grown old, you see, that's for sure. She had the waist of Venus!"

"The games, the laughs, the favors..."

"And the *amours*! Turner, I drink to your health!"

"Robinson, it's my pleasure to return the compliment. To yours, with all my heart."

They drank, and their hands reached across the table to one another, meeting above the Britannia-metal plate, where no shellfish now remained.

"Waiter!" called Mr. Turner, languidly.

James Davy was at his post behind the partition. He appeared immediately at the opening of the box. Sadly, Mr. Robinson said: "Our fish, if you please?"

Davy, as nimble and eager as if he had never had any other job in his life, went away. He came back with a platter bearing a pot of tea, a boiled salmon larded with ham and anchovies, slices of sturgeon on a bed of minced shrimps and two brochettes of jellied eels. The two foreign spies immediately attacked the broth with an equal appetite.

The time for secrets of State had obviously not yet come, for Robinson went on, while tipping a drop of brandy into his tea: "Common sense dictates that there can no longer be any question of rivalry between us, worthy friend and parent. The dear creature remained two decades in suspense; that is established. I affirm for my part that I desire to remember her thus. I refute the idea that she ever wished for a single instant to deceive us."

"I believe it wholeheartedly!" exclaimed Mr. Turner, warmly, with his mouth full. "That would be an insult to the tomb that has scarcely been sealed. It takes a long time to make up one's mind, doesn't it?"

"Certainly, particularly when the decision is so very important."

"She saw in us two gentlemen of the same age, whose fortunes were equal, or very nearly, of manifest honorability. I would have hesitated myself, I assure you."

"Me too, for God's sake!"

"All the more so as she was a prudent woman..."

"Yes, yes... and clear-sighted!"

"And discreet!"

"And worldly-wise!"

"Robinson, my worthy friend and cousin," said Mr. Turner, in a voice a-quiver with emotion, "I feel that I might pour out my heart upon your breast: a draught of bitterness, mingled with sensuality!"

"Why should I be ashamed to make the same confession to you, my good man and old comrade? We have been associated formerly in business; destiny has now brought us together in an affair of sentiment... We should have no secrets between ourselves, don't you agree? Let us drink the cup of confidences to the dregs."

"So be it. I'm ready. Ask me anything."

"Well," said Robinson, "I would not be sorry to know exactly when poor Constance promised to become Mrs. Turner."

"In May 1809... Precious memory!"

"As for me," Robinson said, with a sigh, "it was in May 1808 that she consented to be my wife."

"Always the month of May!" Turner said, with feeling. "It's the most favorable time for loving transactions. The spring..."

"The reawakening of nature..."

"The season of fresh violets and the first roses!"

As one, they ceded a truce to the boiled salmon, and reached for their portfolios as if in a single movement. Robinson's cigar-box was already on the table beside Turner's snuff-box; both were decorated with the same smiling portrait of the sultana. Their two notebooks were soon side-by-side, and our two cousins simultaneously pulled out two pieces of glossy paper of identical texture and hue, seemingly taken from the same stock.

At that moment, James Davy was peering through a crack in the partition. His mouth, as pure and beautiful as a woman's, formed a mocking smile.

"*I promise*," read the fat man, raising his voice, scarcely able to contain his emotion, "*to give my hand, as soon as I quit the theater, to Mr. William Robinson, brewer of Lyon in France, to whom my heart already belongs.*"

"*I promise*," the tall man, spelled out, his voice trembling, "*to give my hand, as soon as I quit the theater, to Mr. Frank Turner, brewer of Brussels in the Low Countries, to whom my heart belongs already.*"

Both of them, at the same time, deciphered the signature: *Constance Bartolozzi.*

Each of them wiped away a sincere but furtive tear. Then they looked at one another with slightly troubled expressions, each one afraid that he might encounter a smile on his rival's lips.

"Do you know something, cousin?" the brewer from Lyon continued, hesitantly. "In similar circumstances, Frenchmen fight to the death."

"Brabantines strangle one another with all their might," replied the brewer from Brussels.

"Between the two of us, on the other hand, who are Englishmen..."

"True Englishmen, damn it!"

"Gentlemen, God damn me!"

"When I die! Saxons of the old rock, Robinson!"

"There's a stronger tie between us, isn't there, Turner?"

By way of a dignified response to this chivalrous appeal, Turner got up, came around the table, pressed Robinson to his breast and solemnly said: "A bond as strong as steel!"

They remained thus for a moment, one hand in a clasp and the other on the heart, forming a tableau. Then they took their seats again.

"I want to tell you everything," Robinson said, putting a thick slice of salmon on his plate. "I don't want to keep anything secret. In exchange for that cherished promise, in due course, I sent her a sealed envelope containing my handwritten will, in which I made her, very sensibly, my sole heir."

"Very sensibly," Turner echoed. "Having judged it appropriate to do exactly the same thing, I can only approve of your conduct."

Davy was no longer peering through the crack. He was standing up straight, his arms crossed. He was listening attentively, but coolly.

Robinson and Turner resumed eating, their eyes lowered, as if each of them now sought to avoid the eyes of his accomplice. An observer would have guessed that the storehouse of their confessions was still not emptied, and that the greater part of the confidences had yet to be shared.

"Well!" said Robinson, who was certainly the most decisive, all of a sudden. "You may think what you will, but Constance gave me to understand that our relationship–do you understand me?–had not been sterile... And that a charming child..."

"A fair-haired cherub!" Turner sighed.

"Waiting," the fat man went on, "for the day of our wedding to call me father."

"That was exactly the manner–very modest but precise–in which she put it to me," murmured the taller man.

"In such a way..." Robinson contrived, "I think you understand... My will extended to that delicate offspring..."

"As did mine, obviously. I drink to your prosperity, cousin!"

"And to yours, cousin!"

"But consider for a moment," Turner went on, in a piercing tone, "the points of similarity between us: the sons of two sisters..."

"Both of us brewers."

"Both of us millionaires, thank God."

"Admirers of the same woman..."

"Treated in the same fashion..."

"In the same honorable fashion, Mr. Turner!"

"Oh, to be sure, Mr. Robinson! From the bottom of my heart, I believe it... Honorable to all three of us... Then widowers at the same time..."

"The same *amours*..."

"And co-fathers, if I can express it thus..."

"Of the same frail creature. Turner, a Frenchman would jeer..."

"A Belgian would laugh heartily. As for me, I say: we are not cousins, but brothers!"

"Twin brothers, in my judgment."

"If you will permit me, Robinson, I shall henceforth address you simply as William."

"Me too, Frank—it's simple and convenient. But tell me, these details are flavorsome... At what time of the year did you come to see her?"

"Always in the month of May, my good William. I had the first fortnight. And you?"

"Similarly in the month of May, worthy Frank. She gave me the second fortnight."

They clinked their glasses.

"What would a Frenchman say, my dear Frank?" Robinson asked, looking at his partner over the rim of his glass.

"What would a Belgian reply, my dear William?"

"A Frenchman has no respect for anything," the fat man said. "A displaced Frenchman would make the observation that there are 22 other fortnights in the year."

Turner shrugged his shoulders disdainfully, saying: "And the Belgian could not help adding, stupidly, that by that count we might have 22 rivals taking up the 11 surplus months... But we're Englishmen, God damn it!"

"Loyal Englishmen!"

"May Heaven confound the Low Countries!"

"And may the Devil take France!"

"Up with merry England!"

"Merry England forever!"

This matter being settled and the salmon displaying its spine, perfectly dissected, Mr. Turner asked Mr. Robinson—who was fully in accord—if he might pass him a slice of sturgeon.

"From the heights of Heaven," he said, shifting the minced shrimps sprinkled with curry powder, "poor Constance is very likely watching us."

"So that she might be content with me," Robinson said, "I will make you a sacrifice in honor of her memory." He adopted a noble pose. "Turner!" he went on, "Take note of my solemn declaration: I concede to you the totality of the child!"

Turner withdrew his hand as if he had been struck by a martinet and the table-spoon fell into the mince. "Do you think, brother," he said, "that I could wish to fall behind you in generosity of the heart? You do not know me!"

"Indeed, indeed," Robinson put in, laughing. "I understand you, and I approve of you, as always. Anything for poor Constance, no? But as far as the offspring... Well, it's understood that no more will be said. We'll cut it short. So, then, Frank, you have no heir?"

"The same as you, William, I suppose?"

"I've some four millions, honestly amassed, Frank."

"I have a fraction more; the way the money's coming in, it'll be five million."

"Nine million!" calculated James Davy, who was still at his post.

"The Devil!" said Robinson. "And have you considered this? If we were to die tomorrow, as chance would have it, one of two things might happen. Either the wills could take effect, in which case the offspring that we've both cut in would come into eight or ten millions. Or we could annul the wills, in which case your millions and mine would go directly to that creature that we kicked out of London long ago for dishonoring our family."

"To the son of Helen Brown," Turner murmured, in a voice that was subtly changed. "To that scoundrel, Tom Brown." He added: "It's said that the mother died in Sydney, after a birching."

"I'm convinced that the son will die on the scaffold, at Tyburn," Robinson said.

James Davy was now pressed up against the other side of the partition-wall, listening. He stood as motionless as a statue—except when the name of Helen Brown was mentioned, when he shuddered briefly from top to toe and his eyelids lowered, drawing a veil over the light in his eyes.

"Waiter!" Turner shouted.

"Gentlemen?"

"A gingered crayfish for a toothpick and a jug of the old sherry that you served me here in May last year."

"And tea, waiter," Robinson added, "and French brandy, and be quick about it!"

Davy crossed the room like an arrow, for he did not doubt that the most important part of the conversation was imminent. He did well to hurry; when he returned, the discussion had moved on.

Our two friends were hunched over the table and seemed more deeply engrossed than before in their mutual confidences.

"If poor Constance had lived," Robinson said, emotionally, "I would never have considered it, I give you my solemn word on that."

"And I offer you the same," Turner replied. "It was necessary, I admit... that irreparable loss."

"That's the very word—irreparable. But listen, then! Is it forbidden to think about impending old age?"

"Certainly not!"

"A memory, no matter how tender it might be, is no company for long winter evenings."

"Assuredly. One needs someone beside the hearth."

"I can't say," the fat man sighed, "that I could ever hope to replace her..."

"Oh, never!" the tall man put in.

"But in the end," Robinson continued, taking his cigar-box and slipping it into his pocket as if he were fearful of the Turkish portrait, the mute witness to his apostasy, "but in the end—there you are!"

"There you are!" echoed Turner, who made his snuff-box disappear with an equally furtive and remorseful gesture. Then, lowering his voice, he asked:

"How old is yours? Mine's a little too young–in her 18th year. But sensible, mind you–and experienced... An angel!"

"Mine's only 16," admitted stout Robinson, blushing like a girl, "but you might reckon her 30, at least, for her prudence."

"And you're engaged?"

"Very nearly–promised, as they say. You?"

"Decidedly–with a penalty. I'm marrying her on my return."

"Gad!" exclaimed Robinson. "You're what I call a fine fellow, cousin Frank, and you've found the right way to dispose of your millions! I ask you formally for your permission to drink to the health of Mrs. Turner."

"On the express condition that I can empty my glass to the health of Mrs. Robinson, by all the devils!"

"Bravo! I reckon to quit Lyon afterwards."

"I shall leave Brussels."

"To return to London, I hope?"

"Naturally! These ladies will be the best of friends."

"And sometimes," Robinson murmured, with a tear in his eyes, "we shall take them to visit poor Constance's grave."

"We shall teach them," Turner mumbled, damply, "to love the one who... that which... from the height of the empyrean..."

"Potted mignonettes... garlands of flowers..."

"And a little picnic on the grass!"

They were so drunk that they had difficulty getting to their feet.

"To the ladies! All three of them!" Robinson cried, emptying the jug into their glasses.

"And that our wretched nephew, Tom Brown, will hang!" added Turner, wildly.

A few minutes later, the pale figure of James Davy came to life on the other side of the partition and a smile of satisfaction was born on his lips. Had he come here to find out exactly when William Robinson and Frank Turner intended to marry?

When the two faithful brewers finally quit the table where they had completed their Homeric feast, Davy guided their staggering steps to the street door. Then he went back into the parlor, where Master Grant was continuing to roast his apoplectic face. "The foreign spies have gone," he said.

"Did they pay?" asked Master Grant.

Davy threw four sovereigns on the table, adding in a grave voice: "Tonight, we have saved the house of Hanover and the Protestant succession."

"I'm a Scot and an Anabaptist," Master Grant replied, pocketing the enemy's money without a qualm. "To me, all that's just mockery and misfortune."

Behind Covent Garden, in the middle of that inextricable labyrinth named Storegate—nowadays partially demolished—there used to be a narrow back street, long and tortuous, which the wretched inhabitants of the district called Low Lane, although it had no official name. In the middle of that thoroughfare, where it was at its widest, there was a fairly large building whose frontage was an incomplete wall that stopped abruptly halfway up the second story. It was said that it had been constructed as the first establishment of the famous schoolmaster Joseph Lancaster, the pioneer of the mutual system of education.[20] The masonry-work had never been finished, abandoned before serving its purpose, and London's black breath had already dyed it with soot.

At the door of this newly-built ruin hung a little sign, fixed to an iron rod, bearing the words: *Will Sharper's Spirit Shop.* One might have said without any exaggeration that this sign was a hundred leagues away from any civilized region. London, at the beginning of the century, was host to such strange depths and such incredible barbarities that one is tended to wonder whether our own Paris ever descended so low, even in the Middle Ages. Certain parts of the City, St Giles's, Spitalfields and the shameful limbs that have become the richer part of the docks, utterly defied description; there were hundreds of streets barred to the police. At midday, when it was foggy, passers-by were strangled behind the Tower and, in this very street, some 50 yards from the theater where our own Talma [21] played Shakespeare, the rain had to fall from the heavens to wash the blood from the gutters.

London had no knowledge then of that humble providence of the streets, the warden for whom the word "policeman" was coined; there were only sergeants, watchmen and constables. The British policeman had never yet displayed the epic bulge of his fortified helmet in this place—where I saw, with my own eyes, in 1845, the shameless label Will Sharper's Spirit Shop.[22]

In front of the facade, on the other side of the street, there were broken-down cottages that served as dormitories for hundreds of prowlers. A single cast of a net, purposefully disposed in that horrid place, would have filled Newgate from top to bottom. The two houses situated to the left and right of the ruined cottages similarly gave shelter to an industry without a name. They were accustomed to armed clashes; from dusk to dawn, within and without, there was an interminable orgy of savage brawls. Two pawnbrokers' stalls clung to the soiled walls, whose famished proprietors traded loans for pledges, never letting up until their usurious pillage had stripped a man of his skin.

The bar-room that extended from this vestibule of infamy was almost as vast as the interior of a church, but its very breadth seemed hideous because the pine-board ceiling was only six inches above the heads of its customers. A half-dozen smoky lamps, some of them set on the barrels that served as tables and others on the ground, moderated the darkness with a vague and ruddy glow. A veritable human ant-hive swarmed over a floor scattered with damp straw and litter: men, women and children–many women and many children.

Only the front wall, as we have said, was masonry, cracked and rickety; the rest had the appearance of an evil boathouse, diabolically framed on uneven ground. There were huge holes in the floor, at the bottom of which particular societies were comfortably established, playing cards. This must once have been a garden, for thin tree-trunks, sawn-off two feet from the ground, were still rooted therein, taking the place of stools.

To the right of the main door, whose threshold was three steps down from the mire of the street, four empty barrels supported a pine plank serving as a counter, surrounded by a palisade of unseasoned wood, such as one might see in an open field. On the counter, mingled in calculated disarray, were jugs, bottles, pitchers and even little barrels containing the spirits favored by the people of London: raki, Irish porter, Scotch whisky and gin, the last-named being a notoriously poisonous beverage which kills three times as fast as other strong liquors. That is the drink of preference, over there; we have absinthe here. In the establishments where gin is the master, one cannot ordinarily get porter, ale or wine, but at Sharper's everything was sold. Jenny Paddock, the widow of John Devil, would serve Johannisberger in a broken glass if necessary, or Lachryma Christi in a bowl.[23]

Jenny Paddock was a five-foot-six-inch Scotswoman, still strong and as solidly built as a man, but haggard and tremulous with brightly-burning eyes. She was situated behind the counter, for the royal heritage of Sharper's inn had fallen to the distaff line. Two ugly rogues and two 14-year-old girls carried out her sovereign orders. Under the counter, between the four casks, a sharp-nosed little Jew served as Jenny Paddock's foot-warmer while selling contraband tobacco. The little Jew was then 12 years old; he was thrifty and already knew many useful things; Jehovah having blessed his commerce, he became an honest moneylender when he grew up.

Facing the counter, to the left of the entrance door, a 40-square-foot enclosure surrounded by slats embedded in the mud contained tables and stools. This was the parlor, expressly reserved for gentlemen and ladies of high society–swells, to employ the technical term. Entry to this parlor cost a penny a couple, when anyone was sufficiently proud to pay so dear solely to satisfy his self-respect. From the entrance to the depths, which disappeared into a thick cloud of smoke, was a good 60 paces. Halfway along that route, one found the dining room, an enclosure as privileged as the parlor and similarly barricaded. Like Master Grant's establishment, the dining room had boxes, but Sharper's boxes, tottering and horribly worm-eaten, never played host to foreign spies. Everyone therein was English, from their rimless hats to their soleless shoes, not to mention their sleeveless coats. Hurrah for the conquerors plying their ladies with drink! A boxing ring faced the dining room, maintained in a state of relative privacy. The stakes to which the circular cord was attached had slates hanging stakes to which the circular cord was attached had slates hanging on them on which bets could be recorded.

On the far side of the ring and dining room, the ceiling rose up abruptly, as the ground sloped upwards, to create a sort of amphitheater. Amphitheater is the right word, make no mistake: we are in an illustrious spot here, which has left its name in the archives of London low-life. For more than 20 years, twice a week, on Mondays and Fridays–saving absence caused by imprisonment–Thomas Paddock, nicknamed John Devil, gave public lessons in artful swindling. The police, who know everything, were perfectly well aware of it, but Low Lane was an inviolable refuge, and Thomas Paddock could never fall into a trap beneath the smoke-stained boards of Sharper's.

Thomas Paddock, or John Devil, had a reputation of the highest order. In Low Lane, this strange professor had triumphantly replaced the other, Joseph Lancaster, who taught only good things–without result, naturally enough. Merry England has much more of its renowned eccentricity than one might readily believe; she is rather reminiscent of one of those unfortunate children who drive themselves crazy making believe that they are debauched. John Bull will be immediately and completely entranced by any man who stands on his head.

It was not only budding thieves who contributed to Thomas Paddock's curriculum; his courses were, in fact, a direct response to Gregory Temple's book entitled *The Art of Discovering the Guilty*, and one might ask whether the originality of Gregory Temple might not have been even more dangerous than the originality of John Devil. Neither one of them was infallible. We have observed the fall of Gregory Temple; for his part, John Devil–the first of that name–permitted himself to be led to Tyburn, where the gallows still stood, and had made no provision for his return. The Low Lane inn, supervised by his inconsolable widow, was deep in mourning for an entire night; the gin ran in torrents and left all the guests at the funerary orgy dead drunk in the mud. Then, because the death of one man cannot kill an institution, Thomas Paddock's chair of philosophy was taken by a successor–and whenever a malefactor, elevated by his genius to a higher level, accomplished some series of great exploits and acquired legendary status, the admiration of vulgar rogues would bestow upon him the sobriquet of John Devil.

About an hour before midnight, that evening, Sharper's was as full as one of those tin-plate caskets in which the fishermen who catch gudgeon along the banks of the Seine keep their live bait. From one end of the great hall to the other, wallowing in the straw and the filth, groups of drunkards could be seen sleeping off their gin. In the parlor, a few knights of industry of low degree, a little less wretched than the common run of the stupefied rabble, were playing the duke with the night-birds. The greater number of the latter–a horrible thing to relate, which is one of the most awful curses of English vice–had not yet attained the full figure of womanhood; within the uniform mask that gin pastes over the faces of all its victims, the naive smiles of children sometimes broke forth.

Pipe-smoke, trapped by the excessively low ceiling, filed the air with a cloud so utterly opaque that the most piercing gaze could not have penetrated ten steps from the entrance; only confused movements and vague luminosities were perceptible through those suffocating vapors. The noise was not quite as intense as we, who are accustomed to French smoking-dens, would have supposed; it was a dull and earnest murmur, mingled with the clinking of pewter and brass. The oceanic grumbling was occasionally punctuated by a sudden blasphemy, or a threat, or the demented exclamation of a gambler. There were solitary drunken women singing monotonously and lugubriously to themselves; others suffered fits of coughs brought on by the gin.

To those familiar with the refrains of our own popular pleasures, that bizarre boutique of London pleasures would, in sum, have resembled a hospital ward where relaxed supervision had allowed an insidious orgy to take hold of the dying. It was an obscene temple to the dance of death.

There were, however, some healthier specimens. Consider Noll Green, the boxer from Southwark, and Lochaber Dick, the ale-drinker, who earned his living swilling beer from buckets in Trafalgar Square. In addition to their avowed professions, they were two audacious bandits. Dick and Noll had recently returned from distant parts, both of them having been deported to New South Wales, from which they had succeeded in escaping in the company of the son of the famous Helen Brown, who had died in Sydney under the birch. Noll had a Herculean build; odds of seven to one were offered on him at the boxing hall in Whitechapel. Dick, who was not so tall or broad, had an elastic stomach–a precious property that had made his fortune since he had begun to exploit it. There was not a single rubberneck in the whole of London who would not willingly pay a penny to see Dick visibly swell up while drinking a bucket of beer without drawing breath. Noll and Dick had been convicted of murder at one time, and the police had locked them up in close confinement. Dick was considered cleverer and more dangerous than Noll, who dared not take him on in spite of his athleticism.

They were at the same table in the parlor, drinking punch with a child of 15 or 16, whose blinking eyes and furrowed face contrasted with their robust and healthy appearance. The child had a singularly intelligent face, simultaneously impudent and sly. In his hand he held the pamphlet that was all the rage: *The Book of the Adventures of John Devil the Quaker*. His name was Ned Knob. The regulars at Sharper's had made a meal of this rag, as the biography of John Devil was known in their common parlance.

The majority of the assembly did not know how to read; most of them had bought the pamphlet purely for the engraving that had generated such fury. The engraving was already stuck up all over the dividing walls, even above the head of Jenny Paddock, the tall Scotswoman who reigned over the counter. Those who had some slight hint of literary learning were painfully spelling out the text in their corners, but little Ned Knob, who had been a solicitor's clerk before being dismissed for theft–a true savant, this one–was reading the most interesting passages in a loud and intelligible voice for the edification of the boxer and the beer-swiller. All around the parlor balustrade, the curious assembled to listen.

"...Satan once came to the parish of St. Giles," the little clerk read, his voice sharp and broken, "to see about carrying off some wretched trifle to his inferno–for the inferno is the equivalent of St. Giles. Satan found an Irishwoman, drunk but starving, because she had been drinking for a week without eating. She was comfortably seated in a mud-heap, nibbling the jawbone of a dog that had died of rabies. Satan thought her so beautiful that he paid court to her, while holding his nose. Thus it came about that John Devil was born nine months afterwards, in an empty gin-barrel, with 32 wolf's-teeth in his mouth and a Quaker's hat on his head.

"At three months, he stole his nurse's pipe–she was from the Isle of Man, and gave apple-brandy instead of milk. At four months, he set fire to the house of the Temperance Society. At six months, he mounted a donkey to take himself off to Oxford University, where he was received with open arms thanks to his mount, which consorted amorously with all the doctors.

"At one year, he sold the rector for a shilling and sixpence at Cambridge Fair, and the King desired to see him.

"He went to St. James's on his donkey. The Prince of Wales said to him: 'Little fellow, what is the biggest thing in the three kingdoms?'

" 'It's your royal highness's nightcap,' John Devil replied.

"The Prince of Wales was curious. He wanted to know why there was nothing as big as his nightcap in England, Scotland and Ireland–but the King said 'Sssh!' and the Princesses put on a show of blushing.

"John Devil saluted His Majesty and asked him in his turn: 'Gracious sovereign, do you know what costs the least and what brings in the most?'

" 'It's Ireland,' replied the King, as a first guess.

" 'It's Bengal!' cried the royal Prince.

" 'It's the tax on gin!' Princess Caroline put in, who was still laughing at the thought of her august husband's nightcap.

"John Devil shrugged his shoulders and said: 'Dogs wouldn't want your tongues... It's the paper on which the false notes of the Bank of England are issued.'

"The King, seeing that John Devil had such spirit and modesty, blacked his eye with a blow of his fist and appointed him turnspit at Windsor Castle, with the right of access to the cellars and the title of a Scottish baronet. The King, as you see, was a generous prince; he also went mad.

"At the age of two, John Devil finally became tall enough to be admitted to the stables. Princess Caroline, seeing so handsome a soldier, sent him her gilder, in order to make a frame for him.[24] It was agreed that John would have his meals served, a suite of 18 rooms and 100,000 pounds for necessities; but the Prince of Wales, the Princess' husband, emerged from the wardrobe where he had been hiding with several witnesses at five shillings apiece, two barristers, a solicitor, a bailiff and a judge, assisted by his clerk. He had to go to the Court of Common Pleas, and John Devil would have been condemned to pay a fine if his certificate of baptism had not proved his extreme youth.

"When it was seen that he had got past the law into the bargain, in spite of his six soleless feet, all the women of the court sent him their gilders, with frames at the ready. At that time, he would have been able to make his fortune and become Archbishop of Canterbury, but experience is the fruit of years. He got it into his head to be Secretary of State, and went up into the dome of St. Paul's to see something of where the political wind was coming from. When he got up there, he found that he had forgotten his spectacles; the verger fetched him those of the great Isaac Newton, who is buried somewhere nearby, and John Devil saw two innumerable armies whose soldiers, from such a height and distance, seemed like ants in the dust. One of these armies, led by Fox and Canning, was called the Whigs; the other, commanded by Castlereagh and Wellington, named themselves Tories.[25]

"John Devil, having noticed the Regent making much of the Whigs, naturally concluded that the loyal Prince had the intention of favoring the Tories, and he was coming down the steps four at a time to offer himself to Wellington when he met his venerable father, Satan, who guided him into the cathedral choir, arm-in-arm with the Dean. Satan grabbed him by the ear, and made him the gift of a new Quaker's hat, saying:

" 'You're four years old; it's time you knew what's what. All that glitters isn't gold, and a good deal of evil isn't profitable. The floors of courts are slippery; bliss isn't to be found in palaces; on the other hand, one's badly lodged in thatched cottages. Make yourself a member of the confederacy of London thieves, if you want to hold on to your innocence.'

"That was easier to say than to do. Anyone can obtain a doctor's diploma, but it's necessary to pass examinations to be received into the company of the great family. John Devil spent seven years in the school of Thomas Paddock, even though, from the very first day, he stole his breakfast, dinner and supper from his master's pocket. When he was questioned on his thesis, his examiners were Jack Sheppard, Robin Lewis and Jeremy Drummer [26] and the president was Thomas Paddock himself. He was given two hours to steal the Speaker's silver bell from the House of Commons; after an hour and 20 minutes, he came back carrying the orator's very table, with the bell on top of it. The four examiners pressed him to their breasts–after which Jeremy, searching in his pocket for his handkerchief, found Jack Sheppard's tobacco-pouch, while Jack let out a cry as he pulled Robin Lewis's watch from his waistcoat; Robin was holding Thomas Paddock's purse, who had Jeremy's silk handkerchief in his turn. John Devil was carried in triumph to Finch Lane for three days, and the Supreme Council caused a medal to be struck in memory of that fine trick.

"John Devil was 14 when he hit upon the idea of taking a trip overseas. He embarked for New South Wales in the capacity of a convict; he had paid for his passage by delivering three hammer-blows to the head of an alderman, who died of them. When he became bored down in the hold, he cut through his manacles with a hair steeped in vinegar and indoctrinated his companions so thoroughly and so well that the crew was put in irons while the passengers took over the ship. John Devil was made captain, as was only reasonable, and the vessel landed at Port Jackson, where the former captain, his officers and his sailors were passed off as assassins and put to work in the docks. In the meantime, John Devil and his companions led the high life, feted everywhere as if they had been officers of the Admiralty.

"The governor of the colony was in a nice position. John Devil immediately thought of procuring it for himself, because he had to settle down sooner or later, but he fell in love with a beautiful Scotswoman, his mistress—who cost the eyes from a King's head out there, because the governor, the attorney general, the sheriffs, the judges, the deputies, the supervisors, the commissioners and the supernumeraries tore out their own. There was no woman but her in the entire colony under 50 years of age.

"It's one thing to carry the desk of the speaker of the House of Commons away on one's head, but another matter entirely to steal a woman from Sydney. Women are so rare out there that they're guarded like the exotic animals in our Zoological Gardens. John Devil hid the beautiful Scotswoman in a bale of wool and took ship; he was homesick. En route, he read for the first time the sublime work of Gregory Temple, Superintendent of Police, which is like a practitioner's manual—and which ought to have been titled *The Art of Stealing Without Ever Being Discovered*, for it mounts placards over every pitfall-trap and fairy lights around every taut net.

"John Devil's twentieth birthday arrived as he made landfall at Plymouth; he came to London with the beautiful Scotswoman, who was now Lady John Devil, and delivered himself entirely to free trade. Thomas Paddock had said as he died: 'My successor is the Quaker'—for John Devil always wore the huge hat that Satan, his father, had given him in the choir of St. Paul's. He did not give the lie to Thomas's prediction, and brought about incontestable progress in the science..."

Here the story of the principal exploits of John Devil was recounted: a story in which truths mingled with fables, in which the chronicler had placed a number of absurd boasts among bloody and all-too-real misdeeds. The crowd around the balustrade had swollen, and the parlor itself had filled up by degrees. From every corner of the den the audience had assembled. Wide-open eyes and gaping mouths were visible all around the little clerk.

To give an idea of the success obtained by Ned Knob, the reader of this entrancing poem, we may say that at one point, Jenny Paddock, the five-foot-six-inch Scotswoman herself, left her counter, jumped over the balustrade, lifted the clerk from his seat, and sat him on her knee so that she could hear better. Dick and Noll were extremely proud to be the companions of little Ned Knob.

"One night," the reader resumed, "a month and a few days ago, Gregory Temple's pretty daughter, Suzanne, came into his bedroom carrying a warm beer..."[27]

"Listen! Listen!" The injunction went round as if in a full sitting of Parliament, while others added: "The story of the actress is beginning" or "The story of Constance Bartolozzi!"

"...for Suzanne Temple is as pretty as a love-affair," Ned went on, "and the Superintendent of Police is in the habit of drinking a half-pint of warm ale every night before going to sleep. The doors of the house were firmly shut and securely locked; the bolts had all been shot, and the Superintendent, who is a cautious man, had lifted the battens inside the chimneys and looked under the beds.

"Get into the home of a man endowed with such prudence, if you can!

"It must have been two hours after midnight when Gregory Temple saw a tall individual suddenly appear at the head of his bed, dressed in black and wearing a Quaker's hat. You will have guessed who this individual was; Gregory Temple was no more incompetent than you; he recognized John Devil without ever having seen him before.

" 'How did you get in here?' he cried, seizing the loaded pistol that he kept on his night-stand.

"Whether the stranger thought this question indiscreet, or had some other reason, he did not judge it worthy of a reply. Gregory Temple was a cool customer; seeing a smile beneath the folded-down rim of the huge hat, he aimed for the heart and pulled the trigger. The pistol sputtered like a tinderbox throwing out a futile spark as the stone is struck: the fuse and the bullet had been removed.

"The Superintendent of Police wanted to leap from his bed, but a hand of steel restrained him.

" 'Gregory Temple,' the stranger said to him, 'I am the son of a woman you have killed, and I promised my mother that I would avenge her...' "

"Listen! Listen!" repeated the quivering assembly, while Ned Knob, the reader, got his breath back.

Before resuming his reading, the solicitor's clerk boldly surveyed the curious and avid crowd surrounding him. "Pack of brutes," he said, chewing a wad of tobacco that made his young cheek bulge. "You believe that John Devil will kill the Police Superintendent, no? This happened five weeks ago, but Gregory Temple is still alive!"

"Get on with it, little one!" ordered the boxer and the beer-swiller, as one.

" '...and I promised my mother that I would avenge her!'

"The Superintendent tried to struggle, but the stranger's grip was vice-like.

" 'It would be easy for me to strangle you,' the latter went on, emotionlessly. 'You know that perfectly well; I see it in your frightened eyes–but that's not the way I intend to finish you, Mr. Temple. I would rather use your pride to destroy you. You have the reputation of being the king of detectives: a bloodhound with piercing eyes, a keen ear and infallible wit; that is the honor you value more than life itself. Mr. Temple, I shall amuse myself with the game of proving to London and England that your skill is charlatanry, your wit obtuse, your ear deaf and your eye blind.'

" 'I challenge you to do it!' cried the Superintendent, his vanity more powerful than his terror.

"The stranger, still smiling, replied: 'The challenge is already accepted. I am John Devil the Quaker. This evening, between eleven o'clock and midnight, I killed Signora Constance Bartolozzi, prima donna at the Princess Theater. I left her diamond-encrusted golden casket on her bedside table, to give you firm proof that profit means nothing to me. The blow is aimed at you; I am sorry that the poor woman has suffered in consequence, but I chose her because she was in the public view and the murder will generate a lot of noise. Anyway, we're all mortal. You will find the mark of my thumb on her throat, a letter of mine in her portfolio, and my own bloodstained handkerchief on the bedspread: these are the points I concede to you as the contest begins, and the gallery, our judge, will know soon enough that I have given them to you. Now, Gregory Temple, celebrity detective, expert calculator of probabilities, illustrious deductionist, put yourself to work: I give you 40 days to blow your brains out!'

"The vision disappeared as suddenly as it had arrived. The following morning, after a night full of feverish nightmares, the Chief Superintendent was woken up by the commissioner from Marylebone, who had come to deliver his report of the murder of Constance Bartolozzi.

"Thirty-eight days have passed. Gregory Temple works from dawn to dusk and from dusk to dawn: he digs; he sniffs; he flounders; he calculates with savage desperation; he moves mountains of deductions and probabilities–and Constance Bartolozzi's murderer walks untroubled through London's streets.

Gregory Temple's *Art of Discovering the Guilty* has reached its 30th edition, but he discovers nothing. The Lord Chief Justice has already said, in public, 'He's going under'–see the engraving! La Bartolozzi is waiting–see the engraving! And John Devil is in on top–see the engraving!

"That is the state of affairs today, March 14, 1817. The author of this important document, who is perhaps John Devil himself, will wager 100 guineas against sixpence that Gregory Temple will go mad, if he does not die of apoplexy."

This conclusion was welcomed by loud applause and wild laughter.

Cries of "He's going under!" were heard on every side as the engraving was studied.

"And the actress is waiting, see!"

"And John Devil's having a ball at the top of the plank!"

Little Ned Knob was reflective as he drank a glass of gin that was certainly well-earned.

Suddenly, two sharp whistle-blasts sounded outside, cutting through the tumult. Dick the ale-swiller and Noll the boxer leapt to their feet as one. The turbulent murmurs that had filled the inn a few moments before were succeeded by a glacial silence.

"What's that?" Ned demanded, having got up in his turn. "Damn me if there isn't something fishy going on!" [28]

Dick and Noll looked at one another uncertainly. There was not an eye in the place that was not fixed upon them, curiously. In the silence, two more seeming whistle-blasts sounded, which had something more imperious about them.

The boxer and the beer-swiller used their elbows to plough a course through the surrounding crowd towards the door. Before crossing the threshold, Dick turned and said: "If anyone's thinking of following us..."

"...I'll brain him!" Noll finished.

Ned Knob's piercing grey eyes shone beneath his tousled hair.

The door closed behind the two convicts.

The crowd, whose apathy had been briefly alleviated, soon returned to its state of stupefaction. Its members returned to their former occupations: groups reformed; the herd of tattered sybarites retired to the damp straw once again, wallowing like pigs; the card-games resumed in the depths of the wells; the poisoned fountain poured out gin, and the blackened pipes burned. Evidently, no one had any intention of facing up to Noll and Dick's threats.

Ned Knob, however, had gone to the counter. Jenny Paddock turned to look at him. Standing on tiptoe, he took hold of her arm and said: "Is it him?"

"Who?" growled the innkeeper, in a surly manner.

"The Quaker?"

She shrugged her shoulders. "Go take a look," she replied.

Ned Knob made a move towards the door, but he dared not go out. His cheeks were very pale, and his lips were tremulous with fear. He was obviously moved by more than curiosity, for the battle between his terror and his desire to know was making him sweat.

Suddenly, his course seemed to be decided. He slipped silently through the crowd, detouring around the wells and stepping over the creatures heaped up pell-mell upon the floor. In the back wall of the inn, there was an oblong gap, formed by the removal of a plank, which served to ventilate some of that sewer's noxiousness. No one but the little clerk could have passed through that hole. First, he put his head through, then his body followed, leaving scraps of cloth behind on the badly finished edges.

As soon as Ned Knob was outside, he moved on purposefully, muffling the sound of his steps as best he could, rapidly making his way around the exterior wall of the shanty. He crossed the lane and found himself in the midst of the ruined cottages which served as permanent lodgings for the greater number of the inn's guests. The tenants were getting to grips with the gin on the other side of the street; no one remained in the lodgings. Ned slid through the debris like a cat, stopping from time to time to listen. Eventually, the sound of voices that seemed to rise out of the ground reached his ears.

"The cellar!" he murmured.

Instead of continuing on his way, he went back several paces, and soon found himself on the very edge of the street, in front of the only section of wall that was still standing. At the base of his wall, there was a little ventilation grille. Unhesitatingly, Ned got down into the mire and laid his head at floor level, against the grille. The first words that he caught informed him that he had arrived too late and that he had missed at least a part of the conversation's revelations.

The voice that was talking was very soft—so soft that Ned took it for a woman's, in spite of the masculine sonority of certain inflections. He squinted, trying to pierce the gloom, but he could see nothing, even though the vault of the cellar was half-collapsed.

"I thought of you because you're old hands," the remarkably harmonious voice was saying.

The little clerk drew back slightly; it seemed to him that he could have touched the speaker if he had extended his arm. *Where have I heard that voice before?* he thought.

As the boxer and the ale-drinker made no reply, the mystery man continued: "Comrades, I have a job for you tonight, but for old hands you seem to be taking a long time to choose between your fortune and the gallows!"

He's threatening them, Ned Knob said to himself. *He must be a hard nut to threaten Noll Green and Lochaber Dick!*

"If we were able to work together," the beer-swiller said, "but Noll here, me there..."

"How much do we get paid?" asked the boxer.

"A hundred pounds each, cash down. Four hundred pounds in Paris, once the job's done."

In Paris! echoed the clerk. Then he added: *A thousand pounds! Why pay a thousand pounds to those two, who'd set fire to London for ten guineas?*

"It's like this, you see, sir," Noll said, reluctantly. "I've already tried to leave the country. That wretched villain Temple has men on every packet-boat now..."

"I nearly fell into a wasps' nest!" said Dick. "There's a whole pack prowling around London Bridge–it's impossible to get aboard."

"We needn't worry about London Bridge, comrades," the stranger replied, "and we need have nothing to do with packet-boats. I've a nice little boat of my own, out at Blackfriars..."

"For crossing the Channel?" the two bandits cried, as one.

"Haven't we done better than that once in our lives, out in Sydney? But it's not for crossing the Channel; it's for going down the Thames with the ebb-tide, very gently and without any trouble, as far as Exmouth,[29] beyond Greenwich. There'll be a smuggler's sloop there, which will take us on past Kent for the continent. Your passage is paid–yours, Noll, as far as Andresolle, on the far side of Calais, and yours, Dick, to the bay of Alikerque, south of Ostend... and here are passports issued by the French ambassador and the legation of the Low Countries."

Well, well! Ned said to himself. *I hope that this business is all above board!* He heard the sound of a flint being struck close at hand. A sulphur-match was touched to the tinder and burst into flame. By that sudden light, Ned caught a glimpse of his two friends with a third person, dressed in black, whose face was entirely hidden from his high vantage-point beneath the rim of a Quaker's hat.

Dick was holding a matchbox in his hand. The stranger was holding two passports in his pale and slender fingers, which he was in the process of opening up. "The descriptions," he continued, "are crafted to fit anyone in the world. Here's your way-bill, Noll, and I can assure you that you never had any as good. You're a nobleman over there, my friend, and you understand that's necessary to dress and behave accordingly... The Comte de Belcamp, you hear me?"

"The Comte de Belcamp," repeated the boxer, as a child might in committing a lesson to his head.

Ned shivered at that name, and his feline eyes brightened. *Helen Brown's husband called himself the Marquis of Belcamp!* he thought. *We had a file on him in the office.*

"Comte Henri de Belcamp," the Quaker repeated, his voice slow and distinct, "the son of a French émigré, raised in England... repeat it!"

Noll did as he was told.

"You repeat it too, Dick."

"What! The same thing?" said the astonished beer-swiller, as the Quaker handed him the second passport. "Are Noll and I to be the same man?"

"The very same," the stranger replied, calmly. "You shall be the same man."

Indeed, by the light of another match, Ned Knob could read the same name on both passports: Comte Henri de Belcamp.

The boxer and the beer-swiller repeated in unison, laboriously: "Comte Henri de Belcamp, son of a French *émigré*..."

Each of them added, with a broad smile: "That's funny!"

"I swear that I'll see the light in all this," the little clerk said to himself, feverishly. He pressed his head to the bars of the grille.

"And now?" asked the Quaker.

"The boat at Blackfriars," Noll replied.

"The smuggler at Exmouth, beyond Greenwich," added Dick.

"I go to Andresolle."

"I to the bay of Alikerque."

"There," the boozer continued, "we go our separate ways... me to..."

"All right!" the Quaker interrupted. "I'm quite certain that you won't forget the rest."

The rest, alas, was exactly what the little clerk wanted to know.

The last match went out. Ned heard the clink of gold coins.

"Not right now, I hope, Master Tom!" the boxer exclaimed.

Tom, echoed Ned. *Tom Brown*! Then, as if a ray of light had struck him: *I knew I'd heard that voice... it only remains to see the face.*

"Let's at least go back into Sharper's for five minutes," the beer-swiller went on. "Time to say a few words to Ned Knob... And we've got women..."

"On your way!" the Quaker said, imperiously.

Ned only just had time to throw himself behind a heap of debris. The three companions left the cellar through the foundations and passed by him to get out into the street. The stranger was walking between Dick and Noll, taller and leaner than either, enveloped by a black cloak whose collar was touching the rim of his hat. It was a dark night; Ned could not see his face.

They turned right at Sharper's and went down together towards the Thames, through the network of narrow streets that made the ancient district a veritable black forest. Ned, having left his hiding-place, cautiously, followed them at a distance of 20 or 30 paces.

There were a few whispered exchanges between the three companions as they went on their way. As they reached the riverbank at Blackfriars, at the end of a dark and narrow alley, Ned–who had drawn a fraction closer, sliding along the walls–caught a few words.

"What good's a letter, since we don't know how to read?"

"The letter will contain nothing but a blank sheet of paper," the Quaker replied, "but it will speak for itself. When you receive it, this is what it will mean: tonight, between ten o'clock and midnight!"

"And until then?"

"Have a good time, and wait."

The Quaker, taking the lead, followed the shoreline, which was cluttered with vessels of every sort, from monumentally heavy barges to light skiffs that skimmed the surface without leaving any wake, built to carry fur-clad pleasure-seekers to Richmond.

The man with the big hat soon descended one of the black staircases leading down to the water, and opened a padlock securing the chain of a sleek fishing-boat, its oars at the ready.

The tide was going out. Noll and Dick climbed into the boat. "Comte Henri de Belcamp!" they said in unison, one more time.

"And don't make a move until you receive the blank letter."

"Understood. See you soon!"

"In Paris, at the appointed place," the Quaker replied, waving goodbye to them. "Bon voyage!"

The boat was already slipping her moorings, moving out into the stream. The Quaker calmly climbed back up the steps. Ned tried to catch a glimpse of him, at the moment when he was face on, but the banks of the Thames are not lit like the banks of the Seine, and there was still the huge hat and the cloak.

If I have to follow you all the way to Hell, Ned said to himself, furiously, *I'll see your face!*

Instead of going back into the side street, the Quaker went on towards the bridge. At the corner of the wharf, an elegant tilbury was parked, guarded by a very pale and seemingly melancholy young man. The Quaker jumped into the interior, and the enthusiastic horse struck sparks with all four shoes, leaving the bewildered clerk behind on the bank.

"Richard," said he whom we have been calling the Quaker to the pale young man who held the reins, "it's too dangerous for you to stay in London any longer."

The reins quivered in the young man's hands as he replied: "Have you found out anything new, then, James?"

"I've labored on your behalf all day, Richard, and God is witness to my belief that you are innocent, in spite of the appearances stacked against you."

"Bless you, and may Heaven reward you, my generous friend!"

"But everything is against you, my poor Thompson; there's nothing in la Bartolozzi's papers acknowledging the debt owed by your mother, Fanny Thompson. It's absolutely necessary that you flee."

"Without seeing Suzanne again!" stammered the young man, his head dipping towards his breast as his hands dropped the reins.

"Be a man, Richard!" said the Quaker, taking the reins and stopping the carriage at the entrance to a house of modest appearance, situated at the end of the Strand, over whose door was a brass plaque bearing the words: *Office of Mr. Wood*. "We're the same height and the same age; our hair and beards are the same color. You know that my purse is at your disposal. I'll give you my own papers, if necessary... and you can count on me to look after your child!"

Richard Thompson embraced him, tears in his eyes, and raised the knocker of the house with the brass plaque.

A single stroke of the whip set the horse in motion; the tilbury set out again along the road. It turned at Charing Cross and then went along Piccadilly. Beyond Hyde Park Corner, between the hospital and Cadogan Square,[30] stood a newly-constructed building topped by a pyramidal appendage of a kind more common nowadays than it was in those days: a steam vent. The edifice was large and opulent in appearance; it might have accommodated some considerable industrial enterprise. At the front, under an illuminated clock-face, the name of its owner shone in letters of gold: *Percy Balcomb & Co.*

The Quaker jumped down to the pavement.

In London, every visitor advertises his social status in advance by the way he employs a door-knocker; there is a scale that everyone knows, without being aware of it, which descends in tones and semitones from the fulgurant appeal of His Grace the Duke to the hesitant scratching of the poor thing who comes to ask for sixpence. The Quaker's knock was clear, curt and imperious.

The door soon opened. The Quaker was introduced into a workroom, as vast as a dining-hall, where several tables were covered in plans and designs. On the desk that occupied the center of the room, several letters addressed to Percy Balcomb & Co. were still sealed, awaiting the attention of their addressee.

The Quaker opened the envelopes. He glanced over every letter, then rang a bell. A gentleman appeared at the threshold of a side-door.

"Is there any news, Perkins?" the Quaker asked

"Nothing good, milord. The engineers are opposed to my 800-horse-power engine, saying that it's just as impossible as building the Tower of Babel."

"Are you sure of yourself, Perkins?"

"Yes, milord."

"Then let the engineers say what they will, and hire the very best workmen in London."

"The engineers want to know if your lordship intends to equip a war-fleet..."

The Quaker smiled gravely as he interrupted. "Have you news from the African coast?"

"Yes, milord. Some progress is being made on the River Congo, but it's necessary that the wood be brought from the interior, and the local blacks are troublesome. To make the ship—a top-of-the range frigate, of the sort your lordship dreams of commanding—will cost half as much again from an American slipway."

"And Mobile's response?"

"Exactly that! The Yankees are always eager to make money. We have the estimates, in pounds, shillings and pence, for all the armaments, from the 48 cannons to the grappling-hooks. The three brigs are on the slipway... you'll have four million to pay in June, milord."

"We're on schedule, Perkins."

"And four million more in July, if you place the order in the Congo."

"I've placed the order, Perkins, and I'll pay."

The gentleman bowed. "Milord," he went on, "we have to put down 3,500 pounds on account, this week."

The Quaker reopened one of the letters that were scattered on the table and took some bills therefrom, which he studied. "Here's 38,000 Austrian florins from Rothschild," he said.

"From Prague?" Perkins murmured. "With the money you've had from Prague these last 12 months, you could have made a million sterling by constructing 100 or a 150 engines for sale."

The Quaker got up and extended his hand to the gentleman.

"We've come a long way, Perkins," he said. "We have even further to go. Percy Balcomb & Co. wasn't founded to make a million sterling..."

An hour or so later, James Davy, wearing the modest and elegant costume in which we saw him at police headquarters, was climbing the softly-carpeted stairs of the Buckingham Hotel in Grosvenor Square. A liveried valet was waiting for him at the door of the principal apartment on the first floor.

The proprietor of the hotel, in full evening-dress, followed him in, with a register bound in red leather under his arm.

"Monsieur le Comte will surely accept my excuses," he said, in French. "I shall be particularly honored to have your name in my register. England is a free country, thank God, but this Gregory Temple, the Superintendent of Police, pays scant attention to the constitution, and he demands inspection of the passports of all travelers from abroad, since this unfortunate business of Signora Bartolozzi."

James Davy immediately took out his wallet and offered his fully-stamped passport to the hotel-proprietor. While the other was unfolding the paper, he took up a pen and wrote in the register: Comte Henri de Belcamp.

"Comte Henri de Belcamp!" the hotel-proprietor read aloud from the head of the passport. "My thanks to your lordship." He bowed and went out after receiving an order—directly from his lordship—that soup should be served in the room of Madame the Comtesse de Belcamp.

His lordship then crossed the room and entered the magnificent bedchamber of Madame la Comtesse. In the depths of the bed-alcove, among the waves

of lace that were blooming around the pillow, he saw the charming black-haired
head and smiling face of the beautiful Irishwoman, Sarah O'Neil.

Part One: The Chateau de Belcamp

I. The Charabanc

We have crossed the Channel, leaving London and its lugubrious follies far behind. It isn't dust on one's shoes that one shakes off in quitting the English capital;[31] 20,000 brooms and 300 laborers work incessantly upon its filth without ever scouring it clean. Besides, thanks to the happy importation of tarmacadam, Paris has been acquainted for five years with the splendid mud that seems inherent on the shores of the Thames; our boulevards, entombed beneath their honest coatings, are returning to the moat-like state of their infancy, triumphantly defending–in spite of an impotent army of sweepers–the Paris of Notre-Dame, the Bourse and the Tuileries against that other Paris which is ten paces, but a hundred leagues, away on the opposite bank of the great yellow river.

At the moment when our history resumes, we are no more in Paris than in London; it is a pleasant countryside on the banks of the Oise, three hours from the Opera in a rickety cart, that brightens before our eyes in the joyous sunlight of the first days of May. We ask permission not to reveal the actual name of this tranquil region, which will be the theater of a violent drama. Although some of the actors in this drama are dead, others–thank God–are still full of life, and even the dead are still honored and respected by their families.

It was eight o'clock in the morning. A horseman, dressed in an elegant hunting-costume over which a light cloak was draped, was galloping on a handsome English mare along the road from Paris to l'Isle-Adam. The horseman seemed very young: curly blond hair framed his handsome face, and the horse's motion brought out the suppleness of his graceful form. At first glance, one would have thought him scarcely 20 years old, but his calm and profound expression suggested more.

The air was fresh. The morning wind was sighing in the still-defoliated branches of the tall trees, whose forest perfume was returning, while it stirred the brambles garlanding the long hedgerows, which were already in leaf, and shook snowy blossom from the rounded apple-trees on to the hopeful vines beneath. There was not a single cloud in the blue vault of the sky, but in the depths of the grey valleys that made bizarre and capricious circuits around the hills white mists, as light and transparent as the veil that hides the smile of a young bride, rolled before the breeze, altering their position and level at every instant, bathing, covering and re-exposing the low-lying ground. Sometimes, when there were stronger gusts of wind, a gleaming meadow would suddenly display its green carpet or a pond its rippling silver surface.

Everything, as you know, is seductive in the paradise of the banks of the Oise, where one can find beautiful rocks, peaceful grass and waters that are still and foaming at the same time—and ancient chateaux, the pride of the country, and quiet forests, offering refuges for thought.

Two leagues from Saint-Leu-Taverny, not far from a village that we shall call Miremont for reasons of discretion, the road that runs through the forest comes to a goose-foot junction, where six hunting-paths meet, not counting the main thoroughfare. There is a sturdy signpost at the center of this star, but—as is the custom of signposts—it indicates precisely nothing. Our young stranger made a tour of the post, trying in vain to decipher inscriptions effaced by time and the rain; only two names still stood out: Paris and l'Isle-Adam.

"It must be on the right," he thought, turning towards the north-east, "but there are two paths going in that direction, and to judge by the angles at which they are set, either of them might lead me astray. Hold on."

He released his mount's bridle. The noble animal, rather than grazing—for the grass was thick on the side of the road—kept her head high, a certain sign of irreproachable education. It was a fair bet that the traveler's patience would not be severely tested, because he had passed a number of carts and pedestrians on the road—but he had no need to wait for a waggoner's cart, clad in canvas and hooped like an enormous barrel, to appear over the brow of the hill. The sound of wheels, mingled with merry chatter and bursts of laughter, was audible in the trees to the left of the road. An instant afterwards, a charabanc carrying three young girls was disgorged into the goose-foot, hurtling across it like a whirl-wind. The traveler raised his hat and opened his mouth to speak, but there was no time; three pretty smiling faces greeted him, responding to his gesture, and the charabanc, drawn by a horse whose mane and tail were flying, vanished at the gallop into one of the hunting-paths.

More hoofbeats sounded under the trees and more bursts of laughter. This time, it was three young men who arrived, pushing and whipping three stubborn farm-horses covered in sweat, which could go no faster.

"Hey, Monsieur!" shouted one of them, when he perceived our traveler. "Which way did they go?" It was a tall fellow with an alert attitude, who had something military in his bearing. One could not say that his was an old mous-tache, for he could not have been more than 25 years old, but since the end of the century we have become used to seeing many young men sporting whiskers. Every revolution, like every restoration, has its victors and its vanquished. Our fine fellow was a victim, even though he did not give that appearance; he had been a sub-lieutenant in the old army, and merited the title of "brigand of the Loire," as well as many others. For the moment, he was a law student; his name was Robert Surrisy.

The two others followed, clip-clop, at a distance of a few paces. The first of them was a strong and handsome young man with black curly hair and a proud and intelligent face, whose symmetrical features were as melancholy as

Robert's were cheerful. Indeed, he and Surrisy appeared to be perfect and vivid counterparts in every way; Robert seemed to have the monopoly on boldness and insouciance, leaving meditation and timidity to his friend, Laurent Herbet–for they were fast friends, intimate and inseparable. Laurent was a medical student.

The third rider, mounted on a pony that looked like a donkey, was simply Férandeau, a pupil of Louis David, the painter of history, to whom human injustice had so far refused the Grand Prix du Rome.[32] He produced little work, but he had faith in his artistic talent in spite of the unanimity of contrary opinion. He was not exactly handsome, nor well-built, but his appearance made an agreeable impression because of the irrepressible good humor enthroned in his face. The expression of his clear and smiling eyes, separated by the bridge of his excessive nose; his vastly wide grin, exposing gleaming white teeth; his colorless hair, as thick and unruly as a virgin forest; his clothing–a vestment whose name changes over time but which is peculiar to painters who slave away without result–everything in him and about him, in fact, had a homogeneous color that was unfashionable, candid and intellectually myopic. Férandeau could see no further than the end of his nose, which was large but narrow.

That was the entire company at the moment when the charabanc full of girls vanished into the woods, but while we were describing our three friends a fourth person appeared and came into the goose-foot in his turn.

If Férandeau's pony resembled a donkey, Briquet's donkey was a veritable goat. Briquet was also called Bricole, or Trompe-d'Eustache.[33] All three were improvised names, for he had no family name; he had been found, barely an hour old, in the corner of an artist's studio following the departure of a model–a fact of which he was neither proud nor embarrassed. Having been born in a studio, and the studio being situated in the Rue de l'Ouest, facing the Luxembourg Gardens, he was incontestably a Parisian, and that title was sufficient glory for him. He did not hide from anyone the fact that he would not have been able to bear the bitter indignity of a departmental origin.

Briquet, Bricole or Trompe-d'Eustache, had the honor of being manservant to Laurent and Robert, while simultaneously being a student of Férandeau's–currently his entire school. When necessity demanded, he also served the association as cook. He was a little chap, thin but wiry, as lazy as a lizard but capable of heroic bursts of effort. He was very timid, but as impudent as a demon when the devil was in him; as abstemious as a desert camel in times of famine, but known to gnaw a leg of mutton down to the bone after dinner if someone were kind enough to provide one. In sum, he was a cheeky monkey, but a devoted one.

In response to Robert's question, our young traveler pointed to the path that the charabanc had taken. "By way of returning the favor, my dear Monsieur," he added, forthrightly and courteously, "I should like to know which road leads to the Chateau de Belcamp–I'm a stranger in these parts."

Robert, the head of whose horse had already passed through the goose-foot, pulled the bridle to tighten the bit. The others halted at the same time, all looking at the stranger with sudden curiosity. If one can believe the German proverb that says that a bad conscience fears inspection, the young stranger must have had a good and clear conscience, for the gazes turned upon him elicited nothing but a pleasant smile.

Robert and Laurent blushed at the same time, and the former said: "Pardon us, Monsieur, if we are slow to reply. A thought has struck us all at the same time... at least, I presume my comrades have the same idea. Our honorable friend the Marquis de Belcamp is awaiting his son... but that's not a question addressed to you, Monsieur, and as far as the path from the Croix-Moraine, where we are at present, to Miremont is concerned, it's the one you have just indicated to us."

The young traveler raised his hat for the second time. "I am happy, Messieurs," he said, in a voice remarkable for its sonorous softness and harmony, "to discover three friends of my beloved father as soon as I have set foot on the land that was the cradle of my ancestors."

"You are Comte Henri de Belcamp!" cried Robert, his eyes shining with a singular brightness.

Laurent already had the young traveler's hand in his own.

"Well, well!" said Férandeau. "What a turn-up! If your mare has foals, you know, I'll be your academy in return for one."

"Here, Monsieur le Comte," said Robert, who had taken a hand in his turn to shake it warmly, "search as you may, you will not find a single human being who is not devoted, body and soul, to the brave Marquis de Belcamp!"

"I thank you, Monsieur," said the young Comte, with feeling. "I know that my father has a noble heart but I dread, after so long an absence–for his exile lasted 24 years, and I was born in England–I dread, as I say, that political schisms..."

"I would fight for Napoleon tomorrow if it were possible!" Robert put in. "One can say that hereabouts, without objection, even before you, who wear your loyalty to your father in your face. You know that Monsieur le Marquis is ever-ready to die, anywhere, for his King... oh well, I believe it would require the Devil himself to turn the point of my sword against anyone with a drop of Belcamp blood in his veins. Ask him whether he, too, would not spare his brigand, as he calls me. Anyhow, our charming birds have had the time to take flight, and we shall not catch them now. Monsieur le Comte, would you like us to be your guides?"

"I accept wholeheartedly, Messieurs."

Briquet had dismounted to engrave his signature on the signpost with a five-*sou* knife he had bought with his savings. Férandeau took a turn around the English horse, examining the rider after making a close study of his mount.

"Fine linen," he murmured. "If he's bringing foreign coin to the old man, that won't inconvenience him!"

The cavalcade continued on its way.

"Messieurs," said Comte Henri, with his benevolent smile and his truly heart-warming voice, "tell me about my father, I beg you. I'm returning from a greater distance than you might think–from the far side of the world, to tell the truth–and I'm counting on you to fill me in on this place, which I shall love henceforth."

"It isn't Paris... or Peru," Briquet muttered, bestriding his little donkey.

"Monsieur le Marquis returned here three years ago, as you know," replied Robert, who served as spokesman, "When he arrived, he wanted to do as much as possible in a hurry, since his affairs were in some disorder. But what would we think of Providence if she deserted men like him? I don't understand business very well, or I'd be able to explain. The land has increased in value; he has sold some off very advantageously; in brief, you will one day be an heir...if you have no objection? If you've made a fortune in the Indies, so much the better; I would like your father to be surrounded by smiles and good fortune! Since we have met in advance, I should like to say, Monsieur le Comte, that he has been very anxious about you."

Robert was riding the least awful of the three farm-horses. He and the stranger had gained ground without parting company; meanwhile, Laurent kept company with Férandeau fifty paces behind, while Briquet formed a rearguard a further 50 paces distant.

"He's a schemer, that Robert," said Férandeau. "By this evening, he'll be on intimate terms with this story-book hero newly arrived from the antipodes. A handsome chap, all the same, whose cloak hangs well."

"He resembles his father," observed Laurent, always the dreamer. "Strangely enough, although I like his father very much, I don't feel the least attraction to him."

"A question of sentiment, old man. Sympathies are like secret knots. Personally, I'd be happy to accept a few valueless curios from him, such as Iroquois tomahawks, Malay daggers or Chinese lanterns. I once got four packets of cigars for a Patagonian fan. Apart from the gifts he might heap upon me, the young man inspires in me the kind of calm disinterest that one expresses in saying: I don't give a hoot."

"You take that attitude to everything, and you're quite happy!" Laurent murmured. "Myself, I don't look at the world through rose-colored spectacles. Robert worries me; Robert has a secret..."

"That's a laugh!" the artist put in. "He loves Jeanne."

"That's not it. Robert was hiding something from me, even in London."

"That's not possible!"

"Robert's been to Paris twice..."

"Without asking your permission! There's a thing! I'd be off like a shot if I could afford it."

"His old mother, Madeleine, is poor and Robert has no savings," Laurent Herbet thought aloud.

At that very moment, Robert was saying: "My God! Yes, I looked for you in London. We were there, Laurent and I, in connection with a most unfortunate and extraordinary affair, of which you might have heard tell–the murder of Madame Bartolozzi..." As he pronounced that name, he turned a frank and open but singularly penetrating gaze upon his companion.

Comte Henri's horse dipped her head, as if the bit had started suddenly between her teeth, but the rider's face remained impassive and his tone was cool as he replied. "Indeed–everyone was talking about the tragic event while I was in England."

"You are destined to become acquainted with all our histories, Monsieur le Comte," Robert went on. "I have not always been an old law student, and my first vocation did not draw me towards the five codes. Monsieur le Marquis is our adviser, and there is nothing he does not know about our petty affairs. He will tell you that Laurent Herbet, that dear boy behind us, had an interest in that bloody adventure, as had his sister Jeanne. I went with him merely as a strong arm and a good head in case anything went wrong. London was entirely unknown to us, and your father was kind enough to give us an introduction to the famous Gregory Temple, the Chief Superintendent of Police, whom he got to know well while he was in exile. That worked out badly for us; poor Monsieur Temple was completely wrapped up in the Bartolozzi affair, but from another viewpoint than ours, and his mind was already reeling under the impossibility of solving the puzzle... do you know that he went mad?"

"I have had the honor of meeting the eminent man of law myself," said the young Comte, in whom an attentive examination might have revealed a certain successfully-suppressed unease, "but I have not seen him since his resignation and did not know of his illness."

"You met him!" Robert exclaimed, in astonishment. "He told us, when we told him about the anxieties of Monsieur le Marquis as to your whereabouts, that he had no knowledge of your existence!"

Comte Henri touched his forehead with the gloved tip of his finger, but this significant gesture was not the only explanation he offered. "My dear Monsieur," he added, "you are also probably destined to become acquainted with my biography. It is fundamentally simple, but surrounded with details that might seem romantic. There was a time when I served interests that were not those of the English government."

This time, Robert did not look at him. His facial expression changed, and a question rose to his lips, but he suppressed it and said, in a light tone: "Did you also make the acquaintance of Suzanne Temple, the Superintendent's daughter? She was in that charabanc just now...

"I have never had the honor of being introduced to Miss Temple," Comte Henri replied, calmly. Then he added, in that courteous tone that signifies throughout the world the most perfect indifference: "Miss Temple is staying in the neighborhood?"

"Miss Temple is staying at the Chateau de Belcamp," Robert replied.

"And her father?" the young Comte asked, his lip quivering imperceptibly.

"Her father is God knows where–perhaps in London, perhaps in Paris. His madness is not the kind that requires his sequestration. He is obsessive; he drives himself incessantly; he searches..."

"He sometimes comes to visit his daughter at the chateau?"

"Never."

Mental agitation is difficult to conceal, especially in the intimate and unchanging circumstances of an indoor meeting–but in the open air, when the body is in motion, the play of the features has a thousand pretexts. Across a hearth, Robert Surrisy might perhaps have divined the anxiety of his companion, in spite of his admirable self-possession–the young and forthright soldier appeared to be a curious and clear-sighted fellow–but he certainly saw nothing here. At least, he offered his excuses to Henri for having allowed the conversation to stray from matters directly concerning the Marquis de Belcamp.

"Hey!" called Férandeau. "You're missing the viewpoint!"

Comte Henri immediately reined in. All trace of preoccupation had vanished from his face, and it was with a clear expression of satisfaction that he looked out over the pleasant panorama extended before him.

The hunting-path was crossing a heath that formed the eastern extremity of the highest plateau in the region, which was nicknamed "Little Switzerland" although it deserved better. "Little Switzerland" clearly implies a comic opera landscape of waterfalls, chalets with tiled roofs and singing girls named Ketly hesitating between the naive affection of Wilhem and the raw adoration of Max, who meet beneath the dark vault to settle their differences to the tune of the *ranz-des-vaches*.[34] I know nothing more offensive than that abusive caricature; the Swiss are the brave sons of William Tell. They will march on Paris one day to set fire to the Opéra-Comique. There was not a single chalet here, I swear, nor a single Ketly, for all the local girls had honest names like Fanchon, Monique or Madeleine.

The forest, opening out like a fan, displayed three-quarters of the horizon through two large open spaces. We shall concern ourselves only with the estate that ran towards the north-east, because the rest is irrelevant to the scenes of our drama and utility is the only excuse for description in our Age of Iron.

The path descended the precipitous slope of the plateau–which seemed to fall suddenly away into the valley–so tortuously that it was hidden 20 times over behind thickets of birches, chestnuts and oaks. To the left and the right, the heath stretched away like a perforated carpet, pink and yellow set against earth the color of ash. The two wings of the fan that framed the scene to either side were groves of enormous beeches, shaped by recent felling into straight and symmetrical lines.

The lower plane was dominated by the Oise. One arm of the river, narrow and bordered by willows, ran by a mill to empty into a pond, while the main course, slowing down as it crossed the plain, glistened beneath the precocious foliage of alders, and sparkled among rich crops of sword-lilies.

A bridge was directly in front of them–an ancient stone bridge, with the miller's cottage close by, its thatched roof as grassy as a meadow and its wet black wheel incessantly wailing the two notes of its melancholy song. Beyond the bridge the outflow, also singing, threw forth its foamy turbulence.

The valley was separated in two like a river with an island in mid-course. At the center, facing our viewpoint, a marvelously uneven hill reared up. Trimmed and cultured hedges climbed around and around its slopes, arrayed like the steps of a verdant calvary between copses whose round saplings extended their tufted wigs and jutting rocks. At the very summit, in a clearing, there was a windmill with neither roof nor sails, like the last remaining tower of some ancient ruined manor.

The hill extended a gentler slope to the north, as far as a grove of noble oaks planted in alternating rows, which covered a large plateau halfway down. The grove was face-on, extending two large arms at whose center, preceded by an avenue of ten ranks of hundred-year-old elms, stood a chateau built in the time of Henri IV.[35] The north part of the plateau, where the manor stood, was terraced, dominating the surrounding estate. Beneath the terrace, a graceful village, guarded by its bell-tower and long blue spire, displayed all of its houses but the outermost, which were hidden in the valley floor.

The Oise ran happily through the meadows where huge cows were going slowly about their business, widely dispersed and proud of their solitude, amid flocks of sheep compressed and herded by anxious dogs. In the distance, large meres were visible and yet more woodlands. On the slope facing the hill on the other side of the river there was a modern park, dominated by a small new chateau, the Chateau-Neuf, built in the English style, surrounded by groups of large trees and well-manicured velvety lawns.

At the time of writing, this place is still a paradise, although Parisian taste has already occasioned the construction there of a few delightful villas, which have exactly the same effect in that countryside as flies floating in milk–but the other way around, needless to say, faded and white as they are among the rich tones of the verdure.

Robert, after a few minutes silence, extended his arm to point to the old chateau, whose roof, still moist with dew, was glistening in the sunlight.

"Monsieur le Comte," he said, "there is your father's house."

At first, Comte Henri de Belcamp contemplated this landscape–which is the pride of the countryside surrounding Paris, so generously fertile and picturesque–with an appreciative eye. His gaze roamed back and forth between the twin valleys, and then returned to the pleasant hill where Robert Surrisy was recommending the paternal home to his admiration and affection with such benevolent bombast. He saluted his father's house, smiling–but Robert, who was watching him, searched in vain for any sign of emotion in his face.

Laurent and Férandeau caught them up. Laurent had heard Robert's last words–"there is your father's house"–and the instinctive prejudice roused in him against the young Comte were further enhanced, for he saw nothing but coldness in Henri's distracted eyes.

That one has no heart! he thought.

"That's a pretty scene out there," said Férandeau, reining in his mount, which flattened out its long ears and set about browsing noisily. "There's a Claude Lorrain to be made of the far side, an hour before sunset. Look at the road that climbs and snakes from the mill to the chateau. If it weren't unworthy of one of David's principal pupils to abandon the Academy to paint trees and old walls..." Then he added, in an alarmed tone: "I'll be damned, though, if they aren't about to break their necks!"

Halfway up the slope, at a turn in the road that narrowly bordered the prettiest precipice in the world, the charabanc carrying the three young women was climbing the road to the chateau. From a distance, it did indeed seem to be balanced on the edge of the abyss.

"It's Jeanne who's driving," Robert told him. "There's nothing to fear."

"The danger seems imminent from here," the young Comte observed.

"It's Jeanne who's driving," repeated the former Sub-Lieutenant, calmly. Then, turning towards Laurent, who did not seem as completely reassured as he was, he murmured: "The silly things won't prove me wrong."

"You shouldn't have left the charabanc," Laurent replied.

"Comte," said Robert, "I appoint you the judge. I was with three demons in there. This sister of Brother Tranquil here"–he pointed to Laurent–"is three times as mischievous as the other two, and in all probability you are destined to suffer, as we all do, the caprices and devilments of Mademoiselle Jeanne. Laurent, Férandeau and Briquet mounted the three horses. On the long slope a quarter of a league from Pontoise, we found Mignot's little donkey wandering in the wood. Jeanne said to me: 'Aren't you ashamed to overload our poor Cabri like this?' Cabri is the dapple-grey pulling the charabanc. I got down, and Bricole got hold of the donkey to take him back to Mignot. It was agreed that I should walk at the head of the team, but all that was nothing but a conspiracy. The girls wanted to go on by themselves–or, rather, Mademoiselle Jeanne wanted to take them... and the fact is that she has a fine skill. Before I even had my foot in the stirrup, all three cried out together: 'Giddy-up, Cabri!' We were at the top of the Moraine rise. Cabri's like them; he's always ready for mischief. He went off like a hare. They passed close to you, didn't they? You know how fast they were going. We tried to go after them–and the end of the story is that they're still going, as you can see!"

His extended arm pointed to the charabanc, which maintained its merry trot in spite of the steepness of the slope. In the bright sunlight the young women's frocks were clearly visible: two pale and one black.

"The fact is," said the Comte, "that Cabri, from the little I've seen of him, is worth three of Bucephalus...[36] but the danger's past. Let's go on."

The charabanc disappeared behind a mossy rock crowned with misshapen hornbeams, whose grey and vigorous trunks overhung a green cornfield. Henri and the former Sub-Lieutenant began the company's descent, while Laurent and Férandeau remained behind, watching Briquet carve his name into a beech. This was Briquet's hobby: he inscribed his signature everywhere, so that he might one day be famous. The name of Briquet did not belong to any authentic title, and if it had been the property of some powerful family, he would have carved the name Bricole instead. Had the name Bricole designated in its turn some feudal and jealous race, Trompe-d'Eustache would still have remained to him–but what a shame!

"Do you realize, Monsieur le Comte," Robert continued, controlling his horse by the strength of his arms during the rapid descent, "that this whole story was to do with you? It's for your sake that we went to Pontoise today, so early in the morning."

"For my sake?" Henri echoed, astonished.

"For your father's sake, at any rate–it's all one, I suppose... it's his birthday in a few days time..."

"That's right! Saint-Honoré's Day!"[37]

"The sixteenth of the month. It's a long time since you've celebrated it."

"A very long time," murmured the young traveler.

"You shall have your revenge. The rest of us celebrate it every year, and everyone does their utmost to make the best of it. Now, Mademoiselle Jeanne, who is his favorite, got it into her head that it was necessary to let off fireworks this year, on the esplanade in front of the chateau. The idea took off, as all Mademoiselle Jeanne's proposals do... and this was the third trip we've made to Pontoise, our capital, to buy the explosives and apparatus necessary to bring Mademoiselle Jeanne's idea to fruition. The charabanc that you saw pass by is full of rockets, roman candles, sparklers and squibs, like an artillery-chest. There is even a new powder the artificer calls fulminate of mercury,[38] which is said to produce the most curious effects."

"Its use isn't without danger," the Comte said. "In England, where it's already used for priming hunting-rifles, the most careful preparations have to be taken."

"Ours is well wrapped in paper. Hold on! There's the charabanc, stopping up there, under the platform. Suzanne and Germaine are getting down–they're two lovely little dears. Mademoiselle Jeanne's remaining on board by herself, so that she can go across the bridge to deposit this morning's purchases in the arsenal, which is in the cottage of the Chateau-Neuf's lodgekeeper, down there on the left. Steady! There's a good view of the Chateau-Neuf from here; it's a nice house. It's been let–a lawyer from Paris came to visit a few days ago... He mentioned an Englishwoman. So much the better! The more neighbors one has, the more dances there are... and Mademoiselle Jeanne loves to dance. Monsieur le Comte, if you have good eyes, you can see that Mademoiselle Jeanne is even prettier than her companions."

They were halfway down the hill, having come to a halt on a narrow border where the road turned around a rock, which had the semblance of the balcony of a Flemish turret above the river. The hill that we have described was clearly visible from there, between the leafless branches of an old beech, and the farewells of the young women were taking place a few hundred paces away.

"You called her Mademoiselle Jeanne Herbet?" said the Comte de Belcamp.

"You remembered her name," the former Sub-Lieutenant replied, with naive gratitude. "She's even better than she's pretty, and if God owes anyone down here the favor of Heaven, it's her." Robert went on first, because he wanted to hide the emotion that might betray the secret of his heart.

Henri directed one last glance, coldly and indifferently, towards the three young women. "You said something at one point that excited my curiosity..." he said, tentatively.

"I noticed that," Robert interrupted him. "It was the Bartolozzi affair, wasn't it? You're asking yourself what connection there is between those two youngsters, Jeanne and Laurent, and the celebrated Italian singer whose career was so tragically cut short. Ordinarily, I would not tell this to someone I had just met, but your father is our confessor. In London, as in Paris, Italian names contribute a good deal to the success of chanteuses, but Madame Bartolozzi was born in the village that you see beneath the chateau; her real name was Constance Herbet."

If the two companions had been level with one another, Robert could not have helped, this time, noticing the strange expression that suddenly darkened the young Comte's face–but the road was narrow; there was only room for one horse. Henri, who was in the rear, exerted a violent effort of self-control. "I understand," he said, in a voice that he succeeded in making calm. "Madame Bartolozzi is a relative of theirs."

"Yes... a relative," said the former Sub-Lieutenant, in a low voice, "and more than that."

"Their mother?"

"Jeanne knows nothing about it," Robert hastened to say. "Constance Herbet intended to return here, after retiring from the stage, to live honestly on her pension..."

Comte Henri's head was bowed and his brow was deeply furrowed.

At that moment, a dry and brittle explosion echoed through the trees that now, because they had descended so much further, hid the other bank of the Oise more completely. A cry followed the explosion, coming from the same direction. At the same time, a much louder cry–a cry of terrible anguish, emanating from the breast of a man–came from the place where our two riders had just been standing together. Then came rapid whistling noises, confused and intermingled with the brief and vibrationless explosions that accompany a firework display.

Robert struck his horse about the ears with the riding-crop he held in his hand. The pain made the poor beast jump, and launched it into a desperate jolting gallop. Henri whistled softly; his mare immediately followed suit.

There are cascades of events so rapid that the pen cannot communicate their amazing suddenness. It did not require ten seconds to accomplish that which I would not be able to write in an hour, for you to read in two minutes.

The cries and the detonations continued. Laurent, who had a full view, howled in a lamentable voice: "My sister! My sister! Help her, in the name of God!"

Robert and Henri arrived simultaneously at the elbow where the road, abruptly broadening out, descended a gentle slope to the bridge that it crossed to join the road ascending the opposite slope. A terrifying spectacle was offered to their eyes.

As they had both guessed, it was the fireworks contained in the charabanc that had ignited–but there was also the raging horse, maddened by the noise, the heat and the smoke. Cabri was descending the slope in convulsive bounds, his eyes aflame, his nostrils flared and his mane bristling.

There was the fire too, which had spread with frightful rapidity to the young woman's clothing.

She was leaning over the guardrail, livid with astonishment, but she still conserved something of her innate intrepidity and was holding tightly to the reins. The hem of her mourning-dress was already aflame and smoking. Her marvelous beauty was strangely exaggerated by the terrible backcloth, compounded of tormented flames, flashes, scintillant showers and furious whirlwinds of vapor.

At each end of the bridge, which was just large enough to permit the passage of an ordinary carriage, there were two stout corner-posts–or, rather, two portions of uncarved rock. That was the most immediate deadly danger: Jeanne was likely to be smashed into pieces before being burned or drowned.

A dry rattle escaped Robert's throat. He stood upright in his stirrups, and blood jetted from the ears of his horse.

"Hup! Hup! Hup!" Comte Henri said, for the third time, in a low voice. The mare stretched herself, hollowing out her supple back and bringing her belly to the level of the grass. You have doubtless seen, on stormy days, a swallow skimming the ground.

Robert was still halfway down the road when Comte Henri had already crossed the bridge. Henri stopped the mare with a single word and jumped down to the grass on the right of the path. No one had even seen him touch his saddle-bag, but at the moment his foot touched the ground–as the charabanc arrived, hurtling like a stone cast down from a mountain top–a flame erupted from his hand and a shot rang out.

Cabri collapsed like a stone, his muzzle against the boundary-post, in a pool of blood.

Henri threw away his weapon, seized Jeanne–who seemed to be enshrouded in flame–around the waist, and hurled himself, with her in his arms, into the turbulent foam of the outflow from the mill.

Robert and Laurent were already leaning over the parapet of the bridge, their avid eyes probing the foam, desperate for knowledge. Every second seemed to last an hour, but Comte Henri and Jeanne certainly remained under the water far longer than is normal after such a plunge. There is a natural law that regulates the return of immersed bodies to the surfaces; swimming movements hasten the process, but cannot override it. To slow it down requires a material object, an increase in weight, or an effort to dive further down. None but the eye of God could penetrate the mystery of the delay.

Finally, Jeanne and her savior reappeared–a long way from the bridge, because they had had been forced to give way to the force of the current. Jeanne had lost consciousness, but Henri kept her head above water while swimming vigorously towards the bank.

The shortest way back to solid ground was around the mill and along the stream to the point at which it rejoined the current that emptied into the pond, where there was a mound of alluvium planted with willows. The young Comte laid Jeanne down upon the grass. She was half-naked, because the flames had consumed the lower part of her mourning-dress, her puffed-out sleeves and the veil that floated behind her straw hat. She looked, therefore, as if she were dead.

Henri was alone with her; the thick branches of the willows screened them from other eyes. For an instant, here as at the bottom of the stream, Henri had only to take account of the ever-open celestial eye that plumbs the innermost secrets of our conscience.

These are strange words; ordinarily, one only pronounces them when a crime is imminent–and this man, to the contrary, had saved this woman three times over: from the rock, the fire and the water. Even so, just for a moment, Henri's features presented an aspect even stranger than our words. For a moment, while the footsteps of those who were running towards them were still muffled by distance, Comte Henri's implacable and somber face had been frightful to behold. He was kneeling beside the inanimate Jeanne, his left hand supporting the nape of her neck, while his right thumb was touching the exact point on the throat where the corpse of Constance Bartolozzi had displayed the slight blemish as to whose cause the three surgeons of the Royal College had been unable to agree.

And Comte Henri was in the same position that Sarah O'Neil had ascribed to the false Prince Alexis Orloff, leaning over the sleeping Bartolozzi on the night of the murder.

The footsteps were drawing nearer–but how much time had John Devil needed to turn that woman's sleep into death? Jeanne was also asleep, even more deeply...

Comte Henri heard the approaching feet, and his stony smile seemed to say: I have the time; a single second would suffice to accomplish my task.

She was 17 years old. The turbulence of the waterfall had disarranged her hair. Her black tresses streamed from her temples to her shoulders and from her shoulders to the grass; her eyelids were half-open, fringed with silky lashes. Her oval face was delicately formed and a delightful smile was perceptible on her innocent mouth. The pure lines of her body, interrupted by the tatters of her mourning-dress, displayed the chaste and juvenile grace of its contours; her two white hands were crossed upon her breast. She was as beautiful as a saint, and as beautiful as love itself.

Comte Henri slowly abandoned the posture that the assassin had adopted on the night of the third of February at the head of his victim's bed. The muscles of his face relaxed. His right hand drew away and smoothed the hairs veiling her gentle forehead, and he said to himself: *If she loved me...!*

The willow's foliage became agitated. At that moment, Jeanne opened her large eyes, which Comte Henri had imagined to be black but were in fact as blue as the profound azure of a summer sky.

Robert and Laurent hurled themselves out of the bushes just as Jeanne, languidly lifting her gaze to the young man and already smiling, murmured: "You're the one who saved me... thank you!"

Laurent lifted her in his arms, while the weeping Robert kissed her two hands.

"Monsieur de Belcamp," Laurent said, "I have no one in the world but her; every drop of my blood is yours."

"Belcamp!" repeated Jeanne, who had closed her eyes again, too weak to keep them open.

The impassioned Robert dropped her hands to throw his arms about the neck of her savior, clutching him against his breast. "Comte Henri," he stammered, sobbing with joy, "I do not yet have the right to say that I love her, but if ever you have need of...I do not say a hand, and I do not say a purse, I say a heart... understand that you only have to say the word, and you shall see what a soldier's word is worth!

"Comte Henri..." echoed Jeanne, who seemed asleep within her smile.

There was a terrible commotion in the Marquis de Belcamp's kitchen. The night before, trunks had arrived at the chateau bearing the name of Comte Henri, of whom vague mention had occasionally been heard, although no one had ever seen him. Ordinarily, when a man in the Marquis' position is a widower, and has an only son traveling abroad, one can see portraits hanging on his walls–usually more than one–of the dead wife and the absentee, but there was none here. No image remained of the late Marquise, or of the heir. Their names, it is true, often cropped up in evening conversations, but they were always raised in response to the lure of the mystery. Everyone was obliged to admit, in the end, that nothing was known of the dead wife, or anything of the son of the family.

That was strange, it has to be said, but what was even stranger was that in this respect the life of the old nobleman–which was otherwise as clear and limpid as a rock-pool–presented only the shadow of an enigma. The mystery, moreover–if there was a mystery, in the accepted sense of the word–was not one of those maintained by any great effort; it arose quite naturally from the fact that there was a discontinuity in the Marquis' life. His London staff remained unknown to his French staff. On his return from exile, he had brought no one back to the chateau of his fathers but a single manservant, a taciturn dotard who had died peacefully a few months after the crossing. As for the rest of his household, Monsieur le Marquis, desirous of putting his exile behind him, had followed the perfectly natural course of recruiting servants from among the children of those who had served his forefathers.

William, the old English manservant, had not been popular in the neighborhood while he lived; his cold manner and foreign accent had discouraged familiarity. Now that he was dead, though, he was sincerely missed, because–as the excellent cook, Madame Etienne, observed–he would have talked, one way or another. "Now," she added, "it's rather titillating to have no clear or definite knowledge of the misadventures of a master so full of goodwill and intolerance."

Madame Etienne was from Pontoise, where she had rendered 15 years faithful service to the widow of a doctor, who had continued her husband's business clandestinely. Instructed in the school of that illustrious lady, Madame Etienne had an elegant and inquisitive manner that frequently gave her away. By the same token, she was also inclined to include in her discourse a great many words whose precise significance she did not know. She was an elderly fair-haired woman, fat and florid. She was a good cook, and if she ever spoiled the dinner it was only for lack of inattention, as she frankly observed. Her immediate assistants were Julot, a native of Miremont, who was beginning his career in service, and Anille, a pretty girl from l'Isle-Adam, who regarded distant Paris much as the Hebrews dreamed of the promised land. Don't forget that there were no railways in that era, and that tourism was not yet part of our way of life.

Anille and Julot hated one another, and expected to marry some day if they never found anyone better.

The remainder of the household comprised a robust manservant named Pierre, Miss Suzanne's chambermaid Fanchette, the gardener–who also served as coachman–and Briquet, alias Bricole or Trompe-l'Eustache, who had his own covert in the kitchen of the chateau because the overburdened Priory refused him a lodging.

The Priory was a modest habitation not far from the Chateau-Neuf on the other side of the Oise; it accommodated Madame Touchard, *née* Herbet, the aunt of our young friend Laurent and his pretty sister Jeanne. Robert Surrisy passed the greater number of his days there and Férandeau was currently receiving its hospitality. Robert's mother Madeleine lived in an isolated cottage on the bank of the Oise.

The reason for the commotion in the kitchen was that the focal point of three years' general curiosity, the young Comte Henri, had been seen arriving–mounted, so the gardener-coachman swore, on a glorious beast. He was a trifle pale, hatless, and wet through, in spite of the warm Sun, but hearty, to be sure, and ready to favor everyone with a smile.

We know of no event in the world, not even an earthquake or the news of a revolution overwhelming Pontoise that could have brought such animation to the Chateau de Belcamp's kitchen. Madame Etienne was excited and boastful, already talking about introducing the newcomer to the national cuisine. The distracted Anille was scurrying back and forth, breaking a few pots here and there but achieving nothing else. Julot, meanwhile, was talking over the story of the fireworks with his enemy Briquet. Fanchette and the gardener-coachman were correcting them, but no one was listening.

"See here!" cried Madame Etienne, who could muster a commanding voice when she wanted to. "You know impertinently that it titillates me to take charge of any fracas in my own kitchen. As far as I can see, it's a lot easier to stop a galloping horse with a bridle than two pistol-shots, and Cabri wouldn't give a farthing for thirty *pistoles*,[39] but Monsieur le Comte acted for his best, didn't he? And he's a well-set-up young man–there's not a shadow of a doubt about that. There's an incompatible resemblance to Monsieur le Marquis."

"He must have a lot of clothes," Anille observed, "to fill five trunks."

"As far as that's concerned," Madame Etienne replied, stirring a casserole, "my former mistress's brother also went overseas, and he always brought back trunks full of natural history, which took up far more room than his effects and his linen. Monsieur Briquet, don't be always getting in my way like that!"

Madame Etienne did not like Briquet, because he kept writing his name on the kitchen walls in charcoal. This vice, seemingly insignificant at first glance, might be very injurious to the young man's future. Briquet despised Madame Etienne, because she was only from Pontoise.

Briquet had come from the Priory, where everyone was singing the young Comte's praises. Férandeau, in his enthusiasm, had promised to paint his portrait.

"That one," said Madame Etienne, "is what one ostensibly calls an idler. My former mistress also had a cousin who was a painter, but at least he earned good money making signboards and other things. Settle down, Monsieur Briquet!"

"I wish someone would paint my portrait," murmured little Anille.

"You!" gallant Julot riposted. "You aren't pretty enough by half for that!"

Anille lifted up her broom; Julot took up his stool to defend himself. There would have been a battle if Madame Etienne had not stepped between them, loudly defending her leadership of the fracas.

The tinkle of a bell sounded inside the chateau.

"Go see to that, Julot!" Madame Etienne commanded. "Pierre's taking care of the young Monsieur, who has to change from top to toe, thanks to his penchant for submerging himself. As quick as you can!"

Julot took off his clogs and ran barefoot towards the drawing room. When he returned, he said: "It's all a bit funny. One of the masters waiting for the other to get dry before saying hello. Monsieur le Marquis is in the drawing-room, very white, as if he'd been ill. 'Go tell Monsieur le Comte that I'm ready to receive him,' he says to me..."

"My former mistress had an uncle who never said *tu* to his wife," Madame Etienne observed. "That's what's called the etiquette of *haut ton* among the persons of distinction who make up the highest classes of choice society. Remember that!" She stirred her casserole in an aristocratic manner, happy and proud that she had been able to pronounce this series of elitist terms correctly.

Julot was right, though. Monsieur le Marquis de Belcamp was alone in his drawing-room, as pale as an invalid risen from his bed. He had proudly drawn himself up to his full height, and his gaze–which was normally soft and merciful–had an expression of austere severity.

When he had given the order to Julot to inform his son, he remained motionless for a moment, with his eyes lowered. The drawing-room's three windows, which overlooked the open countryside–seen in reverse formation to our earlier description–were open. The Marquis closed them one after the other, slowly and pensively. Then his sad gaze made a circuit of the family portraits hung on the paneling. A hint of red animated the pallor of his cheeks, and he lowered his eyes again.

He was 60 years old, and was every inch the nobleman, his features full of pride and mansuetude; he must have been a very handsome cavalier in his youth. He was two inches taller than his son, and his larger forehead was crowned with fine white hair. Apart from that, there was a strong resemblance between them. The bold and aquiline features of the young man were still recognizable in the old, particularly the almost feminine softness of their smile, which did not detract at all from the masculinity of their gaze. The color of their hair must always have been different, though, for that of the son was fair, while the thinly-pencilled eyebrows of the white-haired father were still as black as jade.

The Marquis paused for a moment after closing the last window. His thoughts, visibly engraved on his features, were melancholy. His right hand slid mechanically into his hunting-jacket and brought forth a large locket, enameled with gold. He opened it.

The locket contained a miniature representing a young and very beautiful woman, dressed like a goddess in a fable, as was the hideous fashion of a certain epoch, particularly in England. The hair crowning her forehead was a kind of red-tinted blonde that seems particular to the Saxon race.

Monsieur le Marquis de Belcamp gazed sadly at the miniature; his eyelid trembled as if a tear were trying to escape from his eye.

"Helen," he murmured, perhaps unaware that he spoke aloud.

He hid the locket hurriedly, because the door was creaking on its hinges. Those who believed that there was no portrait of the late Marquise in the chateau were mistaken.

"Monsieur le Comte," announced the manservant, Pierre, who stood aside to let his young master pass.

Our traveler came in with his head held high and a humorless smile on his lips. He walked towards his father eagerly, but without extending his hand. Having arrived a few paces from the old man, by which time Pierre had closed the door behind him, the Comte came to a halt, bowed respectfully and said: "Monsieur le Marquis, I shall only claim the paternal welcome and greeting that is my due after having proved to my father–my only judge–that I am fit to carry his name and that I am worthy of his goodwill."

The old man remained silent for a moment. His heart seemed to have swollen to fill his breast and take his breath away. *It's her voice*, he thought. *Her voice, which I have never been able to hear without a shudder extending to the very bottom of my soul. Those are her eyes, too; it's she, in her entirety–the dream of my youth, the implacable love of my mature years. She! My joy, my torment, my pride and my shame. She, my remorse; she, my misery. She, the bitter and cherished flower of my memories!*

"Does my father not wish to hear me?" asked the young Comte, whose remarkably harmonious voice seemed to be searching for a softer and more melancholy tone.

The old man made a supreme effort to master his profound emotion, and replied: "Speak, Monsieur. I'm listening."

In London, in the year 1786, there was a rich company of brewers, very experienced in the beer trade and famous for the excellence of its products. The name of this establishment, which was inscribed on the red placards gleaming in the windows of every tavern in the metropolis, was Brown, Turner, Robinson & Co. Nicholas Brown, the senior partner and managing director of the brewery, which occupied three acres in Pimlico, was the only one to be married, and had only one daughter, who was destined in his mind for one or other of his two partners and cousins, William Robinson and Frank Turner. Both of them were an appropriate age to become his son-in-law, and they loyally disputed the affection of the lovely Helen when Nicholas Brown came to die.

Helen was 16. She was beautiful enough to create a storm when she entered a room, and her education had been that of the richest heirs of the aristocracy. Old Nicholas Brown, who was a widower with none but his daughter to love, had been her slave for a long time; she never had time to work up a desire.

Certain natures, either too vigorous or entirely neutral, can resist the slow poison of paternal indulgence; in others, more numerous, a mortal seed is planted thereby, which may require time to develop but always bursts forth sooner or later.

In Helen, the seed was brought to fruit by her father's death. She wept; then, seeking to deaden the pain, she delivered herself into the hands of an impoverished *grande dame*, who set about enthusiastically opening the doors of aristocratic society for her. Because English law does not permit a minor's business-partner to become her guardian, Turner and Robinson were automatically set aside, and the guardianship of the heiress was placed in the hands of the exceedingly skillful and capable solicitor who had handled the dead man's affairs.

Lady Edgerton, the impoverished *grande dame*, and Mr. Wood, the retired lawyer, found that they were old acquaintances. Under that austere surface that is the disguise of English life, immorality has strange depths. Britain's own writers, despite the obstinacy of national prejudice, have made repulsive confessions in that regard. We have no intention of following them along that path, and it will suffice for us to say that the French, much less prudish in appearance and ever-ready to laugh at the hypocritical exaggerations of British cant, closes their eyes in disgust on discovering that which it veils. We do not need to learn anything more than the facts established on the first battlefield of the terrible talent of William Hogarth [40] to know that the principal victims of the gangrene of those mores are young women.

Helen Brown, thrown into a new world and systematically separated from the friends who might have been able to protect her with their advice, fell prey to that Lord Bogeyman who is ever-present in the novels of Smollett, Goldsmith and even the prudent Richardson. This lord is invariably a swindler; Helen was ruined in more senses than one. As her nature was not the kind that permits stopping halfway, having fallen victim to bandits, she made a resolute corsair of herself, armed by her youth and her beauty. She swore an oath that she would not die in the straw, like all the pale heroines of the eternal romance of English depravity.

She kept her word, and died on a much harder bed.

In 1788, she had her first brush with the law. She was convicted of stealing diamonds from the home of the Duchess of Devonshire, whose adolescent son had imprudently opened the door of the house to her. The affair was so loudly publicized that Turner and Robinson resolved to remove the dishonored name of Brown from the company's name. The establishment in Pimlico was dissolved and the two associates, having divided the considerable proceeds, left England, where there remained henceforth an indelible stain on their commercial reputation.

Turner established himself in Lyon, Robinson in Brussels, and neither of them lost any time in further augmenting his fortune.

Helen Brown was pardoned, as a minor who had not realized the seriousness of her action. The appeal for mercy was carried to the King by the Duchess of Devonshire herself, who had been touched by Helen's youth and her marvelous beauty. After securing her release from prison, the duchess took her into her home. In one of those sudden changes of fortune so common in London, Helen suddenly became a celebrity in the most exclusive earthly circles, a star in the most inaccessible of firmaments. With the Queen protecting her, it became good form to proclaim her a victim and heap loud scorn upon the alleged hardness of her father's former associates. Indeed, had these merchants not been so cruel as to compromise their fortune and expatriate themselves, in order not to hear her name spoken?

This lasted several months, and while it lasted, unfortunate circumstance brought to London the last of the Knights of France, a heroic companion of Lafayette, the Marquis de Belcamp, outgoing colonel of the first regiment to march on Paris on the 11th July, after the fall of Necker.[41]

The Marquis met Helen Brown and fell in love with her. He was still one of the most handsome cavaliers of the time, even though he had passed the bounds of youth. The Duchess of Devonshire, whose enthusiasm was probably declining and was perhaps already growing weary of the romance of her generosity, favored his suit. Helen consented. She was married with great ceremony, as befitted the apple of the eye of the entire English aristocracy. The Duchess, bitter with jealousy for the idol that she had offered to the shiftless cult of her caste, said: "What more could have been done for my poor daughter?"

Helen had no lack of cleverness or will-power. During her sojourn in her protector's town house, she had withdrawn into charming modesty and perfect decency. The world was, quite frankly, at her feet, waiting for her inspection—but there was a cloud hanging over her, a fatality or a calumny. A demon does not become an angel again, and that gentle young woman was an angel, whose become an angel again, and that gentle young woman was an angel, whose beauty recalled the virgins Reynolds copied from Raphael. Her voice, her soft voice, diffused like a vibrant perfume into the innermost recesses of the heart. The Duchess was said thereafter to be cold, and was freely accused of capriciousness in every quarter of high society.

A child arrived after a year of marriage, a cherub as radiant as love in his mother's arms, and who compelled admiration, even in that land of handsome children where Sir Thomas Lawrence has found the models for his smiling families. Everyone knows what effort the English spouse and mother puts into the accomplishment of her duties, but Helen was an exceptional wife and exceptional mother. Hers was a reputation of earthly sanctity; she was crowned in the drawing-room chatter of Brighton and canonized at Almack's.[42] There was no one in the entire world of men as happy as the Marquis de Belcamp.

One day, the Marquis stopped receiving the revenues from his French estates. Inevitably, he had been categorized as an *émigré* and his possessions had been sequestered. Nothing remained of his fortune but a sum of money deposited in an English bank. He was so sure of his wife that he did not even try to prepare the ground before issuing the proposal that they must give up their social life. It was at the height of the season, in 1793. Helen was charmingly resigned; she did not shed a tear. What could they possibly need outside the walls that contained their love? Her only request was to finish the season, in order to retire inconspicuously, with honor intact, from the battlefield.

A few days later, a certain Charles Cook, of whom the Marquis had never heard, died in Northumberland. The old solicitor, Mr. Wood, who had been the Marquise's guardian when she was Miss Brown, presented himself with a will by which the dead man named her his sole legatee. Their circumstances were comfortable again; there was no longer any question of quitting society. Mr. Charles Cook, the unknown kinsman, had been worth 3,000 pounds.

From this moment on, however, Helen occasionally seemed sad and preoccupied. At other times, she had fits of sudden gaiety that seemed somewhat exaggerated. She became devout, and often went out alone to go to church. Her zeal took her across other boundaries; she joined a temperance society for the moral uplift of the poor, and her elegant costumes sometimes exuded a perfume of gin and tobacco; it was evidently necessary to seek out the victims that she wished to extract from vice in their natural habitat.

After a splendid end-of-season party given by Lady Breadalbane, one of Helen's friends and mentors, some very valuable diamonds were stolen from the drawing-room. The following day, Helen received the first installment of her payments from Northumberland.

Some revelations appear by slow degrees, each day that passes dissipating a little corner of the concealing cloud; others burst like a thunderclap. One evening, Helen came home drunk.

(If anyone is tempted to exclaim upon the implausibility of this point, it is only necessary to read a few pages of any biography of the Prince of Wales, who became George IV. It is not only daughters of brewers who have become Marquises who return home drunk. Remember that England hides its vices with the same care that we devote to putting ours on show. Would we not have publicized that wretched regency with shameless gossip, more boastful than vicious? London immediately put it in the cellar, then set about blocking all the air-holes. In a hundred years time, London will be talking about the austerities to which the regency piously devoted itself within that cell.)

Monsieur de Belcamp thought, at first, that he was the victim of a bad dream. He did not want to believe his eyes. The testimony of the senses cannot contend with the impossible. He demanded an explanation–and obtained one that was far too complete. The young Marquise threw propriety to the winds; that pink and charming mouth vomited forth appalling blasphemies. The mud of the city was concealed beneath that satin skin. The son of crusaders, the companion of Lafayette, had married A THIEF who was henceforth inured to every ignominy!

Monsieur Belcamp fell dangerously ill and was carried as far as the very gates of death. When he awoke from his long and terrible delirium, his wife had left his house, taking her son with her; the nest was empty.

Madame la Marquise, making the most of the time left to her, had committed several bold thefts by way of bidding farewell to the aristocracy; then she had thrown herself head-first into that abyss of filth into which the London Police sometimes plunge at their peril, but which, for the most part, is an unassailable refuge.

It was in this period that the relationship was established between Monsieur de Belcamp and Gregory Temple, then a mere detective at Scotland Yard. Whatever your opinion or mine might be of Gregory Temple's trade, as a person he was gentle, serious, loyal and good. He was, moreover, what the English call "a true gentleman"–a title that does not correspond to our word *gentilhomme,* but which signifies a certain self-respect and various honorable delicacies. Gregory Temple found Monsieur de Belcamp in frightful circumstances, harried in the very depths of his misfortune by personal disquiet, and rendered him invaluable assistance. Thanks to him, the Marquis was at least able to detach his own honor from his wife's shame, and keep his position intact.

In addition, Gregory Temple made every effort to recover the Marquis' son. He did not succeed. The end of the last century was the epic era of the great association of London thieves, who were literally masters of a substantial sector of the city and who, protected by barbarous custom, boldly snapped their fingers at authority behind the walls of their feudal citadel. The Marquise was in the very heart of this darkness; she had, of course, changed her name. It is not necessary to go to England to see analogous falls, and the prodigious depravity–not merely of the heart but of taste–that permits one to live in a sewer when one has breathed the pure air of aristocratic elegance, cannot even be considered exceptional. We have all seen brilliant meteors extinguished by sensuality in the gutters of our own fatherland.

In 1805, a woman named Helen Brown, who was a member of the gang run by John Devil–who was then Thomas Paddock–was seized and condemned to deportation for life. Gregory Temple had arrested her. There is nothing strange in the fact that the law was satisfied with the name Helen Brown; Thomas Paddock's lieutenant was by then notorious in the Inner Temple and St. Giles's; the name was as illustrious as Jack Sheppard's.

On the very day that sentence was passed, a boy of 11 or 12, as pretty and as modest as a girl, came to ask for Monsieur de Belcamp at his town house and handed him a letter. The letter read:

Monsieur,
One often remains rancorous against those one has offended. Personally, I am only sorry about one thing in the world, and that was doing wrong to you. You have a noble heart, and you deserved as good a wife as the Earth could provide. I do not ask you for the forgiveness that you could not in all conscience offer me; I would not know what to do with it in my present circumstances–but I send you Henri, our son, whom I have kept worthy of you. This is the little corner of my soul by which something of God's mercy has entered into me. For his sake, I have respected your name, which I might have dragged behind me into my ignominy. The child is pure; raise him well, and do not teach him to despise his mother.

Helen Brown.

That man, as good in his weakness as he was brave and strong in his heroism, had tears in his eyes as he read this strange epistle. Helen was wrong when she said that he could never have forgiven her. No one knows how far such hearts might be able to descend–or climb–on the slope of merciful folly!

Monsieur de Belcamp opened his arms to the child and held him clasped against his breast for several minutes. The child manifested no other sentiment than surprise, more because of a politeness that was certainly extraordinary than from any other motive. Helen had told him only that he was bound for the house of a protector; it was left to the Marquis himself to say to him: "I am your father."

The child displayed respect and affection then.

He resembled Helen in his hair, his eyes and most particularly his voice; one might have believed that one was hearing Helen's soft and vibrant speech–but he was a Belcamp in the shape of his face and the aquiline design of his features.

The first time the Marquis called him Henri he made no response and the Marquis said: "My son, do you have another name?"

The child hesitated, blushed and finally replied: "No, milord. My name is Henri."

"Henri Brown?"

"Yes, milord, Henri Brown."

"Who is the young boy named as Tom Brown in your mother's trial?" asked the Marquis.

"I know nothing about my mother's trial, milord," the child replied, innocently.

The Marquis, continuing his inquiries, learned that Henri had been a pupil in a school in Southwark, where his mother came to visit him. He only went out once a week. The headmaster of the Southwark school fully confirmed the child's testimony. Helen Brown, in the depths of her degradation, has retained sufficient conscience to safeguard this young soul.

Misfortune remains mysterious; those who suffer strive incessantly to deceive eyes desirous of interrogating their hearts' wounds. Monsieur de Belcamp said nothing at all about this event to the very few friends who still crossed the sad threshold of his house on rare occasions. Even Gregory Temple never saw the child, who was placed at the University of Edinburgh [43] since his studies proved to be sufficiently advanced. There was no sham, however; at the University, Henri bore the name de Belcamp. His intelligence, precocious and already cultivated, developed rapidly in that illustrious milieu. He was soon one of the most remarkable pupils of Professor Dugald Stewart,[44] a follower of the doctrines of Reid,[45] from whom Jouffroy,[46] Cousin [47] and the eclectics drew numerous principles that were slightly spoiled by the appropriation. In 1810, the 17-year-old Henri de Belcamp submitted his degree thesis on the *Methods of Investigation Applied to the Metaphysical Sciences*, and scored a veritable triumph.

At about that time, the Regent of the University wrote to inform the Marquis that a woman, still young and very beautiful, had come several times asking for her son. The Marquis consulted his oracle, Gregory Temple, who told him that Helen Brown, having escaped and committed numerous crimes since her escape, had now assumed—even in London—the name of Lady Rowley. In the wake of that interview, the Marquis caught a mail-coach and departed for Edinburgh.

During the journey, the Marquis experienced dire forebodings. He reproached himself for not having kept the child who was his only future closer to home. On arrival, he found the city of Edinburgh excited by an audacious theft from the Lord Lieutenant's house. Lady Rowley had vanished and the young Comte Henri de Belcamp was no longer at the University.

A letter was waiting for the Marquis when he returned from London. It must be remembered that the young man was supposed to be ignorant of his mother's infamy; he wrote quite frankly to inform the Marquis that she had furnished the means of allowing him to satisfy his passionate desire to visit the continent. The letter had been sent from Calais.

Since that time–which is to say, for seven years–Monsieur de Belcamp had not seen his son again. During the first few years, he had received frequent letters, which were veritable models of filial duty; they indicated a precise and subtle mind ardent for knowledge. They never asked for money, save for one occasion when his father–grasping the nettle, so to speak–apprised him in a letter that it was not permissible, in all honor and conscience, for him to accept the money furnished by his mother. Henri replied by claiming a small sum in order to pay his hotel expenses in Vienna, where he was then staying. "I have put what remains of my mother's money in the poor box at the Cathedral," he added. "As for the future, I am in the German lands, which are infatuated with all kinds of philosophy, and I have what I learned from my master, Dugald Stewart."

It was certainly not the sort of correspondence that should displease a father's heart. In our day, and until the knell of the century sounds, he who leaves his useless Gothic sword to rust in its scabbard may still play the knight in his speech and his handwriting. Even as these letters were speaking of hope and honor, however, there were strange threats hovering around the Marquis de Belcamp, persistently troubling his tranquillity.

This proud young man, embarked in distant lands on adventures of intelligence, had a double of some sort. The exploits of Helen Brown and her son–Tom Brown, that is; not Henri's son but his counterpart, for he was the same age–were making her career as notorious as that of any actress or queen. So far as history knew, she had given birth to but one child; Helen Brown's son, it was said, was in London, following in his mother's footsteps with great flair. He was already becoming famous in the criminal underworld, evading the pursuit of Gregory Temple–the march of whose career had led to the Lord Chief Justice appointing him Chief Superintendent–as if it were mere child's play.

Already, people were beginning to call Tom Brown "John Devil."

As for Helen herself, she continued her war against society with extraordinary valor. She responded to the warrants issued against her with further audacious, almost fantastic, thefts; sergeants and constables pursued her in vain. It was not until two months after the Emperor's fall, when the Marquis of Belcamp had already returned to France, that Helen and her son Tom were arrested at a feast in an oyster-house in the best part of Oxford Street, carried off to Newgate, and shipped from there to New South Wales. Helen was treated with mercy by virtue of her sex, Tom by virtue of his age.

As soon as the affair was reported in the newspapers, the Marquis wrote to Gregory Temple, but the heroic Superintendent, laid low by an unknown malady the doctors named Asiatic cholera or morbid cholera, was hovering between life and death. By the time he was convalescent, Helen and Tom were already en route for Sydney; he saw neither the mother, nor the son.

After this time, Monsieur de Belcamp ceased to receive further news of his son; the latter's correspondence dried up, and that fact added considerably to the doubts and fears of the unhappy father. The last letter had been written in Warsaw five months before.

Monsieur de Belcamp was on the point of deciding to go to Poland when he received a missive from London that rendered his departure futile.

"Father," said the letter, which tackled the question frankly, "instead of finding you in London, as I had hoped, I understand, as I stand at the door of your empty house, that the final misfortune has fallen upon me, if not upon you. The mother that God gave me has fallen into the hands of the law and set sail for that Australian territory about which one hears so many horror stories.

"In addressing you, whose heart is so great and noble, I do not believe there is any need to take oratory precautions in avowing that everyone maintains in the depths of his soul, no matter what, an invincible love for her who delivers him into the light of day. I still love my mother–but it is not, however, for my mother alone that I intend to undertake a long hard voyage.

"It is for you, Father, for whom I have a proper regard and wish to spare from a supreme unhappiness. Helen Brown issued a threat as she departed. Was she awaiting an intervention on your part, or on the part of the Chief Superintendent of Police, whom she knows to be your friend? I do not know what it was, but your name has been mentioned, and you know that she is carrying with her an infallible means of revision, since it is Helen Brown who has been sentenced and my mother's legal title is the Marquise de Belcamp..."

An hour after receiving this letter, Monsieur de Belcamp was en route for London. In London, he found no trace of Comte Henri. He only learned that Helen and her son Tom Brown had departed for Australia on a State vessel three days before.

The Marquis de Belcamp had no confidant. He enclosed within himself the nagging doubts born of these coincidences. In speaking of another man, we would have substituted the word "certainty" for the word "doubts," but we are dealing with one of those noble minds that will only think evil as a last resort. He returned to France, cherishing a *residuum* of hope that could not help but diminish with every subsequent day that passed.

In three years, two items of news penetrated his solitude by way of Gregory Temple: Helen's death, and the escape of Tom Brown, who had fought and killed three guards with his own hands before going over the wall of the Port Jackson Penitentiary. There were indications that Tom Brown had returned to London, and was now–according to the Superintendent–the most redoubtable bandit in the three kingdoms.

This, therefore, was the state of affairs when the Marquis de Belcamp, after three years of silence, had received a letter from London–which informed him, purely and simply, of the imminent arrival of his son.

For a little over three weeks, the solitude of the old man had been alleviated; he had given shelter to Suzanne Temple, whose father, pursued by a dark obsession, seemed to be on the verge of madness.

Comte Henri de Belcamp followed swiftly behind his letter.

This story will enable to reader to comprehend the strange gravity of the explanation of all that had happened between father and son.

They were there in the drawing-room, facing one another, surrounded by the portraits of their forefathers. The Belcamps were not one of those families whose histories had begun by eavesdropping in some antechamber or by lifting the curtain of a conjugal bed with a cowardly adulterous hand. They were of another sort, and the infamous legendry of French courtesanship is no longer or broader than that of the glories of France.

From Honoré II de Belcamp, who laid down his body like a rampart before Louis IX at Damietta, to Lieutenant-General Henri de Belcamp, the father of the present Marquis, who was killed at Rossbach in the year of his birth,[48] there had been none in the family but simple and loyal soldiers–not a single courtier. Versailles knew little of them, but everyone knew their name at the front.

Father and son alike presented to one another faces full of character. They were handsome in the same way; beneath the fair hair of the young man the same proudly gentle features of the white-haired old man were perceptible.

A ray of sunlight passing through the panes of the tall window played upon the faded embroidery of the antique tapestries, striking a spark here and there from the gilded corner of a picture-frame. Nothing in here was new; everything spoke of times past. Silence, extended to the point of meditation, reigned in that vast room, which was somber in spite of the sunlight. Outside, the same calm lay upon the lonely lawns, bordered by the grey stones of the sunken fence. The only sounds that disturbed it momentarily were the raw and distant voices of farm animals calling in the pastureland, the patient plaint of the mill and the murmur of the wind in the giant trees of the avenue.

The Marquis had his back to the window and his face remained shadowed; the young man's noble head, on the other hand, was fully lit. They both remained standing, staring one another in the face.

"Father," said Comte Henri, whose voice lowered involuntarily as the solemn interview commenced, "it's seven years since I left the University of Edinburgh, disobeying you for the first and last time. Two years after that, you apprised me of the necessity of not buying my bread with the money supplied by my mother. Two years after that, at the moment when I was returning to you, my path was diverted by duty. My journey to New South Wales has lasted more than three years. I shall only tell you today about that journey, which has left me with a memory that is sad and consolatory at the same time. I have heard my mother's last sigh, who died a Christian, reconciled with God."

These words trembled on the old man's mouth: "Died a Christian..."

"Father," the young Comte continued, "I believed for a long time that you and my mother were split apart by a lack of sympathy. She gave me an upbringing so religious and so pure that I would never have guessed the truth for myself. I owe you a confession: until the day when your letter awakened a suspicion in me, I took my mother's side."

"That is natural, my son," the Marquis said. "Woe betide those children who cleave to the more powerful side!"

"I had come to you in the first place," Comte Henri went on, "because my mother instructed me to do it. I did not know why she sent me into exile, and I said to myself: my father is rich; my mother is poor. That seemed unjust to me. Later, it seemed cruel to me that my mother was obliged to change her name in order to come to see me at the University of Edinburgh... I know now that that was not the true motive for her disguise. It was with her that I went to France after quitting the university. We remained together for a month, the shortest and happiest time of my life. She showed me nothing of herself but the tenderness of her heart and the graciousness of her spirit."

A profound sigh rose up from the old nobleman's breast; Henri looked at him with controlled affection, murmuring: "You loved her very much!" Then he continued, as he saw the old man's eyelids trembling: "Thank you, father! It was only in London, following my return, that I became acquainted with the full extent of our misfortune. The city resounded with the name of my mother, who had been condemned to criminal punishment after a scandalous trial. My studies and my travels had made me numerous friends, but I only knew one man in London of whom I had heard my mother speak. This man was a retired solicitor, who had formerly been her guardian and who, I had reason to suppose, had not been uninvolved in her fall. In spite of a certain repugnance left over from my childhood memories, I went to see Mr. Wood. He said to me: 'She will come back; I'm waiting for her to authorize me to enter an appeal. There was a procedural fault: it was Helen Brown that was sentenced but it is the Marquise de Belcamp who is out there.'

"He added, while rubbing his hands: 'It will turn the tables on old Gregory Temple, who–before taking to his bed, may the Devil take his soul!–laid the trap into which poor Helen fell. It will also turn the tables on that Frenchman, the Marquis de Belcamp. If Helen had had the time, the business would already be in hand, but they sent her out before her turn, and the Marquis had a hand in that.'

"Father, I wrote you that letter–the last that you received from me–and I embarked on the *Tonnant*, which was sailing for New South Wales. The crossing seemed to take forever. After making landfall in Sydney, it was a further year before I found myself in my mother's presence. I do not know what the future of that country will be, which seems to be a molded block of heterogeneous matter is the middle of our terrestrial creation, but I can affirm that its present is hideous and shameful.

"It is 800 leagues from Cape York to Cape Wilson, and no one knows the extent of the colony that extends along the coast to the west, where the Blue Mountains are no boundary. Without setting any precise limit to it, England has designated that immense extent on the map of the world as a prison; she has expelled the aborigines to the interior, where the arid and infecund soil can neither nourish a man nor slake his thirst. Every place that is host to a drop of water is guarded by an English rifle, with the result that the former owners of the land have no alternative but to steal.

"This water, refused to humans, is drunk by animals: England's sheep and horses. Without water, all creatures of monetary value die. One discovers black men dead of thirst on the sand–but they were free men, and were consequently worthless. They avenge themselves by assassinating white men when they can, by means of their long and needle-sharp hunting spears. The English say that they are ferocious beasts; they hunt them assiduously in that capacity. Such is the march of civilization. No, I'm mistaken: the last governor of Port Jackson has caused Bibles to be printed in a hybrid language that neither the blacks not the whites comprehend, and he has enlisted–or rather collected–a thousand aborigines to track down escaped convicts, in order that they might be devoured when they are found. They bring back nothing but their scalps, and are paid an official bounty on presentation of each hairpiece.

"Women are not transported, save for very rare and seemingly arbitrary exceptions.[49] That enormous expanse of land is devoid of women, which condition undoubtedly augments the somber ferocity of its population. The voluntary settlers, whose number increases incessantly, are very often bachelor adventurers who come seeking their fortune. Even so, there are fathers with families, but as the squatters' stations–as the farmers and their farms are called–are disseminated over vast distances, their wives and daughters are isolated from the society of the towns. None of them goes there to stay permanently; everyone makes haste to raise, shear and kill their sheep in order to return to Europe enriched, to live like a gentleman. A petticoat is a curiosity in the streets of Sydney, and Sydney has more women than anywhere else in Australia.

"During my stay, it happened that I assisted in the disembarkation of a cargo of women at Port Jackson. In the Australian colony, it is strictly forbidden to buy human flesh, to strike anyone, or to blaspheme, but all these unfortunates were sold in broad daylight, on a harbor-side steaming with blood, in the midst of a tempest of punches and oaths.

"Father, I do not tell you this so that you will know what a curious place New Holland is; I tell you this because Helen Brown, my mother, was still beautiful, and died a martyr..."

Henri paused. His face was pale and his eyes downcast. Beads of cold sweat were forming beneath the Marquis' grey hair. What description can be made, what name bestowed upon the sentiment that was tormenting his soul? His son was now a man. For more than 20 years, this Helen Brown, who had wed shame to his honor, had wallowed in vice and infamy. Why did he shiver in every fiber of his being, as if she had acted the part of one of those noble women whose portraits smiled around the paneling–as if it had been a question of a pure and stainless Belcamp fallen through misfortune into the hands of a gang of drunken brigands?

She was dead. Death rehabilitates. Is that enough? No, for the common run of men; yes, for the exception. The Marquis de Belcamp was the exception; he had one of those hearts that is loving and devoted, which forgives according to the law of its nature, as light illuminates and life respires.

"Helen Brown was still beautiful," the young Comte continued, slowly. "Very beautiful. The principal objective of my journey was to safeguard your name. I had left your name in London, and I was going under the name Henry Brown. I promptly set about searching for my mother.

"At Sydney, within an hour of disembarking, I discovered the first chapter of a lamentable history. The Sheriff of the county had disputed possession of Helen Brown with the Overseer of the port. They had fought a duel. Helen had asked the Crown Magistrate for protection against her two persecutors, and then begged for Commodore Banks to protect her from the Magistrate. All of them—the Sheriff, the Overseer, the Magistrate and the Commodore–surrounded her like the obscene monsters that came out of the sea to devour Andromeda.[50] They laughed when they told me that. It was the way of things. I longed to load my pistols and to run to the town to kill those four mad dogs, but I had a mission and I sealed my wrath within my heart.

"It was up to me to defend my mother against the entire world–except for you, Monsieur. Before you, I bow and I acknowledge with a groan the depths to which she had sunk. It is certain, however, that Helen Brown, having fallen so low from such a height, rose up again from the very depths of her misery and misfortune. Those who no are longer equipped with the Aegis of honor ordinarily accept infamy as their lot; my mother could have bought comfort merely by remaining at her allotted level, but she stood up straight and refused, at the risk of her life. I have called her martyr; Mary Magdalene, who is a saint, also left a scrap of her nuptial robe on every thorn along her path..."

"Don't plead, child," the Marquis de Belcamp interrupted, his eyes moist and his voice husky. "Your cause is already won, and I forgave her a long time ago. If I had known that Helen was repentant–listen well in order to know me well–I would have been out there searching for my wife, as Orpheus sought his in Hades. I would have bought her back with my money or my blood. I would have led her by the hand, here to this house, and I would have forced all the portraits that surround us to look at her, doubly rehabilitated by her penitence and her pardon."

The young Comte took both his hands and pressed them to his lips, murmuring: "She hears you, and I thank you!" Then, he continued: "Helen Brown, forcefully hardening the tone of her failing voice, was beaten for the first time, in Sydney, for giving way beneath her burden. She tried to kill herself. She was put in manacles and conducted to Paramatta [51] to put an end to the indecent quarrels fomented in the capital by her presence. At Paramatta, another pack of jackals came barking around her. A noble young man, the father of a family and owner of a station on the Macquarie River, claimed her out of compassion, in order to abstract her from the ignominious treatment that awaited her. His flocks were stolen by night and his house set alight. The Sheriff of Paramatta took Helen on as a housekeeper, for reasons that it would be odious to repeat. It is always the same in these parts when a woman is concerned; the men become wild beasts. Helen, accused of trying to murder him, was taken with a noose around her neck aboard the vessel that conveys recalcitrant convicts to Norfolk Island.

"Norfolk Island is the inferno; one only talks to its prisoners with a dagger or a pistol in one's hand. Its inhabitants are nothing but chained tigers held in check by demons.

"Helen was on Norfolk Island when I landed in Australia. To discover that simple fact, I was obliged to cover 300 leagues and to lose three months. I was sent from town to town, station to station, and it was only in Bathurst, in the interior, that I chanced to discover my mother's fate.

"Norfolk is a fortified island. No one is admitted to that Tophet [52] but the damned and their demonic tempters. In spite of all my best efforts, I could not obtain permission to visit my mother there. I bought two blacks and a convict freed on license. We constructed a boat in a deserted creek off the Castelreagh river, built with the wood of the giant myrtles that cover the hills of muddy sand. A young fir-tree served as a mast, thickly-braided rushes as a sail. One night, we rowed down the Castlereagh and bravely set out into the equinoctial ocean. The breeze was blowing from the west; by day, we could not longer see anything of the coast but a blur, and the nameless islets scattered about the sea presented the same appearance to us. On the third night, we obtained fresh water and food at Middleton Reef, [53] halfway to Norfolk.

"On the sixth day, at five o'clock in the evening, we sighted the grey rocks of the island. Perkins, my convict, rowed ashore that very night, and contrived to discover, at the risk of his life, in which of the three compounds or camps Helen was imprisoned. As soon as he returned to the shore, we distanced ourselves from the coast and spent the following day out of sight. As the Sun went down, we came back to the land in spite of a northeast wind which pushed us back towards the open sea, and with the aid of our oars we reached the point at the south of the island. The camp, with its little fortress of tree-trunks, was no more than 300 yards away from the place where our boat was moored, with a rock serving as an anchor, in God's safekeeping.

"We needed all our resources. Perkins and I each had a double-barreled rifle and a pair of pistols; the blacks were armed with English hatchets, to cut into the palisades if we needed to, and long Malay daggers, whose utility was unfortunately less certain. There was a European sentry at the gate of the fort; the two aborigines squirmed across the sand like serpents and the sentry was stabbed without releasing a single cry.

"Perkins, who knew how these citadels were guarded, had brought two packets of fresh meat, by means of which two enormous mastiffs, as thin and long-legged as wolves, were enticed to approach. Perkins seized each of them by the tongue and the throat, and stabbed them in the heart. Then, he set out to find the sleeping-cabin where my mother might be hidden.

"As we crept across the first open space, I perceived by the feeble light of the clouded Moon an immobile and indistinct form in the very center of the yard. I went nearer; it was the trunk of a eucalyptus planted in the ground to serve as a pillory. Raised around it, resting on two feet of soil, was a small platform of planks to which a human being was attached. I went even closer. A hand of iron clamped upon my heart. I distinguished the form of a woman covered in rags and attached to the trunk by four cords, one of which held her neck, the second her wrists, which were bound behind her, the third her waist, and the fourth her ankles. One last step brought me so close to this woman that I could have touched her with my hand, had my arm not been paralyzed at my side.

"As soon as I saw it, I knew that this was my mother!

"In the inferno of Norfolk, as in the purgatories of continental Australia, she had found that same pack, always that terrible pack of savage suitors, mad dogs clad in red or in black, baring their teeth at one another and barking their lust, whip or dagger in hand. My mother had been subjected, from dusk to dawn, to the ignoble torture of the whip, as a punishment for 'rebellion.' From dusk to dawn, she had lain there, exposed like the hanged men left on the gibbets of feudal scaffolds.

"I thought she was dead, but she was asleep.

"She was asleep, harassed by fatigue and pain. At the first contact with my horrified hand, which touched the still-moist wounds on her bare shoulders, she shuddered and tried to fight. For six months, every one of her awakenings had been a hideous struggle. Her bonds restrained her; I put my handkerchief over her mouth to stifle her cry, and I whispered into her ear: 'It's me, mother. I've come to save you.'

"She murmured, with a weak discouraged sigh that I shall remember all my life: 'Still the dream pursues me!'

"In her sleep, she very often saw her son, who had come to rescue her.

"In less time that it takes me to tell you now, father, Helen was released from her bonds; Perkins and I placed her between us, to sustain her without staggering. While we were returning to the boat in this fashion, we lost sight of the two blacks, who rejoined us on the shore. We lifted the anchor. The wind was in our favor; we were already some way distant and no alarm had yet been raised on the island.

"My mother had my two hands upon her lips; I listened to her, as she spoke of God through her tears.

"Suddenly, a thick red flame sprang up behind us, like a lighthouse. All three of us were struck by the same thought: it was the fort that was burning.

The blacks had only escaped our surveillance for a minute, but a minute had been sufficient for those incendiary virtuosos. If any doubt had remained, two cannon shots that resounded in the night would have convinced us, followed soon afterwards by the explosion of the powder magazine. The aborigines, who were lying in the bottom of the boat, leapt to their feet at the noise of the detonation, and contemplated their work with a mute smile. It was a great misfortune for us, which excited a great deal of legitimate wrath and set an implacable pursuit upon our heels.

"Having avoided the first phase of the hunt, we set sail for New Zealand. We had no compass; Perkins was steering with the aid of the Sun and my watch. On the second day out, the sky darkened; we continued at hazard for more than a hundred hours. At the end of that time, we were hungry and thirsty, and on the following morning, we searched the horizon avidly for any sign of land. Perkins thought we were close to Cape Otou, the northernmost tip of New Zealand. The risen dawn showed us a rocky islet to port, in which direction the wind was blowing–and a naval schooner, that was being carried directly towards us by that same wind.

"We shipped our oars and added their force to that of the weakening breeze, and were able to hide our boat among the rocks without being seen. The schooner passed us by. We found rainwater in hollows in the rocks, and kangaroos in abundance to appease our hunger. My mother was pained by her wounds, but no word of complaint ever passed between us.

"None of us doubted that we were on one of the reefs south of Lord Howe Island–and, in consequence, quite near to the Australian coast that we wished to avoid. After two more days of tentative progress, the wind freshened, blowing eastwards, and drove us on to the most densely-inhabited stretch of coast, between Port Jackson and Newcastle. We happened, however, to land two hours after nightfall, and we went deep into the plain of sand that precede the prairie of dwarf myrtles–the bush, to employ the colonial term–whose immense mat extends over thousands of square miles. An hour from the sea, the bush takes on the appearance of a tea plantation, in which every plant is less than three feet tall. We called a halt beneath that Lilliputian cover.

"The two blacks went to Newcastle, while Perkins set off to walk to Sydney to attempt to obtain a passage for us on some merchant ship setting sail for Europe. We never saw the blacks again. Perkins returned on horseback, leading two other horses by the bridle. He had bought a compass at a neighboring station, not for a sea voyage now, but to steer us through the immensities of the bush. News had reached Port Jackson from Norfolk; there was a price on our heads. Mounted police were already scouring the coast for us.

"Perkins' plan, if one might call such a desperate enterprise a plan, was to get into the mountains, to cross them, and to reach the Macquarie River before attempting to penetrate the interior. He had only the vaguest idea of the breadth of the continent, and thought that it might not be impossible to reach Van

Diemen's Land across the desert. That night, we were at least 15 leagues into the bush.

"At daybreak, we saw–for the first time, in my case–the prodigious scene of desolation that is the uniform and terrible physiognomy of the land of Australia. The bush extended to the horizon in every side: a motionless ocean; a sea of dull and greying vegetation with a few islets formed by mountains of sand. As far as the eye could see, there was not a single salient point to break the mortal monotony of that aspect. The distant hills looked like waves suddenly frozen by a mysterious curse. Our eyes searched involuntarily for the petrified vessels that were the natural inhabitants of those paralyzed spaces.

"Nothing moved. There was no breach in the implacable line of that horizon. There was not a single four-legged creature, nor any bird, nor any snake.

"Our horses were tired. The morning wind got up at the same time as the Sun, whose disc was like a livid veil. The dirty sands were already charging the breeze with an impalpable dust that can blind travelers lost in those homicidal steppes within a few days. We allowed our mounts to browse the young shoots in peace while we lay down under the myrtles, where fatigue soon delivered us to sleep.

"The wind that burned our eyelids had at least one advantage. In a few hours, the wind would fill in the deep impressions left in the sand by our horses' hooves. It would require the noses of hunting-dogs trained by bush-rangers–as escaped convicts are called–to discover a trail beneath that fine dust. Often, if the wind was strong, even the dogs could not do it–but the blacks, much superior to dogs, separate the dust from the sand with hairs from an opossum's tail, as a skilled antiquary may uncover the finesse of a bas-relief beneath a thick layer of plaster, and it is by no means rare to see them sweep out a track in this way for several leagues. Without dogs and blacks, the bush would be an inviolable refuge for fugitives.

"We covered ten leagues on the second night. For 48 hours we had not seen a drop of water, but Perkins knew the secrets of these deserts. That morning, he exposed the roots of a sort of herbaceous myrtle, whose shoots were as dry as heather and also had an acrid odor; the obese roots, on the other hand, were rather like salsify, their tissues being swollen by watery sap and presenting a spongy texture. It was a supreme effort of nature in the inhospitable climate. Even here, the vegetable kingdom produces bread and wine, forcing acknowledgement of God's greatness. Why? Because here is a strange plant, comparable to the stomach of an African dromedary, that stores the water of the last rainfall for weeks on end, and delivers to your desiccated lips–in the middle of a desert where the very air is sufficiently charged with salt to irritate thirst to a feverish extreme–exactly what is necessary to avoid an agonizing death.

"On the fourth night, our exhausted horses collapsed. Perkins butchered the least emaciated, and we made a good meal; afterwards, we went on our way on foot.

"Our journey had lasted a week, during which the bush had changed its appearance little by little. There were a few tufts of grass between the bushes, which attained a slightly greater height themselves. The providential roots that supplied us with water were becoming rarer and drier; a few fir-trees showed up here and there, and a black line in the distance announced the presence of gum-trees.

" 'We're coming to a river,' Perkins said–and my poor mother regained courage.

"The neighborhood of a river, however, brought us even more danger than aid. It is invariably along the rivers that the squatters build their stations, because it is only there that sheep may graze. The mounted police also distribute their posts along the rivers, with their kennels and stables of aborigines.

"One Sunday evening, after nine hours on the march, we came into a region where the bush resembled recently-pruned shrubs, among which enormous saplings had been allowed to grow for centuries. These were eucalyptus trees, relatives of the myrtles: the tallest trees in the world, which attain a height of 220 or 230 feet, while their dwarf brothers barely raise a cubit above the soil. There were also groups of pines and acacias, vaguely reminiscent of the managed copses in English parks. We saw smoke between the trees, and the wind carried animal odors to us. We were close to a station.

"We waited for nightfall. Perkins gathered his strength, intending to procure us fresh horses and nourishment. He departed an hour after sunset. We heard dogs barking in the distance, then a gunshot. Perkins didn't come back.

"For two days, we had eaten nothing. In the same interval, the roots, progressively less moist, had refused us miraculous drops of water. The gunshot struck me as if it had penetrated my own heart. Perkins was our last hope.

"We could not think of taking flight. My mother was reduced to a state of extreme weakness and it had already become necessary for us both to support her as she walked.

" 'Carry me to that large tree, Henri,' my mother said.

"I obeyed. She sat down with her back to the trunk of the eucalyptus, and closed her eyes.

" 'I have every hope that you will be able to save yourself when you are alone,' she murmured. And as my lips opened to utter a word of reproach, she added, softly and calmly: 'Henri, my beloved child, it's here that I shall die.'

"That thought had never entered my head, father. The poor woman had had no parent to safeguard her youth. In her life of sin, what part had the mercy of God played in her misfortune? The same Providence that has placed that tear in the root of an arid plant, in the middle of the dirty sands, has placed in the heart of a child a source of love that nothing can dry up. Nothing! I loved my mother as though I had been the son of a saint..."

He stopped, covering his face with his trembling hands. The Marquis de Belcamp allowed himself to collapse into an armchair, his sad head bowed over is breast.

"No," Comte Henri went on, suddenly, "broken and weak as she was, that thought had never entered my head! Death surrounded us on every side, and Perkins' corpse had to be out there somewhere on the outskirts of the neighboring station. Hunger brings us death, as do thirst, fever and fatigue. There was death in the howls of those ferocious dogs and the raucous cries of the blacks in the woods. So what? I had not thought about death—my mother's, at least.

"I did not believe it. I dismissed the word and the idea, as one would a suggestion of delirium. It seemed to me to be impossible.

"But it was true. By the first light of day, I saw that pale face in which life as already no more than a fugitive and uncertain reflection. Her beautiful smile was upon her colorless lips. She said: 'Say a prayer for me, my son.'

"Her hands came together on her breast, and her enlarged eyes closed. I saw that her mouth was moving slowly, as if she were repeating after me the words of the orison. My voice could scarcely rise from my throat.

" 'My Lord,' she said, when I had finished, 'I shall not make my confession to my son, for fear of soiling his mind. I make my confession to you, in myself, to you who have said: my mercy is greater than their perversity...'

"She paused for a moment, immersed in the depths of her conscience.

"There was a blast of wind. The sand flew up everywhere. Around us, our recent tracks were already covered. The eucalyptus at whose foot we crouched was growing, as is often the case, in a sort of rounded basin whose rim was covered with thicker brush.

"I heard the barking of hunting dogs in the woods, and the ground occasionally reverberated with galloping hoofbeats. Whether Perkins had escaped or whether he was already dead, they had come running to search the bush—and if it had not been for the protective wind, the bloodhounds would have already bounded into the interior of our refuge.

" 'It is another master that I have offended,' my mother continued, after a long silence. 'You have reason to weep over me, Henri, my poor child, for I die without the forgiveness of the one who was the victim of my life. To him, I returned evil for good—and yet, I swear by that faith that is reborn in my soul and which is the flower of my final agony, that I have never had anything but profound respect and sincere love for him. In the very bosom of my folly, the image of my husband came to search me out. How many times have I been on the point of dragging myself to his knees?'

" 'Henri,' she went on, as a spark of enthusiasm reanimated her dying gaze for a moment, 'the hour is nigh; don't dispute my will. I want you to help me to get up.'

"I obeyed mechanically, and to prevent her from raising her voice–for the noise of the chase was drawing closer and the dogs were howling in the wind now.

"I took her in my arms. She could hardly breathe any longer. As soon as she was upright, she fell to her knees, murmuring: 'Let me go.'

"Then she clasped her hands together, extending them towards me. 'Comte de Belcamp,' she said to me, 'you are the son and heir of the one that I have so cruelly offended. His quarrel is yours, for I have insulted you in your father. I am kneeling before you, and I extend towards you my clasped hands to implore and beseech you. Comte Henri de Belcamp, in the name of your father, to forgive me and bless me!' "

A sob escaped the old Marquis' breast.

"Father," continued the young man, whose voice caught in his throat, "in your name, I blessed and I forgave..."

"And you did well, child," cried the old man, "for I was not there to pardon and bless in your place, was I?"

Henri threw himself into his arms, and they clasped one another to their bosoms while he finished, tearfully: "May God give you recompense, father! And may she hear you, who died so far away with your name upon her lips. She died without getting up, as befits a repentant sinner. She died with her hands joined together. She died on her knees."

The father and the son remained in one another's arms for some time. The son felt a loyal and gentle heart beating against his breast, full of love. If you had seen their tears mingling together, you would surely have found it impossible to think that those two sets of tears were not equally sincere.

The rest of the story was, in fact, of scant importance. As it provided an explanation, though, Comte Henri related how it came about that the owner of the station happened to be exactly the same young farmer who had formerly attempted to provide his mother with a home, how Helen Brown was given a Christian burial, and how the generous squatter facilitated Henri's embarkation for England.

"And that, father," he continued, "is how these last years, during which you have heard no word of me, have been spent. I bring mourning to a merciful and good man, the head of a family; but to the son upon whom these austere portraits gaze, I bring the security of honor and a solemn guarantee. The name of Belcamp emerges unstained from this whole trial. It shall not resound in the English courts; it is not written in a single register of infamy; it is not graven on that poor distant tombstone..."

"Henri," said the Marquis, after a long pause. "I believe you, and I shall prove it. It was for me–or, rather, for both of us, since we constitute a single and whole family–that you made that long hard voyage; it was for me, equally, that you adopted the name of Brown for that purpose. Have you ever used the name Brown before, Henri?"

"I used it continually until the day when I presented myself at your house, for 15 years, father."

"And never again?"

"Never."

"I hesitate to ask you another question, my son," the old man continued, visibly embarrassed.

"Don't hesitate to ask me, father, any more than I shall hesitate to answer."

"There is a strange coincidence. I have often heard talk, in London, of a son of Helen Brown, but no one ever calls him Henry Brown."

"Tom Brown!" exclaimed the young Comte.

"Exactly," replied the Marquis. "Tom Brown."

"Father," Henri said, in that clear and candid tone which suited his noble visage so well, "there are two distinct phases in the life of Helen Brown: one of crime and one of expiation. Even in the criminal phase, she respected your name, and that is surely the proof that there remained a vestige of honesty in the depths of her heart–but she was surrounded by wretches who were past the experience of any scruple.

"Tom Brown was a scarecrow designed to hold you at arm's length, an engine of war directed uniquely against you. I do not know Tom Brown. Perhaps it is not a false name, for there are as many Browns as there are paving-stones in the city of London. What is false, and imaginary, is the notion that he is Helen's son. It is evident that this Tom Brown has been made into a phantom of my own personality. Perhaps it is his own doing, since he is said to be a precocious bandit of singular intelligence, reliant on his status as the son of a lord—these words were quoted in a trial that I followed attentively at the time—to deceive or sow fear in the lower ranks of the police."

"This Tom Brown," the old man persisted, "departed for Sydney on the same ship as his pretended mother."

"I remember that distinctly."

"Did you hear talk of him in Australia?"

"Often."

"Did he not escape?"

"He did, in the most skillful and audacious fashion."

"And does anyone know what has become of him?"

"He has become the King of London's malefactors. He has killed la Bartolozzi and driven Superintendent Gregory Temple mad. He calls himself John Devil the Quaker."

"And have we anything to fear from him?"

"No, since he is deluded. Only Helen knew the truth, and it is all over with her."

The old Marquis remained pensive for a moment, then he got up abruptly, as if he had been seized by a bothersome thought.

"In any case, Henri, my son," he said, his voice suddenly changing, "this is your heritage. You are brave, you are strong, you are young, you are learned, and you know the world. By God, if you are attacked, you will defend yourself!" He took the young man's hand and looked him in the face, good-humoredly. "In consequence, we shall be able to ride our high horse until the end of time," he continued, smiling. "Monsieur le Comte de Belcamp, we have said and done that which we owed to one another. I am content with you and with myself—and, all things considered, with our old manor and its thousands of *écus* of rents, although it will not permit us to live like princes. Our name is safe, God be praised! But let's get out of this drawing-room, Henri, my dear son, and since all these proud crusaders will no longer be able to see me, I shall show you that I am just a poor old man, too feeble even to bear any grudge regarding his own misfortune."

He crossed the room and went out first. Following him, the young Comte caught sight of his own face in the mirror, and saw that it wore an expression of mistrust. Evidently, this change in his father's manner presented him with a puzzle to be solved.

The Marquis had scarcely crossed the threshold, however, when he turned round, his hand plunged into the breast of his hunting-jacket. It extracted the locket with which we are already familiar–and Henri saw the portrait of his mother.

Henri felt a kind of confusion, because this surpassed his expectations. He kissed the hand that held the locket, and murmured in a penetrating tone: "You shall be thanked, father, more than in words."

"I shall love you very much, Henri," replied the old man. "Don't thank me, love me. If you only knew how I have needed affection! Come and see your farm and your fields, my boy. We are not very great lords, now."

It is truly disgraceful not to have enough to give. We are all actors, and excellent hearts also have their innocent deceits. At that moment, the Marquis became bourgeois with pleasure, and sought what many people call communal feelings, not merely to let the matter of the conserved locket fall from a lesser height, but also to excuse the modesty of his domain. He passed his arm beneath Henri's, who was even more emotional now than he had been during his solemn explanation.

As they went down the steps of the chateau, Henri paused, as if the marvelous panorama of the Oise valley had struck him for the first time.

"To be sure, to be sure," murmured the Marquis, with a slightly constrained smile. "There's a pleasure that you'll be able to take in its full abundance, Belcamp. As the proverb says, the view costs nothing!" He took a few steps towards the windows and shouted: "Hey, Pierre, Madame Etienne and all the rest!"

Immediately, little Julot–jostling past Anille in order to be first–threw himself into the courtyard, cap in hand. Anille followed, thumping him in the back. Then came Fanchette the chambermaid, Pierre the chamberlain, François the coachman-gardener, and finally Madame Etienne, the most considerable functionary of the petty empire. They had all been waiting for this moment, and had queued up at the kitchen-door, the men with their caps in hand and the women with their hands in their apron pockets. Madame Etienne had made a formal promise that the Marquis would make a speech.

"My children," said the old man, "this is the Comte de Belcamp, your master."

"Good day to you, my friends, good day," Henri added, smiling affably.

That was all.

Briquet, who had stayed by the window–whose sill he had already cut into in order to engrave the first letter of his name–declared that one would have thought him capable of handing out a coin or two. The others, without making light of the possibility of a gratuity, were more disappointed by the lack of ceremony.

"In my former mistress's place," said Madame Etienne, returning to her casserole, "when the young man came home, Uncle Gruel–who was the curate at

Saint-Brice–addressed all the domestics for a quarter of an hour with the eloquence of his heart.”

“Isn’t he a dainty chap, though, our Henri?” sighed Anille–which earned her a thump in the back from Julot.

“You should see the ones in Paris!” said Briquet.

“Are they all like you, Monsieur Trompe-d’Eustache?” asked Fanchette, a pretty girl with her wits about her.

The Parisian replied with prideful modesty: “They’re bigger, and I don’t have the clothes.” Then he added: “Mademoiselle Fanchette, you have insufficient education to speak of scientific matters like my nickname Trompe-d’Eustache. If you wish, I’ll explain its significance to you in private. Briquet is my formal mode of address, Bricole is what my friends call me.”

“And Trompe-d’Eustache is like saying Bobèche or Galimafré,”[54] Madame Etienne put in, rudely, having just seen the freshly-engraved window-sill. “You’re titillating, and you’re good for nothing but doing damage to my kitchen; it’s because of you that I wasn’t able to invite Monsieur le Comte to come in here so that it might pass the inspection of a master’s eye.”

At that moment, the old man was opening the little door to the right of the gate, saying: “Those were all the servants that remain to us; there are six in all, for the entire Chateau de Belcamp!”

“In that not enough, father?” Henri asked.

“For me, quite... but since your trunks have arrived, Henri, I am ambitious. Your grandfather was the Lieutenant-General of the King’s armies, and before departing for London, I was closely related to four ducal families. Would you have any objection to serving the King, Monsieur le Comte?”

“I shall leave my plans and my vocation to you, father; your advice shall be my determination. There are immense fortunes to be made in Australia.”

“Trade!” murmured the old man, knitting his eyebrows and blushing. “I don’t remember any Belcamp ever having exposed himself to the risk of bankruptcy... here is our farm.”

“There are farms in Australia too,” observed the young Comte, softly. “All is commerce in today’s world–and Rohan, the greatest name in France, was once a bankrupt.”

“Here is our farm,” repeated the old man, already smiling.

There was a magnificent small holding adjacent to the wall of the park, whose carefully-cultivated acreage extended as far as the river.

“It brings in 18,000 *livres* after taxes,” the Marquis said. “Outside of that, we don’t have an *écu*, Monsieur le Comte, and the chateau has to be maintained. The park wall cost me 50 *louis* last year. Listen, boy, you do well to consult me, because you’ll never find a better friend than me, but if I am scornful, don’t take offense. When I was your age, my mother owned all the land you see on the far side of the river, as far as l’Isle-Adam. It’s me that has ruined you, by disobeying the King without taking the side of the people. I was for the King and I am still for the King, but my sword broke in my hand when it became necessary to direct its point against Frenchmen. My mother told me that I was a woman, and she had good reason; it was necessary to be one thing or the other; there's no middle route between devotion to duty and rebellion. I was worthless; it was just that I should be broken like my sword. If that's what you want, my boy, I'll sell the farm and give you the money to make millions in Australia."

"If you'll go with me, father!" Henri said, clasping the arm that he was holding to his breast.

"By damn!" the Marquis replied. "It wouldn't make me any less of a gentleman! Our four ducal cousins have each come to see me once–with their duchesses, no less. I don't know how they've done it, but they've lost none of their lands or chateaux. They all said to me, and their duchesses too: 'Cousin, it's a matter of making a good marriage'...the implication being: 'Since you haven't a *sou...*' " He interrupted himself, raising a finger to point along a side-path to a gracious mansion, halfway up a hill, among clumps of trees. "Hold on, Henri– there's the Priory, where that dear child you saved this morning resides."

"Mademoiselle Jeanne," said Henri. "A charming person."

"And as good as, or better than, she is charming–a little further on, to the left, is the cottage of my brigand, Robert Surrisy."

"Is that a noble name?"

"We're not the only ones to hide our history," murmured the old Marquis, "and nobility is rare in Miremont. Old Madeleine says, however, that their ancestors were gentlefolk. She's a poor woman, who works with her hands to make a living, and who..." He paused, then continued, abruptly: "Go into trade, Henri! Go into trade, damn it, and don't listen to an old fool! Do you know who my friends are, apart from Madeleine's son? They're the Herbets, the Besnards, the Chaumerons, my two deputies, Morin and Potel–for I'm Mayor of my constituency–and two or three other families of retired merchants. My pride makes me laugh. And what would my four dukes and their duchesses do in the midst of these good folk? These people like me, and I like them. What I am afraid of, my boy, is that you expected to find yourself heir to the grandeur of our ancestors."

His anxiety was manifest, for his words were too humble and too bitter by turns.

"I came to find my father," Henri replied, simply. His gaze wandered involuntarily towards that modest and pretty house whose blue roof was half-visible behind the trees. "Are the Herbets rich?" he asked.

"The aunt, Madame Touchard, has a small income," the Marquis replied, "but the two children are in her care now that their mother is dead."

"Has Madame Bartolozzi left nothing to her children?"

The Marquis turned around, astonished. "How did you know...?" he began.

"I came from London," Henri put in, "and I chatted this morning with that young man, Robert Surrisy."

"A noble and loyal creature! His mother has been unfortunate, and I have a genuine affection for them. For your guidance, it's generally believed hereabouts that Constance Herbet was married in England. Robert and Laurent have been over there to look into her affairs, but la Bartolozzi left nothing but debts."

"So do they all!" Henri observed, in a tone of perfect indifference.

Eighteen thousand *livres* in rent from a single tenant with a park of a hundred-and-some acres, overlooked by a stylish chateau in good order, was not, at the commencement of the Restoration, quite as humble an estate as the Marquis de Belcamp was trying to make out. The great fortunes of the landowners had not yet been reconstituted and the great fortunes of the industrialists had not yet been made. It was ambition that made him speak in these terms, and his newly-born ambition was for his son. He was already dreading having done too little for the one who would be the joy of his life.

Henri's mind was on very different things. There were many questions pressing upon his lips, but which he would not allow to escape, so imperious was his self-possession. These questions had nothing to do with his father's fortune. Comte Henri was playing a much bigger game than that.

At the midday meal, which was called dinner in those days, Henri was presented to a sweet and beautiful young woman, Suzanne Temple.

Since her father's illness, Suzanne had effectively become the Marquis' ward. She immediately thanked Henri for having saved her dearest friend, Jeanne; then, when the young Comte said a few words in reply–commonplaces of the sort that the modesty of convention matches to praise–she shivered at the sound of his voice. When he looked at her, smiling, she lowered her eyes and went pale. During the meal, she made an effort to be pleasant. The Marquis, full of joy, was arranging his new life and wanted everyone in the world to be happy.

When the meal was over, horsemen, carriages and pedestrians began trooping through the wide-open gate. In the country, certain kinds of news spread with singular rapidity. The entire district knew about Henri's arrival, and everyone wanted to see him.

An old couple were the first to cross the courtyard: a solemnly marching husband and a fat woman, rather embarrassed, in her best clothes. Inscribed upon their persons, in easily readable characters, were the words that no bleach has the power to efface: retired from trade.

"Those are the Morins du Reposoir,"[55] said the Marquis. "Good people." He added, furtively squeezing his son's hand: "All that they are bears witness to their affection for me. This isn't your world, Henri, but be pleasant for my sake. This exhibition, as we say in London, is a bill that only has to be paid once..."

"Oh, father," Henri replied, happily, "if you were not so generous I would think that you were making fun of me. I haven't come from the court, and I dare say that beside your four dukes and their duchesses, I would cut a rather miserable figure..."

"You, boy!" exclaimed the Marquis. "In the midst of 20 dukes, you would have the air of a king! Ah, for example..." He moved closer to the window. "Here are two that might interest you, the Bondon de la Perrière twins. Come see, Henri—it would cost you two *sous* at a fairground but it's free here."

As he obeyed, the young Comte passed close to Suzanne Temple, who got up from the table. The Marquis had his back turned. Henri took Suzanne's hand, touched it lightly to his lips, and murmured: "Mademoiselle, I am your friend; you have nothing to fear from me."

"That's easy for you to say!" Suzanne murmured, her white cheeks reddening.

"Come on," said the Marquis, "You'll miss the view!"

Henri put a finger to his lips and joined his father. Two hearty fellows of about 40, their heads squarely planted on their thin necks, with broad noses, full lips, thick joined-up eyebrows and enormous shoulders, were walking staidly, keeping in step, separated by a slight and sallow woman whose raised-up silk dress displayed the legs of a wading bird. She wriggled between the perfectly equal and symmetrical Hercules on her right and left flanks, both of them growling at her while she smiled at both of them—although only one of them was her husband, for the law is strict. Florian Bondon de la Perrière—the left-hand Bondon, as he was generally called—wore a lilac ribbon on his arm to avoid the possibility of unwitting adultery.

There was a touching story attached to these two fair-haired beauties, whose resemblance deceived even their mother's eyes, and who could only be distinguished from one another by ribbons of different colors; if some mischievous hand effected an exchange of ribbons, the exquisite and divine sensibility of maternal love itself fell into error. In their youth, Célestin and Florian Bondon had been the heroes of that graceful poem. They remembered it with pleasure, and Madame Célestin loved to recount at great length her mother-in-law's numerous mistakes. They were Siamese twins, save for the cumbersome and prodigious connection that might actually have conjoined them. Célestin then adopted the color pink, while lilac was reserved for Florian—who, in addition, always took the left-hand side. Mother Bondon was methodical; when she was deceived, she whipped both hands and both colors, in consequence of which she induced the two little ones to avoid mischief.

When they grew up, Célestin and Florian, the two lambs of the sheep-fold, became strong and rather plain rams. Célestin remained honest, but Florian was passionate, and achieved a profitable revival of the infamous drama of *The Menaechmes*.[56] Célestin was obliged on several occasions, in spite of his pink ribbon, to pay his brother's debts—and, according to rumor, to receive several stern warnings delivered with the aid of a stick by anxious spouses. When he married, the local comedians called his wife Madame Jumeaux. There were even worse anecdotes, because Férandeau took it into his head one day to attach the lilac ribbon—which he had obtained clandestinely from the bachelor—to the hus-

and's arm. That walk in the moonlight was talked about for a long time, but Madame Célestin never complained about it, and the two Bondons de la Perrière always presented to all and sundry the image of a perfect union.

In addition to his position as a spouse, Célestin was a member of the municipal council: Florian took his left-hand side and commanded the National Guard, with the rank of Sergeant. Mademoiselle Chaumeron, the eldest daughter of the great Chaumeron family, had paid court to him, but Madame Célestin did not want another woman in her house.

The right-hand Bondon, the left-hand Bondon and Madame Célestin had a collective nickname, the pupil of David having compared the remarkable trio to two colossal candlesticks flanking a diminutive clock: the trinity was designated "the Bondon garniture."[57]

The family Chaumeron were 13 at table, but none of them had died all year. Those received at the Chateau de Belcamp were the father, the mother and the eldest daughter; the others only came to outdoor parties on the lawn.

Monsieur Potel, the Second Deputy–a learned man of means who secretly aspired to a sub-prefecture–had a light cart, and his chestnut horse was prancing into the courtyard at that moment. His main distinction was to have proved in a pamphlet that Miremont (*Mons mirabilis*)[58] was a town even more ancient than Paris. He was a hearty countryman, a widow and the father of one of the three young women in the charabanc. Mademoiselle Germaine Potel was a happy and humorous 16-year-old. Her big black eyes moistened whenever there was talk of a good deed done or to do, but she was an incorrigible mischief-maker who thought of nothing but amusement when she was not working for the poor: a veritable imp, more lively, crazy and scatterbrained than the age in which she lived. She had been the lovely Jeanne's only friend until Miss Temple had arrived at the manor.

We need itemize only one more family, composed of Madame Besnard–the widow of a former steward of pre-Revolutionary Belcamp–and her son, Monsieur Besnard junior, a local beau and rustic Don Juan.

Monsieur de Belcamp came into the drawing-room arm-in-arm with the son whom everyone had come to see, as if he were some exotic beast. The Morins, the Chaumerons and the Bondons had already been shown in by Pierre.

"Monsieur le Maire," said Morin–for that title completely effaces that of Marquis from the viewpoint of a First Deputy–"my wife and I wished, on this solemn occasion, to offer you our sincere felicitations, motivated by the happy event that has brought this assembly together. I refer to the return of Monsieur le Comte de Belcamp, your son." This speech was made in a firm and clear voice honed to perfection by municipal harangues.

Madame Morin added: "Many apologies... many apologies..." She was a timid wife, unable to shake off the habits of counter-service and humble circumstance.

"Your turn, Célestin!" murmured Madame Bondon.

Célestin raised his right arm, and Florian's arm immediately reproduced the gesture, as if the twins were connected by an invisible thread. At the same time and in the same voice, both brothers said: "Monsieur le Marquis, I have come with my brother..."

"...and my wife..." added Célestin, solo.

"...to give you my heartiest congratulations," they finished in unison.

The two arms fell back. Madame Bondon divided a haughtily approving glance between the two of them.

"Yes indeed!" said Papa Chaumeron, who was the most cheerful man in the district, unceremoniously. "Me, I wear my heart on my sleeve, you know; allusions evade me; can't do compliments. We shall love the son as we love the father, that's it! All done, Papa Chaumeron. Let's go."

"What lovely fair hair," Mademoiselle whispered in her mother's ear. In Miremont, when anyone said "Mademoiselle" without further addition, the reference was to the eldest of the Chaumerons; she was one of those mature daughters who had had the beauty of the devil for a dowry, but had lost it some time ago.

"Be very dainty and don't smoke," her mother replied, "and I dare say he'll notice you."

Comte Henri was charming. You might have thought that he was a candidate for office, such was the grace and bonhomie with which he responded to his welcome. The Marquis was grateful, almost tearful, as he watched the young man waste such cordiality on such a poor company for love of him. As for Miremontese "society," it was over the Moon. Morin had received three well-crafted compliments on his famous oratory; Madame Célestin, between her two caryatids, had been gratified by a smile; Papa Chaumeron's fingers were still tingling from a handshake akin to his own, but superior; and Mademoiselle's heart was still racing five minutes after the particularly friendly greeting she had obtained.

The pretty Germaine only met his eyes, but her lovely black eyes lowered while her rosy cheeks became more vivid; she sat down beside Miss Suzanne and whispered in her ear: "How frightened Jeanne must have been in his arms!"

Jeanne and her brother Laurent were doubly entitled to be the favorite topic of conversation today, and everyone had something to say about them. Madame Many-Apologies Morin set her timidity aside to whisper that they would soon have neither parent nor place. Madame Célestin emphasized the fact by adding that the widow Touchard, the aunt, was on the point of showing them the door—in support of which the Bondon twins made the same gesture and proffered the same smile.

"I'm a plain speaker, me," muttered Papa Chaumeron. "The income they had from Heaven knows where has dried up, and the widow's practically penniless. Hey ho!"

"They'll go to Madeleine's," Mademoiselle insinuated, in a bittersweet tone. "Monsieur Robert won't leave them wanting, that's for sure!"

"Hardly!" said Besnard junior, miserably. "La Surrisy hasn't a *sou!*"

Provincial pity is the heaviest bludgeon of all. In the house of the Marquis–whose sympathies were well-known–the general commiseration had become even more offensive than usual.

"Jeanne has good friends," said Germaine, however, indignation making her even prettier.

"Let us go to see," concluded the Marquis, getting to his feet. "I'm eager to have more news from the Priory."

Comte Henri had said nothing. He went to Suzanne, who seemed to be stricken by some strange malaise, and offered her his arm.

Suzanne shivered, and gave him her trembling hand. "Come with us, Germaine!" she begged.

Germaine was afraid of the newcomer, whom she thought as beautiful as a star, but she was curious and young women like to be afraid. Comte Henri, Suzanne and Germaine formed a group in the middle of the caravan, which went out through the gate to take the path leading to the riverbank. The others gravitated about this center, dispersing along the route, everyone talking about the same subject and singing the various parts of an enthusiastic chorus in celebratory praise of Henri. One voice alone opposed this unanimity: that of Besnard junior, the Lovelace [59] of the commune.

They arrived at the bridge, at the very spot where the event had taken place. Comte Henri was kind enough to offer a detailed account of the adventure–a story that was even more interesting when one had the scene before one's eyes. The mill-workers came to their doorstep and tipped their caps, furnishing their own brief but energetic explanations to all and sundry.

When the march resumed, Monsieur Besnard muttered between his teeth: "What a mighty feat! All of 25 strokes!"

This jealous utterance remained unechoed, however. Ten contrary voices intoned yet again the canticle of admiration, and the eldest Mademoiselle Chaumeron said to her mother: "That little Jeanne has had her share of luck!"

There was only room to cross the bridge two abreast. Germaine was obliged to drop in behind Suzanne and Henri. She saw Henri seize the opportunity to say a single word in private. When she resumed her place, Suzanne was as pale as a corpse.

Jeanne soon came into view, not quite herself but smiling, advancing to meet the caravan on her brother's arm. The old Marquis embraced her in heartfelt fashion. He loved her all the more now that she owed her life to Henri.

The widow Touchard, her aunt, came to thank the savior of her niece, but those thanks were a long way short of matching those that Robert and Laurent had rendered in the clump of willows, and Madame Touchard finished up by saying dryly: "Perhaps my niece needed to be taught a lesson regarding her imprudence."

Comte Henri saw the young woman change color, and that her eyelids were tremulous. Her eyes became brighter as the widow Touchard continued: "She has not even said a proper thank you to Monsieur le Comte."

"That's true," Jeanne murmured, so softly that even those standing next to her could hardly hear her, "but I'm by no means ungrateful!"

In the context of our habitual effusiveness, these words said very little, but they said too much for Laurent, who looked at his sister with astonishment and disquiet.

"That's a heavy cargo you have there, my poor Madame Touchard," said Mademoiselle to the aunt.

The aunt, stiff and tight-lipped, shrugged her shoulders as she replied: "It can't last long, as you well know... if it hadn't been for the accident, I'd have let it go today."

Within ten seconds, the entire company knew what the aunt had said. Laurent and Jeanne were definitely under sentence.

At that moment, Robert seized the hand of Comte Henri, who greeted Jeanne, saying: "Would you permit me to feel your pulse, mademoiselle?"

"Are you a doctor of medicine, Henri?" asked the Marquis, merrily.

"I would not venture to say of medicine," the young Comte replied, in the same tone, "but doctor, yes, by diploma of the faculty of Tubingen. Regarding the particular circumstances in which Mademoiselle Jeanne finds herself, I have had other experience, in a less civilized context."

While speaking he had taken the young woman's arm; the touch of his hand made her grow pale.

She, too, is afraid! thought Germaine.

A circle had formed around them, and everyone was looking on curiously. Mademoiselle and Besnard junior exchanged a knowing wink.

"Will you trust me, Mademoiselle Jeanne?" Henri asked, with a softer smile.

"Yes," she replied, very quietly.

"Then, I shall give you something that will calm your fever and lighten the burden within your breast."

"That's true," murmured Jeanne. "It's as if I had a weight upon my heart."

Henri gave her poor trembling hand to Robert and instructed that the invalid must be put to bed immediately. Then, taking a step towards the aunt, he said, emphasizing every word: "It is imperative, Madame, that your niece must not be subjected to any distress or disquiet of any sort for several days."

"That cannot be guaranteed," the widow replied, almost brutally.

"Indeed, Madame," Henri said, lowering his voice but speaking sternly, "when you have heard me out, you will guarantee everything!" Having subjugated her with his gaze, he added: "We have legal matters to discuss, Madame."

Robert, Laurent and Jeanne went slowly back to the house with Germaine and Miss Temple. The widow stayed where she was, looking at Henri open-mouthed. The astonished circle of onlookers had only heard the last few words: *legal matters to discuss.*

"Are you a lawyer too, Monsieur le Comte?" asked the Marquis, whose astonishment was at least equal to theirs.

Henri nodded his head diffidently. "Licenciate of Jena, father," he replied, lightly, "and doctor of law of the University of Cambridge." As he spoke, he took the widow's arm and led her away.

The consequent scene was arranged and conducted without reference to anyone else; no one but the principal actor was in on the secret. All gazes followed the couple as they drew away; there was a singular contrast between the noble figure of the young cavalier and the gross awkwardness of the widow.

Monsieur Potel, a Second Deputy and orderly man who liked to keep track of things, consulted his watch; the interview, according to him, lasted exactly a minute and a half. The widow, when she returned, seemed transfigured: the disagreeable expression on her face had completely disappeared. In the gallant features of Monsieur le Comte, on the other hand, nothing was discernible but a lightly mocking smile. He headed toward the house, doubtless to complete his medical duties.

Don Juan Besnard sidled up to Mademoiselle Chaumeron in order to compare notes. They were unanimous in declaring that there was something shady about the business.

"Come in, Mesdames and Messieurs," said the widow Touchard, in an entirely amiable manner. "I can't imagine why I let you remain outside. It was distress. My sister's children are my entire family, thank God! I have no one on Earth to love but them, and when I saw my dear little Jeanne return this morning... ah, Lord knows, I break out into a cold sweat just thinking about it!"

"Mademoiselle Jeanne has no other needs henceforth but solitude and silence, my good woman," Comte Henri said, as he descended the steps with Suzanne and Germaine. "We shall all take leave of you; but first, in the name of those who have the right to watch over your wards, my dear Madame Touchard, I congratulate you and thank you."

A ripple of astonishment ran around the circle, which was still continuing as everyone came to the riverbank again. There, horses, carts and charabancs were waiting to be boarded, like the wagons that follow an army. Never had the sphinx posed such a riddle to Miremontese society. It was no more and no less than a miracle. The aunt had been touched by a magic wand. The people on foot and on horseback, in charabancs or carts, were all of the same opinion: it was a miracle!

"My boy," said the Marquis, as they climbed the winding path that was taking them back to the chateau, "you must acquaint me with your other talents, for even I seem to be a mere yokel from Pontoise... isn't that so, Suzanne?"

"Monsieur le Comte de Belcamp knows many things," murmured the young woman, attempting to smile.

"And what the Devil did you say to that she-wolf to change her into a lamb?" the old man went on, veiling his genuine and vibrant curiosity with the tone of pleasantry.

"My father," said Henri, even more gaily, "I have so far only rendered count of three of my seven years of absence. I still owe you the rest, and I shall discharge my obligation over a period of time. You can see that I have not totally wasted my time during my travels. I am ambitious, as you said. If it were sufficient to come to the fore in life, as it used to be, to equip oneself with arms and deliver telling blows with axe or lance, I would endeavor to choose the best lance, the best axe and the best armor; then I would harden my muscles in order to bear them. But those days are gone; I have therefore equipped myself with other arms."

The old man put his right arm around his son's neck and they walked on in this manner, shoulder-to-shoulder. "Son," he said, in a soft voice tremulous with inexpressible affection, "I firmly believe that you have a higher destiny than this place. I have a great deal of pride, but just as much pain. You have placed yourself within arm's reach of these good people, and within mine, and I thank you—but some day, fame and fortune will come to fetch you, and I shall be alone once more. If you have to leave us again, my son, it might be better if you did not return."

After the evening meal, when the young Comte and Suzanne had retired to their rooms, the Marquis slowly made his way to his own bedchamber. He sent Pierre away to prevent him chattering. He went to bed, but his joy was like a fever that chased sleep away. When he finally went to sleep, he dreamed that he saw a petite wife, gentle and beautiful, surrounded by little children who resembled his beloved Henri.

VII. *A Busy Night*

There were logs blazing in the large fireplace, in order to drive the lingering damp out of the empty apartments. Slanting moonlight projected the diamond-shaped checkered shadows of the leaded windows on to the long white curtains, still folded, that had been brought out of the wardrobe. The night was calm; no noise was audible outside save for the breeze singing its chromatic scale in the branches and the miserly mill encroaching upon the hour of slumber.

Comte Henri was sitting at a writing desk on whose lid were set his open portfolio, his pistols and several opened letters. The lamplight fell vertically upon his head, so young but admirably pensive, which he supported with his hand. His fingers, delicate but firm, were half-hidden by his blond curls. His eyes were lowered, and the profile that descended from his forehead to his eyelashes, following the curve of his long eyelid, was exquisitely pure. His large forehead was thoughtful, the partitions of his skull stretched by the power of his will. An adept of phrenological science might perhaps have divined, between those harmonious ears that seemed sculpted in white marble and beneath those silken curls, the twin mounds in which Gall has placed conjectural promises of military glory–and the threat of murder.

Not everyone is a follower of Gall, and not all Gall's followers are in perfect accord with one another. An ordinary man, instead of searching for these problematic hillocks, would have directed his gaze upon the almost feminine delicacy of those temples, on the elegant and vigorous musculature of that neck, and most of all upon those clean-cut lips, upon which a pensive smile was presently playing.

"What's old Gregory doing now?" he murmured, as his smile broadened. "How many paces has he taken along the trail? And how do I come out on the balance-sheet on a day when I have had such a major part to play? Have I profited or lost? Should I increase or decrease my score?"

He took a blank sheet of paper and dipped his pen in the ink.

"My poor devil of a master," he continued, "is an intelligent and learned man, after all. His misfortune is to have encountered someone even more learned and intelligent than he. The Thompson business is a stroke of genius! If I had not been able to divert his hounds along that track, I think that old Gregory, in spite of his own calculations–which I have countered move for move– would have remained on the right track."

He divided the blank sheet in two with a long vertical line. To the right, he rapidly inscribed three names: *Jeanne, Suzanne, Madame Touchard.* To the left, he wrote only one: *Belcamp.* Then, he became meditative, as if he had laboriously worked out in his head the unknown quantity of some mysterious equation.

"Multiplying obstacles, incessantly retreating further into the impossible," he pronounced, slowly. "That is the law posited by Gregory Temple himself. Is it strictly true? I don't know, and it scarcely matters. I have gone into the ring to do battle, and I must concentrate my tactics there. If I should chance to be defeated, if some furious madman—for that is what it would take—comes to say to me: 'You are an assassin,' I shall counter that disloyal or extravagant accusation with the absolute, philosophical and mathematical sincerity of my table of alibis. If I were still defeated in the aftermath of the accusation, contrary to justice, it would not be unprecedented... Indeed, I have often asked myself why, down there in Seville, the bull always waits in the arena for the matador's sword. I remember wanting to cry to the bull: 'disembowel or flee!' I shall follow that advice, and with one bound I shall find freedom outside the arena."

His hand gently caressed his forehead.

"Multiplying obstacles, incessantly retreating further into the impossible," he quoted, for a second time, as if a light had sprung forth from those words. "An ingenious formula, but puerile, as all formulas are. Every time some Archimedes takes the bit in his teeth and cries: '*Eureka!*' the Devil laughs. What is the impossible, humanly speaking? It's what the makers of theorems call the absurd. Gregory's entire theory rests on a series of demonstrations of absurdity. Are you accused of having talked too much? Prove that you are mute. Of having bitten? Open your mouth and show that you have no teeth. If the crime has left the imprint of a bloody foot on a floor, have yourself carried there and let everyone see your two wooden legs. How can the mute be convicted of speech, the deaf of having listened at the door, the blind for having taken aim at a target? The absent, in sum, for it is in the alibi that the theory is consummated. How can the absent be convicted of doing something that requires his actual presence?

"If I were a judge, and had ten worthy witnesses swear on oath before me: 'This man has killed; I saw him do it,' I might doubt it—but I could have no further doubt if that man responded to ten other witnesses with his own testimony: 'I have not killed, for I have neither dagger, nor hand, nor arm, nor shoulder.' The certitude is in the impossibility. The testimony of the senses themselves cannot create the absolute that does not exist. It requires a bold individual to occupy a seat of judgment!"

While he was talking, he had written in the left-hand column, beneath the name of *Belcamp*, two other names—*Laurent* and *Jeanne*—with the result that the table was now configured thus:

Marquis de Belcamp	*Jeanne*
Laurent	*Suzanne*
Jeanne	*Madame Touchard*

"I have gained this," he continued, "And I have lost that... I have gained my father, and that was the most difficult, for circumstances were united against me. I have gained that which is of incomparable value to me: the precise knowledge of the two final obstacles that stand between myself and my goal. I knew that Constance Bartolozzi had heirs; I searched for them; they are here!"

His finger indicated the names of *Laurent* and *Jeanne*.

"I have gained much," he continued. "I have lost much, too–perhaps voluntarily, as one sacrifices pieces in a game of chess, perhaps by a misfortune that even the best moves could not have countered entirely. How could I have expected to find Gregory Temple's daughter, Suzanne, here? A bad card, that one, if it cannot be played with supreme skill! But a major trump nevertheless, if it can be played at the right time... which shall it be?"

His slightly furrowed eyebrows relaxed, and a sad smile played upon his lips, while he murmured: "Poor Suzanne! I have seen her before, radiant with youth and happiness. I have seen her so joyful and so beautiful that her mere appearance enlivened the heart like the Sun in spring. At present, her eyelids fall languidly, like a veil accustomed to catching tears. If she had not encountered me on her path through life..."

He sighed, and remained silent for a moment.

"Get on! Get on!" he murmured. "The Wandering Jew isn't the only one to whom Fate has spoken thus. She says it to everyone enslaved by a tyrannical thought, the greatest that man... Suzanne is a weapon directed against me; if I cannot redirect her, I must break her! That's the law.

"To this one," he went on, turning his gaze upon the name of *Madame Touchard*, "I have given part of my secret. She will let it out in time, I know, and perhaps it will be better for everyone in France to remain in complete ignorance regarding the Bartolozzi affair... but old Temple and Dr. John Devil agree that it is necessary to seize the bull by the horns when difficulties arise. *I cannot be guilty*, that is the principle. Should I conduct myself like those who dread their conscience? Imprudence is only for the criminal. I have done well. And so we come to my beautiful Jeanne!"

For a few seconds, his pen sketched out, with a singular facility and a remarkable vigor of execution, the silhouette of a young woman with her eyes closed and her head overrun by the beautiful mass of her hair. It was a masterly piece of work; anyone who had seen Jeanne Herbet, even once, would have recognized her at first glance.

"Jeanne!" he repeated, his voice as gentle and sonorous as a song. "Was the name ever so charming? Why does it wake an echo in the depths of my being? Her death is worth nine million, and I have saved her twice in one day. Is that calculated? It is. Laurent and Jeanne are like a double screen in front of me, which will arrest the gaze of Gregory Temple. I am far away, retreating further into the impossible, and still I multiply the obstacles behind me..."

The sketch took shape beneath his practiced hand. It was definitely Jeanne, in a faint, at the precise moment when the first breath had forced her colorless lips apart. The Oise ran by the edge of the meadow, and the grove of willows was there.

"If she loved me..." he thought, aloud. "If all those millions came to me as a dowry... if the world's imbecilic eye saw me as the hero of that banal drama: the wedding of the ruined gentleman and the wealthy but illegitimate heiress...?"

He forced a laugh, and crossed out the adorable sketch with three strokes of his pen.

"She is a thousand times more beautiful than that!" he said. "A thousand times! I believe that I might love her in spite of myself, even if I do not intend to love her. Since I came into the world, I have done what I wished. I require an incomparable love to enjoy incomparable good fortune. I desire to love as I have fought, to excess! She will be my creation if I am destroyed. She will have everything that could be set at the feet of an idol, and will not even know that I am the enchanter whose wand has changed her misery into a fortune."

The piece of paper touched the top of the lamp-glass and burst into flames. Comte Henri was still laughing, but there was no sarcasm in his laughter, which was the joyful and manly expression of an anticipated triumph. While the flame obliterated Jeanne's name and features, he added: "Is it enough to make her a Comtesse? There are still kingdoms to found... and where I shall be going, I would not have so far to travel to found a kingdom than I have already covered between my dungeon in Norfolk and here! Laugh who will, but I can intoxicate myself without gin; I would become a King to make her a Queen!"

The ashen remains of the burnt paper took flight, blown away by his breath; then, the set of his features changed abruptly. He seemed to be alert to some distant sound that was neither the voice of the mill nor the plaint of the nocturnal breeze. He had come from a land where hearing acquires strange sensibilities; on that calm night and in that sleeping household, no other ear but his own could have perceived aught but silence.

"She had closed her window," he murmured. "She is not in bed."

He placed a pad of notepaper in front of him but his pen, newly furnished with ink, remained suspended, as happens sometimes to those who cannot decide how to begin a letter–but that was not the case. He was listening.

A distant and scarcely perceptible sound echoed in the corridor. Comte Henri stopped listening. He smiled coldly, and said: "It's the door. She's gone out."

At the same time, his pen ran across the paper, hastily tracing the following words:

Dear master,
Richard Thompson is in Paris under a false name. Nothing else to report.
James Davy.

He selected from his portfolio an envelope stamped in advance with a London postmark, but in such a manner that the faint and blurred imprint seemed to have been accidentally effaced at the point where the date should have been legible. It was a veritable masterpiece of engraving. The letter was placed in an envelope to which the following superscription was added:

Gregory Temple, esq.
19 Rue Dauphine
Paris.

When Comte Henri's pen paused, he listened again. A light but distinct step was audible in the corridor. He closed his portfolio, having put the letter into it, then he lowered the shade of his lamp and stretched himself out with his eyes closed and his head resting on the back of his armchair.

There was a discreet knock on the door. Comte Henri made no movement. There was a second knock, then a third. The key grated in the lock as if a timid and feeble hand had hesitated to turn it, then the door rotated slowly on its hinges. Suzanne appeared on the threshold, clad in the same clothes she had been wearing during the walk; she had only taken off her straw hat, and her lovely blonde curls were scattered on her high-necked dress, buttoned in the English style.

She was so painfully nervous that she did not see Comte Henri next to his writing desk. Her frightened eyes looked round the seemingly empty chamber several times over. She swept her hand across her forehead, whose dull pallor seemed leaden. The effort that she was making to collect her thoughts was evident in her distressed expression.

When she finally discovered the young Comte asleep, a vivid red replaced the livid white of her cheeks. She closed the door behind her, and marched purposefully towards the writing desk. She lifted the shade from the lamp, in order to shine the light directly upon the features of the sleeper,

She examined him for a long time.

Henri's face expressed a profound tranquillity. His lips retained the frank and friendly smile that conferred such charm upon his features.

Suzanne's eyes turned away from him and scanned the objects on the lid of the writing desk. She started on seeing the pistols, and took hold of one of them.

Not a muscle stirred in the Comte's face, but the dry double click of the pistol being cocked caused his eyes to open nonchalantly.

"Is that intended for me, Miss Suzanne?" he asked, calmly.

"No," the young woman replied, lowering her eyes.

"I suspected as much. You have a soft and noble heart. I know more than one woman–more than one Christian woman–in whom a misfortune like yours

113

might indeed inspire the thought of suicide. I am not asleep, Miss Suzanne, and I would not have let you pick up that weapon if it had been loaded."

Suzanne put the pistol down on the desk-lid.

"That's the one that I used to stop Jeanne's horse," Henri went on.

"You were waiting for me?" Suzanne murmured.

"A mother always comes to someone who can tell her about her child," he replied, in a low voice.

Miss Temple hid her head between her hands. It seemed that she wanted to speak, but the words caught in her throat.

"The night when I assisted Richard was dark," Henri said, "and I had placed myself in the shadow of a pillar in the chapel, which was lit by a single lamp. How did you recognize me, Suzanne?"

"Your features are unfamiliar to me," Miss Temple replied, "but I had heard your voice."

Henri smiled. "My voice!" he said. "Fair enough. No disguise would have done me any good, and I am happy to have nothing to hide."

"Have you really nothing to hide, James Davy?" Suzanne said, very quietly. "I had heard your voice on two occasions."

"Mrs. Thompson," the young Comte replied, without any bitterness or annoyance, but with cool firmness, "I have done you a good turn; never try to do me a bad one!"

At the pronunciation of the name of Mrs. Thompson, a sob rose from Suzanne's breast. Comte Henri went on in a softer tone: "We are alone, Madame, and I shall not reveal your secret to anyone else. As far as the name James Davy is concerned, your own experience informs you that there are occasions when an honest woman may be forced to throw a veil over her life. The same may apply to a man of honor. I have retaken the name of my father; I sincerely hope that you will soon be able to take that of your husband."

"My husband! My husband!" Suzanne repeated, letting herself fall back on to a chair as she found that her face was bathed in tears. "My father! My poor little child!"

The Comte took up her cold hand, and warmed it between his own. "Why did you threaten me, Suzanne?" he murmured.

"Threaten–me?" she said, from the depths of her distress. "Can I threaten you? Can I implore you? Is there a single reasonable or sane thought within me? Richard Thompson told me, once when he went away: 'James Davy will take care of the child.' Then, in his last letter, he said again: 'You will see James Davy, who will tell you about the child.' My father often pronounced the name James Davy too, and one morning, I thought I heard in his bedroom the voice of the unknown person who had been a witness to our wedding...

"I was afraid, because my father was already the enemy of Richard Thompson. 'It is his assistant, James Davy,' was the reply I received to my questions. At the chateau de Belcamp, I witnessed the arrival of the master's on—a gentleman, a Comte—and I did not think straight away that this could be James Davy, the policeman... but your voice made me shiver to the utmost depths of my being. I, a woman and an Englishwoman, have come in the middle of the night to a man's room! I did not doubt that you could tell me about those who are dear to me, since you have spoken the name of my husband twice today... but I am surrounded by dangers, and it is in James Davy and not in the Comte de Belcamp that Richard had told me I could trust. I only wanted to know... don't punish me!"

Henri reflected, having heard this explanation, which would perhaps have seemed confused to anyone else but was superabundantly clear to him. This woman, whom he had recently placed in the passive column while filling in the balance sheet of his situation, had changed places and swollen the active one by sole virtue of the weapon that she had against him. This weapon was the *casus belli* that a powerful State might require to conquer a petty neighbor. The explanation was innocent but it removed none of the danger; no, she had not intentionally threatened him, but what is more terrible than an involuntary threat? It is the kind of threat posed by loaded cannons, which must either be destroyed or turned against the enemy. Suzanne was the daughter of Gregory Temple; it was Gregory Temple and James Davy who seemed to be engaged in a strange and mortal duel, the prelude to a greater battle. Suzanne did not know anything, but she knew precisely what was required to introduce the enemy into the Chateau de Belcamp, the center of his operations and the pivot of his maneuvers. It was necessary that Suzanne should be broken—or that she should become an instrument in the hands of the young Comte.

He looked at her more sadly than before. She was very far from following his train of thought, for she cried in a fit of anguish and impatience: "But you know nothing, after all, since you have nothing more to say to me?"

"I admire the fate that pursues certain existences," Henri replied, gravely. "I can indeed tell you about those who are dear to you—and in order not to prolong a needless torment, I shall tell you immediately that Richard is still at liberty, and that the child has been entrusted to safe hands."

"My dear beloved!" Suzanne stammered, lifting her clasped hands towards heaven. "Oh, the sacred name of God be blessed!" Then she added, wiping away her tears and avid to know: "What else, Monsieur le Comte? What else?"

Henry rose abruptly to his feet, as if he were trying to suppress an emotion. He walked around the room two or three times, then came suddenly to a halt before the frightened Suzanne, who had revealed a great deal about her fears and maternal hopes. "Do you think, Madame," he asked, "that the Comte de Belcamp would have adopted an abject disguise and a false name for any frivolous motive?"

His eyes were shining and his lips trembled. Suzanne looked at him open-mouthed. "I had not thought about that," she murmured.

"And it's of little importance to you, isn't it?" Henri went on, his smile full of compassion. "Suffering and love see nothing but themselves. You are in love and you are suffering; you are doubly entitled to be an egotist. There are other interests, Madame, that man places still higher in his reason, if not in his heart. The secret of these noble efforts is not mine to divulge; I can tell you only that they will be manifest one day in world history.

"I'm not asking you to divulge any secrets..." the poor young woman began.

"Then thank God that you have not inadvertently caused me to reveal any, Suzanne!" Comte Henri interrupted, whose voice was becoming more and more earnest. "Drowned as you are in the depths of your personal distress, however, you must know that the great ideas of the future are rumbling beneath the apathetic surface of nations in chains. Whether I am an officer or a soldier in the army that is marching on that mysterious crusade does not concern you; what you need to know is that I am devoted to it with all the strength in my body and all the passion in my heart. Listen to me, Suzanne, because your very life depends on my words—your life, through that of the beloved child who is your soul. Hear this: if my father stood in my way on the route that I must follow implacably, I would thrust him aside; if the woman I love barred my way, I would break her; if my shadow were an obstacle, I would annihilate the man in order to destroy the shadow."

Suzanne still did not understand, but she was possessed by mortal dread.

"What I have done," the young Comte went on, "is between my conscience and God. Henri de Belcamp is not ashamed of the actions of James Davy, and those days of humble heroism when my coat-of-arms was concealed by the detested manhunter's badge will count double in my memories, as a campaign against enemy forces. The police are not solely directed against malefactors; if I deceived your father, it was not in the service of crime..."

"You deceived my father!" echoed Suzanne.

"I could offer these simple words in reply," said the young Comte. "I was under the command of your father, who was pursuing Richard Thompson, and Richard Thompson found a refuge with me. Was that not already a betrayal?" He lifted his handsome head proudly. "But I was a traitor in other ways too. In London, I was a spy for the great army whose invincible battalions await the hour to conquer or die."

"Why do you tell me that?" asked Suzanne, in a low voice. "Wasn't the first confession sufficient?"

"I tell you that because I must put a cruel gag upon your mouth, Madame," the young Comte replied, slowly, "and I need to show you the necessity that forces my hand. You alone know that Comte Henri de Belcamp calls himself James Davy in London."

"And you think that I would give you away?" cried Suzanne. "You—my husband's savior!"

"You are Gregory Temple's daughter," Henri said, looking away. "You are Richard Thompson's wife. Some very strange things will soon occur here, which might draw my secret out of you in spite of yourself. You cannot tell, nor can I estimate accurately myself, what incalculable misfortunes might transpire as a result. Madame, I came here to tell you that Thompson is saved and that you would see your child again. Now I must say something different, because you make me afraid and I require hostages. Hear my words: as Richard Thompson's life depends on me, Richard Thompson is not yet saved; and as your child is my ward, you shall not see your child again..."

The breath caught in Suzanne's throat. She went down on her knees.

Henri went on: "...unless, as I give you my word as a gentleman, you give me yours in return."

"Richard... the little one... my beloved child," Suzanne murmured. "Where is he? For pity's sake, where is he?"

"In France."

"And Thompson?"

"In Paris."

"What do you want from me?"

"First of all, silence. Absolute silence, with no exceptions."

"I shall be as silent as the dead. What more do you want?"

"Your help."

"To do what?"

"Anything."

"You shall have my help, to do anything and against anyone."

He drew her to her feet and took her clasped hands between his own. "Suzanne," he said to her, "I respect your father, I like your husband, and your child is the first that I have held in my arms. You have nothing to fear if you keep your word."

There was something in his voice that penetrated the heart. Suzanne smiled through her tears. "You have held him?" she said. "Not long ago?"

"Yesterday," Henri replied.

Before he could defend himself, she pressed her lips to his hands with reckless ardor.

"This hand that has touched him..." she stammered, laughing and sobbing. "Has he grown much? Is he beautiful? Has he begun to call for his mother?"

"He is beautiful," Henri replied, complacently. "He looks like you, Suzanne. He is growing well. He calls distinctly for his mother. But..." His tone changed as he continued: "...my nights are no more my own than my days, and we must part now, Madame."

"One more word," the young mother begged. "Is he far from here? Will it be long before I see him again?"

"He is in Paris," the Comte replied, "and the whole thing might be over in a month."

"A month!" Suzanne murmured, as she headed for the door. "An age...!"

Henri accompanied her to the threshold. His gaze, in which admiration mingled with pity, followed her down the corridor. When the young woman's hunched shadow vanished into the darkness, he closed the door again, double-locking it this time.

There was sweat on his temples.

He sat down at his writing desk and dashed off two pages of densely-packed handwriting. He folded the paper into the form of a letter and addressed it: *To Lady Frances Elphinstone.*

"Tomorrow..." he said, thinking aloud. He consulted his watch, whose hand stood at half past midnight. "Get on! Get on!" he murmured, perhaps unaware that he was speaking.

The window was open. His room was at the eastern extremity of the ground floor. He called out softly to the guard-dog that was loose in the court-yard, which responded hesitantly to his voice, rubbing its belly on the grass. He threw it a piece of bread that he had carried away from the table at the evening meal. Then, he put his hat on his head and tightened his belt. He looked at his pistols, but did not take them up, saying: "We're not in the bush now!"

An instant afterwards, he was in the courtyard, stroking the dog that bounded along at his side. He went straight to the sunken fence. The Moon was shining. He examined the terrain, took 20 steps backwards, then hurled himself forward like a bullet, crossing the enormous ditch with a single bound. The dog dared not jump.

There is a particular pace that the Americans associate with Red Indians on the warpath, that Arabs employ when they are not on horseback, and that the African Rifles have adopted for their soldiers. It is not quite a run but it is not exactly a military march; the knee is not straightened, the heel does not touch the ground, and both legs maintain their spring as if running. It is the human trot; at that pace, an Arab can follow a hired carriage and an Indian can cover 30 leagues in a day. Comte Henri maintained this pace while he crossed the grassy expanse that extended beyond the sunken fence. He took the winding path that led to the mill, crossed the bridge and went past the silent miller's hut. From the several routes that presented themselves to him on the other side of the Oise, he selected the hunting-path by which he had arrived that morning. His light and nimble tread did not even wake the miller's dog, which stretched out in its sleep and let out a dull growl.

Comte Henri climbed the hunting-path without relenting his pace, and came within a few minutes to the belvedere from which Robert Surrisy had shown him the Chateau de Belcamp. He paused and looked behind him. The moonlit countryside was blurred by shadows; all was silent and peaceful. Within the large tableau framed by the black woods bordering the double valley, two lights were perceptible. One came from the chateau, the other from the direction of the Priory. Henri looked pensively at the latter for a moment, then resumed his march through the forest.

He soon came to the crossroads where the charabanc loaded with laughing girls had passed him at the gallop. He paused against at the spot where Robert, preceding his companions, had joined him politely to indicate the route that led from the Croix Moraine to Miremont.

At the foot of the signpost that lacked nothing but inscriptions, a sort of grey mass was visible, shapeless and immobile. Comte Henri went towards it. It was a prostrate human being, curled up like a caterpillar, deeply asleep.

"Hey, Billy!" said the Comte, prodding him with his foot.

Billy uncoiled like a spring and leapt to his feet, saying: "There you are, milord!"

Billy was only four feet tall, but he had the figure of a Herculean dwarf. His short legs and muscular arms could have served as a model for the design of a diminutive athlete. He wore the tight-fitting breeches and long jacket of a London groom–a costume that was then much rarer in France than it is today, when every lucky owner of an old nag and a wheelbarrow allows himself the luxury of an animated sausage who knows how to grunt "Yes sir" and comb his sorry steed in English. It was obvious, however, that Billy was no false groom born in the Rue Saint-Martin or Picardy; he had the ruddy face and big ears typical of his race.

"You were asleep, Billy?" Henri said.

"No, milord."

"Where's your horse?"

"Here, milord." He pointed to a covert on the left.

"How is milady?" was the Comte's next question.

"Gone dancing, milord," Billy replied.

Henri burst out laughing. "Billy, my boy," he said, taking two folded papers from his portfolio, "this letter to milady, the other in the box at rue Dauphine, number 19, and don't take your time about it! Tomorrow morning, when you get back, you stop the coachman right here, and you tell him to turn right." His extended finger indicated the hunting-path that led to Miremont.

"Yes, milord," Billy answered.

"My compliments to milady, Billy, and mount up!"

"Very good, milord."

A moment later, the mounted groom disappeared at the gallop into the night.

Comte Henri had not concluded his excursion; instead of turning towards the chateau he resumed his trot and followed the distant Billy along the Paris road. He proceeded thus along the edge of the forest for 200 or 300 yards, then turned west along a descending path rutted by cart-tracks, which led through recently-ploughed fields. He was now more than two leagues from the chateau. The bell-tower of a village further along the highway sounded half past one.

To the right of the track, beyond the ploughed fields, in a rocky hollow where ferns mingled with deformed thin-boled oaks, stood a woodcutter's hut. At this hour of the night, and despite the moonlight, anyone who had no advance knowledge of the exact position of the dwelling would certainly have passed by without noticing it, for it was backed up against a rock-face of similar hue, and its misshapen thatched roof blended in with the surrounding terrain.

Comte Henri quit the cart track without hesitation and took the little path that led into the rocks. In front of the cabin was a yard ten feet square, littered with debris. The Comte took up a piece of wood and knocked on the worm-ridden planks of the door. Nothing stirred inside. The Comte redoubled his efforts and heard the plaintive cries that accompany the awakening of a child. At the same time, the hoarse voice of a man demanded: "Are there so many houses in the clearing that you've come to the wrong door, drunkard?"

"I haven't come to the wrong door, Pierre Louchet," Henri replied. "Open up—I have to talk to you."

"Oh, indeed," grumbled the woodcutter. "Let's have your name, so that we know who's speaking."

"Richard Thompson."

"Oh! Very well, Monsieur Richard," said the man, who could be heard leaping from his bed and putting on his huge clogs. "Damn me if these Englishers don't do everything the wrong way round. It's one o'clock, isn't it? And the brat'll go back to sleep of its own accord, will it? Believe that and drink water!"

The clogs sounded dully on the trodden earth, the bar of unseasoned wood grated, and the door swung open, creaking on its hinges.

"Your servant, all the same, Monsieur Richard," said an old greybeard, whose round face was displayed by rays of moonlight. "I always forget your other name, which is English, but I don't mean any offense. You're in the neighborhood tonight, then?"

"I've left my carriage up there on the highway," Henri replied. "I'm returning to Paris. Is the child well?"

The child whimpered in his cradle, already falling asleep again.

"Well enough. He's got a good voice—listen! Although he'd be pampered more if my wife was still alive... but my daughter comes to feed him pap three times a day... and me, I like kids!"

"I chose you for that reason, Pierre. Has anyone come?"

"Yes, yes, to be sure... the young man, you know... he wept like a child, all the time."

"Did he say anything?"

"He ate him up with kisses. That's his uncle? And he mumbled away: 'Richard, my little Richard, you, you will see your mother again.' Apparently, you've given the kid the same name as you. Then he said: 'I must go away... far away... I won't see you again.' And he was all wet, because I started crying with him. The mother's no longer in these parts, I suppose?"

"You shall see her tomorrow, Pierre," Henri replied, pensively.

"The mother?" exclaimed the woodcutter. "Well and good. That'll please me."

"She will come in the morning to take back her child."

The woodcutter fell silent. His honest and candid face took on a sad expression. There was no sound within the hut; the child was peacefully asleep.

"That's how it goes," said the old man, with a sigh. "One soon gets attached to these creatures. Me, I've got used to him, and I like rocking him to sleep... but it's much better if his mother comes to look for him; his mother will think even more of him than I do, that's for sure. What's she called? I'll need to know, won't I?"

"Of course. The woman who will come, who is his mother, is called Lady Frances Elphinstone."

"Lady–how about that! I'll have to learn my catechism all over again! It's funny, the names people have over there in England!"

"Can you read, my friend?"

"I can't, but my daughter can."

"Will she be here?"

"If you wish. She lives on a farm, not far from here."

"Give me some paper and light the candle."

"The candle I can do, Monsieur Richard," the woodcutter replied, "but the paper... I always take a plate with me when I go to buy cheese."

After this solemn homage to the utility of paper, old Pierre Louchet took a piece of white chalk from a hole in the wall behind the door and held it out to his visitor. "Write the name on the door, Monsieur Richard," he said. "My daughter will read it, if she can, when she comes.

By the light of the moon, on the badly fitted planks, Henri wrote in large letters: *Lady Frances Elphinstone*. Then he returned the chalk to the woodcutter, along with a gold piece.

"That won't prevent the mother from paying you, Pierre," he said, as he took his leave. "Thanks, and good night!"

Twenty *sous* every time, thought the woodcutter, closing the door. Before going back to bed, however, he rubbed his thickly bristling beard against the child's cheek, and muttered: "I'd marry anyone to have a cherub like you."

Henri went back to the highway at a slower pace. It was nearly four o'clock when he reached the grounds of the chateau, after a nonchalant and thoughtful stroll. He came as far as the sunken fence, whistled to Sultan, the guard-dog, spoke to him in order to be recognized, and threw him another piece of bread. Then, he took off and came down lightly beside the animal, which licked his hand as if acknowledging his master in agility and audacity.

A few minutes later, the light behind the young Comte's windows went out; he was sleeping peacefully in his bed.

Billy, the four-foot Hercules, worked as a groom for Lady Frances Elphinstone, a young widow of the English aristocracy.[60]

The English aristocracy, which is much more grandiose than ours, is a citadel whose door cannot be forced by any "mediocrity" (as its inhabitants, and the extremely mediocre writers who sing its praises, invariably put it). Within this sanctuary, compared to which our Faubourg Saint-Germain could pass for a mere pleasure garden, there is no one but admirably distinguished lords and marvelously refined ladies. Each of the latter is united, by the grace of the feminine senate that presides over the great elections of Almack's, with a heroic sportsman, a renowned singer, an eloquent barrister, a briefly-fashionable Byronic poet, an innovative fastener of cravats, a splendid stomach capable of containing 50 dozen oysters, or a doctor bound by an oath to the memory of his ancestors not to reveal the secret of the universal panacea that he carries discreetly about his person.

A lord of the English aristocracy ordinarily has but two arms, and rarely has more than two legs on which to walk. He dines several times a day, it is true, but his stomach complains about it. In the street he is, at present, obliged to breathe the same air as his tailor, but I do not doubt that free England will some day invent a more dignified and decent atmosphere for the exclusive use of its aristocracy; it is offensive and humiliating to certain privileged lungs that they should have to take in air that the public has already inhaled and exhaled.

Never forget that in London, the word public is an insult.

The lords and ladies of the English aristocracy are not very numerous in England; abroad, they are found in profusion. It is the reverse of our own domestic situation, where everyone has a little of the Vicomte in him, by virtue of his own fantasy, and can decide for himself to play the petty lord. Over there, the mania of selection is inveterate; there is such a desperate need to examine, to categorize and to exclude, that even the dancers at the glorious balls at Almack's, who already bear noble names, are chosen by scrutiny. It is necessary to provide proofs to be admitted to that picnic, the aim of all the imbecile vanities of elegant society, as it was once necessary to provide proofs to be a Knight of Malta or a Canoness of some noble chapter. And John Bull, with that beam in his apoplectic eye, heaps abundant and weighty scorn upon any aristocracy that does not have such a foot upon its own breast.

Lady Frances Elphinstone was an English aristocrat, and that was it. She said so, and we have no entitlement to put her to the proof. She had a sufficiently well-equipped household, and her Paris apartment had been furnished at considerable expense. Her conduct was irreproachable. She received few visitors–and, in fact, seemed not so much a common mortal as a princess traveling incognito.

In her chosen quarter, on the edge of the Tuileries, the English were well-known. English distinction exists; it even offers, occasionally, specimens of exquisite perfection. It rarely possesses the charm of French elegance, but the correctness of its lineaments can achieve splendor when its reserve stops short of prudery and its pride does not turn into stiffness. There is an axiom: "Nothing is as beautiful as a beautiful Englishwoman." To which one might add: "Nothing is as noble as an English noblewoman who escapes the gross prejudices, petty ridiculousness and comical weaknesses of her race."

Pure English blood, when it is successful, realizes the fine dream of majesty experienced by children and poets, combining statuesque grace with regal politeness.

Lady Frances, we are forced to admit, was not at all like that. One could not discover her brilliance in fair-haired serenity, or in the tepid calm of Britannic symmetry. She was a strong and lively brunette, like the daughters of those magical shores where Ireland opposes its basalt dikes to the fury of western storms.

In the county of Connaught, whose strange horizons sometimes resemble Norway and sometimes Italy; on that coast where the torment of the waves has hollowed out the most beautiful grottos in the world; within the shelter of those prodigious colonnades attributed by popular superstition to a dynasty of giants; along those scintillant beaches, which the Celtic proverb calls the flower of the Earth and the pearl of the sea; beside those enchanted lakes that mirror ruins and forests like silent poems; on those gentle mountain slopes, where the Sun plays upon the blue heather perfumed with incense; out there, finally, out there in the emerald isle where the last Gaels speak the language of ancient Erin, at the extremity of green and joyous Ireland... misery, famine and every vice that proceed therefrom, have not yet completed the annihilation of the most magnificent race of men ever to glorify the Earth.

The genealogy of that race is like a song of the Homeric lyre that accompanied the chords of Ossian's harp. The beautiful daughters of Ierna arrived one day with the merchants of Miletus, the rival of Tyre;[61] they married giant sons of the sea whose heads rose above the great waves on the September tide: Neil, Brien, Connor and Diarmid. From this union came Erin, daughter of Aspasia the Milesian,[62] exile of the land of light, and the giant of the Hibernian mists, whose feet were on the bottom of the sea while his head was in the clouds.

O'Neil, O'Brien, O'Connor and MacDiarmid, the children of Erin, became the Kings of the four tribes of Ireland. After many centuries and many misfortunes, you will find these names dispersed among the crowd, like fragments of an immense rock scattered in the soil. These are not Scottish clans, the images of families, which–in spite of their endurance of extraordinary persecution–still protect the liberty of the Highlands against London; this is the terrible dispersion that follows the explosion of a mine or a lightning strike. Here, the limbs are disconnected from the body; one O'Brien does not know another; one

O'Connor, for a copper coin, will fight another. The moral degeneration is complete; nothing remains of the tall and proud crag but pebbles, and the noble edifice in ruins is naught but a heap of vile debris.

And yet, on the summits of those prodigious columns of black porphyry which are the pipes of the Giants' Organ, or on the octagonal paving-stones of that basalt mosaic which extends for a league into the ocean, meriting the name of the Giant's Causeway–the giants are still everywhere, you see–I have sometimes stopped, stupefied, before some young beggar who resembles, in spite of the insult of his rags, the Greeks of the Iliad. It has happened more often still that I have leaned on my elbows on the embankment of some path to contemplate, as she descended the slopes of Mamturk [63] or followed the green paths along the shore of Lough Corrib, some bare-legged girl with plaited hair who was a Minerva by Phidias, an Athenian detached from a bas-relief on the Parthenon: tall, correct and bold; proudly bearing on her left shoulder a jug with the profile of an amphora, while her gently-flapping mantle floated behind her on the wind of her progress. Alas, the Homeric young man was more thief than beggar, and would sell his false testimony for sixpence to anyone who wished, and the Athenian of Phidias had not a single feature, apart from her beauty, in common with Aspasia.

Lady Frances Elphinstone was exactly the kind of magnificent flower that blooms out there among the ruins and balances the arrogance of its corolla above the maledictions of misery. Everyone who has had the opportunity to admire these marvelous flowers has been struck by the fanciful dream of placing them in the midst of all the elegance of London or Paris, of placing the crown of nobility on their pure foreheads, of sliding into their silken tresses the milky smile of pearls or the flamboyant gaze of diamonds, and of throwing upon their harmonious shoulders the mantle of luxury that is so often dishonored by ugly platforms; Lady Frances Elphinstone was that dream realized, and everything that the dream promised Lady Frances had.

There is nothing–absolutely nothing–English in the Irish race. One can understand the hatred that separates the two families by their dissimilarity alone. It has often been said that the Irish are more closely akin to the French; the assertion has the semblance of truth only when the English are taken as the standard of comparison. The Irishman is much closer to the Frenchman than the Englishman, who has the glory or misfortune of being the only one of his kind in the universe. Lady Frances was every bit as beautiful as a Greek, an Italian, or even a Frenchwoman, but she possessed a richness of blood that excluded her at first glance from Saxon provenance. Her accent and her name alone made her English to the Parisians.

Her accent was real; her name was not. We have already encountered Lady Frances Elphinstone twice within this story, at the hotel in Grosvenor Square where she called herself Madame la Comtesse, and at police headquarters in Scotland Yard, where she was named Sarah O'Neil. We have heard talk of her on a third occasion, in the fantastic biography of John Devil, where she was described as the Irish Beauty.[64]

We are confronted here by a singular nature, much less familiar to our readers than the banal eccentricities of the English character. We know little about Ireland but what England tells us, and we know well what a sovereign injustice it would be to inform ourselves about Poland by means of Russian literature. Entire nations have become human sacrifices; Ireland, the jewel of creation, excites little sympathy and no one any longer reads the terrible poem of its torments.

Lady Frances was not yet 20; she was in the full bloom of her luxurious youth. Her black eyes promised more than her heart could perhaps deliver: an ardent and indomitable passion. Her gaze had a charming temerity, but was also often timid and modest. We do not know her history as yet, but the mistress of John Devil had nothing in common with the damned of London's Inferno. The charm of her smile had a naive finesse reminiscent of a child's smile. One only had to glance at her to deduce, from the bold profile of her head and the solid design of her features, that she had a great intelligence and a vigorous will. Such, at least, her nature must have been in its seed: great, in every opulent and select sense of the word.

There is, however, a racial decadence that makes itself evident in a manner quite distinct from the personal decadence of each individual. In Ireland, where that decadence is profound and universal, the toxic effect–if one might express it thus–of the slow and mortal poison expresses itself as a diminution of specific gravity in the moral condition of individuals. The envelope no longer has its normal contents; there is a failure and impoverishment of the entire system. To sum it up in a single telling and painful word, the Irish have much of the frivolity of the negro.[65] It is a singular thing that the American, who is an Englishman-and-a-half, whether he be from the North or the South, slave-owner or abolitionist, detests the Irishman as he hates the negro. The American recognizes in the Irishman the white negro, and abhors him instinctively, in consequence of the aversion for misfortune that is the distinctive mark of the Saxon race.

In London, the cruelest insult that one can inflict on a man is to call him poor.

This ravishing young woman, Lady Frances, was white. The qualities that God had put into her were still there; no personal vice had stifled them. At a given moment, perhaps, they might have erupted explosively and torn away the mysterious envelope that kept them imprisoned–but at this hour, when her corporeal beauty had acquired full perfection, her intelligence and her heart lagged behind in the limbo of infancy. In many respects, she was still a little girl, variable in response to any gust of wind, defenseless against any caprice. She had been conquered, and was under dominion; she obeyed, playing with infinite skill the role that her master had blown in her direction. She loved according to her fashion: she was a devotee–or, rather, a slave, since we have already said the word. Did she know the secret of her own future? No. Did that disturb her? Not at all. She went through life like a brilliant butterfly fluttering through the air. Any fantasy that appealed to her turned her from her route without effort and without remorse. She was happy; she had the ambitions of a *grande dame* and the desires of a *grisette*.[66] Paris enchanted her, even though she had observed it only through her window; she dreamed of the enchantments of Paris day and night. What else had she to do? Her master thought for her.

There was nothing questionable in her household, which consisted of a Presbyterian chambermaid, as stiff as a rod, two seamstresses, a footman, a coachman and Billy.

Let us go back several hours, to five o'clock in the afternoon on the day that Comte Henri de Belcamp made his entrance at his paternal home. Lady Frances, dressed in fashionable clothes, was dining *tête-à-tête* with a quiet and sad young man who was nevertheless able, occasionally, to partake of her communicable gaiety. Prudence, the serious and discreet Presbyterian chambermaid, was serving, slowly dragging her large stoutly-shod feet, but even the affected austerity of her crow's face could not reduce the little dining-room to mourning in the radiant presence of milady. Milady dined in the French fashion, without tea, dishwater masquerading as coffee, ham or stewed apples. From time to time, she moistened her rosy lips with a glass of champagne.

"Richard," she said, "if you had not been obliged to depart, you could have been my cavalier in Paris, since I am here alone. You could have taken me to the Opera... can you imagine that I have not yet been to the Opera!"

"Is it possible," murmured the young man, smiling.

Prudence coughed.

"I'm shocking you, my good woman," Lady Frances said to her, handing over her plate by way of retaliation. "You are my witness, Prudence, that I have only gone out once, to Saint-Roch."

"I have my religion as milady has hers," Prudence replied, as if a wooden doll had suddenly spoken. "I am tolerant, thank the Lord... but I've as much liking for the Opera as for Saint Roch."

"As chance would have it, Prudence, we're of the same opinion for once," said the young woman, displaying all her beautiful teeth in a broad smile. "Serve the dessert, my girl, then have your own meal."

When Prudence had gone out, Lady Frances said: "You're sad, Richard. "Have you any news of Suzanne Temple?"

"That's why I'm sad, Frances," the young man replied. "Everything is getting on top of me, and I'm more desperate than ever to return to London. I became certain today that Suzanne came over with her father, but she has never crossed the threshold of his Paris lodgings. Has he put her in some convent? There are times when I'm afraid that she must be dead."

"That's madness!" milady exclaimed.

"Where can she be? If old Temple has discovered our secret..."

"He adores his daughter, and he's an honorable man."

"Yes... an honorable man," Thompson repeated, blushing and lowering his eyes. "A man of honor... implacable honor."

"How did he first become suspicious of you?" Frances asked.

"By a fatal combination of circumstances," murmured the young man, defeatedly. "In the first place, Mr. Temple found himself in opposition to my mother and me. On the very day of the murder, my mother had had a violent confrontation with Constance Bartolozzi, and I had threatened her, because the woman's stubbornness had reduced us to despair. When James Davy came to me and said: 'Constance Bartolozzi has been assassinated,' I felt dizzy... yes, as if the curses that had come out of my mouth were able to kill her! And when Davy then said to me: 'Nothing has been taken, neither papers nor valuables; nothing is missing but the bond signed by your mother,' I was chilled to the marrow of my bones. A few hours earlier, my mother had taken that bond in her hand... a mist fell in front of my eyes... I became mad, and had a vision of my mother, guilty. Instead of going straight to Mr. Temple, I hid that night, and that was my downfall..."

"Where did you hide?"

"In James Davy's house, while you were traveling."

"And was it James who advised you to hide?"

"James was afraid for me. He had seen my distress. I had been Mr. Temple's secretary for three years. I know his methods, and the influence exerted upon him by certain coincidences. James went so far as to ask me whether I had done it! If Mr. Temple had interrogated me at that moment, I would have been bedded down in Newgate."

"But the following day..."

"The following day, I learned that Mr. Temple had gone through my papers and that his agents had been sent to my mother's house. All London was talking about the murder. Davy told me that I was lost."

"Ah," said the young woman. "Davy told you that." And she added, as if talking to herself: "And yet, James Davy is not your enemy, I know that."

"My enemy!" cried the astonished Thompson.

"He brought me before Mr. Temple at Scotland Yard as a witness," Frances continued, thoughtfully, "and that was to deflect his suspicions. I lied that day, Richard. I wasn't there on the night of the murder, and yet I swore that I had seen... but this Gregory Temple is an extraordinary man. He saw through the lie!"

"Was it James Davy who placed you with la Bartolozzi?" Thompson asked.

"Yes," the young woman replied.

"To find out whether she was faithfully keeping the secret of the meetings that took place in her house?"

Frances made no reply, but then she said: "With respect to a man like Gregory Temple, it's madness to attempt deception. You were mad twice over: first in hiding your marriage, second in taking flight after the murder." Other words hovered on her lips, but she suppressed them by drinking another glass of champagne. You might have thought that a foreign gaze was fixed upon her at that moment, dominating her will. "There are times," she said, suddenly, "when I become weary–very weary–of groping my way through these mysteries. If I were a man, like you, I would break my chain and go forth with the grace of God."

"Are you referring to James?" asked Thompson, astonished again. "We know that he is mixed up in important political matters..."

"Do we know that?" asked milady, very quietly.

Richard looked at her reproachfully.

"He certainly fights," she murmured, letting loose a sigh. "He certainly strives..."

"Frances," Thompson interrupted, in a penetrating tone that was almost severe, "James Davy has a heart of gold!"

"Have you seen your child today?" the young woman asked, brusquely changing the subject.

"For the last time," Thompson murmured, lowering his eyelids.

Frances traced the gentle and noble features of her young companion with the gaze of her black eyes. It was an intelligent but timid face, on which misfortune had already set its mark.

"You're brave, Richard," Frances whispered, "you're brave... but you're not steadfast. Let's not talk about all that any longer. Would you like to take me to the ball at the Colisée?"

Richard thought he had misheard her. She tried to laugh.

"To the ball!" Thompson repeated. "I'm going away tomorrow, Frances, without having seen my wife, and I'm leaving my child behind... do you think that I could possibly amuse myself at a ball?"

"We'll find your wife, and we'll watch over your child," Frances said, affecting a light tone. "When someone is sad, it's necessary to soothe his pain. I have a great desire to go to that ball."

"A public ball, I suppose?" Richard asked.

"Yes–a ball where one pays an entry fee."

"And do you think that you belong in such a place, Frances?"

She finished her glass of champagne, and said, insubordinately: "Why should I, too, not have my secrets? Perhaps I am involved in some great conspiracy..."

"James is not here," Richard murmured. "You at a ball!"

"Oh," she replied, smiling sadly, "James isn't worried about me." Then she added, resolutely: "If you don't want to take me, Richard, I'll go alone."

Dusk was falling; Prudence came back in with the candlesticks. The two table companions kept silent until she had gone. Then, Richard said: "Are you hoping to meet someone at this ball?"

"Vaguely..." the young woman replied, her cheeks suddenly reddening.

"So you've been there already?"

"Never."

"Is it a *rendez-vous*?"

Milady tapped her foot by way of reply and held out her champagne glass. "You're mad, Richard," she said. "Pour!" But she quickly added, lowering her voice: "Even if I did have a rendez-vous... James has not told you everything, Richard... James is an important man..."

"I suspected as much!" Gregory Temple's former secretary exclaimed.

"I shall never be James Davy's wife," Milady concluded.

"I won't ask you to tell me your friend's real name..." Richard began.

"I'm only a poor girl," Frances interrupted, "even though I have the blood of kings in my veins... there are races doomed to decline, always to decline, the bottom of the abyss alone able to arrest their decadence. Are you going to take me to the ball, Richard?"

"If I knew..."

"You shall know all that I know myself. In recent times, the supreme council of the Knights of the Deliverance has met at Constance Bartolozzi's house. I don't know what lies at the bottom of that mystery, but I've believed for a long time that it intends to deliver Ireland from the English yoke... but that's another matter. What I can say with certainty is that la Bartolozzi was afraid, and that her intention was either to quit London or reveal something. Have you ever heard an unfamiliar name spoken that made your heart quicken, Richard?"

"Yes," Richard replied. "Suzanne's."

"They took account of their army one evening," Lady Frances went on, "in la Bartolozzi's drawing-room..."

"And you were there?"

"I was there—don't interrupt. There are things that I can't explain to you. I listened indifferently to the tedious list of conspirators until a French delegate said: 'Robert Surrisy, Sub-Lieutenant of the Imperial army, as brave and strong as a lion...' "

Her eyelids were half-closed, while her eyes steeped themselves in the reverie. She was no longer speaking. Her delightful face partook of both the charm of a young girl and the allure of a woman. While still the flower, it was already the fruit. Ignorance was no longer there, but something similar to the lovely radiance of innocence filtered through those long lowered eyelashes.

"What then?" Richard asked.

"My heart beat faster," Frances replied. "That was all."

"That tells me nothing..."

"Wait! I left London alone; James had gone ahead of me to France. On boarding the packet-boat at London Bridge, I noticed two young people, both noble and fair of face. One of them was sad and dressed in mourning, the other wore that resolute gaiety typical of the French–which I love, Richard, out of hatred for the cold and clumsy English who have killed my homeland and my people. Our eyes met. I laughed, and Prudence growled. In the meantime, while I was leaning over the rail to look at the troubled waters of the Thames, the velvet notecase I was carrying slipped out of my hand. There was a movement beside me; a gloved hand touched the rail, and my cry of surprise resounded with the splash of a man plunging into the turbulent water. A moment later, the handsome young man–the one who was so brave and so cheerful–brought my notecase back to me, smiling."

"It takes shape," murmured Thompson, who was also smiling in spite of his sadness. "I've read more than one novel that began in exactly that fashion." He emptied his full champagne glass in a single draught.

"Shut up!" milady said, threatening him with her charming finger. "And drink on, Thompson–I want you to have a good evening before going away. I spent the first few hours of the crossing in my cabin. When I finally went to the saloon, half a dozen young men were sitting down to dinner in the French manner, and the fizz of champagne was mingled with the clink of glasses. In the middle of the joyful troop, I recognized the hero of my novel–since you have put it thus–the savior of my velvet notecase. I can still see his face, as lively and sparkling as the froth in his glass, among the weighty physiognomies that surrounded him.

"He spoke up, proposing a toast. 'Messieurs,' he said. 'I love the English because they are free. It is necessary to live and die for something worthwhile: I shall live and I shall die for liberty. The luck of the voyage that brings men together sometimes makes for solid amity. We are unknown to one another; let us introduce ourselves before drinking to the future that might perhaps reunite us. I am a Frenchman; I have been a soldier for the Emperor and am now a student, and when the occasion arises, I snap my fingers at melancholy. My name is trying to say smile, according to the interpretation of my college professors: I am Robert Surrisy...'[67]

"I've forgotten the other names, Richard; I only remember the name that was trying to say smile..."

"And have you seen this handsome young man again?" Thompson asked.

"I would like to," the young woman replied.

"To talk to him?"

"No, merely to rest my gaze on the joyful valor of that forehead, to admire the frank boldness of those eyes. As he left the packet-boat, I remember that he said to his new friends: '*Messieurs les Anglais*, we shall see one another again at the Colisée' "[68]

"Then let's go to the Colisée," cried Thompson, rising to his feet. "What woman wants, God wants, and there will be time tomorrow to take up the burden of my melancholy."

Lady Frances jumped for joy. She rang for Prudence, asked for her scarf and hat, ordered that the horses be harnessed and was impatient until she was sitting beside Richard on the cushions of the coach. Prudence, who had put on her shawl and her big straw hat to accompany her mistress, was summarily rebuffed. Billy, instead of climbing on the back of the carriage, presented himself at the door and recalled that he had orders from Monsieur le Comte to execute that night.

"Fine!" said the young woman. "Perfectly fine. Go wherever you please, Billy, and good luck to you."

"Do I take it that I should say nothing to Monsieur le Comte about milady going out?" Billy asked.

"Quite right... get going, Sam!"

The coachman cracked his whip.

Lady Frances, changing her mind, put her mischievous head out of the carriage window and shouted: "Billy! Tell him I've gone dancing!"

Instead of steering towards the Roule district, where the establishment known as the Colisée–a ballroom, theater and permanent funfair destined to dethrone the imperial glory of old Tivoli–was situated, the rig plunged deep into the old city, not stopping until it reached the doors of the main stage-coach office. Richard Thompson got out in order to book his place in the diligence that was departing the following morning for Calais. A recent ordinance required every traveler to sign a register and show his passport; Richard had no passport but he provided a permit from the foreign office, in the name of James Davy, assistant inspector of the Metropolitan Police, and signed the same name in the register.

When he climbed back into the carriage, he found Lady Frances very pale and all a-tremble. Richard interrogated her, but she did not want to explain. Halfway along their route, however, she suddenly asked: "What would Gregory Temple be able to do, if he discovered your presence in Paris?"

"Gregory Temple has left Paris for London," Richard replied. "James told me that."

"In that case," Frances murmured, "I must be mistaken."

As they approached the Colisée, whose brightly-lit portal projected the glare of its illumination into the distance, the young woman abruptly went on: "I ought to tell you, though. I had closed my eyes while I was waiting for you back there, when a sudden noise caused me to open one eye. There was a face framed in the window of the carriage door. I thought it was you who had already come back. I have only seen Gregory Temple on one occasion, but he seemed to recognize me, although he was much changed..."

"In a few hours, I'll be far away from Paris," Thompson replied. Then, he added, pensively: "Every time Davy speaks, one must pay heed. He's a dependable prophet. He gave me strict instructions not to go out with you."

"He told me the opposite..." Frances began, excitedly–but she went pale again, and stopped, as if she were afraid.

Richard immediately understood what she was implying.

"I trust him," he murmured. "James Davy has even given me his name! More than that–he has taken mine in order to protect my wife and my child." Then, he added, in a somber voice: "In God's name, I'm innocent. My life is no longer my own. Woe betide anyone who desires to make my wife a widow and my son an orphan!"

The carriage came to a stop at the end of a long rank of equipages ranged in front of the Colisée, a vast enclosure occupying the greater part of the former Beaujon Garden, containing various constructions analogous to those which make our present-day Pré-Catelan the very image of Paradise, according to the faith of gay women and young men clad in their Sunday best. Paris invents nothing; in certain periodic epochs it moves back its pleasures along with its enclosing wall, and invariably cries: "Miracle! Miracle!"

The Colisée was a miracle because it replaced Tivoli, and its Russian mountains were a little higher; because its flags fluttered upon freshly-gilded poles; because one could see marionettes of wood and flesh there; because one could get very good ice-cream there; and because it had a magician who dwelt in the depths of a brick-lined cavern, who would tell your fortune for 15 *sous*.

In a hundred years, Paris, having attained its virile stature, will dispatch its enclosing wall to Melun and build its miracle in the middle of the forest of Fontainebleau. It will say: "Look at these rocks that I have made and these 900-year old oaks that I have planted in clods of earth! I have something like a palace here, which isn't bad for something built with materials other than planks and plaster. I have the orchestra of Musard XIV, transatlantic balloons and natural animals, if you count vipers!" In those days, the site of the Pré-Catelan will already be an ancient and unfashionable district, so ancient that the Prefect of the Seine will be ashamed to pass along its boulevard, across its corpse.

The Colisée was quite new. Its vogue, which had scarcely begun, promised to be splendid. It must be admitted that Parisian mores have changed since then, and that the upper strata of society have completely forsaken fixed-price rejoicings, but in the first years of the Restoration the aristocracy did go to Tivoli, Marbeuf and the Colisée, as it was subsequently to patronize Ranelagh, descending so low as to concoct an instant carnival in our streets and make the European fortune of the Opera balls. Now, the aristocracy, having aged, has become a hermit; only the lower orders, always as restless as the cobbler in the fable, raise the Devil to amuse themselves and throw their obols into collection boxes "for the upkeep of the Parisian Paradises."

The first strains of the orchestra made Lady Frances' heart leap. She was a child–a frivolous child, avid for pleasure. No sooner had she crossed the threshold of those enchantments than the festival atmosphere took hold of her and intoxicated her. Even Richard could not hold that fever at bay. He was English, and Paris makes the English crazy. The movement, the noise, the laughter, the perfumes, the harmony, the pell-mell of flowers and flirtatious women stunned him to the same degree as his companion. For an hour, they were a hundred leagues away from real life. For all their preoccupations–and each of them had a distinct set–they forgot everything save for the intimate and obstinate thoughts that was the very life of their separate hearts. As she smiled at the young cavaliers who greeted her, Frances dreamed of Robert Surrisy; in passing his bewitched gaze over the brilliant swarm of pretty women, Richard was searching for Suzanne. Of disquiet or dread, however, there was henceforth no trace.

Fundamentally, and despite the awful weight of his destiny, Richard was almost as much a child as Frances. She wanted to see everything and try everything. He allowed himself to be led. Carried along by the crowd, as noisy and tumultuous as a sea-wave, they arrived at an octagonal enclosure placed almost at the center of the garden. It was there that the crowd pressed most tightly around a kind of monument of bizarre appearance, composed of two Chinese temples, both very tall but unequal in height, with an inverted arcade strung between them, whose broad curve formed a valley between two mountains.

They were indeed mountains: the Russian Mountains–the contemporary "craze," as the modish expression put it. I know duchesses of a respectable age who confessed to me–a long time ago, alas!–their passionate desire to risk a descent from the Russian mountains. Things that cost a *sou* in a funfair are no longer comprehensible; the Russian Mountains, having become despicable, are like those wastrels who end up as rag-and-bone men; nothing is duller than fashionability's relics, whose life is essentially ephemeral. In those days, however, noble, distinguished and virtuous wives would slip out of the conjugal home by the window in order to lose their breath and win dizziness on those prestigious slopes.

At the moment when Richard and Frances arrived in front of that suspended valley, whose slopes hid behind a lavishly gilded mantle decked in capricious arabesques, the crowd raised an enthusiastic shout. An entire flotilla of sleighs, hurled from the larger temple with indescribable ardor, descended like a whirlwind, slid to the bottom of the curve, and were borne upwards again by their own momentum to land gracefully on the platform of the smaller temple. Steam-power has made us blasé with regard to spectacular velocity, but railways had not yet been invented then. The crowd watched open-mouthed, agitated by long waves and murmurous expressions. Then another convoy passed through, and another, incessantly, accompanied by the laughter of the joyous and the brave, the wild cries of the fearful, the comical contortions of the game's devotees and the sickly pallor of the novices.

Frances dragged her cavalier along, already reddening with puerile desire, crying: "I want a go!"

They climbed the fragile staircase leading to the temple of departure, which bent under the weight of amusement-seekers. On the landing that preceded the platform there was a mob obscuring sight and sound alike. Lady Frances, impatient to get to the sleigh that would make her so happy, pushed and shoved like all the other children and laughed wholeheartedly at the petty incidents of the confusion.

Richard finally got his hands on a two-seater sleigh, decorated with such audacious flourishes that it might have served the Great Mogul as a palanquin. Frances was moving triumphantly to climb into it when she heard a voice behind her distinctly pronounce the name Sarah O'Neil...

She turned as if she had been bitten on the heel by a snake. Her sharp gaze pierced the crowd that surrounded her, in every direction. She saw nothing but unfamiliar faces, which laughed at her distress, attributing it to fright.

"Get off, if you daren't go!" they cried to her. "Give up your place and go down!"

Her clenched fingers dug into Richard's arm. He turned to face her, and was alarmed by her pallor. "Has someone insulted you?" he asked, excitedly.

"No," she replied. Then she added, lowering her voice to a murmur: "You didn't hear anything, then?"

"Hear what?"

Instead of replying, Frances' eyes grew brighter and her trembling finger pointed to the front of the platform, where the first rank of sleighs was balanced for the moment of departure. Richard's eye followed the gesture, and he tried to stifle an exclamation.

"Suzanne!" he ejaculated, in spite of his efforts.

"Robert!" murmured Frances.

The sleigh contained a young man and a young woman, who disappeared at that exact moment, precipitated down the rapid slope.

"We must follow them," said Frances, reverting to her original intention.

Richard seized her in his arms and set her down on the leather seat of the sleigh, amid general laughter provoked by the thought that the young foreigner was dying of fright.

"Push!" he commanded, putting a silver coin into the hand of the operative charged with regulating the departures. "Push hard!"

He added, as the sleigh accelerated: "This is the shortest route!"

Frances saw the lights racing past to the left and right with extravagant velocity. It seemed that her heart skipped a beat. Her breath was reduced to a gasp. She closed her eyes to avoid measuring the depth of the abyss into which she plunged. Such is the exact sensation procured by a sleigh-ride in the Russian Mountains.

It lasted a tenth of a minute, after which the movement ceased with a gentle shock. Richard leapt out of the sleigh and threw himself towards the exit door without waiting for his companion–but the crowd was as dense here as everywhere else. All he could make out, at the very bottom of the staircase, was the blue hat of the young woman he had taken for Suzanne Temple.

"Did you see him?" Frances asked, when he came back. "He had a green coat with gold buttons..."

"I know how she's dressed now," Richard replied. "We'll find them, if we have to scour the whole garden!"

They scoured the whole garden. Blue hats and green coats with gold buttons were in fashion. They found many such hats and many such coats. After two long hours of fruitless searching, Frances sat down, exhausted, on a grassy bank at the foot of a clump of lilacs.

"It was definitely him!" she said, sadly.

And Richard added, in consternation: "I could have sworn that it was her!"

At that moment, a green coat and a blue hat turned the corner of the shrubbery.

"It's them!" Frances cried.

Richard got up, his heart sinking. It was, indeed, the young couple from the sleigh. The glare of a street-lamp struck their faces fully as they passed by. Richard released a long sigh of relief, while Frances burst out laughing. It was not Robert Surrisy, and it was not Suzanne Temple–but Lady Frances' laughter choked on a cry of terror, while Richard froze as he was sitting down again, speechless.

There were now three people on the bank. Between the two of them was an old man, thin and white-faced, who had placed his hat between his knees to display the disordered wisps of his grey hair. He took a handkerchief from the depths of his hat and passed it slowly over his forehead three or four times. He said nothing. His eyes, which shone with a somber clarity, went back and forth between Richard and Frances.

Richard and Frances were dumbstruck.

After a long silence, the old man murmured: "Sarah O'Neil." He had a soft smile now, and was rubbing his two sets of fingertips together. "Did you ever hear talk of Gregory Temple, who boasted of catching thieves?" he asked, in a whisper. And when no one made any reply, he added, bowing his grey head: "There is a great secret. Old Temple had a secretary named Richard Thompson. He loved him like a son. Richard Thompson has been found with Sarah O'Neil. God sees everything; justice will be done..." He placed his dry and trembling hand on Richard's shoulder, in order to get to his feet. When he was upright, he looked around in a timorous fashion.

Madness expresses itself in a man's features, his gestures and his bearing just as much as his eyes. One might have said with total confidence that this man was mad, from head to toe.

He replaced his handkerchief in his hat and moved stealthily towards the clump of lilacs, whose branches he parted. He disappeared, almost creeping, behind young shoots already in leaf.

"That was true," Thompson murmured, with tears in his eyes. "For a long time, he treated me like a son, and I loved him as if he were my father..."

"His madness is to seek," Frances thought, aloud, "always to seek. He will die seeking."

The murmurs of the fairground were fading in the distance, and the periodic thunder of the Russian Mountains was no longer audible. Gaslight, which makes today's smallest popular gatherings more dazzling than the most brilliant of Versailles' halls in the ostentatious times of Louis XIV, is never exhausted, but in those days the oil dried up in the lamps, announcing the advent of the hour of retreat. While Lady Frances Elphinstone and her cavalier went back along the alleyways the day faded around them, and it was obvious that the Sun of those pleasures was setting. They were no longer talking; they were each occupied with their own thoughts.

"Thompson," said Lady Frances, suddenly. "You are unfortunate, and you are good. I feel a sisterly affection for you. Tell me honestly: what tie binds you to James Davy?"

Gregory Temple's former secretary stopped, astonished; "Don't you understand how much he's done for me?" he murmured. "The history of my secret marriage? The help that he's given me since the birth of my little Richard? It's thanks to him that I knew about the Superintendent's first suspicions. It's thanks to him that I'm able to flee, and it's he who will look after my son in my absence. I have his own pass in my portfolio, and I am only here because he has lent me his own name, for they are looking out for me at every port of embarkation. I don't look like James, but my age, the color of my hair and eyes, my complexion and the shape of my face tally with his, and our heights are similar. It's his money that will take me back to England."

"And why are you returning to England, Richard?" Frances asked.

"Because James' pass was stamped for ten days only, and in 48 hours it will be necessary to have it renewed at Scotland Yard."

"What will you do over there?"

"I have my mother."

"Wouldn't you be much safer in France?"

"That's not James's opinion..." Richard began.

"And you have a mission to fulfil for James, in London," Frances put in. Lowering her voice, she added: "You're like me, Richard. You do as he says."

Thompson remained silent.

"And like me," the young woman went on, "you know nothing about his secrets."

Thompson looked at her. "Why are you saying this to me, Frances?" he asked, with a hint of severity in his voice. "Don't you trust James Davy? Isn't he your friend?"

Lady Elphinstone opened her mouth, as if an angry reply was hovering on her lips, but her eyelids lowered while her face became red.

"Richard," she said, in a strained and strangely resigned tone, "James Davy has done even more for me than he has done for you. I owe him my liberty, perhaps my life... I owe him everything. I shall remain faithful and devoted; I shall obey until the end. But why hide it? I'm becoming afraid of the night into which I'm marching. For a moment, I hoped that you might shine a light into that night... Let's go, Richard, I'm deceiving myself. You've known him for less time than I have... and we shall both die as we are, as that man's slaves and instruments, without having guessed his secret."

She moved rapidly towards the exit gate, where impatient employees were urging the throng to move faster. Richard woke Sam the coachman, who was sleeping on his bench, and hoisted his companion into the carriage.

Before letting the high-stepping, head-tossing horses off the bridle, Sam cracked his whip half a dozen times, the sounds echoing from the body of the coach as the tip of the whip reached back to the station normally occupied by our friend Billy. "Do you see the coachman with those two white horses?" he said, without any prompting, using his hand to indicate an equipage that was moving towards the Champs-Elysées. "Two beasts fine enough for any Frenchman! Well, he came in behind us, and he was making fun of me because I had carried an old monkey all the way from the stage-coach office."

"An old monkey?" Richard echoed, while Frances put her head out of the door.

"I'm not a cab for ferrying poor folk, am I?" the indignant Sam went on. "If he gets on again, I'll set him straight... hold on, though!" His wrath increased as he pointed with the stick of his whip at the silhouette of an old man, thin and bent over, who was moving unsteadily and uncertainly through a flood of pedestrians. "There he is—my old monkey! He's still prowling around. He reckons to go home the way he came!"

The rig moved off. Thompson and Frances looked at one another silently. They had both recognized the former Chief Superintendent of the Metropolitan Police.

After a few moments, Thompson murmured: "Madmen play strange tricks..."

Frances, as if talking to herself, said: "If he weren't mad..."

Thompson shuddered.

Frances went on: "You know Paris better than I do. Can you name a place a long way from here?"

"The farthest is the Barrière du Trône," Richard replied.

Lady Frances lowered the glass partition to say to Sam: "I need to go to the Barrière du Trône."

"It's one o'clock in the morning..." the coachman began.

"Don't spare the horses!" the young woman instructed, peremptorily, as she closed the glass again.

The thin old man, bent nearly double–Gregory Temple, since we have easily recognized him–immediately mingled with the crowd of pedestrians, concealing himself as best he could behind the couples returning merrily from the fairground. He threw an occasional cat-like glance towards the coach, which was hindered from taking flight by its load and the heavy traffic.

He had a perfect view of the glass being lowered and the coachman turning to listen to his orders. He made an instinctive movement towards the equipage then, but at that moment Sam, dissatisfied with the order he had received and wanting to take out his anger on something, directed two violent blows of his whip at Billy's empty place.

The old man plunged more deeply into the crowd, trotting along and arching his spine. Despite the unsteadiness of his step, he moved faster than all the young couples, wriggling between them like an eel.

The coach, leaving the rough ground that is now pierced by the magnificent streets of the Beaujon district, reached the paved roads of Roule. Sam soon set his horses trotting. The old man, left behind, stood up straight again, blowing out his hollow cheeks in annoyance; his prey was escaping him. His unsteady legs became firm, and he continued on his way with a vigor and agility of which one would never have thought him capable. After a further hundred paces, he took off his hat, which he set resolutely under his arm, knotted his cravat around his waist, and broke into a run, not without uttering a few dull sounds of complaint. Incredible as it would have seemed to anyone who had seen him a little while ago on the bank between Lady Frances and Richard, he did not lose an inch of ground on Sam's team until they reached the Place de la Madeleine.

At that point, he came across a cab that was returning home empty. He hailed it, opened the door convulsively, and collapsed on the seat.

"The coach!" he cried, desperately. "Ten francs!–a *louis*!–whatever you want, if you don't lose sight of that coach!" He put his handkerchief over his mouth to interrupt the airflow that was tearing his lungs.

The coachman took his whip by the thin end and cracked the thicker one about the ears of his nags, which leapt forward. The coach had already reached the top of the Rue Caumartin.

Gregory Temple seized the damp and greasy cloth of his seat in his fist. His nerves, violently over-exerted, were terribly agitated. His eyes, whose light had been extinguished by a bleak and somnolent apathy not long ago, burned like a pair of incandescent coals. He was pressed into the corner of the cab, stiff and motionless. His gaze followed the route, visible beneath the coachman's elbow. At that moment, you might have taken him for a dog, with his unblinking eye fixed as if cast in bronze. The intensity of that stare had something frightful about it, by comparison with the trembling of his poor frame and the white spareness of his face.

If he weren't mad? Frances had said.

Obviously, this man had been playing a part in the Colisée garden. He had put on an act; he had assumed a disguise, exaggerating his weakness and emphasizing his decrepitude. Even so, he was in reality old, weak and decrepit, for the effort of running had left him exhausted. A few paces more and he might perhaps have fallen dead on the pavement, like a used-up machine whose spring had finally snapped.

As Thompson had said: *Madmen play strange tricks.*

Madmen can play the actor. There are those *who feign madness* by masking the symptoms of their own malady with others. Madness develops through innumerable stages; each inferior stage can simulate the next, and it happens to be the case that the reverse is also true. Gregory Temple's stare was mad. Gregory Temple was one of those madmen who play mad. He had feigned imbecility a little while ago, although his illness was the fixity of his obsession.

The cab's two horses, exhausted by a full day's work, were worn out. They went along the boulevard, which was full of potholes, as if they were performing epileptic somersaults–falling, then getting up, then falling again–but they went. The former Police Superintendent could still see the coach ahead of him. He let out a joyful grunt every time the coachman put his heart into his unfortunate beasts with another blow of his cudgel.

As they passed the Passage des Panoramas, which was still under construction, the boulevard–which was as badly maintained as a second-rate country road–put a stop to the spirited trot of Lady Frances' horses. They slowed down, and the two nags regained their breath. Gregory Temple wiped his forehead with his handkerchief, and stretched his limbs, which had been as stiff as if he had suffered a cataleptic fit.

He took a pinch of tobacco from a large box whose ivory lid was encrusted in black letters with the word *memento*, the date *February 3, 1817*, and the name of *Constance Bartolozzi*. For the first time since he he got into the cab, his lips moved. He whispered: "Where are they going?"

They passed the Porte Montmartre, then the Portes Saint-Denis and Saint-Martin. Beyond the Temple, the boulevard was no more than a high road running through meadows. The coach accelerated again. The former Superintendent placed his finger on his forehead.

They're trying to put me off the track, he thought.

One of the horses fell at the junction with the Rue Saint-Sébastien, and time was lost in getting it up again. Despite the blows inflicted by the coachman, who would have clubbed a dozen horses to death for 20 francs, it was impossible to make up an inch of ground. The other horse, by way of emulation, did a belly-flop as it reached the Place Royal. Gregory Temple opened the door, jumped down into the clotted dust, threw a *louis* to the coachman and took to his heels.

As he arrived at the Place de la Bastille, the coach disappeared behind the corner of the Faubourg Saint-Antoine. He crossed the square, already out of breath. He did not lack courage, but he had presumed too much of his strength.

"If only James Davy were with me!" he murmured.

When he reached the corner, the coach was no longer to be seen.

Gregory let himself down on a milestone. When he applied his handkerchief to his mouth, it came away red with blood.

He remained where he was, as motionless as the dead—but he had not entirely lost hope. The character of his state of mind changed instantaneously from suspicion to certainty. Many maniacs are prophets; their obsessive fixity is like a telescope before their eyes; in a given direction, they see much further than other men.

Gregory said to himself: *They'll be back*!

And he stayed where he was. As calculation was second nature to him, he had picked the right milestone to fall upon; it was exactly at the junction of the Rue de la Roquette and the Rue du Faubourg. When one makes up one's mind to put hunters of the track, the A B C of procedure is not to take the same path twice. The fugitives had gone towards the Barrière du Trône; they had to come back by the Rue de Roquette or the Rue de Charenton, cut across the Place de la Bastille, and re-enter the city center by the Rue Saint-Antoine; Gregory Temple was certain of that.

He kept watch on both the Rue de Charenton and the Rue de la Roquette, recovering his breath and his strength in case there was need for one last race. Sweat ran down his brow; his chest and sides were aching. He sat down gingerly on the damp ground, placing his back against the cold stone. His eyes closed, voluntarily, because he wanted to get as much rest as might be possible in the time he had. His ears remained alert; he said to himself, sternly: *stay awake...*

Fatigue, entwining him in its mute and invisible bonds, was already numbing his limbs—but not his mind, which was busy reasoning.

It was no longer a suspicion of guilt that weighed upon Richard Thompson, his former secretary; his liaison with Sarah O'Neil cast new evidential light upon the whole affair. Gregory Temple had earlier left this Sarah O'Neil at liberty precisely in order to arrive at his present destination. Sooner or later, infallibly, she would put him on the track, unless the very foundations of his science were false—and were not the foundations of his science as solid as mathematical truth itself?

With his hand on the most painful wound he had ever received in his life, he thought: *I am not going under*!

He took pride in his algebraic victory. One more step, and the exercise of his intelligence would light a candle within this darkness. He said to himself: *I am alone, and am more powerful than in the days when I had my army*!

He lay in wait, wide awake, general and soldier at the same time...

But he was still resting against the stone when the triumph of his realized calculation should have brought him to his feet with a single bound. All came to pass as he had foreseen: the noise of wheels was audible in the distance, not in the Rue du Faubourg but beyond the sharp bend in the Rue de la Roquette. It was definitely the fugitives' coach. It went past at a trot, drawn by its two fine horses. Gregory Temple heard it, because he stirred and murmured confused words, but it was in a dream that he heard it. It was in a dream that he said henceforth: *I am awake...*

He was asleep, his head slumped on his chest. Slumber, toying with his thoughts, had taken him by surprise. Who among us has not fallen victim to that bizarre trick, pursuing the chimera of meditation into the land of dreams?

Gregory Temple slept, while his insatiable brain continued its efforts to stay awake; he worked as he slept.

The coach crossed the Place de la Bastille and took the Rue Saint-Antoine. It stopped near the Palais-Royal. Richard stepped down to the ground and Lady Frances extended her hand to him, saying: "Bon voyage!"

It was two o'clock in the morning when Lady Frances Elphinstone re-entered her town house in the Place Vendôme. It was much later, when the day was already brightening, when Gregory Temple arrived at No. 19 in the Rue Dauphine, on the arm of an obliging suburban laborer who had lifted his chilled body from the milestone.

This No. 19 was an ancient town house with only three windows in the front. In compensation, the narrow and gloomy alley that led to the courtyard was a good 30 paces long. The courtyard was a well, inhabited by a porter of the primitive school, who was now lame, one-armed and deaf. He lived in a wooden hut at the bottom of the well. It was his home; he had tried several times to raise dogs there, but they had all died. His children were alive, though: a one-eyed daughter and a son who limped along with the aid of a crutch. On all four sides of the courtyard the house rose up to the height of six stories; the court itself was barely 12 feet long and 12 feet broad, counting the space taken up by the hut. When one looked up at the sky from its bowels, one felt dizzy.

The porter at No. 19 was called Fortuné. It was more than ten years since his wife had last set foot outside the hut where she was growing fat, afflicted as she was by rheumatism. Rheumatism makes one fat. She cooked for a swarm of students nesting on the various floors. Bijou, the one-eyed daughter, carried the plates; Coquinet, the son with the crutch, carried out commissions with an extraordinary celerity. Father Fortuné was a pawnbroker, and had plenty of money. The rents were not expensive at No. 19, and Mother Fortuné's cooking had a well-deserved reputation. It rarely happened that a room remained vacant for more than 24 hours, and there was often a waiting list of candidates for tenancy. Father Fortuné charged ten *sous* for admission to the queue to enter his Eden.

Such houses have gone now. There is no longer any such thing as a porter, and some concierges are already inscribing Doorkeeper on their front doors.

The suburban worthy stoutly refused the coin offered to him by Gregory Temple, but finished up putting it in his pocket with pleasure, saying: "It's not worth it. You had one too many, didn't you? If I had an *écu* for every time I'd been gathered up like that on the Vincennes road, I'd have six *livres*..."

"When would you like someone to come up and do your room, Monsieur Gregory?" asked Father Fortuné, as his tenant went past his hut.

"My letters!" said the old man brusquely, instead of answering the question.

He was handed a rather voluminous package, composed of his correspondence.

"Any callers?" he asked.

"No more today than any other day, Monsieur Gregory," Father Fortuné replied, having turned towards him his less deaf ear. Since you took the third floor back, you haven't had a visit from a cat–not even a cat!"

The old man went on his way and climbed up the stairs.

The porter turned towards his gout-ridden wife, whose frightful rotundity filled the depths of the hut. "The English," he said, shaking his bald head, as dry as old parchment, "aren't made the same way as the rest of us."

"His gold coins fetch eight *sous* at the jeweler's," Madame Fortuné replied.

While going upstairs, Gregory Temple examined his letters. He picked out one that bore a slightly smudged London postmark.

"James Davy," he murmured. "He never sent word that Richard Thompson had left London!"

These words constituted a reproach. He opened the letter, and after darting a single glance at it his expression cleared.

"Well done!" he cried. "I can count on this one; he's never mistaken."

The letter contained these three lines:

Dear master,
Richard Thompson is in Paris under a false name. Nothing else to report.
James Davy.

The former Police Superintendent put his key into the lock on his chamber door and opened it with an expression that was almost cheerful. As soon as he was inside, the key was turned the other way, to double-lock the door again. The door was never to be found unlocked, at any hour of the day or night, whether he was in it or out of it–and Bijou would be able to tell you from experience that it was impossible to catch the least glimpse of anything through the keyhole. Whether the tenant was present or absent, his room was rigorously defended; no one ever got into it, even to bring him his meals.

Bijou was curious, and the one eye she had was as sharp as an owl. She had posted herself on the far side of the courtyard more than once, at one or other of the third-floor windows, hoping to take advantage of a joint, an interstice or a crevice by means of which to penetrate the tenant's perpetually-closed curtains with her inquisitive gaze—but the rampart remained opaque. A faint light was easily perceptible when he spent the night in his room, but one could not see the lamp or candle that produced the light.

On the day of his arrival, he had summoned a carpenter, who brought planks with him. For several hours, the carpenter had been sawing, planing and hammering, The next day, that tenant had brought in a bucket as black as oil under his great-coat, from which a house-painter's brush projected. Three weeks had gone by since then; Bijou was withering away. Ordinarily, it did not take her 24 hours to have her tenants at her fingertips. By way of revenge, Bijou had nicknamed this one the Mole. She detested him; she suspected him of being a fabricator of fake money or living on the proceeds of some other punishable trade.

The Mole was, however, a generous guest. He paid his rent weekly, according to the custom of the hive, and always added five francs "for service," even though he received absolutely none. He brought in all the necessities of his existence himself, under his great-coat, and no one in the house could boast of ever having done anything for him. This was precisely what Bijou had against him: once, she had tried to put on a show of zeal and bring him up his correspondence; through the closed door, the Englishman had instructed her rudely to leave him in peace.

He received a great many letters, and Father Fortuné, in imitation of many solicitors, notaries and bankers, added a third to the postal charges, to cover errors or omissions—which did not prevent the mysterious tenant from adding a gratuity to the sum reclaimed. With respect to profits, the Mole was worth more than the rest of the house, but Bijou remained implacable: she wanted his secret as well as his money.

He had a secret, this Englishman who never ate Mother Fortuné's cooking and brought back bread in his pockets; he had a secret, this old man who made his own bed and put a plug in his keyhole—a great secret, perhaps an abominable one! What was he hiding in the room that he had made into a citadel? Was it a living person, or was it a treasure?

It might have been a living person, for Bijou had often heard talking while she loitered by the door. Sometimes, she thought she could make out two distinct voices. But how had the Englishman smuggled the other one in? And what was he up to? It might be a woman, or a stolen child, or perhaps a cousin whom he had imprisoned and put in irons, as was commonplace in theatrical melodrama.

One night, when the room directly below was momentarily vacant, Bijou had installed herself there. At about midnight, she had woken her father, who vent up with her; then, her brother Coquinet had arrived on his crutch. They heard soft and furtive footsteps, apparently those of a woman–not, at least, those of a child–moving back and forth in the Mole's room. It was so curious that they went down to fetch Madame Fortuné, who made a great effort to get out but found that the door of the hut had long ago become too narrow for her. Have you seen the miracle of the watermelon sown in a glass globe, which grows just sufficiently to fill the globe–whose narrow neck always provokes naive individuals to ask how the melon could possibly have got in there? It was the same with Madame Fortuné; Don Juan himself, the stealer of women, could not have plundered that conjugal domicile without demolishing the hut.

That night, the family Fortuné listened until daybreak to the soft and discreet footsteps marching back and forth in the Englishman's room.

Usually, the Englishman went out at eight o'clock in the morning, taking his key with him. He was remarkably proper in his manners and his clothing: he invariably dressed entirely in black, with silk stockings and buckled shoes. Over this ensemble, he draped an ample great-coat, brown in color, whose gaping pockets were always full of provisions when he returned. Since arriving in Paris, he had twice been absent for four days at a time. On the other hand, he had once spent four entire days without going out of his room. During these four days, Bijou had heard nothing behind the door. She had sniffed the draught that escaped through the cracks, hoping that the odor of a cadaver might reveal an accomplished suicide. She did not sleep at all on the last night, thinking of the locksmith who would come to open the door with his skeleton key and display the corpse in the midst of the chamber's mysteries; the fever of curiosity had reached ferocious extremes. The following morning, however, the Mole–the damned Mole!–appeared in the corridor with his neatly brushed black suit beneath his brown great-coat. Bijou's good eye had wept.

What would she not have given to do as we do–to go in this morning behind Gregory Temple, while he turned the key twice in its lock?

The Englishman's room, as everyone in the house called it, was situated at the end of the third-floor corridor, and was numbered 21. There were seven rooms on each floor. This was a fairly large room, even though it only had a single window overlooking the courtyard. The furniture consisted of a white-painted wooden cot, three similarly treated chairs and a recently varnished writing desk in the Empire style. It also housed a small chest of drawers and a slender clock set between two decorated porcelain vases on the mantelpiece. The walls were covered in yellowish paper, dampened and loosened by humidity.

Under the Restoration, students' lodgings were no more sumptuous than this–and luxury has not made very much progress since, in similar circumstances. The splendid gaiety of youth has to be robust to resist the depression sweated by the walls of these cold slums, but this is the home of the love and laughter of 20-year-olds. Poor and cold as it may be, hope gives birth to palatial furnishings and redresses lusterless lanterns with the mantle of the Sun. This is the home of the boastful and prodigal health that recklessly dispenses its inexhaustible treasure. In here, the human chrysalis that sleeps benumbed by collegiate ice warms up in the wind of liberty; can you not see the sprouting of its wings? In here, the plant, stunted because it has been set in a cellar, emerges in response to the first breath of Heaven's air, and one can see that it will soon come into flower. This is the home where the adolescent gives birth to the man, in the midst of a noisy and hectic party; it is the temple of smiles and song, the mysterious granary of the poet, the first dream of the lilac hat or the white dress, the little rose-bush in the window... who knows? All the beloved wretchedness that tearful luxury will look back on with regret much later is the honeymoon of the amorous child who celebrates his marriage to life.

What does the envelope matter, anyhow? What exterior magnificence could add to the astonishments of the awakening soul? What would you give for riches like these? Youth itself is gold!

But dismiss youth summarily from the nest that it furnishes and decorates; break the enchantment; bend that white head over that hollow chest; reduce the smile to the wrinkle that is its skeleton, and hope to its cadaver, regret...

Everything on Earth has its place and setting. The soldier who retires, wearied and perhaps wounded by life's battles, has need of more than the austerities that gladden the heart of he conscript. Battle supposes conquest. Go forth naked, happy children, but don't come back without the cloak that will warm up your old age!

An old man in these cells furnished by dreams and hopes is a sad sight, because an old man has neither hopes nor dreams. But that's not the only reason you'd have a chill in your veins as you crossed the threshold of the Englishman's room. The fear and compassion produced by contact with madness, that mysterious punishment dreaded by all, would have clutched at your heart. Here are the lodgings of a madman: the impression of dementia seizes you as you enter, as if the maniac himself, laughing and frolicking, had jumped at your throat.

The bed was in the middle of the room. On the white-painted boards that formed its foot, the following date was inscribed in black: *February 3, 1817.* That date was repeated on the bedhead, above the pillow. To the right and the left, on the yellow wallpaper, that date was legible again, traced in large letters.

On the mirror above the fireplace a wide stripe bore the legend: *February 3, 1817.* Each drawer in the chest, placed face-to-face with it, replied: *February 3, 1817. February 3, 1817* was written on the lid of the writing desk. Enormous letters and numbers, traced in chalk on a blackboard standing in front of the window, shouted as if raising their voice to be heard over a murmur: *FEBRUARY 3, 1817.*

Everywhere that date was inscribed, so that it filled the room as an obsessive idea fills and fatigues the sick brain, there was beneath it the word *Memento,* and beneath that, the name *Constance Bartolozzi.*

That was what caught the eye at first, but one passes naturally from the general ensemble to the detail. After having perceived the form of the tree, you study the arrangement of the larger branches, then the branches ramifying therefrom, from the twig to the leaf, and in the leaf itself you trace the delicate weave of the veins. A similar gradation presented itself here, and the prodigious work of the obsession, like the sap of the tree, ramified and became slimmer, going from great to small to produce a kind of threatening net whose every strand, made up of the same words and the same figures, enveloped you and oppressed you, driving the breath back into your lungs, and weighing upon your skull like a leaden cap.

They were everywhere, those words and figures–everywhere! They were engraved on the top of the little table, traced on bookplates and on all the floorboards; various utensils bore them like labels; they reconstructed, in characters as subtle and delicate as the strands of a spider web, the washed-out pattern of the wallpaper; they leapt out violently from the door, which was filled with huge letters and figures: the same ones, engraved with the point of a knife, murmuring the same frightful drivel:

Memento – February 3, 1817 – Constance Bartolozzi.

The madman must have had a head of bronze to bear the terrible pressure of that word, date and name–which surrounded him like an atmosphere–without falling into a depression that would lift into furious delirium. It must have been like a church bell perpetually sounding in his ear, wearying his eye in the same manner, never permitting his distraught spirit to rest upon another thought. There was no means of escape; the imperious instruction that it must not be forgotten was reasserted everywhere. The pitiless memento worked unceasingly upon his mind like the insistent strands of a penitent's hair shirt. It was a torture without remission, a moral prison that burned like molten lead, a vulture that devoured the very matter of the denuded brain instead of the heart.

Inevitable, implacable, those words were to the right and the left, in front and behind, above and below, black on white and white on black, somber in the light and bright in the darkness, visible and legible, speaking in high and low voices at the same time, incessantly probing the same wound, patiently and incessantly picking at the same scab.

Could anyone but a madman inflict upon himself that futile and incredible refinement of torture?

The madman crossed the threshold of his Inferno with a smile on his lips; as he turned the key in the lock to seal himself in, he released a great sigh of relief. He let himself fall rather than sit down at the foot of his bed, for he was literally exhausted, but not without casting a gaze of profound and loving affection all around him, upon those friendly objects and walls that spoke the same language as his fever.

No young painter, happy and enthusiastic in the consciousness of his talent, ever cast a gaze more tender upon the sketch-embellished canvases in his studio, after a long absence. No father ever looked with greater passion upon his growing child whose birthday had come. Gregory Temple was at home; he had made a dwelling of his thought. The tyranny of that obsession, which is fearful and repulsive to us, he breathed in by choice, plunging back into it with a kind of sensuous rapture.

Was he utterly mad? His expression was calm, his forehead luminous, his smile both firm and peaceful. Or was there at the core of his madness, when it did not collide with exotic motivation, something equivalent to rationality?

How should we define the words reason and madness?

Has not every one of us encountered, at some stage in his life, some thief of sacred fire too close to Heaven and too distant from the Earth, indicted—in the legal sense—by a court of idiot sages? Where does it begin and end? Who is to judge? Is not the six-foot man deformed from the viewpoint of the dwarf? Would not Punch replace Apollo in a conclave of hunchbacks?

For a few moments, Gregory Temple savored the delight of resting after his long fatigue. He had dropped his packet of letters beside him on the bed. His hands—which were a little dry but white and regular, affecting the delicate form that the experts consider a sign of a subtle and searching mind—were rubbing gently one against the other. He did not speak.

After five minutes, he got up and took some bread, wine and a plate of cold meat from a cupboard. He set them out on the mantelpiece and ate standing up, eating moderately but with a hearty appetite. If he had been a German madman instead of an English one, he would have lived on next to nothing, but among the Anglo-Saxons, even the mind draws nourishment from roast beef.

When Gregory Temple had finished his meal, he filled his glass to a moderate level, lifted it as if it were the bearer of mystical health, and drained it in a single gulp. After that he put everything back in place and went back to the bed to sit down again.

He stayed there, pensive and silent, for at least half an hour. The working of his brain was almost legible in his mobile and expressive features. He collated and he calculated. From time to time, his smile or an approving tilt of his head, announced the satisfactory results of his mental labor.

When he got up, he took a piece of white chalk from the mantelpiece and turned towards the blackboard standing before the window. This blackboard, which we have mentioned previously in passing, was surely the most interesting of the Englishman's movable effects. This was what made a screen for Bijou's good eye when she stood at one of the windows on the far side of the courtyard, and it was to fabricate this that the carpenter had sawed, planed and hammered on the day of Gregory's arrival. Gregory had painted it black himself, and left it to dry during his first four-day absence.

At the top of the blackboard, as we have said, were the word, the date and the name that were reproduced throughout the room. Under that heading, which was placed like a title above the frontispiece of a book, four vertical lines had been drawn, dividing the totality of the surface into five columns of equal width.

The first column was subtitled: *Gregory Temple*.

The second was subtitled: *Her Enemies*.

The third: *Those to whom she was an obstacle*.

The fourth: *Those who have profited from her death*.

The fifth: *The Impossible*.

The second, third and fourth columns were connected by a horizontal bracket, indicating that all three of them referred to Constance Bartolozzi. The first and the fifth, both isolated, thus became appendices.

Each column contained a number of notes written in chalk, some encrypted, others in plain English. The traces of chalk, perceptible beneath the writing, testified that many earlier inscriptions had been erased, replaced and erased again, so that the present draft of this strange showcard was the result of painstaking reconstruction. As the layout now stood, the five columns were closed off at two thirds of the total height by a horizontal line. Underneath this line were three compartments, one of which bore the title *Counterproof* while the others opened their accounts with two pairs of initials: *R.T.* and *S.O.*

If, by some miracle, Bijou's good eye had been able to see through obstacles and dart a glance into the room's interior, her curiosity would have been tested here by bitter disappointment. For her, the blackboard charged with hieroglyphs would have been an enigma even more impenetrable than the Englishman's conduct–and it would not have been sufficient, in order to get out of it, to say "It's the bedroom of a madman." Even admitting the madness, something remained: something provocative and tenacious that excited the mind like the challenge of some terrible charade. The idea of crime would spring to mind, even in the absence of comprehension. That name, *Constance Bartolozzi*, together with the word *memento* and the date, could not be anything but the name of a murder victim. There was no other choice than between two suppositions: the Englishman was either an assassin, or an avenger.

The tabulation, which will soon be as clear to the reader as the bill for some commercial transaction, was the subject matter of the first chapter of *The Art of Discovering the Guilty*, and embodied a key element of Gregory Temple's methodology. His theory of the impossible was only represented in the layout by a single column because–convinced as he was that his own science had been turned against him–he had scant hope for this final key, which was ordinarily so powerful, and had made him victorious on so many occasions. In fact, the fifth column, subtitled *The Impossible*, was empty and virginal; no word had been written there, nor had any been erased.

The first column, *Gregory Temple*, had three subdivisions, labeled as follows: *1. Ingrates; 2. Enemies and the Envious; 3. Heirs.* This was a reproduction of the system applied to la Bartolozzi herself.

Under the heading *Heirs* there was: *R.T., my ward since infancy, my secretary, my pupil–the age-old story of the serpent that one nurtures in one's bosom.*

Under the rubric *Enemies and the Envious: R.T. owes me too much; crushed by my superiority, detests his subordinate role; mediocre intelligence; does not understand his master at all, and jeers at that which he cannot understand.*

Under *Heirs: R.T. believes that my responsibilities will revert to him; made ambitious by love, and, doubtless to become worthy of the woman he loves, boasts of being my successor.*

A horizontal bracket placed under these three subdivisions recombined them, preceding this corollary: *The crime has been a challenge to my infallibility; an attack on my renown; a means to bring me down. Proofs: the publicity given to the words of the Lord Chief Justice, HE'S GOING UNDER, and the pamphlet entitled* The Life and Adventures of John Devil the Quaker, *purely directed against me and published in an edition of 80,000 copies.*

Beneath this was written: *N.B.: R.T. is incapable of having written the pamphlet, but in the world of English letters, just as certain geniuses of obtuseness are rolling in money, other intelligent men are dying of hunger: the pamphlet's intelligence could have been purchased for three or four guineas.*

We pass on to the main part of the table, to the three columns joined in the middle beneath the sinister sign:

Memento – February 3, 1817 – Constance Bartolozzi.

The first column, *Her Enemies*, included: *Fanny T., mother of R.T., singer like her at the Princess Theater–mediocre talent–relegated to the second rank after having occupied the first–seized by rancor and depression–disorder dissipation, great needs–a part of R.T.'s salary sent there–obligations contracted; Fanny T. owed Constance more than 1,000 pounds–inquiry at theater: Fanny T. mounted conspiracy against her enemy.*

There was also a fairly considerable list of names, containing almost all of la Bartolozzi's colleagues. (This is not directed against theatrical folk, who are indeed deplorably jealous of one another–but not much more than lawyers, doctors, men of letters, millionaires and rag-and-bone men; it is the flower produced by the tree of confraternity.)

The second column, *Those to whom she was an obstacle: Obliging, but a businesswoman, la Bartolozzi, touched the interests of almost all those who became her associates. Fanny T... paid her 60 pounds a year. Fanny T... often said that Constance would soon quit the theater, and that she would take over her osition. R.T., his mother's fool, took up her quarrel, insulted la Bartolozzi in the street (being drunk) in May 1815. La Bartolozzi's lawyer came to R.T.'s office at Scotland Yard in December 1816, regarding a check for 30 pounds that he had signed on his mother's behalf.*

Tom Brown, son of Helen Brown (the Comtesse de Belcamp), heir to his two uncles, Mr. Robinson and Mr. Turner, both very rich and both having made a will in favor of la Bartolozzi–Fact of the utmost importance in the discharge of R.T.

These last words were heavily underlined. Then there was another list of names. Then this note: *La Bartolozzi plays host to the Knights of the Deliverance. Did she possess dangerous secrets? Simple question.*

The second column, *Those who have profited from her death: NO ONE, actually and definitely; the assassin stole nothing. S.O. took nothing but her wages. The assets were adequate to pay the dead woman's debts.*

1. Indirectly, Fanny T., and thus R.T., both discharged from their annual interest–and of the principal debt, since no record of the obligation was found among the dead woman's papers.

2. Eventually, Tom Brown (I note this to the discharge of R.T., for I would wish to find him innocent of the full balance that has been so cruelly debited from his account); this Tom Brown, although still very young, is a hardened and highly-skilled criminal; escaped from Sydney with exceptional audacity; murderer several times over; returned to England, according to every appearance, but not officially sighted. By virtue of the la Bartolozzi's decease, Tom Brown becomes the natural heir of Frank Turner and William Robinson.

N.B. The paragraph relating to him in the John Devil *pamphlet must, however, be considered–according to its appearance–as the beginning of a false trail or pure nonsense.*

3. Ultimately, if the wills of Robinson and Turner are not revoked (which seems improbable), the natural son and daughter of the dead woman, resident with the widow Touchard at the Priory, in Miremont, Seine-et-Oise.

4. Finally, Turner and Robinson themselves, or one of them–mere conjecture. Tiresome burden of an old liaison–promises of marriage weighing upon them–to follow.

This was everything in the upper part of the blackboard, the column of *The Impossible* remaining empty at present. We pass on to the lower part labeled *R.T.–Counterproof–S.O.*

R.T.–For me, ingrate, enemy and envious, heir; for Bartolozzi, enemy on his own behalf and his mother's. The first of those who stood in her way; the only one–with his mother–actually to profit from her death.

Counterproof–Flight of R.T., clumsiness (but he is clumsy). Objects of value left on the victim's night-stand, clumsiness of man who is not professional thief; he is clumsy and not professional thief.

Same fact: cleverness on the part of Tom Brown, who is professional thief (he is skillful).

Bloody handkerchief, marked R.T., letter signed with same initials: coarse means, but which brings in the premises of my book, just as much as the creation of the phantom John Devil. (R.T. knows my book by heart.)

Alibi, journey to visit his mother in Surrey, some leagues from London; infantile impossibility, naive attempt on my method well within R.T.'s reach.

N.B. It is proved by witnesses that R.T. and Fanny T. had visited Constance Bartolozzi at home the day before the murder.

Child mysteriously lodged in the mother's home, proof of son's amorous intrigue: sharpener of ambition.

Embarrassment with respect to me, for a long time; emotions without cause, desire inhibited by terror of confiding in me, preoccupations, absences, absolute neglect of work.

At this moment, Gregory Temple was doing exactly what we have been doing: reading each of these paragraphs, but with an extreme and passionate attention. Each of these phrases was for him a knot in an immense net into which his prey must sooner or later fall. He had reduced several weeks of arduous and oft-corrected labor, replete with amendments and corrections, to a skeleton. Gregory Temple still lacked the key to the patiently buttressed vault, but he had hewn it from the solid rock. Worn down by his life's work, he went on his way with a firm step, like the Indian with war-paint on his skin who moves along forest trails following the mysterious but ineradicable track of a doomed enemy.

"There's one strange thing," he murmured to himself, as his pensive gaze remained fixed on the phrase he had just read. "It was about the time that James Davy came to work at Scotland Yard. Suzanne changed too. Poor Suzanne! Such a candid and joyful child... but girls often undergo these transformations at the age when the child becomes a woman. Suzanne! The fortune of my heart! My final happiness! The image of her blessed mother!"

He remained still for a moment, overwhelmed by the weight of his reverie. His burning gaze softened and became damp; his head was bowed. But the moment was brief. In that room, one would have to have been blind to dream for long. The voice of the walls that spoke to the eyes was a constant clamor—and it was he himself, who did not want ever to pause in his progress, who had given them their voice!

Memento – February 3, 1817 – Constance Bartolozzi.

"To work!" he murmured, shivering. "When you have attained your goal, you will become a father again!"

The last paragraph contained in the column entitled *Counterproof* had an overwhelming significance. It was constructed thus:

The absence of traces, according to my theory, which I so patiently taught to R.T.; the protection of the Lord Chief Justice, who is self-accused by the insolence of the words Gregory Temple is going under. SURGICAL STRIKE, wound having occasioned death by an internal lesion, without leaving any external mark. R.T. has been assistant surgeon on His Majesty's brig Neptune.

The old man's finger pointed at this line, while the light furrowing of his eyebrows betrayed his mental effort.

Under the rubric *S.O.*, there were these lines:

Has seen nothing; statement false, given under the orders of an unknown master–hook cast on a line–intimate relationship with this one proves nothing; a single word exchanged with that one would prove everything... if ever I acquire certitude that R.T. and S.O. know one another, I have the answer to the riddle, and the affair Bartolozzi is another feather in my cap!

While Gregory Temple read these words, a smile of triumph was born upon his lips; his eyes shone and the pallor of his cheeks was tinted with red.

"That's true," he said, straightening his bent back. "Strictly true... no, Milord Chief Justice, I'm not going under! No, no–Gregory Temple isn't the kind of madman whose brain is too desiccated to calculate impossible numbers. Gregory Temple is an inventor, milord, like Galileo or Newton! Your lordship has often deigned to mock, saying that the sole result of his method has been to force malefactors to obtain degrees from Oxford or Cambridge, and that it will henceforth be necessary to have passed examinations for doctorates of philosophy in law and medicine to be a successful thief... you are a noble idiot, milord! I shall have the honor of telling you to your face before I die. Is there nothing else, then, if your lordship pleases, other than that sole result?

"Even if it were true, what Chancellor of the Exchequer would dare to boast of a similar achievement? If I had only added to the barriers that the law opposes to criminals the same obstacles that are set between honest men and their fortune, would that count for nothing? I would have made the least crime as difficult as the most glorious action, and you mock! I would have erected on the road of infamy, in addition to the familiar obstacles of conscience and the law, all the obstacles that bar the path of virtue, and you smile beneath your powdered wig! Is the following reasoning, milord, above or below your illustrious intelligence?

"Why does this Christian parable sew the high road to Hell with flowers, while the narrow pathway to Heaven is strewn with thorns? Is it not that everyone in the world would go to Heaven if the way were comfortable, and that no one would go to Hell if the avenues leading there were anything but easy? Being unable to make the road to Heaven any easier, I make the road to Hell more difficult–and I ask you, milord, whether the result is not the same?

"And coming back to reality–as befits a serious man before your lordship– I ask again: don't you think that studies undertaken to an evil end might nevertheless prove a good influence? Don't you think that the unfortunate moving into the shadows while going to the bad might turn back halfway if he receives the benefit of light? What is conversion, if not the conquest of night by day?

"And finally, I ask you: do you think that once turned back towards the summit, that man, armed henceforth for loyal combat and reinvested with all the credentials that open the doors of glory and honor, would simply choose to go down again into the vault of our social mire? That can certainly happen, because perversity, like valor and genius, has its prodigious exceptions–but do you think that it can happen routinely and frequently? For myself, I say no! And as for the exception, if it should present itself, we shall commit ourselves to its subjection to a supreme examination that is not in the Oxford syllabus... we who are going under, milord, we who are become a poor lunatic, we who have crossed the strait rather than go to Bedlam!"

His nostrils were wildly flared; ten years had been lifted from his shoulders, and his proud eyes challenged the absent Lord Chief Justice.

He went to the blackboard and applied his chalk to it, level with the line that was labeled *R.T.–Counterproof–S.O.* Filling in the blank spaces that followed the initials, he first completed the baptismal and family names: *Richard Thompson, Sarah O'Neil.* Then he drew two diagonal lines from the two names, which came together under the *Counterproof* column, and wrote at the junction: *Key fact: both surprised together at the Paris Colisée, May 8, 1817!*

Then, Gregory Temple threw the chalk away and crossed his arms upon his raised breast. For a moment, triumphant enthusiasm illuminated his whole frame, and his face was radiant.

Soon, though, the sound of his anxious footfalls was audible again; the wrinkles had returned to his temples and the pallor to his cheeks. Every time he passed in front of the blackboard he glanced at it rapidly, and little by little he became suspicious.

Doubt is the malady of the learned. No evident cause had given birth to this doubt and no new fact had produced it, save for the incessant mental effort that was hammering away in that indefatigable brain. The sequence of conclusions, formerly so clear and plain, became troubled: fog rose up in the midst of the light. That which had previously dazzled Gregory Temple like the Sun of evidence itself, faded now into confusion.

"That's it, though," he said, stopping in front of the blackboard in a sudden fit of anger. "I needed nothing more than that glimmer, and I have caused it to appear! What else do I need to be certain? Whence comes this blind doubt in the midst of my conviction, which is founded in logic itself?"

But doubt is a mute adversary, which does not take the trouble to reply to such arguments, and whose powerful silence disparages certainty.

"I doubt!" murmured Gregory Temple, lowering his head again. "Is it the affection I had for that young man? Oh, I like him, of course. I was halfway to giving him a place in my dreams of the future... and sometimes I thought that my poor Suzanne. Of course, of course, there is the frustration of a great hope smashed... and Suzanne's unhappiness has redoubled my anger. I saw that they liked one another right away, like a brother and sister... did I not repent of once having said: My daughter shall never marry the son of an actress? Wasn't it then that everything began to go wrong? But all that ought to reinforce my certainty, and yet I doubt! Is it the absence of material proof? I'm not a judge; others would have to absolve or convict him. I no longer have any affection for him. What does the absence of material proof matter when the chain of deduction has all its links? I doubt... I'm getting old... my faith in myself is weakening... and I shall soon give reason to the Lord Chief Justice, for if I doubt, I go under!"

He turned his back on the blackboard and went back to the foot of his bed, where he sat down. Time had moved on; the Sun, already at its zenith, penetrated the narrow courtyard with its light, extending its rays as far as the former Superintendent's retreat. The letters and figures traced on the wall stood out with a new clarity, throwing forth their eternal reminder. Gregory Temple's head was aching; it was at that moment that the weary brain repelled odious meditation with all its strength. He closed his eyes in order to flee, if only for a minute, from the pitiless obsession of the silent scream that he heard in the sight–but through his closed eyelids he could still see the word, the date, the name written in his mind even more legibly than on his walls.

In the darkness where he took refuge, letters and figures appeared to him as large as phantoms, and his two hands rose convulsively, clinging in distress to his moist face.

"John Devil!" he murmured, after a few seconds of veritable torture. "That name pursues me. It was not my own impulse that took me to the stage-coach office yesterday evening. A note delivered by an unknown hand bid me: *Go to the stage-coach office*. Who wrote it? Why? Is it a trap? Richard Thompson is innocent... I know nothing...

"John Devil! John Devil! Someone is beneath that mask and behind that lie! Who? Will I die mad before strangling my executioner?"

He leapt to his feet in one of those transports of wrath that only emerge in their full dementia from the depths of solitude, when a man has no one else but himself, and the teeth of his passion have nothing to bite but his own substance.

They are indescribable, these powerful scenes that no one can imagine unless he has been the sole actor of one, or until the day when some madman roaring in his padded cell can take up his pen and write the memoirs of his delirium. It is a horrible drama that world knows only in its denouement, which is often suicide; it is the hideous single combat of the abandoned against the demon Despair; it is the epilepsy of the soul.

There was blood on Gregory Temple's fingernails; he was insensible of the fact that he was clawing at his temples. Beneath the convulsion of his eyebrows, his ardent and somber eyes issued an absurd challenge to the heavens. All his limbs were shaking; his grey hair was standing on end; a line of foam flecked his clenched lips. His clenched fists–which were no longer wrinkled but displayed their thin, fleshless tendons as taut as violin-strings on the point on breaking–struck at his face by turns, and the numb cheeks reverberated with a flaccid noise. Three more times he growled that name, which sounded like some futile fracas in the painful void of his brain.

"John Devil! John Devil! John Devil!"

Then he cried: "I must get him! My blood will deliver him to me! More than my blood, my daughter's bread! The last of my mother's line! I shall put a price on his head!... And besides, have I sunk so low? Has the Prince Regent paid his debt to me? Do I no longer have my army? Am I not a thousand times stronger than his shadow in which I'm hiding? I shall go to Windsor; I shall speak to Prince George..."

He had been striding back and forth, but he stopped suddenly, and the strength of his animated voice died into a sarcastic laugh.

"I'm going under," he whispered, collapsing on his cot, whose worm-eaten frame groaned under the weight of his body. "They are all in league against me. All around me, there is now a rampart. And I'm an accomplice to their perfidy; I allow myself to take the bait that they throw to me; I believe in the phantoms they evoke; I release my prey to chase their shadow; I seek John Devil, the mannequin set by them upon my route, when my rigorous and infallible calculation has already discovered the real guilty party... Richard Thompson would laugh heartily if he could come in through the window with the draught..."

With sudden coldness, he continued: "That one cannot make haste enough, for the crisis has arrived. I have his head beneath my hand, and his life is mine! John Devil is a murderer, as I well know, but John Devil is named Richard Thompson, and the noose that will hang Richard will tighten about the neck of John Devil!"

He snatched up the packet of letters that was next to him on the bed. James Davy's letter was the first to fall under his gaze, and he smiled in satisfaction.

"This one won't let me down," he murmured. "My choice is made. It's to him that I'll confide everything I know and believe. Him in London, me in Paris; I to depart, he to arrive. We shall see whether John Devil, since there is a John Devil, will escape this time!"

His face lit up again, and he even had an ironic smile on his face–an invariable sign, in him, of triumph. He sat down at the writing desk and dipped his pen in the inkwell. He wrote:

To James Davy, esquire, Assistant Inspector of the Metropolitan Police, Scotland Yard, London.
My very dear friend...

His pen stopped abruptly, doubtless because he was searching for the right word or phrase. While he searched–or perhaps because his brain, having resolved the problem of perpetual motion, was already following another train of thought–his gaze chanced to fall upon the envelope of the letter signed by James Davy.

For more than a minute, he looked at it without seeing it, his blindly staring eye lost the void. His pen remained suspended above the paper.

At the end of a minute, his eyelid quivered, as it does when the interruption of distraction restores the faculty of sight to the pupil.

He was looking directly at the London postmark.

Another minute went by. Gregory Temple did not stir.

After yet another minute, Gregory Temple reddened slightly, and his lips were imperceptibly puckered. He put his pen down on the desktop. He closed his eyes, while the color in his cheeks gave way to pallor duller than before.

When he reopened his eyes, he picked up the envelope and examined it closely and attentively. From a drawer he took a magnifying glass and wiped it carefully; he examined the postmark with the aid of the lens.

He was still silent, but a nervous twitch in his hand betrayed his emotion.

Under the desk, he had a basket containing a heap of letters arranged in packets. Gregory Temple rummaged therein and took out a packet of four or five letters bound together by a piece of string. He untied the string with an awkward and tremulous hand. He set out the letters on the desktop. They were all postmarked London, and the characters of the postmarks were blurred, as is often the case with postal dispatches that are rubbed and stained, either by the hands of sorters or the vicissitudes of their journey.

Gregory Temple, armed with his magnifying glass, subjected each stamp in its turn to a minute examination. They were all similar–and, by a singular coincidence, the accidents that had partly-effaced or stained them had produced an identical result: not one of them retained a legible date.

Gregory Temple set his lens down beside his pen. His eyes were lowered. He remained so still for a while that one might have taken him for a statue. Then, he got up and marched stiffly towards his blackboard. He took up the chalk.

He hesitated. The pallor of his cheek was livid, and the muscles of his mouth were taut. He hesitated for a long time.

Finally, however, the chalk slowly approached the virginal column that was entirely black–the fifth–at the top of which was inscribed the bizarre subtitle: *The Impossible.*

With a jerky hand, Gregory Temple wrote the following words:

James Davy, false London postmarks.

Then he went back to his writing desk and finished, as if nothing had occurred, the letter he had begun to that same James Davy. Then he wrote another one, this one addressed to Monsieur Robert Surrisy, at Miremont, near l'Isle Adam, Seine-et-Oise.

"If milady had not got to bed so late," Prudence said, gravely and stiffly, "she would have had a more agreeable awakening. I always get up with a contented heart, thank God, because when I turn my eye to the day ahead, I see nothing there–neither thought, nor word, nor deed–contrary to the Lord's command-ments."

The maid's hands were full of Lady Elphinstone's rich and lustrous hair. Lady Frances had slight circles around her beautiful eyes, evidence of fatigue and sleep-deprivation; she had only had a few hours sleep. Prudence had woken her in the middle of her first dream to give her the missive brought back by the faithful Billy–who, as we have seen, had also slipped into the box at No. 19 Rue de Dauphine the letter addressed to Gregory Temple.

The message destined for Frances was as long and rich in detail as the one with the London postmark was simple and laconic. It was not so much a letter as a set of diplomatic instructions–or, rather, an entire part in a play whose stage directions were specified in advance with particular care. Frances had been yawning while she read the letter, but not at all diffidently. Even though the no-ble and charming Frances belonged to that congress of queens that is London's high society, she obeyed the orders of Comte Henri Belcamp punctiliously and rigorously.

Love sometimes produces these enslavements, and we do not suggest hat there is anything marvelous in the fact.

While the virtuous Prudence, whose Presbyterian perfume would have cut to the heart of anyone within pistol-range, plaited and rolled up her abundant tresses, Lady Frances was yawning wholeheartedly; that was what had prompted the maid's harangue. All around them was movement and disorder; the trunks were being packed for a journey, and the confusion of the unexpected departure was encroaching upon milady's toilette.

"Sam told me to say to you, milady," Prudence continued, "that we've been obliged to hire post-horses, not just for the wagon but the coach. God only knows what ours were doing last night!"

Lady Frances smiled.

"And this country house where we're going," Prudence went on. "Is it to milady's taste?"

"Entirely," Frances replied, yawning.

"When did milady visit it, then?"

"I don't remember, my dear–but speaking of dear, would you like to look after a child, Prudence?"

Curiosity paralyzed Prudence's fingers and she paused in her work to say. "A child? What child?"

"What child?" Frances echoed, pursing her lips. "My son, the very honorable Edward, Viscount Elphinstone, I suppose."

Prudence looked at her open-mouthed. "I've never heard anything about that!" she murmured.

"You'd have to find 50 guineas a year on top of your wages, my dear," said Frances, still smiling, "to have the right to know my entire history."

Prudence immediately returned to work. "I would be as devoted to milady's son as to Her Ladyship herself," she said, coldly. "Her Ladyship, as a widow, can certainly have a child."

"And you can see that I'm using that permission, Prudence."

"But where is the dear little one?" asked the maid, in an even frostier tone.

"On our way... we'll pick him up in passing."

"And how old is he?"

An observer who had examined milady's pretty features at that point would have thought: Here's a young mother who isn't at all sure of the age of her son–but the Presbyterian, busy knotting her mistress' chignon, could not see her face, and Frances replied: "My little Edward was born not long before milord's death... but I beg you, my dear, to get a move on. It's vital that we make an early start."

"How many leagues away is this chateau?"

"I don't know. Get on with it!"

This response was the simple truth, but it was made in such a way that Prudence could deem it a way of breaking off the conversation. She shut up, pursing her pale lips and continuing her task in a fit of pique.

Half an hour later, Lady Frances Elphinstone and her household left the house in the Place Vendôme. Milady, wearing an elegant traveling costume, and the grey-clad and straw-hatted Prudence, climbed into the coach, while Lisbeth, one of the seamstresses, took her place beside the coachman; this was by express instruction of milady, who had been giving orders all morning like the general of an army. Billy climbed up on the rear banquette.

The second seamstress, the footman and the cook got into the wagon, loaded with baggage and driven by a postillion.

As soon as she was ensconced in the coach, Lady Frances retreated into her corner and unfolded the letter that Billy had brought to her in order to re-read it and study it attentively. Prudence, looking at it sideways, could not decipher a single word.

The post-horses set a vigorous pace. In less than two hours, they were in the forest. Sam, on the instruction of his mistress, asked the name of every village they passed through.

Lady Frances still had the open letter in her hand. Finally, a peasant responded to Sam's interrogation with the name he was waiting for. Lady Frances ordered him to continue along the highway, but watched the left hand side of the road more attentively. An eighth of a league beyond the village, she called the coach to a halt, while the wagon continued on its way. She stepped down to the ground; to Prudence's considerable annoyance, it was Lisbeth who was recruited to accompany her, along with Billy. We should say that the choice was not Lady Frances's, and that it was specified in the letter. Neither Billy nor Lisbeth knew a word of French.

Milady, Billy and Lisbeth went on foot along a deeply rutted cart-track, which ran westwards through recently-ploughed fields. The undergrowth, made up of chestnuts and oaks, encroached up on the grey heath covered in rosy flowers, while the soil, excavated more deeply here and there by the extraction of a tree-stump, displayed the bright and gritty ochre of its entrails.

A few hundred paces along the route, the path descended abruptly into a gully to which cultivation had not yet extended. The soil here was damp and stony, and ferns displayed their long fronds amid the white trunks of birch trees. Lady Frances stopped to look around, seemingly astonished that nothing was to be seen. She consulted the letter again.

"There ought to be a hut near here, Billy," the young woman said.

Billy immediately set forth on a quest. Within a minute, he had discovered the path leading to the woodcutter's dwelling, whose grassy roof and grey walls scarcely stood out from the neutral and somber tones of the surrounding terrain. As she went towards it, Lady Frances saw that the door was closed.

The gully was isolated; the noise of an axe, which carries for a long way, can be heard at a considerable distance. A brown goat, perched with its four feet together at the summit of the crag that overhung the little house, stretched out its bearded chin and let out a thin bleat. A peasant's head was visible through the hut's only bull's-eye window, to the right of the door. Billy had no need to knock.

"She's like a dog, that Cocotte," said Pierre Louchet, as he opened the door. "She's on guard. Your servant, Madame and company. I got up late, because the little mite, forgive the expression, was awake all night. Are you his mother, who has come to take him away from me?"

"Yes, my friend," the young woman replied. "I'm in a great hurry to see the dear child."

"I think he looks like you!" Pierre Louchet murmured, looking at milady with admiration. "You make a pretty fine mother, meaning no offense, and he's a little Jesus. Come and see him!"

He stood to one side to allow Frances to come past him into the hut. Between the old ink-colored wardrobe and the bull's-eye was Pierre's bed: a straw mattress, a ragged grey sheet and a soldier's coverlet. The child, however, had a nice little mattress in a basket and gleaming white linen. He was white himself, as fresh as a rose in his sleep.

Lady Frances leaned over him and kissed him.

"He's a lively one," Pierre went on. "Crying, already scampering around, soon be talking... it's the pap we make him from Cocotte's milk. Goats give milk like quicksilver."

"I'd like to take him away without waking him," the young woman said.

"Take him away!" Pierre exclaimed. "You've only kissed him once! And, while I think of it, there's a word you have to say–your name–before giving orders."

"Lady Frances Elphinstone."

Pierre Louchet scratched his ear.

"It was certainly something like that," he muttered, "but you'll have to wait here a while, with our daughter being gone on an errand this morning, so she can't tell me what's written behind the door... I've heard tell of beautiful ladies who steal children..."

Milady turned round to call Lisbeth.

Pierre Louchet suddenly clapped his hands, as if an idea had struck him. "That's all right!" he cried. "You must know how to read as well as our daughter. Let's see how you say the words written on the back of the door." He took milady by the arms, unceremoniously, and drew her to the door, which he closed, saying: "What's written there?"

"Lady Frances Elphinstone," replied the young woman, reading the words traced in chalk the night before by Comte Henri. "My name, exactly."

The woodcutter went back to the basket where the child was sleeping.

"Our daughter will give me another," he murmured, while a large tear ran down a furrow in his cheek.

He gave the basket to Lisbeth, who had just come in, and he asked:

"Are you taking him very far?"

"England," milady replied.

"Goodbye, little one," said Pierre Louchet, in a tremulous voice. "Who'll wake me up at night now to annoy me?"

Frances set three *louis* on the table. "By way of thanks, my good friend," she said.

When she had gone, Pierre Louchet sat down on the doorstep with his head in his hands. "She only kissed him once!" he thought, aloud. Then he got up and went to look at the empty place where the basket had been. The hut seemed to have grown, like a desert.

The goat bleated on its crag; Pierre Louchet began to weep warm tears. He seized his axe, closed the door of the hut and set off into the forest at a rapid pace.

Only once! he thought. *His mother! She didn't touch him at all, except once!*

The coach had caught up with the wagon and they went on together at a rapid trot. Prudence looked at the child sleeping in his basket, then at Lady Frances, who did not seem to be overly preoccupied with her sole heir. Prudence may not have been of the same opinion as Pierre Louchet in finding any considerable resemblance between the mother and the son, but the Presbyterian maid and the woodcutter were in perfect agreement on one point, at least: in observing that the young mother was singularly undemonstrative in the matter of caresses.

Billy shouted stop as they arrived at the Croix Moraine signpost and made the coach turn on to the hunting-path leading to Miremont. Lady Frances scarcely cast a distracted glance at the splendid view as they passed the relevant point. The sight of the sleeping child, which should have warmed a mother's heart, awoke in her a world of melancholy thoughts. Perhaps she was feeling an unwonted pang of jealousy towards those happy souls whose life is passed in the paradise of conjugal tenderness sanctified by maternal love...

"Do we turn right or left at the mill?" asked Sam, at the bottom of the slope. "Or should we go past the bridge?"

Lady Frances, waking up with a start, glanced down at her letter. Prudence smiled tartly.

"To the left!" milady shouted. Then, as if she had suddenly remembered that she was a mother, she took the basket from Lisbeth's hands and deposited a smiling kiss upon the child's forehead.

The coach was now going along the wide and well-graveled path that ran along the bank of the Oise. Fifty paces or so from the mill, not far from the clump of willows where Comte Henri had taken the unconscious Jeanne into his arms, two men—one old and one young—were walking. They turned at the same time when they heard the sound of wheels.

"Monsieur le Comte!" said Prudence.

"Oh!" cried the Marquis de Belcamp, who was one of the walkers, at that moment. "I'll wager that this is our new neighbor, the Englishwoman who has rented the Chateau-Neuf. It might well be someone I know, since she has come from London."

Henri looked at the coach, indifferently.

"A pretty woman, to be sure," the older man said, bowing politely.

"Isn't he going to recognize us?" grumbled Prudence. "Would my lady like to tell me the password?"

"The order of the day, my dear," Frances replied, staring her down, "is never to try to be impertinent with me." She gracefully inclined her head at the same time, to acknowledge the Marquis' bow.

"Well, well!" said Henri, swiftly crossing the road. "It's Lady Frances Elphinstone! What fortunate coincidence...?"

He came to the carriage door, his hat in his hand. A few compliments were exchanged and then the coach went on its way again, while Comte Henri rejoined his father.

"We are acquainted, then," Prudence said, in a neutral voice, "but not very well..."

"I give you my full permission, my dear girl," milady interrupted, dryly, "to publish everything bad that you know about me hereabouts. I would even yield–voluntarily, since I have a helpful disposition–to the desire you have to know my secrets, if I had any. Here, as in Paris, Monsieur le Comte de Belcamp, an old friend of my husband's, will be a resource and a companion... as he was in London, and will be everywhere that I have the good fortune to run into him again."

"That really is the tenant at the Chateau-Neuf?" the old Marquis was asking his son.

"You know everything that happens hereabouts!" replied Henri, laughing. "Our friend Robert had already mentioned it to me yesterday, but I didn't expect to discover in the newcomer one of the most charming and honorable stars of high society. Lady Frances had a magnificent success two years running, until her husband's death."

"Ah–so she's a widow?"

"For a year now."

"Then her success took place while you were away?"

"Exactly. She was still deep in mourning when I was introduced to her, on my return. She's a very distinguished young woman, who lives modestly since the Viscount's death, bringing up her child as a good mother should."

"A Vicomtesse, eh!" said the Marquis. "But those English Viscounts aren't at all like our Vicomtes! I never knew of a Viscount Elphinstone in the House of Lords. There was Baron Elphinstone of Elphinstone, Governor of Madras. Outside the peerage, I also know of Sir Howard Elphinstone of Sowerby, who became a Baronet in 1815, and the Elphinstone branch of the Earls of Stair..."

"The late Mortimer Elphinstone, Viscount of Elphinstone of the Scottish peerage," Henri replied, in the distinct tone of a man who could talk about titles and genealogy with all due authority, "never sat in Parliament. He was the third son of the Baron John Elphinstone or Elphinstone, Governor of Madras, that you mentioned, who also bore the title of Earl of Tresham. His lordship also served the East India Company in the capacity of Resident at Mysore. After his death, in London in 1816, his peerage..."

"Another time, another time!" the old Marquis interrupted, laughing. "You have all that at your fingertips, just like everything else, my boy. I'm the father of a encyclopaedia! Good God! Doctor in law, doctor in medicine, doctor of literature, a genealogist like my late friend Hozier...[69] soon you'll be arguing agriculture better than a book..." He paused, while a cloud descended over his face, then continued: "What's certain, my dear child, is that I've no hope of keeping you in this poor place. You haven't dug into such sciences to bury yourself in our ignorant countryside, have you?"

"You see me through the lens of your affection, father," the young Comte replied. "In today's world, everyone knows a lot, but doesn't do much digging. I shan't ask anything more of Heaven if it has given me a permanent share in your beneficent and tranquil existence."

The old man stifled a sigh and glanced sideways at his son. "You have a secret?" he murmured. Then, before Henri had time to reply, making a sudden effort to recover his natural bonhomie, he said: "Comte, you have turned everyone's head towards us. I must take precautions and say to you: don't let all my eagerness, anxiety and jealousy disturb you. With respect to you, I am like a mother who becomes tiresome by the force of her affection."

"Father!" cried the young man, taking his hand to press it to his heart. "If you only knew how much I have needed to be loved!"

They walked in silence, one beside the other, for a little while. The old man waited, but Henri said no more.

"Well then, my son," said the Marquis, replying to his own thought, "perhaps you don't have a secret and I'm just an old lunatic." Then, pointing at the wagon, whose turn it was to take the road along the riverbank, he added: "Here's your star's luggage. Do you think that beautiful heavenly body might condescend to illuminate our little world?"

"I've told you that she is very distinguished, father–that implies, in my usage, simplicity and good will."

"Then again, Belcamp is worth as much as Elphinstone! We went to the Holy Land long before there were Governors of Madras, Mysore and Bombay. I prefer Jerusalem to Calcutta. You?"

"Good day, Bob!" the young Comte shouted to milady's red-faced and thick-set cook, who was enthroned on the wagon's banquette. "How do you like our French sauces?"

"Not much, milord, not much," Bob replied, without touching his hat. "I've eaten turtle soup in Paris. One is proud to be English, milord!"

The wagon went on. Bob maintained his triumphant pose, and did not turn round to see what effect his speech had had.

"There's someone," Henri said, "who prefers Calcutta to Jerusalem, father."

"I spent 20 years in England, my boy. I was talking about you, not about kitchen-dwellers."

Henri lowered his eyes. "Would you still love me, father," he murmured, "if everything you believed in, I denied? If I were to attack all that you defend? If the object of your devotion were the object of my hatred? And if I had in my hand and axe that might shatter your idols?"

The old man replied without hesitation: "I can't tell, my son, whether you're being serious or mocking me. Only wait till I am dead..." Then, pressing Henri to his heart in a fit of inexpressible tenderness, he added: "Remember these words that I say to you; they are not carelessly spoken; I am in full possession of my reason and my honor: I would have loved you if you were guilty of murder!"

"And would you have punished me, father?"

The Marquis stood back, and put his hand on Henri's shoulder. "Comte," he said, slowly, "are you studying your father too? So that you may be a doctor in this faculty as in all the rest, know this of me: I would have exacted capital punishment."

"Father," Henri went on, "it is a noble science to know a heart like yours. You would not have been worthy of your name or your faith had you said anything else." He continued in a strange tone, whose quality no delicacy of language could render precisely, which was serious and bantering at the same time, full of both serene softness and indomitable pride, which said much more than the words themselves. "But since you are so good and so strong; since–a rare thing–you would, without ceasing to love me, render me to the justice of Brutus, never ask me my secret. For I, too, may have my inflexible conscience, my faith dearer than life, my honor that would bind me to death as yours would bind you to kill!"

"Can you not do as I asked, my son," murmured the old man, "and wait until I am dead?"

"No, father."

"Then be free. I have nothing to dread, for there is but one honor, one faith and one conscience."

They walked slowly towards the Priory. Henri had attained–at the cost of a few mysterious words calculated with admirable correctness, it is true–the position of a man with a secret: a secret admitted and respectable, at least so far as his father was concerned. He had arrived on the previous evening with the difficult task of making the Sun shine in the middle of the night and giving a full explanation of the enigma of a life on which terrible suspicions had weighed. He had come through that test as if it were child's play. His haughty manner had faltered just once; in the balance–and even in the face–of the chivalrous allegiances of the old man, his own allegiance had been successfully established as a counterweight. Now and henceforth, after that first victory, he could demand the benefit that is accorded only–and not invariably–to enduring confidence, to proven honor and to the infallibility of the heart, as one might almost say: the privilege, of having a secret.

Of all the concessions that can be made in life to amity, love and devotion, this is the largest by far; to characterize such a case–even by comparison with sanctity or heroism–the word exorbitant is not too strong.

There are magnificent examples proving that honor can put its trust in honor in this way; they are rare, but they exist. There are others, far more numerous, in both ancient and recent history, which cry: Beware! Do not tempt human fallibility! There is, if we may be permitted to stress the fact, a complete absence here of any control or any barrier: the talisman that becomes invisible or the armor that becomes invulnerable. There is a character in a Régnard play [70] upon whose head anyone can put a foot, saying: "it's your lethargy!" No response is possible to that magic word. Here, the opposite is the case; the man who has a secret, and who was won the right to act in virtue of such unknown obligations, possesses a cabalistic spell capable of shutting the mouth of the entire universe. Whatever he might do, there is a secret that motivates his action. Whatever he might say, his secret is his excuse.

"After all," said the old Marquis, putting a brave face on it, "I already have some dealings with the camp of the Emperor's friends. My brigand, Robert Surrisy, is one of the best men I know..."

"I have not said that I am in the camp of the Emperor's friends," Henri interrupted. "I have said nothing, and who knows if there is anything in that to put a cloud over the gaiety of your excellent heart, father? Take me as I am, and don't lose your way in that forest of conjectures in which one always goes further than is necessary. What you say is true: there is but one honor, one faith and one science. I did not lie when I told you yesterday that I was worthy of your name."

"I remember now," the old man murmured, "that you made no reply yesterday, when I asked you if you wanted to serve the King."

"Your sword was of my generation, father, when it returned to its scabbard of its own accord, in order not to redden itself with the blood of the conquerors of the Bastille."

"Is it still a question, then, of a war between the people and the King?" asked the Marquis, anxiously.

The young man replied to his worried expression with a calm smile. "It is a question," he said, "of giving a medical consultation to the heroine of the most bizarre novel that whimsical imagination could ever have invented."

"Do you already have clients other than Jeanne, then?"

"I was referring to Jeanne, father."

"And you bracket the word novel with the name of our poor wild flower?"

"A charming flower and a curious novel–comic and dramatic at the same time–whose eventual denouement is a fortune!"

"What are you saying, Henri?" the old Marquis asked.

"Not one fortune," the young Comte continued, tranquilly, "but two... four millions on one side, five millions on the other."

"Oh, you're a dreamer!"

"Often, but not on this occasion. You haven't asked me, father, by means of what charm I changed Madame Touchard's attitude so abruptly."

"Who would dare to interrogate a man of as many mysteries as you?" countered the old man, half-seriously and half in jest. "One would always be afraid of falling upon some terrible secret."

"I beg you never to be constrained with me, father," said Henri, whose tone was becoming more and more cheerful. "If a question should embarrass me, I shall simply ask you, quite frankly, for permission to refrain from answering it. In the meantime, what would you like to know about pretty Jeanne's novel?"

"Perhaps la Bartolozzi left more than is generally believed?"

"A few jewels, a little money–including some owed to her by her friends–and a great many debts. But one does not only inherit from one's mother..."

"Is the father known?"

"I shall tell you a bizarre story. Four years ago, at the beginning of 1813, I was studying medicine, science and theology at the Catholic University of Munich. Germany is a naive and solemn country conscious of its own ponderousness, which wants to make progress in order to convince itself that it is not stagnating. Everything is growing and everything speaks of growth on the other bank of the Rhine, where the richest and most pedantic language in the world is spoken. Among every five men, you will find four doctors; among every ten buildings, you will count a theater, an academy, a museum, a library, a glyptotheque, a pinacotheque,[71] a polytechnic institute, an athenaeum and a military school. Ladies write Greek verse, children compose tragedies; everyone there knows his lexicon and does his homework–even the drinking-songs sung in the kitchens are in Latin.

"There, everything ordinary is shameful and is raised to the superlative. Every fête becomes a *festival*, and there are festivals of everything: music, poetry, white wine, cabbages, pipes and beer. It was at the great beer festival held in the Munich Odeon that Mademoiselle Jeanne's novel begins. You're laughing? Mademoiselle Jeanne has never left Miremont? I'm serious, though: her fortune, or rather her two fortunes, were there and I met them, one of them carrying off the first prize for Belgian beer and the other the first prize for French beer: a brewer from Brussels and a brewer from Lyon, both Englishmen whose names cannot be unfamiliar to you, father."

"I do not remember ever having been acquainted with any brewers," said the old man.

"These you knew well. One was named Frank Turner, the other William Robinson."

"Mr. Brown's associates."

"My mother's two cousins, who became expatriates after the Duchess of Devonshire affair. They were at the festival, each one intent on demonstrating the excellence of his national beer-glass in the spotlight of a jury selected from every social class. I was the judge for the University of Munich. The brewer from Lyon and the brewer from Brussels were able to read my name in the list of jurors displayed at the entrance to the great hall. They came to see me, and called me cousin. They were two staunch Englishmen, gentle and polite; I was their judge. They told me about their millions–which, if their celibacy were to be indefinitely prolonged, would one day become my inheritance. After the prizes had been given, the question of inheritance was put to one side, but they wanted to continue confiding in me, and I was able to discover that they were each in a similar situation. Mr. Turner and Mr. Robinson each had a natural child, which each of them anticipated legitimizing by an eventual marriage. There were obstacles to both these marriages that could not be explained to me at that time, but which would disappear in due course.

"Once Mr. Robinson and Mr. Turner had left Munich, you will understand that their affairs of the heart did not loom large in my thoughts. I left Germany myself a short time afterwards to return to London and I had then to undertake my journey to Australia. In Australia, I made the acquaintance of a very eminent gentleman who gave me considerable help in the accomplishment of my mission: Sir Paulus MacAllan, the Commissioner-General of the Sydney Police. It is he who has now replaced Mr. Temple at Scotland Yard, in the position of Chief Superintendent. I was determined to find out everything for myself and passionate, perhaps insanely, to know everything. Mr. Temple's book, which seemed to make policing into a science–or, rather, an ensemble of sciences–a grandiose mathematics driving the criminal into a warren whose exits were all logically sealed, might have its fair share of utopian hopes and dreams, but it opened a horizon. It established a sort of closed field into which society must henceforth lure and tempt crime; it lit up the lists and sounded the trumpet to begin the tourney. I would probably make a pitiful sergeant, but thanks to Sir Paulus I can say that I understand the mechanism of English detection clearly and completely–another doctorate that it was necessary to add to my collection of diplomas. I have a purpose in telling you this, father: you might find yourself in the company of people who have seen the Comte de Belcamp, your son, seated at the secretary's table in the office of the Chief of the Metropolitan Police...

"While I followed the syllabus of this new faculty, the second chapter of our lovely Jeanne's novel unrolled before my eyes. The two first prize-winners from Munich, Mr. William Robinson and Mr. Frank Turner, came together, dressed in mourning and with tears in their eyes, to ask for information as to the details of the murder of Constance Bartolozzi, which had deprived each of them of a fiancée. La Bartolozzi, in effect, had promised marriage to both of them. They had been waiting patiently for her to retire from the theater, in order to give them a home with a ready-made family–a wife and child at the same time– for a number of years, Robinson in Brussels, Turner in Lyon.

"Each of them, of course, knew himself to be a father–to the extent that their two wills, deposited with a lawyer named Daws at No. 4 Regent Street, specify Constance Bartolozzi as sole heir, and her daughter after her, in almost exactly the same words. That is the talisman with which I was equipped with respect to Madame Touchard."

"Poor Jeanne!" murmured the Marquis, whose delicacy was severely wounded by the whiff of baseness given off by this anecdote.

"My God, father," said Henri. "It all depends on how the tale is told. You'd laugh at it in the theater."

"Certainly... and I'm no more stiff-necked than necessary, my boy... although I'd have wanted to die if I'd had any conception of your taste for Police-work! But my little Jeanne has such a noble and pure heart! God preserve me from saying anything against that unfortunate woman who was her mother..."

"She was an actress," said the young Comte, in a coolly contemptuous fashion.

"I've known actresses who had beautiful souls..." the old man replied, then changed tack: "But I'd like to know one thing. During your voyage of exploration in the land of the Police, haven't you ever encountered my old friend Temple himself?"

"That is part of my secret, father," Henri replied, without lowering his limpid gaze or losing his smile. "I can only tell you that Gregory Temple knows neither Henry Brown nor Henri de Belcamp."

"Do you have a third name?" exclaimed the old man.

The young man's smile faded by degrees and his face took on a melancholy expression. "The person I love best here is my father," he said, slowly, "although I have seen since my return to France, and for the first time, a young woman whose angelic gaze has caused a mute chord to vibrate in the depths of my heart. The best day of my life will be that on which I can say to my father, showing him my heart laid bare: this is what I kept secret."

The Marquis extended his hand, saying: "I shall have no more confidence in you when that day comes than I have today."

"Today," Henri echoed, as a painful sigh elevated his breast. "But tomorrow..." With his head high, as though dead set on the thought that seemed to obsess him, he continued: "Tomorrow is still uncertain, and each day's troubles are sufficient to itself. Let's go into the Priory, where I have two things to do."

They passed over the threshold of that gracious and tranquil house. The widow Touchard came to meet them, and the Marquis was able to hear what she said to Henri in a confidential tone: "I have the birth-certificates ready."

"How is my brigand? And Laurent? And Férandeau?" asked the Marquis. "For I can see in your face, my dear lady, that you have good news of our lovely little invalid?."

"Jeanne had an excellent night," the widow replied, "but as she still needs rest. I've sent the young men away. They'd be kicking up an infernal racket all day long. You can come in; my niece is up."

Jeanne was indeed still very pale, and her eyes were languid with fever. She was sitting on a divan in the drawing-room. When the young Comte appeared, her cheeks became vividly pink. She tried to smile at the old man, but her charming mouth twitched as if she were trying to hold back tears.

Henri felt her pulse, watch in hand, and said: "We're better. Don't you feel the weight on your heart any longer, Mademoiselle Jeanne?"

"Yes," she replied. "Always."

"This evening," Henri instructed, "two spoonfuls..."

"And a strict diet, I think?" the widow put in.

"Mademoiselle Jeanne can eat as she pleases. The rest of the medicine can be thrown away. The fever won't reappear tonight.

"Well, Jeanne," Madame Touchard said, "you can thank Monsieur le Comte for that!"

Two tears quivered in the corners of the young woman's eyes, shown up by the timid smile formed by her pale lips. She was adorably beautiful.

"A strict diet of words!" Henri observed, cheerfully. Then he added: "My good lady, I'm at your disposal."

The widow took the hand that he offered her, and they left the room together.

The Marquis followed them with his eyes. When he turned back to his young companion, the two detached tears were rolling slowly down Jeanne's cheeks. "Oh, little one," he said, "I've seen you in worse condition than this, and you didn't cry. Have we had some news?"

Jeanne shook her head and lowered her eyes.

"Has my brigand Robert told you his...?" Monsieur de Belcamp continued.

Jeanne's breast heaved under the pressure of a sob.

The old man sat down beside her on the divan, to examine her more closely.

"It's been a very long time," he murmured, "since I could read the eyes of young women... but I've seen something similar quite recently. There was a happy and cheerful child in London for whom life was nothing but a long series of wishes fulfilled, who sang to the birds and offered the curls of her long blonde hair to the caresses of the breeze, innocent of all cares. Her 18th birthday arrived, and she became pale and serious, dreaming while people talked to her and frequently–very frequently–turning away to hide a tear that rolled from her poor swollen eyes. If Robert Surrisy were able..."

"Robert has a loyal and worthy heart," Jeanne put in.

"And yet you're weeping, little one? Your aunt..."

"Since yesterday, my aunt treats me as if she were my mother."

"And yet, you're weeping?"

Jeanne lifted her beautiful moist eyes to look at him again. "Monsieur le Comte," she murmured, "has promised that he will take away the weight that I have on my heart."

Madame Touchard came in again on Henri's arm. Henri immediately picked up his hat, explaining his abrupt departure to Jeanne by saying: "I must take my father away from you, Mademoiselle Jeanne. One more day of solitude, and tomorrow you will no longer know that you have been ill."

The widow went to her niece and embraced her tenderly. "If we had lost this treasure," she murmured.

"Henri," said the Marquis, after a period of silence, as they went back along the bank of the Oise, "why did you mention only one child for both fathers, when we have a brother and a sister here in Laurent and Jeanne?"

"Because my two first prizes for beer did not take me into their confidence by halves," replied the young Comte. "I have left them over there, promising each of them to find out what I can... and I certainly did not expect that my research would come so swiftly to fruition. In order to carry out this mission, I required very precise information. The first encounter of one of them with la Bartolozzi was in May 1798. For the other, it was a year later, in 1799. Even before seeing the birth-certificates that Madame Touchard showed me just now, I was sure that Jeanne was the only one within the relevant age limit."

"And may I ask you what you intend to do, Henri?"

"Write immediately to Mr. Turner and Mr. Robinson."

"Who will choose?"

"Nature, perhaps... or perhaps caprice. My role ends when my duty is fulfilled."

When they went back into the chateau, Comte Henri ordered that his horse should be saddled at eight that evening. The Marquis heard him give the order, but dared not ask the reason.

At the conclusion of the evening meal, Henri said to Suzanne Temple: "Tomorrow morning, I'll bring you news of your child."

He returned to his room and wrote two letters, one addressed to Turner, Brewer, at Lyon, the other to Robinson, Brewer, at Brussels. Then he slid two sheets of blank paper into two other envelopes. On one of these envelopes he wrote, disguising his handwriting with remarkable skill: *To Comte Henri de Belcamp, Poste Restante, Brussels*; on the other: *To Comte Henri de Belcamp, Poste Restante, Lyon.*

He gave the first two letters to Pierre, instructing him to post them in l'Isle Adam. He put the others–those containing the blank sheets–into his portfolio.

His handsome mare was waiting for him at the stable door. He leapt into the saddle and trotted rapidly away down the road to the mill.

Scarcely had Comte Henri and his English mare disappeared round a corner when an astonishing mechanism, pulled by two valetudinary horses, emerged on to the esplanade. It resembled one of those cabs dating from the first years of their manufacture, which filled our childhood with wonder. The upper part, shaped like a pie, had a bulge in the middle pierced by a hole, which might have served as a sheath for the brass root of a black plume in a funeral ceremony. The doors were as wide as the *Morality in Action* engraved on the windows of the coach from which Ravaillac assassinated Henri IV.[72] The steps had been set in place before the invention of hinges, for they descended in four stages, each as high and broad as four ordinary steps.

This monument stopped at the gate of the chateau; the coachman, in rustic costume, descended to the ground while the two horses coughed in a sad and discouraged manner.

"Many apologies, Madam Etienne, many apologies," said a high-pitched, wheezing voice to the powerful cook, who deigned to open the gate herself.

"All alone, Madame Deputy!" said the cook. "Monsieur Morin's coming up the hill on foot, I presume."

"No, Madame Etienne, no," replied the stout companion of Monsieur Morin du Reposoir, First Deputy of Miremont. "Many apologies. Loiseau, watch out for my foot; it's easily sprained. Monsieur Morin isn't coming, but it's necessary that I talk to Monsieur le Maire."

The cook hesitated. "If Mademoiselle Suzanne will do," she said, "I'd much rather fetch her than report to Monsieur le Marquis after dinner to tell him that he has work to do. He signified that he wanted to sleep, and that visits are incoherent and titillating to him at the moment."

"Many apologies, my good Madame Etienne," the First Deputy's wife interrupted, loftily, "but it concerns affairs of State!"

Madame Etienne took off her apron and offered her arm, on which the Deputy's stout wife leaned gratefully, while also accepting Loiseau's. They arrived in this manner at the steps of the chateau; while they were climbing up, not without difficulty, the old Marquis displayed his benevolent smile at the open window of the vestibule.

"Have you some news, my dear Madame?" he asked.

"Ah, Monsieur le Maire," replied the breathless woman, "very serious circumstances make it necessary... it's been 22 years since I last went out without Monsieur Morin. Many apologies! Go away, Loiseau, and don't give the horses water that's too cold. Monsieur le Marquis, grant me a private interview..."

At a sign from her master, Madame Etienne went back to her kitchen, where she said to her subordinates: "War must have been declared against England, and Monsieur le Comte will be Deputy instead of Monsieur Morin."

"Where's Monsieur Henri gone off like that, tonight?" asked little Anille.

"Stupid!" said Julot. "That's none of your business."

"Me, I'm going to look for a place," said Fanchette, the chambermaid. "I'm sick of looking after someone like Miss Suzanne, whose eyes are always red from weeping, though no one known the reason why."

A tousled head appeared at the window and Briquet cried: "Bonaparte's escaped from Elba!"

Everyone shivered. Briquet, delighted, burst out laughing. "You still don't know that, after three years?" he said. "In Paris, they'd put you out to grass!"

"You're a naughty boy just the same, Monsieur Trompe-d'Eustache!" said the cook, severely. Then she went on: "When I was with my former mistress–it was in the days of the Directory and the three Consuls–I knew better than the impudence of youth. There is, as they say, something fishy going on.[73] But that doesn't mean that masters needn't always pay the wages of their staff regularly."

Meanwhile, in the drawing room, the Deputy's wife collapsed into an easy-chair, saying: "Many apologies! I'm only a woman... and while I think of it, I met the postman while I was coming past the mill. He came to my carriage door and said: 'Good day, Madame Morin du Reposoir, how are you? Are you going as far as the chateau? I mean the Chateau de Belcamp, for we have a worldly one at the Chateau-Neuf–the wife of an English lord. If that's the case, you can save me a trip up the hill.' "

She put two letters on the table. "One helps out whenever one can, isn't that so?" she added. "Although a postman has no right to hand over his letters like that... but a person in place... that's how my poor Saturnin came to be laid up, stricken by an anonymous communication he received that the enemies of public tranquillity were in Miremont..."

"The enemies of public tranquillity!" echoed the Marquis, smiling.

"Yes, Monsieur le Maire–and of the King! Holding secret meetings in the fields... and all the brigands of the Loire in the vicinity, disguised as peaceful laborers."

Monsieur de Belcamp's gaze fell at that moment upon the two letters that the stout woman had deposited on the table. One of them bore the stamp of the Commissariat of Police in Pontoise; the other the stamp of the Prefecture of Versailles. The sight of these two seals made a much greater impression on him than the words of the Deputy's wife. He tore open the first envelope without asking her permission, which was totally contrary to his habitual courtesy. He had read scarcely three lines when he pulled urgently at his bell-cord.

The Deputy's wife shivered from top to toe.

"Many apologies," she stammered, hardly knowing what she said. "Many apologies... are we in danger?"

"Send someone to fetch the local Constable!" the Marquis instructed Pierre, who came in response to the summons. "The Constable and Florian Bondon... immediately!"

"The armed forces in their entirety!" murmured the Deputy's wife, taking a small wicker-encased bottle from her pocket. She kept her smelling-salts in it. "I'm only a woman, Monsieur le Maire... do you fear an immediate invasion?"

The Marquis opened the envelope containing the Prefectorial missive.

"Madame, and good neighbor," he said, smiling as he finished reading, "it appears that we have a club in Miremont. The administration is worried. I cannot share these fears entirely. Once, Miremont was in the power of the insurgents; there would still be a few small things to accomplish to complete the Revolution... but I must do my duty and take all necessary precautions. The Miremontese army must be put on a war footing. We have the local Constable and eight National Guardsmen–all very badly armed, alas, but there's not the shadow of a doubt regarding their courage, and that will surely be necessary to combat the danger that threatens us. Return to your husband, my good lady, thank him on my behalf, and tell him that he must have a good night's sleep, in order to be fit and ready for the coming battle."

The Deputy's wife could not disobey her Mayor. She rose unsteadily to her feet, murmuring "Many apologies!" in a tearful voice. "I'm only a woman," she said, in the doorway. "If I wait for the armed forces, they will be able to escort me to the conjugal domicile."

The Marquis gave her his word of honor that she had time to get back to Miremont before the Revolution.

The local Constable arrived a short time afterwards, along with the Bondon garniture: the slender clock and her two stout companions. This trinity formed a complete and inseparable whole; to summon one was to bring out the others. Blondeau, the local Constable, had a state-issued rifle and was the manifest elite of the Miremontese army. Madame Célestin, speaking on behalf of her Bondons, replied on behalf of the National Guard and promised a review of the troops for the following morning, which was a Sunday. One of these imposing demonstrations is sufficient anywhere to discourage evildoers lurking in the shadows.

After leaving the chateau, Blondeau went to the inn. While drinking from his half-liter mug and smoking his pipe, he admitted that he would give a good ten *sous* to see the return of the other one. As regards the Bondons' allegiance, Madame Célestin, in spite of their solemn engagements, had turned their coats on the march to the cause of the altar and the throne. "Men in your position have no other duty but to protect their family," she said to the compassionate twins. "I have no one but you two."

The old Marquis turned over in bed more than once that night before he could get to sleep. "The commune is neither broad nor long," he thought. "Since Master Henri has taken the trouble to have his fine horse saddled, his rendezvous can't be as close to us as all that."

It was not the letter from the Prefect of Versailles that preoccupied him, nor that from the Commissioner of the Pontoise Police. Monsieur de Belcamp was perhaps more scornful than was necessary of the fears that those two dispatches had expressed. The one idea that filled up his brain was: what could Henri's secret be?

The two administrative letters alleged the presence in the vicinity of a mysterious person, a sort of ambassador representing secret societies that were already functional in Italy, England and Germany. In 1817, opposition was brewing; the various factions of the army that had broken up into distinct parties after the victory were now reuniting under the flag of Bonapartism. The presumed goal of all conspiracy was the Emperor's recall. Was Henri the alleged conjuror? And had Henri chosen for a battlefield the peaceful village where his father represented the threatened government?

Monsieur de Belcamp, wearied by his attempts to sleep, had relit his lamp and was deep in thought, listening to the sounds of the night. Had it been fully lit, you would have seen sadness in the handsome and gentle face supported by his hand, but no trace of anger.

"They have as their talismans," he murmured, while his veiled gaze lost itself in the half-light, "the two words that sound most highly in the imagination and the heart after the name of God. They speak of glory and liberty at the same time. They have the man to personify glory, the great hero of the modern epic. For liberty, the word itself is sufficient. And this impassioned and ardent child, who has drunk the new science avidly, who is intoxicated by his battle against the unknown, who seeks–fearlessly, and thus far without reproach–to lift the lid of Pandora's box... this child whose strength I admire and whose gentle beauty I adore... this child, my son, my priceless treasure, my only hope in life... by what right may I say to him: 'You shall not go where your inclination leads you! Born today, you must conceive a passion for yesterday! Wisdom consists of looking backwards! I forbid you the future, because it is a lie! I order you to be old, because I am no longer young...' "

His smile was impregnated with a hint of bitterness. "By what right?" he repeated. "I have known but one: the right of the strongest. Would I use it, if I had it? And has anyone ever had that right, against a head and a heart like the head and the heart of Comte Henri de Belcamp?"

Already, he thought he had heard–several times–the sound of horses in the distance. The night was calm and the last breath of the evening had faded away. Even the monotonous plaint of the mill had fallen silent.

"When one listens," the old man thought, "every noise changes its aspect. Ten times over I've heard the hoofbeats of Henri's horse on the gravel of the bridge..." Then he sat up, and went on: "but I'm not mistaken this time! The miller's dog has woken up!"

The nocturnal breeze was indeed carrying the sound of irritated barking, evoking a response in kind from the unchained Sultan, who was prowling in the courtyard. But that was all, and the Marquis waited in vain for the nearer sound of horseshoes on the stony terrain of the hill's summit. While he waited, an almost joyful smile–which was almost malicious, too–lit up the noble features of his visage.

"There is one right that is always the most powerful," he murmured. "The right of the heart. Love is what's required to chain the handsome lion that frightens me with his very gentleness and tranquillity. Suzanne is lovely, but she is weeping already... Jeanne! A dear enchantress who–for the first time–would not let me see into the depths of her heart today... but Robert, my poor brigand, would die; it's unthinkable. There's Germaine, a veritable bouquet of grace, gaiety and perfume... pity about Jeanne, though. If I could only say to Henri: 'Choose between Jeanne and Germaine...' " He sighed. "Ah, once I would have had all the flowers of Versailles and the Trianon! Those proud tribunes yielded willingly to the smiles of princesses; inside every conspirator there's a knight errant... but we have no princesses at Miremont!"

He closed his eyes; sleep was on its way. All things considered, Germaine and Jeanne were worth as much as princesses. The miller's mastiff was no longer barking, and Sultan was asleep. The old Marquis' head fell sideways, while the names of Germaine and Jeanne died upon his lips.

It was not Henri's horse that had troubled the silence of the Oise valley that night. The Marquis had guessed correctly; Henri was a long way away. Even so, the Marquis had been mistaken, for it was not necessary to go as far as the limits of the commune–which were neither broad nor long–to discover the goal to which the Comte's nocturnal course had been directed.

As regards the noises heard in that waking hour, when dreams very often take the place of reality, the Marquis de Belcamp had not been in error. There had been more than one traveler along the riverbank, which was normally deserted after nightfall. Horses' hoofbeats had sounded on the gravel of the bridge and the miller's dog had barked, defiantly and angrily, having scented a passing stranger.

The dust of the forest paths had been stirred up by galloping horses coming from various directions. Solitary riders had glided along the hunting-paths. The countryside was strangely busy that night, and the miller's dog was not the only one to howl.

Henri galloped too, but in the first instance, he went in the opposite direction to the mysterious riders. After leaving the chateau, he descended the winding path in a leisurely manner, then climbed the hunting-path leading to the forest belvedere. The night was not yet completely dark. Having arrived at the signpost at the Croix Moraine on the l'Isle-Adam road, he turned towards Paris and gently urged his horse to the gallop. Less than two hours afterwards, he crossed the Barrière de la Chapelle and went into the Faubourg.

It was a journey of seven or eight leagues, whose goal might have seemed quite frivolous. Henri stepped down in front of the nearest post office to which he could obtain directions. He deposited in the letterbox one of those letters whose envelopes contained blank paper, one of which was addressed to the Comte de Belcamp in Lyon, and the other to the Comte de Belcamp in Brussels. Then, he jumped on to his horse and left the Faubourg, without giving his horse time to draw breath. He left Paris again, and maintained the same pace as before until he reached Saint-Denis, where he deposited the second letter in the post-box at the town hall.

It was definitely for the sole purpose of accomplishing this task that he had put 15 leagues beneath the legs of his handsome horse. From Saint-Denis to the Croix Moraine, the valiant beast ran flat out, without once altering her quick and easy gait. No spur ever touched her flanks. Henri spoke a few words to her from time to time, while caressing her sweating neck. It was necessary to slow down to follow the steep path that led from the belvedere to the bridge, but once in the valley Henri murmured *hup*! and the noble creature leapt forward as if she were leaving the stable.

Henri did not cross the bridge. Instead of steering towards his father's house, he followed the route along the riverbank. He passed the Chateau-Neuf and the Priory, all of whose windows were dark. A quarter of a league from the Priory, on the very edge of the woods that stretched to l'Isle-Adam, and directly opposite the Belcamp park–whose final trees bathed their roots in the water–on the other bank, a light shone among clumps of elders that were already in leaf.

Henri went into the copse for a hundred paces before stopping and dismounting. He unfolded a large blanket rolled up behind his saddle and put it over the fuming flanks of his horse, whose bridle he tied securely to an oak-branch. Having done that, he unfastened his cravat and put it over his face like a veil, using the pressure of his hat to hold it at the temples. Then, he enveloped himself in his cloak.

It was one o'clock in the morning. The light was shining in the window of a very modest house a few hundred paces from the bank of the Oise, already half-hidden by the trees on the edge of the forest. In front of it, there was a little garden bordered by elders. This was the house of Madeleine Surrisy, Robert's mother.

Four men, armed to the teeth, had been hiding since ten o'clock in the evening, two in the elders and two in the trees, standing sentinel at the four points of the compass. A fifth, similarly armed, was standing outside the door of the house.

Madeleine Surrisy's house was been the destination towards which the mysterious travelers had made their various ways through the surrounding countryside from every direction. They had arrived separately, all on horseback, except for one old man wearing the cassock of a Catholic priest, whose carriage had stopped on the Paris-l'Isle-Adam Road not far from the signpost at the Croix Moraine. He had come the rest of the way in a sedan-chair.

Apart from the old man, all the horsemen wore bourgeois clothing under capacious cloaks.

The little bell-tower at Miremont had been sounding eleven o'clock when the first horseman arrived at the bridge by the mill. He had presumably had his itinerary mapped out up to that point but no further, for he had stopped his horse a hundred paces from the outflow, just opposite the cluster of willows where Comte Henri had come ashore the previous day with Jeanne unconscious in his arms.

The horseman, without dismounting, whispered these words: *"For the best!"*

A shadow stood up to the side of his horse. The shadow wore the costume of the local peasantry, but under the battered hat the two tips of a long and bushy moustache were visible.

"What do you seek, good cousin?" he asked.

"I seek the road to the fountain."

The peasant extended his hand, which the traveler touched. The contact lasted longer than an ordinary handshake. When the prescribed signs had been exchanged, the peasant stepped back and gave a military salute.

"My General," he said, "I don't need of all this rigmarole to recognize you. I'm Sergeant-Major Foucault; I served in your brigade at Wagram."[74]

"That was warm, comrade," the horseman replied. Then, offering his hand again, he added: "Sergeant Foucault, the old army is not dead and its time will come. Forward march!"

The peasant obeyed, and marched at the double towards the Priory, which he passed by. At some distance from the edge of the wood, he stopped in his turn and said: *"For the best!"*

A voice from behind the elders replied: *"There are no wolves in the forest."* Then the same voice added: *"Good cousin, have you come to seek the fountain?"*

The peasant had stepped behind the horseman, who replied in Italian because the majority of these formulas originate in Italy: *"Fede, speranza e carita"*–which means "faith, hope and charity."

"Enter," said the voice. *"This is the fountain."*

The rider dismounted. Two men took his horse while a third led him by the hand towards the house.

As we have said, there was an armed man outside the door. He and the horseman touched hands; then, the guardian of the door held up to the moonlight half of a playing card that had been haphazardly torn in two. The cavalier set another half-card against its jagged edge, the two of them forming a complete ace of hearts.

The guard took off his hat and led the way across the threshold. "Welcome to my mother's house, General," he said.

"Ah!" said the rider, whose proud and martial visage was now illuminated by lamplight. "Lieutenant Surrisy!" He threw his arms around Robert's neck and added: "A young man and an old soldier!"

Robert's eyes filled with tears. Outside, a *"For the best!"* was heard, followed by *"There are no wolves in the forest."*

It was a new arrival–another *good cousin*, since that was the title which the Knights of the Deliverance gave one another throughout Europe. Much later, the efforts of Carbonarism [75] would render that denomination historic.

There was a change in the reception of the latecomers. The horseman whom Sergeant Foucault and Robert had called General assumed the office of examiner, and it was he who subsequently conducted the ceremony of the combination of the playing-cards.

The widow Surrisy's house was as cramped inside as its humble external appearance suggested. The furnishings remained as they were, no special preparation having been made to enhance the solemnity of the gathering. The assembly was held in a downstairs room that served simultaneously as the widow's kitchen, dining room and bedroom. The company was seated on the two benches that accompanied the long table. A stack of logs was burning in the blackened and capacious hearth. The alcove had two beds draped in serge mounted one atop the other. The bread was on the shelf and the poor crockery behind the rails of the dresser. A pendulum-clock was ticking in its cherry-wood case.

When the clock chimed midnight, there were nine around the table: three grey heads, four men at the peak of their strength and two younger men. Of the nine, five had the kind of military bearing that civilian dress exaggerates as it attempts to disguise it; three were bourgeois; there was a single ecclesiastic. Of the five military men, two were old and three were in the full bloom of their virility; both young men were of the other sort.

The priest seemed to be the oldest of them all. His long white hair framed the pallor of his thin cheeks. Over his simple black cassock he wore the red sash of the Legion of Honor.

The others had nothing in their dress to distinguish them, but five of them were wearing supplementary badges like the priest: two wore the sashes of senior officers, three the saltires of commanders. Strictly speaking, there would have been no need of such signs to declare that an assembly of highly placed people had gathered within this poor hut for some solemn purpose. Around the broad table, the faces spoke, all calm and serious, some of them animated by contained enthusiasm, other bearing the seal of resignation to duty–a sentiment more solid, more indomitable and, above all, more redoubtable than the dash of ordinary valor.

Everyone in France–and everywhere else, to tell the truth–has a soldier's courage, but the other courage is rare throughout the world, even in France.

There were four Generals there–one of whom had been a Commander-in-Chief who had governed his armies like a minister and deserved a ducal title–one Admiral, one Secretary of State, one Senator, two Princes and an Archbishop. The Archbishop was the only foreigner; it was, however, he who spoke first, opening the session and taking the role of chairman.

"My lords," he said, with a pronounced Italian accent, "would you care to stand up while I offer a prayer to the Most High, asking him to send down his Holy Spirit upon our assembly?"

They all got up, and the priest recited the *Veni, Sancte Spiritus*.

"My lords," he continued, as he sat down again after having made the sign of the cross, "several of us were unknown to one another before this evening, at least with respect to our faces–for everyone except me possesses the renown that posterity will transform into fame. For the first time, in this land of France–which the Emperor Napoleon, with God's aid, set at the head of the nations of Europe and the world–we have gathered together the Supreme Council of the Deliverance.

"We might restrict our powers to our patriotism and our conscience, and that would be sufficient–but they will raise us higher still. On the door of our house is inscribed the divine motto, the entire catechism in three words: *faith, hope, charity*. To all those who will come to draw water from our symbolic fountain, we may say: Peace be with you, for our work is not war, and we shall not encroach upon God's designs.

"Without prejudice to our various personal projects, the Supreme Council has come together for the sole and definitive purpose of contriving the deliverance of an illustrious captive whose odious chains are an insult to religion, civilization and human rights. How to break the Emperor's chains and put an end to his cowardly torture–that is the problem we must resolve. Ultimately, when he is free, it will be for Napoleon alone to choose the route he will follow to his destiny."

An approving silence followed these words.

General B***, who would die at a later date trespassing over the boundaries of this peaceful program, asked: "Who summoned us together?"

"The Emperor," replied the priest.

The General Duc de **** added: "England, Hudson Lowe,[76] France, the shame of our enemies and the honor of our Fatherland!"

"By what means was the Emperor's appeal made manifest?" queried the Senator Comte de ****.

The formula of the *good cousins* in the forest was heard outside, this time pronounced by a female voice. Most of the assembly's members pricked up their ears in astonishment; the priest was the only one who was not surprised.

"My lords," he said, "the arm of God has to stretch a long way to reach that reef lost in the immensity of the ocean. The hatred of the English has hollowed out a prodigious moat around the prison where the august martyr is suffering, as broad as half the world and as deep as the Inferno–but the Ark was also lost in the incommensurable solitude of the waters, and the dove was nevertheless able to reach it, bearing its message of hope. Every one of us knows the name of the cherished and noble Irish surgeon who was the first comforter of the giant fallen aboard the *Bellerophon*..."

"O'Meara!" they cried, "Barry Edward O'Meara."[77]

Five raps spaced in a particular fashion were heard at the door. The priest got up, went around the table and took up a position at the threshold.

"*What do you seek at the fountain?*" he asked, through the closed door.

"*Fede, speranza e carita!*" was the response.

The priest opened the door, saying: "*Enter, the fountain is here.*"

A veiled woman appeared in the doorway. The priest kissed her hand and presented her with half of a playing card, which the unknown completed. Then, he said: "In the name of the one who is dearest to our hearts, Françoise O'Meara, be welcome!"

The stranger threw back her veil, She was a young woman rendered very pale by emotion, but whose noble beauty every one of them could appreciate. She remained silent for a moment, looking at each of the men surrounding her in turn. No one among them could put to that pure and charming face either of the names that we have already pronounced so frequently: Sarah O'Neil or Lady Frances Elphinstone–who were no less entitled than she to the appellation "the beautiful Irishwoman."

She took from her bosom a long letter, which she unfolded, saying: "Stoke up the fire."

General B*** went to the hearth and got down on his knees to blow air at the dying embers. Lady Frances handed the open letter to the priest, and added: "My brother's correspondence is closely examined. Sir Hudson Lowe will not allow a word to pass that concerns the Emperor. Furthermore, these letters arrive having been stripped from their envelopes and passed through many grubby hands. Even that is insufficient for the government of free England... in order to come this far, I had to flee like a criminal; my brother's name halted me at every step, and attracted a swarm of spies. I am in France under a false name, Messieurs."

General B*** got up. The logs were burning brightly.

Lady Frances took a flask full of colorless liquid from her pocket. "Underneath the insignificant lines of these four long pages," she said, "there is a cry of agony. Disperse a few drops of this in the middle of the first page, Monsignor, and then dry it with the flame."

The priest obeyed; his hand trembled. When he had moistened the paper, he went to the fire and leaned over avidly, watching out for the completion of the miracle.

Scarcely had the damp page begun to warm up, emitting the subtle odor of some chemical concoction, than the large and forceful strokes of a pen became visible through the doctor's fine handwriting, vividly red beneath the black ink.

"The Emperor's handwriting!" murmured the priest, in a choked voice. He put his hand to his heaving breast.

Everyone was standing up; the silence was so solemn that you could have heard a child breathing.

"There are only four words," the old man continued, weakly. He recited rather than read them, slowly, for his eyes were blinded by tears.

"*THEY ARE KILLING ME!*"

Then he put the paper to his lips.

The paper was then passed from hand to hand, and every mouth kissed it religiously, while a tear formed at the corner of every eye.

The inscription was already fading, through, and when the letter was returned to Lady Frances, the four words traced by the Emperor had completely disappeared.

A profound silence reigned over Madeleine Surrisy's downstairs room. All Europe was by then aware of the invidious treatment that England inflicted upon the vanquished enemy, to whom she played host in order to inflict the slow death of a thousand cuts within the misery of a foul prison. Despite the precautions of the jailer burdened with such despicable fame, letters were received from Longwood [78] and the correspondence of the English officers themselves was full of melancholy revelations. The ferocious treatment meted out to the Comte de Las-Cases [79] in consequence of a few modest complaints sickened every heart, and the very barbarity of the conquerors gave birth to compassion for that fallen grandeur.

"What are we going to do, Messieurs?" General B*** was the first to ask, his teeth gritted and his fists clenched.

"Even if we had soldiers," replied the Senator Comte ****, in a discouraged tone, "it would be necessary to equip them with wings."

"If we had earthbound soldiers," General B*** said, brusquely, "we would only have to proclaim that he had escaped his prison to make a sail for Europe; that which is false today would be true tomorrow and we would have the French fleet to seek out Napoleon in St. Helena!"

No one supported or opposed this opinion. The priest said: "We are here to free a captive, not to proclaim an Emperor."

"And we are too old," added Major-General F***, "to waste time listening to fairy tales.

"Speak, then!" said B***. "What should we do?" And as no one was in any haste to reply, he leapt up on his bench, adding: "Nothing? Will you pretend that you have not heard that cry of distress? Will you fold your arms? Will you wait for the article in the *Moniteur* that has been drafted in advance, which will appear within years, perhaps within months, as if it were it were fresh news, saying: *Napoleon Bonaparte has died on St. Helena, following a long illness.* Long indeed, Messieurs, and cruel! On reflection, I don't have as much reason as you for becoming emotional. My true master, the god whose apostle I have appointed myself, is not called Napoleon but Liberty! It is not liberty that is in chains out there; it is not even an Emperor... if I have a fever, you should have a rapture."

"General," said the former Minister, the Duc de ****, "no one here deserves your reproaches. The mere fact of our meeting, which has cost so much trouble and risks so many dangers, is proof enough that our devotion has no need of any spur. Let us speak calmly before acting with audacity and firmness, because fever and rapture are worthless and unproductive. Let us remember that the Emperor's ear is listening to our deliberation, which is supreme in more than one sense, for every one of us has come a long way, and has a long way to return. The authorities are already on the alert–who knows when the hour or day will come when we shall no longer be able to meet again? At least, let the echo of our speech be a consolation and a hope for the one who is in exile, and whose eagle eye still looks across the vast expanse of space at France. At least, do not compel the sister of the noble O'Meara, reporting on our assembly by this mysterious process of transmission, to say: Discord is in the camp of the despairing!"

General B*** offered his hand, emotionally, in the midst of murmurous applause.

The password was heard yet again outside, and several voices asked: "Aren't we all here?"

Françoise O'Meara let her veil down again and asked: "Milords, which of you is Commodore James Davy?"

Everyone looked at her in surprise. The clock chimed one, its noisy tick beating the pulse of time in its sonorous casket.

Outside, the sentinel said: "*What do you seek, good cousin?*"

A vibrant masculine voice replied, in English: "*I seek the fountain.*"

"If no one among us is named James Davy," O'Meara's sister went on, "open the door to the newcomer."

"We only speak French here!" replied the sentinel outside, rudely. "Who are you and what do you want?"

The black veils were brought down over every face.

The priest said, in an anxious tone: "My lords, the Grand Master is appointed by the Emperor..."

"Our lives are at stake..." murmured the Minister, Comte ****.

"It only requires one traitor..." added Major-General F***.

But the smiling General B*** replied: "It's precisely because we have put our lives on the table that we must play... and I'll take care of the traitor."

"You are my prisoner!" cried the voice of Robert Surrisy, outside.

"Your hand!" the other voice pronounced, imperiously, in French, adding almost immediately: "Knock five times!"

There was now a deep silence in the interior. At the five raps, the priest went to the door and pronounced the sacramental question: "*Good cousin, what do you seek at the fountain?*"

The voice replied, switching into English again and putting a singular emphasis on each word: "*Faith, hope, charity.*"

"From which forest do you come?"
"From the forest of Ireland."
"The first, second third or fourth?"
"The fifth and only."

A murmur ran through the assembly and the priest opened the door, saying: *"Enter, Master; the fountain is here."* At the same time, the priest drew away the veil that covered the pallor and fatigue of his face.

All those around the table–who were standing now, with their faces turned towards the door–did likewise.

The new arrival alone kept his black mask, which descended from his forehead to his breast, in the midst of the uncovered faces. We know him too well to have to describe yet again the proudness of his stance and the nobility of his manner. His gaze made a slow tour of the table. He took time to examine each member of the assembly attentively.

"My lords," he said, eventually, in a firm and respectful tone, "I am hiding an obscure face and you are showing me illustrious ones. I have crossed the sea to say to you God be with you: I have the means of liberating your Emperor! Just as I have crossed the sea to say to your Emperor: 'Sire, with God's help, I shall save Your Majesty!' "

"You have seen the Emperor!" This cry burst forth simultaneously from every mouth–then there was silence; doubt was already replacing enthusiasm in the expressions of certain faces.

Admiral Baron **** said in a low voice: "Everyone who knows the island of St. Helena believes it impossible to penetrate as far as the prisoner of Longwood."

"It is the prisoner of Longwood," the newcomer replied, "who has expunged the word impossible from the French dictionary. The route I took to reach the Emperor is my secret, as is the means that I shall employ to keep my promise. My life is a secret; my work is a secret. I wanted to be master of this association, so many of whose members are above me, in order to have the right to keep my secret. As there is only one sanction in the world capable for forcing people like you to follow an unknown route in a blindfold, I went in peril of my life to obtain that sanction–and I received it."

He walked towards Lady Frances, bowed to her, and said in English: "Are you Françoise O'Meara?"

"Yes, milord," the young woman replied. "I've been waiting for you."

"To give me a message?"

"This one, milord. I will give it to you if you can give me a sign to demonstrate that you are Commodore James Davy."

The stranger took off his cloak and extended his left arm, pointing with his right hand to the cuff of his black dress-coat. The thread of silk that formed the seam had a knot with a double bow, which delicate fingers could easily grasp.

"Withdraw the thread, if you please," said the stranger.

Lady Frances pulled the knot and the entire seam came undone. A thin leaf of silky paper was set between the two pieces of material.

"Read it," said the stranger.

Lady Frances read it, nodded her head, and took from her bosom a box of the kind in which sweets are packed, which she gave to him. The stranger opened it and broke through an inner cover; the false bottom enclosed a second leaf of paper similar to the first.

The stranger gave the two papers to the priest, who acquainted himself with their contents, kissed them, and passed them to the man standing next to him.

The two papers made a tour of the table in this fashion. Then, the priest, having consulted the faces of his associates—each of whom nodded by way of assent—said: "Let the Emperor's will be done!" He stepped towards Davy, adding: "Commodore Davy, will you kneel down...?"

The stranger obeyed.

"Commodore Davy," the old man continued, slowly and solemnly, in God's name and by the Emperor's command, I appoint you Knight; Officer; Commander; Senior Officer; Grand Cross of the Legion of Honor." He had taken his own sash in his hand, which he passed around the stranger's neck while pronouncing these final words. He gave him the accolade, then raised him up by the hand and conducted him to the central position that he had formerly occupied.

"Commodore Davy," he went on, "Grand Cross of the Imperial Order of the Legion of Honor and Grand Master of the Knights of the Deliverance, assume the presidency of our Supreme Council here, which is yours by right. Tell us what we need to know about your projects; give us our individual tasks in that common and pacific endeavor. We are ready to listen to you, and ready to obey you."

It was about three o'clock in the morning. All around Madeleine Surrisy's house there was a noisy confusion of voices and footsteps. The interior lights had been extinguished. The Moon was hidden behind the wooded slopes of the hills in the direction of Pontoise. On every side, people were talking in the shadows and horses pawed the ground. The Commodore and Françoise O'Meara had left first, in opposite directions, both on horseback. Nothing disturbed the hastily exchanged *adieux*. Everyone was possessed by a sort of contained enthusiasm.

General B*** kissed Robert on both cheeks before mounting his horse and saying: "The Devil only knows whether we'll give you time to become an advocate, Surrisy! I hope that your epaulette will have its partner before next spring. Don't ask me any questions, lieutenant! It's witchcraft; we're going to make St. Helena into a conjuror's thimble."[80] He saluted as he put on his hat.

Half an hour later, all was silence and solitude along the banks of the Oise.

At the Croix Moraine signpost, the old priest, General Duc de *** and Admiral Baron **** paused, the first on the point of returning to the carriage which awaited him a few paces further along the Paris-l'Isle-Adam road, the two others just as they were turning to continue on their separate ways.

"Admiral," said the Duc, "you alone are truly competent to assess this business. What's your opinion?"

"General," the glorious mariner replied, thoughtfully, "steam-power has not yet revealed its secret to us. We old sailors have no liking for an innovation that would make a sunken wreck of our artistry. Among every ten mariners of my era, nine would say 'The man is mad!' For myself, given the applications to which steam had already been put, I'm only surprised that the fellow's idea has taken such a long time to materialize... but so it is with everything simple and great."

"You're confident, then?"

"Confident?" echoed the Admiral, hesitantly. Then, he added: "You have to be a seaman to see the obstacles. Listen, Messieurs, if Commodore James Davy has the enormous sums of which he speaks at his disposal–and agents on the coast of Guinea, at the Cape and even in New Orleans–this is a dream so brilliant that one would willingly awaken it. I, for one, am ready to do everything in my power to serve the enterprise."

They embraced one another and went their separate ways.

At the same moment, or very nearly, Lady Frances and Comte Henri de Belcamp were riding together along one of the gravel paths cutting through the Chateau-Neuf's little park. The night was remarkably calm and quiet; no sound could be heard in the valley save for the distant and perpetual murmur of the mill-race.

"No, you're not my slave, Sarah," the Comte was saying in that gravely melodious voice which cut so easily to the heart. "I've chosen you to march beside me on a difficult road. I chose you because I love you and because I see in you an Irishwoman, the enemy of everything that I hate. Have I not always respected you as a cherished sister, Sarah?"

"You told me that I would be your wife one day," murmured Lady Frances, in a strange tone, in which reproach was perceptible but no regret.

Comte Henri's moral insight was too keen for that nuance to escape him. "At that time," he replied, "I thought that you loved me truly."

"And have I not acted as if I were entirely yours, Henri?"

The two horses were moving side-by-side at an equal pace. The young Comte put his arm around Frances' shoulders and pulled her gently towards him so that he might kiss her forehead. "Before you knew it yourself," he murmured, "I read what was in the very depths of your heart."

She shivered, at the sound of Henri's voice rather than the contact of his lips. Her eyes strove to pierce the darkness to read what was written in her companion's features. Henri smiled. "What could you read in my heart?" she whispered.

Henri hesitated before replying. "I never heard your voice so tremulous, Sarah," he said, finally, his expression changing. "The heart is a book to which a new page is added every day. I stopped reading at yesterday's page, and I see that more leaves have been written today. Now I understand your anxieties and scruples, which astonished me at first because they were new to me. I treated them as infantilism because I had not guessed their source, but now I see that it's worth taking the trouble to calm them. I read in your heart, Sarah, when you believed that you were everything to me, the tenderness of a sister rather than the passion of a lover."

"A sisterly tenderness that would go as far as dying for you, Henri!" Lady Frances said, very softly.

"And will always go as far, I suppose," the young Comte replied, in a tone that was becoming stern, "at least until our pact is overtly and honorably dissolved."

Frances gave him her hand. "I need a master," she said, abruptly reining in her horse.

It was Henri's turn to peer at her through the darkness.

She added: "When I speak to you of slavery, it's neither a complaint nor a reproach. I'm afraid of liberty."

"How many times have you been in love, Sarah?" the young Comte asked, almost cheerfully.

"Have I told you that I've been in love, Henri? Myself, I'm not sure that I can."

"I know it, good and lovely little sister. There's a bizarre and fatal sympathy between us: you ought to be in love, since I am."

"Ah," Frances murmured, not even trying to conceal her sadness. "You're in love?"

"And that makes you feel a strange melancholy? It seems to me, too, that this unknown who has entered into your thoughts so long after me takes part of my well-being and my joy. Our souls are sisters, dear child, and will only be separated, I believe, by death!" He kissed Frances' hand and released it. The two horses resumed their slow walk, leaving the open ground and passing beneath the vaulted foliage of the oakwood. "No, you have nothing to fear," the young Comte went on, after a pause, "and I don't want you to experience the kind of fright that used to be so foreign to your nature. You must follow in my footsteps, enthusiastic and confident. My goal, whose luminous splendor you cannot glimpse, calls to you in the night, and you must not ask for any other leadership than the loving hand of your guide. Now that you know more about it..."

"And I admire it all the more!" she put in.

"But you have less belief in it, Sarah. Why should your faith be stronger than mine, when I am often obliged to stifle the voice of my reason, crying out and demanding: Is it a dream?"

"It's not your power that I doubt, Henri," the young woman murmured.

"God forgive you if you have doubted my will!"

"I have carried out your orders in the matter of Richard Thompson," she said, so quietly that Henri had difficulty hearing her.

"And you have seen that I have drawn Richard into a trap," said the young Comte, whose voice also weakened as his head slumped forwards. "One who loves and trusts me... and you have held a poor little child in your arms, who cries for his father and his mother!" There was profound and painful emotion in his voice.

"Only tell me," stammered Lady Frances, with tears in her eyes, "tell me that Richard Thompson's wife will not be a widow. Tell me that poor gentle creature... it's the first time that I've held a child in my arms, Henri... tell me that the dear little creature won't be an orphan!"

"Sarah, Sarah!" murmured Comte Henri, slowly, while his proud and handsome head, accepting her suspicion, raised itself gradually into a shadow that formed a veil in which there was not the least hint of sacrifice. "I have, thank God, felt the weight of my cross before placing it upon my shoulders–but until now, you have helped me to bear it."

"And I shall still help you, Henri! I'm only a woman; I beg you to have pity on me. Tell me that Richard Thompson will not pay with his life for the trust he put in you..."

"What have I done, Sarah O'Neil?" Henri cried, with such heightened bitterness that the young woman dropped the bridle of her horse to bring her hands together and extend them towards him. "What have I done, between that first hour when you encountered me providentially on your road, and tonight, when you are breaking my heart beneath the outrage of your ingratitude, to merit any suspicion of dastardliness?"

Lady Frances retreated into dismal silence. The young Comte heard her sobbing, and went on in a gentler voice: "You are in love, Sarah. I have already lost within your heart that which another has won there. I am in love too... at least, I feel within me that long-awaited tremor that my terribly occupied youth knew only in hope and in dreams. I am in love–but my affection for you is in no way diminished. I hear you weeping; I am a man and you are a woman: I forgive you before you have asked my pardon. In addition, Sarah, I too say to you: have mercy, my sister! I need you; the road is too long to be traveled in complete isolation. For a long time you have been half my strength and confidence. I beg you, Sarah, don't abandon me!"

She threw her two arms around his neck and he clutched her to his heart, while the two horses waited, motionless.

"Never, Henri, never!" she exclaimed between her tears. "I am with you, entirely. If you forbade me to love, I would obey, at the risk of breaking my heart!"

They held the embrace for a moment. What does it require to kill nascent love in the heart, to fill it with another passion more ardent, more vivid, more profound, which is often already demanding to be born? It only requires the will of the dominator. The other love is still no more than a tepid glow or a romantic gleam, caressing the threshold of an infant heart–and the heart, perhaps, remains infantile in spite of itself. But once that spark is admitted, it will set fire to the heart!

Besides, Henri was driven, his destiny incorporate in the inflexible line of the route he had already traced. He had no choice, and it was the eleventh hour.

"My dear little sister," he said, thrusting her back into her saddle with his vigorous arms, "We're both mad. A little while ago, I didn't ask enough; now you want to give me too much. Listen to me, for my suffering and your tears must not be in vain. Because of me, the threat of death is suspended over the head of Richard Thompson. I have drawn him into a trap. Every step he takes is ruled by my will, of which he recently became the accomplice. I shall go further along that path, because it is impossible to stop without repudiating my entire plan–and death alone, as you well know, is capable of barring my way. Richard Thompson will be imprisoned in my place, tried in my place, condemned in my place..."

"Condemned!" echoed Sarah, shuddering.

"Condemned, with the aid of my own testimony. But his wife shall not be a widow, nor his child an orphan–I give you my word! Let nothing inhibit you from smiling over that little crib, Sarah; love the child generously, caress him fondly, tell him, if you wish, the names of his father and his mother, as soon as he is ready."

"Have you forgiven me completely, Henri?" Lady Frances murmured, smiling through her tears.

"Yes and no, little sister. Yes, because I must give you your task; no, because I have inflicted the punishment of an explanation upon you–the first that has been necessary between us, Sarah! The role that you have played tonight, which has admitted you so far into my secret, will not place you in any danger. You will never meet the people you have seen again. If it happens, it cannot happen until our great cause is won, and then the role you have played will be your fame and fortune. Those you have seen–all of them, without exception– came a long way, and the place of our assembly was chosen expressly for that reason. Some are outlaws, others highly-placed individuals who are risking their fortunes and their lives in this conspiratorial game, and have only one aim in consequence: to hide. They are now en route to the north or the south; some of them will even cross the border. Here you are only exposed to encounters with the soldiers of that army whose chiefs alone have seen your face. Françoise O'Meara has returned to England; there is no longer anyone here but Lady Frances Elphinstone, who will be the reigning beauty of local society, who will eventually live and smile, and fully satisfy her taste for pleasure. I do not even ask of Lady Frances Elphinstone the name of the lucky mortal who has attracted her gaze. If Lady Frances wishes to tell me that name, I shall refuse to hear it, because the suspicions she has evidenced on the subject of Richard..."

"Henri!" murmured the young woman, in a supplicatory tone.

"It's the last time I shall allude to that, Sarah, but I must add one thing in all seriousness. The man that you love will perhaps be jealous, in time to come, of my influence over you. The nature of a relationship like ours is indefinable and incomprehensible. If that is so, he will fight me like an invisible enemy. It is possible that he will get in my way, and then... I don't want to know his name."

Lady Frances became thoughtful as she heard these final words.

"And my task?"

"The role of a great coquette, this time," the young Comte replied, laughing. "We are quitting the somber paths of drama to take in a comedy: a theater-pit strewn with flowers. There is a handsome fiancé here, whose engagement must be broken off. I shall take care of the young woman; a few of Lady Frances' smiles will render the young man drunk and foolish..."

"The young woman..." said Frances. "Henri, is it the one you're in love with"

"It's the one I shall be in love with, Sarah."

"And the young man?"

"Tomorrow–or, rather, today, for the day is already four hours old–I shall show you your conquest as we come out of church after mass."

They had reached the Chateau-Neuf, whose white facade was vaguely outlined in the first light of dawn. Lady Frances attempted to smile. Henri kissed her hand, bidding her farewell and urging his horse to a trot in order to descend the path that led to the river.

Frances followed him with a thoughtful gaze until his confused form was lost in obscurity.

She woke Sam and gave him her horse. Then, instead of going back to the apartment she had chosen for herself, she slipped into Lisbeth's room, where the child was accommodated. Lisbeth was asleep. Frances sat down silently next to the crib. She stayed there for a long time, studying little Richard as he slept, as calm and happy as a beautiful angel.

"To love! To love!" she murmured. "To see the birth of that dear flower of good fortune... to be the Holy Spirit of that Trinity, all three bearing the same name, breathing as one, living one and the same life!"

She leaned over. The long lashes of her eyelid released a single tear upon the forehead of the little child. Then she went away slowly, her head bowed.

It was a Sunday in May. At 4 p.m., the Sun was peeping through pink clouds, gilding the summits of the hills whose contours were blurred by light mist. The birds were issuing an energetic wake-up call and the swinging bell of the little church was chiming its meager carillon. No vestige of the night's events remained in the peaceful countryside. You would have searched in vain for any trace of the passing of those mysterious reminders of a great and terrible past, who had taken advantage of the cover of darkness to play with the destiny of nations.

The humble abode of Madeleine Surrisy was tranquil and serene. The willows in its meadow were mirrored in the Oise, unstirred by any breath of wind. On the other bank, the Belcamp park extended its woods as far as the Henri IV chateau, as clement and honest and semi-bourgeois as the Bourbon greybeard, giving not the least impression of feudal insolence or oppressive brutality. The mill was on holiday, in honor of the dominical day of rest. The Chateau-Neuf, very white in the midst of its verdant lawns and sharing with the old chateau the monarchy of the neighborhood, spoke of temporal conquest and the accepted rights of new aristocracies–the first step towards the long-anticipated epoch when thatched cottages would command insane prices because there would no longer be any palaces.

The riverside path where so many seditious feet had left their imprint was not like the pathways of North America, treasonous chatterboxes that could not be relied on to keep the secret of a trail. We are too civilized; there are too many tracks on our roads to permit the reading of footprints in the dust and mud that we cultivate here. Our bloodhounds have other skills. No one, not even that subtle amateur Blondeau, the local Constable, would have been able to follow the trail left by Robert Surrisy, Laurent Herbet and Férandeau–three conspirators–as they returned to the Priory, where they spent the rest of the night in their beds. If the incorrigible Briquet had not been so imprudent as to engrave his name on the wall of the little house, all the Police of France and Navarre would have been unable to figure out whether or not that natural child of Parisian gaiety had stood guard with his cudgel for the Knights of the Deliverance.

It is reasonable to suppose that this Briquet, like so many others, had had a prodigal father, for this father–who may not have been a poor man–would not have been obliged to abandon the mother and child had he handled his economic affairs wisely and secured an income. The mother, for her part, was a model by trade, but not of good behavior; and it reflects well on Briquet, whose education had been totally neglected, that he had learned to engrave his name without ever having been to school. Who can say what heights Briquet might have scaled if he had had the opportunity to study literature or arithmetic?

At five o'clock, the first mass had taken place, as usual. At six o'clock, Blondeau came to wake Monsieur le Maire to tell him that his active surveillance had discovered nothing suspicious in the territory of the commune on the previous night. Blondeau had been in his bed, enjoying the sleep of the just; he was not a wolf, to gad about in the moonlight because the Prefect had had a bad dream about conspirators. Blondeau gave the government a full measure of zeal for his six francs, and never went out after dusk except to pull a hare from its hiding-place. Monsieur le Maire kept his own feet warm; colds in the head were for gendarmes.

At seven o'clock, Madame Célestin, in her church clothes and flanked by her two Bondons, reviewed the Miremontese National Guard in front of the town hall. It would have been difficult to find nine soldiers as well turned-out. When Florian Bondon, according to his duty, had given a few military commands, echoed in a whisper by the right-hand Bondon, Madame Célestin gave a speech to bestow on this devoted militia the felicitations of France. Our conspirators would have been very impressed!

At eight o'clock, the Bondon garniture came to make their report to the Mayor, testifying to the solid and excellent spirit of the community. It was made by Madame Célestin.

At nine o'clock, Madame Etienne served breakfast personally, complaining that she had not yet had any compliments, even though she had surpassed herself since the arrival of Monsieur le Comte. Henri won her over at a single stroke by telling her that he had never eaten better cooking. Henri was in a very good mood this morning, and his cheerfulness was singularly expressive; his frankness and certain allusions to a very dear subject even forced a smile from poor Suzanne.

As for the Marquis, his nocturnal anxieties could not hold out for a minute against the cheerful disposition of his beloved son. In addition, he still had his plan, and he brought up Germaine's name several times in the course of the meal. Then it was time to leave for mass; Henri offered his arm to Suzanne to lead her to the harnessed carriage that was waiting in the courtyard.

As they went down the steps he had time to say: "He looks like you; he's charming. I've embraced him on your behalf and said goodbye on your behalf."

"Goodbye!" the poor young mother repeated, as her moist gaze thanked him.

Everyone was smiling that morning. The servants went down the hill in their Sunday clothes, slapping one another on the back. Anille's hair was in slight disarray and Julot had a black eye. Briquet, as a Voltairean, was scornful of worship, but went to church to visit a pillar whose soft stone already displayed the first four letters of his name; he had no special clothes for the Lord's day, but he had replaced his peaked cap with an old hat that he had waxed on Saturday evening. Madame Etienne, by contrast, gleamed like a Sun in the spoils of her former employment: a Valenciennes lace bonnet, a merino wool dress and a patched-up shawl. She put on a fancy accent when she wore this costume, and the solemnity of her bearing knew no bounds.

"All that has gone up in smoke," she said, measuring her processional pace. "The risk of attacking the commune, whose political opinions favor the throne the altar and the fatherland, would not be inconsequential. You'd have to go as far as l'Isle-Adam or the Faubourgs of Paris to find a Bonapartist, Monsieur Trompe-d'Eustache excepted."

"If one had not been sworn on oath to keep secrets..." Briquet began.

"What secrets, Monsieur Bricole?" Fanchette asked.

"I could explain it to you if we were to meet *tête-à-tête*," Briquet replied, in a low voice. A Parisian understands the language of the heart.

All the prodigious vehicles whose descriptions we have already sketched out were reunited in the church square, from the square chest where the three Bondons sat facing forwards to the funereal chariot of the Morin ménage, including the delivery-van in which the 13 Chaumerons were stacked, the charabanc belonging to Germaine's father and five or six carts of more-or-less original architecture. Don Juan Besnard had a little item that he called a tilbury, which Mademoiselle the eldest commended as a kind of elegance. Until today, the paragon of Miremontese equipages had been the old Marquis' stout and solid *berline*, but today every eye was drawn to an elegant coach pulled by two frisky horses, which snorted and pawed the ground in front of the town hall door. The entire village, instead of going into mass, gathered around this coach, whose coachman–who did not understand a single word of French–stared sleepily and apathetically at the crowd.

As soon as she arrived, Madame Etienne came to look at the coachman, saying scornfully: "That's the English for you!"

"There are enough of them in Paris!" Briquet added. "They're not so dear."

Successes that arrive too close together detract from one another. There were three successes in Miremont, any one of which would have set the commune alight in normal circumstances. Firstly, there was the lovely Jeanne, who was appearing in public for the first time since her accident at the mill bridge, and upon whom the widow Touchard was lavishing every maternal attention. Secondly, there was the Comte, the darling of the district. Finally, there was the rich foreigner whom no one had yet seen, and whose name was already being mangled by everyone.

There are two ways in which a rich Englishwoman may be represented: either as something round, obese, red, blue, shapeless and monstrous, bizarrely decked in burlesque furbelows; or as something tall, thin, black, bony, mounted on legs like rickety stilts, in a vast checked cloak, topped by a ridiculous straw hat, with a green veil flapping in the wind. There's no escaping it; rich Englishwomen who are represented in any other fashion have no authenticity. It is axiomatic, above all else, that a rich Englishwoman is never young.

The success of Lady Frances Elphinstone was prodigious, and utterly effaced all others. On going into the church and seeing that adorable young woman, dressed with supreme simplicity, modestly and piously kneeling at the end of a bench, Miremontese society almost lost the respect due to the holy place. The peasants, who had already had an opportunity to stare at her as she got down from her carriage, were far from according her the same importance as her horses. By contrast, Madame Morin du Reposoir, the First Deputy's wife, Madame Célestin of the Municipal Council, Besnard the seducer, all the little Chaumerons under the command of Mademoiselle the eldest, Monsieur and Madame Chaumeron themselves, Potel the learned Second Deputy and his daughter Germaine, who was as fresh as a rosebud this morning, the two proofs of the same caricature who were Bondons, and Férandeau—who represented the high ideals of Art within this slightly bourgeois world—all partook distractedly of the holy water and disputed the places that offered the best view of this ravishing stranger.

There were official benches ranged behind the Marquis' station. The accommodation of these benches had lately been on the point of prompting a civil war. On that occasion the gentle Deputy's wife, Madame Morin du Reposoir, nicknamed Many-Apologies because of her politeness, had addressed some very lively words to Madame Besnard, the Don Juan's mother, and Madame Célestin. Now, those benches were deserted. Madame Morin knelt down beside the local constable, who was already drunk from his Sunday celebrations, and Madame Célestin, gritting her teeth, reined in her team under the pulpit. Mademoiselle and the lively flock of little Chaumerons—all thin and sharp, throwing fearful glances at the mother who guided them through life with a handful of whips—dispersed themselves around Lady Frances with wild curiosity. The Verger, we are obliged to say, turned round three times while lighting the candles, and Monsieur le Curé, himself, good and worthy priest that he was, was slightly distracted as he came out of the sacristy.

There was no one on the bourgeois—which is to say, the seigneurial—benches except the two Messieurs de Belcamp with Suzanne, the lovely Germaine beside her father, and Jeanne Herbet with Aunt Touchard and side her father, and Jeanne Herbet with Aunt Touchard and Laurent. Jeanne was still very pale, but she had come through the nave with a firm step, leaning on her brother's arm, and had been able to say to Germaine, under cover of a kiss: "He has cured me."

Robert–who was normally certain to be found everywhere that Jeanne's smile was displayed–was not among the curious swarm. You would have been able to observe, at the very moment when the bell signaled the entrance of the priest, a movement at the back of the nave among the peasants grouped around the door. There were young boys there, a few farmers, and also a few sunburned faces with short-cropped hair and large moustaches, conserved in spite of all good advice–every parish, at that time, had its bellicose contingent, and the sol-dier-laborer is a distinctive species. This company moved aside in order to give amicable and respectful passage to a couple who were coming in: a proud and handsome young man who also sported a moustache and retained a military ele-gance beneath his bourgeois clothing, and a tall woman dressed in black, in the peasant style but with a certain strictness. The old woman was calm, sad and proud beneath her hooded cape–doubtless proudest of all of the dear and noble son who was not ashamed of her and who led her carefully and lovingly by the hand. They were Robert Surrisy and his mother, Madeleine.

To honor one's mother no matter what her social position might be is surely the simplest virtue in the world. It is a singular thing, which seemingly indicates that this natural and necessary worship often displays its apostates, that we are always affected by the sight of such a couple: an elegant young man publicly cherishing the poor good woman who is his mother. It is not our fault if the lax stupidity of certain vanities, inflated at the expense of an emaciated heart, have made that payment of a strict debt into something resembling hero-ism.

Two moustache-bearers who had exchanged nods of the head and smiles worth more than any Masonic handshakes with Robert, made room for them on a bench near the middle of the nave. Mother and son knelt down side by side.

The mass began.

To see is a good thing, but what is incomparably better is to be seen. The members of Miremontese society grouped behind Lady Frances began to feel the sharpness of the latter appetite. Mademoiselle, who had a brand new ruched green hat made out of an old dress, on which the entire family had worked, felt a legitimate desire to humiliate the Englishwoman, whose hat was not ruched at all. Madame Célestin, for her part, was seized by the fantasy of showing her wedding-shawl to the Englishwoman: a memorable shawl that had faithfully re-tained its label for two years in order that everyone would be able to see its price.

Mademoiselle said to her mother: "We're making a spectacle of ourselves here. We ought to resume our usual places."

Perhaps Madame Chaumeron had something to demonstrate. She pushed Papa Chaumeron, a frank and rounded man, who immediately began to march off. All the little Chaumerons started off at the same time, happy to make a fuss. The Bondon garniture followed, then Madame Morin du Reposoir, making many apologies to the feet she trampled as she passed. During the gospel, the entirety of Miremontese society took up its proper place in front of the English-woman, whose exclusive attention every one of its members secretly hoped to capture.

The Englishwoman prayed. I would not go as far as to say that she did not see Miremontese society, but her admiration was exempt from all disturbance. Mademoiselle's hat excited no envy; she was not jealous of Madame Célestin's wedding-shawl. If her distracted gaze strayed from her missal once or twice, it was not to study the splendor of all those outmoded costumes. One or twice, her eye made a rapid review of the benches between her and the choir. She seemed to be searching for something she could not find.

The previous night, at the threshold of the mysterious house that she had entered under the name of Françoise O'Meara, Lady Elphinstone had had a vi-sion. She had believed that she recognized, in the young man who pronounced the mystical formula, the handsome young man whose image had pursued her since London Bridge: the reckless and merry cavalier who was the cause of her escapade at the Colisée; the madman who had taken a bath in the Thames on a cold April morning for the express purpose of saving her dainty notecase; the hero of the novel, whose name wanted to say smile.

But she thought she saw him everywhere!

As she left the cottage, her avid gaze had made a review of all the faces half-hidden in the shadows, but none resembled that of Robert Surrisy. Here again, in the church that she had entered with a vague hope, nothing.

The mass came to an end and Frances, after a curt sign of the cross, made her way all alone towards the parish door. Very close to the threshold, through the crowd of villagers, she saw an old peasant woman hanging on the arm of an elegant cavalier; her heart beat faster, but the crowd thickened between them— and Lady Frances had been so often deceived already!

At the door, Comte Henri de Belcamp came to offer her holy water, and offered her his arm for the return to her carriage. Before the reawakened Sam had whipped his horses, Lady Frances was able to bow graciously to the whole of Miremontese society, formed in groups in the square.

Soon after her departure, the various groups came together again, pos-sessed by an immense need for slander.

"She's not so much!" Mademoiselle said, disdainfully.

"She isn't that well dressed!" added Madame Célestin.

"A bad sort," said Madame Besnard, who gave the exact impression of an apple-seller dressed for a gala.

"Many apologies," said Deputy Morin's wife, "but I'm of the same opinion. The affronted air..."

"Stuck-up and worn out!" concluded the mother of all the Chaumerons.

"Well," cried Germaine, who had joined up with Laurent and Jeanne, "if that one isn't as beautiful as an angel!"

"She's certainly very beautiful," said Jeanne, whose pale cheek had taken on a red tint as she returned Comte Henri's greeting.

"And her outfit," the easily excited Germaine went on, "is ravishing in its taste, distinction and..."

"Sheer perfection!" Mademoiselle put in.

"I think she's rather pretty, myself," said the Lovelace Besnard.

"I think she..." the two Bondons began at the same time–but Madame Célestin had acquired by assiduous practice the skill of pinching as hard with her right hand as with her left. Neither of the two Bondons completed the sentence, because the sharp claws of their housekeeper dug into the flesh of their arms with equal energy.

"Well, Mesdames," the Marquis said as he came up to them, "chance could not have served us better, I think. You have a charming neighbor there."

"Many apologies," the Deputy's wife immediately murmured, "but I agree with Monsieur le Maire."

"There's something pleasing about her," Madame Célestin put in.

"A *je ne sais quoi*, as they say," added Mademoiselle.

"What's that?" concluded Chaumeron. "I don't mince my words, me. The Mayor's said it: she's charming."

As the session concluded, it was unanimously, if unexpectedly, agreed by all the members of Miremontese society that it was not necessary to maintain rigorous etiquette with a person so accomplished. The custom, throughout the land, is that the first visit should be made by the newcomer, but once Comte Henri–in whom everyone had total confidence–had explained something of English society, to which Lady Frances Elphinstone belonged, the question arose as to who should inform her that all Miremont, as a body, would present its respects to the noble foreigner.

Comte Henri was dispatched as an ambassador to convey this important news to Madame–after which all the members of that society, some on foot and others in carriages, took the road to the Chateau-Neuf. Robert Surrisy, after taking his mother back to her house, encountered the caravan on the riverbank and joined it.

The Chateau-Neuf, a lovely modern house, had one of those obese rotundas so dear to lovers of the Pompadour style in front of its facade. They have pretty rooms inside, and excrescences on the outside that fill every passer-by with the desire to exterminate them. Outside this rotunda was a broad terrace overlooking the valley, displaying to the fauns of the forest its border of stucco nymphs, the proprietor's lovers. To marry a terrace like that, Mademoiselle would gladly have sold her soul.

Lady Frances Elphinstone and Comte Henri went up on to this terrace to enjoy the view. We are not talking about the landscape here, but about the imposing aspect offered by the entire society of a rural commune marching in a body, in formal dress and with honorable intentions. At the moment when they leaned on the balcony, between two *immortelles*, one of whom was dancing under the slight influence of wine while the other was playing a double flute with her nose, the tail of the caravan was just coming into the shade of the oaks in the avenue.

"...And if Miss Temple sees the child?" Frances said, continuing a conversation that had already begun.

"She won't recognize him," Henri replied. "She hasn't seen him since the day he was born."

"Poor mother!" murmured the young woman.

"Hold on!" said the Comte. "The advance guard's about to come up. Take a good look, Sarah, and you'll be forced to agree that I've chosen you a handsome cavalier."

Frances was very pensive. "To make him fall in love," she murmured. "And if that cost me the one that I love...?"

Henri did not hear, or pretended not to hear. Miremont came out of the avenue and arrived at the gate on foot; they had left their vehicles at the bottom of the hill.

"Here's my father," Henri said.

"I recognize him. I've seen him twice already–he's a fine old man."

"Do you see the couple following him, Sarah?"

Lady Frances did not reply. Her cheeks were as white as alabaster; all her blood was flowing back towards her heart.

The couple following Monsieur de Belcamp comprised Robert Surrisy and Jeanne. Lady Frances' soul was in her eyes. Occupied as he was in greeting the newcomers, the young Comte did not see that.

"Did you see?" he asked, eventually.

Frances passed both hands over her face as one does when waking from a light sleep. Robert and Jeanne were going into the house, arm in arm.

"I saw," she stammered. Then she added, in a different tone: "How beautiful she is! And how she must love him!"

"Who do you mean?" Henri asked, turning back to look at her in astonishment.

The color returned to Frances' cheeks in a rush. "Am I as beautiful myself?" she murmured, lowering her eyes.

"There's nothing in the world as beautiful as you," Henri replied, looking at her with vivid and profound admiration.

He was telling the truth. At that moment, when her beauty was infused by a soul, there was an almost supernatural charm in her. She looked at him with eyes moistened by an emotion that he did not understand, or perhaps attributed to regret regarding their own past relationship. A spark sprang from the pupils that burned behind the tears, bright enough to dazzle.

"I shall act according to your will, Henri," she said, from the depths of some strange self-communion, "and if it is possible for me to do it, I swear that he will fall in love with me."

There was an enchantment abroad, which had in truth rendered Miremont mad, from its head, the Mayor, to its four huge feet, the Bondon team. Never had that society experienced a celebration like it. The arrival of Comte Henri was already an unexpected windfall; the advent of Lady Frances Elphinstone, Viscountess [81] of English high society, completed the measure. Miremont felt that it had become a capital; it was feverish. Madame Morin, already vast by nature, visibly swelled and offered so many apologies that her husband, ordinarily patient, ordered her to be silent. The plain speaker Monsieur Chaumeron proposed the establishment of a conversation room like those at spas, and the left-hand Bondon, taking the bit in his teeth, spoke in favor of instituting sea-baths at the mill bridge.

Buffon's *Natural History* teaches us that the lowest rank of the animal kingdom whose summit is man is the sponge; the two Bondons were madrepores, and that meager backbone Madame Célestin had one foot on each of them, like the Colossus of Rhodes. In her judgment, the left-hand Bondon was guilty of talking too much, and the right-hand one of having kept silent.

All the young Chaumerons had, of course, been left at the door. They found work to do uprooting tulips from the flowerbeds–the younger ones out of a pure necessity to be hurtful; the older ones with discernment and with the objective of presenting the bulbs to their father, who was a keen gardener.

Lady Frances won every heart with a single stroke. Whether she really belonged to the aristocracy or not is scarcely important, and we have no hesitation in affirming that no similar advent among the patrons of Almack's could have obtained the same success as she at Miremont. The lovely Suzanne was not a Viscountess, it is true, but she was pretty, good and spiritual; even so, her sojourn at the chateau had passed almost unnoticed. The charm of pure English origin is worthless in France as an instrument of seduction; we are beyond its reach. An Irish enchantress is another matter; she has more in common with us. She has, when she wishes, our elegance and our petulance; she warms up when she is rubbed, sparkles and bubbles.

Lady Frances had left her melancholy on the terrace. When she entered the drawing-room, everyone was struck by her gentle gaiety, her affable simplicity and her aristocratic benevolence, The old Marquis de Belcamp, who was certainly not as lacking in good taste as his honest administrators, was literally dazzled. This young woman, so marvelously beautiful and pretty at the same time–a rare combination–seemed to him to be grace, spirit, bounty and frankness personified: the very incarnation of everything attractive and seductive. It seemed that he would not have to search far afield to realize the dream that he had conceived the night before. He wished to restrain Henri by means of love; here was love herself.

One thing that pleased him, more than any other, was milady's conduct towards Jeanne, his *protégée*. Milady showed exquisite kindness to everyone, but with Jeanne it extended as far as tenderness. There was a pretext–the terrible accident to which Jeanne had almost fallen victim. Lady Frances crossed the room and set herself next to Jeanne, who was seated between Robert and Laurent. She took the astonished and somewhat confused Jeanne's hands in her own, and spoke to her softly and politely–and her tone became a caress in itself. While she spoke, her smiling gaze happened to meet Robert's, and Robert would not have been able to say why his heart beat so forcefully within his breast.

"I have thanked the Comte," Frances said, as she took her leave of Jeanne, kissing her on the forehead like a child, "and I said to him, though I don't know why: 'It seems to me as though you have saved my dear little sister.' "

But if there was a single moment of triumph, it was the one when Lady Frances, at the first overture from the Marquis de Belcamp, accepted–without any ceremony and with the most adorable alacrity (that being the expression of Monsieur Morin du Reposoir)–his invitation to Sunday dinner. Every Sunday, in fact, the Marquis received Miremontese society at his table. One might have hoped that milady might join them on the following Sunday, but today! A last-minute invitation! The word employed by the first deputy was not, in truth, an overstatement. Adorable!

Mademoiselle, heartily annoyed by this turn of events, whispered in Madame Besnard's ear that this was tantamount to throwing herself at people's heads; Madame Célestin would have given a week of each Bondon's life to be able to take her down a peg or two; and Many-Apologies herself confessed to Madame Chaumeron that such off-handedness strayed very close to effrontery– but all this was kept quiet. Out loud, the four worthy individuals applauded wholeheartedly.

They went down the hill together, and Lady Frances took her place in the Marquis' *berline*. The courtesans of Louis XIV were doubtless very ardent in disputing the privilege of climbing into the King's coaches, but no capricious favour improperly accorded to a newcomer by the Sun of Marly [82] ever excited such muffled jealousy. What increased the rage of the ladies was the laxity of their men-folk, all of whom were quite shameless.

The young Chaumerons were herded towards their father's house. For years, they had been promised that when they were old enough and wise enough they would eat at the chateau, but they had never attained that status. The young Chaumerons hated Sundays because, in the absence of their father, mother and Mademoiselle, the cooking left a lot to be desired–and while they ate their excessively frugal repast, they would dream about all the good things that were abundantly spread upon the table at the chateau.

The Chaumerons were pilferers by nature. The father, in addition to his plain speaking, had large and deep pockets in which he accumulated sugar-lumps, pieces of nougat, biscuits, cakes and even pastry-crusts. Madame and the eldest Mademoiselle also did what they could. All of it was carried off for the children, who did not get their hands on much of it. The emptied pockets furnished desserts for a week.

The eldest of the supernumerary Chaumerons could not have been less than 17, although she was still dressed in baby-clothes. Don Juan Besnard was already looking her over, in spite of the thin legs that projected extensively from dresses that were too short. The youngest of the others, whose ages were distributed at regular intervals, was seven. Férandeau had designed a pediment for a Greek temple made up of two Chaumeron families, bracketed by massive end-pieces.

Briquet lent a hand at the chateau on Sundays to get a place there, and his name was now engraved in three places under the table. Today, everything was up in the air: Pierre, Julot, Anille, Fanchette and even the gardener-coachman were helping to figure out symmetrical placings that would bring the young Monsieur together with the English milady.

Madame Etienne suffered cruelly, as you might imagine, at the sight of Monsieur le Marquis with such a petty entourage. There had been better company in the home of her former mistress, who was only a doctor's wife, and she complained bitterly to Briquet about the leftovers that constituted Miremontese elegance. "It's the effect of his inclemency," she said, talking about her master, "and his never being able to break the habit of being generous with his cake. On top of all that he's the Mayor of the town council, compelled on that account to represent all the indigenous bourgeois in the commune."

Today, though, she was proud. All the starvelings of Miremont could come, even the three idlers of the Touchard household; at least, there were respectable mouths to feed. Madame Etienne had seen the Englishwoman's coach in front of the church—what a sight! And everyone in the world knew already that she had a male cook! It was a question of surpassing. Madame Etienne's kitchen had the appearance of a battlefield; half of the devastated and plundered poultry-yard was there.

The monumental roasting-spit, which was turned with the aid of a capstan, was unreeling its cable noisily. The huge cooking-pot was singing on its hook. Scintillating casseroles warbled on the boilers. Julot and Anille, seated amid heaps of feathers, were arguing and hitting one another. There were plucked fowls everywhere, draped with bacon or dismembered; the chopping-board resounded; frying butter sizzled—and in that tropical temperature, in the heart of all the carnage and fabulous disorder, Madame Etienne did battle, disheveled but calm, scarlet-faced but collected. She had said: "This must be a memorable dinner!" and she had no wish to be made a liar.

There was, in consequence, a great spectacle when more than 20 guests, including Monsieur le Curé and the old Schoolmaster, took their places around the large table groaning under its load. Lady Frances was seated as was appropriate, to the Marquis' right. Like Madame Etienne, Comte Henri surpassed himself and his liveliness infected the entire company. The meal was exceedingly merry, despite the unexpected but habitual indisposition of Many-Apologies. The stout Deputy's wife was accustomed to attack the food with such voracity that she became uncomfortable two thirds of the way through the meal, after which she plied her fork in the loyal service of Monday's indigestion.

The Bondon garniture remained inseparable, Madame Célestin perennially enthroned between her two coral reefs and indulging in innocent commerce with both. She loved mushrooms, chicken-skin, olives and other dainties; throughout dinner the left-hand and right-hand Bondons picked various delicacies from their plates to place them on hers. They ate even more heartily than the Deputy's wife, but were never discomfited. As far as appetite was concerned, the only ones better equipped than the Bondons were the Chaumerons. The father, the mother and the eldest daughter were like the abyss; they engulfed everything. You could have choked a dozen men in the full bloom of maturity with what they stuffed into their stomachs and pockets. Férandeau credited them with the pelican's facility of employing its oesophagus as the feeding-trough of its family. He had made a sketch in the antique style, in which the ten little Chaumerons foraged with their snouts in that natural rack.

The Marquis greatly admired the scintillating wit of his right-hand neighbor, which maintained a continual fusillade of fine repartee with the Comte, whose place faced hers—a battle in which Robert played the part of sharpshooter. He did not, however, forget his left-hand neighbor, who was our lovely Jeanne. Jeanne ate little and seemed to be laboring under some strange oppression. A veil of melancholy sometimes descended upon the charming delicacy of her features; at others, her natural gaiety took fitful hold of her and her soft and joyous laughter, familiar to every ear, could be heard. The pallor of recent days was replaced by a hectic vermilion; her large blue eyes flashed and languished by turns.

There were two people whom her gaze continually sought out: Robert and Comte Henri. Her eyes flickered from one to the other.

Germaine, on the other hand, to whom Laurent was talking in a low voice, had neither enough ears to listen to Comte Henri nor enough eyes—laughing but naive—to contemplate him. When, by chance, she returned her attention to Laurent, it was to respond to some question put forward for consideration by Henri—until Laurent finally said to her, impatiently: "So you like him a great deal, Germaine!"

"Oh, certainly not," she replied. "He's too handsome, too bold, too sarcastic."

"But he hasn't been sarcastic to anyone."

"That's right... but he still frightens me."

Laurent sighed. That was obvious.

During the last entrée, the Marquis rang for Madame Etienne. The puissant cook responded promptly to the call; with her apron coquettishly set aside, her hair pushed back under her well-bleached head-dress, hands clean and a proud smile on her lips she was waiting behind the dining-room door, having entrusted the roast to Julot and Anille. This is an old French custom, and more than one among us can still see it observed in some family that clings to the old ways. This comment embodies none of the mistrust of the preliminary essay on food and wine; it is a fortunate souvenir of patriarchal life.

The Marquis filled a full plate, while the Comte poured out a full glass of wine.

"Madame Etienne," said the Marquis to the chef, who listened to him with her head held high and a frank expression, "Everyone here is content with you. Taste your food and drink to your health."

Madame Etienne took the glass in one hand, the plate in the other. She was so emotional that her cheeks would have put a dish of tomatoes to shame. She bowed all round and her voice trembled slightly as she replied: "Thanking you, Monsieur le Marquis and Monsieur le Comte. When one has proper masters such as you, who are the cream of the good world, one does what one can to be intolerable."

That said, she bowed again and went out proudly. The Chaumerons followed the plate and the glass with envious eyes. If their pockets were only tin-plated, people could carry food home in their juices, with their accompanying wines.

At dessert, they drank to the health of Jeanne first of all, Lady Frances next, and then all the ladies. Férandeau recited verses, Mademoiselle a romance entitled *Rosita, or the Calabrian Brigand,* and the Garniture Bondon rose as one to act out Iphigenia's confrontation with Achilles and Agamemnon. This overshot the bounds of the comic to attain splendor. The right-hand Bondon was Agamemnon, the left-hand Bondon Achilles. They often made mistakes, and when they did, Madame Célestin would correct them gently and firmly.

That was the climax; they left the table to take coffee in the enclosed garden. Comte Henri, even though he had the advantage of his status, did not dispute Jeanne's arm with Robert, but offered his own to Miss Temple as usual. Monsieur de Belcamp, who felt 15 years younger today, took possession of Lady Frances.

"I received a letter from my father this morning," Suzanne said to Henri as they went down the steps. "He will come to visit me when he returns from London."

"Ah," said the young Comte, lightly. "Gregory Temple is in London? When did he leave?"

"Yesterday evening."

"And when is he coming back?"

"I don't know."

"Madame," he said, in a very low voice which brought a chill to Suzanne's veins, "you were wise to warn me and I thank you. It may be that when Mr. Temple returns, I shall be able to meet him face to face without any danger to either of us. The opposite is also possible; that depends on circumstances. In consequence, should those circumstances arise, your role in all this will be subject to change. I shall give you my instructions."

He bowed and withdrew.

The old Marquis had escorted Lady Frances Elphinstone to the rustic table where the coffee had been set out. Henri seized the opportunity to slide adroitly between them, and said to the young woman: "It's necessary that I talk to Jeanne alone."

Frances, surprised, looked at him questioningly.

"And it's necessary that you have a *tête-à-tête* with Robert," he added.

Frances blushed, and murmured: "How do I do that?"

"Tell my father that I'm a fine storyteller, and when I've made these good people into an audience... is it necessary to remind you that you are a woman, and deliciously beautiful?"

"No," Frances murmured. "I know that now." Then, accepting a cup from the Marquis, she pointed a finger at Henri, who withdrew. "My dear neighbor," she said, "I'll wager that you don't know all the talents of your son Monsieur le Comte."

"Can he sing?" said the Marquis. "Does he play an instrument? We have a violin here, and a harpsichord of Jean-Jacques' time,[83] to whose music we dance every Sunday. We even have a guitar..."

"There's no need for any of that! In London, he was one of the delights of last season; he had only to tell us a story."

"Henri," called the Marquis, loudly, drawing a little way away from the table.

Every gaze followed his. The Chaumerons took advantage of the favorable circumstance to stock up on sugar. No one can be under the delusion that he can see into a mother's heart; Madame Chaumeron had more than a kilogram of comestibles in her pockets. Among these foodstuffs was a set of nutcrackers for Mimi, her last-born. The poor child had wanted some nutcrackers for a long time. Monsieur Chaumeron would not approve of that; he was a strict man, who never took any silverware.

"Henri," the Marquis went on, "milady tells me that you had all London running after you, this spring..."

"Good God! How would I do that, father?"

"Don't be modest... with your stories?"

"Do you know any ghost stories, Monsieur le Comte?" Mademoiselle exclaimed. "I know one in which a steward disguised himself as the Devil, to buy a chateau at a better price."

"Many apologies," murmured the Deputy's wife. "Stories of that unpleasant sort make me nauseous when I've just eaten. I'm only a woman..."

"A story about thieves!" suggested Germaine.

"Do you know the story of Cartouche?" [84] Madame Célestin asked. As one, the two Bondons added: "He was a wine-merchant from Courtille."

Tongues were beginning to wag. Lady Frances said: "No one else knows Monsieur le Comte's stories. Like him, they come from the other end of the world..."

"Let's see, son!"

"I'm ready, father. I only need to know whether you want to laugh..."

"Laughter does no harm after dinner," the Curé observed, sagely.

"A few gentle tears..." Madame Chaumeron began.

"Terrify us, Monsieur le Comte," Germaine pleaded.

Having taken two cups of coffee, Besnard the seducer said to his mother: "The fellow's a bore; I'd rather take a stroll than stay here for his sake."

"Well, Mesdames," Henri said, "at least I have your goodwill. While I was sitting at that table, around which so much wit and good taste was brought together with so much youth and beauty, I could not help thinking that out in Australia I often shared very different repasts. I left London nearly three years ago, with the intention of making something of a tour of the world. Our ship sprang a considerable leak while passing the isle of St. Helena, where we put into port.

"You have seen St. Helena!" the cry went up on every side.

"Twice, Mesdames," Henri replied.

"But Bonaparte wasn't yet there?"

"The first time, no. The second time, the Emperor was already installed in his poor hermitage at Longwood."

"And did you see him, Henri?" the Marquis asked.

"Yes, father."

Comte Henri de Belcamp rarely wasted words. His rapid glance assured him that these were no exception, since Robert Surrisy, Laurent Herbet and Férandeau were all listening. He continued, as if nothing had happened. "That first time, St. Helena still belonged to the East India Company. I was ill when I arrived there, and I was cared for in the house of Sir Edmund Balcomb, an English merchant, who lent that very house to Napoleon at a later date, while the residence of Longwood was being fitted out. The merchant's family was troubled; news from London brought by our ship had informed the unfortunate mother that Percy Balcomb, her son—a young man of whom she had entertained high hopes—had been convicted of a crime in England and deported to New South Wales.

"I had business in New South Wales, and in recognition of my debt to these good folk, I promised that I would do everything possible to see their son and ameliorate his situation. We set sail again and landed at Port Jackson after a long and difficult crossing.

"All of you are aware, Mesdames, that New South Wales is part of New Holland, or Australia, colonized by the English, which transports its convicts there. It is not exactly a paradise. The English administration does whatever it can to catch potential colonists in the various states of Europe; it advertises in newspapers like those pharmacists who invent patent medicines; it prints books that represent the soil and climate of that distant country in the brightest colors—but, in brief, I never met an Australian colonist who was content with his lot.

"By way of revenge, the former inhabitants of the county—the aborigines—are hunted through the woods as if they were wild beasts, under the pretext that they prowl around their forefathers' lands and that they steal an occasional sheep from the immense flocks that live off their own pasture.

"In theory, the convicts are treated with a certain humanity, but in practice they are subject to the most deplorably arbitrary law. I suppose my story will not seem to you to be cheerful thus far, but every story requires an introduction and my introduction is done.

"At midday, on a torrid day at the beginning of autumn, I was introduced into the summer-house of Sir Alexander Turkey, the Governor of Newcastle Penitentiary. I had letters of recommendation, which are indispensable in every country that is held by England. In Australia, as in London, a man who has not been properly introduced might as well be an Irishman or a dog. The Governor received me courteously, because my letters of credit were good, and I asked him for news of young Percy Balcomb, who was in his workshop.

" 'Oh, certainly,' he said. 'Percy Balcomb, indeed! A fellow who plays innocent and will end up badly! You see, Monsieur, I'd rather have a dozen self-confessed out-and-out rogues than one of those pale rascals that you adore in Europe and who are the heroes of your absurd bourgeois tragedies. Do you get my drift? I'd prefer a hundred murderers to one innocent criminal.'

" 'If, however, justice has been deceived...' I suggested.

"The Governor shrugged his shoulders gravely and asked me if I were personally interested in this Percy Balcomb, condemned by a jury for having withdrawn considerable sums on several different occasions from the business of one of his uncles, whose cashier he was. When I replied in the affirmative, he took up his great straw hat and asked me to follow him.

"He was a perfect gentleman. He opened his cigar-box for me, and asked me the names of the winners at the last Epsom races. The penitentiary, situated half a league from Newcastle, connected to the Governor's house by a ropewalk, which leads to a little isthmus beyond, giving passage to the Morris peninsula. The latter is a rectangular mound of earth on which no tree or blade of grass grows; there a little fortress has been built as a temporary lodging for recalcitrants.

"As we crossed the isthmus, the Governor pointed out two barriers and two sets of guardsmen, plus two ranks of kennels. There were two human garrisons and two garrisons of dogs to guard that tongue of sand. The fortress was situated at the center of the peninsula. All around it, along the beaches, there were sentry boxes and kennels. Out there, the dog is man's best friend, when the man is a jailer. All the dogs come from England, a free country. They are precious, especially for hunting the natives.

"We went into the fort, which appeared to me to be very well-organized, formed as it was of a double edifice, abundantly protected by four sets of guardsmen and enclosed by two sets of ramparts made of the trunks of gum-trees. I asked the Governor why the precautions were so luxurious, and he said: 'The rogues escape all the same!' Then, he asked a bare-legged black Corporal who was patrolling the area between the bastions for the prisoner Percy Balcomb. The Corporal's shirt, it is true, had large stripes on each of its ragged sleeves, and he also wore a policeman's hat. Percy Balcomb was led out: a handsome young man with a proud and intelligent face, whose features bore the imprint of a terrible despair. I have read furious diatribes in English books against the ball-and-chain that our convicts drag behind them; I do not defend those balls, but Percy Balcomb had manacles of steel around his bruised wrists and his neck was enclosed by an iron collar. My opinion is that the English diatribes are and always will be bad jokes.

"With his watch in his hand, the Governor very politely gave me permission to speak to the convict alone for five minutes. I told Percy Balcomb that I had come on his mother's behalf. His eyes filled with tears. I asked him if there was anything I could do for him. He shrugged his shoulders as if to accompany a negative and discouraged response, but in contradiction to that gesture he replied: 'I swear on the name of God that I am innocent, and I would rather die than suffer the tortures inflicted upon me. If you are a friend of my father and mother, I beg you to have a horse ready tonight in the thicket at the southern point of the ropewalk.'

" 'It will be done,' I replied, in a whisper. The Governor was already coming back; I added in a much louder voice: 'Courage and patience!.' Then, I touched his hand and left.

" 'I'll wager that he told you he was innocent,' the Governor said, taking me by the arm. 'A good chap would have asked you for a pound of tobacco and a bottle of rum. I can't stand these weak-kneed victims. Would you like to see the place where John Smith was overpowered by our dogs? They're fine beasts.'

" 'Does overpowered mean devoured?' I asked.

" 'Not at all–the blacks saved the carcass. Ah, damn me if John Smith wasn't a strapping lad. He was in the dungeon for having sworn... do you know anything about London's old hands?'

"I confessed my ignorance.

" 'Pity! It would have amused you to know that John Smith was the son-in-law and successor of the famous Thomas Paddock of Sharper's and, like him, adopted the name John Devil. The news will be published in the European papers, and some other old hand will take the name John Devil. There you are!'

"The last phrase was to indicate a place where the sand had been recently disturbed. It was John Devil's grave.

" 'He had succeeded in getting past the sentries and the two walls,' the Governor went on. 'He was only missing a set of wings to reach the coast or cross the causeway when the dogs brought him down. Naiu-Dweru, the Corporal in the shirt whose get-up we were admiring just now, smashed his head in just as his arms and legs were being eaten. Poor John! At least, that one never bored us with his innocence.'

"Such was the funeral oration of John Smith, old hand or hardened recidivist, one of the famous bearers of the nickname John Devil, so celebrated in the prisons of London.

"As we went back I examined much more attentively the elaborate and formidable defenses surrounding the establishment on the Morris peninsula. It was the first time I had seen Percy, and all the prisoners are liable to swear that they are innocent. I don't know why I had confidence in him, but it was absolute. It seemed to me impossible that his noble face could belong to a malefactor. Perhaps that sentiment had its ultimate origin in the gratitude and amity I retained for Balcomb of St. Helena, but it was already sharper and more profound than that. All my thoughts were focused on Percy; I was wholeheartedly committed to his cause. It would not be overstating the case to say that I loved him like a brother. That is the way I am made: my heart does not tarry.

"Even so, I almost regretted having promised to help poor Percy, because an escape that could not be carried through was inevitable death in that place.

"The Governor, delighted with the new interest I devoted to his barriers, his dogs and his soldiers, complacently explained to me the excellence of its theory, whose inventor he was. The dogs had already eaten three old hands for him, and it had only increased their appetite.

" 'Unless they can get hold of a balloon,' he concluded, 'my inmates are nailed down.'

"He left me in order to arrange for a consignment of recalcitrants to be taken to Norfolk Island the following day, one of whom was poor Percy Balcomb.

"At about nine o'clock that evening, I left for Newcastle. I had bought not one horse but two, fine strong animals. I headed across country in the opposite direction to the ropewalk. Then, once I was in that desert savannah, planted with dwarf myrtles that are known locally as tea-bushes, I promptly doubled back and made for the actual goal of my nocturnal expedition. I was in position by ten o'clock, 200 paces from the southern point of the ropewalk's enclosure, an equal distance from the shore. A little acacia wood served to hide me and my two horses. I was resigned to a long wait, for we were still a long way from the most propitious hour for an escape. In the black night, I could see the lights of the Morris peninsula shining, and when the wind was right, I could even hear the wild laughter of the black soldiers mingled with the barking of the dogs.

"I had seen those huge dogs, thin because they were systematically starved. It seemed that I could still see them, and measure their lean flanks. Would those wolves dine on human flesh tonight?

"The sky was laden with dark clouds. A warm and heavy breeze was blowing from the southeast. About eleven o'clock, the first lightning-flash split the horizon. The lights on the peninsula were already being extinguished.

"At midnight, there were no more lights. Dogs and men alike had fallen silent. Torrential rain began to fall, as abruptly as the opening of a tap, piercing the light foliage of the acacias and soaking me to the skin within the blink of an eye. At the same time, the darkness caught fire and thunderbursts rent the sky in every direction. The echoes persisted for a long time and silence was not restored, for as soon as the rumbling of the thunder died away in the distance the shouts of men, the howling of dogs, the call of a clarion and several shots resounded in the direction of the peninsula. I didn't see the muzzle-flashes of the guns; the rain enveloped me like a sheet.

"A mad impulse took hold of me, to hurl myself to the aid of the man who was alone against so many frightful perils. I would have given in to that impulse, which drew me with irresistible force, if the idea of duty had not restrained me. I had a position to maintain and a promise to keep. At the end of a few minutes, the distant noises coming from the peninsula died down, and were drowned by the closer noises of the tempest. The sea had been instantaneously whipped up, and its waves were breaking furiously. It was no longer a commonplace downpour but a waterspout that was descending upon us.

"The fort now seemed to be between me and the howling pack. The chase was continuing on the point of the peninsula most distant from the shore. Percy had not yet succumbed.

"Half an hour passed. Oh, how much more terrible silence can be than noise! I would have given blood to hear a human cry, a dog's bark–even a gunshot!

"That silence was the end. The hunters cease to urge the pack on, and the dogs no longer howl when the prey is dead. My two hands clenched upon my breast as if to suppress the beating of my heart.

"Suddenly, hoofbeats sounded dully on the sand. A troop of horsemen went past the acacia like a whirlwind and made for the beach, and I heard: 'He's killed the Corporal...! He's in the water...! There's 25 pounds for whoever gets hold of him!' Generous England has retained the practice of putting prices on men's heads.

"A moment later, there was a black line along the shore. A moment after that, a pack of dogs arrived from the isthmus and hurled themselves along the waterline.

"I leapt into the saddle, because as soon as the dogs had arrived on the scene, I was under threat myself. I spurred the horses, seeking to clarify the instinctive idea that had sprung into my mind. It was necessary, at all costs, to keep the rendez-vous point clear. I left the wood, holding one of my horses by the bridle, and galloped southwards in a straight line.

"The cordon of soldiers extended no more than 500 paces. I was soon beyond it. After dismounting, I tied my horses to the branches of a bush and ran towards the shore. I had four pistols in my belt, and I took two in my hands. I ran into the water, making a lot of noise, and immediately saw the black line moving some 50 paces away from me. I fired all four of my pistols one by one, as if shots were being exchanged. The line broke in several places; no more than a minute had passed when a crowd gathered at the very place where I had discharged my weapons, calling the dogs to get on the trail–but by then I was already on horseback, galloping back to the acacia wood.

"I had gambled on a chance so remote that it must seem absurd to any cool-headed man. The whole maneuver was calculated to give Percy the time to get ashore. In order that my ruse should succeed, it was necessary that Percy had been able to swim strongly through that frightful sea, and that he had arrived at precisely the right moment, ready to profit from a diversion that could not be prolonged. If he were late, the dogs would already be on my trail; the time remaining to us was measurable in seconds.

"I passed between the acacia wood and the shore, where no one was any longer to be seen, and I shouted with all the force of my lungs: 'Percy! Percy Balcomb!' Further caution seemed to me to be futile.

" 'Shhh!' murmured a voice very close to me, low and calm.

"I turned. There was someone in the saddle of the second horse.

" 'Is that you. Percy?' I asked, paralyzed by surprise.

" 'It's me, and may God thank you!'

"My arms opened instinctively. He pressed me to his bosom, and for an instant–at a time when instants were priceless–we remained in a tight embrace.

" 'Adieu!' he said to me, shivering at the first howls of the pack.

" 'Let's go,' I replied.

"And the two horses, immediately accelerating to full speed, rattled through the myrtle branches.

"Thus I became, in following the criminal by my own free will, a criminal myself. Why did I do it? I don't know. There are times when one is strangely drawn. The idea never entered my head to do otherwise. I had a heart full of joy, and I went into those unknown dangers as if to a fête..."

Comte Henri paused to draw breath. His mouth, so frank and so young, bore a dreamy smile–but beneath the lashes of his lowered eyelids his gaze darted rapidly around his audience. He saw Lady Frances disappearing as she turned on to the path leading down to the park. Her companion was Robert Sur-risy.

The enclosed garden presented a curious spectacle at that moment. The members of the audience were standing motionless at the places they had taken at the beginning of the story. With the exception of Robert and Lady Frances–whose absence had passed completely unnoticed–no one had budged.

Three-quarters of the interest of a story, it goes without saying, is in the personality of the teller. Certain well-endowed individuals know how to lend a supreme charm to the most trivial narration; everyone knows some sorcerous orator who has the masterful gift of moving or astonishing his audience as if he were playing them like a musical instrument, making them sad or making them laugh as he pleases, acting out his drama, changing scene with a glance, clearing his sky with a smile, bringing forth passion, gaiety and laughter by turns. Comte Henri was one of these fortunate people, and the fact that he himself was the hero of the adventure he was narrating added immeasurably to the savor of his tale. It was he who impassioned the audience, because it was he who brought the drama to life.

All the women were listening with profound attention–even Many-Apologies, who was suffering from the imprudent generosity with which she had overburdened her stomach. Madame Besnard, Madame Célestin, Madame Touchard, Madame and Mademoiselle Chaumeron were all ears. Germaine was pallid with pleasure. Jeanne was staring open-mouthed at the storyteller, coloring sometimes as she briefly looked away.

As for the men, the Marquis manifested the same naive avidity as Jeanne or Germaine; he loved and admired wholeheartedly. Férandeau was entertained, but he refreshed his pleasure from time to time by sipping from his glass at appropriate moments, as if by way of punctuation. Laurent appeared to be astonished; there seemed to be some resentment and mistrust in the glances he darted at Germaine and Jeanne by turns. The Deputies, Messieurs Morin du Reposoir and Potel were digesting their meal awake, but the Bondons had fallen asleep while digesting theirs.

When Comte Henri paused, the whole assembly breathed out loudly; then there was silence, save for the precisely matched masculine snoring of the married Bondon and the bachelor Bondon. There was nothing astonishing in the fact that the sleep of the former was tranquil; he had always been virtuous–but as for the second, one can only conclude that the indiscretions of his youth had been forgiven.

"Well, son," the old Marquis murmured, "one day or another, you'll tell me your entire history, won't you?"

"Whenever you wish, father."

The left-hand Bondon muttered in his sleep: "The two hunchbacks, 33!" And the right-hand Bondon: "My uncle's legs, 11!" They were both enthusiasts of the ingenious pleasures of the *jeu-de-l'oie* [85] and lotto [86] was equally dear to them. This time, however, their dreams came to a painful conclusion as Madame Célestin's fingers pinched them both–a punishment familiar to them. They opened they eyes without complaint, and twiddled their thumbs resignedly.

The young Comte continued his story.

"For three mortal hours, we heard the pack behind us. Our horses' hoof-beats were muffled by the rain-soaked sand, so we could keep track of their running. We had a dozen white policemen and a swarm of blacks on our heels. The storm, far from diminishing, grew even more violent; sometimes the light of the gigantic tropical lightning-bolts brought the entire horizon leaping to our eyes.

"We headed directly westwards to get out of the undergrowth that hindered our passage and into the eucalyptus forest. In the absence of starlight, the wind–which had been blowing from the south as we set off–was our only guide. We kept it on our left cheeks, thus exposing ourselves to the risk of doubling back on our course if the wind happened to change. We had not yet said anything to one another. We felt our strong and willing horses between our legs. We were certain of gaining ground, slowly but surely.

"As the first three hours ended, we came into a completely open space, and the storm blasted a hole in the clouds. Momentarily, we saw the firmament, and that was enough to confirm that we were heading in the right direction. Our brave horses set themselves to gallop across the favorable terrain and when we paused, having sustained that pace for a further three-quarters of an hour, there was total silence around us.

"We came to a halt. The rain had stopped. Our horses drank from pools of rainwater and browsed moist grass.

" 'Have you also reason to flee?' Percy asked me. When I replied in he negative, he urged me to return to Newcastle while there was still time.

" 'When I get back to St. Helena,' I told him, 'I want to be able to tell your mother that I have put you aboard a ship bound for Europe.'

" 'What have they done for you?' he murmured.

"It was not the time for relaxation. I remember that I replied: 'Soup and herbal tea. Let's go.'

"We reloaded our pistols on the move, and ate on the move as well, for there were provisions in the saddlebags. Our horses, returned to a moderate pace, gave no sign of fatigue until daybreak. First light showed us evidence of cultivation, or at least of attempts at cultivation, on the banks of a little stream leading towards some rather large buildings. It was a squatter's station. I knocked back the bolt on the stable door with a single kick and, in the presence of a frightened groom, I made an exchange between our two valiant mounts and the squatter's two best horses. The squatter got the best of it, but we had to have fresh mounts to cover 15 leagues that day.

"Have I told you how Percy and I got on together? We were very nearly the same age. From the morning of that first day, we were singing to one another at the top of our voices as we crossed the bleak desert of dirty sand. The pale, drawn young man of the peninsula had undergone a genuine change, and Sir Alexander Turkey would not have recognized him. He was as happy as I was–for I was gaiety itself in those days. Like me, he had traveled a great deal. Neither of us had the slightest doubt of the other, and we contemplated that impossible journey with smiling faces. I don't believe that we would have wanted to be anywhere other than where we were. We thought of ourselves as tourists traveling for the pleasure of it, discovering the interior of Australia into the bargain. There are immense expanses of unknown country there, perhaps destined one day to be called Belcamp Land or Balcombia.

"You will notice that our names also resembled one another; they had the same skeleton, if the grammarians are right to declare that the consonants are the bony frames of words.

"The truth is that we loved one another, like two brothers who had never been apart. I was certain of Percy Balcomb's innocence before he had told me his story. The astonishing frequency of judiciary errors on the part of our neighbors has the good side-effect that everyone convicted there retains some measure of the benefit of the doubt, but that was not why I came out in favor of Percy. I saw into his heart; I had far more faith in that noble soul than any tribunal to which he had been subject. A criminal, no matter how skillful an actor he may be, sometimes lets his mask slip, then displaying a providential stain, scar or furrow that is the mysterious but sure sign written by the hand of God, warning others to be on their guard. Percy had no such mask.

"A criminal may be shameless, able to laugh in the face of conscience and brave remorse in the artificial merriment of his carousing, but he cannot be calmly cheerful, partaking of the intimate joy that is born as soon as one awakes and brightens the sleep-wearied eye. Percy was cheerful. He woke up as joyously as a child. I wished that Percy's judges had consciences as good as his.

"As I speak to you now, Percy is free and rehabilitated, and more powerful than people of his age usually are. He is the head of one of the most prestigious business establishments in London, and the magistrates who sentenced him can no longer hold a candle to him. That proves little, but you shall see him soon, Mesdames, and will agree with me that in the very depths of a prison that frank knightly smile already spoke clearly of more than rehabilitation."

"We shall see him, my son?" the Marquis put in.

"He knows that I have come back to be with you," Henri replied, "And his last letter said: 'I shall take a week's vacation for the express purpose of embracing your father...' " He added, with a smile: "And perhaps you will be glad that I have praised the happy and honest character of his physiognomy, for we resemble one another very closely... not in the romantic fashion of being able to be mistaken for one another, but enough to astonish people who hardly know us, when we are seen separately. If Balcomb had fair hair, or I had brown hair like his, the similarity would be almost complete, and we should be able to rival the Messieurs Bondon de la Perrière."

He bowed to Madame Célestin–who, profoundly flattered, smiled as she contemplated the two pendants whose centerpiece she was.

"Is he married?" asked Mademoiselle–but the question, asked with the best of intentions, went unheard.

"For eight days," the young Comte continued, "we headed due west. We did not encounter a station every evening where we could exchange our horses, but Percy already had faith in his destiny. 'Life has its lucky streaks,' he said. 'As soon as I saw you back there, I thought: good fortune has arrived. Nothing will stop us; I can guarantee that. We shall fall into a bottomless abyss from which we shall emerge at the antipodes!'

"Luck did indeed seem to be guiding us by the hand; if there was a house in the desert, we headed straight for it, and its owner would say to us: 'Who showed you the way?'

"On the ninth day, we found a Sydney newspaper in the home of a squatter on the Rhode-Stream,[87] 80 leagues from Newcastle; the price on Percy's head was 100 guineas. That astonished us. Who could possibly have traveled any faster than us? The Rhode-Stream is a small tributary of the River Macquarie. Our squatter told us that the newspaper had been brought by a company of nomadic aborigines who had recently come down the Macquarie. We ate at his table and accepted his hospitality for the night, in order to give the blacks time to get further away. We exchanged our horses for the best two in his stable, paying ten guineas for the privilege, and went on our way.

"Those two horses would come to a terrible end!

"We had to choose between two courses: to cut across the entire breadth of Australia from southeast to northwest, across unknown territory, in order to reach Port Keats; or to turn southwards, avoiding the town of Bathurst, cross the Macquarie River and make for the Lachlan, which would put us on the Murray River heading for Adelaide. We settled on the latter alternative, and began our journey with our saddlebags completely replenished, our hearts light and a song on our lips.

"We thought that the wandering tribesmen would now be far behind us, but on the first day we saw columns of smoke ascending from the bush, white against the leaden sky. We urged our mounts forward. The tribesmen were on foot; we should make much faster progress. Such, indeed, was the case; we crossed the Macquarie 15 or 20 leagues from Bathurst without any anxiety and without seeing the slightest sign of a black man–but every morning, as we awoke, we could see smoke in the distance behind us, which seemed to be pursuing us. It became evident that the blacks were on our trail.

"We had our pistols and plenty of ammunition. While our horses were able to carry us, it would be possible to fight and perhaps to win–but we understood well enough that our pursuers were waiting for the precise moment when our horses would no longer be able to carry us.

"Percy's mount gave up the ghost five days after our departure from the Rhode-Stream station. In the previous 48 hours, we had traveled 30 leagues without seeing a single blade of grass. Percy got up on the rump of my horse, carrying his saddlebag, and my brave mare walked for two more days under that double load. We buried her when she died in her turn, and we continued on our way, burdened by our saddlebags. We thought that we were close to the Lachlan, where a good many stations were already established.

"The following day, towards nightfall, we stopped on the edge of a clump of pines, overwhelmed by hunger and fatigue. I chanced to turn around, and saw black dots standing out against the sandy plain. I pointed them out to Percy, who laughed as he said: 'This is our Austerlitz![88] Tomorrow, we fight. Let's find a good bed to sleep on.'

"There was half an hour of daylight left. We knew that we were running no risk by night, because they could not follow our trail once the Sun went down. To the south, we perceived a black line of gum trees, which told us that there was water nearby.

"We waited for dusk, picked up our saddlebags, in spite of our fatigue, and headed towards the forest. Two hours later we were beneath a vault three times as high as the tallest cathedral. We stopped at the foot of a giant eucalyptus whose glossy trunk was too broad to be embraced by six men.

" 'If we could only get into the crown of this monster,' Percy said, 'we could withstand a siege by all the blacks in Australia.'

"I took from my saddlebag a pair of steel gloves armed with talons, and a pair of spurs with their straps. I had bought these objects on my arrival in Sydney, with the idea of making a expedition into the interior. I buckled on the spurs first, then I put on the gloves. Three minutes later, I was astride the first branch, 90 feet above the ground. I threw my equipment down on to the sand, and Percy joined me.

"At the place where the major branches of the eucalyptus projected from the trunk, there were deep armpits, large enough for a man to lie down in at full stretch. We ate the last of our provisions and lay down placidly on mattresses made from our cloaks.

"As we awoke on the following day, we saw that the large circle that the shade of our gum-tree kept clear of vegetation was swarming with blacks. It was broad daylight; the tribesmen had followed our tracks. There were at least 200, including men, women and children. They had about 20 dogs, which were hairless, thin and unhealthy but as tall on their legs as wolves; their appearance indicated a terrible ferocity.

"The blacks saw us as soon as we leaned over our balconies to look at them curiously. They all began talking at once, and those who had bows took aim at us. An arrow embedded itself a few inches above my head but the danger was not great; the spreading branches provided all the cover we could wish. In any case, we were still more than 40 feet from the top of the tree, whose crown offered us a safe haven.

"My first task, on disembarking at Port Jackson, had been to study the indigenous language. I understood everything that the blacks were saying. They had come a long way, crossing the Blue Mountains to come after us. They were talking about money, using the English word. They were in the process of becoming civilized, since they already understood that it is acceptable to sell the blood of two human beings for a fistful of pounds sterling. They were promising one another that they would return to Sydney with our heads and buy 100 pounds' worth of brandy.

"Our heads, however–which probably seem to you, Mesdames, to be in considerable danger–were not so easy to cut off as all that. There was a complete blockade, which is a terrible thing for a destitute garrison to face in any country, but in this case the besiegers too were threatened by famine, and we had our firearms.

" 'I can see at least 30 strong men,' Percy said to me, having made a count of the tribe's combatants. How many shots can we fire with the powder in the flasks?'

" 'Twice as many,' I said, 'and there are 15 cartridges at the bottom of my saddlebag.

" 'That's two and a half times what we need,' Percy murmured. 'Are you a good shot, Henri?'

"The blacks had lit their fire and were dancing around it, celebrating in advance the brandy that would cost us so dear.

"In addition to the 30 warriors, the tribe comprised 20 old men, 50 or 60 children, about 40 women of various ages and a class of individuals unique to Australia, whom the English call 'cripples' or 'the infirm.' These were unfortunates who had one or more horribly withered limbs, while the remainder of their bodies remained perfectly healthy. On the other hand, there were others whose thick legs supported massive torsos, and whose arms attained extraordinary proportions. The English doctors have not yet determined the causes of these two afflictions–which the blacks, according to their own wisdom, attribute to the vengeance of airborne spirits.

"The infirm generally enjoy the same influence within their tribes that certain primitive countries of Europe afford to those other victims of supernatural punishment, madmen and idiots.

"I told Percy that I thought I could be sure of my shot in spite of our disadvantageous position–firing from directly overhead is the most difficult shot of all.

" 'That's good, Henri,' he said, with a forced smile, 'but would you have the heart to put down all those poor devils at the foot of the tree!'

" 'Indeed!' I said. 'I follow your thinking and I admire your humanity, Balcomb, but I have other things to do here than sell my skin to buy hard liquor for these brutes. I don't mind waiting for hunger to make me ravenous, but they won't set foot in this tree, I promise you that!'

" 'The Devil with your tree!' cried my companion, angrily. 'If it's necessary to fight these fellows hand-to-hand, I shan't be sentimental about it.'

"Two hatchet-blows resounding against the trunk cut short his speech. Eucalyptus wood is hard and very resistant. We thought at first that they were trying to fell the tree–an enterprise that would have required at least a week–but they were only cutting off large pieces of bark to form the roofs of their tents. This work lasted about an hour, after which their camp was established. A fire was lit beneath each individual tent. Dinner time came and they began cooking.

"There is no other country in the world whose terrain is so miserly with comestible products. Apart from kangaroos, whose numbers are constantly diminishing, wild dogs or dingoes, squirrels, opossums, a few species of monkeys, parakeets and rare water-birds, the endless forests of New Holland are devoid of game.[89] The ungenerous soil, covered everywhere by large or small myrtles, gives birth to not a single native legume. The bushes produce berries like bits of wood; the trees themselves–God's splendid generosity!–bear fruit like stones.

"Even so, our hopes of seeing our besiegers stricken by famine were cruelly deceived. Each fire, reduced to ardent embers, was covered with large and appetizing slices of meat that seemed to have been cut from a very large animal. The smoke from these grills drifted up to us and only served to sharpen our increasing hunger. The rogues had disinterred my horse, and all the steaks sizzling on the charcoal were my property.

"One of the infirm was directly beneath me. His household consisted of a woman with bristling hair and three children who climbed over him like lizards. His swollen arms were as thick as stovepipes, while his emaciated legs resembled two flails. His head was symmetrical, though, and he had the torso of an athlete. His share of my horse was five pieces, which he ate heartily, brutally throwing the bones to his wife and children; they gnawed them in their turn before throwing them to the lean dogs, whose bloodshot eyes were devouring the spitting embers beneath the dripping fat.

"It was the same in every tent. The man ate his fill, then gave the rest to his family, who yielded any surplus to their beasts.

"The meal was not made up entirely of horsemeat; that was combined with the produce of the hunt, which consisted of two dingoes reduced to skeletons, a dozen parakeets, a basket of little batrachians resembling our toads, several bowls of living earthworms, snakes and scorpions, and a rosary of magnificent spiders. These last delicacies were eaten raw, sometimes even alive, for we could see the long earthworms writhing in the mouths like animated macaroni. The women had none of that. Our infirm neighbor, a gastronome of the first rank, had for dessert an entire brochette of hairy caterpillars, while his wife watched him with the dead and hungry eyes of a she-wolf.

"After the meal, there was more dancing, then fighting. The most eager conflict was between two invalids for a mouthful of my horse. One of them, a cripple–I remember this horrible and comical detail–had his leg broken like a dry stick of wood. The morsel fell to the ground, where it was immediately devoured by famished dogs.

"These clowns took no notice at all of us, seeming to understand perfectly that they had only to wait. At about two o'clock in the afternoon, they sent a volley of arrows at us, and stretched out their feet in front of the fires to take a nap.

"Percy said: 'I'm hungry, and I'm going hunting.'

"He climbed up. I followed him from branch to branch, desirous of at least discovering the extent of our domain. As we arrived at the summit of the tree, which formed a platform above our neighbors–for chance had placed us in the oldest tree in the forest–an unexpected spectacle presented itself to our eyes. We were no more than 400 paces from the Lachlan, in whose rain-swollen bed the blackened water was flowing impetuously. The forest ran along its banks, at least a mile thick. A mile southwards, the Lachlan abruptly changed course, disappearing behind a hill. To the right of the elbow, the woodland had been cleared and tall buildings were visible, whose numerous chimneys were smoking.

"If we had kept going for half an hour longer the previous evening, we would have been saved! Saved from the blacks, at least–for the inhabitants of the station might also have thought it well worthwhile to earn 100 pounds.

"While I was looking at this dwelling-place, so close and yet so far away, a pistol-shot fired close to my ear almost sent me tumbling down from the top of the tree to the bottom. A cry of triumph from Percy followed the shot, while a diabolical clamor went up from the suddenly awakened camp.

"Percy had killed an opossum of the largest kind within its nest, in a hole in a thick branch. It must have weighed almost as much as a hare. There was no lack of dead wood around us. The opossum was dismembered with the aid of my hunting-knife, and was soon roasting in front of a fire lighted in the armpit of a green branch. It was our turn to dine, which we did with a healthy appetite– after which we repaired to our balcony to smoke our cigars.

"There was a terrible hullabaloo at the foot of the tree, which was attacked by axes on every side. The blacks were trying to notch the trunk to form a kind of ladder, which they undoubtedly intended to scale. In the midst of this disorder, a council was held, and our neighbor, the infirm caterpillar-eater, shouted at the top of his voice that if we were allowed to lie up for too long, we would lose our butter.

"The Australian aborigines call human fat butter, especially that around the kidneys. They are not cannibals–not many of them, at least–but they use this butter to anoint and rub on their bodies, in the belief that all the vigor of the dead person will thus pass into them, redoubling their own strength.

"The first attempt to scale the trunk was made that evening. A dozen men tried to climb up at the same time, clinging to the tree by means of cords and carrying long spears in their mouths–but we did not even need our pistols to repel that primitive attack; two wooden poles served us as lances, and we sent the assailants down much faster than they had come up. I think that if we had broken half a dozen heads, the others might have withdrawn, but the disgust those miserable creatures aroused in us was mingled with pity. For my part, I aimed my pistol 20 times without having the resolution to pull the trigger.

"We had time in hand. The recent rain had left pools of water in all the gum-tree's coverts, and we still had half the opossum for the next day. Night fell. We were on the point of taking to our beds again when a particular odor attracted our attention: the odor of green wood burning.

"I leaned over, and saw that the blacks were adopting a new strategy, and a powerful one. They had piled up dry wood around the trunk of the tree and were evidently trying to set fire to our refuge. For certain resinous trees, that would have been a matter of several hours; for others, as with our own oak-trees, it would have required several days, given the enormous girth of the trunk. The eucalyptus was probably somewhere between the two extremes; by my estimate, we had about 24 hours.

"There was no time for hesitation. We had to stop the fire spreading, no matter what the cost. Percy and I took aim simultaneously, and two of the blacks, shot in the skull from above, collapsed as if struck by lightning. The others disappeared in the blink of an eye, and a lament as long and mournful as the howl of a wild beast resounded from the deep shadows of the forest for more than an hour. At the end of this interval, the wives of the two dead men came in search of the bodies, which they dragged away by the hair, howling. Then the funereal hymn began again.

"But the fire did not die out. Little children came to throw armfuls of dead wood on it. We could not fire on little children.

"Towards midnight, I was able to see by leaning over that the bark of the tree was scarcely eaten away, but there was a subdued menace working away in the interior of the trunk. We could hear a sort of bellyache within that giant of the vegetable kingdom as its desiccated fibers were tortured; it was sweating out its agony.

"Sweating was the right word. The branch on which I was lodged became moist and sticky, while the trunk oozed great drops of gum like vast tears. Long sighs were emerging from fissures and strips of bark groaned as they detached themselves.

"Shortly before daybreak, there was a crackling in the very roots, and we felt our beds shaking. I shouted to the blacks: 'I'll kill the children if they come near.'

"The little ones fled. The men tried to force them to return to their work but the women defended the children. When dawn came, we saw female bodies lying on the sand.

"As midday approached, the trunk was burning strongly; the bark was aflame. We ate the rest of our opossum and then we discussed our predicament. There were only two alternatives: to allow ourselves to be grilled like cutlets or to attempt general carnage.

"We were looking at our pistols in a somber fashion, our hands gripping the butts firmly, when I suddenly saw Percy's eyes brighten. I followed the direction of his gaze, which was fixed on a major branch whose near-horizontal projection was more extensive than the height of one of our tall European poplars. On the branch, there was an opossum, doubtless the mate of the one we had killed the previous evening.

" 'We won't have time to eat that, Balcomb!' I said, laughing sardonically.

"He put his finger to his lips.

"My laughter froze and I shivered, because I had guessed what he was thinking. We both remained perfectly still.

"The opossum knew that it had nothing to fear from the people down below, who were 100 feet away. Because it did not see us move, it glided along the branch, as light and graceful as a bird. From the branch, it passed to the trunk, whose summit it attained with a bound. We watched its undulant tail while its muzzle disappeared into the hole that was its nest. We heard a little cry; then the charming animal came back down, this time nervous and anxious. It went around the trunk, looked up and down, let out a soft and plaintive cry, then took to its branch again, showing us the route to safety—us, who had killed its mate!

"As I said, I shivered. Lost hope that is reborn, contrary to all expectation, makes one tremble just like terror. The route that the opossum showed us was very narrow and very difficult–and one would certainly have to conclude that it was more suitable, as a matter of practicality, for a squirrel than a man. Even so, we both followed the little quadruped's retreat with avid attention, and when it leapt from the end of the branch into the neighboring tree, 50 feet from the trunk, we looked at one another. A plan of escape was coming into view. The odds against its success might have been a hundred to one against, but we were desperate.

"We had to wait for nightfall. From that moment on, all through the evening, our tree went through a series of incendiary phases. The majority of the roots burst, making a noise similar to musket-fire; the trunk was cleft in several different places, at various heights. It still remained firm at the base, but it was already dying; the withered foliage hung limply down around us. We could no longer see its thinned base, above which the place where the fire's effect stopped formed a kind of circular excrescence. We were certain nevertheless that the fire was making rapid progress, for the blacks were no longer taking the trouble to feed the flames. The trunk itself was now burning, like a profoundly penetrated log. The attentive faces of the blacks, ranged in a circle, were illuminated ruddily by the fire's reflections. They were waiting for the collapse, evidently expecting that it would happen soon.

"As dusk fell, the infirm, the women and the children withdrew to the shade of another tree, carrying their cooking-utensils. The tents were broken up and reassembled some distance away. The night darkened. There was a hissing sound and we saw an enormous shower of sparks emerge from the trunk at the impact of a log that one of the blacks had thrown. A joyful cry went up, and our enemies–men, women and children, reconciled by the approaching celebration–began an infernal dance around the fire.

"The moment had come. We exchanged a silent handshake and tightened our belts, where our loaded pistols were wedged. Each of us took a single glove and a spurred boot. We had had time during the final hours of daylight to engrave on our memories the shape of the branch that might serve us as a bridge. I, for one, would have been able to describe every curve and every knot, from its emergence from the trunk to the point at which its tip was lost among the branches of the other eucalyptus.

"One thing remained impossible to calculate, though, and that was the strength that the branch might possess at a distance of 40 or 50 feet from its attachment.

"Would it support the weight of a man? That was the question that the passage of the opossum could not possibly resolve. One certain fact was that it would be madness to burden it with the weight of two men at the same time. I climbed on to the branch alone.

"Complete darkness was now necessary; the light of the embers, masked by the swollen trunk, no longer reached us. I slid gently along the length of the branch, which remained inflexible beneath my weight for 30 feet or so. I advanced with infinite caution; the blacks had no suspicion of what was happening above them.

"Forty feet from the trunk, I felt the branch bend; a little more and I would find myself within the range of the firelight. The tree was a frightful thing to see; it was now hollowed out all around, and its thinned-out trunk was like a vault burning as red as a furnace. The blacks were throwing pieces of wood from a distance, which immediately burst into flame within that ardent brazier.

"One step further on, I felt the branch quiver, disengaging its tangled extremities from those of the higher branches. It made little noise, because the withered foliage was not yet dry. I was about six feet, horizontally, from a fairly thick branch of the neighboring tree; vertically, the distance was 12 or 15 feet.

"I hesitated, because the diameter of the trembling bridge that sustained me was diminishing with a rapid progression; I could already encircle it with my arms. On the other hand, to attempt a jump or even a sudden movement would immediately attract the attention of all the tribesmen. The branch, solid and flexible, bend gradually downwards, reducing the distance along both axes.

"I extended a foot into the neighboring tree without a single black head being raised.

"Balcomb and I had agreed a signal; I would imitate the feeble and plaintive cry of the opossum, and immediately afterwards would make my way to the trunk of the second tree. I would then be 40 paces beyond the last of the blacks, and the bulk of their company would be three times as far away, because the new camp had been set up on the far side of the tree.

"No black head turned in my direction as I made the opossum's call, but several became very still and as stiff as ebony statues. They were waiting for the call to be repeated. Everyone knows what exquisitely subtle senses humankind has in its savage state; I was under no illusion. The attention of my enemies had been awakened, and Balcomb's task would be even more difficult than mine.

"Five minutes later, my ears caught the almost-inaudible sound that my companion-in-adventure was making as he crawled along the branch. Those blacks who had set themselves on guard like dogs scenting prey did not turn in his direction any more than they had turned in mine–but it seemed to me that I saw their ears pricked beneath their bristling hair. The infirm individual whose tent had been nearest to our gum-tree before the fire was lit pronounced a few words in a low voice that I could not hear. Ten warriors rushed towards the camp, from which they took their spears and clubs. I saw them disappear into the forest at an oblique angle. Had they mistaken the nature of the sound? Were they going to scout around at a distance? The line that they were following was taking them further away from me.

"After their departure, the camp resumed its customary aspect: the men wallowing around the fire, the women occupied in the tents, the dogs prowling here and there. The dogs, in my view, were our most dangerous enemies.

"The branch that had served me as a bridge was bending little by little. I felt the one on which I was now set quiver, and I soon saw a dark form creeping towards me.

" 'A dozen of them have gone off I don't know where,' Balcomb said to me, as he arrived safe and sound. 'So many fewer to worry about. Let's take advantage of the opportunity.'

"I darted a last glance at the camp. Apparently, everything there was calm. If we had been dealing with Europeans, I would willingly have bet on the success of our hazardous project–but it was a matter of Australian savages, who were even finer bloodhounds than their starveling dogs. There seemed to me to be something menacing in the immobility of that infirm rogue, our former neighbor with the emaciated legs and elephantine arms,

"It was no time for hesitation. We buckled on our spurs, put on a glove each, took our knives in our other hands to give us a third point of support, and resolutely set about the most difficult part of our endeavor. Although much less stout than our first gum-tree, the one in which we now were had a large enough trunk to make a screen for us, and we were able to effect our descent in convoy.

"The operation itself was difficult in the extreme. Ordinarily, of course, one would embed the talon of a glove or a spur with a single sharp blow, but that was not an option. We had to make the steel bite by means of slow pressure, which necessitated powerful effort; in addition, as one foot remained unequipped, every movement threatened to turn our bodies around. In truth, we maintained our equilibrium by a miracle of will power. All went well, though; we had got more than halfway when Balcomb said: 'What's that on the sand underneath us, Henri?'

"I looked down, and saw dark objects that I would have taken for lumps of stone, clumps of moss or clods of earth if there had been a stone, a sprig of moss or a particle of earth for a hundred leagues around. I was chilled to the marrow of my bones, and if I have ever felt the full anguish of terror in my life, it was at that instant.

"Those dark masses were the ten blacks who had made a detour through the woods, and were waiting for us.

" 'They're bushes,' I said, however. 'Let's go on.' There are moments when the certainty of death in preferable to the prolongation of torture. The idea of climbing back up never entered my head.

"What would we have gained by going back up? Even in our most distant forests, it is perhaps as well to gain time, for there is always hope of rescue–but there, in spite of the proximity of a European station, the sand beneath us had undoubtedly never borne the imprint of a shod foot. There was no grass; the colonists had no business here.

"We would have gained two more nights and one more day of martyrdom, for the blacks would have put us to the proof of fire for a second time, and the miracle of the opossum would not have been repeated to appease the rebellion of our hard-pressed stomachs.

"It was necessary to wager everything we had, in desperation, to bring the game to an end. I went on ahead of Balcomb. Twenty feet above the ground, I held myself steady with the left hand, which wore the steel glove. I planted my knife in like manner to support my knee, and I took one of my pistols from my belt, cocking it with my teeth. When he heard the noise, Balcomb stopped.

" 'Hold hard, Percy,' I shouted to him, while I took aim as best I could at one of the black forms, 'Get ready to jump!'

"I fired. At the same moment, I felt a prick on my shoulder, another in the thigh and another in my back. Spears trembled all around me, embedded in the bark of the tree.

"The black at whom I had aimed jerked and fell back, flat on his belly. My bullet had found his heart. The others, as is their invariable custom–and I had counted on that–had already disappeared behind the neighboring trunks. The Australian savages, like the majority of North American redskins, give ground once there is a dead man beside them. They are always surprised by a battle.

"Balcomb and I reached the ground at almost exactly the same time. For the moment, I did not feel my wounds, and my exhilaration at having firm ground beneath my feet was so great that I imagined our enemies dispersing like seagulls taking flight. Not a soul was any longer visible around the fire: men, women, children and the infirm had disappeared as if by magic. I sat down to unbuckle my spur, which would have hindered my further movement; Balcomb did likewise. I had time to reload my pistol. Balcomb transferred his steel glove to his left hand, and we took up position with our backs to the tree.

"The funeral lament sounded some 50 paces away, under cover. At the moment when men began to intone that monotonous chant, an arrow drove into the bark of the eucalyptus between my right arm and my hip.

" 'Here they come!' I said, at the same time as Balcomb, who was watching the other direction.

"They were indeed coming; a hail of projectiles preceded them. They came from every side at once, with their dogs on leashes made from tree-bark; they were beating the dogs in order to enrage them. The impact of their attack ought to have wiped us out ten times over but, as I have said, there is a timidity in these poor creatures that exceeds their ferocity. Dogs–there were our enemies! The dogs were released ten paces away from us, while the blacks swung their spears and brandished their short clubs. Had it not been for our steel gloves, I believe those dogs would have brought us down, but we were men with lions' claws. We were wounded; we were bitten; I felt the fetid breath of the horrible animals on my face more than once–but we tore their tongues with the stabbing iron fingernails in our right hands, while the claws of the left were embedded in their throats.

"We killed five dogs and four men in that attack. The four men fell at a distance, shot by our pistols. I received two spear-wounds in the breast.

"We reloaded in haste. Percy was less grievously wounded than I. I was losing a good deal of blood and felt myself becoming weak. While packing my second pistol, I felt faint.

" 'My poor friend,' I said to Balcomb, 'I sense that I shall soon abandon you.'

"He looked at me. We were shadowed from the firelight, but he must have seen nevertheless how pale I was, for his arms drooped.

" 'I'd give the rest of my blood for a drop of water!' I murmured.

"Long funeral laments pierced the silence of the night. They came from further away this time. Our pistols had spread terror among the blacks.

"There was a bright flash of light–an immense splendor, I ought to be able to say, for I believed that it was the supreme dazzle of death. The entire roof of the forest lit up above our heads, showing us every minute detail of the branches, the powerful sinews that sustained the thousand delicacies of the great arches of foliage. The tree-trunks sprang out of the shadows like a tall, straight colonnade. I don't know whether it was the suddenness of the sensation or whether my eyesight had already lost the faculty of measuring objects, but the surrounding spaces seemed to me as vast as an unmeasurable horizon, and that somber cupola of vegetation, suddenly illuminated as if a Sun had slipped under its shade, appeared to me to be higher than the sky itself.

"It didn't last long. An almighty crack sundered the silence and the ground shook beneath the weight of the giant gum-tree, which was falling. We were surrounded by debris for a moment, because the tree had fallen towards us. It created a kind of shelter to the left and to the right of us; nothing was left clear but the ground situated directly in front of us, which had been shielded by the trunk against which our backs were resting.

"The night had already become blacker. While the light shone, I had darted a rapid glance at our surroundings, and I had perceived neither blacks nor dogs. I sat down on the sand. Balcomb tried to bandage my wounds, of which there were five.

"We had about a quarter of an hour's respite. The interval did not replenish any of my strength, because I had already lost a great deal of blood. I remember that the ferocity of my thirst left me incapable of clear thought—but I had a dream. One of the blacks, remarkable for the extravagance of the hair that fell upon his shoulders, back and breast to form a sort of beard-cloak, wore a bandolier of cord supporting a bottle. I saw that bottle incessantly, and I desired it madly. We had nicknamed him the lion because of his mane. When cries went up nearby to inform us of the renewal of the assault, I managed to stand up on my trembling legs and say to Balcomb: 'I shall kill the lion, to drink from his bottle.'

"The dogs, pricked by spear-thrusts, threw themselves upon us. I had no time to fire my pistols; I was bowled over by the first impact and I felt the horrible beasts begin to devour me. Balcomb's two pistols were discharged on my behalf and disencumbered me, leaving the corpses of two dogs across my body. He took one of my pistols from my hand, the other from my belt. I had not lost consciousness. I heard two more shots, and Balcomb said to me: 'Take it, Henri! Drink!'

"He had killed the lion. I lifted the bottle to my lips avidly; it was strong liquor. I quaffed a large draught and I got up, seized by a fit of passion. For three or four minutes, I was possessed of prodigious strength. With my glove on one hand and my knife in the other, I created a pool of blood all around me.

"Then, suddenly, I saw red. A club whirled above my head, seemingly on fire, describing a circle of sparks around me. I had no fear, and no hope; my moral insensibility was complete.

"Was I mad? Amid the noise of the fray—for the battle was still going on, and Balcomb was defending me like a demon—I heard hoofbeats and the sound of voices. They were speaking English. There was a volley of musket-fire. The man with the club lost his balance and choked me with his weight..."

At this point, Comte Henri paused, as if in spite of himself, and extended his hand to the old Marquis, who had drawn closer. "Father," he murmured, "At that moment, my only thought was of you, and there was a veil of tears over my eyes."

The old man threw his arms around his son's neck, and kissed him like a mother. "If you had been killed, son!" he murmured.

All around them there was a profound silence.

"Tell us the rest, quickly!" cried Germaine, whose large moist eyes were sparkling through her long eyelashes.

"I have little to add," the young Comte went on, "except that the consciousness of my madness took increasing hold of me. I couldn't bear to die insane—my father is a Frenchman and a soldier! Fear must have made me lose my reason... but I didn't remember being afraid.

"What to believe? A shadow passed before my half-closed eyes. Could it possibly have been anything but a dream? The shadow was an adorable young woman whose gentle and compassionate smile was displayed to me by torch-light...

"Torches? A young woman?

"This is the last vestige I can recover from the depths of my memory. I had closed my eyes. Two trembling arms lifted me up, while a voice—Balcomb's voice—called me by name. I opened my eyes again; Percy's lips were on my forehead, and I heard him say: 'He's still breathing!'

"To whom was he talking?

"I lost consciousness. I never saw Balcomb again in Australia...

"...The sunlight passed through the Indian muslin curtains. Parakeets and songbirds conversed in the lilac crowns that blocked the view from my half-open windows. A fresh breeze impregnated with perfumes fanned my feverish forehead.

"I was vaguely conscious of having already been in that place for several days.

"It was a rather large room, furnished with a certain austere elegance, whose white maple furniture was strongly suggestive of German propriety. The window looked out into a large garden whose young trees seemed like children by comparison with the screen of giant gum-trees obscuring the horizon. A mill-wheel was singing outside, and I heard the bellowing of cattle in the distance.

"Was it my dream, persisting in the submergence of my mind?

"I wasn't dead, because I was suffering. The wound in my breast sent pain shooting through me. I put my hand upon it, and felt a pain in my shoulder. That pain caused a movement that awakened a burning sensation in my back. My memories came back in a flood.

"The battle! Why was I not dead in the midst of devouring dogs and human beasts more ferocious still?

"I put out my hand to take a little bell that was beside me on the bedside table. I didn't have time. From the bosom of a cloud–I express it thus because that was how it seemed–from the bosom of a cloud of white muslin, a delicious smile emerged, like the ray of sunlight that suddenly breaks through an autumn mist, and a soft voice that made my heart vibrate like a lute said: 'Don't move. I'm here to care for you.' "

Comte Henri de Belcamp's last words had a strange effect on the crowd. The old Marquis smiled like an expert listener detecting a romantic adventure, while the majority of the audience-members–men and women alike–brought their chairs closer and redoubled their attention. Germaine blushed excitedly. Jeanne's eyes were lowered and her cheeks were mortally pale; it appeared that an excessively strong emotion was pressing upon her heart, and that she was on the point of becoming ill.

Comte Henri's gaze turned towards her while he paused.

"Well," said Monsieur de Belcamp. "Who was this angelic apparition?"

"Oh, Monsieur le Comte," Germaine put in, "don't leave us in suspense."

Henri smiled at her, and continued in a meditative tone: "It is for that which follows, Mesdames, that I began this story. The more-or-less curious journey across the Australian desert, and that vulgar battle of two well-armed men against a swarm of naked savages, would not have been worthy of any claim on your attention..."

"Bless me!" said Monsieur de Belcamp. "The rest must be very interesting, then!"

"I should like to ask Monsieur le Comte," Monsieur Morin du Reposoir–a keen hunter–put in at this point, "to what specific breed these barbarians' dogs belonged."

"Many apologies!" the Deputy's wife interrupted, severely. "Husband, you should not cut the thread of this fascinating narration for us!"

"There's a fine painting to be made," Férandeau said, "of those two men coming down while the rogues lie in wait for them below."

"The story! The story!" Germaine demanded, as petulant as curiosity itself.

Jeanne rested her charming head upon her hand.

"I had never heard the voice of that young woman before," Comte Henri went on, "and yet I had the sweet and consolatory feeling that one has in recognizing a much-loved voice after a long absence. The young woman was sitting in an easy-chair a few feet from my bed, placed in such a way that the sunlight streaming through the window left all of her face in shadow while illuminating by contrast the admirably pure lines of her profile. It was doubtless because of her position that I had not seen her right away, because my weak eyes had been dazzled by opening for the first time to the broad daylight of a sunny morning. I shut them again to shelter my injured eyesight in darkness, and that angelic profile was imprinted on the interior of my eyelids.

" 'Is Balcomb... dead?' I asked.

" 'Percy Balcomb,' a soft voice assured me, 'embarked yesterday on a Dutch ship and is now sailing towards the United States of America.'

" 'Was it you who saved him, miss?'

" 'It was my father... but he has not yet given you permission to talk. My father is a doctor, and he has strongly recommended rest. To spare you the fatigue of interrogating me, I shall try to tell you everything that you might wish to know...'

"She got up. Her figure was even more graceful than her face. She set aside the wave of muslin that had previously encircled her like a cloud. It was the smooth covering that had protected her from draughts during the night, while she had watched over me. Once disencumbered of that light drapery, she appeared to me as she was: a simple girl from Germany, the country where I had spent the best and happiest years of my life.

" 'You must be as good as you are beautiful...' I murmured, in German.

"She blushed with pleasure.

" 'Yes, yes,' she said, smiling, 'we understand English very well, and we always recognize our own accent of the Thuringian forest... we'll chat in German later. Your wounds aren't dangerous in themselves, but the blacks dip the points of their spears in the sap of some plant or other, which inflames the flesh and makes it swell up. If not for that, you would already be healed. You're in the house of Doctor Schwartz of Saalfeld, who ruined himself back home by building a hospital and came here to rebuild his fortune. I am his daughter. I'm 17 years old, and my name is Georgelle. I have a fiancé who will soon come to join us, who is the same age as you and resembles you... my father believed that it was you...

" 'Now, I shall tell you how it came about that help reached you in that remote place where you were about to die–and that will be all; after that, you must rest...

" 'Since daybreak, we had perceived a great column of smoke in the woodland towards the northwest. Our herdsmen and station-workers all said that it was the blacks. My father had no desire to disturb the blacks–who are, in his view, the legitimate owners of the land. Even so, towards dusk, our cattleman told us that he had heard a gunshot in the woods, near the big bend in the river. There are unfortunates who are more to be feared than the blacks–bushrangers, as escaped convicts are called hereabouts. My father decided that a reconnaissance party should be sent out as far as the bend in the river. I mounted my horse along with the others, because I never leave my father, and we set out as night closed in. As we approached the tall trees, we thought we heard a gunshot in the distance. The wind that was blowing in our faces carried the odor of burning. We had five well-armed men, and my father gave the order to press forward. At the bend of the river, the wind carried vague noises to us, then four shots distinctly spaced. We took to the gallop; by then we were under the tall trees and nothing impeded our progress.

" 'Unfortunately, the noises suddenly died down completely. We lost time in searching for the right direction, and we mistakenly crossed the river. We were on the far bank when a sudden flash lit up the forest a thousand yards away from us, followed almost immediately afterwards by the sound of a battle. We had to return to the ford. My father and his steward, with two domestics, galloped forward at full tilt and fired a volley that scattered the blacks, who will not normally stand up to an attack. You had lost consciousness at the foot of the tree and your friend Balcomb was weeping, saying that you were dead... but here you are, 17 days after your arrival in our house. You have had a fever because of the poison. Mr. Balcomb did not want to leave until he had received my father's assurance that you were safe. That was four days ago. You no longer have any fever or delirium–only an extreme weakness that is still capable of killing you if you are imprudent. You would be wise to sleep now.'

"She drew away from my bed and sat down by the window with a book.

"The effort I had made to follow her story left me exhausted. I had not the least desire to interrogate her. To tell the truth, I felt neither the slightest need nor the slightest suffering. I was unable to express the troubled twilight of my mind. I understood what she had said, but the events which might have led to my demise were still misted with confusion and I tried hard to recover my own memories of them, which were trying to reassert themselves.

"The head of the young woman that I had seen leaning over me as I lay in agony... that must have been Georgelle.

"How can one explain the subtle workings of the mind at times when it is numb and enfeebled, shocked by the least effort? One idea fixed itself in my mind: she had said, 'I have a fiancé who resembles you...'

"That struck me in such a way as to put everything else in shadow. It struck me because I, too, had a fiancée who resembled her...

"No one here knows me, not even my beloved father. It is necessary that I explain myself, like a living and talking enigma who reveals his own inner being. My adventurous and studious youth had, I suppose, included a few passionate intrigues, but I had never fallen in love–and there was within me an ardent and immense need to fall in love.

"Who, then, was this fiancée that I had without knowing it, and who resembled Georgelle? What name can be attached to this false and mistaken memory, which discovered in the past one of those mirages that normally belong exclusively to the future?

"I had no fiancée. I had not yet encountered any woman who had inspired in me the thought of endless affection and an indissoluble union. How could Georgelle be the reflection of a flame that had not been lit–the echo of a sound that I had not heard?

"I beg you to follow me through the story of this bizarre and charming sentiment–which will be, I feel, the story of my entire life–whose birth took place in that bed of agony, in the darkness of my mind and the inertia of my heart. God spoke to me, I assure you; there was something there that was not only incomprehensible but supernatural.

"For this was not a feverish folly. I was calm; it was not a return of my delirium. Through the veiled spaces in which my poor intelligence was swimming, I followed my course tranquilly, and I smiled with welcoming pleasure at the lie my memory provided.

"I had a fiancée who resembled Georgelle, as Georgelle had a fiancé who resembled me. Without that, Georgelle and I might have loved one another. That was it. We were separated by two loves: a barrier that was unbreakable but as transparent as a crystal rampart. Our hearts were close enough to touch, but there was an abyss between them.

"Although I would have had difficulty, at that moment, in following the conversation of a child, I wandered tirelessly, with a sure spirit, in the labyrinth of these subtleties. I understood my incomprehensible romance; I said to myself: here is the strange mystery of the brotherhood of souls: my fiancée and I; she and her fiancé; we are but a single couple..."

"And what happened next, son?" asked the old Marquis, not without a certain impatience.

"Oh, I beg you, let him speak!" murmured Jeanne's soft voice. She was as white and as beautiful as a lily. There were pearls of sweat across her forehead, from temple to temple, at the fringe of her hair.

"Let him speak! Let him speak!" Germaine repeated, enthusiastically. "For myself, I understand all this!"

"I liked the savages better," Férandeau murmured. Then, speaking to Laurent, he added: "Do you fancy playing a game of billiards, old chap?"

Laurent declined with a brusque gesture.

"Nothing happened, father," Comte Henri replied, seemingly having fallen prey to some extraordinary emotion. "Because a dream is nothing, according to common sense... and yet, it's because of that dream that I have seen my fatherland again and am at this moment close to you.

"I went to sleep without losing sight of the objects that surrounded me–or, rather, the dream that I had gave me a distinct perception of those objects. There was a kind of reality in it. I was lying on my bed, with my head turned towards the window, and I saw the leaves quivering in the breeze, throwing their little mobile shadows on the curtains. I breathed the perfume of flowers. Georgelle was reading.

"Georgelle had black hair. I had only previously encountered one woman's face that had the same serene gentleness and the same charm, a naive reflection of angelic youth. Her eyes were black too, bathed in the beautiful languor of virginity. She put down her book and looked at me soulfully. I got up and I went to place myself at her knee.

" 'Is she dead?' I asked her.

"I was talking about the one she resembled. She shook her head, smiling meditatively.

" 'Why have I forgotten her?' I asked, again.

"Her lips never moved, and yet I heard her voice saying to me: 'She is not yet born for you.'

" 'Then what is this inside me, Georgelle?'

" 'It is a memory of the future...'

"The meaning of these words seemed as precise and as simple to me as those of an ordinary conversation. I accepted their nonsense and I said to myself: *That's true; I'm remembering the future.* 'And him?' I murmured.

" 'I've never seen him,' she replied, her smile entirely impregnated with firm certainty, 'but I'm waiting for him. He will come to me as you shall go to her.'

"She closed her book. She put her hands on my shoulders while my elbows were on her knees. We looked into one another's souls.

" 'I see him,' she said to me, eventually, in a voice so low that I could scarcely hear it. 'I see him through you.'

"I made no reply, but my entire being swelled up with an inexpressible charm. I, too, could see her–the other, my fiancée–in her and through her: the same beauty, more transparent, and somehow possessed of an even greater attractiveness. The image was reflected in those same eyes, which were no longer black but tinted with the azure of the heavens... the same smile, which seemed to murmur my name within a kiss...

"There was a man sitting by my bed when I woke up; Georgelle was no longer in my room. The man was a German of mature years, with friendly, intelligent and respectable features. A pronounced family resemblance informed me that this was Georgelle's father. When I opened my eyes, he took my pulse.

" 'Let's see, let's see,' he said. 'All is well. You've come back from a great distance, my dear fellow, and I was a long way ahead when I assured your friend Balcomb that you were out of danger. The poison used by those unfortunate aborigines is not very powerful, but you absorbed it through five wounds. You can eat a little if you have an appetite... and I shall permit you to chat with my poor Georgelle.'

"The last words were pronounced in that sad and tender tone which, in the mouth of a father, is a confession of mortal dread or profound pain. My gaze questioned him. He lowered his eyes and his voice sank to a whisper. 'Has she spoken to you about her fiancé?'

" 'Yes,' I replied. I added nothing further, because I saw a tear trembling in the corner of his eye.

" 'My dear guest,' he went on, his voice becoming firmer, 'with respect to any other subject, her intelligence is clear and lively, her mind precise, her good sense exquisite...' He stopped. His lip quivered as he added: 'Have you guessed?'

" 'Did it go bad?' I murmured–for I had indeed guessed.

" 'From the world's viewpoint,' Monsieur Schwartz continued, 'it's not entirely madness. It's sufficient to accept the fact as real and to make believe to strangers, for example, that we're expecting a young man from Germany who is my daughter's fiancé, to make it impossible for the most piercing gaze to penetrate the secret of her malady–but from the medical point of view, no doubt is possible; it's a case of mental illness.'

"There was a cold sensation in my veins, and my head was aching.

" 'Madness is not a contagious disease,' I thought, aloud.

" 'Has she also told you that you resemble her fiancé?' Monsieur Schwartz asked me, hesitantly.

"I don't know how to describe the gaze that he directed at me as he asked me that question.

" 'She did indeed tell me that,' I replied.

"He was about to say something else, but turned his eyes away and remained silent for a while. 'When you are better acquainted with that refined heart,' he continued, eventually, 'when you come to appreciate the exquisite loyalty of that soul...' He paused again, before continuing, brusquely: 'She is all I have, Monsieur. I've lost her mother. If I knew of a man who had the power to cure her, I would give that man everything: my fortune and my blood.'

"There was a slight noise at the door. Georgelle came back in. She seemed happy; she was very excited.

" 'I've just had some news,' she said, throwing her arms around her father's neck.

"Monsieur Schwartz pressed her to his heart and asked, softly: 'What news, my dear child?'

" 'He has landed at Sydney,' Georgelle replied. 'It will not be long before we see him.'

"The poor father turned his head away and lifted his eyes to Heaven.

"I was left alone. While Monsieur Schwartz had been talking to me, I had been afraid; a sharp doubt had slipped into me. I had asked myself the question: *Am I not also mad?*

"My own symptoms had only existed for a few hours, but they were the same. My mental condition was exactly similar to that of the unfortunate and charming Georgelle.

"Of all the punishments God can inflict, madness seems to me the most cruel. I took refuge, anxiously, in the hope that my own symptoms were a relic of my fever carried over into my healthy state, my convalescence hardly having begun. I racked my brains to discover differences between myself and Georgelle, but the more effort I made the more it seemed to me that the similarity was complete. Georgelle was mad, because she had created in her imagination an entity–a fiancé–who resembled me. How could I not be mad, since I too had created an entity–a fiancée–who resembled Georgelle?

"One singular thing is that even as my reason–for I had my reason, whatever you may think–affirmed these logical conclusions, hauling me in consequence before the tribunal of my conscience, accused of madness, I became calmer and my terror faded. I was soon astonished that I had been afraid.

"There was another way to analyze these questions. I seized it avidly, and I think that all madmen should seize it likewise. What difference is there between the madman and the sane, in the opinion of the madman, but the abuse of the most powerful reason? The madman believes himself sane, and believes in consequence that those who accuse him of madness are mad. I told myself, taking a middle course that would absolve the one without condemning the other, that Monsieur Schwartz was mistaken. He did not understand his daughter. The natural conclusion was that, since Georgelle was not mad, I was not mad either.

"And I plunged back into the depths of my dream, with incomparable delight. I made an ardent and brilliant poem of it. I built a temple to my idol and I worshipped her at its altar.

"I did not call her Georgelle. I did not give her a name.

"Georgelle came back, accompanying the valet who brought me a light meal. When we were left alone, I said: 'I dreamed about you.'

" 'I know,' she replied. 'I went to sleep on my book, because of the many sleepless nights I had passed by your side. You came to kneel in front of me, and you said: *I have seen him...*'

"I was stupefied. 'And who brought you the news about which you spoke to your father?' I asked.

" 'Prayer... when I pray hard, I see him.'

"My sleep that night was long, peaceful and restorative. The following morning, Monsieur Schwartz came to visit me, and said: 'Out of 17 nights, Georgelle spent 11 by your side. She believes that she loves his phantom in you. What does it matter how one loves? I think that you would be able to heal her by marrying her.' When I made no reply, he added: 'My family is respectable; I am a doctor of medicine; in two years, I shall be a rich man; I will give you everything, keeping nothing for myself but my diploma.'

" 'Monsieur Schwartz,' I told him, 'you have saved my life and I love your daughter like a sister. Consult her; whatever she decides, I am ready.'

"He embraced me, and I heard him murmur: 'Your friend Balcomb told me what you had done for him... but for that I would never have dared...' He added: 'Be generous to the end. You alone can obtain her consent.'

"I did as he asked. A few minutes later, holding Georgelle's hand between mine, I asked her if she wanted to be my wife. She looked at me in stupefaction and withdrew her hand. Then, smiling suddenly and offering me her forehead to kiss, she murmured: 'My father thinks I'm mad. I understand, and I thank you: you are better than me.'

"From that moment on, she lavished a sister's caresses upon me.

"Monsieur Schwartz listened in tears to the account I gave him of that scene. The excitement was too much for my enfeebled condition. In the middle of the night, I suffered a bout of fever, after which I passed into a doze. I saw Georgelle at the head of my bed. She said: 'Look to the coast of France.'

"Of all the countries in Europe, France is probably the one of which I have seen the least, for the joyful and laborious years of my youth were spent in Scotland, Germany and Italy. Even so, I have never been able to hear the name of France without passion stirring in my heart. I looked to the coast of France, to repeat my poor Georgelle's expression. I saw a tranquil river running through a happy valley and bathing its bordering meadows, like the fringe of a paradise of crops, flower-beds and shady woodlands. There was a chateau overlooking the valley. I saw an old man. That was you, my beloved father; you were holding Georgelle's hand. Georgelle called me with a smile; your appearance was displayed before me, saying: 'Come to us; you will be happy with us.' "

"Well, son," said the old Marquis, trying to laugh–for he was surprised this time, and ashamed of his emotion–"these clouds into which you have taken us are worth more than those in the air, that's for sure. We'll look out for your Georgelle..."

"Was that Georgelle, then?" murmured Germaine.

Jeanne, who was braver than Germaine, would not have dared ask that question, but she held her breath as she waited for the reply.

Comte Henri's eyes were lowered. After a pause, he replied slowly: "No, it was not Georgelle." Then, his tone changed abruptly. "Mesdames," he went on, "I stayed in Doctor Schwartz's house for three weeks. Several days before my departure, I conceived a whim to revisit the place where Balcomb and I had come so close to finding a grave. For the first time, the doctor allowed me to mount a horse. He wanted to come with me; Georgelle completed the party. We sat down on the giant trunk of the eucalyptus, which was lying full length on the sand. There were bones, already going white, all around us. At the moment when I finished the story of our aerial captivity, pointing to the very branch whose shoulder had served me as a bed, Georgelle touched my arm and said: 'He's there!'

"Monsieur Schwartz squeezed my other arm with a sad smile.

" 'He's there!' Georgelle repeated, getting to her feet. 'He's going into the house. Come and welcome him, father.'

"We had to do as she asked, because she was mounting up and whipping her horse. Halfway along the route we met a valet who called out as soon as he saw us: 'There's a stranger!'

"Doctor Schwartz looked at me, stupefied.

"We went back into the house; a traveler was waiting in the parlor. Monsieur Schwartz remained in the doorway, motionless. The traveler was my age, my height, and carried himself like me. Georgelle went towards him, and took him by the hand to lead him to her father. There was some mysterious harmony between them, I swear it, for the stranger's astonishment equalled and surpassed our own.

" 'You don't know me, Mein Herr,' he said. 'I'm from Germany, and I'm your cousin. My father, Leopold Reibar of Leipzig, died a ruined man. As he lay dying, he told me to go to you. I'm strong and courageous. I can work for my living.'

"Georgelle threw herself upon her father's neck and kissed him, saying: 'I'm not mad. I've never been mad. Tell him you are welcome: no more, no less. It is necessary that he should be here, like Jacob in the house of Laban,[90] and that he shall win his wife... as you shall win your wife, Henri,' she added, enveloping me with a radiant smile."

Comte Henri fell silent. Robert, who had slipped back into the audience, whispered in Laurent's ear; the latter rose to follow him to one side. Germaine and Jeanne thus found themselves sitting next to one another; their eyes met and then were lowered. Germaine was very pink and Jeanne was pale.

Lady Frances was sitting in the last row of chairs, half-hidden by a lilac-bush.

Férandeau clapped his hands upon the plump shoulders of the two Bondons and cried: "Who's for a game of *vingt-quatre*?" [91]

The two Bondons, waking up with a start, looked around, flabbergasted.

"Let's see, son," said the laughing Marquis. "I like your German demoiselle and even her cousin from Leipzig. Here's a denouement: they are married, those two? But you? At the risk of committing a great indiscretion, I ask you, in the name of these ladies, which of them will be obliged to win you?" Bowing all around, he added: "For the prophecy of the dream is definite. It is I who have the duty of presenting my son's mystical fiancée to him. Now, all the ladies that I have presented to Monsieur le Comte are gathered here: my good Suzanne, my lovely Jeanne, my elfin Germaine, Mademoiselle Chaumeron. The stage is set..."

"Except for Lady Elphinstone," Férandeau objected.

The Marquis started, and said: "How could I have neglected the queen of our gathering for so long? Where are you, beautiful lady?" He offered his arm to Frances, gallantly, as he added: "Gentlemen of the orchestra, to your instruments if you please; milady will deign to offer me her hand for the first quadrille."

As had been his invariable habit since arriving at the chateau, Henri played escort to Suzanne Temple. They left the enclosed garden first to take the beautiful avenue of lime-trees that led back to the house.

"Miss Temple," Henri asked, "did you notice anything in my story?"

"Is it a romance?" Suzanne murmured.

"It is a history–which contains, like all histories, a certain amount of romance. I told it for you, Miss Temple."

"For me?" Suzanne repeated, astonished.

"You do not know, Madame, how much you owe to me already, nor how much you will owe me in future," the young Comte said in a low voice, as Pierre opened the double doors of the drawing-room in front of them. "Richard

Thompson may soon have need of a refuge... my father and everyone else here are now expecting a guest called Percy Balcomb, whose portrait you will have recognized."

"Richard has never been a convict, like this Percy Balcomb!" Suzanne said.

"My history is even more of a prediction than a story, Miss Temple," Henri replied, softly. "I can do a great deal, but perhaps not enough to prevent the errors of human justice."

He bowed. Frances and the Marquis de Belcamp were just coming in. Through the window, various groups could be seen crossing the lawn. Henri's rapid but piercing glance made out Robert and Laurent in conversation to one side of the gateway in the hedge. Robert seemed to be speaking heatedly to Laurent, who was listening to him with lowered head and furrowed brow, his face pale. Comte Henri smiled.

In Miremont, everyone danced–even Many-Apologies and Aunt Touchard. The two Bondons had taken the trouble to learn an entire speech on the subject of dancing. Every Sunday, they recited in unison, at the moment when the orchestra struck up: "Dancing was known to the ancients as a pleasant and salutary exercise..."

The orchestra comprised a harpsichord contemporary with the youth of Mozart and a violin. The harpsichord had almost lost its voice, but the violin made noise enough for both of them. The violinists were Férandeau, who played anything that was requested; the left-hand Bondon, hammered into whose fingers and head was something he called his quadrille; and the pretentiously awkward Don Juan Besnard, who was capable of anything–even playing pizzicato. like Paganini.

The harpsichord had formerly devolved to Madame Célestin alone, but the arrival of Suzanne, who was a genuine musician, had thrown her back into the shadow. Férandeau behaved impeccably in Suzanne's vicinity; it was as if there were a magical circle around her that suppressed the recklessness of David's pupil. As soon as Miss Temple came on the scene, Férandeau became as docile as a lamb. He had a genuinely well-developed artistic instinct, and with the exception of historical painting, of which he had an odd notion, he could have done all sorts of things. His voice was good and well-pitched; Suzanne loved to hear him sing.

The Bondon garniture had three ways of working. When she was part of the orchestra, Madame Célestin, seated at the harpsichord, had Florian and his violin on one side and her husband on the other, who beat time badly. When the garniture danced, Madame Célestin divided herself into two equal parts; *l'été* belonged to the right-hand Bondon and *la poule* to the left-hand one, the *pasto-urelle* to the legitimate Bondon and the *chassé-croix*, to the trivial Bondon.[92] Finally, when Madame Célestin, taking a brave decision, waltzed with Don Juan

Besnard, her two melancholy Bondons sat down on either side of her empty chair and kept watch, with equal fidelity, over a folded pocket handkerchief.

Férandeau and Susan were the orchestra. Robert came in with Laurent, and both headed for the smile-filled corner where Jeanne was sitting between Germaine and her aunt. Invitations were offered. Monsieur Potel had obtained the hand of Many-Apologies. Don Juan Besnard, returned to the fold, solicited that of Mademoiselle. Meanwhile, the two Bondons stood guard upon their common treasure.

"Doctor!" cried the old Marquis to his son, who was leaning meditatively against the marble fireplace. "A consultation, if you please? Milady would like our lovely little Jeanne to make up a four. Is Jeanne allowed to dance?"

"We are already fatigued..." the aunt began.

"A single quadrille, in order not to refuse milady," Henri cut in. "And I shall dance with Mademoiselle Jeanne."

He took the young woman's cold and trembling hand. Robert and Laurent exchanged glances. Germaine did not want to dance.

The violin and the harpsichord attacked the quadrille. During the first three figures, Robert and Laurent watched Henri's face and expression vainly from their standpoint in a window-recess. He scarcely exchanged a few words with Jeanne, whose steps he guided and supported with serious solicitude.

At the end of the third figure, Comte Henri said in a low voice: "The one to whom I gave the name of Georgelle was called Jeanne, like you."

Jeanne's hand, which had warmed up again in his, became as cold as marble.

At the commencement of the fourth figure, Comte Henri added: "I did not tell the whole of my dream." She raised her eyes to look at him. He murmured: "In my dream, I saved from fire and water the one I would love for all my life..." She was so pale that he stretched out his arm to support her–but she smiled. As he led her back to her place, he did not say another word.

Immediately afterwards, he went to sit down next to Lady Elphinstone.

"Are you content with me?" she asked him.

"You're an enchantress," the young Comte replied. His gaze was still fixed on Jeanne in spite of himself. "Is he already in love with you?"

"Judge for yourself. In four hours, he'll carry me off."

"Carry you off?" Henri repeated, unable to stop himself smiling.

Lady Frances showed all of her beautiful white teeth, favoring him with her most joyful smile.

"Could he possibly leave me here," she said, "when he returns to Paris to study the law?"

"That's reasonable," the young Comte replied. "And will you be glad to follow him?"

"Are you asking me that question seriously, Henri?"

"That which concerns my best friend will always be serious for me, Sarah."

She hesitated, no longer smiling. "Oh well," she said, after a pause, "I left Paris against my will, obediently; I shall be happy to return to Paris."

"Because our dream is of Paris?"

"Perhaps."

"Then, my dear and beautiful Sarah, since that is your caprice, instead of your chateau in the fields, you shall have your house in the city... and it may be that you shall soon serve me as well in the city as in the fields."

Frances was radiant. "Make up a four with me," she said. "I'll dance with Monsieur Surrisy."

Henri went to offer his hand to Germaine, who immediately left her place to follow him.

No one, in the Marquis de Belcamp's pleasant drawing-room, had any idea of the strange and terrible drama whose threads were being positioned here and there, like the web of a spider that works in silence and seems at first to be fixing its attachments haphazardly. In the midst of that bourgeois atmosphere, among all those ridiculous petty country folk, on that Dead Sea on which the microscopic passions of the village had previously been scarcely able to float, a wind was hovering, saving its breath and already filling its lungs to exhale a mortal tempest.

At the end of the quadrille, Madame Célestin resumed what appeared to be her situation, saying: "The two little ones have had their heads turned."

"Thank God there are still people in Miremont who know how to conduct themselves," Mademoiselle replied.

The left-hand Bondon ventured to pinch her bottom in the greatest secrecy, but the sympathetic sundial's other pointer was obliged to make a parallel gesture, and his hand pinched emptiness. Madame Célestin regathered her flock with a severe expression, shrugged her shoulders, and concluded: "There are those who are pretty and those who aren't." She had a reputation for repartee, but legend has no record of Miremont ever being colonized by the Athenians.

"You're a rude woman, Madame!" exclaimed the eldest Chaumeron, bristling.

"You're a shameless one, Mademoiselle!" riposted Madame Célestin, between her two fearful corals.

"I'm a plain speaker," the stormy voice of Papa Chaumeron thundered, at that moment. "I don't mince my words: Monsieur le Marquis, we have never been better entertained than here today!"

Robert took Laurent outside. There were only the two of them on the lawn. Night was falling.

"Germaine is just like Jeanne," Laurent said, stuttering with anger. "If you won't be my witness, I'll get Férandeau."

Robert seized both his hands and squeezed them hard.

"You will not fight that man!" he said, between clenched teeth.

"Will it be you who'll get in my way?" cried Laurent.

"Yes," Robert replied, coldly. "It will be me, even if it comes to that..." He stopped, and went pale in his turn.

"Even if it comes to that!" Jeanne's brother repeated.

"He has saved your sister's life," Robert said, slowly.

"We could have done that as well as him!"

"He's the son of the Marquis de Belcamp."

"What does that matter to me?"

"Listen brother—for we are brothers, not only by virtue of friendship or my love for your sister, but by virtue of the destiny that makes us children of the same misfortune. Neither one of us has a father's name to wear... your mother has been assassinated, my father perished by the dagger..." He clasped Laurent to his breast and held him hard. "Brother! My brother!" he repeated for a second time, "I have this to say to you in conclusion: Even if it is necessary to use violence to prevent you from fighting Comte Henri de Belcamp, I will do it; on that road, between you and him, you shall find me, sword in hand!"

It was nine o'clock in the evening. The Marquis de Belcamp was climbing back up the hill with Suzanne Temple on his arm, after having accompanied his guests as far as the bridge by the mill.

"I'm not asking you to reveal your secret, my dear," he was saying, in a paternal tone, "but your sadness must be very profound to resist this joyful wind that has blown over our pastures for some days... since the arrival of our Henri, by Heaven—why not say it? Henri is charming to you. For a moment I thought... but I'm obliged to make you a confession, my pretty Suzanne—if I were 40 years younger and a woman, that boy would drive me crazy!"

"You're a fortunate father," Suzanne murmured, with a melancholy and gentle smile.

"And that Lady Frances! She doesn't have the same accent as you, Suzanne. Did you notice how she conducted herself in church? Doesn't it strike you that Lady Frances and Henri would make the most handsome couple that it would ever be possible to see?"

"No," Miss Temple replied. "I never thought about that."

"And our little Jeanne, Suzanne? Have you thought about that?"

"That one deserves to be happy!" the young Englishwoman said, in a low voice. "She's an angelic child."

"Of course, of course... but it wouldn't be such a sad fate to marry Comte Henri de Belcamp... the cock ennobles the hen, you know? There's Robert, you'll tell me? Can't he pay court to Germaine? Yes, but Laurent... Devil take it! We have half a dozen little Chaumerons growing up, without mentioning Mademoiselle the eldest, who stopped growing a long time ago... it would be a capital thing if Henri were to find his wife here. I've got it into my head that it's the only way I have to clip his wings."

"Lady Frances has an adorable little child," said Suzanne, timidly.

"It's amazing how you notice children, my dear. You'd make an admirable young mother. I've never seen milady's child but everything she has is adorable! Believe me, it wouldn't be painless to abandon her to Henri. There's the age, though—is she 20? And would it be proper? The Elphinstone family is particularly well-regarded... but a widow, with a child... Hold on, I think you're right: Germaine is a jewel of a girl, but Jeanne would make a Comtesse a million times better than all the Comtesses in the Faubourg Saint-Germain... have you discovered something? Women have microscopes for eyes..."

"The story of Georgelle..." Suzanne began.

The Marquis let go of her arm and put his hands together admiringly.

"Didn't that carry us away!" he said. "What imagination! What spirit! What heart! There must be truth in it, falsehood, invention, reality... everything, in sum. What is it, Pierre?"

They were on the esplanade and the manservant came up to them, cap in hand. "There's someone in Monsieur le Marquis' room," he said.

"Someone? Who?"

"Monsieur Robert's mother... she's already been there quite a while... before the guests left. She didn't want to come into the drawing-room, and she said that Monsieur le Marquis was expecting her, so I put her in your room."

The Marquis became suddenly concerned.

"You did the right thing, Pierre. I'd forgotten." He took Suzanne's hand to lift it to his lips. "I hope you sleep well, my dear, and dream pleasantly."

Suzanne's hand closed on his, and held on as he moved to withdraw. "One more word," she said. "I'm worried about my father."

"I promise you that we shall go to Paris this week, my girl, and we shall invade my good friend's retreat in spite of all his defenses. *Good night, dear child of mine.*" [93]

The old Marquis went slowly up the steep staircase that led to his apartment.

"Well, Madeleine, my old friend," he said, as he pushed open the door to his room. "Is there news? Why have you come looking for me so late?"

Robert's mother, who was called Madame Surrisy in the neighborhood, was kneeling down in prayer, her hands supported by a chair. At the sound of Monsieur de Belcamp's voice, she hastily got to her feet and stood up straight. She was wearing a peasant costume but there was something in her bearing that was not at all rustic, more suggestive of the cloister. For the moment, though, the hood that ordinarily shielded her face and gave her the appearance of a nun had been thrust back to expose the thick tresses of grey hair that still topped her forehead.

She appeared to be about 50 years old, but suffering had marked her features deeply. It was evident, however, that she must once have been beautiful. There was pride in the regular lines of her face, but the fire had gone out of her eyes and her invariable expression was one of dull resignation.

"Old friend indeed, Armand," she murmured. Then, collecting herself with a bittersweet smile, she added: "I would have come earlier if today had not been Sunday and if I had not been afraid of disrupting your pleasure."

"Have I ever refused to see you, Madeleine?"

"No, never. You have been good to us, Armand; it's thanks to you that I can give bread to the general's son, who thinks he lives on the little that his poor old mother has. His poor old mother has nothing to give him—neither bread by day nor a pillow by night. We owe everything to you, Monsieur de Belcamp; we breathe your air and we eat your money. You owe us nothing, though..." She paused, then added in a low voice: "At least, you don't owe us any more than that..."

The Marquis took her hand. It was rough and wrinkled, because Robert's mother worked from dawn till dusk.

Ordinarily, when a woman like Madeleine talks in this manner to a man like the Marquis of Belcamp, once can read a threat in the woman's eye and hatred or dread in the eye of the man—but there was none of that in this case. Madeleine was sincere in her gratitude, despite the hint of bitterness implicit in her words. The noble and handsome face of the Marquis expressed nothing but affectionate concern, mingled with compassion.

"I shall do more, Madeleine, if you wish," he said, softly. "I have not forgotten the days of yesteryear, and I love your son Robert with all my heart."

The peasant woman blushed and lowered her eyes.

"While he had his sword," she said, responding to a reproach that certainly had not been addressed to her, "we accepted no charity from anyone." Then, she raised her voice. "No, Monsieur de Belcamp, you've done enough for us. If you did more, no matter how little, it would be too much, for the boy would ask himself whence that assistance came. He knows very little about money, but I think he knows well enough what a servant's savings might be. I've come to you for something more important than that. It might be a long story, Armand; have you time to hear me out?"

"If it might be to your benefit, my good Madeleine, we have all night before us."

"It might be to my benefit, for you will give me your advice, and perhaps your help—but before I begin, I must ask you for your word as a gentleman to keep it secret."

"What! It must be very serious, Madeleine," said the Marquis, smiling. He brought two armchairs forward.

"It's serious," the peasant woman said, as she took the seat that the Marquis offered her, while he sat down in the other. "I shall not speak unless I have your formal promise."

"So be it, Madeleine. You have kept more than one painful secret yourself, generously and without any promise. Whatever you tell me will remain between us; I give you my word of honor."

"Thank you, Monsieur le Marquis." Madeleine's voice was firm. There was a sort of emphasis, so to speak, in the very simplicity of her speech. She collected herself for a moment; then, slowly lifting her eyes towards Monsieur de Belcamp, she began: "I am your old friend, but a friend so humble that I ought to thank you, Armand, for continuing to employ that word, which is a memory of your youth and my childhood. You have often told me that the Surrisys once lived as gentlefolk, a long time ago. I believe that certain families are ill-fated, and I fear for my son, who will doubtless be a perpetual loser in the battles of life, as I have been. At 20, he has already seen his career broken, and that was neither his first nor his greatest misfortune. He is happy, though; he marches through life with his head held high and his gaze fixed on the future. When he surprises me weeping sometimes, he sings and he says to me: 'Mother, our name wants to say smile...'

"Good luck brightens, while misfortune is like the night; from that comes the strange circumstance that binds certain people together throughout their lives. I know you but you do not know me. Your very misfortunes, which are great, always left you so far above me that I saw you incessantly, while from your viewpoint I remained perennially lost within my shadow. You know some facts of my history, but you don't know the whole history of my heart. When I left this country for the first time, when I came to rejoin you in London in 1790, my hope was to be your wife..."

"Nonsense!" exclaimed the Marquis. "My good Madeleine!"

"I had taken seriously," the peasant woman continued, unsmilingly, "the vague promises made to a child some years previously. I had the ambition, and was perhaps in love. My illusions soon died, however. I bore no jealousy towards that young woman, so beautiful, who became the Marquise de Belcamp, and I did my best for a long time to protect her against herself."

"That's true, Madeleine," the Marquis put in, emotionally. "And never since then–never, even though you have seen everything that I know by hearsay; even though you have been the merciful witness of those saturnalias which, after so many years, seem to me to be a dream–have you voiced any denunciation with respect to me, or any betrayal with respect to the world."

"While I was in your house, Armand, as paid companion or servant," Madeleine continued, "I was noticed by a Irish nobleman."

"The General!" said Monsieur de Belcamp. "Are you going to tell me things that I know as well as you, my dear?"

"I told you at the start that you know nothing, Monsieur le Marquis, and it is absolutely necessary today that you should know my life page by page. When I was forced to leave your house because I was about to become a mother, I had been legally married for six months. Does that astonish you? You understand, then that what I am telling you is not superfluous."

"But why, then, does Robert not have his father's name?"

"Because he does not have the right."

"And how can he not have the right, if his mother was legally married?"

A few pearls of sweat were visible beneath Madeleine's white hair.

"Maurice O'Brien was neither a General nor rich then," the peasant woman went on. "He wanted to keep our marriage secret in order that it should not impede his promotion. I was obedient to the extent of accepting the appearance of shame, even with respect to those I loved. To you, as to everyone else, Armand, I was an unmarried mother. I remember that I always carried my marriage certificate on my person, and that I pressed it to my heart whenever I felt my face becoming red.

"O'Brien left for Germany, where the Emperor of Austria had offered him an advantageous position; he left us in London, assuring me that he would soon rejoin us. I lived alone with my little Robert. O'Brien's letters brought joy into our solitude. Those letters always spoke of a reunion in the near future.

"While I was afflicted by an illness, I took in the wife of an Irishman who had followed Maurice to help me. She couldn't read. One day, she gave me a letter from her husband so that I could read it to her. It was during the Italian campaign. Peggy's husband, after speaking of battles and the adventures of the campaign, mentioned Maurice, giving him the title of Colonel. I didn't know that he had attained that rank.

"I called my little Robert, who was playing downstairs, to give him the good news–but by the time he had climbed the staircase, he found his mother in a faint. I had continued the letter. It said–every word is engraved on my memory–'In a month, we shall be in our winter quarters beyond Izonso, going back towards Trieste. There, we shall be in the land of milk and honey. The Colonel has found an Austrian countess who is as rich as a gold mine. We shall be at the wedding.'

"I did not wait for the following day to depart. That same day, I took the stage-coach to Plymouth, where several ships were taking in freight for Venice. A month afterwards, I was in Trieste, despite contrary winds and French cruisers.

"Who knows what would have happened if I had been able to take my son with me? O'Brien was good; but I had already had great difficulty meeting the cost of my journey.

"You are mistaken, Armand, if you think you know the truth of my interview with the father of my child. It was one of those scenes that are not at all obvious. I went to seek him out at the chateau of the Countess von Loëve, six leagues from Trieste; he was to be married on the next day but one. His fiancée was a very beautiful woman of 23, Henrietta Boehm, the widow of Count von Loëve, the richest landowner in Germany after the Princes of Liechtenstein.

"Maurice was crushed by the sight of me. I appeared to him as the spectre of a conscience that he believed he had killed. He was a man of iron, but be collapsed into a chair like a woman. I saw his entire body tremble, I saw sweat inundate his brow. I did not say anything. He took my hands and wept.

"The first thing I said was: 'Our little Robert has grown well...'

"He went to his writing-desk and opened it. My heart was constricted, because I thought he was going to offer me money–but I had guessed wrongly. He took out a pistol and put the barrel to his head. The detonator did not fire. I had time to drag myself towards him on my tottering legs before he had loaded his second pistol. I clung to his arms. He looked down at me madly.

" 'You are my wife,' he said, in a staccato voice. 'I love you... yes, I love you, and I love our child. But I'm ambitious. I've had a dazzling dream. I'm only 30 years old. After my marriage, Archduke Charles will make me a General; it's promised. In ten years, I shall be a Field Marshal. You are the awakening from that dream, and I shall kill myself!'

"He made an effort to escape from my grip.

"I loved him. I have loved him all my life. I am here with you now, Monsieur de Belcamp, because I still adore his memory.

"I had on my person–as always–my poor marriage certificate. I took it out and tore it up.

"He fell to his knees before me.

" 'Promise me that you will live, Madeleine!' he cried.

" 'Mothers do not have the right to die,' I replied.

"I returned to London. He married. He became a General. He would have been one anyway. I raised my Robert as best I could. His father's money was anathema to me. To pay for his education, I worked as a servant.

"When my son was old enough to be a soldier, I came back here–long before you, Monsieur de Belcamp. On March 16, 1812, a man crossed the threshold of my house and asked for Madame Surrisy. I recognized him at first glance, but he did not know me. My hair had gone white on the night following my visit to the Chateau von Loëve; I had been old at 25. The man was General O'Brien. When I said to him, 'That's me,' he closed the door and held me in his arms for a long time.

" 'Madeleine,' he said to me, 'I have risked my liberty to enter France and come to you. The world has probably judged you as severely as it has judged me, for you had not the right to sacrifice the name of your son for me. I have committed a crime and you have been its accomplice. I love you for that, Madeleine, and I admire you. To me, you are devotion itself, which closed the eyes of conscience; you are the only woman that I could ever love; you are my wife and the mother of my son. I am a widower and I have come to return to you all that I have taken: my name, my title and my fortune.'

"He lifted me up–a poor, white-haired old woman, whose face was so profoundly hollowed out by tears. He was still young. I thought him handsome and brilliant.

"Henrietta Boehm, on her death, had left him a great part of her immense fortune.

"He was right, Monsieur de Belcamp. The world had included both of us in the same severe judgment. In the depths of my conscience, I could not consider myself worthy to be recompensed thus. I accepted for my son, but in accepting, I retained a doubt and a fear.

"My Robert had been in the Russian campaign. He was a prisoner of war in Breslau. The General wanted him to be at the marriage–whose celebration would have taken place, but for that, as soon as we arrived in Germany. We waited for Robert in Prague, which would henceforth be our place of residence. All the land that Henrietta Boehm, Countess von Loëve, had left the General was in Bohemia. Your brigand, as you call my poor Robert, had become the heir apparent of an annual income exceeding two million florins.

"The University of Prague was then one of the most turbulent in Germany. In 1820, the students had held an armed assembly on the Moldau to receive the

Deputies of the affiliates of Milan, and General O'Brien, who was then the Commandant at Hradshin, had charged them at the head of a Croat regiment. In consequence, the mysterious Society of the Rosy Cross had sworn an oath of eternal vengeance against his name.

"Three Counts Boehm were studying at the University of Prague. Their family had challenged the will made by the Countess von Loëve in favor of the General but lost the case.

"On the evening of the day when my son was due to arrive from Breslau—which was also the day fixed for our solemn marriage, to be celebrated at the city chapel with the Emperor's permission–General Maurice O'Brien was found dead in his bed.

"Robert Surrisy, who arrived happy and joyful, found his mother in tears beside his father's coffin..."

Madeleine paused, and the old Marquis de Belcamp, who was listening intently, murmured: "That's a strange story!"

"Did you ever hear talk in England," the peasant woman asked, suddenly, "of an evildoer called John Devil?"

"Often," the old man replied, "but the bandit was executed at Tyburn long before the time of which you speak."

"He was there, though," Madeleine continued. "Or there was, at least, someone there who used the name John Devil and who came from London. In the criminal inquiry that was held, the mistress of one of the Count Boehms declared that, having come before the appointed hour to play a trick on her lover, she had hidden herself in a wardrobe. From there, she had heard a young man, little more than a child, named George Palmer, demanding 250,000 florins from the Counts as a fee for services rendered. During the discussion, the young man had said: 'It's a very cheap price to pay for a revenue of five millions, French money.' One of the Counts had raised the question of whether they could be certain of the hand that would do the deed, and the young man replied: 'John Devil.' "

"And this John Devil was the assassin?" the Marquis asked.

"That remains a mystery. George Palmer was never found. The young woman was imprisoned for false testimony, and the three Counts were acquitted."

"What weapon did he use to carry out the assassination?"

"No weapon was used. The body had no other trace of violence than a very slight mark on the throat. The judge decided that the General had succumbed to a fit of apoplexy."

"But that is not your opinion?"

"I am certain of the opposite. I am sure of having heard the assassin's voice three times: once on the evening of the murder; once on the night of the murder; once during the night which extended from yesterday, Saturday, to to-day, Sunday."

"Last night!" cried the Marquis, half-rising from his chair.

"The first time, it was at the door of Saint Vitus's Church in Prague, going out of evening service. There were two young men behind me, dressed as University students. One said to the other: 'Make your decision–in 48 hours the marriage will have taken place, and it will be too late.' I turned around, not because I attached any prophetic or threatening meaning to the words, but firstly because the voice–which was gentle, sonorous and virile at the same time–was so striking, and secondly because any bride-to-be, even a white-haired one, takes an interest in the word marriage. The night was dark. The young men appeared to me as a living mass within which I could not distinguish any faces.

"The second time was the following day, an hour after midnight. My room and the General's were separated by a small dressing-room where an old Hungarian Sergeant who served as his valet was bedded down. I was just going to sleep when I heard someone talking. The words that reached my ear entered into my dream, and I saw my husband surrounded by assassins, who were saying to him: '*To you, Maurice O'Brien, from the Rosicrucians of Prague*!' There was only one voice, in reality, which said that: the voice I had heard on the steps of Saint Vitus's.

"The dream did not wake me up. I did not wake from my sleep until the cries of the servants who had found the General already cold between his sheets. The old Sergeant was drunk, sleeping profoundly. There was no trace of forced entry on the doors or the widows. On the dead man's bedside table was a folded parchment bearing the actual words that the voice had pronounced: *To you, Maurice O'Brien, from the Rosicrucians of Prague*! The words were traced in charcoal, beneath a sketchy design representing a rose and a cross.

"The third time... I have your word, Monsieur de Belcamp, so I tell you without hesitation that the Supreme Council of the Knights of the Deliverance met in my house last night."

"What!" cried the Marquis de Belcamp, leaping out of his chair. "That devil Robert..."

"I'm not talking about Robert, Armand," Madeleine interrupted, with the calm hauteur that, at certain moments, made her a great lady in spite of her costume. "I only repeat that my house was chosen for a meeting-place, and that persons of very great importance gathered there."

"You overheard their plotting, Madeleine?"

"It would be useless to question me on that subject, Armand. I know nothing, except that certain secret associations are, at their outset, as noble and grand as chivalry, calm as religion, valiant as love of the Fatherland or the passion for liberty. But all mystery creates darkness, and all darkness calls to malefactors. Crime sometimes takes the opportunity to hide in those shadows. It was not political vengeance that killed Maurice O'Brien; it was cupidity. The mortal blow was purchased.

"The students of Bohemia would not have had 250,000 florins to give to the assassin. The Knights of the Rosy Cross would not have added theft to the murder and stolen from the dead man's own room the marriage-contract bearing a donation in favor of Robert, recognizing his legitimacy. Neither one nor the other, finally, would have contrived the disappearance of a poor child who was not yet 15 years old, and who was abducted from the guardianship of the Imperial and Royal house of Reichstadt, where she was being educated: Sarah O'Brien, Countess Loëve, only daughter and sole heir of the late Henrietta Boehm, my noble and opulent rival.

"It was not the Rosicrucians who inherited our property in Bohemia; the Rosicrucians did not come into possession of the immense domains that were the patrimony of the young Countess Sarah in Tyrol, Vienna, in the crownland of Goritz [94] and in Istria, which would enrich 20 princely families! If the Rosicrucians had wealth like that, they could raise armies and fight pitched battles against the Emperor of Austria! No, there was a murder, a kidnapping and a theft; the murders, kidnappers and thieves have hidden the triple crime under the adventurous mantle of those knights errant who come out of darkness to conquer new worlds. They, who do not exist in the eyes of the law, are like the common dead, who may be accused, outraged and killed without defense.

"I received in my house last night nine heroic devotees and one bandit soul, for it was in my house, last night, that I heard the voice of the General's assassin for the third time."

"So," said Monsieur de Belcamp, "these conspirators you call the Knights of the Deliverance are connected to the Rosicrucians of Germany?"

"It is possible," Madeleine replied. "Certain ideas are not national; they envelop the whole world like a net."

"Do you share these ideas?"

"I am a widow and a mother. On the one hand, there is the memory of my beloved Maurice, who fought against them; on the other, the thought of my son, who would die for them."

"And what do you want from me, since you have obtained my unwitting oath and sworn me to silence?"

"You are rich and I am poor; you are powerful and I am weak. The oath that I extracted from you was useless; don't regret it. You have never been a traitor... and by this time, those who came to my house have been beyond your reach for a long time. I will tell you everything I know, in order that you will be able to help me discover the murderer of Maurice O'Brien. If I knew much more, I wouldn't need you.

"First, this is what has happened. The day before yesterday, at five o'clock in the evening, a man that I didn't know came to find Robert and touched his hand. My son made a sign and went out. He and the man remained together for a quarter of an hour, after which the man got back on his horse. Robert said to me: 'Mother, you must sleep in my bed tonight; I need the downstairs room.'

"Mothers know everything, even when their consent has not been obtained. I guessed immediately why Robert needed my room. On several previous occasions, good men from hereabouts and the surrounding neighborhood–old soldiers and young madmen–had met there to talk about the past and the future. That annoyed me, Armand, not only because of the danger that such meetings always attract but because the poor house in which we live in is yours, and you would have been able to say to me: 'Was it for that, Madeleine, that I–a faithful friend of the King–have given you a shelter?' "

"I would indeed have said that, my old friend," the Marquis said softly, "if they were not so weak and the King so strong."

A word rose to Madeleine's lips, but she lowered her eyes silently. Then she went on: "I let it happen, because of the poor pride that makes me hide my misery. In order to say to my son: 'don't do that,' it would also have been necessary to say we owe the roof over our heads to charity... At nine o'clock, I went up to my upstairs room, believing that it was a meeting like all the others–but before lying down in Robert's bed, I happened to look out of the window and I saw the glitter of a rifle-barrel at the edge of the water."

"They are already armed!" Monsieur de Belcamp exclaimed.

"I swear on my Christian faith, Armand, there is nothing in this to alarm you. It concerns a distant project... strange...and which might have incalculable results. But among the faithful devotees of this mysterious Church, no one dreams of employing force here in France. You'll know soon enough why there were rifles outside, that night. At that moment, I was still totally ignorant, and I was afraid, because I saw armed men posted behind the elders in our garden and shadows moving on the edge of the forest.

"Anxiety kept me up. A little after midnight, hoofbeats sounded on the path along the riverbank; words were exchanged at the door of the house, which opened. I had recognized Robert's voice. Ten minutes afterwards, another noise, another arrival and a similar exchange. Eight horsemen presented themselves thus, plus an old man who was carried in a sedan chair. The tenth arrival was a woman. It was then after midnight. Something that seemed peculiar was that Robert and the armed men remained outside.

"Between midnight and one o'clock, yet more hoofbeats sounded. It was the eleventh arrival, and the last. He spoke in English, and there was an icy chill in my veins. I heard the voice of the steps of Saint Vitus's, in Prague, and the voice of the General's bedroom: the voice that had said 'In 48 hours, the marriage will have taken place, and it will be too late'–words that had undoubtedly killed the last hesitations of those who were still making the purchase; and the voice that had pronounced the words calculated to deflect suspicion: *'To you, Maurice O'Brien, from the Rosicrucians of Prague!'* "

"Could you be perfectly sure after such a long lapse of time?" the old Marquis put in.

"After a thousand years!" cried Madeleine, with extraordinary force. "After a thousand years, if human existence could last so long, I would wager my hope of salvation on a single word pronounced by that man! That voice, once it has been briefly heard, remains in the ear and the memory as if it were a mark graven in the most durable metal. I have told you; it does not resemble others; I shall distinguish its tone in the innumerable crowd assembled for the last judgment, and I shall say to God, if God does not know everything: 'That man's conscience is red with blood!' "

She paused, and then continued pensively: "A voice softer than a woman's song and, at the same time, so masculine that it seems like vibrating steel. I am certain that man is great even in his crime. I hate him–oh, how I hate him–but I fear him and I would not dare to send my Robert to face him...

"My first impulse, when the sound of that voice struck my ear, was to hurl myself out of the room and to call for help. It required all my strength to contain myself. I had lost consciousness of the place where I was and the circumstances surrounding me. My memories, violently evoked, revived the past. I was abruptly transported to that monumental house in the ancient city of Prague; close at hand, I saw again the room where Maurice yielded up his last sigh under the pressure of a criminal hand. It seemed to me that my cries would wake the servants and surprise the assassin *in flagrante delicto*.

"But what could I say? And who were the people to whom I would be crying for help? There were armed men there. Again, I saw the reflection lost in the shadows. These men had sworn, like the others, on the cross and on the dagger, to put traitors to death.

"What treason is there, higher, more manifest, more mortal than that of the initiate who makes his house a refuge of mysteries, and opens a way by which a profane eye may look into its interior? The traitor who would be accused, convicted and punished within the same minute would be Robert, my poor child.

"And even if I had been able to introduce myself into that circle with impunity, what could I say? O'Brien had always been the terrible and ever ready enemy of these affiliations. His entire military career, in Italy as in Germany, had been directed against the adored idol of these temples. What voice, among them, would be raised against the murder of O'Brien, even if my affirmation could have been proven?

"I had no proof. Even the tribunal commissioned to investigate Maurice O'Brien's death had declared the crime chimerical and given the murderer the name of apoplexy!

"You know that house of yours, Armand. You know that Robert's room is connected to the room below by a fixed ladder that descends into the alcove. I had no desire to know these men's secrets. Their secrets were of scant importance to me and I shall hasten to forget what I know of them; but the one who was for me no more than a voice–the trafficker in human blood who had sold the life of his fellow man for 250,000 florins–I had to see, finally, face-to-face.

"There are other tribunals than those of mundane judges, and God's justice sometimes waits for human effort. I wanted to see the assassin, at least to know his features as I knew his voice–and to discover his name, perhaps–in order to have the means of pursuing him henceforth, no matter where he might go, even if it be to the ends of the Earth, and to fight him everywhere.

"I opened the trapdoor above the ladder without making a sound, and I went down. The alcove's curtains were closed. I slid belly-down on to the bed, and I put my eye to the narrow crack left between the two pieces of serge.

"They were all around the table where the lamp was burning. I was four paces away. I could see them–all of them–except that man. Satan protects him!"

"His back was turned to you?" said the Marquis, excitedly.

"I would have waited," Madeleine said. "The least movement would have shown me his profile, the color of his hair–something, at least, some sign... but there was nothing. There were nine uncovered faces; the woman wore a thick lace veil, and the assassin had a square of black silk over his face."

"He was the leader, then!" said Monsieur de Belcamp.

"Yes," the peasant woman replied. "He was the leader."

"A military man?"

"An English naval officer."

"English! What rank?"

"Commodore."

"Impossible!" murmured the old man. "That's one of the most important titles, which corresponds to our rear-admiral."

"Although he was the leader," Madeleine said, slowly, "he had a lesser rank than all his assistants."

Monsieur de Belcamp made a gesture of astonishment.

"There were Generals there," the peasant woman went on, "an Admiral, a former Minister, a Senator, Princes, a Cardinal Archbishop..."

The Marquis got up and strode back and forth across the room. "Already!" he thought, aloud. "Already!" Then, he stopped in front of Madeleine and added: "Can you name these people for me?"

"No," the peasant woman replied. "I can't do that."

"The leader, at least?"

"Yes, that one–because I'm counting on you. They called him Commodore Davy."

"Davy!" repeated the Marquis. "There are Davises in England, and Davies, but Davy... Commodore Davy! But it's not important. Finish your story, Madeleine."

"I have finished," the peasant woman replied, "And I have no further need to explain why there were armed men outside. We shall, perhaps, see them as combatants, but they are only sentinels for now. Monsieur le Marquis, you know everything that that I am permitted to tell you. Do you want to advise me and help me?"

"I want it with all my heart, my good Madeleine," the old man replied, resuming his seat. "Have you made a plan?"

"To find that man, to unmask him, to punish him..."

She stopped. Monsieur de Belcamp's eyes were fixed upon her. "Is that all, Madeleine?" he asked.

She collected herself before his gaze, and said: "No, that's not all, Armand. The name of Surrisy will once again mean smile. I have sometimes dreamed of a fortune for my poor and joyous child."

"Dream is the word!" murmured Monsieur de Belcamp.

"As I said... but who knows? These men rarely take apart a weapon that can still serve them. It is not George Palmer or this Davy who is the true assassin. The Counts Boehm have stolen two inheritances..."

"O'Brien was an educated man," Monsieur de Belcamp thought aloud. "The stolen contract must have been properly drawn up... and it is perfectly certain that this Davy will have kept it, as a key that could keep the Boehm coffers permanently open. The simplest means are the best; I'm on very good terms with the Prefect of Police..."

Madeleine shook her head. "That's impossible," she said. "My son has sworn an oath, and I must keep it."

"Who desires the end, however..." the Marquis began. He stopped to reflect, then went on: "You understand that the man possesses such resources that it will be necessary to go to someone powerful right away. Would you prefer the English Police?"

"No Police," said Madeleine, firmly.

Monsieur de Belcamp was opening his mouth to declare himself powerless when an idea suddenly came into his head. "By all the Devils!" he cried. "We have our man! A friend of poor O'Brien! I'm sure that he's spoken to me about this business before! All the advantages of the Police but nothing that can awaken your aversion. He may already be known to you. Have you ever heard of Gregory Temple?"

"At the time when he could do something," Madeleine replied, "this business was in his hands. Your memory doesn't deceive you. I made a journey to London, and solely on the basis of a description of the body, Gregory Temple told me: 'It's an Englishman who struck the blow. I know that wound and the hand that made it. John Devil is involved. Maintain absolute silence and come back in eight days.' Eight days went by, then several weeks, then a month... then years. Gregory Temple ended up sending me this message: 'Either John Devil does not exist, or he is a veritable demon.' Now it's said that he's gone mad. If he couldn't do anything when he was in full possession of his faculties and head of the world's finest Police force..."

She stopped, because the old Marquis was looking at her, smiling. While she was speaking, he had opened his writing desk and brought out his writing-materials. His pen was already touching the paper.

"I dare not claim to know my old friend Temple perfectly," he said, while writing, "but if there's anyone in all the world who knows him a little, it's me. In all my life, I've never guessed a rebus or a charade, and it may be precisely for that reason that I so admire his subtle mind, toying with difficulties and swimming in an ocean of calculations while I have my two feet solidly planted on the shore. He reminds me, in fact, of a spider ceaselessly spinning its web, and I've amused myself watching him for 25 years.

"I'm ashamed to admit it, but Police matters interest me greatly. I'm still a child in that respect; when I was in London, Gregory was an inexhaustible source of stories, a storyteller in action, who astonished me every day with some new marvel. When he is publicly branded a failure in his contest against la Bartolozzi's assassin, whether it was John Devil or not, whether John Devil exists or whether that is only a name covering up the collective misdeeds of an army of bandits, I say to myself: the assassin must beware!

"When my pretty Suzanne arrived one day in tears, and gave me to understand between her sobs that her father had fallen victim to an obsession, I couldn't help thinking of those clever cats who feign sleep in order to attract mice within the range of their claws. Gregory Temple has not let me into his secret, but he has written me three lines, saying: 'If you have anything to tell me or anything to ask of me, I am not yet dead.' Gregory Temple must be in the grip of a terrible and implacable mission. I would not dare and would not wish to throw an obstacle into his path and take his mind off his goal, but this takes us into his mind. This John Devil might not be a fantastic being after all. Perhaps we shall put Gregory Temple, the king of bloodhounds, back on a trail that he had lost, furnishing him with the spark that will light up his route...

"By God, Madeleine, I don't have the talent to help you in this. I hate this blood-thirsty rogue John Devil, who has made an orphan of my little Jeanne. I'm taking part in this war to the death which he has launched against old Temple, and if ever this monster comes within reach of my hand, no matter that I am the Marquis de Belcamp, I shall seize him by the collar like a gendarme."

He took up the pen again, having set it down while he spoke, and finished his letter in a few lines. He made a copy, then slipped each piece of paper into an envelope, addressing one to the Rue Dauphine in Paris and the other to Leicester Square in London, both in the name of Gregory Temple, esq.

"If anything can be done," he said, handing the two letters to Madeleine, "this will do it. Perhaps he will come to the chateau in answer to your appeal, perhaps he will arrange a meeting. Be ready."

The peasant woman rose to her feet.

"And have you nothing to say to me about my son before you leave?" said Monsieur de Belcamp, with the vivacity of a young man. "Good Heavens! Before he arrived, your son Robert was the cock of the walk–you must be jealous, Madeleine!"

"I saw Monsieur le Comte at mass," the peasant woman replied, smiling. "He is as you were at his age, Armand..."

"That's a lie, my good woman. I have never been half as handsome as that. He resembles his mother, to whom God gave the face of an angel."

"He is as you were at his age," Madeleine repeated, firmly. "I see no other resemblance in him–and, for the sake of the respect I owe him, I need to forget that he is the son of that woman."

"She is dead, Madeleine," the Marquis murmured.

In a low voice, but distinctly, the peasant woman said: "Pray God that all of her is dead, and that the son inherits only from his father."

Monsieur de Belcamp's brows knitted involuntarily.

"He has arrived among us like a good spirit," Madeleine went on, "and my Robert made my heart beast faster telling me the story of the bridge by the mill. That is you, Belcamp! I tell you that I do not want to look beyond that. I do not want to see anything in him but his father, whose name he bears and whose heart he undoubtedly has."

"The child is better than either of us, Madeleine," the old man murmured. "Something tells me that he will be the joy of my old age and the glory of my name. And I forgive her, whom God in his mercy has received–most of all because I owe to her my Henri, my dearest treasure and my last love."

After leaving the chateau, Madeleine went rapidly down the hill, because the mail-coach spent the night at Saint-Leu and it was necessary to go that far in order to throw her letters into the box. She did not want to lose an hour or any opportunity to extract her son from this affair.

When she arrived at the riverbank, she saw two shadows gliding between the willows: a man and a woman. The night was very dark, but Madeleine was able to ascertain that the two shadows were not dressed as villagers.

Softly, she called out: "Robert!"

No one replied.

"Hey, Robert!" she repeated, raising her voice and speaking authoritatively, for her nature was as resolute as a man's and never left a job half-done.

"Hey?" replied a voice from the other side of the river, near the miller's house. "What's up, mother?"

Madeleine stopped, astonished. That was not the bank from which she had expected her son's reply to come.

Who was the other man, then? she asked herself.

It could not be Laurent, because Laurent was striding across the bridge with the former lieutenant–who asked from a distance, in an anxious manner: "Has something happened to you, mother?"

Who was the other man, then?

Madeleine darted a suspicious glance toward the willows.

"Thank God," she said, "it's necessary to take to the road when one has need of one's son. Your bed might soon be sold if you spend your nights under the stars. Good evening, Monsieur Herbet; you haven't kept your sisters outdoors so late, I hope?"

"Jeanne has been in bed for a long time," Laurent replied.

Madeleine pricked up her ears at a sound that the others had not heard.

"All's well then," she said, raising her voice, "for it's no time for a young girl to be running around. Robert, I was looking for you. I have two letters that must be posted tonight."

"Give them to me, mother."

"No, I want to take them myself."

Robert looked at her in surprise. "Let's go, then," he said. "I'm ready to escort you." He and Laurent exchanged a handshake. An instant afterwards, the bank by the bridge was silent and deserted.

This silence was broken by a slight noise. The early foliage of the willows was disturbed, and muffled footsteps sounded in the grass. The two shadows that Madeleine Surrisy had perceived came out of the bush and came slowly through the meadow.

Madeleine had not been mistaken; they were a man and a woman, and they were not villagers.

"They've gone," murmured a voice that was grave, but so soft that a listener would not have been able to tell, at first, whether it was the man or the woman who had spoken.

But another much weaker voice, whose quivering inflexions could only have come from the throat of a young woman, replied: "Let's go back in, I beg you. I don't know why I came. For three days, I've been acting as if I were in a dream. My own fright tells me that I'm doing wrong by being with you. Let's go back in, I beg you, Monsieur le Comte."

Henri's lips brushed the hand of his companion, who stopped, as if she were about to faint.

"Jeanne, my dear beautiful Jeanne," he said, in a low singsong voice. "Beloved promise that God made me, so far away from my homeland, hope and light of my exile! Jeanne, my celestial bride! You came because you are already obedient to the man who will be your guide and your support until your dying breath. You came because there is a link between us that is not yesterday's, and because our destinies were united in Heaven before our souls could encounter one another on Earth. Jeanne, don't tremble when you have me by your side, for you would not be here, pure and saintly as you are, if this were not where you belong. Don't cut short the moments that are, for you as for me, the dawn of happiness–for you love me, Jeanne; the voice that descended from Heaven could not have lied, and if I do not press for that charming confession which will make my heart's joy boundless, it is because your heart itself has whispered to me: 'Since the first moment, I have been thrown towards you as if our souls had recognized one another; I believed that I was in love before I saw you, but I was mistaken, Henri, for it is the sight of you that has shown me existence, hope and the sweet tears of love.' "

"My heart has not said as much to me," murmured Jeanne, who was no longer trembling but smiling. "It speaks more eloquently to you than to me."

"Has it deceived me?"

"I don't know..." she said. Then she stopped, shivering. Her sensations were altering with distressing rapidity. "Ever since you arrived," she said, lowering her voice again, "I've been suffering."

"Do you want be rid of it?"

"No. It seems to me that I can no longer do without that suffering."

He drew her hand towards his heart.

"Yours isn't beating as fast as mine," she observed.

"It's swimming in its own gladness, Jeanne. I'm calmer and happier than you, because I have put away from me, for this moment, what is perhaps the better part of my life–everything that is not you–so that I can sit down free from all care at this feast of joy. Tomorrow will bring its troubles; tomorrow, I shall awaken from this delicious dream, and I shall look into the face of the work that I chose without measuring my strength–but today, my love celebrates its protected feast. I am at rest–I, who normally have none of the peace of the Sabbath...

"No, you're right. My heart isn't beating fast; it fills my breast. A little while ago you said: Why did I come? That's the question that floats incessantly in my mind, and which numbs it like languor or drunkenness. Why did she come? There is only one answer: every fiber of my being murmurs: She loves you! She loves you! Oh, I assure you, the pulse of supreme felicity is tranquil, and the heart that beats too quickly has not yet crossed the threshold of the paradise of love."

"Even so, my poor heart is making me ill, and I love you!" Jeanne sighed, involuntarily.

As soon as she had pronounced the word, she made an effort to withdraw her arms. During that gentle contest, Henri felt burning tears falling on to his hands. His lips touched Jeanne's forehead, and she became cold. He was obliged to support her.

"Let's go back in," she said, again. "Let's go back in, I beg you."

They were in the avenue of ancient oaks that descended from the esplanade to the water's edge–its last trees mirrored in the Oise–facing the Surrisy house. The spring night was so profoundly tranquil that the sound of the river caressing the bank seemed a distant canticle. The breeze could be heard passing slowly through the tops of the trees like long sighs, as sweet and faint as the breath that climbs from the lips of a dear child to a vigilant mother's ear.

There was an old tree, felled by the April tempests, lying in the moss; it still had all its roots. Henri set Jeanne down on this seat and knelt before her. He was one of those known to God alone, whose heart could never be sounded by any human gaze. What was within his soul, surely as great and powerful as the soul of a mortal creature could be, no one knew. He had no confidant and he would probably have died rather than give up his secret unwillingly–but whatever he was, good or evil genius, his eyes were burning at that moment with a youthful, ardent and sincere passion. It was love: true love, which is the enthusiasm and efflorescence of the heart.

Just as the most divine paint-brush cannot give figures grouped on canvas that mysterious complement, that sublime nothing, called life, so the actor who is the incarnation of genius cannot give perfect rendition to that magisterial sentiment, that providential and queenly malady, that miraculous leap of the soul towards the fecundity of happiness.

Lovelace can reheat the appearance of his lukewarm caprice, and Don Juan can apply cosmetic chivalry to the savage brutality of his desire, but neither is permitted to play the great game of love–beautiful love–which, like a man and like gold, has its own face, its own language, its own value and its own title. A man can disguise himself, it is true, and false money is in circulation, just as Don Juan is often a conqueror and Lovelace triumphant–but that is because complicit victims and the willfully blind are plentiful throughout this base world. This man was neither Don Juan nor Lovelace: this man loved and believed; this man possessed, at this particular moment–regardless of his past or his future, or even of himself–that gift of eternal virginity which the great and true words of the poet attribute to love; this man possessed all that he needed of youth, naive faith and ardent certainty to gird himself with the nuptial robe and intone the canticle of canticles.

The night was moonless, but the firmament of stars looked down, unimpeded by a single cloud. All the diamonds of those mysterious eyes, grouped in distinct clusters in the deep blue, let their invisible light fall and smile like the dew, which comes out everywhere at the same time and which–to the eye already accustomed to darkness–outlines the forms of nearby objects better than a ray of light. Jeanne tilted her soft face, pale but radiant in that clear obscurity; Henri clasped his hands together; silence spoke within them; their eyes met and did not part again, uniting their souls in a long mute kiss.

They were as beautiful as youth itself and the first flowering of love. The entire delicious poem of the transfusion of hearts bloomed in the languor of their smile. Jeanne's relaxing curls fell like an opulent veil to the chaste threshold agitated by the beating of her heart; it required no more than a breath of the sleeping breeze to carry them to Henri's lips. Henri seemed to be praying, sheltering in his contemplation, worshipping the idol.

They were as beautiful as the first fruits of ecstasy, which must eventually form the distant lamps of memory, still speaking of youth to a heart numbed by the chill of the years.

"I should like to know this Georgelle," Jeanne said, suddenly, shivering at the sound of her own voice.

"That is what I called you before knowing your name, Jeanne," the young Comte replied. "For a long time now, all my thoughts have been of you. When I saw you appear that night, called forth by my closed eyes, for me you were the other Georgelle–the divine creation of which the actual Georgelle was the charming shadow or reflection."

"And you would have loved her–the actual Georgelle–if it had not been for the strange dream?"

"I would have been searching for you in her. In the very depths of my being, Jeanne, the thought of you existed in a latent state–as witness the joy that I experienced in recognizing Georgelle. But to speak of these things is to give words a significance they do not have. What good does it do to attempt to explain the inexplicable?"

"It will be my happiness to wander always in the infinite field that is ours," Jeanne murmured, "since our souls met therein. You have opened it to me; it is no longer necessary for me to close it. I understand that, Henri, and when I retreat within myself it seems that I too have been waiting for you forever, incessantly. They all told me that I loved Robert Surrisy–and certainly, if you had not come, I would have consented to take him for my husband without any reluctance, for he is good and gentle. I have a sisterly affection for him. But I think I remember that I was always pensive in the midst of my childish cheerfulness... because I was cheerful before being happy, Henri. Why has my happiness made me sad?"

"You will be cheerful again, my dear Jeanne. Every earthly transformation is painful; it is from the depths of malady that the sad chrysalis throws forth the joyous and brilliant butterfly.

"And what did you think," the young woman continued, avid to return to the aerial expanse that is the homeland of love, "When you saw your dream completely realized, like Georgelle's? Were you already impatient? Were you fearful?"

"I was impatient. Jeanne, I was not fearful. At the moment when I hurled myself to your aid, I had not yet recognized you, but while I contemplated you, inanimate within my arms on the bank behind the willows, I felt an upsurge towards God, followed by a mortal moment of weakness. You were my Georgelle, but so marvelously superior and more beautiful! I thought: she is dying! My eyes were hot with tears. I held you up, cold and so pale, as you will never be held again until God leaves your charming corpse on Earth to carry off your spirit to the abode of his angels. I watched out for the breath that was slow to be reborn. I am afraid to tell you what I thought then, Jeanne."

"Oh, tell me! Tell me!"

"I thought–and my delirium made a fervent prayer of the impious wish–I thought: If she will not love me, let her die!"

Jeanne put her hands on Henri's shoulders and her smile was a celestial caress.

"It was not an impious wish," she murmured. "I am glad that you made it."

Henri, still kneeling, leaned on the trunk of the ancient oak; his blond head was thus pillowed on her mourning-dress.

"I had imagined black eyes beneath your ebony lashes," he went on. "Your eyelid slowly lifted; the blue of your irises cut into me like hope. I felt your love even before you did, and I shall ask nothing more from God, except to give you on Earth all the happiness that is promised to you in Heaven."

"Love me constantly," said Jeanne, "and your prayer is granted."

There was a silence then, more eloquent than speech. Jeanne's slender white fingers toyed distractedly with Henri's beautiful hair.

"Comtesse de Belcamp," she thought, aloud.

Henri felt her hand become cold. He lifted his head and saw that her eyes were full of tears.

"Why weep, Jeanne?"

"If all this is nothing but a dream...!" she murmured.

"Why should you say that?"

"Comtesse de Belcamp!" the young woman repeated, with childish solemnity. Then, lowering her head, she added: "No, no, I would have no right; there are things which are impossible." She avoided the Comte's eyes, which were looking at her tenderly, and continued in a different voice; "Monsieur le Comte, it is necessary that you know my history..."

"I know your history, Jeanne," Henri put in.

She looked at him; this time, her astonishment bordered on incredulity. "Did your vision tell you...?" she began.

"No," the young Comte replied, smiling even more tenderly and protectively. "Visions have little to say, and do not concern themselves with genealogy. But there are other things between us than the vision, and our destinies are crossed at more than one point on life's highway. You know nothing about me, save for appearances, but I repeat that I know your history: that which you know yourself, and that of which you are ignorant."

"From your father?"

"I have educated my father on that subject."

"From my aunt?"

"I have told your aunt things she did not know."

"From my mother?" Jeanne said, so quietly that Henri could hardly hear her.

He hesitated for a moment; when he finally replied, his voice betrayed profound emotion. "Jeanne," he said, "you are at this moment... you understand me perfectly: I mean the only being to whom I would expose the depths of my heart. I have friends and I have my father, but my secret, my beloved Jeanne, will be yours alone. Others in my place might perhaps think that the secret is of a kind that cannot touch the heart of a woman... but I shall educate your heart. I shall not elevate it at all; it is at the level of all that is noble, but I shall teach it that which every woman's heart knew in the days of chivalry. It beats, that dear heart, with the same pulse as my generous hatreds and my ardent ambitions."

"You hate, Henri? You!"

"No man, but a nation."

"And you are ambitious?"

"As the one sent by God to liberate the world."

Jeanne's eyes sparkled in the night, for it is the souls of young women that comprehend–or believe they comprehend–these great temerities we call madness. Every audacious spirit that moves beyond the merely human level has its living shadow, the echo and refuge of its idea, and it is always a woman.

Jeanne put her lovely little hands together, and said as if in prayer: "Henri, how I should love to die with you!"

"It's to live that's necessary, Jeanne," the young Comte cried. "To live to conquer. You shall temper my sword, so that it will last out the conflict. After the victory, you shall be the sweet crown of my triumph."

"Henri, Henri!" cried the young woman, lifting eyes radiant with enthusiasm towards the heavens. "Could it be that I have been chosen for this? I don't know what your work is... do I need to know? I believe in you, as I believe in God, and I would follow you with blindfold eyes even though the by-passers on the road were shouting in my ear: 'Turn around, this is the road to Hell!' "

The young Comte drew her towards him, until her inclined forehead touched his lips. There he placed a kiss.

"May Heaven determine that it is always thus!" he murmured, with a hint of melancholy. "But let's get back to you, Jeanne. I did, indeed, know your mother, whose home in London was a meeting place for the soldiers of an army that does not march towards my goal but whose passage will clear a part of my road. There are redoubtable paths where every backward step is punished by death. Human justice will never lift the veil covering that murder."

"Could you lift it, Henri?" Jeanne asked, in a different tone.

"There are ties that cannot be broken, Jeanne," Henri replied calmly. "If I were able to lift that veil, I would not do it at your knees, for it is not permissible for a daughter to repudiate the memory of her mother, and he who has sworn an oath like ours has no right to listen to his heart; my ignorance is my salvation."

"If you knew the assassin's name, you would not be able to reveal it?"

"God, who desires our union, has permitted me not to know it," was all that Henri said.

Jeanne covered her face with her hands.

"Such is the law whose slave I am twice over," the young Comte continued, his soft and serious voice bearing a dolorous inflection. "Or, rather, such are the two similar laws that I must obey blindly: the law of the association that condemned your mother, and my own law, determined by myself and for myself alone–which is the supreme law, because my work, which is worth a thousand times more than my life, depends on its fulfillment."

Jeanne was weeping quietly.

"Before that law," Henri continued further, "which seems to impose the duty of supporting and underlining every word, we have neither brothers nor sisters, neither mother nor father, neither wife nor lover; the law is everything."

"A terrible law!" Jeanne murmured. "Is there anything in the world so great as to motivate such a pact?"

"Two immensities: love and hatred."

"Neither sister, not mother, nor wife!" the young woman recited, slowly. "You would have been able to be the instrument that made me an orphan?"

"That was possible."

"Even if you had already been acquainted with me? Even if you were in love with me!"

"I would have had to choose between obedience and death."

"In choosing death, you would have killed me!" Jeanne sobbed.

"Just now," Henri said, in a firm voice, "you said: how I should love to die with you!"

"In combat, that's true, although I'm only a poor child!" Jeanne said. "Yes, in the ardor of battle, in the enthusiasm of the assault."

"Jeanne," Henri put in, "the martyr too has his ardor and his enthusiasm. The martyr is still a combatant."

The young woman slumped forward in discouragement, sighing as she stammered: "Oh, why did you save me?" And when Henri tried to take her hands, she pushed him away violently. "You who asked of God," she cried, with all the force of despair, "the power to give me on Earth all the happiness that is reserved for the angels in Heaven; you who pronounced those very words–for I may remember yours if you may cite mine, Henri–Henri, have you nothing to offer me but a choice between a parricide and a suicide?"

The young Comte got up and crossed his arms. His handsome head was proudly raised. His metallic and vibrant voice had a timbre that Jeanne had never heard before.

"Yesterday we were friends," he said. "Far from being espoused, we have not yet agreed to be engaged. Oh well! I feel anguish in my heart that the simple renunciation of that which I do not yet possess will be as cruel and destructive for me as the divorce of the agonized from life. It was not chance that led our conversation on to its present ground. These subjects were voluntarily broached by me. You needed a clarification and I needed a proof. I have often put a blindfold over the eyes of someone who asked to be admitted to the sanctuary... but you were the one I chose, above all others, to be the sustenance of my virtue and the guiding light of my soul. To me, you were above all others, since I gave myself to you in exchange for yourself. I could not introduce you into the temple in any other fashion than with you face bare and your eyes wide open. I have done that; I have done well. If it is necessary that I carry my dead hope and my extinguished dream away from here, and if it is necessary that I leave this place with tears in my heart and live the rest of my life in mourning because of you, then I have done well, since I have done my duty.

"Don't interrupt me, Jeanne, for this is a vital speech. Between us, there is no place for the vain skirmishes with which vulgar lovers kill time. I cannot be content with part of you; I want nothing less than the whole of you. When I have finished, you shall either say to me: 'I am the Comtesse de Belcamp,' or, poor beautiful angel, you shall give me your hand to kiss, and we shall separate forever...

"I am what I have told you I am. I have not said enough. I am much better than that, or much worse. I have made too little of the dangers that envelop me like a shroud–from which Lazarus will perhaps be reborn! I am an outlaw ten times over, perhaps 20; I no longer keep count. Every Police force in Europe is looking for me; every court in Europe would convict me. For me, every inch of ground might conceal a trap; every friendly hand might suddenly close upon mine like steel handcuffs. You have seen howling mobs of armed villagers surround a rabid dog–that's me. I have no refuge but within myself. When I search for a point of comparison within the records of historians and the fictions of poets, I can find none, for Marius is left wandering peacefully through the ruins of Carthage and Satan rebelling against the lightning in Hell.[95]

"This may seem grandiose and seductive to your womanly imagination; I must strip the truth bare. Let's go down! To the fallen archangel there remains a spark of the splendor drowned out by the thunder. If there is anything more loathsome than Hell, it is the mire black with shame and red with blood. I have so many enemies that I am sustained in my march by the imprudent effort of their hatred. Were one to strike me in the riot, I should fall upon another; the blind mob would not be able to contrive a gap into which I might fall.

"Tomorrow, though, you who are ashamed of your birth, someone will say to you while pointing a finger at me: 'He has married her millions to redecorate his wretched coat-of-arms...' Don't interrupt! I've told you that I know your own history better than you do. You are rich and I am poor, I assure you of that. Accept it as the truth. Another will cry out to you: 'His coat-of-arms is false; his title is not his; he's the son of a London thief!' Yet another: 'He is a thief himself!' Another: 'He's an assassin!' And to cap it all, perhaps in the middle of a feast, perhaps as we leave the church where the candles lighting our wedding ceremony are still smoking, a black army might present itself, whose leader will put a hand on my shoulder, saying: 'I arrest you in the name of the King!'

"Listen to me! 'I arrest you, not because some flag has fluttered above some tower, nor because some traitor has sold out some bold conspiracy, but because a treasure-chest has been opened here with a false key, and a dead man has been found there in his bloody sheets! I arrest you–not you, Bryan of Glencoe [96] who threw his gauntlet at George II on his throne; not you, Mallet [97] or Cadoudal;[98] not even you, delirious fanatics, Jacques Clément,[99] Ravaillac or Damiens;[100] but you, Mandrin,[101] you, Cartouche, you, Poulailler,[102] John Devil or Jack Sheppard! You cutthroat, bandit, forger...' "

Comte Henri de Belcamp paused to wipe away the sweat that was running down his face. Jeanne had been listening, breathless. She opened her mouth, but he bade her be silent with an imperious gesture.

"It's the truth," he continued, while the fervor of his voice was reduced to a murmur. "It's neither the frivolous emphasis of amorous spleen nor the bitter exaggeration of despair. It's the exact and scrupulous truth. These things might have happened yesterday, as they might happen tomorrow. Even so, I have come to a child who is happy in her pleasant mediocrity; her angelic gaiety is the joy of all around her; she has a friend who is almost a fiancé, brave, honest and good, not as saintly and beautiful as she is but adequate to give her the vulgar happiness that is the best we can hope for on Earth. God preserve me from mockery! That happiness calls itself the peace of the soul. I have come, and the young woman is unfaithful to her fiancé; the neighborhood listens and watches in vain, unable any longer to hear the song or see the smile; she now knows how to weep. Why did I come? What will become of her? Of what vengeance have I been the pitiless minister?

"Oh! I have come because I am young and my heart has lost none of the suave virginity that has become so rare in the world! I have come because there is a force more powerful than us, which some call God and others love! I have come because that unknown force led me by the hand through the hatreds of men and the tempests of the sea. I have come because I am in love!

"I am obliged to confess in all humility that I am the lowest of the low; but in my pride I also add that I am the highest of the high! While my heel is embedded in the mire where my enemies lie crushed, my head is above the clouds and my eye stares the Sun in the face. I have made Kings tremble; I have made nations shiver. For all the scorn amassed around me, I shall have heaps of glory. Behind my scaffold, my triumphal chariot waits. I fight; I am not defeated, since I exist; I fight alone against everyone; I feel myself growing larger in my darkness and my solitude; nothing shall stop me; I make light of battles lost and am intoxicated by my victories...and I march onwards incessantly, incessantly, climbing a new rung every day. Tomorrow, I shall have the scaffold beneath my feet... my head will surpass the level of thrones... Europe, with a great cheer, will proclaim my name...

"Jeanne, my crown was large enough for two heads; Jeanne, my dear love, the terrible secret known only to myself I would have sheltered in your bosom, knowing that I would not be forsworn, for you would have been me, the best of me, my joy, my strength, my conscience. Jeanne, there are treasures of tenderness in me that I would have wanted to pour into you. Jeanne, for him who is alone, a moment of weakness might be fatal; I wanted to lean on you. You were worthy of me; I believed that I alone was worthy of you. I would have given you everything: all my sadness and all my joy; I would have taken everything from you: your tears as well as your smiles. Jeanne, I have built castles in the air for us. Although my task is that of a giant, my love is that of a demigod. I love you... I love you as no woman has ever been able to want to be loved on Earth... I cannot love anyone but you; without you, my life will henceforth be widowhood. Jeanne, for me there is not even the refuge of death; I belong to my work, and I would have given you my work; you can only condemn me to mourning for the rest of my life...

"Jeanne, I'm finished, and my heart is breaking. Depending on your decision, I shall rise to my feet invincible... or resume my route, unflinchingly, resignedly, but sadly: weaker because I had dared to hope, more alone because I had dared to love!"

He went down on his knees again.

For a moment, there were only two voices audible in the darkness: the whisper of the water lapping the bank and the murmur of the trees caressed by the breeze. Then Jeanne yielded a long sigh. After that she threw her arms around Henri's neck and hid her head within his bosom.

As if she were speaking to the very heart of her lover, which she felt palpitating beneath her lips, she said:

"I want to live and die with you!"

XVIII. The Patache [103]

It was nine o'clock in the morning, three days after the Sunday when Lady Frances Elphistone had made her entrance into Miremontese society. The l'Isle-Adam *patache* was going back towards Paris empty, for the sole purpose of not having failed to do it.

Railways have given the world an appetite for locomotion that was completely non-existent in 1817. Along the eternal latticework that borders our iron roads, everyone has noticed a vast number of melancholy old men watching the steam pass by. They are all retired *patache*-conductors or directors of little stage-coach offices who have returned to private life. As their envious eyes follow the cloud of smoke that carries so many impatient travelers, they are saying to themselves: "They ended up somewhere else just the same!"

Nowadays, one starts off there.

The conductor of the l'Isle-Adam had closed the curtains of his compartment to hide its wretchedness. He drove two poor beasts as sad as he was at a sickly trot, occasionally putting to his dry lips–in the absence of any tips–a cornet that he would have held with much better grace if it had only been a glass of purple wine, sending forth his morose fanfare to echo in the forest.

This conductor was, however, a winner. Last winter, he had killed off "the competition"–that monster which sucked the blood of ancient messengers. The competition was dead in its fireless office; its four phantom horses and two worm-eaten carriages had been sold at public auction–but the "main stage-coach office" was dying in its turn. Such is the way of the world.

Today, however, the defunct deity that presided over these lugubrious enterprises had an unexpected godsend in reserve for our conductor. While he scrutinized the distant reaches of the deserted route, searching with a discouraged eye for that white blackbird, the Paris-bound traveler, a numerous and choice company was gathering at the Croix Moraine, which was the nearest thing Miremont had to a station. Around the inscriptionless signpost that marked the middle of the star, there was a circle of grassy turf; resting on this bank was a considerable quantity of overnight bags, baskets and packages belonging to the Bondon garniture, Madame Morin du Reposoir and the Chaumeron family. These individuals accompanied their baggage, all in traveling costume, wearing the particular expression that is reserved for pleasure-parties.

On such occasions the weather is usually rainy, and all their umbrellas were open. There was one made of blue cotton, which serves to indicate the degree of civilization attained there. The blue cotton umbrella was carried by Cécile Chaumeron, the long-suffering second daughter, who was beginning to put up barricades in order to claim her place in the Sun. Mademoiselle was still downtrodden; her umbrella was green floss-silk.

Papa Chaumeron was enjoying himself under a portable kiosk, a veritable family monument, which was made of pink silk and dated from the days of the Directory.[104] Many-Apologies sheltered her traveling clothes beneath a movable olive-tree with strong iron struts, whose handle was modeled on the head of Prince Eugene; she had bought it when she was in trade. Madame Célestin had no umbrella; placed between her two twins, armed with similar utensils, she was doubly protected; like an abundance of dark riches she received drips from the right and drips from the left on her antiquated crêpe hat, which was wry and sharp as her own face.

Mademoiselle was still asking herself why the Bondons had united their destinies with such an old crone, as she mischievously thought of her. She would not have disdained the social position of Madame Célestin.

"Beleuil is late," said Papa Chaumeron, taking a watch as large as an umbrella from his waistcoat pocket. "It's past nine o'clock, damn it!"

They all took out their watches, except for the second Chaumeron, who was still waiting for one of her own. She was only 18; there is no need to hasten the blunting of children by the vicissitudes of life.

It is rare to find unanimity among watches in the countryside. The watches of Miremont, however, found themselves in agreement, give or take half an hour; it was past nine, and Beleuil was late.

"He's capable of having had an accident," observed Madame Célestin. "I'm not so lucky! Célestin, bring that umbrella closer!"

The two Bondons obeyed simultaneously, for no command ever applied only to one. The two umbrellas, brought forcefully together, rebounded, releasing a shower of droplets on to Madame Célestin's shawl.

"Many apologies," said the Deputy's wife. "You haven't asked for my opinion, but if you only had one escort, you would only have one umbrella, and you would be underneath it."

"If you think that everything is rosy in my position..." Madame Célestin retorted, sharply.

"Now, now!" exclaimed Chaumeron. "I'm a plain speaker, me. I'll wash that Beleuil's head... eleven minutes late?"

"And if he doesn't have a seat left..." said Mademoiselle.

"He's capable of that!" sighed Queen Bondon. "We've no luck in our house."

It was obvious that the two madrepores were about to speak, for they raised their short fat arms at the same time. Indeed, they said as one: "We have none in our house."

"Bah!" said Cécile. "The l'Isle-Adam carriage always goes back empty."

"There's no need to speak to say nothing," Mademoiselle observed. "When there are passengers, it doesn't go back empty."

"Many apologies," said the Deputy's wife. "That's fair."

"There you are!" Cécile continued, laughing surreptitiously. "Those who have their own carriage to go to Paris are very lucky."

Everyone looked at her sideways, and Papa Chaumeron, who never minced his words, said: "Shut up, you! Do you want your bill? Oh, but..."

"It seems to me, Mademoiselle," Many-Apologies added, dryly, "that I have my carriage just like the Mayor and the Englishwoman."

"And me, just like you," said Madame Célestin.

"And us!" cried Mademoiselle.

"That takes three days to get to Paris," Cécile riposted, drawing away from her father, whose hand was sometimes as frank as his tongue. At least Monsieur le Marquis and milady have horses that aren't made of wood."

Alas, alas! That Arcadia, Miremont! If looks were daggers, the second Chaumeron daughter would have been stabbed many times over.

"Papa," cried Mademoiselle. "Tell her, one more remark and she'll stay at home."

"At any rate," Many-Apologies muttered, "Monsieur Morin du Reposoir has a position..."

"And he's not the only one!" Madame Célestin put in. "There are those who have better things to do with their money than throw it out of the window."

"And I'd rather be here," added Mademoiselle "than ride around in carriages that aren't mine, like Miss Suzanne and Mademoiselle Jeanne, and Mademoiselle Germaine..."

"With a foreigner!" bid the Bondons' suzerain.

"That no one knows from Adam or Eve," concluded the Deputy's wife, inadvertently offering her snuff-box to Mademoiselle, who plunged into it up to her elbow.

"Eighteen minutes late," Chaumeron intoned. "Excuse me!"

"Young girls with an Englishwoman," Madame Célestin continued, "who has a child! And no husband, to boot!"

"Did you notice yesterday," asked Cécile, "how Miss Suzanne caressed the little child?"

"Hush!" said Papa. "You're too young to be talking about that!"

"Even so," insinuated the Deputy's wife, a stout serpent who had a better bite than her humble appearance suggested, "Many apologies, and I say it without malice... even so, I don't like sad and distraught young girls who can't ever keep up with table-talk and who throw themselves on little children like a poor man on a loaf of bread."

This was a great success.

"Too right!" Chaumeron exclaimed. "Bitchy! I'm a plain speaker, but not as much as that!"

Madame Célestin attempted to blush. Mademoiselle lowered her eyes. The two Bondons, seeing that Chaumeron was laughing, came apart like a pair of springs, and Cécile's astonished eyes made a tour of the circle in the hope of divining the cause of the incomprehensible merriment.

"I don't know why you're laughing," continued the perfidious Deputy's wife. "You know very well that I respect the Mayor's house, and his son is certainly a nice-looking boy who tells good stories, but... many apologies! Not to mention the political affairs in which we're embroiled–and Madame Célestin can tell you whether we had a review of the national guard for nothing–it wouldn't surprise me much if the three idlers weren't mixed up in all that... many apologies! Without looking for trouble where there isn't any, there are some funny things going on. Old Touchard dotes on her niece since Monsieur le Comte whispered in her ear; Jeanne Herbet hasn't laughed since she's been fondled... and you know what they say about she who has, holds...! Milady was chatting with the brigand in the woods for two hours last Sunday, while Monsieur le Comte sent us to sleep standing up. Mademoiselle Germaine, of whom I don't want to speak ill, since she's the daughter of a colleague, devours Monsieur le Comte with her eyes... there! I've gone to great pains on her behalf... and Laurent Herbet has a good mind to jump on Monsieur le Comte. Many apologies! There's something fishy going on, and we'll soon see what it is."

The "three idlers" to whom she referred were Robert Surrisy, Laurent Herbet and Férandeau.

"Something fishy!" exclaimed Chaumeron. "Fat ones, too! Damn it! Twenty-five minutes late."

The rain came down harder. On the other side of the hill there was an inn, where Beleuil had stopped to drown his sorrows in a half-liter of Sannois wine, the best in France after Suresnes.[105]

Impatience embitters the sunniest spirits. The fraction of Miremontese society surrounding the signpost was definitely beginning to lose the gentle amenity that procures, so it is said, the peaceful life of the fields. Each of them sought something to complain about. They abused the sky and the earth; they wondered why all Miremont had left home at once to go to Paris.

"There are things to be done, that's all!" said the inundated Madame Célestin. "It's the last time I'll go. Little gifts maintain amity, but the Mayor never gives us any, and every year one has to go out of one's way to search for everything his party requires..."

"When you include the journey," Chaumeron said, by way of support, "it's a costly business."

"Many apologies! The Mayor never gives us anything... and last year I had ten *sous* change out of 14 *livres*."

"And you can be perfectly sure," Cécile added, pitilessly, "that Monsieur le Comte's and milady's gifts will put everyone else's in the shade."

"We ought to go back home!" said Madame Célestin. "What do you think, Monsieur Chaumeron, who speaks plainly?"

The two corals exchanged an anxious look. They loved Paris. Why? That was their secret. They would have vegetated quite comfortably a hundred feet underground, but they loved Paris. What an enchanter Paris is! It doesn't need Orpheus to make its stones dance.

As for Monsieur Chaumeron, he was at that greying and slightly apoplectic age when the fathers of provincial families adore the idea of a little trip to "the capital." Let us draw a pious veil over the naive rascality of our uncles.

On the other hand, Mademoiselle and Cécile, who had no fingers on the family purse-strings, made an occasion of the journey. There was the promise of the Opéra-Comique. Even the Deputy's wife, liberated from the Deputy, would not have given up her few hours of widowhood without regret.

"Victory!" cried Chaumeron, instead of responding to Madame Célestin's insidious overture. "Here's Beleuil. Trump!"[106]

His gloved hand pointed at the very top of the hill, where a ray of sunlight piercing the clouds seemed to surround Beleuil's patache with glory. The two Bondons hauled themselves upright and shook their umbrellas. Pointing to Madame Célestin's scowl, Madame Morin said to Mademoiselle: "It's just as well–many apologies!–journeys are tiresome when one is shepherdess to a flock like that."

"Monsieur Florian is a handsome man!" the eldest Chaumeron retorted, sharply.

"Is he the left-hand one?" the Deputy's wife asked. "Many apologies. She'll never let him marry, my dear."

"There are three people on top," Chaumeron announced. "The interior must be as full as an egg. Damn!"

"Bonjour, Monsieur Chaumeron! Bonjour, Madame Morin du Reposoir! Bonjour Madame and Messieurs Bondon!" shouted a joyous voice in the distance, as three hats were raised in the air. "All aboard, Mesdames! All aboard, Messieurs! All aboard, Mesdemoiselles!"

"The three idlers!" groaned the stout Deputy's wife. "They're going to cramp our style!"

Beleuil, seeing the manna that God had sent him, had given his nags two generous strokes of the whip, Monsieur Chaumeron was waiting for him in the middle of the road, watch in hand.

"Thirty-one minutes late, my boy," he said, sternly. "When we get to Paris, we'll sign a letter of complaint addressed to your managing director."

"Have you got directors, Beleuil?" Férandeau asked.

The conductor stepped down.

"How much is the fare?" Madame Célestin asked.

"Always the same: 2.50 francs, not including the tip."

"And for three?"

"Three times 2.50 francs and three tips," Férandeau replied.

Madame Célestin's yellow cheeks were tinted pink.

"That will be two francs for me," said the Deputy's wife. "You know..."

"Half fares for children and military personnel!" murmured the pupil of David.

Chaumeron was speaking in his turn: "Beleuil, four francs for me and my eldest, the little one thrown in. Up we go!"

"Thrown in!" echoed the indignant conductor. "She's as tall as a flag-pole!"

"Five francs for me and my two Messieurs?" Madame Célestin offered.

"I'm the wife of a Deputy: two francs just for me–you'll earn the rest on the weight of my luggage."

"Four francs for my eldest and me, ten *sous* for the little one! Last offer!"

From the height of the top deck, Férandeau solemnly intoned: "All aboard, Mesdames! All aboard, Messieurs! All aboard, Mesdemoiselles!" Although the expressions worn by Robert and Laurent indicated serious preoccupation, they could not help smiling. Meanwhile, Madame Célestin remarked on the perennial contrariness of chance; the rain had stopped at exactly the moment when she was about to be sheltered. That wretch Beleuil still wanted his fare. The Deputy's wife offered the opinion that they ought to cut through the woods to the Pontoise road, where the diligence would pass by at ten o'clock. Férandeau advised Beleuil to be careful, as they were capable of it.

In the end, after a long, horrible and embarrassing discussion, in which pleas and threats were invoked by turns and every device was employed that was capable of frightening or tenderizing, Beleuil opened his box in order to cram in the gentlemen, ladies, young women, umbrellas, overnight bags and packages of Miremontese society. They were contented, having obtained a discount of 25 *sous* for the whole party; tomorrow would be rosy; they could go forth to dine with their acquaintances and bed down with their friends. Their expenses would be confined to strict necessities: tickets for the Opéra-Comique–less expensive than glove-merchants–the gratification of the candlestick [107] and the purchase of some little surprise for the Marquis' birthday celebration.

The Bondon garniture occupied the entirety of one of the seats; one could not see the joints. Facing them, Papa Chaumeron tried to accommodate himself between his eldest and Madame Morin du Reposoir, whose transportation was really worth considerably more than 2.50 francs. The damp umbrellas, the overnight bags and the second Chaumeron daughter were in the middle. Florian had generously offered to let Cécile sit on his knee, but that proposition had had no other consequence than a pinch from Madame Célestin.

On the top deck, Férandeau was smoking his pipe in bright sunlight, the clouds having been swept away, undoubtedly for the sole purpose of annoying Madame Bondon. For several days, Férandeau had been making himself ill with suppressed laughter and evil pleasantries that he could not let out.

Until now, in spite of the differences in their personalities, the three idlers had had a common desire to amuse themselves and to take life as it came, always in good part. They were not, by any means, bad fellows–but we must confess, however, that circumstances have introduced them to our readers in an idyllic and rustic appearance that is not entirely reliable. The student on vacation is not at all the student in Paris; in the country, there is always some Jeanne or Germaine to subdue the fast friends of punch and the pipe for a little while. The artist is something of an exception, especially if his destiny is to be a pupil of David, in spite of the muse that presides over academic painting. There is more obduracy in the artist–who cannot, like Alcibiades,[108] change the temperature of his mores at a moment's notice. Generally, he celebrates his carnival [109] with a straight face, using it to disguise his second nature.

If anyone should object that I am confusing the artist with the dauber at this point, my response is to challenge him to show me an artist who has not something of the dauber in him. Every artist has been a dauber; that is the law, just as every butterfly has been a caterpillar. The student, after all, is everyman. He is your future notary or your discreet doctor, riveted to his white cravat and not daring to wear a beard any longer for fear that he be mistaken for a male; he is your advocate pleading none but the most richly-lined briefs, the judge who is virtuous despite public slander and who has certainly left his last prank under the school bench; he is your local Counselor or departmental Prefect, or even His Excellency the Minister. In a word, he is a member of society in the most general and most banal sense; he will, of necessity, marry and have children, submissive to all convention and slave to every hypocrisy–but not the artist.

Granted that grandeur is a chain, the artist remains free, no matter how great you might imagine him to be. That liberty, amid our servitude, is as beautiful and as ugly as anything in the world. Certain people even find that the ugly enormously outweighs the beautiful, because there are artists in that number who are named neither Mozart nor Michelangelo. In the country, the artist takes a malign pleasure in standing out like a fly in the milk. He poses with an indescribable delight, proud of the genius whose proof is in his hat. He mystifies, if no one takes the trouble to mystify him, and–strangely enough–he is wont to take Germaine or Jeanne for those good girls, protectresses of arts and scholarship, who are dotted about certain districts of Paris like faded blossoms in a flower-bed. When he does not make this mistake with respect to Jeanne or Germaine, the thesis changes: he is positively afraid of them. Anyway, as they say in vaudeville–the most deceptive of the beasts of the Apocalypse–young women don't like artists. (With respect to Paris, of course, I make an exception in favor of the kind of doll who has a local reputation as a pianist; such dolls are neither free nor artistic.)

Férandeau, a very honest fellow and possessor of a talent of which he was quite unaware, came to Miremont to have fun. He admitted it. He was not in love with anyone. The Bondons, the Morins du Reposoir, the Chaumerons and Don Juan Besnard were extremely amusing. He had a sketch-book dedicated to the naked gladiators–Romulus, Tatius,[110] the Sabines, the three Horatii condemned 20 centuries and more before to raise their muscular arms in swearing to destroy their cousins and friends, the Curiaces. One evening, while returning to the Priory, where Madame Touchard saw nothing in favorable terms, he drew the diverse figures of Miremontese society in this sketch-book, in various poses, thus taking his first groping step towards renown–for the excellent Férandeau, who persisted in painting Roman and Homeric history deplorably, eventually came to use his brush as Beaumarchais used his pen, and found his true vocation in caricature.

But he despaired of his friends Robert and Laurent; he had consented to become a villager so as not to be parted from them; to keep company with them, he had become a conspirator! He needed his friends, who understood his studio jargon and could reply in kind: two little saints in the country, but two madmen in Paris, who had taken wholeheartedly to the joys of student life in spite of their habitual lack of funds. Robert was a stalwart of the Latin Quarter and Laurent a tear-away in the Chaumière. What fun they had! What exploits! What devil-ment! There had to be something in Robert and Laurent to motivate Férandeau's devotion.

Several days ago, however–upon the romantic advent of young Comte Henri de Belcamp–a sudden and complete transformation had overtaken Robert and Laurent. Férandeau's two friends deserted him at the same time; they no longer understood; his best jokes fell flat without the slightest response. Laurent and Robert were forever exchanging confidences in which he had no part to play. He was alone and he felt surrounded by mystery.

"Now then," Férandeau said, shaking the ashes from his pipe, not without a certain solemnity, "when the Miremontese contingent is crammed into the in-terior, amity is a gift of the gods, but I'm tried of bearing the burden of the con-versation all on my own. You've hardly laughed at any of my droll remarks, and I haven't even voiced a quarter of those that came to mind, because we three have gone to the Devil. If you've got problems, I want a share in them; if you've got secrets, tell me frankly that I'm in your way; if there's something to be done, give me my task."

Robert offered him his hand, but Laurent replied, rudely: "There's nothing you can do, Férandeau. Robert's running after that foreigner, Lady Frances El-phinstone. Jeanne and Germaine have gone mad. I want to run someone through with my sword–I don't know whether it's Robert or Comte Henri de Belcamp."

"Robert–with your sword!" repeated Férandeau, stupefied.

"Because his sister no longer loves me," Robert said with a sad smile, "and because I cannot yet furnish him with an explanation that I haven't yet worked out."

Férandeau's astounded gaze went from one to the other. "Is that how it is, my poor fellows?" he murmured, "And I'm complaining! I have a suspicion that your quarrel is stupid. Don't worry about that–some stupid quarrels are emi-nently respectable. So, Laurent, you're thirsty for Robert's blood?"

"Imbecile!" muttered Jeanne's brother, with a smile

"Very well!" Férandeau exclaimed. "Get it off your chest! You should suffer, since it's you that's wrong.

Laurent and Robert looked at one another. Laurent took Robert's hands. "Give me your word of honor that you will always love Jeanne," he said, brusquely.

"So long as I live and breathe, I shall love her," the former Sub-Lieutenant replied. "I swear it."

Laurent threw himself into Robert's arms, murmuring: "It needed Férandeau to say the word." He laughed, but he had tears in his eyes.

"What word?" said the artist. "Stupid? It's better than wishing that he was dead."

"Have you forgiven me?" Laurent asked.

"Continue this affectionate scene while I relight my pipe," Férandeau advised.

"On condition that you will let me follow my intended route," Robert replied. "It's not for you or me to interfere. Your role–our role–is to be ready for the moment when we are needed."

"Hold on!" said Férandeau. "I prefer non-speaking roles–but permit me one motion: when a quarrel is made up, it's customary to dine; that seems to have been handed down from he remotest origins of society. We have the wherewithal for dinner at the *Veau-qui-tette* [111] if we forego the Opéra-Comique. I propose we do away with the insipid Feydeau Theater, [112] having already seen enough of *Le Calife de Badgad* or *Ma Tante Aurora*, replacing the aforesaid theater with a particular hostelry where we can celebrate the happy circumstance with glass in hand..."

"Hey, Lieutenant!" shouted a rough voice from the right-hand side of the road.

Robert immediately turned round, and Férandeau looked angrily at the unfortunate interrupter. It was a peasant walking along the road with his staff in his hand and his haversack on his back.

They were about a hundred yards from the village of ***, whose bell-tower was visible through the trees, beyond a bend in the road. The *patache* was coming up to the side-road that led through ploughed field towards Pierre Louchet's hut. The peasant who was heading towards Paris, dressed for a long journey, was Pierre Louchet himself.

"Where are you off to dressed like that, Corporal?" Robert asked.

"To London," the peasant replied.

"Without saying anything to me?"

"Indeed not. I would have gone to Miremont if I hadn't recognized you on the carriage."

"Stop!" Robert instructed the conductor.

"Is it settled," Férandeau asked, "that we're all eating at the *Veau-qui-tette*?"

Robert already had his foot on the iron steps. "Let your horses draw breath in the village, Beleuil," he said. "I'll run." To his two companions, he added: "If I don't catch up with you, I'll meet you tonight at eight o'clock in the Passage Feydeau, at the theater entrance." Without waiting for a reply, he jumped on to the road and fell into step with the peasant.

"Always mysteries," murmured Laurent, while the carriage began moving again.

"The hope of a feast at the *Veau-qui-tette* seems to have faded away," Férandeau replied, sadly.

At that moment, Surrisy was saying: "What the Devil are you going to do in London, Pierre?"

"I don't know, Lieutenant," the peasant said. "I'm under orders."

"Whose orders?"

"Whose? Oh, it's an English name. It's all I can do to remember it... on... on... ton... son..."

"Thompson, perhaps?"

"Yes, Thompson... perhaps. Or something like it... no matter. He's a good tipper... and he must be living out your way, to be sure!"

"Have you much to tell me?" Surrisy asked, darting a glance at the carriage that was already disappearing in a cloud of dust.

"Quite a lot," the woodcutter relied, "if you've time to listen."

"Why didn't you come to Miremont?"

"That's part of the story. It's already a week since I should have left for London with a package to give to a gentleman of that country. I have the name in my sack... so I came up one morning to say a few words to you about what was happening, and to ask you if all went well the other night at the fountain..."

"Yes, very well!"

"Good. The old uniform's in the lavender with the worms; we'll give it a good shake-out some day so that it doesn't get eaten away. So, I came up one morning, and as I arrived at the Croix Moraine I met... ton... son... the Englishman–a handsome chap, fair-haired! 'Why haven't you gone?' he said to me. 'You've no business here. Quick march–you'll be suspected of being a spy.'"

"You–Pierre Louchet?"

"That's what I said to him. 'Me, a spy!' Ah, but I ought to add that I had ideas about this and that, to tell you about the child and the 20 *sou* tip, in gold..."

"What child?" Robert interrupted.

"That's right, you don't know. He put his hand on my shoulder in the fashion that you know..."

"What!" the former lieutenant exclaimed. "He's one of ours?"

"A bit... and high up... you'll see. After putting his hand on me that way, he said very low: 'You know what happens to traitors? If you aren't gone tomorrow, watch out!' That was the day before yesterday. I haven't slept in the house. This morning, I was going to send my daughter to Miremont to let you know, when I saw the lady who said: 'I'm leaving for England with the child' pass by in a nice coach. And I thought she was a long way away, I did!"

"What lady?"

"Ah, yes," said Pierre. "You don't know... but if it's all the same to you, Lieutenant, let's go into the woods, in case we bump into... look, it must be shady in there... and my daughter's only gone and told me that she'll have to have a husband to keep her."

Robert Surrisy knew Pierre Louchet well enough not to try to rectify his manner of communication. He followed the honest woodcutter into the trees, and said, simply; "Go on!"

"Shady as a carriage, eh? And do you know who that lady was with in the coach? With the girl from the Chateau de Belcamp, Jeanne Herbet and the daughter of Potel, the Deputy..."

"That's all right," Robert said. "Go on."

"Well, a moment later, the blond chap went by in his turn, on horseback... oh, I raise my hand to a thousand-*écu* animal like that! When he'd gone by, I said to myself: 'I'll run up to Miremont and tell the Lieutenant, before starting off...' But everyone's out and about today. I spotted you on top of the *patache*. Where was I?"

"You haven't even started, my poor Pierre."

"That's right. Let's begin at the beginning. See here, that must be the child of an important person that I was feeding my goat's milk to... and if the King of Rome wasn't already..." He stopped short and appeared to be making a supreme effort to untangle the threads of his thought. "So it was about three weeks ago," he went on, "one night in late April. I'd walked my daughter back to her master's house and I was going to bed when I heard knocking at my door and someone shouting: 'For the best!' All well and good. I gave the response and lit my candle.

"It was the fair-haired chap whose name you said... Ton... Son. He had a nice little child in milk-white swaddling-clothes. He touched me on the shoulder like a Master and said: 'He's weaned, but he needs a woman to look after him. Where's your daughter.' Who knows who told him how to get to my hole, and that I had a daughter? I said: 'My daughter's in service, but I've raised her since she was a mite after the loss of my dead wife, and I know about all that.' He told me that he was in need of a mother and gave me a coin, which I put in the money-box that's my daughter's dowry. He went away.

"I looked after the child–a little lamb that made me laugh and was as pleased with his basket as if it had been a diamond-studded crib. I made him pap with the goat's milk, which wakes children up and makes them strong. All right... two days later, one morning, someone thumps on my door with his fist:

'For the best!'–'What do you want, good cousin?'–'Pierre Louchet, woodcutter'–'That's me'–'I want to see the child.'

"It wasn't the same man. Well-dressed and good looking, but seemed sad. He went to the crib and took my little child in his arms... I say 'my' child because it doesn't take me long to get attached, and it happened right away. As soon as he smiled at me, that was it. The other one hadn't a miserable face, I suppose, but this one was hiding his tears, and I saw him fondling the little one and smothering him with kisses. That would make you think he was the father, wouldn't it? The idea struck me, but no... the father was the other one... and I don't know whether I saw him hug the poor little creature once, what you'd call wholeheartedly. That's the way it went for 12 days; sometimes one came, sometimes the other, never together. The one that cherished the child so much wasn't rich; he never gave anything, but the other left me a tip every time, which went into my money-box. Oddly enough, I liked the one who didn't pay me better. So it goes.

"The last time he came–the one who didn't pay–he cried a lot. He sat beside the crib and took a little portrait out of his shirt, framed in gold, which he looked at crying all the while. He put it to the baby's mouth, who kissed it as best he could, poor dear mite. I said: 'Show me.' He let me look at it–the prettiest lass one could ever see, that one! 'Is it his mother?' I asked him. He put his hands over his eyes. That time, he gave me two five franc pieces, and said: 'I shan't come back again.' I thought: 'In one go he's laid out as much as the other did in half a dozen,' but I'd counted wrong. The other had made six visits in all and when I opened my money-box, having had an idea, I found six English sovereigns, which is worth 150 francs give or take a *sou*...and three 20-franc *louis* that I had from the woman, which makes a dowry of 300 francs for Madeleine, counting the two *écus* and 80 francs that I put together bit by bit.

"You can see that it was a good deal. The other only came one more time–when I say the other, I mean the first... the handsome blond, the father. He arrived, as always, in the middle of the night, and told me that the mother would collect her child the next day. That was a blow–I was attached to him like a grandfather... and my daughter loved him too, make no mistake. So, the next day, in broad daylight, a beautiful woman came, with a little bit of a lackey, haughty as you like, and an English peasant who seemed like a good chap. 'Pierre Louchet?'–'That's me.'–'I'm looking for my child.'–'That's all right.' But, as you know, Lieutenant, these aren't the old days. I'd taken my precautions, and as the beautiful woman had the Devil of an English name..."

"Lady Frances Elphinstone?" Robert put in.

"Something like that... but I can't be absolutely sure; all these English names are alike. We'll have to go to the house, where the woman's is written out in full. I can tell you that the little one hadn't grown thin in my house. No! He was fat, he was pretty, he was wriggling, thanks to the goat's milk. Good! The mother didn't look at him much and gave him one half-hearted kiss. Is that fishy? And yet she didn't seem crooked. At any rate, I had to give her the little creature; I could have cried!

"When she'd gone, I was all alone, thinking. I wasn't proud. The goat came prowling around looking for the child. I turned it away, poor beast. I had an idea. The beautiful woman didn't look like the little gold-framed portrait at all.

"It was the day after next when the fair-haired chap sang out 'For the best!' again and gave me the order to go. On the Tuesday I went to see you at Miremont, and ran into my blond chap again... but before running into him, I'd seen something funny: my little one, who was supposed to be in London. It was in the woods, to the right of the Croix Moraine, and the coach was waiting in the hunting-path. The child was rolling in the grass, watched by the English peasant... and the demoiselle that's living at the Chateau de Belcamp was with them. That one leapt to my eye, as they say. I stopped in amazement to look at her. That demoiselle is the one in the little gold-framed portrait, I swear to it–only a little paler, with sadder eyes. But she was smothering the child with the force of her kisses. That's right–just like the other one, who isn't the father. It's fishy, I tell you.

"Fishy or not, that's what happened. I said to myself: the Lieutenant gave me an order the other day that if I see anything, no matter what, in the surrounding area, in the woods or on the road; I have to make my report. Obedience! The soldier has no need to know the secrets of the strategy. So I've made my sincere and truthful deposition."

Robert Surrisy did not reply immediately. He seemed to be lost in a labyrinth of reflection. Eventually, he said: "You've done well, Pierre, my friend, and I thank you."

"Not at all... is it any use to you, Lieutenant?"

"Perhaps," Robert murmured, having fallen back into his reverie.

"So much the better... although you have, as they say, the expression of one who doesn't see any clearer than me..."

The former Lieutenant cut him off. "Let's go to your house, Pierre!"

The woodcutter marched off immediately.

Robert accompanied him in silence; after they had taken a few paces, he raised his bowed head again and shook it brusquely. "Damn it, this isn't our sort of business, Corporal," he said. "It needs better field-glasses than ours to see through it."

Pierre Louchet opened the door of his house and they went in together. The former Lieutenant was obliged to let his eyes become accustomed to the gloom before deciphering the characters scrawled on the inside of the door. After having read them, he dipped a cloth into a pot full of water, and carefully erased all traces of the name of Frances Elphinstone. The woodcutter watched him do it with surprise, but he did not permit himself any observation.

"To whom is the letter addressed that was entrusted to you?" Robert Surrisy asked.

Pierre promptly unbuckled his haversack and unrolled a little packet of cloth, within which was a letter bearing the inscription: *To J. H. Wood, esq., 4 The Strand, London.* Robert wrote the name and address in his notebook.

"What should I do now?" the woodcutter asked,

"Obey," Robert replied. "The order was given to you in accordance with the rite, my man, and you must not question it. Be on your way–and not a word of what you have told me to anyone else in the world!"

At six o'clock in the evening, Miremontese faces were on display in the Passage Feydeau, a dark alleyway off the Rue des Filles-Saint-Thomas, one of whose forks leads to one side of the Rue Feydeau, the other to the Rue des Colonnes.

The appearance of the neighborhood has changed completely since 1817. The old haunts of singers and vaudevillians–friends of gaiety, as one said frankly, in the days when share prices were not the only national literature and everyone's sole concern–have disappeared from the extension of the Rue Vivienne. There is scarcely a veteran of the wings remaining who can still talk about those old glories, the Café Chéron and Mother Camus' restaurant. Under the Restoration, the Café Chéron was as lively a place as the Café Procope had formerly been; as for Mother Camus' establishment, the provincials preferred it to Véfour's, because the portions were larger and the prices more modest. It was famous.

The remainder of the passage was occupied by scabrous booksellers, dingy milliners, glove-merchants celebrated for their good character, a flower-shop, a costumier's, a tobacconist's and a shop selling phosphor matches. Everything was uniformly grey, dusty and ugly. Paris is still not entirely free of shops where things are displayed that no one buys, and whose merchants have no intention of selling them because their real business is another kind, but it must be confessed that such mysterious trafficking flourished remarkably under the Restoration, when the entire Palais-Royal had displays full of pretexts and surprises.

The milliners smiled at fortune behind a half-dozen old hats that Mademoiselle would not have wanted; the flower-shop brazenly shook its violets under the noses of passers-by, displaying twin rows of Savoyard teeth that seemed enameled in snow; the glove-merchants, less bold, restricted themselves to picking their noses–a Masonic sign understood throughout the universe; the costumier had changing-rooms; the tobacconist managed a mythical marriage-bureau; the match-seller, finally, had contacts in the theater and was responsible, in exchange for a small consideration, for obtaining audiences with princesses, with or without *roulades*.[114]

No one believed any of it; such holes are as necessary to these industries as to night-flying birds. The least ray of light puts them to flight. The species never becomes entirely extinct, but every demolition crushes enormous quantities of them. When the fresh air penetrates the last noxious passage, when light inundates the last disreputable gallery and dries up the cavernous dampness of the last peristyle, virtue will surely reign over the health-filled world–and the English, wandering like shadows, will ask our doorstep uncles in vain where the playground is nowadays to be found.

All the merchants in the passage sold theater tickets. What a trade! Madame Morin du Reposoir, flanked by another fat lady who had taken over her business, bought hers in the bookshop. The Chaumerons struck theirs from the man with the phosphor matches, and the Bondon garniture, via the medium of Madame Célestin, purchased their coupons at the costumier's. That took an hour. Terrible efforts were expended on both sides for the sake of two *sous*. The vocabulary of the Passage Feydeau was then celebrated throughout Europe, but Miremont replaced eloquence with bravura, and richness of language by heroic tenacity. Miremont was the conqueror and landed triumphantly in the peristyle of the theater with the tickets they had plundered.

Joconde, the beloved of Pontoise, was playing; Monsieur Etienne [115] was then the great poet of the Passage Feydeau. Martin, Elleviou and Madame Gavaudan were singing.[116] There was a crowd, but one could have said that Miremont made a considerable proportionate contribution to the success of these excellent artistes; Miremont, that evening, filled out the Feydeau hall. From the foremost boxes to the flies, Miremont was enthroned in full dress. The two Bondons wore gloves; the left-hand one also wore a brand new blue ribbon on his arm, for it is on days of celebration above all that it is necessary to post a warning-light on the brink of the abyss.

The packages, baskets and overnight bags that we saw piled up at the foot of the Croix Moraine signpost were full of Sunday dresses, fresh ribbons, imitation Valenciennes lace, and those dear cotton velvets that one mounts in metal on one's forehead when one fancies something original and is a long way from home. Miremont was striving for effect; Miremont was under arms; Paris had better watch out!

Among the first-tier boxes was one as bright as a basket of flowers: Lady Frances Elphinstone's, which contained Suzanne, Jeanne and Germaine. Suzanne had chosen a seat in the back row, with the result that the front was lit up by three delightful faces: Frances, Jeanne and Germaine. Frances was as happy as all innocent worshippers of Paris are when they receive a caress from their idol. Jeanne, who was in love and beloved, was as beautiful as the contemplation of happiness; she sensed the emotional gaze of Comte Henri behind her.

Henri was, indeed, there, in the same row as Suzanne. Deputy Potel was also there, looking like a bodyguard. Madame Morin du Reposoir had not waited for any such invitation. Disregarding the expense, she had bought upper circle seats, so that she was sure at least of being in first place after milady's box. The Bondon garniture was displayed in the gallery; Madame Célestin was keeping a close watch on Florian, who had a woman sitting next to him. With his flighty character, that Florian brought many worries into Madame Célestin's household.

In the fourth circle sat Chaumeron and his two daughters. He had won his case; Cécile had only paid half price in spite of her size. In the fifth, Briquet, knife in hand, was craftily inscribing his name on the balustrade. There were indeed five circles in the Feydeau auditorium, which had already been condemned twice by architects for its immeasurable height but had reopened both times by virtue of speculation and did not actually collapse until 1830.

Robert Surrisy, Laurent and Férandeau were in the orchestra stalls. Robert was seated at the end of a row next to the ground-floor boxes, placed so that he could keep watch on milady's box without turning round.

It would require an entire page to record the meaningful glances and gestures, the acknowledgements and pleasant grimaces exchanged between the various members of Miremontese society. The Chaumerons were slightly put out to find themselves higher up than the Bondons, and Madame Célestin cursed roundly at seeing the Deputy's wife below her, but they saw one another's annoyance and consoled themselves with that.

Briquet was not at all annoyed. Férandeau held the Opéra-Comique in contempt, wishing that he was at the *Veau-qui-Tette*.

We have no comment to make on the play, because our drama unfolds outside the theater.

Towards the end of the first act, Henri leaned close to Lady Frances' ear and said, loud enough to be heard by everyone in the box: "I see Lord Seyton down there. It's necessary that I speak to him." Jeanne turned round; Henri gave her a smile and added: "I'll be back shortly." He left the box.

Robert slipped inconspicuously along the aisle and left the orchestra stalls by the door facing the box. Jeanne looked around the auditorium seeking to identify the man named Lord Seyton.

In the corridor, Robert broke into a run. This precaution was not superfluous, for by the time he arrived in the theater foyer, Comte Henri de Belcamp was already disappearing into the depths of the Passage Feydeau. He was alone; Lord Seyton was not waiting by the exit. Robert, who put his best foot forward, saw him climb into a cab, still alone, at the corner of the Rue des Colonnes.

The cab's two horses broke into a trot and turned the corner of the Rue de Richelieu; Robert had no difficulty in following it.

The cab went down the Rue de Richelieu and stopped in front of the Passage Hulot, not far from the corner of the Rue Traversière, where the Molière fountain has since been erected. Robert slid into the shelter of a doorway. Monsieur de Belcamp got down, said a few words to the coachman, and without looking right or left, went into the passage leading down to the Rue Montpensier.

Robert immediately left his refuge.

"Are you booked, friend?" he asked, as he passed alongside the cab.

"Yes, sir, I am," the coachman replied, "and paid in advance to remain at this very spot."

Robert went down the steps four at a time and crossed the Rue Montpensier into the alleyway that ran behind the Café Hollandais into a cobbled street, which he surveyed with a piercing glance. Comte Henri was already walking in the garden–at a rapid pace, to be sure, but with an easy manner that certainly betrayed no suspicion that he was being followed.

The garden was still laid out like a labyrinth, full of hedges concealing verdant closets, which made the Palais-Royal the most renowned pleasure-garden in the universe. Henri passed through the pleasure-seeking crowd without once stopping or turning round. Robert was following him more closely now, by courtesy of the gaudy laughing swarm, watching him attentively.

Henri was obviously not looking for anyone here. He was passing through. He went to the right of the fountain, whose newly-restored jet was designed to fall in a very distinct pattern that some said was a rose, others the star of the Legion of Honor. The star and the rose, equally famous in the province and abroad, each had their respective partisans;[117] the two things do not resemble one another in nature, but where jets of water are concerned, faith was their salvation. Duels had been fought to settle the question, and it was said that a regular at the Café Valois died without fear or reproach crying: "But it is a rose."

Comte Henri, cutting straight through groups of elegant young men and flocks of pompously-undressed women, arrived at that other glory: the Palais-Royal cannon. Robert expected some mysterious meeting to take place at any moment, and he kept his man closely covered–but Comte Henri exchanged not a single word or glance as he went along. He kept to his course. Where was he going? Had he left the box in the middle of an act merely to take a walk? When he reached the cannon, he changed direction abruptly. Instead of continuing towards the Palais, he went back into the garden, pressing his pace. Robert was on the point of losing him two or three times, and would indeed have lost him if he had not suddenly realized that he was not the only one on Monsieur de Belcamp's track. Since they had been among the hedges, a little man of bizarre appearance had been pushing or brushing his way through the crowd.

At first, Robert had taken him for a child, because of his height and the thinness of his limbs, but the lamplight had illuminated the face of a little man, monkey-like, jaundiced, worn and wrinkled, with blinking eyes hurt by the light. This little man was dressed entirely in black. His coat, waistcoat and trousers were coming apart at the seams and very dirty. His black hat was bald, crooked and squashed. He had enormous shoes that gave him the appearance of Hop o'my Thumb [118] clad in seven-league boots.

French poverty is not expressed thus. For anyone who was no stranger to English life, it was as plain as the nose on his face that this little man was a Londoner. At every step along the muddy shires of the Thames, one encounters fashionable clothes thus reduced to tatters, a hundred times more hideous than authentic rags. Now, Madeleine Surrisy's son knew London much better than he would have cared to admit. It was the obvious Englishness of the little man that attracted his attention. His maneuvers soon left no more doubt; he too was after Comte Henri. In order to remain on Comte Henri's heels–who had not paid him the slightest attention–the little man went straight through the crowd like a dog shooting between people's legs, using his elbows in an entirely British verve.

At the far side of the garden, facing the gambling den at No. 113, Robert suddenly lost sight of the Comte. It is only necessary to hesitate for a second to lose a man in a crowd and not know which way to go. Robert was in that situation when he saw the sordid black hat slipping between two milk-white shoulders surging forth from beneath the veils of married women. The two women, to each of whom one of these shoulders belonged, issued their complaints in harmony, but the little man was not in the least discomfited, even though they expressed their outrage in the finest vocabulary of the marketplace.

Robert followed the direction of the hat, which served as his lighthouse, and caught sight of Comte Henri's profile at the moment when, having crossed the street, he was disappearing into the alleyway beside No. 113.

The little man threw himself into that alley, with Robert after him.

Henri did not climb the stairway to the gaming house; he took the Rue de Valois, which ran down to the Passage Radziwill–which was slightly less repulsive then than it is now, but was already one of the most shameful streets in a quarter than counted its shames by the hundred.

At the far end of the Passage Radziwill, in the Rue des Bons-Enfants, a carriage was waiting. The Comte climbed into it. The carriage set off just as the little man emerged from the passage.

When Robert came out in his turn, the carriage was already turning past the guardhouse of the Bank. The horses seemed to be strong; Robert did not think for a minute that he could match their speed. He looked round for a cab but found none. He stopped at the corner of the Rue de la Vrillière, along which Comte Henri's carriage was moving at a rapid trot.

He saw this: the little man in black was not as discouraged as he. As the carriage passed the guardhouse, the little man leapt forward with an agility unexpected in one of his wretched appearance. In a few strides, he had reached the carriage, and one audacious and fortunate acrobatic leap carried him on to the rear seat, where he huddled like a monkey.

The carriage disappeared into the distance.

Robert went back into the Palais-Royal and ordered a dish of Bavarian cream at one of the tables hidden in the bushes. From that table, through the meager foliage, he had a view of the alley beside the Café Hollandais, through which Comte Henri would have to go to reach the cab that was waiting for him at the other end of the Passage Hulot.

Henri, however, was nonchalantly lounging on the seat of his carriage. He lit a cigar. His hand, white and exquisitely formed, was firm. While the match lit up his face, though, you would have been able to observe darker rings around his eyes. His cheeks, forehead and lips were very pale.

The carriage went the long way round before stopping in front of the main entrance of a large house in the Rue Meslay. As he got down, Henri darted a glance at the rear seat, which was empty–but there was a little man at the door of the house, and it was he who lifted up the door-knocker. When the cord had been pulled, the little man humbly touched his old hat and stood aside. The Comte went in without taking any notice of the little man, who came in behind him.

The Comte went straight to the concierge. The little man remained hidden under the arch.

"Mr. Warren?" Henri asked, putting his head into the lodge.

"Don't know him."

"What! Isn't this no, 24?"

"That's right–but we don't have any Monsieur... what did you say?"

"Warren–William Warren."

"An Englishman?"

"That's right."

"Who does he represent?"

"The Commission for London and the United States."

"Don't know him."

Henri took a letter out of his pocket and read the address aloud: "Mr. W. Warren, 24 Rue Bondy."

The concierge shrugged his shoulders and pulled the cord. "Go out by the boulevard and the street facing," he said.

Henri thanked him, and took the door opposite the one by which he had entered. He thus found himself in the Boulevard Saint-Martin. Scarcely had he closed the door when a high-pitched voice with a strong English accent cried out from the arch: "The cord, if you please!" A few seconds later, the little man in black walked in his turn into the boulevard behind Comte Henri–who made no move to find out whether Mr. W. Warren, Commissioner for London and the United States, was in residence at No. 24 Rue de Bondy. He wanted nothing but carriages tonight, and his precautions for avoiding all possible pursuit were so superabundant that he went on his way without hesitation or anxiety. His trail, cut at each juncture, could not be followed. He was sure of this, to the extent that the fair-haired and charming cavalier, Comte Henri de Belcamp, had been left behind in the covered coach of the Rue Meslay. He now had black hair, and thick side-whiskers of the same hue; the disguise was so perfect that he could have passed before his father with impunity.

It could not have been any motive of scant importance that compelled Comte Henri to adopt this masquerade and these inexplicable detours; nor could it have been any preoccupation of ordinary life that engraved circles round his eyes and made his lips pallid. Nevertheless, he remained calm; he held his head high. He was one of those men who can control the beating of their hearts.

He climbed into a cab in the Place du Château-d'Eau-Saint-Martin and was taken to the Barrière Saint-Denis, where he got out. He ran along the exterior boulevard to the Barrière Poissonière, where he took a public coach back towards the center. All this must have been planned in advance, because he left the public vehicle at the Conservatoire to throw himself into a coach that was obviously waiting for him, which departed at the gallop, taking him in no time at all to those joyous latitudes where the old Tivoli opened its gardens on to the Rue Saint-Lazare, at the end of the Chaussée d'Antin.

The district was already being built up, but still presented a suburban aspect. On the eventual site of the Gare de Rouen, where the streets are now so well-aligned and sad that they have imprinted their names on every capital in Europe, there were only a few buildings, villas surrounded by gardens, and large tracts of rough ground. Around Tivoli–which retained an excellent appearance in spite of its decadence–was a world of pleasure-gardens arranged in rows, where bourgeois traitors and bold speculators nourished at their own risk the habitual criminals who befriend holiday-makers. There one could see everything that can still be seen, alas! A little further away, seemingly to flatter the aspirations of certain Parisians towards nature, were groups of sickly chestnut-trees, poisoned by the dust, and beds of those frightful acacias whose flowers and leaves smell of brandy saturated with tobacco-smoke.

Comte Henri's driver stopped his sweating horses not far from the present-day entrance to the Salle Sainte-Cécile. The Comte immediately lunged into a back street running parallel to the Rue de Clichy, along the wall of Tivoli.

You have seen the madness of a runaway stallion, doing its utmost to shake off a horsefly stuck beneath its mane. It comes and goes, galloping and kicking, its mane and tail whipping back and forth in harmony. It hurls itself through bushes; it plunges into ponds; it whinnies, trembling and stiffening on its legs of steel; it rolls in the grass or the sand; the wind tears flecks of foam from its mouth and sweat runs along the black gutters of its smarting flanks. But is the fly worried by any of that? It pumps its quota of blood. When the stallion collapses, exhausted, the fly travels peacefully in the wrinkles of its hide. The noble animal's efforts achieve nothing; it carries its microscopic enemy with it wherever it goes. If the fly goes away, it is because it is no longer thirsty.

Twenty paces behind Comte Henri, the little man in black was running along the side street.

We need to go back a little less than an hour, for Comte Henri was running his laps with singular rapidity. While he was still sitting in Lady Frances Elphinstone's box, next to Deputy Potel, two couples stopped at the door of a well-known house in the vicinity of Tivoli, whose sign bore an image of a fat man dressed like King Louis XVIII, surrounded by everything edible: meats, fish, fowl, game, vegetables, pâtés, tarts, fruits and preserves. The legend read: *Le Gourmand du jour.*

Two placards were stuck on the windows of the ground-floor room, through which red-and-white-check cotton curtains were visible. The first represented the funeral procession of Credit, killed by bad debts; the second displayed a table superabundantly laden, behind which a cook was smiling, saying to the public: *Cheap today, free tomorrow.*

The two couples looked like this: two hearty fellows of evil appearance, both Herculean in stature; and two poor girls clad in cheap finery–wretched luxury–who bore the vivid stigmata of their misfortune in every part of their bodies. They were beautiful, but only at a distance, and like flowers from a bouquet thrown on a dung-heap. They both had brand new sashes over their faded dresses, gifts of the evening before or the same day, bright hats, poor shoes, and jewelry too large to be genuine. Their escorts, on the other hand, were clad in the finest cloth and furnished with good linen; their big feet stretched the varnished morocco of their boots, free of all mud-spatter. Skin the color of ox-blood was visible in the gaps between their cuffs and their gloves.

To tell the truth, they resembled neither workmen on holiday nor seamen strayed into Paris under pressure to pay their bills; but in spite of the elegance of their costumes they bore even less resemblance to gentlemen.

"You to wait outside," one of them said, extracting himself from the arms of his companion. "We to go in, here, Miss Josephine." [119]

"*Await*," added the other. "Wait... *wait a little, yonder*, Miss Celina."

"And to think that they're French!" exclaimed Josephine, putting her hands together.

"And Comtes!" added Celina.

"*Yes, my dear child...* French... *émigrés*... parents dead... *'tis so*... poor émigrés... to have forgot the language..."

" *'Tis so!*" repeated the other, raising his large eyes to heaven. "Poor little *émigrés*! Forgot the French language!"

The two hussies burst out laughing. Noll Green, the boxer from Southwark, frowned, while Lochaber Dick, the beer-swiller, clenched his fist in a threatening manner. They had been in Paris since the morning, and God knows what infernal omelet of broken bottles was already cooking in their stomachs.

"Talk to them, Josephine–you know English!" cried Celina. "They're going to hit us!"

"Sweethearts," Josephine said, immediately. "*Sweethearts of ours*, we're going, *we go...* to wait for you at the dance-hall over there... *wait for you...* while you attend to *your little business... do you love me, rogue?*"

Dick lifted her off the ground to embrace her fervently.

"What did you say?" Celina asked.

"I said, do you love me, rogue?"

"How do you pronounce that?"

"*Half a guinea for drinking your health, you sharpers!*"

Celina did her best to murder the phrase; her answer was a punch and two six-*livre* coins–after which they took flight, with the promise that they would rejoin the two men when their *business* was concluded.

Noll and Dick went into the *Gourmand du jour* and asked for a private room where they could chat comfortably. They both knew the name of things to eat and things to drink, so they were served an ample supper.

"To come here... *here*... a gentleman, this evening." Noll told the waiter.

"To ask for you? It's all right... I understand English."

"*Here*," Dick repeated.

"Let him in? Fine. Ring if you need anything."

Dick and Noll sat down and started with a friendly handshake across the table. They had not been suffering since their departure from London; their appearance was superb, and each of them had put on several pounds. On their large coarse faces, however–which the journey's libations had already tinted deep red–there was a certain expression of anxiety and ill-ease. Any Parisian villain would have described their moral state in this fashion: they were afraid.

They looked at one another in silence.

Noll uncorked a bottle of Bordeaux and sighed profoundly. Dick responded with a similar sigh, extending his glass.

"We haven't had time to chat, old Green," he said. "Time flies in Paris."

"So does money!" Noll put in.

"Bah!" said the beer-swiller. "Tom Brown will bring us more... money, that is. If that were all..."

The boxer swallowed the entire contents of his full glass in a single draught. "Yes, yes... if that were all," he echoed. "I would give a lot, old hand, to be sitting in the parlor at Sharper's, even though we'd only have a pot of beer instead of this damned claret. What have you done with the passport?"

"Lit my pipe with it, this morning. You?"

"I tore mine up and threw it in the river... but that won't get us to the other side of the Channel, will it?"

"No, we should have left by the mail-coach this morning."

"Without money?"

"Tom Brown reckoned on that. He's holding on to us."

The boxer pinched the cork of a second bottle with the tips of his fingers and extracted it effortlessly. "The good life in Brussels!" he went on, in a melancholy tone.

"To Lyon, too, by God!" exclaimed the beer-swiller. "I could have worked there on my own account very comfortably. I'd already made some useful contacts, when that Devil of a letter arrived."

"The blank letter!" groaned Noll, who had a sort of pale cloud on the scarlet backcloth of his face.

"It arrived at midday... for eleven o'clock in the evening. A bad day!"

Noll's glass clicked on his teeth when he tried to drink.

Dick looked at him, surprised. "You aren't a *greenhorn*, though," he said, employing the word used in Australia and throughout North America to charac-

terize new conscripts to the adventurous life. "Me, I can still drink like a man...
cheers!"

He did indeed swallow the rest of the bottle, valiantly.

"What do you expect?" murmured the boxer. That fat brewer in Brussels
took me for a friend. He had good wine–and Hollands gin like you've never
drunk, old hand!" This was said with real feeling.

"Oh," said Dick, "it's easy to see that you don't know my brewer in Lyon.
It wasn't Hollands gin he had, it was balm! Do you think I don't regret it?"

"Give us a cup of brandy," Noll said. "I'm sick at heart." Having drunk,
he continued: "When eleven o'clock chimed, he was talking to me about his
marriage. He said: 'My dear Comte...' "

"Hold on!" the beer-swiller interrupted. "So he was getting married too?
My man in Lyon, Mr. Turner, had already had his wedding-presents... a pretty
little thing, who'd have led him a merry dance!"

"He was drinking the wine that I'd poured him," Noll went on, in a somber voice, "when I felled him like an ox with a blow of my fist. He never uttered
a sound... but he was breathing... and he looked at me with his eyes bulging out
of his head." Noll passed his hands over his forehead, becoming almost pale.

"God damn me!" Dick exclaimed. "You're not very merry tonight."

"No," the boxer replied. "The day when Joshua Bone died drinking with
Tom Brown... I remember he was like that."

"And had he done something for Tom?" Dick asked.

"Yes... and Tom Brown paid for it handsomely."

There was a silence. The plates making up their meal were untouched;
they had done nothing but drink since they sat down.

Dick spoke first. "The Devil with it!" he said. "You could make Tom
Brown jump with your thumb..."

The boxer shook his head.

"I'll bet ten pounds that I could lay him out in six passes," cried the beer-
swiller. "You're ill, old hand!"

"Yes," Noll said, very quietly. "I believe I'm ill."

"Hadn't you ever seen a dead man before?"

"Yes, I've killed... you know very well that I've killed."

"How many times?"

"Many times."

"And how old are you, Noll?"

"Twenty-one next birthday."

"I'm only 20, and I seem to be your master. To the Devil with these dark
thoughts, mate! The two brewers are where we'll all be, a little sooner or a little
later. Is that anything to put us in a bad humor? Put me three or four good
pinches of pepper in a glass of brandy and your heart will be back in its place,
like a good fellow. God damn me! We must be able to stand up straight, old
hand... in my opinion, we'll have work to do tonight."

The beer-swiller took the trouble to prepare the terrible medicine whose formula he had prescribed personally. He poured half the pepper into a wine-glass full to the brim with brandy, stirred the beverage with the handle of his fork, and presented it to Noll, who gulped it down in one.

"That's warm," he said, breaking the empty glass between his fingers, which did not bleed at all. "I feel better, and that's enough chitchat, friend! We barely have time to get our business straight."

"Right!" said Dick. "That's the ticket! Our business. You're the oldest—what's your opinion?"

"My opinion," said the boxer, who was sitting up straight, having been revived by that diabolical potion, which might have killed a horse, "my opinion hasn't changed. Tom Brown is using us like a couple of tools to be broken when the need arises."

"The need's arisen, then; we're on the point of being broken."

"Exactly."

"Have you worked out why the two murders were done?"

"No. It must be the beginning of some devilish scheme. Trying to work out Tom Brown is a lost cause. What good would it do, anyway? What matters to us is that Tom Brown never leaves evidence behind him; all those who've done his work are dead."

"You're talking like a book now, Old Noll."

"It's warm, your medicine, but it's good. I'm going to swallow our man like a chicken... if he comes alone."

"He'll come alone," Dick said. "He doesn't trust anyone but himself to carry out certain executions."

"Don't drink any more then, old hand. We're in tune."

"Not only will he come," continued the beer-swiller, "but he'll bring the money and the new passports he promised. He always keeps his word. It's only the final blow that breaks the bargain."

"He's a tricky fellow," murmured the boxer.

"There's two of us, and we're worth our price. Who'll begin?"

"Where can we put the body?"

These two questions were voiced at the same time.

As is the custom in certain suburban drinking-dens, which serve as lodg-ings if the need arises, there was a bed in the room furnished with bleached cot-ton curtains. The curtains were shut. Noll and Dick got up at the same time. Noll went to draw the bed-curtains and Dick opened the window.

The bed had no sheets. The window overlooked the rough ground of which we have spoken. It was pitch dark outside.

"It's jumpable," said the beer-swiller.

"And we could stash him in there," Noll added. Then he turned in alarm towards his companion, who had stifled an exclamation of surprise. "What is it, old hand?"

Dick closed the window again. "It's amazing what you think you see on a dark night," he murmured. "Do you remember Ned Knob–solicitor Wood's little clerk?"

"A funny little chap–crafty. So what?"

"So what? It seemed to me that I saw a little chap creeping along under the window–very short, very thin, and very like Ned Knob."

"You're dreaming... but so am I, by God, or else there's someone behind the door." He lifted the catch swiftly and threw it wide open. The corridor into which he threw himself was empty.

As he closed the door again, the clock made the dull click by which old clocks signal the approach of the hour, a minute or two early.

They moved towards one another. They were somber but resolute–and certainly, to see them thus, side by side and hand in hand, both young, athletic in build and broken in by all manner of violent crimes, it was impossible to have any doubt about the result of the imminent conflict.

"Is it agreed?" Dick murmured.

"It's agreed," Noll replied. "I'll begin by stunning him with a punch... you know that I won't make any mistake." He clenched his powerful fist, whose muscles stood out.

"I'll finish it," Dick added, "by stabbing him with a Bowie knife. You know that I won't make any mistake with that, either."

"When?"

"When he's paid, and takes the passports out of his pocket."

"So the signal will be...?"

"His wallet in his hand. Aim true."

"And strike hard!"

The clock chimed. As the first stroke of nine o'clock sounded, the door opened and Comte Henri de Belcamp appeared on the threshold.

Comte Henri de Belcamp consulted his watch as he got back to the carriage that was waiting for him in the Rue Saint-Lazare. It showed half past nine. He had certainly lost no time in straightening out his business with Noll Green, the Southwark boxer, and Lochaber Dick, the beer-swiller, at the *Gourmand du jour* restaurant. He returned as coolly and calmly as he had departed, although his face was very pale in the light of the coach's lanterns. He woke the sleeping coachman and leapt nimbly over the step, saying: "To the gallop!"

He threw himself on the seat and tore off his thick beard and black hair with a single movement of his hand, like an actor ripping off his stage-jewelry after having wiped away the feverish sweat that triumph and defeat alike set upon the brow.

All the calmness–or, rather, all the statue-like coldness–that had formerly been set upon the young Comte's face like some strange seal had vanished now that he felt screened from all scrutiny. There was an extraordinary emotion in his face now–and, it must be said, in the entire attitude of his body. He put his hand on his heart repeatedly; it was beating so hard against the walls of his chest-cavity that it was hurting. His face was radiant with some powerful exaltation; his eyes were savagely bright; the deep breath pumped by his straining lungs was noisy.

Words fell from his lips, perhaps unwittingly. "Remorse!" he murmured. "What does it want with me? I defy it! I am my own path: it's fate that kills. My hatred is as pure as love, since it was not born of the spirit of vengeance. I seek my weapons in the shadows, but I shall do battle in the light of the Sun. I have the right to be implacable, since my name is Punishment. The Hell with re-morse!"

He smiled proudly, challenging God to do likewise.

"And that's the final blow," he continued. "The path is open wide and free; the last obstacle is removed. I shall march henceforth with head held high, sweeping the crowd with my eyes, at which none shall have the right to be of-fended. No one in the world–no one but a liar–will be able to point at me and say: 'there is one of those men that the world calls criminals.'

"Not only do I have my conscience for my refuge, but I have made that refuge into a citadel whose rampart is the law. God was with me; I shall have the world. Nothing stands any longer between me and the millions that will be the sinews of my war. They are mine–and as if my road to victory were already blessed by good fortune, it is love that has given me my weapons!"

These last words burst forth involuntarily, and were followed by a silence.

"And for that, my good lord," said a high-pitched voice, in English–which struck his ear like a supernatural visitation–"poor Dick has drunk his last bucket of ale and Noll Green won't knock out any more boxers at Covent Garden, eh?"

Comte Henri's head experienced a shock and a shooting pain. The idea that he had suddenly been struck by madness went through his brain like a sharp cold needle. He looked at the right-hand door and the left-hand door, which were shut. The coach was empty. The noise of the wheels on the roadway made it impossible to tell whether the voice had come from above, below, in front or behind.

He remained motionless for a moment, holding his breath–the bold man who had never been afraid of man or demon in his entire life.

His eyes strayed by chance to the front seat, where he had carelessly thrown his cloak after waking the coachman. The cloak was moving.

Comte Henri contemplated this mystery with a sort of horror. He had confronted two Herculean assassins alone; here, there was not even room for a man!

Precisely for that reason, Henri's nerves rebelled. He would not have been afraid of a man.

It was, however, the head of a man that emerged from the folds of the cloak: a poor head, thin and pale, with sharp features and bloodshot eyes; the head of the little man dressed in black rags whom we have observed following the Comte with such imperturbable relentlessness.

Henri's eyes were no longer expressing anything but surprise.

The little man stared at him with a singular mixture of terror and effrontery. "I presume that it's John Devil to whom I have the honor of speaking?" he murmured, tremulously–but with a smile that was by no means free of irony.

Henri shivered at the name of John Devil, and his eyes flashed.

"Don't strangle me right away," the little man went on, hastily. "It would be a pity, for you and for me... for me because I count on making my fortune, for you because it would be the end of your story. My life isn't worth a shilling, but I take my precautions as if I were a millionaire."

"Who are you and what do you want?" Henri demanded, rudely.

"I'll tell you all that, my good lord," the little man replied, "but first, I'd like to acquaint you with the precautions that I've taken against being strangled by you. I haven't the strength of a fly; it's a matter of having an avid intelligence. So this is how I arrange my petty affairs: I have my mother in London and my mistress in Paris. My mother and my mistress each have a copy of a little testament I've written. My mother must open hers if she doesn't hear from me for four days, and it's three days since I last wrote to her. My mistress must do likewise the very next morning if I don't return one night. Now, following my orders, my mother and my mistress have taken the same precautions as me– with the result that if, after doing away with me, you set out to do away with my mother and mistress too, according to your habit, you would still have to deal with two unknown denouncers who would be able to have your head cut off in France or see you hanged in England, according to your lordship's choice. That's all."

The young Comte had recovered his coolness and considered his interlocutor with curious eyes.

"What do you say to that, my good lord?" the little man continued, throwing the cloak to one side in order to make himself entirely comfortable.

"Nothing, as yet," Henri replied.

"That's fine–you need to know what my little testaments contain. I know how to make them: I was once a solicitor's clerk, and I'd have carried it through if it hadn't been for the gin, my good lord, for I've an eye as sharp as a pen-knife and a light-fingered hand. My testaments contain, apart from a list of my bequests, a very curious anecdote relating to Tom Brown, Noll Green and Lochaber Dick–not the anecdote that came to pass at the *Gourmand du jour* but another one: the distribution of passports in the name of Comte Henri de Belcamp, in the cellar of the demolished house opposite Sharper's in London."

The young Comte's stare became fixed.

"And do you know who I am?" he asked, in a low voice.

"You're Tom Brown," the little man replied, without hesitation, "at Sharper's and in other places. You're James Davy at Scotland Yard. My former employer, old Wood, calls you Henri–Henri de Belcamp, I suppose."

Henri put his hand over his eyes. "You worked for Wood?" he said, in an even lower voice.

"And I knew your mother well. Ned Knob... little Ned Knob. Like all pickpockets, Mr. Wood loves no one but himself: he kicked me out because I took a shilling here and there. Your lordship has his mother's voice... a lovely voice, to be sure. It's the voice that I recognized in the cellar, over the road from Sharper's. It's also the voice that I recognized this evening, at the end of the Passage Hulot, when you paid for your cab. There was another gentleman following you, but he lost us at the guardhouse outside the Bank. I've been looking for you in Paris, eating dry bread, for a fortnight."

"How did it come about that the other gentleman was following me, Ned Knob, my friend?" Comte Henri asked, softly.

In a few words, the little clerk gave a description of Robert Surrisy that was so precise and detailed that it was impossible to mistake him.

The young Comte smiled. He opened the carriage door and spoke to the coachman in a language that was neither English nor French. Ned Knob did not remember ever having heard a similar language. The carriage was on a boulevard, and the coachman urged the horses to go faster.

The little clerk began to tremble.

"Ned Knob, my friend," Henri said, fixing him with a cold stare, "You know how things stand and you're a brave lad, but your precautions are vain. When one wagers all against all, it's necessary to be sure of one's ground, and you need more than stage-armor to confront John Devil."

"Are you really John Devil, then?" Ned stammered, terrified.

The carriage stopped abruptly. Ned, whose eyes had been fixed on the Comte for some time, glanced sideways out of the windows. There was a black wall on one side, silent and still water on the other. There was not a soul to be seen in the vicinity.

The little clerk went white, and his face became distressed. "I knew that I was risking my life," he said, between chattering teeth, "but I wasn't lying; if you kill me, you're finished."

Footsteps were audible in the distance on the solitary quay. Instinctively, Ned opened his mouth to call for help. The Comte raised his hand. The cry died in Ned's throat and he slipped to his knees, stammering: "I told the truth, I told the truth. If you kill me, you're dead!"

Henri set his notepad on his knees and handed a pencil to Ned, whose eyes regained their spark.

"Write!" the young Comte instructed.

Ned looked up at him, then his wretched body gave way, while he moaned: "I've broken my head on a rock!"

Henri studied him carefully. "Write!" he repeated, in an imperious tone. And he began to dictate, while the little clerk took the pencil. It ran over the paper with amazing rapidity. Two sheets were completed in an instant. Ned tore them off and gave them to Henri, who read them. The first said:

Mother,
The package that I left in your hands must be put in the post today, addressed to the Comte de Belcamp. It's a matter of life or death.

Your son, Ned.

The second said:

My poor Molly,
If you want to save my life, send the package I entrusted to you to the Comte de Belcamp. My salvation depends on you.

Ned.

When he had finished reading these notes, Henri looked at the little man, who was looking back at him, staring at him with wide-open eyes, somber and resolute.

"You guessed what I was going to dictate to you," he said.

"I have met my master," Ned replied. "Question me before you kill me, milord. Perhaps you have need of a slave?"

Henri did not reply.

"Or a dog," added Ned. "I want to live."

Henri tore up the two sheets of paper, and threw them out of the window. "To the boulevard!" he said to the coachman.

Ned embraced his knees, and there was a tear in his bloodshot eye. "Milord," he said, "until this moment, you would not have been my conqueror, for I would have died avenged."

Henri's shoulders made an imperceptible movement. "There were specific formulations agreed with your two depositories beforehand that should have been in these letters, weren't there, Ned?" he murmured, smiling.

"Yes, milord. As soon as the letters were received, my two depositions would have been in the hands of the law in London and Paris."

The young Comte put his gloved hand on the little man's meager shoulder, while he spoke in a negligent fashion. "Unless John Devil has stolen his reputation, I think it more probable that your mother and mistress would both have been visited by John Devil. Ned, my friend, you owe me nothing for the life that I have given you; I need neither a dog or a slave; those who serve me are rewarded for their devotion..."

"My body and my soul are yours, milord!" said Ned, forcefully.

Comte Henri got out of the carriage at the corner of the Rue du Temple and the boulevard. He put a dozen gold pieces in Ned's hand.

"You must be a very clever chap." he said, "to have followed me all the way from the Palais-Royal. Go to a tailor and get yourself a complete outfit of new clothes. This is my address in Paris; tomorrow morning, you'll be at my disposal, ready for anything."

"Anything, milord!" echoed the little clerk.

Henri watched him go into a neighboring clothes-merchant's, then went quickly away in the direction of the Rue Meslay.

The little clerk chose himself a complete suit of clothes and changed into it immediately. He looked at himself in several mirrors, quite satisfied, and went out, carrying his former wretchedness under his arm.

Ned was not without a domicile. In the Faubourg Montmartre, a few steps from the boulevard, there was then a farm belonging to the hospitals of Paris; the Rue Geoffroy-Marie runs through the site now. The neighborhood of that farm, which was reached by way of a tortuous passage whose entrance was on the Faubourg itself, was one of the curiosities of the great city. All the dirty accoutrements of country life were there, without fields: a colony of pig-sties, stables, chicken-runs, manure heaps, little lakes of asphalt yawning on the edges of pathways. Save for the trees, the air and the water, the frightful village lacked nothing; it produced milk, eggs and rabbits; its cockerels woke the whole of the Bergère district in the middle of the night, and every evening one could see its skinny cows drinking from the filthy gutters of the Rue de Boule-Rouge.

It is not so far removed in the night of time; the farm lasted until 1838.

There were roads there as poor as any in Brittany, heaths where the thistles–Paris's heather–grew to gigantic heights. By day, bric-a-brac was sold in the mud; by night, the darkness was alive with vermin.

Numerous houses of ill-repute were distributed along the principal passage, which ran as capriciously as the River Meander [120] from the Faubourg Montmartre to the present corner of the Rues de Trevise and Richer. The branch that went back towards the Rue Bergère via the Passage Hamel was overflowing with dustbin-rakers. The Opéra sang and danced 50 paces away to the west; to the south, another 50 paces away, the Bourse displayed its civic virtues and proverbial honor. Fifty paces: a hundred leagues! Nowadays the Boule-Rouge district is home to so many clerks and fancy goods, and so many women of means inscribed in the ledger of Paphos [121] that we can scarcely believe the legends of the monstrous past. How near to barbarity the pure flowers of civilization can bloom!

Ned had a sixth share in a little shed in the Passage Hamel. (When I say a sixth, I am only counting humans.) In his corner, Ned had two bundles of straw, which he shared with a large and robust woman of 40, who had been a coal-heaver at Rotherhithe and a giantess at Greenwich Fair—his pretty Molly, as he called her. Another bundle was the resting-place of a Jewish family of scrap-iron merchants. The final heap accommodated a Savoyard couple on in the full fervor of their honeymoon, who bred rabbits in the hope of making an income of three thousand francs therefrom.

Molly was the legal wife of a carrier of portable bridges for spanning gutters, and Ned had bought her from her husband, in a perfectly honorable transaction conducted in Lower Thames Street, for a shilling. That fashion of divorce retains something noble and truly English; the resultant unions are generally amicable. Ned and Molly's love for one another was founded in mutual esteem.

Everyone in the shed was asleep save for the hungry rabbits, which where prowling their wooden hutches in a melancholy fashion. Ned came in, making as little noise as possible as he made his way to the straw where Molly was snoring. He put an uncorked bottle of brandy under her nose and the valiant woman, believing herself to be in the most delightful dream, opened her large mouth to receive the celestial dew. When she had drunk enough, Ned woke her up with a kick in the ribs.

"It's your man, my love," he said.

Molly put out both hands to grab the brandy bottle.

"Get up, I beg you, my heart," said Ned, with polite gravity. "Your man has done some good business this evening, and it's your turn to do some work."

For a long time, Molly had earned her living unloading coal-barges; she was by no means lazy, and immediately got to her feet. When she stood up, the top of Ned's head was level with her chin. She took an old straw hat with a green veil that was hanging from a joist and put it on. The rest of her clothing consisted of a torn calico dress, over which a man's waistcoat was buttoned. When she went out like that, the Parisian street-urchins followed her through the streets, making carnival calls; Ned was proud of this success.

"A swig, Master Knob," she said, "to warm my heart. A swig!"

Ned allowed her to take two large gulps; then he went to get a shovel and a pickaxe from the sleeping Jew's scrap, which he placed in Molly's hands.

"You can't see how I'm dressed now in here, my beloved," he said. "Let's go out, and one look will be sufficient for you to understand why I can't carry these things through the city."

Pretty Molly followed him meekly. He stopped under the first street-lamp and went on affectionately: "Look at me, my love. Look at your man!"

She opened her large stupid eyes. "Haven't you found me a new skirt as well, Master Knob?" she asked.

"A skirt, Molly," the little clerk replied, lifting his hand to fondle her chin, "and a spencer [122] too... and good shoes for your little feet... and a silk scarf... and a fine linen chemise!"

"A swig, Master Knob!" said the coal-heaver, overcome by emotion. "A swig to drink!"

Master Knob had his bottle under his arm. They drank a tribute to their marriage.

Under the Restoration, the Palais-Royal district, where the life of pleasure was concentrated, and the areas around the theaters went to bed much later than we do today, but the rest of the city damped down its fires early. Beyond the boulevards, in particular, active traffic ceased at ten o'clock, and in the northern districts that are now centers of business and pleasure, those abroad could not be sure of their safety after a certain hour. Ned Knob walked ahead, his head high and his hands in his pockets. Molly followed him with her pickaxe and shovel. They did not find a single urchin in the whole of the Faubourg Montmartre to give them cheek. Molly did not ask where she was going; she could see the glitter of the bottle-glass in "her man's" armpit and that was sufficient.

From the Faubourg Montmartre, at whose extremity Notre-Dame-de-Lorette had not yet been built, Ned and his wife passed into the Rue Saint-Lazare, which was even more deserted and poorly lit. The Tivoli's gates were closed and the lamps within extinguished. Ned turned the corner of the garden and too the side-road along which the Comte had gone two hours earlier—but instead of going past the front of the *Gourmand du jour*, whose windows were now all dark and closed, Ned turned left into the rough ground.

After taking a hundred paces, he stopped abruptly, at the foot of a bush, and said with pride: "See, my love, what I do to those who cross swords with me!"

Molly came to join him. A man's corpse was lying at the foot of the bush, illuminated by moonlight. Molly leaned on her spade and looked at him. "A swig, Master Knob," she said. Then she added, tranquilly: "It looks like Lochaber Dick, who drank buckets of ale for four shillings."

"Come on, Molly, my darling." Ned took another 30 paces into the brambles, and stopped again in a gully where the grass grew tall. A second dead man was half-hidden in the grass. "Would you have believed that your man was even stronger than Noll Green the boxer, my love?" Ned asked, crossing his arms upon his breast and posing like a winner at the Olympic games.

"Give us a swig, Master Knob... did you really take them both on alone?"

"And I still didn't use all my strength!" the little clerk replied. "You could easily have searched London and Paris for ten years for a chap like me and not found him, Molly my sweetheart. Wrap Noll up, I beg you, while I wind up poor Dick's affairs... I'm sorry, my love, for I'm a reasonable man–but why did they resist me?"

Molly knelt down beside Noll, who still retained a vestige of his natural warmth. He was stripped in a trice. He had been struck in the eye by a fist and his face was soiled with blood, but there was no trace of any wound on his body. Dick had a bloody Bowie knife beside him. An enormous gash in his right hand had left a pool of blood under his body, but that was all–and one would not ordinarily die of a cut hand or a black eye.

"Dig a ditch here, wife, I beg you," said Ned, indicating a place equidistant between the two corpses. "I'll cut the grass." He took the spade away while Molly attacked the ground vigorously with the pickaxe.

Ned returned after a few minutes, carrying an armful of grassy turf and a few thistles furnished with their roots. Pretty Molly seized the spade then, and cleared away the earth loosened by her pickaxe. From time to time, she asked for a swig of brandy, while Master Knob watched her work with affectionate admiration.

"There you are!" she said, eventually, wiping her forehead with the back of her sleeve. "They'll both be comfortable in there!"

She took the leather pouch in which Noll Green had kept his chewing-tobacco from her lap and bit off a plug. While Ned tried in vain to drag Dick, who was the lighter and more manageable of the two, she picked up the boxer and carried him in her arms.

"Always forget something," she murmured. "I've left him his ring. Have you noticed that he only has four fingers on his right hand, Master Knob?"

"He was bitten by a guard dog in Botany Bay the night he escaped with Tom Brown," the little man replied. "I know everything, me. Poor Dick had his head cut open by an iron bar in Newgate, fighting with a turnkey. If they hadn't met me, my love, I doubt they'd ever have found their master."

"But why did you kill them, Master Knob?" the giantess asked.

"Work, wife, I beg you," the little man relied, sternly. "Will you need to know as much as me from now on? Well then, take my place and be John Devil's right hand!"

Molly, who had already hoisted Dick on to her shoulders, let him fall back heavily to earth.

"Give us a swig, Master Knob," she stammered. "Did you find who you were looking for?"

Ned took the spade and turned the first spadeful of earth upon the two poor devils lying at the bottom of the hole, with an air of importance. Molly took over the job thereafter. When she had finished, Ned distributed the pieces of turf, planting a thistle here and there in the gaps. This was done with a good deal of intelligence and art.

"It only needs a few drops of rain," he said, "and all that will be bedded down like a charm. Now, my love, bring the two packages, the pickaxe and the spade. You'll not sleep any longer in suspect places. I'm a gentleman, you're a lady, and we'll live in a hotel, like royalty."

By the time Comte Henri set foot on the pavement of the Passage Feydeau, the Bourse clock was chiming half past ten. He went along the passage rapidly, but just as he reached the theater, he suddenly turned around. Robert Surrisy was behind him.

They both stopped dead at the same instant and looked at one another in surprise. Their stares were frank and bold, neither able to look down before the other.

"Have you been ordered to keep watch on me, Monsieur Surrisy?" Henri asked, his smile very haughty and very soft at the same time.

The former Sub-Lieutenant's cheeks reddened, but he kept calm nevertheless, and coolly replied: "Yes, Monsieur le Comte."

Henri's smile took on a slight hint of irony. "Are we enemies, then?" he murmured.

"Monsieur le Comte," Robert replied, "you know that I have, indeed, more than one reason to be your enemy. Perhaps I have others still, which you do not know."

"Monsieur Surrisy," Henri de Belcamp said, slowly and seriously, "I give you my word of honor that I would rather be your friend."

Robert bowed silently.

"Would you permit me to ask a question?" the young Comte went on, changing his tone once again.

"I am at your disposal, Monsieur."

"Since you came out of the theater at the same time as me, have you been back in, or have you maintained your post opposite the entrance of the Hollandais tap-room?"

Robert rubbed his eyebrow.

"I am addressing a man of honor, Monsieur, and I would be grateful for a reply."

"I have not gone back into the theater, Monsieur."

Henri offered him his hand, briskly. When the former Lieutenant hesitated, Henri took a step towards him and said in a low tone, while fixing him with a stare: *For the best!*"

Robert became deathly pale, lowered his gaze, and murmured: "I have already recognized the voice." He extended his arm in his turn, and Henri touched it.

"Yes... yes..." Robert stammered, in some distress. "You are a Master."

Henri released his hand and went on: "*Good cousin*, I came out to do the work of the Deliverance, and other eyes than yours were upon me. Remember this: you have not left me since I crossed the threshold of Lady Frances Elphinstone's box."

"I have not left you," Robert repeated. Then, he added: "If I have not left you, Monsieur le Comte..."

"Monsieur," Henri interrupted him, "under pain of violating your sworn oath, you would have helped me in the work that I came out to do! Your arm, if you please! We shall go back to milady's box together, and I require you to support my words with your testimony." He put his arm under the former Sub-Lieutenant's.

When they arrived in the box, the curtain was coming down on the last act of *Joconde*. All the ladies were expressing their admiration, and Jeanne said, reproachfully: "Monsieur le Comte should only have been gone a minute."

"Here is the real guilty party," Henri replied, lightly, smiling as he indicated Robert, who bowed silently.

Suzanne touched the Comte's arm and whispered: "My father is in the audience."

"Is he coming here?" Henri asked, his voice equally low.

Suzanne shook her head.

Then, as insistently as any child, Germaine reintroduced the subject of his absence, exclaiming: "Three whole hours! Three hours by the clock!"

All the ladies turned around, making a drawing-room of the box. Frances tried to meet Robert's eyes, but he remained by the door, cold and disconsolate.

Comte Henri, desirous of protesting against Germaine's assertion, swiftly unbuttoned his coat to take out his watch. Jeanne, whose wide and pensive eyes were following his every movement, changed color and let out a cry as she drew back: "Blood!"

"Blood!" echoed Germaine, Suzanne and Monsieur Potel.

Frances put her fan over her eyes.

There was, indeed, blood: two fresh bloodstains, still moist. One was on Henri's cuff; the other, larger in size, was on his white quilted waistcoat.

Henri looked at his waistcoat, then at his cuff. Not a muscle wavered in his tranquil face, and the smile never left his lips.

"That's true," he said, surveying all the frightened faces with a clear eye. He let his most affectionate gaze linger on Jeanne's forehead as she said: "It's true: there's blood!"

Henri turned slowly to Robert, who stood stiff and motionless, like a man of bronze, with his eyes downcast and his brow furrowed. "Did I get all of it, Monsieur Surrisy?" he asked, merrily. "Or do you have a few droplets too?"

Robert lifted his rebellious gaze to look at him, but although the radiance of his eyes was angry, Robert lowered them again in response to the proud and calm will of his adversary.

"Mesdames," Henri went on, with perfect ease and elegance, "Monsieur Surrisy and I had planned to be modest... and you saw that we tried to keep to it, since we submitted to your reproaches without complaint. But chance has denounced us pitilessly, and here I am like Rosine,[123] whose ink-stained fingers could not deny her pen. We have been fortunate enough, Monsieur Surrisy and I, to save a poor child who was about to be crushed by a carriage after falling over. Be reassured, Mesdames, that the blood is not mine."

"Can we be sure of that, Monsieur Robert?"

"We can be absolutely sure," Surrisy replied, "that it is not Monsieur le Comte's blood."

"But the child...?" Jeanne asked.

"Mere scratches."

"Dear heart," said Frances, embracing Jeanne. "She has tears in her eyes."

"It's just that I too have been saved from death," murmured the young woman.

The curtain rose on the short play. Robert left the box. Once in the corridor, he clutched his breast with both hands; he was choking. Instead of rejoining his two friends in the orchestra stalls, he went around the auditorium and knocked on the door of a facing box in the second rank, which was opened to him. Its sole occupant was an old man, who resumed his place while gesturing with his hand towards a chair.

The light of the chandelier, shining through the panes of the grille, made a bizarre mask of the man–beneath which we shall, however, recognize the deep wrinkles and white hair of Gregory Temple, the former Chief Superintendent of Scotland Yard.

"Well?" he said, fixing Robert with eyes that still sparkled feverishly.

One might have thought that a flood of words was pressing upon the lips of the young soldier of the Empire, but that a steel gag held them captive, crowded in his throat. He replied, in a strangled voice: "I did my best; it's not my trade."

"You haven't discovered anything about the man?"

"Nothing else."

"And about the child?"

"Nothing more."

"And the young woman using the name of Lady Frances Elphinstone?"

"Nothing."

XXI. The Impossible

The Sun itself was celebrating. Today, it had selected as a setting that pompous couch draped in gold and purple from which the king of the world might rise. The Orient scintillated beneath its powerful gaze like a chaos of precious stones as it radiated its divine and vivid fire while still emerging from the splendid opulence of its bed.

In the distance, throughout the fortunate countryside where the stream of the Oise slowed down in calculated leisure–a ruse that enabled it not to quit, until the last possible moment, the caresses of that gentle landscape–everything was smiling, singing the glorious mute canticle of awakening: all the woodlands flecked with cloudy white; all the pearl-clad ploughed fields; all the velvet, dew-spattered meadows; everything, from the youngest shoots of grass to the oldest giant oaks, from the water droplet suspended on the bush–daughter of nocturnal vapor that would become vaporous again with the advent of morning–to the colossal robe contemporary with the birth of the world, which would endure until creation's last sigh.

As if the light too were following an official schedule, the Chateau de Belcamp–where the heroes of the fête were asleep–emerged from the shadows with its proud forest-plumed facade well before the mist had lifted from the cradle of the river and the double valley. The morning radiance set its windows ablaze and brought out the sharp lines of its roof, which formed is aristocratic head-dress.

It was the great day, the feast of Saint Honoré: the day of universal feasting;[124] the day of endless dancing and fireworks: the birthday of Monsieur le Maire, the excellent man who had the love and respect of the entire district.

The most subtle minds in Miremont asked themselves repeatedly, always in vain, how Blondeau, the local Constable, could be drunk before the inns opened. The phenomenon belonged to the category of those that had to be accepted without their causes being known. At six o'clock, the local Constable, provisionally drunk already, crossed the esplanade and solemnly discharged his rifle, which was the most incorrigible poacher in the commune. At this signal, the bells of Miremont sounded in full flight, and the National Guard–in spite of the absence of Madame Célestin, their honorary Commandant–fired a volley in front of the town hall.

Monsieur Morin du Reposoir, the First Deputy, came out on the balcony and said a few prudently-phrased words exhorting the Miremontese population to the concord that embellishes enthusiasm. "At this time last year," he said, "there were some deplorable instances of disorderly conduct, which owed their origin to the barrels broached on the esplanade of the chateau in consequence of the family rejoicing. Mix moderation artfully with pleasure, according to the dictates of wisdom. You will then find yourself doubly blessed by health and order. Long live Monsieur le Maire and his son!"

"Long live Monsieur le Maire and his son!" Miremont repeated, on an empty stomach.

Monsieur Morin du Reposoir's servant, an apostate among the crowd, added, "and long live the First Deputy!" but the spontaneous cry went without echo, because Miremont was already heading for the esplanade, calling for the barrels to be broached. Rumor had it that there would be two barrels this year, the second in honor of Monsieur le Comte.

The population left the town hall square, therefore, and took the path that led to the chateau. You might have thought that a thicket was on the march. Men, women and children alike carried enormous sheaves of lilac, for that joy of springtime always flourished for Monsieur le Marquis' birthday party.

On the esplanade, Miremont found Madame Etienne, who was already a little ahead of the First Deputy. Madame Etienne received the people generously, permitting them to decorate the gate with sprigs of lilac and telling them about the solemn ceremonies that had taken place at the home of her old lady on Saint Joseph's Day. Why? Because he was her patron saint, she having been named Josephine.

"My children," she added, "everything will soon be roasting and boiling here for the usual commemoration, complicated, as is only right, by that of Monsieur le Comte. You'll be able to drink as deep as hunchbacks of an abundance of two sorts of wine, red and white, as you may please! Each of you is obliged to lend a hand in putting up and setting the trestle-tables for your own personal festivities, scheduled from midday, food provided, until the Sun descends into the mist. Here, things are done aristocratically, without counting sous and pennies like a rat in some little bourgeois house shearing its lice by way of economy. This is Gamache's wedding,[125] as they say, and a horn of plenty containing everything you could wish: sausages, black puddings, pork crackling, all sorts of rissoles, the famous soup in which you can stand your spoon up straight, and sauces that will make you lick your fingers all the way to the elbow, with lard, pepper, salt and mustard! Not to mention dancing till you drop to the fiddler's violin, the coffee, the liqueurs, the flags and Bengal fireworks in every color, silver and gold, launched from the windows and better than at Saint-Louis de Pontoise! Long live Monsieur le Marquis and Monsieur le Comte!"

"Long live Monsieur le Marquis and Monsieur le Comte!" howled Miremont, as all of its hats were hurled into the air. And this time, of its own free will, it added: "Long live Madame Etienne!"

The Deputy and the cook had the same style, to be sure–except that the cook had the divinely ordained gift of speaking to a crowd. She knew how to deliver words that were truly inspiring: sausages, black puddings and so on. Quintillian is merely eloquent, but Cicero speaks to the heart.

Madame Etienne was flattered, for popularity is akin to an intoxicating beverage. She turned towards the colleagues and subordinates arrayed behind her and said: "That's the way to tickle their fancy, isn't it? It's their own language. They use to shout for my long life in my old lady's house, and again at Pontoise!"

Then her oratory talent expanded again, and she added: "But the moment of delight and general diversion has not yet arrived, because of the partial absence of more than three-quarters of the principal village authorities, the fair sex and young people: the Bondons and their lady, the First Deputy's wife, the Second Deputy and his daughter, Mademoiselle Suzanne, Mademoiselle Jeanne, Monsieur Robert and friends, and the master of all, Monsieur Henri, without whom everything else would amount to nothing. It will begin, by general fixation, when this society returns from Paris–which cannot be long delayed. To take the edge off your impatience, wander as you will, helping with your table, cutting the grass for the ball, girls and boys together–which isn't a sin on Monsieur le Marquis' birthday!

The last was said with a final smile, and Madame Etienne went back to her kitchen in the midst of a veritable ovation.

The old Marquis had not yet got up. His milky coffee, which Pierre had brought up, was fuming on his bedside table. He was sitting up in bed holding a letter in his hand. The shouts and applause from outside carried as far as his bedroom, but he took no notice of them. The letter had been read. He was no longer looking at it; he was deep in thought. Other letters, still unopened, lay scattered about his coverlet.

At that moment, you would have had difficulty discerning the clear and frank expression that his features usually wore. He was smiling, but his smile was somewhat pained–or, rather, a nascent anxiety was detectable in the effort.

"By God!" he murmured. "I know what his secret is! The game of conspiracy has always seduced the young... and one would have to be blind not to agree that the man out there on that rock, St. Helena, has all the grandeur of a giant struck by lightning. The King is secure on his throne now, thank God, and the peace of Europe won't be shaken by the chatter of that nocturnal gathering in poor Madeleine's hovel." His smile became bitter, and he shrugged his shoulders, then continued after a moment of meditation. "My son! My Henri! It was bound to happen. Why do these great and generous natures always turn to rebellion? To what destiny could he not aspire? What step on the social ladder is too elevated for him? Have I ever encountered in my entire life–I, who am already old–a single man as fortunately, brilliantly and magnificently endowed?"

There is no knowing how enthusiastic his affection was when he evoked the image of his beloved son in his way.

His attention returned abruptly to the paper he was holding in his hand.

"But why did this letter make me think of Henri?" he said, with a sort of surprise. "It says nothing about Henri. It only speaks of things that are completely unconnected with him. There are strange associations between our thoughts and the beating of our hearts!" He unfolded the letter again, perhaps without taking account of his own action. "After this," he went on again, "as long as his smile becomes gentle again, everything will make me think of him—everything! I love him as I adored his mother."

The open letter was in front of his eyes, which ran over it mechanically.

It said:

My dear and respectable friend,

You have come to my aid without knowing it, in the terrible wager I have laid against a demon incarnate—the product of my imagination, perhaps, who is perhaps undiscoverable only because he does not exist. I believe that I still have my reason; at any rate, it has brought me to the conclusion of calculations whose enormity astounds me. There are, however, fissures in my mind where I no longer sense life. May God bless you for the paternal shelter that you have given to my poor child!

I love my Suzanne; she is the last refuge of my thoughts, and the desire very often takes hold of me to abandon everything to hurry to her—but an instant afterwards, it seems to me that it would be a desertion, if not an apostasy. Is that my madness? Does it consist in regarding the mortal effort of my existence as the most sacred of all duties? I don't know... but it is more than a duty in my eyes: it is the ultimate aim of my existence. It seems to me that I was created for this, and for nothing but this.

No, I have not forgotten the O'Brien affair: it was my first step into the labyrinth where I might die. I have delayed my response to you because I sent a request to the office at Scotland Yard for the file relating to the murder. It has been refused. That matters little; my memory of the affair is in better shape than my reason; my memory is a book from which nothing is erased.

I shall be at the Chateau de Belcamp one day this week. I shall see the woman of whom you speak. God's justice sometimes moves in strange ways. Who knows whether this woman might be the instrument I have sought so feverishly?

Love to my dear daughter. Respectful compliments to the Comte de Belcamp, of whose return I have been informed.

Your old friend,

Gregory Temple.

"There's nothing but that final mention that could make me think of Henri, though," murmured the Marquis. "It has escaped me... no... but every time there is something mysterious I am, alas, like poor old Gregory: I have my obsession... oh, Master Henri, you have posed a challenge to your father!" He threw aside Temple's letter to take up the first that came to hand from among those that were scattered on his bed, and went on: "You move like Jupiter, surrounded by a cloud! But for our age, we still have rather good eyesight. Monsieur le Comte, your cloud is pierced by daylight... and for all your grandiose pretence of deep darkness, we shall see through you!"

The seal of the second letter was broken.

"Our red-robed cousin," said the old Marquis, reading the signature, "Monsieur le Vicomte de Boisruel, Counselor at the Royal Court in Paris... 'The pressure of business... makes it impossible to meet, as usual, to celebrate the birthday of a kinsman that he loves with all his heart...' What a pity! Judge that he is, Boisruel still has something of the swordsman in him, and he's a good companion. What does Godinot want?"

The third letter, a heavy missive in a grey envelope, bore a solemn stamp with the legend: Commissioner of Police, l'Isle-Adam. Godinot, the son of a Miremontese peasant, had learned to read alongside the Marquis long before the Revolution. He was, by virtue of that, the Marquis' oldest friend, and often visited the chateau.

" 'The pressure of business...' Monsieur de Belcamp read, 'the duties of my office...' No Godinot! He would have told me for the hundred-and-first time how my tutor found that he had more aptitude than me... on to another!"

He took the fourth letter out of its envelope. Its first page had nothing written on it. He looked further; the other pages were like the first, nothing but pieces of blank paper. The idea occurred to him that it was a joke. He scrutinized the envelope to see whether he knew the handwriting. The envelope was postmarked London, and was addressed to Monsieur le Comte de Belcamp.

"Well, well!" he murmured. "Yet another part of the mystery. A blank letter! If I put my son in contact with Gregory Temple, they could play hide-and-seek all their lives with an entirely new pleasure."

Rendered more circumspect by this mistake, he looked at the addresses on the other letters before opening them. There were four, three from London and one from Liverpool. The one from Liverpool and two of those from London were for the Marquis. The fourth was addressed to Miss Suzanne Temple.

He rang the bell. Pierre appeared in the doorway with a bunch of flowers at his side, like a pageboy at a wedding. "My devout wish is that Monsieur le Marquis should enjoy lifelong happiness," he said, in a penetrating tone, "before going to paradise with as much delay as possible..."

"Villain!" cried the old man. "You are capable of consigning me to 20 years of purgatory!"

Without hesitation, Pierre concluded: "...and no purgatory at all!"

Monsieur de Belcamp offered him his hand, in which he held a coin—but he did not release the coin without a firm handshake that was worth ten times as much.

"Thank you, Pierre, my friend," he said. "You're a good chap, and Monsieur le Comte is pleased with you. Let's see—we have some time to spare; you must help me smarten myself up. I want to look ten years younger today than I did yesterday!"

And, as he had said, he did look ten years younger when he walked out some time afterwards into the area prepared for the party, lending his two arms to two friends who had returned to the fold, Jeanne and Germaine. He was young, he was charming–not because his curled and perfumed hair fell upon his shining silk dress-coat, nor because his frilled shirt, dazzling like snow, fluffed out its lace amid the gold embroidery of his waistcoat, nor because he wore all his diamonds on his fingers and his medals on his chest, but because his noble figure was braced with a new vigor; because there was a suppleness in him that gave the lie to age, because his mouth was smiling, because his eyes were shining, and because the enduring firmness of his features radiated the health, life and happiness that are youth itself.

I do not know quite how to put this: he was flirting with the two dear children who leaned on his arms like two plush fruits, more beautiful than two flowers swinging beneath a strong branch, both turning their radiant faces towards him at the same time; he was flirting, not for himself, but for his son, whom he could not get out of his mind. And they, too, who had loved him for a long time, but who seemed at this moment to cherish him a thousand times better, were so affectionate and so sweetly tender that they seemed to constitute between them an assault of filial caresses. They, too, were flirting, and their flirtatiousness was as naively deceptive as the old man's. Their caresses were certainly for him, but they also extended beyond him. On the part of Monsieur de Belcamp, as on their part, all the love they exchanged passed through an intermediary idea that was Henri: the Henri that was the old man's adored son; the Henri that was Jeanne's declared lover; the Henri that was still the dream of the other child, who did not know herself...

Henri was the center and the deity for which the incense of all this tenderness burned.

No one mentioned Henri.

When the guests came to break up the three-way *tête-à-tête*, Monsieur de Belcamp felt a surplus of happiness oppressing his soul. Neither of them had given up her secret, but he asked himself nevertheless, carried away by his uncertainty: Which of them will be my daughter...?

He guessed, for the heart has the gift of second sight, that here was a love divided; love exuded its perfume into the air and the old man felt its intoxication. The future he had glimpsed was like a blue sky behind the lifted corner of a curtain: a delightful future; the family reborn around him like roses blooming on an old bush in spring.

At the end of the path, Suzanne Temple went by, carrying Lady Frances Elphinstone's child in her arms–another of love's deceits!

Monsieur de Belcamp's eyes were full of tears

There were traditions to be observed. The general fixation, to use Madame Etienne's phrase, was rigorously regulated by habit. No one, except Pierre, had yet offered the Marquis many happy returns. The signs indicated, however, that the moment was approaching.

Miremontese society assembled, muttering, in the bushes. Their number was augmented by a number of foreigners whose presence marked the solemnity of the occasion. The people who were due to speak collected themselves. Numerous pockets were bulging with voluminous gifts, carefully concealed so as not to compromise the cherished element of surprise. The Marquis put on a good show of having no anxieties, but every noise caused him to shiver involuntarily; he was like a man awaiting an unexpected blow.

If there had only been one blow! The previous year, the good wishes had lasted a good hour at least. He watched from the corner of his eye, not without a certain entirely natural horror, the eight little Chaumerons foraging in the bushes. They had the right to come in for major festivals. Irrespective of the consequent damage, they brought forth every insensate compliment they could find in the confusion of their scarcely-cultivated memories for the recitation for which Mademoiselle the eldest served as deliverer.

In addition, they had been promised that they could eat at the table.

The table was immense, dressed in the great cloth. Monsieur de Belcamp looked at his watch, which told him that there were still five minutes to go. He wagged his finger at Henri, who arrived on the arm of Lady Frances Elphinstone. Henri immediately came over.

"We know your news, son," the old man said, extending his hand. "You are the last knight errant. Have you saved anyone this morning?" He drew his son towards him and spoke into his ear, saying: "And would you also like to tell us, Monsieur le Comte, if you please, how the precious health of the members of your supreme council is?"

"Well, father," Henri replied, softly. "Thank you for asking."

The Marquis had counted on that question bringing forth a warm counterpoint. His son's imperturbable coolness inspired him to feel admiration. "Why aren't you with us?" he murmured.

"I'm with no one and against no one, father," Henri replied. His smile had, indeed, a calm sovereignty. He added, in a lower and more serious tone: "Every time you think you have seen through me, you will be disappointed and hurt. No one can acquaint you with the truth but me, and I do not have the right to speak to you."

"You're trickier than Prince de Talleyrand,[126] son," the Marquis replied, "but we know what we know!" Then he raised his voice to say: "Mesdames, we have neither the magistrature nor the police; my old friend Godinot and our cousin de Boisruel, the Counselor, are busy elsewhere. It seems that in our Golden Age, justice and its commissioners are still occupied with thieves and litigants."

"We have no one to arrest or judge, I think," said Henri.

"In compensation," Monsieur de Belcamp continued, "I'm expecting, at any moment, the father of our dear Suzanne..."

An imperceptible movement agitated the young Comte's face. It was as rapid as a lightning-flash. He said, with an expression of tranquil contentment: "For my part, I shall lose nothing by the substitution. I shall be pleased to renew my acquaintance with that eminent man, who is–in every sense of the term–what the English call a perfect gentleman."

Lady Frances' eyes were downcast, and her charming cheeks were a little more vividly colored.

A formidable discharge of musket-fire sent echoes ricocheting through the park. The main door at the top of the steps opened, giving passage to the Curé of Miremont, followed by his Curate, his Verger and his choirboy. Behind the clergy came the administration: Monsieur and Madame Morin du Reposoir, the First Deputy and his wife; Monsieur Potel, the Second Deputy; and a poor hunchback, the clerk at the town hall. In the third rank was the Municipal Council, composed of the Bondon garniture in full and five peasants in their Sunday clothes.

Florian Bondon, a little in arrears but holding his left-hand position, doubly ornamented by his uniform and his blue ribbon, served as a hyphen between the municipality and the armed force, His amiable gentleness belonged to the former institution; his weight and corpulence suited the latter. Madame Célestin turned from time to time to keep watch over his conduct.

The local Constable, who had left his hat somewhere or other, and his reason at the bottom of a bottle, completed the march of the constitutional authorities, describing prodigious flourishes.

Madame Etienne opened the procession of domestic servants and farmers. At the same time, the peasants of Miremont, led on one side by Pierre and on the other by Briquet–who was scarcely worthy of the honor–emerged from the right and the left through the lateral doors on to the lawn, which was instantaneously inundated.

Everyone–the clergy, the administration, the municipality, the civic guard, the third estate, the people–had bouquets, and the young women were balancing garlands of ivy-leaves in addition.

Things had been exactly the same the preceding year, to the general satisfaction; the year before, the ceremony had been identical. There was a unanimous cry: "Oh, isn't it nice, this year?"

Because he was a plain speaker, Chaumeron added: "It's never been so well-orchestrated!" He took an oath on it.

Meanwhile, Jeanne and Germaine, taking Monsieur de Belcamp by the hand, had conducted him to a verdant canopy erected in front of the table, under which he sat. Comte Henri came to stand beside him, while Miremontese society in its entirety arranged itself like a fan to the right and the left. We should add the observation that when the musket-fire had given the signal, each member of that society, irrespective of age or sex, had been furnished–as if by magic–with an enormous bouquet.

The Curé offered his good wishes in three simple and suitable words, which had no success. Morin du Reposoir, making use of his well-known eloquence, produced an academico-tradesmanlike [127] harangue that seemed very powerful to Many-Apologies. The two Bondons took up position next to provide the gestures for the discourse that Madame Célestin recited without a single error. Following this morsel, the National Guardsmen raised their rifles, but the Marquis strictly forbade their firing; Miremont's weapons of war were poor quality. Madame Célestin made a sign to Florian, who–with the voice of his twin in simultaneous support–immediately gave the order for the arms to be lowered again. How these two phenomena of Miremontese vegetation had been able to learn all this no one knew, but Madame Célestin was a bit of a witch. [128]

The local Constable also had the right to be eloquent, but he did not deign to use it. He preferred throwing his cap in the air and shouting at the top of his voice: "Long live the King! Long live the Imperial Family! Long live the First Consul!"[129] Madame Célestin unsheathed the military Bondon's sword in order to curb this sedition, but Blondeau continued: "Long live Monsieur le Maire! Long live Monsieur le Curé! Long live everyone who wants to, and the two barrels!"

Enthusiasm is a contagious thing, no matter how lacking in sincerity it might be. The peasants began shouting and shaking their foliage–and Madame Etienne, whose turn it was, had enormous difficulty in obtaining silence. She went to stand before her master, with one hand on her apron and the other holding a bouquet as broad as she was.

"I have the circumstance," she said, with the false modesty of an orator accustomed to success, "I have the circumstance of seizing this importunate occasion to offer Monsieur le Marquis herewith the respects and amenity of all his household, of which I am today the interpreter of all the unanimous and various sentiments, by the authorization that they have given me, with their confidence in my age and my feeble talents! After 30 years of cooking for my former mistress and others, I wasn't born yesterday; as maiden, wife and widow I have always been in houses where it was customary to fry for the midday meal and evening meal alike, as all the certificates in my cupboard, stamped and legalized by the government, will attest. This is why, as the season of spring restores to the present month of May the rejoicings of Saint Honoré, I have granted myself the indulgence of making a Pontoise gâteau for Monsieur le Marquis with his name inscribed in sugar, and Monsieur le Comte's too, to whom I offer my excuses for taking the liberty, ending as always, as the years and the company pass, by embracing Monsieur le Marquis on behalf of all the domestic staff, without ever omitting Monsieur le Comte!"

She took a deep breath, like a diver emerging from the water; then she stepped forward pompously and offered her ruddy and well-washed cheek to Monsieur de Belcamp, who gave her the accolade. The Comte followed suit with similar good grace, and Madame Etienne went back, transfigured, stifling Anille and Julot with the same spasmodic embrace. The brigades headed by Pierre and Briquet deposited their bouquets in heaps on either side of the canopy.

The Marquis thanked them with a few well-chosen words; there was an immense *hurrah*! and everyone took a step back, because a squib exploded on the esplanade announced the tapping of the two barrels of wine.

It was the turn of the society, whose members formed a circle around the canopy. Several pages could be written here in the form of a Homeric enumeration because, in addition to the esteemed individuals that we have already put on the map, Miremont contained a dozen others less salient, who were all there, stuffing the depths of the tableau. We shall leave them in their favorable shade; the light belongs to the strong. Isn't it enough for a single village to possess a Morin du Reposoir retired from business and his wife; an austere Latinist Potel; a Besnard to represent the spirit of rustic gallantry; a Bondon team, who would have been a remarkable curiosity even in Pontoise; and a Chaumeron nursery?

Bouquets, speeches, little gifts bought with regret and at a discount, once the mutual invective of merchant and customer had reached a compromise, and offered with that grace that departs from the heart...

Madame Célestin was charming in offering her match-holder, for which each Bondon had paid half. The deputy's wife gave a "new model"–to use her own expression; it was a silvered turkey-cock whose extended [130] tail had little holes for toothpicks. Chaumeron, via the hand of the eldest Mademoiselle, presented a shelf-ornament consisting of a Tréport fisherman made out of shells, and said: "If words have to be minced, they might as well be minced with pleasure. I would like to be rich enough to offer objects garnished with diamonds, but that wouldn't come from the heart: there: all done, Papa Chaumeron!" He released the little ones, who had crowns of primulas. After the compliments, the youngest was lifted up in Mademoiselle's arms to deposit a diadem of flowers on the head of Monsieur de Belcamp, whose gentle resignation never wavered for an instant.

Férandeau unrolled a naked Spartan, which made the Bondons laugh and the ladies cry. There was a general embrace thereafter, certain painful details of which caused the excellent Marquis to feel nostalgic for the scarlet cheek of Madame Etienne. He let out sigh of profound relief when, to take the taste away after having drunk three-quarters of a bitter brew, he found himself in the midst of a smiling and charming circle comprising Frances, Suzanne, Jeanne and Germaine.

The last kiss was given to him by Henri, whom he held for a long time clasped to his breast. He said to him in a low voice, stifled by emotion: "Son, I am not alone here in loving you." Then, he added, with a motherly caress: "Do you know the gift I would most like to receive from you?"

"I would like to know, father," Henri replied. "For if it is within the power of man..."

"It's only a word, son," interrupted the old man, whose voice was tremulous and pleading. "The promise that you won't abandon your father."

Henri embraced him, and replied: "Saving the will of God that leads us, my desire is to stay with you always."

Henri did not hear the thanks that tumbled murmurously from his father's mouth: a dazzling sight had passed before his eyes. As he and the Marquis separated, he had turned back towards the bulk of the guests who were watching the scene, some with curiosity, others with a vague inclination to sneer, and yet others–the smallest number–with genuine tenderness. At first glance, he had distinguished in the midst of the crowd a gaze that drew him as if mesmerically: a clear, sure, piercing gaze whose profound penetration was as cold and painful as a blade cutting into flesh.

It was a man for whom Comte Henri was waiting–but as one awaits one's adversary at the appointed hour of a duel to the death, knowing in advance that the sword will come flashing from its sheath. The bravest of the brave represses a shiver as the first spark springs forth. It was the only man that he himself had not placed on the stage of his drama, and yet one could not say that this man acted freely outside the mysterious sphere where his will held dominion. Among those who came close to Comte Henri, none was capable of escaping his influence entirely.

For any other, this man would have been the head of Medusa. He had accepted a terrible challenge. He had the reach and the strength to prevail against the most terrible and skillful opponents. Until now, Henri had taken care to avoid him; to deflect his pursuit he had dispensed a wealth of feints and calculations. It was to hide his tracks from this man that he had created confusion, cleverly knotted ten times over, between himself, James Davy and Richard Thompson; it was to deceive this man that he carried a London franking-machine in his luggage; it was to establish one more barrier between himself and this man that he had patiently and cruelly oppressed the heart of Suzanne, the unfortunate young mother.

Even so, his encounter with this man had been anticipated from the very beginning. This man was definitely a card in his game–but the game of the miner who intends to blast a mountain of rock also involves a fuse, and the miner keeps his fuse to one side; he watches over it; he reaches for it only at the precise moment when he sets it alight; then, he flees.

The man we are talking about was the former Chief Superintendent of the London Police, Gregory Temple. He had come in without any fuss, as is the custom of animals and men who hunt by stealth. The cat and the detective have the same velvet tread. No one in the chateau was as yet aware of his presence; even his daughter had not been warned.

He was wearing a new set of black clothes. The rebelliousness of his white hair had been curbed by a barber's hand and his closely-shaven cheeks had lost the wild tones that had contributed more than a little to his appearance as an escapee from Bedlam. He had, in sum, recovered the image of an old gentleman of pleasant and distinguished character.

At the moment when Henri's gaze met his own, his eye lost the strange gleam that seemed to be the conductor of a hypnotic power. His eyelid was not lowered at all, but his pupil suddenly became dull. Henri had felt a *frisson*, but no evident external sign betrayed any trace of the emotion that vibrated in the very marrow of his bones. The eyes of the audience, converging on the heroes of the fête, could not have discovered anything in his gentle and handsome face even had they been more piercing and subtle than those which ordinarily peered through Miremontese spectacles.

Groups were forming to kill the few awkward minutes before dinner. Comte Henri, profiting from this movement, headed through the crowd unaffectedly, directly for Gregory Temple.

At that moment, the old Marquis was holding the fingertips of Jeanne's and Germaine's hands. "Which side do you want at the table?" he was asking them, as mischievous as a child.

While Comte Henri came towards him, Gregory Temple's heart leapt within his breast. It was as if a dazzling light had suddenly burst forth in the midst of the night that surrounded him. He saw nothing further, for sudden lights are as blinding as darkness itself, but he sensed that here, immediately in front of him, was the solution to his problem.

Comte Henri immediately offered him his hand, and Temple took it without hesitation.

"James, my dear chap," he said, "I didn't expect to find you here. Would you show me, please, the young Comte de Belcamp?"

"For my own part, Monsieur Temple," Henri replied, "I was expecting you, but I would have liked it better if you had come a little later. We have no time for an exchange of equivocations or a battle of wits. I am Comte Henri de Belcamp."

The detective felt blood mounting in his cheeks, and half-closed his eyes to hide the fire that was lit in his eyes. His astonishment did not betray itself in speech.

"I know you well enough," Henri went on, "to guess the thoughts that are crowding your head at this moment, and the calculations that you are already making. I repeat that I would rather you had delayed your coming, but here you are! You must believe yourself betrayed; nothing else could have got in the way of your thunder, for you don't love your daughter!"

Temple stared at him again. This was the gaze that had hurled its myrmidons upon the defeated, cornered, resourceless bandit–but it had no handcuffs now.

There was a clump of lilacs encroaching upon the lawn like a graceful promontory. Henri's extended hand pointed to it. Suzanne Temple was sitting on a bench, cradling Lady Frances Elphinstone's child in her arms.

The former Chief Superintendent became livid; his legs were giving way beneath him. Between such men as these, explanations often proceed thus, by way of ellipses so large that each word seems like the footfall of a giant crossing an abyss.

Lady Frances was on the arm of Robert Surrisy. Temple shivered at the sight of him.

"No doubt, no doubt," he murmured, as if talking to himself. "Sarah O'Neil is also an aristocratic lady now."

"Sarah O'Neil does not know your family secrets," Henri replied. "She came to your aid because I wanted her to."

"She came to my aid!" Temple replied, requiring all his strength to contain his anger.

"If not yours, at least your daughter's, who has never had a father!" Henri said, in a bitterly provocative tone.

They were alone now on the lawn. Everyone had gone into the shrubbery. The verdant canopy and the immense arbor that had been built to shelter the table from the Sun remained between them and the bulk of the guests. Lady Frances and her cavalier were coming towards the bushes where Suzanne was sitting. Lady Frances had not even seen her child sleeping in Suzanne's arms–and Suzanne, who had not seen Lady Frances because she saw nothing other than her dream of an angelic smile, was leaning over the dear slumbering creature. Her beautiful pale face, inundated by blonde hair, was a study in ecstasy.

Gregory's anguished gaze turned towards her.

"Mr. Temple," the young Comte continued, "great minds have unfortunate lacunae, and there are strange legions of ignorance within the bosom of science itself. I have deceived you, but I have not betrayed you. When you know the facts well enough to understand the language of dates, I shall tell you my reasons. I have two of them; either one of them might be granted by a gentleman."

"Henri!" called the Marquis de Belcamp from a distance.

"Who is that child?" Gregory demanded, abruptly.

"It's your grand-daughter," Henri replied.

"And who knows that?"

"No one."

"Henri! Henri!" the old Marquis called, for a second time.

"I'm coming, father," the young Comte replied.

"Father!" echoed the voice of Suzanne, who had just noticed Gregory.

The former Police Superintendent was a man whom nothing could astonish, but he was confounded by the calmness with which Henri said: "I need to know whether you're going to attack me and whether I must defend myself. Cards on the table, if you please, Mr. Temple!"

Suzanne came towards them, still holding the child in her arms.

"I grant you a truce, James Davy," said the Police Superintendent between clenched teeth. "A truce that will last until tonight."

"Then I shall grant you a respite, Gregory Temple," riposted the young Comte, in a haughty manner. "A respite even longer than your truce."

As she approached, Suzanne questioned Henri with an anxious glance that was not lost on the Police Superintendent. Henri's mute response reassured the young woman, who offered her forehead to her father. Temple kissed her and asked for the second time: "Who is that child?"

"It's the son of Lady Frances Elphinstone," Suzanne replied.

"Miss Suzanne will make a good mother," Henri remarked, in a serious and fond tone. Then, linking arms with Temple in a familiar fashion, he added: "Master, don't you want to give your good wishes to my father?"

The Marquis de Belcamp and his guests, seeing them come across the lawn towards the shrubbery, wanted to meet them halfway, and no one was within a thousand leagues of suspecting the terrible imbroglio in which those coming towards them were the actors. Suzanne was playing placidly with the child. Gregory Temple and Comte Henri were chatting and smiling at one another.

But strange as the drama already begun might be, another that promised to be even stranger was in prospect. At this very moment, by two different routes and marching in opposite directions, two men were approaching whose meeting here would add the most bizarre and unexpected scene to the play...

"Be welcome, my excellent friend!" said Monsieur de Belcamp, as soon as his voice would carry. "I thought I'd heard it said that you did not know my Henri; Henri claimed the opposite. It's I who was wrong, as usual..." He interrupted himself as he saw Temple greet Frances, whose cheeks became pinker. "Lady Elphinstone too! Well, so much the better. I have only one introduction to make, save for my brigand, Robert Surrisy, and the young Herbets... do you know...?"

"I do indeed know your son, Monsieur le Marquis," Temple replied, "who has decidedly resumed the ease of a man of the world—and I have also had the honor of milady's acquaintance." As he said it, he bowed to Robert with polite indifference.

"I have not hidden from you, father," Henri went on, in a pert manner, "that you still had much to learn about me. I have other stories than my adventures in Australia. My relationship with Mr. Temple is one of the most curious episodes of my life..."

"These ladies will expect a contribution after dinner, son," Monsieur de Belcamp put in. "Their mouths are already watering... Hey, boy! What do you call your manservant, Férandeau?"

"Trompe-d'Eustache in my studio," the pupil of David replied, "but Laurent calls him Bricole and Robert, Briquet."

"Hey! Briquet!"

Instead of helping in the kitchen, the individual in question had completed the design of a heart in the bark of a beech tree, which contained no other name than his. He answered the summons.

"My friend," the Marquis said to him, "go down to Madame Surrisy's house, and tell her that Gregory Temple is here, waiting for her."

Scarcely had Briquet departed when Pierre was seen, napkin in hand, opening the drawing-room door and crossing the lawn at full speed. This sight cleared a good number of faces, and Chaumeron said with his customary frankness: "Trump! If that's dinner... I've no reason to hide my opinion, I could crack a crust with pleasure."

At the word dinner, the eight little Chaumerons, who were seated at the great table for this day alone, let out a ferocious cry of joy.

Pierre arrived as devoid of breath as the Lacedemonian who died after announcing the victory of the 300 at Thermopylae.[131] "The Judge," he said, brokenly. "Monsieur de Boisruel...!"

The Marquis interrupted him joyfully. "Has my red-robed cousin changed his mind?"

"With his clerk..." Pierre continued.

"His clerk!" Monsieur de Belcamp repeated.

"And gendarmes!"

Everyone burst out laughing except Gregory Temple, whose eager eyes made a singularly rapid tour of the circle. Men like him never laughed because something seemed implausible. He knew too much even to believe in the word. His gaze concluded by fixing itself on Comte Henri, who met it squarely with smiling eyes.

"Let's go meet my cousin de Boisruel," Henri said.

"Look!" cried Monsieur de Belcamp, while everyone began walking. "He's left his clerk and his gendarmes behind."

"His clerk is in the drawing-room," Pierre replied, somewhat reassured by the general merriment, "and the gendarmes are on the other side of the gate."

Gregory Temple observed that Monsieur de Boisruel was very pale. The Magistrate responded to the joyous welcome extended to him with a bow that was affectionate, but grave. He was a man of about 40, very elegant and distinguished. Temple, accustomed to analyzing everything, and whose observational acumen was as sharp as it was subtle, was perhaps alone in discerning the embarrassment–one might almost say suffering–that he was hiding behind his apparent austerity, softened by the easy manner that is second nature to a man of the world.

The others joked about the clerk and the gendarmes. Chaumeron had already said several times, with that frankness that made him so likeable: "The more madmen, the more laughter!" He added: "Nothing's lacking but Godinot, the Commissioner. It'll put the cap on things if he comes."

Pierre struck himself on the forehead. "I forgot to tell Monsieur le Marquis!" he said. "Monsieur Godinot is down at the inn on the Church Square."

"Godinot! At the inn!" repeated the Marquis, astonished this time. "He has a room here! But he's an odd chap, and perhaps he's cooking up some specialty for my fête. Meanwhile, cousin, let's embrace. Come here, Henri. Cousin, the Comte de Belcamp."

Monsieur de Boisruel hesitated imperceptibly before taking the hand that Comte Henri held out to him.

Has he come for him? Gregory Temple was already asking himself, his bloodhound's nostrils flaring.

"Cousin," said Henri in his turn, "I would have come to pay my respects while I was passing through Paris if my father had not wanted to reserve the pleasure of presenting me to you."

Even the Magistrate's lips were pale. He stammered rather than replying, and even the least clear-sighted were finally able to see his distress. He let go of Henri's hand and made an abrupt effort to pull himself together.

"Monsieur le Marquis," he said, "you are not only a man to whom I am honored to be linked by kinship, you are my very dear friend... I ask you as a favor to let me speak to you alone for a few minutes."

"With all my heart, cousin, with all my heart," replied Monsieur de Belcamp, linking arms with him.

"It appears that there are secrets," Henri said, with such perfect serenity that even Temple's suspicions were momentarily allayed.

Nevertheless, a general curiosity had been awakened. Glances and pouts were already being exchanged.

"He hasn't come to the chateau for dinner," Robert Surrisy was the first to say; he seemed to be conducting himself with unusual seriousness today.

"We're within the jurisdiction of the Royal Court of Versailles here," pointed out Monsieur Potel, who appreciated legal niceties. "It seems to me that Monsieur Boisruel, belonging to the Royal Court of Paris, cannot..."

"Except in the case of a rogatory commission," Laurent put in, "as newly written into the law."[132]

"Rogatory commission or not," Chaumeron concluded, "I'll come straight to the point: it's farcical to come here like that on Saint Honoré's day. There you are!"

Meanwhile, the Magistrate was saying in a low but penetrating voice: "My dearest cousin, I know that your house is full today, and I would have given anything in the world to wait until tomorrow, but you know that we cannot choose the day or the hour. I am here for Comte Henri de Belcamp."

The old man felt a chill in his veins as the thought of the Supreme Council crossed his mind. He remained immobile and mute.

"A murder was committed on the night of the 12th and 13th of this May in Brussels," Monsieur de Boisruel continued, "and the most serious presumptions..."

The breath that the old Marquis had been holding for a full minute escaped in a loud sigh. He withdrew the arm that was linked with the Counselor's and took a step backwards, crossing his arms over his breast.

"Henri!" he cried, explosively. "The Comte de Belcamp! My son!"

"Take care!" Monsieur de Boisruel said, softly.

"Take care!" repeated the old man, vehemently. "Take care yourself, Monsieur!" Then, as if all his proud anger had suddenly turned to calm, he let out a mocking laugh and added: "Henri, come defend yourself–you're accused of sorcery."

Another voice whispered in his ear: "Take care!" He turned round. Temple was at his side.

At the old gentleman's call, the curious circle had tightened. The word that he had pronounced explained nothing, but emotion is transmitted by other means than words at such times, and the air that everyone breathed was feverish.

There was only calmness–absolute calmness–in the way that the smiling Henri de Belcamp released Germaine's arm to go to his father.

"Son," the Marquis went on, "you left me on Saturday–last Saturday–at ten o'clock in the evening; you mounted your broomstick and assassinated a man in Brussels. Was it a man or a woman, Counselor? And you came back the same day to take your coffee with me on the following Sunday morning."

"I don't understand, father," Henri said, simply.

"Monsieur le Marquis," Boisruel said, sternly, "men of your age and position rarely commit the sin of mocking the law."

"If the law is mad, cousin..." began the old man, growing increasingly excited.

"It is madder still to defy it, in this case, Monsieur!" the Magistrate interrupted.

And Temple repeated "Take care!" as if it were a refrain.

There was considerable agitation in the circle. Madame Morin du Reposoir had already said: "Many apologies! There are things so astonishing... personally, I'm not going to get mixed up in this."

The word assassination was bandied back and forth. The men, for the most part, sensed the absurdity of the accusation, and even though absurdity was not normally an obstacle in Miremont, the unanimous tendency was still to do their duty to Monsieur le Maire by showing the law the door, if necessary.

It was Henri himself who imposed silence with a few scarcely audible words, and who then, turning towards the magistrate, asked for an explanation in the most courteous and respectful fashion.

The crowd carped, and the little Chaumerons, reassembled in a surly group, sang an elegy for the delayed dinner. Very various sentiments were expressed.

"Of course, of course," said Madame Célestin, to whom the Comte had paid too little attention, "he hasn't left for eight days... but I've read stories..."

"They're so clever!" added Mademoiselle. "It's not Monsieur le Comte I'm talking about, you understand..."

"It's not up to us to protect him!" her mother added.

Madame Besnard, widow of the Administrator and mother of Don Juan, was as spiteful as those who live on stolen bread. "We've only known him for eight hours," she said.

"There are people," Germaine riposted, hotly, "that we've known for ten years, and don't think any the better of for that... isn't that so Jeanne?"

Jeanne was as tranquil and serene as Comte Henri himself.

"Well," said Madame Célestin. "I shall leave it to these gentlemen to look into it." The gentlemen in question were the madrepores, who were puffing out their cheeks, and in the matter of opinions favored those of the little Chaumerons.

"That's Pontius Pilate's method!" cried Germaine.

"Anyone who refuses to testify that Monsieur le Comte de Belcamp has not left the country for eight days is committing an infamous act," Robert Surrisy pronounced, gravely. Jeanne held out her hand to him; he touched it smiling sadly and coldly. At the same time, he turned towards Laurent, whose satisfied rancor was perceptible beneath his apparent indifference. He drew him to one side and signaled to Férandeau to follow. "My little ones," he said to them, in a deliberate tone, "we have nothing to discuss. It may be that he"–he pointed at the Comte–"will need our help this evening. Are we ready?"

"I'm ready," Férandeau replied. "I've always dreamed about knocking over a gendarme."

"And you, Laurent?"

"I'm ready... without prejudice to the sword-thrust that I intend to give him in the appropriate time and place."

Meanwhile, Henri was saying, without any emphasis but very distinctly, so that everyone might hear: "My cousin, I don't want anything from you. I put myself entirely at your disposal to answer any questions you care to put to me, and to follow you if you wish to arrest me..."

Confused noises interrupted him. Godinot was coming down the steps of the house accompanied by a poor devil with a flat belly and a hollow chest, whose black clothes–too short in the sleeves and shiny at the cuffs–were stained and sullied by more fat than graced the body of his employer. Godinot was wearing his sash. He was a stout fellow with a stale, startled, fussy manner, full of the importance of the mission that had brought him to the mundane sphere.

"There was no need for the Commissioner of Police," Henri said, in a reproachful tone whose moderation only made it more forceful.

"This is a shameful indignity...!" began the old Marquis.

"On my honor, I gave no such order," Monsieur de Boisruel protested.

Within the circle, curiosity was redoubled. Madame and Mademoiselle Chaumeron, Madame Besnard, Madame Célestin and the deputy's wife hit on the same idea simultaneously, which perhaps expressed a hope. In unison, they said: "It's going wrong! It's going wrong!"

"Good day, Messieurs, good day mesdames," said Godinot, who arrived sweating and panting. "One cannot always do as one wishes, and the higher one's place the greater is one's responsibility. I met the local Constable; there's a happy creature who has no bad blood. I've brought Moisiet, my secretary. Why? Because I haven't come to enjoy myself. Good day, Monsieur le Marquis... A word in private, immediately, if you please; I haven't time to wait."

"You don't usually use that tone with me," said the master of the house. "When I obtained for you the position that you occupy..."

"No impropriety regarding the magistrature!" cried Godinot. "Do you want me to say it out loud? I'm trying to avoid a scandal. I give you the choice: talk in private or do our business in public. It's not me who's afraid of listeners!"

"Speak publicly, Monsieur!" the Marquis instructed.

"And speak prudently," added Monsieur de Boisruel. "I am a Counselor at the Royal Court in Paris."

"No one can remove me from office!" cried Godinot, who was not in the least disconcerted. "Moisiet will testify that I have done my duty, however painful it may be, to an old school-friend. I wanted to do it quietly, the proof of which is that my gendarmes are waiting on the path in the park."

"Gendarmes!" murmured the guests, clamorously.

The former Chief Superintendent's eyes flashed. "*The Impossible*!" he murmured, alone.

"Monsieur the Marquis desires publicity," Godinot went on, "On his instructions, let's get on! The papers, Moisiet! Very well! On the night of the 12th and 13th of this May, a murder was committed in Lyon..."

"In Brussels," Monsieur de Boisruel corrected.

"Excuse me, Monsieur the Counselor," said Godinot, frankly. "I can still read without spectacles, and I'm speaking on behalf of the Department of Seine-et-Oise. The order by virtue of which I am acting came from Versailles."

"From Versailles!" Boisruel repeated, stupefied.

Most of the guests had lost track, and no longer understood what was happening.

"Is it my son who is the guilty party again?" the Marquis asked, sarcastically.

"What do you mean, again?" Godinot said. "Isn't one murder enough? I'll finish... committed at Lyon... I mean Lyon, in the Department of the Rhone... the most serious presumptions weigh upon Monsieur le Comte de Belcamp..."

"Capital!" the old Marquis put in, executing a pirouette worthy of a 14-year-old.

"That's certainly very strange!" murmured Monsieur de Boisruel.

"Absurd!" said Robert, who had been listening with the utmost attention.

"*Impossible*!" repeated Gregory Temple, in a singularly expressive tone.

Monsieur de Belcamp turned towards him and shook his hand, for he had great confidence in his judgment.

Miremontese society was beginning to understand. Even the ill-will of ladies of a certain age could not hold against a solution as clear as day, which fell at hazard from the sky.

"The fact is," said Many-Apologies, regretfully, "that it seems difficult..."

"In Lyon and in Brussels!" Férandeau put in. "The same night! The word difficult is hardly adequate!"

"A night when Monsieur le Comte was here in Miremont, as all those present saw and knew," added Madame Célestin added, abruptly changing tack. "These Messieurs will testify, whenever anyone wants."

"That's obvious," Potel decided.

"For my part, without holding back," Chaumeron grumbled, "I say that the law is wrong to play this sort of game! Tricky!"

"Why is everyone talking about Brussels?" Godinot demanded, crimson with anger. "What's the meaning of this charade?"

"Take off your sash, you booby!" Monsieur de Belcamp replied. "You'll dine with us."

The word dine ran murmurously from one end of the crowd to the other. It neatly encapsulated the intimate sentiment of every heart.

Comte Henri explained to Godinot himself, with benevolent politeness, why his declaration, though fundamentally serious, had excited such hilarity in the audience. As he finished, he added, without the least hint of irony: "I am at the disposal of my cousin, Counselor de Boisruel; I am equally at yours, Monsieur, inasmuch as you represent the law. As this is not a case to which the judgment of Solomon can be applied, I only beg you to come to some agreement."

The dinner bell sounded its joyous carillon, while the fuming plates were carried across the lawn. Counselor de Boisruel remained pensive; Godinot was utterly crushed. The scent of soup sharpened the renewed gaiety of Miremontese society; gloating remarks and outbursts of laughter sprang forth in sheaves. They had never seen such a farce. The Deputy's wife, Madame Célestin and the Chaumeron mother and daughter pulverized the statue of Themis [133] beneath the weight of their pleasantries. The two Bondons were unable to understand it all until the following day, but they laughed all the same, and their twin bellies shook with equal vigor like the udders of a mastodon.

The gendarmes from Paris and Versailles ate; the clerk and the secretary ate; Monsieur Boisruel and Godinot ate. As for the others... not only had the duplicate adventure brought no sadness to the party, it even seemed to have seasoned the merriment of the meal. Comte Henri was dazzling. Gregory Temple, having shaken off his obsession, told stories about the English Police that were enough to make hair stand on end. It was with great enthusiasm that Monsieur de Boisruel and Godinot toasted the health of the Marquis and his son "the prisoner" as the dessert was brought forth–for Henri was a prisoner on parole, and that was the truth! Monsieur de Boisruel, who had the powers of an Examining Magistrate, certainly had the authority to close the case and prepare a report to the effect that there was no case to pursue, but Godinot–a mere functionary charged with executing an arrest warrant–could make no such concession. After coffee, however, Godinot asked for the heads of the Versaillles tribunal, that he might give them all the same ass's head as a bonnet; he proclaimed the obviousness of the facts ten times louder than anyone else.

The journey to Versailles, moreover, was to be an ovation. Lady Frances' coach and the Marquis' *berline* were all ready. Half of Miremont was to follow the prisoner in carriages, while the two deputies and others on horseback would form a guard of honor. Monsieur de Boisruel himself would join the triumphal escort in his post-chaise.

As night fell and the table was being cleared, Gregory Temple came to take Comte Henri's hand and shake it forcefully. "James Davy," he said, "the truce is over."

"Won't you come as far as Versailles, Master?" asked Henri, whose audacious smile was a more audacious challenge than the words.

"I shall be there before you," Temple replied.

"Don't you believe the evidence, then, Master–you of all people!"

"I believe that the two assassins arrived in Paris yesterday. Tom Brown was there–or John Devil the Quaker, if you like that name better. I saw him; he had a drop of blood on his cuff, another on his breast. The two assassins must be dead."

Comte Henri never lost his smile. As he was called to the harnessed carriages he raised his hand in salute and said: "Master, you have taught me to fence; attack, and we shall defend ourselves."

"You believe," Temple said, "that you are secure behind a secret lock whose name is *the impossible*. But I can open it; I was the one who made it!"

"I have changed its combination, Master. Try your keys!"

Jeanne and Germaine came to meet Comte Henri, who added, in a low and rapid voice: "The father of that poor angel who was asleep in your daughter

Suzanne's arms just now has been arrested in London this very day, according to your indications and on your instructions..."

"Richard Thompson!"

"He will hang, if you wish, Master–and you'll make a widow of your daughter. *Au revoir*, Master!" He fell lightly into step with the two young women, who each took him by the hand, while the Marquis followed in his traveling clothes.

Gregory Temple remained motionless, as if thunderstruck. He covered his dazzled eyes. Henri and he had separated halfway between the table and the chateau steps, very close to the lilac bushes where Suzanne had recently been sitting, cradling the little child in her arms. The darkness was profound. The noises of the prisoner's strange departure, the triumphal conclusion to the party, sounded in his ears like some ironic and bitter challenge. A tall dark shape came out of the bushes, walking slowly, and Temple shuddered at the contact of a hand that touched his shoulder.

"I am Madeleine Surrisy," someone close to him said, in a low voice,

"And did you hear the voice of the man who just left me?" the detective demanded, excitedly.

"Yes, for the fourth time in my life, I heard and recognized it."

"Is that man the one whom you formerly described to me under the name of John Devil?"

"He is the one who promised to kill the General for 250,000 florins, and the one who said as he stood at the assassinated General's bedhead: *To you, Maurice O'Brien, from the Rosicrucians of Prague*!"

Part Two: The Criminal Trial [134]

I. Puppet Justice [135]

The Puppet Judge, the merriest man in London, was sitting on his seat. His seat was a sawn-off barrel, whose wide-open belly formed an armchair as comfortable as it was majestic. Before him was his desk: an old plank on two trestles, supporting a tremendous glass of gin. For a cassock, he had a coal-heaver's tarred jacket; for a wig, he wore the head of a mop that must have done long service swabbing the decks of a great many barges. His pipe and tobacco-pouch were beside him, as was his hat, which was furnished with an appendage as long and broad as the beaver's tail beloved by all naturalists. The tail was not, in this case, a trowel but a shield protecting the bare skin of the Herculean coalman from the caresses of his weighty baskets.

To his right sat his clerk; to his left, on another barrel, the King's Prosecutor. The Advocates were on their benches, the accused on his stool of repentance, the audience standing in the mud.

All of them–Judge, Prosecutor, Clerk, Advocates–were playing their various roles with impeccable seriousness. This was the Mock Tribunal [136] of Low Lane, the Puppet Tribunal, one of the most cherished amusements of the English lower orders, who take perpetual delight in mocking the clownish legal system which statesmen proclaim as the finest in the world.

The Puppet Judge and the Puppet Prosecutor, the Clerk, the Jury, the witnesses and the Advocates–the entire Mock Tribunal–were also known as the Irish Court, for implacable London never loses any opportunity to hurl mockery or insult at Ireland. Its auditorium was the far end of Sharper's inn–which is to say, the same amphitheater in which Thomas Paddock, in his career as John Devil, had allowed a younger generation of thieves to drink in his wisdom.

Thomas's widow, Jenny Paddock, was an industrious woman. She was making considerable efforts, and going to a great deal of trouble, with a view to marrying the little Jew who sold contraband tobacco under her counter as soon as the young tradesman was old enough. She was only 20 years older than him, and such unions are commonplace on the other side of the Channel, even among gentlefolk, as the upper middle classes modestly term themselves. Jenny Paddock's specific ambition was one day to be part of the gentlefolk; to arrive at that end, she faithfully executed her various duties as a thief, receiver of stolen goods, fraudster and poisoner. She was the veritable mother of the family of rogues that encumbered her hovel. Mothers like to keep their brood's meager savings in a safe place, and Jenny Paddock never left a farthing in the pockets of her chicks; all the fruits of pillage passed into her wallet. She already had the best part of a thousand pounds, which represented a tithe levied on a million sins. There was not a pickpocket in all London she had not peeled, a picker of locks she had not fleeced, an assassin she had not scalped.

Titus, the delight of humankind, and his father Vespasian, the patron of an industry more useful than agreeable, said money has no odor.[137] In our era, when consideration is the daughter of money, public opinion has gone one better. Money does have an odor, like roses whose stalks emit fumes; money smells good; money carries within itself the most noble and intoxicating of all perfumes. Jenny Paddock was not wrong, and her enterprise was far from being foolish. In the depths of her Inferno, she already belonged to the gentlefolk, because she had money.

She was happy too, partly because she had contrived the ruination of Thomas Paddock, who had beaten her black and blue. The Puppet Tribunal, or Irish Court, having had a bone to pick with its former impresario–the master of St. Anthony's behind Lincoln's Inn Fields–had found refuge with her, bringing at a single stroke the custom of its numerous and select clientele, and the witnesses who followed it everywhere. Covent Garden, Drury Lane and the abandoned Shakespearean theaters would dearly have loved to entertain all the gentlemen turned away from the doors of Sharper's.

It was nine o'clock in the evening and the hall, full of asphyxiating warmth, growled joyously as it followed the eternal trial of Jack Simple, who had stolen his aunt's turkey-cocks. This trial is as famous and legendary among our neighbors as the adventures of Hop o'my Thumb or the misfortunes of Genevieve of Brabant [138] are here.

Jack Simple is the godchild of the squire and the nephew of old Maud, who speaks in Biblical verses. He loves the shepherdess Suzy, but Suzy, as usual, runs after a bad lot. Jack goes to find Peg the witch and asks her for a potion to make Suzy incline towards him. Peg tells him that in order you make up the potion she needs a fat turkey-cock, so Jack Simple goes to his aunt's house that night to steal the king of her back yard. Peg devours the turkey-cock and makes up the potion. Jack Simple, having drunk it, tries to kiss Suzy and gets a black eye, which astonishes and wounds him. He goes to complain to Peg, who has digested the bird, and who asks him sternly whether he drank the potion on an empty stomach. When he says no, Peg gives him a moralistic lecture on the sin of gluttony, which ends with her ordering him to bring her another turkey-cock.

Jack Simple climbs into his aunt's yard again. A second cock is devoured by Peg, who makes up a second potion, and Jack Simple, full of confidence–having made sure this time to drink the potion before dinner–runs to present his cheek to Suzy, who blacks his other eye. Carried away by righteous anger, he cuts a sprig of green wood and gives Peg a good thrashing. Peg secretly swears to avenge herself. The opportunity is not long in coming; Aunt Maud arrives at the witch's house wanting to know the name of the wretch who has stolen two fine turkey-cocks from her yard. Peg boils a cow's head in her magic cauldron and says: "Neighbor, at midnight tonight the thief will climb over the wall of your back yard."

Old Maud, having recited a few apposite verses by way of payment, goes home and gets together with her neighbors. They prepare a strong rope with a slip-knot. In the meantime, the perfidious Peg goes to find Jack Simple and says: "I've boiled my cow's head for you; Suzy will follow you everywhere like a dog if you succeed in wringing the neck of a third turkey-cock exactly at midnight."

You can guess the rest, alas, but what is impossible for you to imagine is the pleasure of the select rabble that crowds into St. Anthony's or Sharper's at the representation of this naive morality play. When Old Maud recognizes the half-strangled thief as her nephew, the storm of joy makes the walls tremble.

Now Jack Simple, with the rope around his neck, is brought before the Squire, who is only pretending to be his godfather. From the Squire's viewpoint, Jack Simple is a living tax; he receives five shillings every Christmas and five shillings every birthday, making half a guinea in all. The Squire, delighted to put an end to this rent, sends Jack to the county assizes. Here begins the macaronic procedure, as old as the heavy merriment of England herself, but to which each stage-director adds new details.

First, there is the interrogation by the shirt-sleeved Coroner, who shaves and sings a Scottish ballad while the unfortunate Jack replies to his questions. Then follows the consignment to prison, the inventory of his pockets, and the division of the poor spoils between the turnkeys. Finally, some Prosperpine of that dark Tartarus comes to play the role of Mrs. Potiphar next to the terrified Jack.[139]

The Circuit Court–the ambulatory court that tours England with its army and camp-followers, its Ministerial Officers, Crown Prosecutors, clerks, employees and lawyers–arrives with a great fuss: a veritable company, as Scarron describes in his Roman comique: a complete troop, in which the advocate Destiny nobly defends widows and orphans, supported by the solicitor Spite. It produces a town in revolt–every Ragotin and Madame Bouvillon is aroused.[140] There are even people so passionate for justice that they follow the Circuit Court from town to town, like those street-urchins in our own land who follow the drums beating the retreat from the parade-ground to the barracks.

The jury is constituted: a dozen brave men who talk cotton thread, dirty fish and molten iron. The Chief Justice takes his place on his august seat; the King's Solicitor puts on his robe; the Advocates adjust their wigs–and the audience admires the fine manner of the ushers, who periodically let loose, even when no one is talking, their famous call for silence, pronounced: "Si-i-ilen-n-nce."

The list of charges, which accuse the unfortunate Jack Simple of every vice and every crime, is read in a high voice; then the Chief Justice gives the order to summon the first witness. Enter Paddy, whose toes stick out of his boots, and whose abundantly bristling red hair supports a tiny hat without a bottom or rim, into whose ribbon a short black pipe is wedged. Paddy walks quickly, in an anxious manner, darting wild glances at the audience; he's an Irishman with an excess of hatred.

"I swear that I saw him, Your Honor! I swear that he took the animal! I swear that he's a villain! I swear that he's a heathen! He's got a grey jacket with holes in the elbows, I swear it! And the poor creature cried out so loudly that I felt a chill in my armpits! I swear that I'm from Ardagh, where there never was a liar! I swear..."

Up steps Murphy, another Irishman! He has seen everything, and he will swear it by his right hand, his left hand and both feet if necessary. What a scoundrel! He has a white linen jacket and he is carrying a living turkey under his arm, which clucks softly and miserably.

Here's Murdoch now, yet another Irishman: "Lying is a sin, Your Honors, God bless your little children! The villainous wretch had a black jacket, as sure as the tongues of all impostors should be pierced with red-hot iron. I swear on my salvation and that of my wife that it wasn't the criminal's first offense, for he knew how to choke the unfortunate creature without letting out a sound. May I go to Hell, my true friends, if I haven't told the truth."

And more Irishmen, one after another: heaps of rags and perjury. No deposition bears any resemblance to any another, but all of them are true, sworn by the most terrible oaths.

The Puppet Judge says: "What jolly fellows! Here's to the health of Ireland!" He drinks an enormous glass, and everyone else does likewise. The ushers, wiping their gin-moistened lips with their wigs, call out: "Si-i-ilen-n-nce, gentlemen!"

The Crown Prosecutor springs to his feet. "Milord, gentlemen!" he cries, in the furious tone the gentle Cicero would adopt to pronounce the *quousque tandem*,[141] "For a long time, a gangrenous and contagious wound has been decimating the population of the country that, I dare to claim, is the greatest in the entire world, as much in respect of its moral institutions as from the viewpoint of its political system. For too long, a baleful evil–whose origin, it seems, must remain a mystery forever–has gnawed at the very heart of the free citizens of our land. If one consults statistics–that eminently English science which, in the view of many great minds, ought to replace all others in due time–one discovers with terror mingled with horror that in the county of Middlesex alone, which is the center of the United Kingdom and hence the pivot of the universe, 772 cases of this morbid affliction have revealed themselves in only 43 years. Far from diminishing, the number is growing; last year's figure surpassed the previous one by 29 per cent–and no one knows or can predict where that frightful progression will end.

"Milord, gentlemen, the first duty of an orator before an audience as illustrious as the one surrounding me is to be economical with his words. I have no puzzle to put to you. I shall call things by their proper names, and I shall say without any ambiguities or frivolous circumlocutions that the evil about which I am speaking–a profound evil; an evil which threatens to become endemic throughout the extent of our three kingdoms–is the nocturnal theft of turkey-cocks..."

For as long as the Mock Tribunal has existed, this has always brought the house down. For almost a century it has brought forth the same tempestuous applause every evening. We have no such durable success on the continent.

When the usher's nasal tones have demanded "si-i-ilen-n-nce" and the storm has slightly dampened down, the Prosecutor's friends come to shake him passionately by the hand. The jurors blow him kisses, as does the Judge. He returns to his indictment, demanding swift, severe and pitiless justice. "Evil must be turn up by the roots. The Institutes of Gaius come straight to the point, and the Pandects of Justinian [142] are categorical in their provisions. Chancellor Stair favors the death penalty; Blackstone–the immortal guiding light of English jurisprudence–has no other opinion in his prodigious *Commentaries*; Christian, in his *Notices*, and Glamorgan, in his *Syntagma*, clamor loudly for the ultimate penalty. [143] All these aristocratic intelligences understand that one vigorous medicine alone can halt the progress of this deplorable cancer of modern society."

The Prosecutor goes on, in a voice rendered tremulous and faint by emotion: "It is time; it is high time! Turkeys, as you know, milord and gentlemen, are of foreign origin, naturalized here. They are fully entitled to the greatest benefits of the law of hospitality. There are those here today who will tell you– via the voice of the Crown's Advocate–yet again that they have not asked for your protection. They will ask you, and I myself will end by asking you, this question: Do you want the family of turkeys to continue to live in your back yards–yes or no–or would you prefer to strike them out of the great chain of being and relegate them to the status of those extinct species whose names are known today to science alone? Of what crime to you accuse them, in order thus to condemn them? Have they committed murder, or even theft? If your hearts have no memory, what about your stomachs? Within ten years, the statistics proclaim, the last turkey will perish, victim of this muted but savage war. To reduce the question to clear evidence that leaves no room for doubt, you have to choose between the turkeys and the thieves, between good and evil, between innocence and crime. God preserve me, milord and gentlemen, from adding another word! The fate of an entire race is within your hands: I leave you to consult your consciences, and may the accused hang!"

Glasses are emptied everywhere, while the friends of the Public's Representative embrace him effusively.

But the Puppet Advocate has a multitude of dirty scraps of paper set out in front of him, and a pile of tatty old books to his right. He puts down his pipe, he adjusts his wig, he smoothes his soiled waistcoat and the scrap of toweling that serves as his gown; everything about him is suggestive of the mental labor that is the precursor of a thunderous exordium.

Suddenly, he reaches out a black hand to seize the thickest of his books, filthier than all the rest.

"Si-i-ilen-n-nce!" sings the usher, slowly.

"And we too," cries the advocate, brandishing his book excitedly, "we too possess the divine Blackstone! The Sun shines for the whole world! Unworthy as we are, your light illuminates us! Blackstone! William Blackstone, sword and torch of the English Themis, we have you, not only in our library, but still in our memory and in our heart; we have your incomparable work, we have it in its virgin state, disencumbered of the impure notes of this Christian that our adversary has no hesitation in citing! Milord and gentlemen, I ask you: does not the candle glow more brightly when it is about to go out? And what possible use is a snuffed-out candle in the dark? The honorable magistrate who attacks us has taken a snuffer named Christian, set him upon William Blackstone, the torch, and cries out: Can you see clearly?

"No, we do not see clearly, because the property of the snuffer, according to Gottlieb Heineccius,[144] the German legal expert, whose wisdom no one here today can contest–one might as well deny the daylight itself–the property of the snuffer, I say, is to suppress light momentarily. I ask the eloquent advocate of the King if he denies the fact?

The Prosecutor shrugs his shoulders disdainfully.

"He does not deny the fact!" the triumphant defender resumes. "And I beg all those who are listening to me to notice one thing: I pronounced the word momentarily. Why? Because to make a snuffed-out candle brighten again, one only needs to relight it. It's elementary, but it's capital! I have the strength to lift up the snuffer; I shall render to our Blackstone the chandelier by means of which he may be analyzed at leisure, and it will only require one of its rays to dissipate the factitious darkness–if I might express myself thus–into whose bosom we have been plunged!"

Jack Simple, the Puppet Accused, was here represented by a fat fool who had been eating spotted dick and drinking stout since the opening of the hearing. The Advocate turned towards him just as he was swallowing a magisterial mouthful that filled out his cheeks.

"Do you think, milord and gentlemen," the advocate continued, "that it is permissible in a free country for an unfortunate child to be torn away from his family under a pretext that I would call futile, if it were not both shocking and odious? Do you think that it is legitimate to substitute mourning for the peace of a citizen, to render nights sleepless and days devoid of appetite, to replace roundness with emaciation and the pink cheeks of youth with pallor? Cast a glance, if you please, judges, jurors, audience, at this deplorable victim of imprudent legislation, and tell me why turkey-cocks should require such torture!"

Our Jack Simple, having finished his pudding, chewed a wad of tobacco and quietly crossed his arms before the eyes of the audience.

"Youth!" proclaimed the Advocate, impetuously. "The gift of the immortal gods: flower of life; treasure of nature! Love, providential aim of existence; splendid law, superior to any law enacted by parliament; superior and anterior, since Philemon loved Baucis [145] and vice versa, well before the installation of the parliamentary regime! Smiles; kisses; dances on the green, to the sound of a rustic violin! Sweet accomplishment of the precept be fruitful and multiply; seed bed of humanity; preservation of the world; elixir of life, which ceaselessly restores new blood to the exhausted veins of the universe! Three turkeys!–only two, in actuality, since the third still graces the aunt's back yard–two turkeys that were sacrificed on the altar of love. Behold the crime! Can the King's Attorney swear here and now that no turkey has ever been immolated for his gourmandizing?

"Would you like to know a deplorable fact? It is the superstition that still reigns over our countryside. We have heard talk here, quite matter-of-factly, of a witch. I ask the gentlemen of the jury: why are there still witches? What has the government done to exterminate witchcraft? The witch ate the turkey-cocks; it's the fable of Bertrand and Raton;[146] my client has extracted the turkeys, not from the fire but from the back yard, and the witch alone has profited. Hang the witch! Hang all the witches! Do a little, the tiniest fraction, of your duty as moralizers, and it will then be time to boast in pompous terms of the excellence of your moral institutions. For myself, I suggest that it is you, government, who have stolen the turkeys, and that my client Jack Simple is a martyr!

"In fact, milord and gentlemen, we plead not guilty. There is no proof that two turkey-cocks have been taken from Aunt Maud, who has taken the trouble to found a sect in which it is sworn on oath. Aunt Maud is the only member of her sect, as is usual in our happy land where there are as many sects as there are copies of the Bible. The neighbors saw Jack Simple arrive at his aunt's house by climbing over the wall. At my client's age, one swims rivers rather than looking for a bridge. I can see only one culpable action, and that is the slip-knot that was put around his neck, and I make my application for damages. Outside of that, we have ten witnesses who say that black is white, that for is against, that hot is cold: that is the Irish! A broom!

"Have we reached the point of risking the rope every time we do our duty to relatives who have back yards? Perish the turkeys, rather than the principles assaulted by this perverse procedure! I like turkeys, milord and gentlemen, but I suppress my appetite before my character.

"In law, the legislation of Lycurgus of Sparta and those of the decemvirs of Rome,[147] the Hebraic law and what we know of Brahmin jurisprudence are in perfect agreement with the body of Roman law, the codes of the Nordic peoples–Silberradt in Germany, Loe in England, Pothier and Ferrière in France [148]–in offering the example of an admirable ensemble. The text *si quis gallinam* [149] cannot apply to turkey-cocks; there is a visible root in each of the two determinative nouns: turkey speaks of the East [150] as Gallina speaks of the Gauls. Turkeys were not subjects of the Emperor Justinian.”

Here the Advocate paused in the midst of murmurs of approval. There were drinks all round, and Jenny Paddock renewed the provision of gin to every table. Then the defender, gathering his scattered notes into a pile and audibly depositing the whole on the stained volume of Blackstone’s divine commentaries, pulled up his sleeves like a man about to deliver a mighty blow.

“Gentlemen of the jury,” he went on, in a changed, hollow voice, “I have said that you are free men; don’t be put off by any unnecessary fear of displeasing the Court. You are the Court. Your verdict is between you and God. On one side, there are two domestic fowls that no human power can resuscitate; on the other, a young Christian soul, a man, the masterpiece of Creation. Out there, on the verdant banks of a stream, on the edge of a large and profoundly green meadow, stands a modest cottage. The large cows ruminating in the meadow do not belong to the unfortunate woman in mourning-dress leaning on the window-sill, her head bowed and her eyes moist. She is poor; she has only one thing on Earth, and that is her son. She is waiting. What is she waiting for? Her husband? No. Her dress is black and the wind stirs the widow’s veil over her face. Her husband will never come back. She is waiting for her son, her only treasure; her son, who supports her; her son, who consoles her; her son, who sometimes makes her smile again through her tears. She is Jack Simple’s mother. You have his life or death in your hands. May God enlighten your reason and breathe mercy into you!”

He let himself fall back, choked by emotion. His friends crowded around him incontinently, feeding him a beer-glass full of gin–after which they lifted him up triumphantly.

“Accused!” cried the Puppet Judge. “Have you anything to say to the Tribunal?”

Jack Simple got up slowly and came to the bar, after having stretched his limbs like a lazy dog waking from sleep. His dull eyes look first at the Tribunal, then the jurors, then the audience–who applaud such a superb idiot!

“I have to say,” he replies, in a drawl, “that if I get away with this, I’ll take care of Peg and Aunt Maud.”

“Wretch!” cried the Advocate.

“Same to you,” Jack Simple replied. “You’re nothing but an idler. My mother’s not in a cottage. She’s banged up in the Bridewell!”

“Wretch!” the defender repeated, tearing the stuffing from his wig.

“And as for the turkeys,” Jack Simple continued, amiably, “they were the first two I ever took; before that, I only stole chickens...” He interrupted himself angrily: “And they’re liars who say that I made the turkeys cry out! I’m not as stupid as that. If you want, I can tell you how to carry them away without making them cry out..."

The Advocate had not a strand of oakum left in his wig.

This is the time for the stamping of feet and wild applause. Jack Simple's explanation, demolishing the work of his defender, is the fifth act of the play–which terminates, needless to say, with a good hanging. The gaieties of John Bull always come to a lugubrious end.

Today, though, the drama was not to have its tragicomic denouement. Jack Simple's explanation was interrupted by a loud noise that came from the door, whose opening and reclosing had provoked a fracas. The faithful spectators shouted, "Listen! Listen" and the howls and cheers that went up at the other end of the inn drowned out the voice of the principal actor, who ended up turning round and abandoning his role. The public, with nothing to restrain them any longer, launched themselves towards the counter, which was still veiled by the thick cloud of smoke.

Beyond the cloud the tumult grew, dominated by a hundred joyous voices shouting in chorus: "Ned Knob! Little Ned and his pretty Molly have come to Sharper's in a carriage!"

It was a rarity, to be sure. There was indeed a hired carriage stationed at Sharper's door, in front of the demolished barracks that served the Bohemians of the London poor as a dormitory. And it was indeed Ned, with his thin, wrinkled face and his sickly eyes, clad from head to toe in new clothes, his hat glossy and his boots as shiny as two mirrors, with white gloves and a malacca cane with a gold pommel. Tiny Ned was hanging from the arm of his pretty Molly, bearded and rolling her eyes, dulled by the somnolence of intoxication but proud in her red silk dress with flounces. Molly was carrying aloft a straw hat surmounted by a sheaf of feathers, already faded, and brandishing a superb umbrella that seemed to her to be the most flattering part of her costume.

Ned stopped a few steps from the door and posed to permit himself to be admired. Vanity is the folly of great negroes and little men. When he had excited enough surprise and general amazement, instead of replying to the confused questions that were coming from all directions, he rummaged in his pocket, where the clink of gold was audible, and threw a French double *louis* on the counter, saying: "Punch all round!"

Men and women alike let out a long cheer.

"Keep your distance!" Ned shouted, while Molly twirled her fine umbrella. "Don't touch my suit or milady's silk, if you please. All that was bought with honestly gained money. You're glad to see me–that's natural; I understand your attachment–but familiarity between us wouldn't be appropriate. We don't belong to the same social class."

There are numerous rogues in France, unfortunately, and it would, in consequence–excepting certain differences of custom and physiognomy–be possible to find in Paris or elsewhere some den of vice equivalent to Sharper's of Low

Lane. Imagine, however, the laughter and jeers that would have greeted a speech like Ned Knob's in our country. In London, it is not the same; the mania of castes, distinctions and categories is so profoundly inveterate there that it penetrates to the utmost depths, where disgrace, at least, must find its level. Among rogues, as among honest men, any insolent pretension may be acceptable, provided that it is accompanied by money in the pocket. The mire of the City, like the radiant West End, has its nobility, its gentry, its public.

No one laughed openly at little Ned Knob and the powerful Molly, who had fine linen and silk on their backs; a circle formed around them–at a distance, as instructed–and the Puppet Judge, expressing the general opinion, said: "We know well enough that you're above us, Master Knob."

Jenny Paddock, not without a slight hint of mockery, added: "Come into the parlor, gentle sir, with your lady; put the balustrade between yourselves and the common people."

The little clerk turned to his companion, and in the naivete of his vain-glory, cried: "See how I am treated, I beg you, Molly my dear child! Isn't it flattering for a woman to have such a cavalier as me!"

"Give us a swig, Ned," Molly replied. "I'll consent to be damned if you aren't a proper gentleman!"

Ned opened the rickety hurdle that served as a gate to the parlor and pushed Molly ahead of him with protective seriousness. He sat down at a table. "Hey, Bab!" he shouted, gesturing to one of the miserable creatures who served John Devil's widow as aides-de-camp. "Come and wipe this tabletop with your napkin, my girl, so that I can rest my elbows on it and chat informally with all these old companions. Do you remember, Bab? I courted you once and you put on airs–see what you have lost, my girl. You could have been the one wearing Molly's dress today!"

Molly seized Bab by the shoulder and shook her roughly. "A swig to drink," she ordered, "or I'll break you in two, hussy!"

"Look!" murmured the enchanted Ned. "My pretty Molly is jealous of her man!"

Jenny Paddock was almost as tall as Molly, but she had fewer hairs on her chin. By virtue of that fact, although every wretch there could have envied Molly her good fortune, jealousy itself was forced to admit that Molly deserved her happiness. In the whole of London, Ned Knob would not have found anyone ready to replace him. Molly took in both hands the bottle of brandy that Bab brought and stuck the neck in her mouth. At carnival time, we have seen more than one Auvergnian disguised as a countess, but for the sickly tint of her flesh, the odor of garlic and the sturdiness of her hair, Molly would have won hands down. While she drank, Ned Knob contemplated the tanned and muscular neck projecting from a sky-blue scarf knotted over her red dress, the bronzed face brushed by the pink ribbons of her hat, the large fishlike eyes cutting into the bottle. God might damn little Ned Knob; he had his paradise on Earth!

"Just like that, Master Ned," said the widow Paddock, who brought their glasses herself on a tray. "Just like that. Yes indeed, you've hit the bull's eye!"

Ned caressed her chin paternally.

"Your sex was created for pleasure, not for business, my pretty Jenny," the little clerk replied. "Man is fickle. If ever I repudiate Molly, my wife. I'll think about you. Let's go! What's up, boys?"

The waiters and serving-girls had delivered pots of burning punch to every part, casting livid reflections on the faces of all the bandits. The actors of the judicial comedy were in the front row, around a cauldron full of flaming spirit, with wives and children who were theirs or someone else's. They were all filling their glasses, drinking a double toast to the health of Gentleman Ned and his lady, amid enthusiastic cheers.

Then Gentleman Ned put down his glass and said, in a serious manner: "My children, you'll understand well enough that, in the advantageous position in which I now find myself, I haven't come here to drink your sorry punch and sniff the fumes of your vile tobacco. I'm the member of a club and I frequent the cigar-couches of Oxford Street–say no more!–but I have 30 pounds to split between a few good fellows, and I thought of you, comrades... a hurrah for me and pretty Molly!"

He was given three hurrahs instead of one, and he went on, addressing the Puppet Judge: "Come here, Sawney,[151] old hand–I'll let you into the parlor."

Sawney, genuinely honored to be chosen, threw away his oakum wig, put his pipe in his pocket and stepped over the barrier. Gentleman Ned left his table and led him to the far side of the enclosure, saying emphatically: "Even my wife doesn't know my secrets!"

This was of scant importance to pretty Molly, who threw her plumed hat behind her back to give herself some air, thus revealing her titus,[152] as bristly as a brush for hunting spiders. She seized her three-quarters-empty bottle in both hands, put her umbrella between her knees, and began singing a lugubrious shanty in a sailor's voice.

Gentleman Ned, his hands in his pockets and standing on tiptoe to raise his head to the level of Sawney's chin, whispered; "Old hand, what's the current price for witnesses in criminal proceedings?"

Apple whisky was burning in every part of the drinking-den, mingling its bitter perfumes with all the infamous odors that made the atmosphere viscous. Jenny Paddock had resumed her place at the counter; the wells had their groups of players; a few drunken girls were dancing alone, pale and haggard, while consumptive children coughed as they crawled and played in the mud; here and there, solitary stupefied drunks stared into the void. A little further away, Paddy the Irishman, an incurable chatterer, told stories of his homeland threaded with oaths, although no one was listening. There were (*infandum*)[153] amorous couples talking in hushed voices. And what, Lord, is the language of love in the depths of such unsoundable sewers? Others were silently exchanging sideways punches; yet others asleep, wallowing in the aisles. Pretty Molly, like the barrel of the Danaides,[154] was trying in vain to fill herself up, and pressed on with her sinister song like one possessed.

It was a long time since there had been such great amusement at Sharper's!

"Merry England forever!" said Gentleman Ned, who was surveying the scene affectionately. "I've come back from France, and I need something to warm my heart!"

"Yes, yes," said Sawney, the Puppet Judge. "There's still no place like London for honest amusement among friends. Have you seen the old hands of Paris, Master Ned?"

The little clerk shrugged his shoulders with sovereign scorn. "Miserable place!" he murmured. "The Police have the right to go everywhere."

Sawney opened his astonished eyed wide, as if some barbaric custom of the Chinese Empire had been mentioned. "Police everywhere!" he echoed. "How are the comrades doing?"

"Miserable place!" repeated Ned, in his turn. "The French aren't men, you know. I fought four of them myself, all alone, without taking pretty Molly's umbrella from under my arm. And Molly is a head taller than their soldiers. Miserable place! Their wine is weaker than our petty ale, their brandy as pale as Thames water, their meat doesn't bleed on the table; you pass a hundred men in the street without seeing a single cheek bulging with a good wad of tobacco, and when my sweet Molly lights her pipe in their taverns all their laughing monkey-women hold their noses. Miserable place! If London ever became well known on the continent, there wouldn't be a single Parisian left in Paris! But we aren't here to chat, old hand. If the price of witnesses doesn't suit me, I'll need time to get to the spirit shop in the Inner Temple."

"You wouldn't really be so heartless as to get your witnesses from the Inner Temple, Master Ned!" Sawney protested. "Business isn't going well here, and we have a living to earn. There are witnesses and witnesses, you know."

"I must have the best; it's a great scheme. And I can tell you that it will be so much the worse for anyone who gets in our way."

"Who are you working for now, Master Ned?"

The little clerk gave him a mocking wink. "If anyone asks, old hand," he said, "I strongly advise you to say that you don't know anything."

"That's all right, Mr. Knob," muttered the Puppet Judge. "Everyone has his own business. It's just a matter of having news of Noll Green the boxer and Lochaber Dick the beer-swiller, who are surely mixed up in it."

Ned lowered his eyes, and the wrinkles on his forehead deepened. "They're both stuck in France," he murmured.

"No one's heard the two whistle-blasts since," Sawney went on. "You know–the night when you read the history of John Devil the Quaker on this very spot. All the same, Gregory Temple has been sunk without trace!"

The little clerk seemed to snap out of an unwelcome preoccupation, and spoke brusquely: "All that's as old as Herod, my man! John Devil's a long way away, Dick and Noll too; Gregory Temple lived before the Deluge. There's no one here but me, who has become a gentleman and who expects to be well served, since I'm paying handsomely. Whether I'm working for someone else or as master of the shop isn't important. Have you got witnesses, yes or no?"

"Yes, by God!" Sawney exclaimed. "Five, ten or a hundred if need be. But you've been in the game, Master Ned, and you know..."

"I know that you're bargaining like a horse-trader, friend! Name your price; I'll either take it or leave it."

"Name yours, Master Ned," the Puppet Judge countered. "There are witnesses and witnesses. For the Hundred,[155] you can get them for six shillings, obviously... and for a civil suit in the Court of Common Pleas [156] I'll cut my margin and offer six at a pound apiece–that's for Irishmen, of course; it's two pounds if you need Scotsmen, four if you have to have authentic Englishmen. But at the criminal court...! You understand well enough, Master Ned, that no one likes to show the corner of his mouth to a sheriff!"

"It has to be the assizes," the little clerk put in.

"Lord Above!" said Sawney. "And you spoke of 30 pounds for half a dozen! If old Peter Duck of the Inner Temple can supply them to Your Honor at that rate, I think you'd do well to agree. The assizes, by God!"

Gentleman Ned smiled because he had been addressed as Your Honor–but that was all. Beneath his infantile vanity he was genuinely clever. The man who had chosen him knew what he was doing, and could sum up a man at a glance. Ned was not lying when he said that even Molly did not know his secret. "My old Sawney," he went on. "For 30 pounds, I could lead the entire society that now surrounds us to the assizes, with Jenny Paddock at its head, even though she's as rich as Croesus. Jenny cost three shillings when I was working in Mr. Wood's office, and her testimony was worth as much as three men's, because the judges liked to look at her. She once robbed a judge who had a 60-guinea watch. How much do you want per head of cattle to testify at the assizes?"

"What kind of business?"

"Serious business."

"Theft?"

"Murder."

Sawney shook his head, as if he were seriously worried. "You'll need *maiden chickens* [157] for that," he said.

Maiden chickens are the exact opposite of old hands. The term is applied in the jargon of London thieves to those rare individuals who have never been up in court, and whose names are consequently unknown to all the members of the tribunals. Maiden chickens can easily offer false testimony in any fairground.

We assume that no one is unfamiliar with the peculiar prosperity that the industry of false testimony has long enjoyed in England, which is far from having said its last word at the time of writing. In the civil suit of the brothers Gartner against the house of Hodgson, Marybury and Hodgson in 1821, the appeal to the King's Bench revealed that the brothers Gartner had received 673 pounds sterling to refresh testimony. 673 pounds is 16,825 French francs. We record the fact without comment, merely adding that in London, no one was surprised. In the years that followed, justice set its hand on several hundred instances of false testimony, but pruning does no harm to a forest and the interesting sellers of free evidence, as they call their trade, have continued quietly to flourish.

"Well, Sawney, my friend," the little clerk said, "You'll supply three pairs of maiden chickens. How much per pair?"

The Puppet Judge seemed to be considering the matter. "Is the accused an old hand?" he asked, after a long silence.

"No, the accused is the most virginal chicken of them all."

"So he killed unintentionally?"

"No, intentionally."

"After a brawl, perhaps?"

"No, in cold blood."

"To steal?"

"He stole nothing."

"Because he couldn't?"

"Because he wouldn't."

"Then why the murder?"

"A whim perhaps, Sawney my friend; we don't have to debate the question ourselves.

"Mr. Knob," the Puppet Judge replied, with calm and serious firmness, because he was for the moment merely a businessman conducting an important affair, "I don't have to tell you that these questions are strictly necessary."

"That's why I reply to them precisely and concisely, Sawney, my friend."

"The price of our testimony is determined by the risk involved."

"As is only fair."

"And there are some circumstances in which the danger is so great that our witnesses wouldn't want to expose themselves to it, for silver or for gold."

"I understand that." The little clerk raised his voice at this point. "Don't be impatient, Molly, my love," he shouted. "We'll be in time for the second show at the Olympic Theater, and we'll spend the rest of the evening there."

Pretty Molly was not impatient; she had slid off her seat and was snoring under the table.

"Is the incident recent?" Sawney asked.

"February last."

"Damn! That's practically yesterday. When it's a matter of years, witnesses are more at ease. The affair didn't make a lot of noise?"

"An enormous amount."

"A pity! The circumstances of these overly famous cases are so well-known! How would our men fare, for instance, in an affair like that of Madame Bartolozzi?"

Ned smiled and ruffled the frill of his shirt in a comic gesture. "So you'd back out, old hand, if it were in fact the Bartolozzi affair?"

"Has Tom Brown been arrested?" asked Sawney, excitedly.

Ned Knob did not reply.

"To testify in favor of Tom Brown," Sawney continued, agitatedly, "would be putting one's head in the noose."

"Is Tom Brown a maiden chicken, then?" the little clerk asked, mockingly. "I told you..."

"All right, all right!" muttered the Puppet Judge. "You've said what you wanted to say, Master Ned... but you won't swear on your thumb that your master isn't named John Devil."

The little clerk looked him in the face, and his eyes gleamed strangely behind their sickly lids. "Old hand," he said, in a low but penetrating voice, "it'll cost a lot to spin the cord that hangs Tom Brown. When Tom Brown is in prison, he won't turn to you or me... but Tom Brown isn't in prison. Don't lower your eyes: would you dare to bargain with me if I came in the name of Tom Brown?"

It was Sawney's turn to be silent. His face, which had earlier been bold and good-humored, now expressed fear. After several seconds, he murmured: "Are Dick and Noll coming back?"

"Never," replied the little clerk, whose grimacing face had also taken on a somber expression. Then, while Sawney was still hesitating, he added: "Man, it isn't a question of John Devil, nor is it a matter of compromising oneself trying to save some unfortunate in spite of the King's justices. It's entirely the opposite; we want to take the hand of the tribunal, which is in difficulty, and give it the means to condemn the man who strangled Constance Bartolozzi."

Sawney looked at him in stupefaction. "Then, it's witnesses for the prosecution you need, Master Knob?"

"Precisely... and good ones."

"May God punish me if I ever do that sort of business!"

"There's a first time for everything, old hand. Name your price."

"But would our fellows want...?"

"We have only to ask them. Your price?"

The Puppet Judge's hesitation grew longer and longer. "It's a matter of a stab in the back, in the dark, and then going home to sleep," he muttered.

"You've been talking to me for too long to refuse, man!" the little clerk said, dryly. "If you're afraid of stabbing, I advise you to think about it."

The threat was not even disguised, and poor, frail Ned Knob was obviously not alluding to himself when he spoke of violence.

"Does the fellow that has to be found guilty belong to the great family?" Sawney asked next, as if he were looking for a means of escape from a terrible necessity. It was well known that the general association of malefactors–the so-called "great family"–had a very powerful organization, and laws that could not be infringed without danger.

But Ned replied peremptorily: "He doesn't belong to the great family."

"Has he ever mixed with us?"

"As an enemy, perhaps; he's worked for Scotland Yard."

"Do we know him?"

"As the hare knows the greyhound."

Sawney's head sagged; he was beaten. "Give me 30 guineas, Ned," he said, "and take your pick of my lot. I've five boys and a woman, all in a fit state to do the job, never having been convicted of anything. If there's a difficult deposition to be made, there's the man." He pointed at the actor who had played Jack Simple. "The Puppet Advocate would also have been useful, but he's going straight back to Sydney."

"Hey, Jenny Paddock, my darling!" Ned shouted. "Light a nice fire in your bedroom to give it a good airing. I'll rent it for a shilling an hour, and give it back to you when it's time to go to bed. We've business to do for the next sheep-market. Send up some rum, of aristocratic quality, white sugar, lemons and cinnamon; I don't like the punch the little people drink! And no one's to disturb us, for any reason! If my dear Molly wakes up, give her a drink. Whoever loves me, follow me!"

He went through the inn, strutting as best he could, and reached the door of the widow's private apartment, situated behind the counter. Sawney called to his flock and followed him, head bowed.

In Sharper's communal hall, a few dull gazes followed this movement, but the apple brandy, aided by the asphyxiating atmosphere, had taken effect and all the heads were made of lead.

A short while later, Ned Knob was installed in Jenny Paddock's own armchair, in front of a bed garnished in olive serge and guarded by a somber crowd of brass-framed Irish saints, facing a coal fire whose burning sent forth opaque spirals of grey smoke. Ranged in front of him, on stools, was Sawney's army, and Sawney himself, slightly reheartened by the flame of a punch that he was stirring with an iron ladle. The former clerk had a paper in his hand, on which the flock was listed.

"Boys and girls," he began, in the important tone that came to him so easily, "this is the first time you have had the opportunity to co-operate in a useful task. Instead of opening a false path to justice, which could easily go wrong without you, today you shall come the aid of a society in trouble. It's not unknown to you that I'm well-versed in the study of the law. You need have no fear, therefore; we're marching on solid ground, and in addition to the agreed price, I shall recompense each one of you according to his merits."

The last part of the statement cleared every face that the ideas of working for the cause of justice had visibly darkened.

"We shall say," Ned continued, consulting his list, "that this dear child is called Jeanie, this jolly fellow Sam, this jaundiced chap William. That won't be enough, since, as the proverb says, in every three Englishmen, there are two Wills and a John, so here's our John! Then we have Toby and Numph;[158] that's very good! Here's the story: you don't know the gentleman's name, understand?"

"It's your lesson," Sawney put in. "Try to pay attention, my ewes."

"We're here," said Miss or Mrs. Jeanie, extending her glass to the burning punch.

Sawney the shepherd added: "They're all remarkably intelligent, except Numph."

"So much the better," Ned went on. "You don't know the gentleman's name and you don't know what he's done. You're witnesses for the prosecution. You're going to ask me: 'What do we say if we don't know anything?' I'll tell you: on February 3 this year, a crime was committed in a nice house in Regent Street, bearing the number 19. The Police and the Justices know perfectly well who committed it, but they can't get a verdict for want of evidence. You, who know nothing, will furnish the evidence. You'll say: 'I saw this, I saw that,' innocent things in themselves, for the most part. The Justice will draw the conclusions. When you're shown the accused, you'll say: 'that's him.' Understand? Not the one who committed the crime–you don't know that–but the one I saw pass by on this day, at this hour, in this place; the one who spoke these words, who lost this coin, who was obviously in trouble...

"My children, you're looking at a person who has drawn up statements, who was charged with exactly that role in the office of one of the busiest solicitors in the Strand. Oh, we put on some comedies in our time, at the Court of

Common Pleas, and I regret that it was all cut short. Miss Jeanie, my jewel, open your ears; I'll begin with you, to give pride of place to the fair sex."

Jeanie Bird, a pale and slender girl with a sweet face and eyes already dulled by gin, put down her glass and assumed the stance of a child listening to a schoolmaster.

"Very well," said the former clerk. "In the play, you're a embroiderer of fine linen and you're familiar with all the cheap prints sold on the street. It's your job! In January last, at your employer's, you were given a dozen cambric handkerchiefs to initial *R.T.*, for which task you received a shilling and six pence. That's all. And pay attention keenly, my good fellows, because you have to learn my words by heart without leaving anything out and without adding anything. It's Shakespeare, damn it! If you change a single word, you'll be vilified! So there you were, Miss Jeanie, my treasure, with your shilling and sixpence, no longer giving a thought to the dozen handkerchiefs, when in February, you paid a penny for *The Adventures of John Devil the Quaker*, a very well-written and highly historic book. You discovered therein, among other things, the assassination of the singer Bartolozzi, and the circumstance that the murderer had left his cambric handkerchief beside the bed, initialed *R.T.*, stained by a drop of blood. My God! There are 10,000 gentlemen in London with the initials *R.T.*, but who knows why certain things strike you? Providence has a part to play. You remain troubled and you try to find out where the handkerchief is kept. It's kept in the shop at Scotland Yard. You run along there; you're shown the handkerchief; it's one of those that you marked. You say so—to whom? To Gregory Temple himself. He won't come back from Paris to contradict you. And be sure to remember this: Gregory Temple made you promise on oath to keep silent until the day the justice interrogates you. Is that understood?"

"Understood," Jeanie replied.

"We can go through it a second time, and a third, if you wish."

"I'd rather get to the punch, but I've got something to say."

"Speak!" said the little clerk, magisterially.

"What if someone asks me the name and address of my employer?"

"I love intelligent minds!" cried Ned. "Come and kiss me, my lovely maiden chicken. Your observation is eminently sensible..."

"I tell you," Sawney put in, "for maiden chickens, they're astounding. Except for poor Numph, they'd sell their father and their mother too!"

"My little beauty," Ned went on, "we have an answer to everything; what we're doing here is the result of careful calculation. If anyone asks you the name and address of the embroiderer's, you say straight out: Mistress Spencer, 13 Haymarket."

"And if they check it out?"

"Mistress Spencer died at the end of March."

There was a ripple of approval among the maiden chickens, and even Sawney could not restrain the smile of artistic satisfaction.

"Let's see, Numph," cried the little clerk. "You're the weakest, it appears. You can manage a commission for a shilling, though, can't you?"

"Oh! Yes, Your Honor," Numph replied, "If it's not too far off." Numph was a Welshman with a face that was frank but brutal, with his hair styled in the mode of Caerbran,[159] which resembles that of our Finistère peasants.

Ned nodded his head amicably, and continued: "Attention. You're an errand-boy earning a living carrying things here and there. On February 3, a gentleman came up to you and put a shilling in your hand with a letter addressed to Madame Constance Bartolozzi, 19 Regent Street, and an order to get a response. You did your duty and came back to tell him: no reply. The gentleman went white, and muttered a curse. That's it!"

"I could say more than that!" protested the humiliated Numph.

"It's all that's necessary. Now, in contrast to our Jeanie, who only has to recognize the handkerchief, when you're asked 'Do you recognize this man?' you answer: 'I recognize him; it's the gentleman who gave me the shilling and the letter.' Can you play that role?"

"My God!" Numph grumbled. "I'm no stupider than the next man, and I was the cock of my family. I can do better."

"That's up to you, friend. One word more and you'll go to the Circuit Court as a false witness. You're young, and people sometimes come back from New South Wales. Think on it!"

"We'll go over his lines with him," Sawney said. "Take Sam now, Master Ned, if you need a good one."

Sam was the Jack Simple of the Irish Court. Master Ned declared that he would keep him for dessert and called Will.

"You, friend," he said, "are an Englishman born in Ulster, lazy as a snake and a bold liar; we'll give you appropriate provisions. You're always out walking. You were out walking that day, the fourth or fifth of February–you can't remember exactly–in St. James's Park, looking at the melting snow on the roof of the palace. A group formed around a young man who fell down unconscious. Someone asked you whether you're a doctor, by any chance, in order that you might bleed the unfortunate man, who was holding a copy of the *Morning Post* reporting the sudden death of Signora Bartolozzi. When the accused is asked to stand up, you say: 'Well, this man resembles the young chap, but one needs to be sure to give evidence that might be the death of a Christian. The young man had a winter coat... and he was paler than this gentleman... I can say no more than that he resembles him.' "

"There's a damnable little villain!" muttered Sawney.

"Well," said the former clerk, putting his thumbs in the armholes of his waistcoat. "I think he has style enough."

The maiden chickens looked at him henceforth with respectful admiration.

"To you, Toby," he went on. "You seem to me to be a resolute fellow who knows what's what. You might be a Police agent if the need arose. Where are you from?"

"Dover."

"You can talk French, then?"

"Quite well."

"Perfect! You come from France, where you were a hired detective under the orders and at the expense of a certain James Davy, Assistant Commissioner at Scotland Yard and right-hand man of the former Chief Superintendent, Gregory Temple. Take notes, my friend, this is beginning to get complicated. Dogs know what prey they're hunting, and are more advanced in that respect than subaltern detectives. You were in Paris to find the trail of a person whose real name you did not know, who had avoided the surveillance of the English Police by stealing the identity card of this James Davy–a card that would serve as an excellent passport in foreign parts, having been certified by the Foreign Office. You were wasting your time in Paris; you searched the city from top to bottom but could not find the false James Davy. Finally, weary of the struggle, you wanted to return to London. At the stage-coach office, you ran into another Englishman who was also booking a seat for London. On being asked for his passport, he offers James Davy's card. What luck! You get into the diligence with him, then on to the ferry, but on arrival at Dover, he gives you the slip. Have you got it, Toby?"

"I've got it–but what about my agent's card?"

"You shall have one, in the name of James Davy."

"And if I'm confronted by men from Scotland Yard?"

"That's the beauty of it!" Ned said. "Listen to this, Sawney! The false Davy is a Scotland Yard man himself; in consequence, to hunt him, it required a bloodhound whose muzzle was unknown in that establishment. If there were anyone in the world less familiar than you to the army of which Gregory Temple was the General, the true James Davy would have chosen him in your place. That's your answer, Toby."

"Demon child!" muttered the Puppet Judge.

"So you think we definitely have talent, old hand?"

"And will it be necessary to recognize the accused?" Toby asked.

"Fully. You're still annoyed, since he made a mockery of you at Dover, where you thought you had him. You'll get your own back by answering: 'I have memorized his description. That's him! That's the man who had James Davy's identity card!' And now, let's have a swig, children, as my Pretty Molly says. Why isn't there a bottle for every desk in the communal room? Open your ears, John, old chap. You must be a maiden chicken, since our friend Sawney says so, but you look more like a five-year-old cock, good to put in the pot to stretch the soup. What? That isn't worth a laugh? You're mourning your *écus*?

"The owl's business is to fly by night along ancient walls. On February 4, at two o'clock in the morning, you were taking a stroll in the Quadrant, at the end of Regent Street, thinking about the high price of gin and the troubles of the times. The arcades were deserted and you could hear the piano in the Great Hall, where young country squires were drinking sherry and watching French waltzes. Suddenly, a man runs past you, jostling your shoulder–although it was, thank God, in the circular space in the gallery. The man lurched to the left and the right, staggering while he ran as if he were drunk. You saw him fall down, then get up again, and you saw a piece of paper where he fell down. You called out to him; 'Hey, you!' but your voice seemed to alarm him; it had the same effect on him as a spur in the belly of a tired horse. He got a second wind and disappeared around the Quadrant. You picked up the paper, which was an acknowledgement of a debt of 1,000 pounds, signed by Fanny Thompson, the actress, to the advantage of her colleague, Constance Bartolozzi."

Silence reigned in Jenny Paddock's room, where the noises of the inn were reduced to a muffled murmur. Sawney and his flock were listening now in somber immobility.

"Take notes, John, my friend," Ned Knob broke off to say. "You have a nice role, and your deposition will be reproduced at length in the newspapers. As you're a thoroughly honest chap, in spite of your funereal manner, and as an IOU in the hands of a third party is no use at all, you took it to Madame Bartolozzi's house the next morning, to return her entitlement in return for an appropriate compensation. Madame Bartolozzi had died that very night. You were sorry for her unfortunate fate, and the idea came to you to seek out Fanny Thompson, from whom the compensation ought to be even greater. Fanny Thompson's son being the secretary and friend of the Chief Superintendent of Police, you ran to Scotland Yard and asked for Richard Thompson. Richard Thompson was out; you waited for him; he didn't come. You went back the following day and waited again–no Richard Thompson! Then, you got a London almanac and you saw that Fanny Thompson, retired from the theater, was living in the country in Surrey. A few hours later, a public coach set you down at her door. The house seemed rather strange. The arrival of a stranger seemed to produce anxiety, even fright. The actress's son wasn't there; no one could say–or would say–where he might be found. As for Fanny Thompson herself, no one could see her because she was ill. You insisted; in the end, she came. It was no lie; she was ill. When she saw the IOU in your hands, she leaned against the wall in order to save herself from falling over, and she said: 'Wretch! Wretched child!' She recovered, however, and gave you five guineas, recommending that you say nothing. John, my friend, have you the strength to bear this load?"

"I have the strength," John answered. "Will I be confronted by Fanny Thompson?"

"At present, Fanny Thompson is appearing in a comedy in New York."

"And will it be necessary to recognize the accused?"

"There's no need. You only saw him briefly, and in the dark. It'll set the seal of stern veracity on your deposition when you say: 'I won't swear that the accused is the man who lost the IOU under the Quadrant's arcades.' "

"By God!" murmured Sawney. "You have enough without that, Mr. Knob. In any case, even if there's no eyewitness evidence, the jury can still draw its own conclusions."

"Now let's see the dominant cock of your back yard, old hand!" said the little clerk, with his vainglorious smile. "You offer me Sam as a first-rate player?"

"There's no better Jack Simple in the entire city!" Sawney replied.

"Jack Simple is a nice job, old hand, but we have a better one. Look us in the face, Sam. Would you like to make your reputation at a stroke, and earn 20 guineas?"

There was a murmur among the other maiden chickens; Sam's eyes shone.

"Calm down, my little ones," Ned said. "Everyone will have cause to be content. We know how to reward merit."

Sam was a very young man, little more than a child. At present, his face still bore traces of the greasepaint and powder with which he had covered his features in order to simulate the accepted character of Jack Simple. By nature, Sam was the direct opposite of that round, heavy-set and foolish type. He had bold features, an intelligent forehead and sharp eyes. He must, therefore, have been a natural actor, and a great one, in order to give a satisfactory performance in the role of Jack Simple the turkey-thief, the mirror of English popular stupidity.

Ned looked at him attentively for some time, then said: "This is high school, my boy; I warn you that there's a danger of breaking one's neck."

"Let's see your high school, little man," Sam replied. When Ned made a face, he added: "I'll call you great man if it's included in the price."

"Let's get on," said Ned. "A director is entirely dependent on his leading actors. Be serious, friend. I'll put the proposition to you; you can refuse it. First of all, you won't get a summons. All your comrades will be called by the Coroner and the Prosecutor. You, on the other hand, will have to present yourself to the Magistrate who is conducting the instruction at this moment. Does that suit you?"

"Go on to the end," Sam answered. "We'll see."

Ned collected himself for a moment and went on. "You're a young provincial idler seized by a mad enthusiasm for the theater..."

"God damn me!" Sam interrupted, blushing to the whites of his eyes. "Who told you that?" Then, without waiting for an answer, he broke out laughing, setting an example that everyone followed.

"A palpable hit!" cried Sawney. "You're a sorcerer, Master Knob."

"That I am, as you well know," Ned said, simply. "I no longer keep count of my achievements in that sphere. Peace, everyone! And pay attention, Sam! At the beginning of this year, you arrived from your village all excited, boiling to make your debut at Drury Lane in *Macbeth* or as Gloucester.[160] The directors had you put out of the door without even wanting to hear you out, because you were badly-dressed and had no recommendation in your pocket from the Court, or a Minister, or a bank. Perhaps that was the reality?"

"That was it," Sam replied.

"So much the better. You'll play your play naturally. This is your role: thrown out everywhere but not discouraged, sustained by the consciousness of your genius, you start running around the taverns neighboring the theaters, and every night a half-pint of gin makes you dream of your first appearance, weighed down by laurels and bouquets, deafened by the cheers. But the two guineas your mother gave you is going fast. You begin to realize that patronage is necessary to get into the theater. On the night when your last shilling sleeps silently in the void of your pocket, an inspiration strikes you: a sublime notion, a mad impulse!

"Next to you, a rejected author happens to mention that Madame Bartolozzi is very powerful...

"You go out, you buy a chipped and rusty dagger with your last silver coin; you climb over a stable wall to get into a courtyard; from the courtyard, you climb up to the balcony; you break a window: you're in the dressing-room of someone who, with a magic word, can bring down those ramparts of steel, the unbreachable barrier between you and the theater!

"Now, you're not an assassin, in spite of your rusty dagger; no more are you a thief; you're merely an artiste. The ferocity of art has taken hold of you. You have scaled these walls and balconies to fall on your knees before the actress of the moment and implore her aid. If she rejects you, well, you shall force her, the dagger at her throat, to listen to you declaim the ambition of Richard or the jealousy of the Moor of Venice. It is essential that she sees what you can do, even if it be in a swoon; it is your right as a madman. Kean [161] would have done the same!"

"God damn me!" cried Sam, who was very pale. "So would I, with all my heart, if the idea had come to me!"

"They'll believe you," continued the former clerk, whose physiognomy did indeed radiate a diabolical intelligence. "More than that, they'll admire you, because that's the English, from top to toe. Besides, extravagant folly is something else. You'll make your debut in eight hours time or you'll have your success in Hell!"

"But what am I doing in the dressing-room?" Sam asked.

"You wait. The queen of the theater receives her court. They play whist in the drawing-room. No opportunity arises. The hours pass and your brain cools down. Madness must be activated while it is hot. The idea of running away has already come to you; you're ashamed of your insensate enterprise, but they're working in the stables and the courtyard is full of grooms combing, brushing, washing, blaspheming. At midnight, la Bartolozzi comes into her room; you take heart again; the time has come... but, wait! She isn't alone! Her chambermaid is helping her. You wait again. The fever mounts again in your brain. This time, you are resolute.

"The clock chimes one. Silence reigns in the bedroom. Your heart beats faster, but your head boils. You press down slowly on the door-handle, which slowly opens halfway without making any sound. A nightlight illuminates the room. Madame Bartolozzi is lying on her bed, asleep. Beside her, on the bedside table, there are diamonds that send forth blue sparks, elongated or foreshortened by the tricks of the tremulous light. You've hesitated for a second–and it is enough.

"On the other side of the room, another door opens and a man comes in. He doesn't hesitate."

Ned Knob's voice became solemn, in spite of himself. "Listen closely to this, young man. Engrave every one of my words on your memory, for in repeating them, you'll be telling the truth. It will be as if the conscience of the murderer were speaking, or as if the dead woman herself had woken up to reveal the circumstances of the unwitnessed crime.

"The man comes straight to the bed, walking as if he has nothing to fear. By the glow of the nightlight, you can see his face vaguely, pale but calm–so calm that you say to yourself: this is merely an amorous intrigue. Even so, you have a chill in your veins. The man is beside the bed, immobile. Why doesn't he wake the sleeper? He leans over. One of his hands passes between the head and the pillow, the other reaches out to the bosom, but the sleeper doesn't wake up.

"What does the man want? He gets up. What has he done? Is this all a dream? He wipes his hand with a handkerchief, which falls, and he crosses the room, heading towards the closet where you are. You hide behind the curtains; he passes very close to you. He has a key to the door communicating with the stairway. He opens that door and disappears.

"What has he done? The diamonds are still on the bedside table, dispersing their moving sparks. You enter in your turn. Nothing wakes that sleeping woman! You draw near; her breath is inaudible. You take her pulse with a trembling hand; there's nothing but a corpse on the bed!"

Ned paused, then resumed abruptly: "And drink, children!" he said, wiping sweat from his temples. Then, he added: "If you aren't capable of telling that story, Sam, we'd better find someone else."

Sam thumped the table with his fist and cried: "It'll have the same effect as a piece of theater. God damn me if I let a role like that get away!"

While Master Ned Knob was enchanting impresario Sawney and his troupe with his cleverness, a new customer had come into Sharper's without attracting any attention. It was a poor little old man who seemed utterly broken down by age–a rare thing in these London dives, where vice and squalor hardly ever permitted old age the time to take effect. The precocious decrepitude that results from excess does not resemble in the least that carefully instilled by the weight of the years; one inspires respect and the other disgust.

This little old man with the tremulous step, wrinkled face and fearful eyes–easily hurt behind their thick shields of blue glass–had had to explain the reason for his presence the first time he had set foot in Sharper's. He had said only one thing, without affectation and perhaps without intention, in asking very politely of Jenny Paddock–who was astonished to see an honest face at close range–whether she had recently heard talk of a young man named Oliver Green, known under the name of Southwark Noll, a boxer.

Jenny Paddock, prudent by nature, did not give out news of her clients to newcomers, but the old man, in response to her questions, had given her to understand that he was the father of the scapegrace–an angry but always loving father–who was looking for his son to pass on a few savings earned by the sweat of his brow.

This had taken place a few days before the present evening. Since then, the old man had come every evening to take a little glass of whisky, diluted with water. He arrived late, because he worked long hours in a copper-stamping factory in Surrey. He had announced right away that he would come back every evening.

At first, the presence of the poor gentleman had caused a certain discomfort among the regulars at Sharper's, and inspired anxious movements even in those implicated in the worst crimes. Ordinarily, in such cases, the man who causes such discomfort and anxiety is not entirely safe among such rough companions, who are unrestrained by faith, law or bit. Over there, making a human being disappear is the least of bagatelles, and it could be said that whoever crosses the redoubtable barriers of these citadels of crime without being an affiliate no longer belongs to the world of the living. In 1817, the same year in which our story is set, two sergeants from Marylebone disguised themselves and went into the Purgatory of Saint Giles on a fishing trip to capture the burker, or body-snatcher, Isaac Burton;[162] they never came back, and that is all that can be said, for not a scrap of their clothing, nor a bone, nor a hair was ever found.

Our old man was, however, the father of Noll Green, and Noll Green, like his comrade Lochaber Dick, possessed a reputation of the highest order in Low Lane. That was a protection in itself. In addition, he took up scant space in his little corner of the parlor; he smiled frankly at tales of villainy; he even made honestly significant allusions to his own young days. It had to be supposed that, if he were not in complete communion with the ideas of the damned who inhabited that Inferno, he was at least possessed of a sufficiently wide and deep indulgence, which had its source in a good stock of ancient peccadilloes.

In that era, retired brigands either boasted of their misdeeds with senile prolixity or hid them carefully, according to character. The latter was doubtless the case, all things considered, with Noll's father, running after his son, quite unable to present a model of stern virtue. He was tolerated; some even went further and became used to his presence. He had paid for two or three glasses of gin, which had won him half a dozen hearts. He called everyone bad lot or scapegrace, but with such gentleness! From the mouth of a woman in love, as they say, the word wretch is a caress. Well, old Solomon Green, the father of Noll, caressed you with smiling insults. It did not need a sorcerer to divine that he much preferred Sharper's bad lots and scapegraces to, for example, the virtuous sergeants of Scotland Yard–of whom he spoke with an entirely appropriate bitterness.

One thing that was certain was that, given his age and stature, if he had posed as an invalid ogre, making light of his ancient rascalities and setting his speech to the level of cynicism that was the very atmosphere of the den, his quavering voice would have cracked and his distinguished face would have protested. Even his clothes, which were certainly not distinguished by symmetry or elegance, would have given the lie to his vain bravado. At the very most, he might have been able to play the role of one of those malefactors who stand in the wings, profiting from crime without committing it, or exploiting the poison of vice without wetting their lips. But such as they are familiar to militant malefactors, who always have need of them, as manufacturers need customers. Usurious pawnbrokers, forgers of banknotes and coins, courtiers sworn to pillage, touts, smelters [163] and fences are in day-to-day contact with their clients, so an old practitioner, even one who did not have the honor of being the father of a first-rate bandit like our friend Noll, could not have been entirely unknown to the regulars at Sharper's. Nothing forces us to the conclusion that the gentleman in the blue spectacles was playing a role, but if he were an actor or a diplomat– the greatest actor or the cleverest diplomat in the world–he could not have chosen the cut of his disguise or the nuances of his character with a more precise or exquisite tact.

Among those who sheltered old Solomon Green, the members of the Puppet Tribunal, and its venerable President Sawney, had to be reckoned the most significant. Old Solomon had an inexhaustible supply of reminiscences of Puppet Trials. He talked about the time when the Irish Court had been held at the Arms of Glencoe, run by the Scotswoman Mona Marie,[164] where the soldiers of the brave 47th line-regiment, the so-called Black Watch, drank–all of them gentlemen highlanders and partisans of "the King over the water." Sergeant Farquhar MacPherson was a Puppet Judge whose like had never been seen and his cousin, the bagpiper Alastair Macpherson, played the role of Jack Simple, giving the audience convulsions when he got up after the Advocate's tearful pleadings to say that his mother was in the Bridewell. Oh, he spoke for a long time! A good third of the army was Jacobite at that time. There were firing squads every week outside the drawbridge at the Tower, and it was a sad sight to see the poor young men marching with the open coffin carried before them by the regimental valets.

Once, it was the turn of Sergeant Farquhar and Alastair the bagpiper. Farquhar commanded the firing squad and Alastair wanted the mouthpiece of his bagpipes to be put to his lips. As his hands were tied behind his back, it was his brother Colquhoun who put his fingers over the holes. Poor Alastair's last breath was, therefore, devoted to the pibroch of the Clan Macpherson: "The King will take back his crown..."[165]

But Old Solomon told lighter tales too. In Lady Marie's place, there were happy souls who were neither for Stuart nor for Brunswick, although they willingly put their hands in their pockets for both parties–Red John, for example, who had talked one day about stealing all the Puppet Tribunal's watches during the performance. He came on as a witness, Paddy the Irishman, and took the purses as well as the watches. He was a handsome lad; when he was hanged at Tyburn, there were many ladies weeping.

In the end, old Solomon had gone as far as promising to play the Puppet Advocate himself, one fine evening, with all the rigor of antique tradition, as soon as a nasty cough he had gave him a moment's respite. Sawney expected a rich harvest of takings on that night.

It was mainly from Sawney that Solomon Green had received the latest news of Noll. The old man only knew that Noll had escaped from the Isle of Norfolk in Australia with the famous Tom Brown and Lochaber Dick. He showed very good taste in taking a certain vanity from that, and expressed a strong desire to see this Tom Brown, who had acquired such celebrity at such a young age. But his information ran out after Noll's return to England. Noll had only come to see him once, the rascal, and then to wheedle a five-pound note out of him! As he left, he had said: 'Father, when you want to see me, come to Sharper's in Low Lane. If anyone looks sideways at you, say that Noll Green, your son, will wash out the mouth of anyone who scowls at you.'

Sawney and the inhabitants of Sharper's had more recent news than that, but not much. Sawney was able to tell him that Noll and Dick had become Tom Brown's mates, helping him out on a regular basis, and that they had done well out of it, drinking the best liquor in the parlor and beating a new woman every night, until a certain day not long after the death of la Bartolozzi; or, to be more precise, the very day that the crestfallen Gregory Temple had quit his office at Scotland Yard. That evening, while someone was reading *John Devil the Quaker*'s book aloud, Tom Brown's whistle had been heard outside. Noll and Dick had gone out, promising to break the head of anyone who followed them.

No one had followed them, and since then no living soul had heard mention of either one of them.

Solomon, on hearing this tale, had shaken his old besotted head. "These bad lots always finish badly, my good friends," he had said, "but after all, the rascal is my son... my only son, moreover... and if he earned good money with this Tom Brown, he might perhaps have set himself up. He's neither in prison nor hanged, we know that for sure. Perhaps this Tom Brown has sent him forth on some important errand. If you run into him here or there, my friends, in the course of your work, tell him that he is wanted at home, and that there are still a few shillings at the bottom of his father's piggy-bank."

Today, old Solomon had arrived even later than usual. "No news of my scapegrace?" he said, bowing to the widow Paddock at her counter.

"Nothing, Mr. Green. John Devil must have carried them off to Hell!"

"Always joking, my good lady! Give me, I beg you, my glass of gin, sugar and water. I've got the taste of copper in my mouth."

"A nasty one, they say, Mr. Green," the widow replied, "but one that'll take time to poison you, for sure. Bab! A little grog for Mr. Green, lazybones."

The old man turned round to go to his usual spot in the parlor, which was exactly where pretty Molly was snoring, sprawled on the moist soil, at the foot of the table he ordinarily occupied. The gentleman favored her with a rapid but attentive glance through his blue lenses. He started slightly, but the tranquil and debonair smile that never left his lips did not fail him. He went into the parlor, circled around the long legs of the former coal-heaver, who had good hobnailed shoes under her red silk, and went to sit at a table wedged into the darkest corner of all. If anyone had been paying attention to him at that moment, they might have noticed that he placed his stool in such a way as to present his profile, obscured by disordered strands of grey hair, to anyone who might sit down at Molly's table. He sat quietly, as was his custom, listening to the confused noises, occasionally catching a distinct word swimming among the murmurs.

Just as Bab was bringing his gin and his water, Jenny Paddock's bedroom door opened noisily and Gentleman Ned, still ebullient and taking up four times as much space as he needed, seized the muscular figure of the widow and stole a treasonous kiss.

"My poor Molly can't see us," he said, with a rascally laugh. "I take care that she doesn't know about my successes with other women. A man of my age and position can't restrict himself to one sole beauty!"

"All men are deceivers," murmured the widow, modestly lowering her bloodshot eyes.

Behind Gentleman Ned came the flock of maiden chickens, escorted by Sawney.

Old Solomon's sharp eyes were looking over the frame of his spectacles, taking inventory of the new arrivals at a glance. At the sight of the little clerk, his smile became rather mocking, gentleman though he was. Ned and pretty

Molly were evidently old acquaintances of his. But it appeared that he had no desire to greet them this evening, for he placed his whole face in shadow and began mixing his water, sugar and gin with infinite care.

"Wake milady up, Bab!" Ned shouted. "Respectfully, if you please, my girl! Mistress Paddock, send one of your waiters to tell my coachman to get the horses ready. We've had difficulty in that wretched alleyway, which wasn't built for vehicles–but a man like me can't go on foot. Oh well! Molly, my little love, have we had pleasant dreams?"

"A swig, if you will, Master Knob," replied the enormous woman, getting laboriously to her feet. As she did so, she readjusted her plumed hat as if it were a peaked cap. Her soiled silk dress had ridden up to her knees. She planted herself squarely on her large hobnailed shoes and filled her pipe while looking around bleakly.

"They followed her through the streets of Paris!" said Gentleman Ned, proudly. "You'll understand that, over there, more than one Countess and Duchess flirted with me. They run after all Englishmen for their good looks and their guineas. But when one is in love with a woman like Molly, my darling, one does not even glance at other women. Give her a swig, Mistress Paddock. Two swigs! As many as she wants! Gallantry is a gentleman's prerogative. If she asks for a barrel of gin, I'll say: roll out the barrel!"

Molly lit her pipe with a candle.

"Treasure!" cried Ned, transported by love. "Come and kiss your man, and don't forget your umbrella."

"Another round of punch, milord?" several hoarse voices inquired from the cloud of smoke.

"Indeed yes, my children, by God!" the former clerk replied, unhesitatingly. "Liberality becomes the great. Serve a punch of the cheapest kind to these poor creatures, so that they might bless the name of a young man who is on his way. Farewell, good Mistress Paddock; I promise you my custom and my protection!"

In the midst of thunderous applause, the waiter came back to say that milord's coachman was waiting.

Ned made an amicable gesture to his maiden chickens and whispered in Sawney's ear: "Tomorrow, at the specified address, for a general rehearsal. Be as silent as the tomb, and you'll experience the fruits of my generosity. After you, my pretty Molly!"

Pretty Molly had the neck of a new bottle between her teeth. "Look after that, Master Knob," she said, as she drew breath again. "We might need a swig on the way."

"The time has come, my little ones," cried Jenny Paddock, going to stand beside the door. "We must make sure that their Lordships come back to see us again. All together, now: Molly and Ned Knob forever!"

"Molly and Ned Knob forever!" was the hearty response.

The little clerk was moved to tears.

Molly was startled at first, but she drew herself up to her full height and her eyes became impregnated with red. She secured her hat over her bristling hair with a single blow of her fist, and took her pipe out of her mouth as if she were about to say something. She looked as if she could have cut a cavalry charge in two.

"Well, my love," Ned asked her, affectionately, "are you content?"

She did not reply, but she seized her man around the waist and gathered him up in her left arm as a wet-nurse holds a baby; then, brandishing her umbrella in her left hand, she made her exit in the midst of tempestuous applause.

The storm took more than a minute to die down, all the more so because the second round of punch was being served. When it did die down, Jenny Paddock said: "It's a great shame to see gold in the holey pocket of a monkey!"

"And silk on the shoulders of an old cab-horse," added Bab, the serving girl, rancorously. "She's three times as old as Master Ned..."

Mistress Paddock, who was Molly's contemporary, interrupted her with a resounding slap in the face.

"The obvious benefit of youth," murmured old Mr. Solomon, who came out to take his usual place on the stool formerly occupied by Molly.

"Father Green," said Sawney, coming up to him with a pensive expression, "those two might have given you news of your Noll."

"Ah, the rascal, my brave friend," the old man sighed. "Must one keep such bad company!"

"Noll Green was a good companion," said Sawney, sadly.

Solomon looked up at him excitedly. A physiognomist would have had difficulty in exactly defining his expression. In that first instant, it was neither paternal anxiety nor sadness, but there was undoubtedly emotion–considerable emotion–and perhaps, even more than that, there was passion. He looked at Sawney open-mouthed; then his eyelids lowered as if he feared that the strange light he felt burning in his pupil might alarm his interlocutor. In a low voice, he said: "You're talking about Noll as if he were dead!"

There are good-hearted rogues; Sawney was one of them. "Father," he answered, uncomfortably, "Noll might not be dead."

Solomon began shivering, and his teeth chattered.

"Listen!" Sawney said. "I thought about you just now, while I was chatting to that dressed-up dog, Knob. May I be hanged–which I probably shall be, whether I wish it or not–if I wouldn't rather lose a guinea from my pocket than see you trembling like that, old man. Noll has gone over there with John Devil..."

"Where's that?" the old man demanded, vehemently. "Where's that?"

"To Paris, damn it! And Ned Knob said that he was never coming back."

"Ah!" said Solomon, letting out a long and profound sigh–but I tell you this: the eyes of a father who learns of the death of his only son never shone in that extraordinary fashion. Sawney did not see that gleam, because the old man was covering his face with his hands.

"Where can I find Ned Knob, as you call him?" he asked, sobbing.

"He has forbidden me..." Sawney began, then interrupted himself. "Hang on, though! It's not him you need to interrogate but Molly, plying her with drink... a lot of drink, for she won't say anything if she's only half-drunk. To-morrow, at 11 a.m., Ned Knob has to go to a meeting; Molly will be alone. Go to 7 Rosemary Lane, Goodman's Field–and don't sell me out!"

Solomon got up, shaking all over, and shook both his hands effusively.

"Thank you!" he murmured, in a halting voice. "Oh, my poor Noll! My dear child! I'll go, my dear friend, and have no fear for yourself!"

He made his way to the door laboriously, and went out. He was scarcely in the street before his entire being seemed to expand and grow. His bent back straightened, his chest inflated, his pace became rapid and firm. You might almost have said that he ran like a young man. And all the while he ran, he muttered between his quivering lips: "Ah! He's dead! Ah! Ah! They're dead! If he hasn't burnt their bodies, I'll find them, even if they're a hundred feet below ground!"

His hands came together and he rubbed them against one another convulsively.

A hundred paces from Sharper's, at a place where the street broadened out to form a kind of square, a cab was waiting. He threw himself into it, pronouncing the name of a hotel in Leicester Square. The horse moved off. The first street-lamp to shed its light through the window lit up a pair of thin hands rolling a round snuff-box with a white lid, on which three lines inscribed in black letters were legible:

Memento – February 3, 1817 – Constance Bartolozzi

At that moment, Gentleman Ned Knob's equipage was arriving in front of Number 7, Rosemary Lane.

"Let us down, coachman," he shouted, knocking as if he were a lord. Seeing the hotel proprietor opening the door a little way, he added: "Mine host! Come and lend your arm to milady. What dinners the embassies lay on! They drank to the health of my wife so often, these Aldermen, Dukes and company Directors, that the poor angel fell asleep in the depths of my carriage. Warm up a pot of heart's-dew [166] to put her right for me, and don't spare the brandy. As for me, I still have two Secretaries of State to see! Let's go, coachman!"

Molly went up the steps as a woman should, her umbrella under her arms, lifting up her dress as if she were fording a river.

"Let's go, coachman, let's go! You know the way to the Court."

They did not, however, go as far as the Court. At about 11 p.m., he cried *Stop*! in front of the house in the Strand where the Quaker's tilbury had stopped to set Richard Thompson down on the night when our story began. The brass plaque mounted beside the door-knocker still said: *Office of Mr. Wood.* Ned got down and adjusted his clothing, as befit a man who wanted to look his best.

We have already observed that every visitor in London indicates his importance by the boldness of his knock; the Prince Regent would have hesitated before hammering like our friend Ned Knob. The door reverberated, and movement was soon heard within the house.

The boss has enough on his conscience to outweigh the dome of Saint Paul's, thought Ned Knob, grimacing like a laughing monkey. *He'll think that the King's envoy has come at last to give him free lodgings in Newgate.*

As soon as the door opened to display two or three frightened servants, who had arrived with candlesticks at the same time, he cried: "Good evening, Kate! Good evening, Daniel! Good evening, unhappy old Loo! So the house hasn't yet been consumed by Hell's fire?"

He strutted along the top step with his hands in his pockets.

The three servants, shaken by the thunderous blows of door-knocker, had expected to see a giant at least. The idea of the little clerk dismissed for theft was so far from their minds that none of them recognized him at first glance. He seemed enormous; it was the gentleman's high-pitched screeching voice that opened their eyes.

"God pardon me, Dan!" said Kate, the first to speak. "Go find the horse-whip, I beg you. It's only that little rogue, Ned Knob, who's drunk and come to sing us filthy songs."

"Ned Knob!" groaned Loo, the housekeeper, who had long been the victim of the errand-boy's pranks. "I've got my broom."

Dan grabbed the handle of the carpet-beater. A bell tinkled impatiently on the upper floor.

Far from recoiling, the former clerk took a step forward, which brought him fully into the light. Kate, Dan and Loo saw that he had well-polished boots, a new hat and complete suit of fine linen. They looked at one another indecisively; all three of them were thinking that Ned might perhaps be a rich man now. In London, insulting a rich man is something akin to sacrilege; Ned had counted on that.

"Look at me, Dame Kate," he said. "Do you know the difference between a rogue and a young man of good family? Haven't you ever heard stories of the sons of lords who finally rediscover their noble parents?" He slapped his pocket, where gold jingled. "Listen to that song, Loo! Death and passion, comrades! We roll around in a carriage now, and we're going to have old Wood as our solicitor. Doesn't it make your hearts rejoice, old pals, to see a handsome youth who has made his fortune?"

Loo put down her broom away and Daniel lowered his carpet-beater.

A second tinkle, angrier and more imperious, was heard from upstairs.

"Don't go up," Ned instructed. "I'd like to give the boss a pleasant surprise. Light the way, Dan! I've got servants now who wouldn't sweep my apartments in your Sunday livery."

"Who dares to knock like that?" demanded a loud voice from the staircase. "And what kind of a secret meeting are you having down there?"

Gentleman Ned put his finger to his lips and slowly climbed the stairs.

On the first floor landing, there was a sort of human bulldog with a bald red head, where a few hanks of coarse grey hair were planted. He was wrapped in a floral-pattern dressing gown, and his hypermetropic spectacles were balanced on his scaly forehead. It was the typical full-blooded Englishman in all his brutal insolence, with blood-red skin and violet veins in the clear blue of his eyes. All the sap of his lost hair had passed into his eyebrows: two tufts of hard fur that jutted out in front of his eyelids by an inch.

This was Mr. Wood, the former solicitor and former guardian of Helen Brown. If his face could be believed, he must have had a long and terrible history behind him. One would have judged him to be nearly 70 years old, but despite his great age, he was bearing up well under the weight of his sanguine temperament and still seemed to enjoy an extraordinary vigor. He could easily have crushed Gentleman Ned's wrist between his thumb and index finger.

Like all long-sighted people, he was able to bring the young man into focus at ten paces. In any case, he was one of those men who thought of everything and was ready for everything. He recognized his former clerk at the first glance, and examined him curiously as he climbed the stair.

"Was it you knocking like that, Master Ned?" he asked, lowering his voice.

"Yes, boss," replied the former clerk. "How've you been all this time? Always as green as holly! You can brag about a ripe old age, but I have only one wish myself, and that's to be as healthy as you are at your age."

"At my age, Ned Knob, you'll have been 50 years in the cemetery where the bodies of hanged men are buried."

"It's your politeness that's no longer diminishing, boss," replied the little man, laughing derisively. "Permit me, however, to hope for better than your prognostication. Since you haven't been hanged, why should I be?"

The solicitor frowned, his massive eyebrows casting a thick shadow over his eyes. The veins in his forehead stood out like cords.

Ned Knob took a step towards him and went on. "You know well enough, boss, that I'm acquainted with the power and weight of your fist. I'm not here to play with you, who could throw me out of the window with a flick of the finger. Let's go into your office and talk reasonably, I beg you, for at present, and meaning no offense, my time is at least as precious as yours."

Mr. Wood turned his back and went back silently into his apartment. Ned Knob followed him. It was Ned who closed the door.

Mr. Wood looked at him anxiously. "You've been my servant," he muttered, anger already making his voice stutter. "You've eaten my bread. I'll give you some advice: Don't threaten me, or I'll crush your head beneath my heel!"

"You'd be perfectly capable of it, boss, but I've no threat to make to you. I've come from Paris and I've come *on his behalf.*"

"You!" said the former solicitor, mistrustfully.

"Only think of me as your pupil, boss," said the little man, briskly, "and you'll no longer be astonished by the road I've taken. What the Devil! Skill is contagious; in order to rub shoulders with a good general, one becomes a good soldier." He ran his fingers through his coarse and frizzy hair, thick as a fleece. He pulled out a scroll of paper, about half the size of a visiting card, and added: "Here are the credentials that will prove to you that I really am an ambassador."

Mr. Wood took the letter. Ned Knob threw himself into an armchair and crossed his legs.

The letter was only two lines long. When Mr. Wood had read them, he looked at his former clerk very attentively.

"There must be something to you, midget," he muttered, "for I've never known Helen's son to be mistaken about a fact or a man. I'm too close to you to judge. If there's intelligence behind your burlesque comedy, so much the better... when you came in, I thought that you'd joined the Police."

Ned shrugged his shoulders with supreme scorn. "A Superintendent only earns 1,000 pounds a year," he said. "I've got passions to satisfy."

The bulldog's face blossomed into a broad laugh.

"That Tom Brown is the very Devil!" he murmured. "Myself, I'd never have seen through the grotesque stupidity that envelops the monkey. Let's get on, my dear Master Knob, since I must deal with you as an equal; the letter is really Tom Brown's. It tells me that you speak as if you were Helen's son himself. You've probably known him even longer than I have, after all, and since Tom has chosen you, I bow to his wisdom. What do you want from me?"

"I want to bring you some news, and obtain other news from you, boss. First, all is going well in Paris; the affair is progressing, and you'll see even less of Helen's son, as you call milord. I was sent to you mainly for matters relating to the young woman..."

"What young woman?"

"Constance Bartolozzi's heir. Do you have the papers establishing that Constance Bartolozzi's real name was Constance Herbet?"

"I have all the papers," the former solicitor replied. "I have Constance Herbet's birth certificate. I have contracts, in which the name Bartolozzi is always followed by the name Herbet in parentheses. I have her declaration to the Commissioner at Waterloo Place. The identity is as clear as day, and there will not be the shadow of a difficulty..."

"Marvelous, boss. For myself, I've brought you the birth certificate of Mademoiselle Jeanne Herbet, emancipated minor, and her power of attorney, with certain other items, such as the power of her guardianship, etc., should the need arise. It's a matter of retrieving the wills deposited with the notary Daws."

"That's what I don't understand!" exclaimed Mr. Wood.

"Why don't you understand it, boss?"

"Because Tom Brown is the sole heir of Frank Turner of Lyon and William Robinson of Brussels, on the authority of Helen Brown, their first cousin, his mother. Because this young woman, Jeanne Herbet, is the only obstacle between Tom Brown and the succession. Because la Bartolozzi carried the secret of her affairs to the grave, and even this notary Daws does not know of the existence of this Jeanne Herbet. In view of these facts, why bring to light that which it is easy to hide under the bushel?"

"We have our reasons, boss. Firstly, our status as an escaped convict, and the fame that illuminates our nickname, John Devil, does not perhaps place us in the best situation in the world to reclaim the inheritance of the two assassinated men legally..."

"That obstacle can be overcome," Mr. Wood replied. "The case would not be argued in London. Would the name Brown, which is as common here as Durand, Lebrun or Martin in France, attract the least attention before the tribunals of Lyon and Brussels?"

"Perhaps. Don't forget that Gregory Temple is over there."

"Does Tom intend to marry the young woman?" the former solicitor asked, abruptly.

"In all probability, boss."

"That's a jolt! I don't like it when a woman gets thrown into calculations as serious as these."

"Oh yes," said Gentleman Ned, confidently. "Love destroyed Troy!"

"And the difficulty here is even greater!" Mr. Wood went on, animatedly. "The Comte de Belcamp is playing an audacious game against the French legal system, which would seem mad to me were the cards in anyone else's hand. It's true that he's possessed of resources no one else has... I don't know what measures he's taken, or will take, over and above the comedy of the double alibi, which is either infantile or a masterpiece, according to the manner in which it is to be exploited; I don't know his latest calculations, and I don't need to know them; I know that he'll win just as he always wins; that's enough for me. But names have been thrown before the French public. Turner's assassin called himself Belcamp, as did Robinson's assassin. When they see Belcamp marrying the heir of Robinson and Turner..."

"Is it Belcamp who'll marry her?" Ned Knob put in.

The former solicitor's eyes brightened. "He's swimming in it!" he murmured. "He juggles with mortal danger like the Chinaman at Astley Circus with his balls and daggers; give him an ocean to jump and he'll measure out his run-up! To him, the impossible... nothing can stop him, except some pebble on the road that everyone but an infant could have avoided. Ned Knob, my friend, you're as puffed up as the frog in the fable who wanted to look like a cow. The role doesn't suit you, but since he's making use of you, if only a little, I remain fully convinced of your merit. Get this truth into your head, though: you know nothing about him; we know nothing about him; no one knows anything about him!"

The little man had a smile full of self-satisfaction, and the bulldog disdainfully turned his gaze aside. He was an old pawn, but at least he knew that he could not see at all clearly, which is a great deal. "Master Knob," he went on, changing his tone. "We'll meet again together at the office of the notary Daws, at the earliest opportunity. The papers you're carrying are in order, as are those in my possession. The wills can be in Paris on the evening of the day after tomorrow."

"One more thing!" cried Gentleman Ned, as if he had achieved a difficult victory. "Now let's pass on to another subject. The Balcomb establishment..."

"Another thing I don't understand!" Mr. Wood put in, coldly.

"Boss," said Ned, "it's agreed that you have no need to know."

"Would you like me to believe that you understand better than I do, little one," murmured the former solicitor, studying him disdainfully. "An enormous sum has already been sunk into it, God knows to what end... God—or the Devil! What is there in common between Tom Brown and that booby-trap they call steam? Steam is fine for amazing 200,000 strollers ranged along the banks of the Thames, watching a boat go past without oars or sails, trailing a mane of smoke. I don't understand, but that's all—I no longer deny it, mind. Behind the charlatanry of steam, Helen Brown's son must have seen a truth, since he's taken a step along that route. If he's seen it, it's there. His is the surest and most infallible eye..."

"Milord is anxious about the Balcomb establishment," the little clerk interrupted.

"If he values the Balcomb establishment, there's reason to be anxious."

"What's going on?"

"The payments have been suspended for three days, and the 800-horsepower machine has been seized."

"And you haven't warned him?"

"He knows why I've stayed silent. I expected the money from Prague today."

"Milord has instructed me to tell you," Ned said, simply and clearly, "that he values the Balcomb establishment and what is done there as highly as his own life."

"So much the worse, lad," was Mr. Wood's only response.

"Do you regard it as a lost cause, then?" Ned exclaimed.

"There's 900,000 francs owing."

"What about the money from Prague?"

"Prague isn't sending any more money."

"The Counts Boehm?"

"Ah, you know that much, my son!" the former solicitor said, astonished. "There's only one Count Boehm now, who'll be in London tomorrow."

"And the two others?"

Mr. Wood reflected for a moment, then plunged his hand into the vast recesses of his dressing gown and pulled out a letter.

"I wouldn't have wanted to confide this to anyone but Helen's son, in person," he said, "but since you have full authority, read it, Master Knob."

Ned unfolded the letter, which was constituted thus:

Mr. Wood, in London

Sir,

I am the youngest and the last surviving of the three sons of Major-General Count Boehm. My elder brother, Count Albrecht, is dead at 25; my second brother, Count Reiner, is dead at 24. I am not yet 21.

Count Albrecht was killed in a duel in Prague; Count Reiner died in Pest of a dagger-blow, in consequence of a terrible mistake.

In his final hour, Count Reiner said to me: "Albrecht and I have been justly punished." Then he said: "For the honor of our name, respond directly to all demands for money addressed to you by the firm of Balcomb & Co. in London."

In the month of February in the present year, I paid into the account of this company, in response to your letter addressed to my brothers, of whose premature deaths you were doubtless unaware, 150,000 florins.

In the month of March, in response to a similar demand, 275,000 florins.

In the month of April, 70,000 florins.

In the month of May, 380,000 florins.

On receipt of a new demand on your part, even more considerable, I was finally obliged to take the advice of those who guide my conscience and my interests. They have told me something I did not know and which grieves my heart: that in the year 1813, suspicion fell upon my noble brothers on the occasion of the murder of General O'Brien. I was very young at that time, newly arrived at the university and not following the same course as my brothers—but, if not by certitude supported by the testimony of my eyes or those of others, at least by the voice of my blood and my conscience, I protest that a Count Boehm cannot be an assassin.

My determination, approved by my spiritual and temporal advisors, is to go as far as I possibly can into the depths of this mystery. I know that there exists in London a man who had the pieces of this murky affair in his hands, after the verdict of acquittal rendered by the court of Prague; he is named Gregory Temple and occupied the position of Chief Superintendent of Police. I have made arrangements to meet with him on the Saturday of this week. If it is a matter of restitution, sir, I shall make a single final settlement. If it is a matter of something else, and the restitution ought to be made to a third party, I shall do my duty.

My address in London will be Mivart's Hotel.[167]

I have the honor to be, etc,

Count Friedrich Boehm.[168]

It was ten o'clock in the morning. The London Sun–which is usually shrouded in dull vapors except for the dozen times a year when it suddenly and capriciously sends forth burning rays worthy of Senegal–was distinct, brilliantly illuminating Gregory Temple's old office in Scotland Yard. The office had changed its appearance at the same time as its old master. It seemed that some flirtatious fairy had breathed over all the severities of the place in which the former Superintendent had spent the best years of his life in solitary meditation. Curtains of Indian muslin fell in fleecy folds, adequately hiding the iron bars that guarded the windows. The simple oaken table had been replaced by a dainty item in Brazilian rosewood, reminiscent of the little writing desks where our mistresses pen their coquettish correspondence. The pompadour armchairs had been reupholstered in finer materials and pastel shades, and even the cabinets where the terrible files slept had been redecorated.

It was, in truth, a pleasure to be interrogated in this amiable boudoir before being plunged into the depths of Newgate or the Fleet.

Gregory Temple's successor, Sir Paulus MacAllan, former subaltern and recently knighted, was an elegant man whom women adored, an enemy of routine and all things Gothic. Backbiters suggested that he owed his post and title to the influence of Miss Clara Clayton, a horsewoman of incontestable merit, much appreciated by the Marquis of Waterford, a close friend of the Prince Regent. Good Prince George and the excellent Marquis of Waterford had been the victims of a veritable avalanche of gossip–but that, of course, never worried them.

In Gregory Temple's time, Sir Paulus MacAllan, who then occupied a position in the Australian Police, had been reputed to be a man of rather slight worth, good for nothing more than recording messages behind a grille. Now, he dined twice a week with the Lord Chief Justice and was reputed to be a genius; Clara Clayton had not suffered so that he might be reckoned as a mere man of talent. In fact, he had neither talent nor genius, but he rendered numerous little services to people of recognized wealth, and the band of rowdy young lords who treated London as a conquered country on a nightly basis willingly proclaimed the superiority of his administration. He had once asked for the hand of Miss Suzanne Temple; perhaps the hauteur with which that step had been greeted had been a trifle too disdainful. One could not say that Gregory Temple was exempt from the sin of pride.

Sir Paulus MacAllan had just come into his office, and his valet was still in the process of putting over his suit a light quilted overcoat of Indian silk, which lent–according to Clara Clayton–a hint of the Orient to his physiognomy. He was a very handsome fair-haired man, whose skin was smooth and a trifle wan, with equine features and a tall stature, well suited to the parade ground. He was no more than 30; his broad face, symmetrical and insignificant, gave precisely that impression. As there is always a reason for a man's success, we shall charitably assume that Sir Paulus possessed some hidden quality. Save for that quality, our eyes shall not be green; we have pronounced a word that is pure gold: insignificant. What victories there are in simple syllables!

A man of fine stature and frank insignificance, decorated moreover with that pale phlegm that England sometimes produces without cultivation, lacking nothing of the elegance fabricated by tailors, boot-makers and shirt-makers, cannot aspire to too high a destiny. The poet who will sing the praises of the goddess Fadeur [169] has yet to be born.

One last feature: Sir Paulus MacAllan was not even corrupt.

"I shall not be in for anyone this morning, Walter," he said to his valet, who had a little office next to his own, "except, of course, for Their Lordships–and Miss Clary, if her fancy brings her. I've a prodigious amount of work. Call the Inspectors and tell them to arrange things between themselves in the hall. I like to leave a certain latitude within institutions. I must be told, however, if there is anything concerning Their Lordships... send Mr. Hoary up."

Mr. Hoary had previously been Sir Paulus' superior. He presented himself coldly and gravely, with his files under his arm.

"Lovely weather, Mr. Hoary!" cried Sir Paulus, on seeing him. "The Sun is shining, to be sure!"

"To be sure, sir," replied Mr. Hoary. "The Sun is shining."

"What's new?"

"An unfortunate watchman grievously wounded, sir."

"In the low quarters, I assume?"

"Portland Place, sir, at the top of Regent Street."[170]

Sir Paulus smoothed his curls. "These watchmen aren't always sober," he murmured.

Mr. Hoary made no response, but his face became redder.

"Was anyone arrested?" asked the Superintendent.

"Three young noblemen, sir, including Viscount B***."

"A peer of England! Leave the file with me, Hoary. Damn it!" He resumed in a lighter tone. "Oh well! We've completely mastered that pyramidal Bartolozzi business. Poor Mr. Temple couldn't make head nor tail of it, but it wasn't too hard. Intelligence has poured in since this Richard Thompson's arrest."

"There's something odd about that," the Inspector replied. "Thompson was a Deputy in my office. He's a worthy young man."

"Of course, of course... but justice has seized him, and the worthy young man has well and truly twisted the neck of that brave Constance. She was getting old..." He touched the pocket of his frock-coat. "I have here a little packet of intercepted letters; it's extremely curious, Mr. Hoary... and terrible, you see. I believe that I've shown some zeal in this matter, and a little skill. I'm not asking you for compliments. I say that it's terrible... and that Mr. Temple did well not to get through the pass."

"Mr. Temple is a respectable and distinguished man, sir, in my opinion."

Of course, of course... I have great respect for your point of view, Hoary. The letters are from Madame Thompson."

"His mother? Fanny Thompson?"

"No," Sir Paulus MacAllan replied, his faded smile becoming triumphant. "Suzanne Thompson–Richard's wife."

"He's married!"

"We've discovered all that, Hoary–not without some trouble, perhaps not without some dexterity... I'm not asking you for compliments. He's married, most certainly... and I'll lay a hundred to one that you can't guess the name of his wife's father. Don't even try–it's not worth the trouble. Mrs. Richard Thompson is Suzanne Temple."

"Sir," said the Inspector, in a stiff and threatening manner, "I've known Suzanne Temple since she was a child; she has a pure heart and a respectable soul."

"Of course, of course... and a lovely person, to be sure. Her letters aren't the least curious aspect of this investigation. His Royal Highness has already asked for copies of them. It might be a novel by Richardson, in truth! Mr. Hoary, I have the honor of offering you my kind regards; you can get on with your work. I believe that you don't need to be told that no one would thank you for making a noise about this business of the injured watchman."

"We've taken up a collection from the staff, sir."

"That's appropriate. Put this shilling in, but don't mention my name. Until I have the pleasure of seeing you again, Mr. Hoary."

The Inspector went out. The valet closed the door. Sir Paulus MacAllan was alone, plunged in the depths of an immense easy-chair placed before the rosewood desk. There was one singular thing about the room that had undergone such a complete transformation: one feature remained the same. On the rosewood desk-lid, in exactly the same place that it had occupied on the old oak boards, the file bearing the name of *Constance Bartolozzi* in capital letters could still be seen. As if to complete the parity, the cambric handkerchief marked *R.T.* and stained by a droplet of blood was next to the file, with the open note signed with the same initials. On the cover or sleeve of the file, however, underneath the name of *Constance Bartolozzi*, separated by a thick line, a new name was inscribed in capital letters: *RICHARD THOMPSON*.

Sir Paulus MacAllan reached for his cigar-box and chose a faultless Havana, whose end he clipped with the utmost care, with the aid of a recently-invented instrument, the cigar guillotine patented by J. H. C. Cook and Son, suppliers to the Prince Regent. Taking his time over it, he thought: *I don't know why Their Lordships take so much pleasure in battering watchmen, who are poor family men, but it seems that one can't cultivate the reputation of a prank-*

*ster without crippling some unfortunate. England is a merry and eccentric land–
one certainly can't argue about that! These young Lords have a devilish spirit in
them. Not only does it take a dozen of them to thrash an old man who can't defend himself, but they turn signposts round, break streetlights and tear knockers
off doors. There's nothing the Regent likes more than tales of such charming es-
capades.*

He lit his cigar, and took a little packet of thin pieces of paper–seemingly
letters gathered into a sheaf–from his pocket. At a certain place in the sheaf,
there was a turned-down corner, such as one might use to mark one's place
while reading a book.

"And here's one," Sir Paulus said to himself, "who refused to be Lady
MacAllan–very clearly, damn it; unceremoniously, even. I was still only a Deputy Inspector on a 125 pounds a year. The silly fool! And how grateful I am for
her foolishness! I would have a disgraced man for a father-in-law. I'd be an Inspector at best, and my wife would inhibit my little transactions with Their
Lordships. Let's look at the romance of Miss Suzanne. I'd rather read it than be
its hero, 'pon my word. Where were we up to? I've done the affair of the Opéra-
Comique with the bloodstained shirt, the arrest of the Comte de Belcamp, who's
a real comedy character... and damned if French justice isn't mad, to arrest a
man for two actions, each of which renders the other impossible! One is forced,
as one advances through life, to agree with oneself that all the intelligence in the
world is concentrated in the land of England, which is its head... and yet there
are men who confess, without blushing, that they're French! But there are Eski-
mos too... letter number 5, in the middle... my business."

He read aloud:

*"How I wish, my poor Richard, that your innocence were as easy to prove
as that of Comte Henri! His arrival at Versailles was a veritable triumph. The
Prefect came to see him in the clerk's office, in spite of the late hour, and the
Examining Magistrate apologized profusely. They wanted to release him immediately. Our good and dear friend the Marquis, his father, was against it, saying
that some reparation was necessary as glaring as the injury itself.*

*"Comte Henri was calm, courteous, insouciant. He called me to him and
said: 'Your father is definitely my enemy, Suzanne, my mortal enemy–perhaps
because I have been a friend to Richard Thompson.' My heart constricted while
I talked to him. I don't know how to express my belief that the man possesses an
almost supernatural power. I was afraid, but not for him.*

*" 'Your father,' he went on, 'declared war on me this evening. He is in the
process of striking the first blow against me. The blows he strikes against me
will only hurt him... or rather hurt you, my poor Suzanne, and him whom you
love even more so.'*

*"He was telling the truth. My father had arrived. I saw him at a distance
with his face pale and his eyes feverish, as they always are nowadays. He was*

speaking to a group composed of Magistrates and Administrators. What was he saying? They listened to him silently?

"I saw the Marquis de Belcamp become suddenly furious, raising his stick at him and calling him liar and wretch. Henri threw himself forward to restrain his father's hand.

"Gregory Temple withdrew, after having looked at Monsieur de Belcamp with an expression whose painful sadness I can't describe. What is there between my father and Comte Henri? My father can make mistakes, but he's neither malicious nor cruel.

"Things have changed. Comte Henri cannot return to the chateau. The Prefect of Seine-et-Oise and the President of the Tribunal of Versailles came in turn to offer their houses to the prisoner, for Comte Henri is a prisoner. He refused, without unnecessary vanity or bravado, but firmly. He even succeeded in calming the wrath of the old Marquis. Everyone who was there for him—and it was a crowd—understood that the legal formalities had to be observed in order that reparation could be exacted with all due solemnity.

"We all accompanied Comte Henri to the jail at Versailles. While thinking on the way, Richard, I lost myself in the labyrinth of mysteries. There were, after all, two murdered men. Where were the murderers? And by what bizarre coincidence had both of them assumed the Comte de Belcamp's name? Isn't this some infernal machination? Or, rather, two machinations: two acts of vengeance that, in order not to miss their aim, had to be carried out in concert. On my salvation, I do not suspect my father. Comte Henri doubtless has other enemies...

"As farewells were said—which were noisy and flamboyant on the part of Comte Henri's friends, calm and grateful on his part—he called me again and found a means of talking to me. He talked to me for longer than he talked to Jeanne Herbet herself!

" 'Suzanne,' he said to me, 'all this is like a theater play, and it will have a final act: there's the curtain.' Smiling, he showed me the prison door. 'If my life is a drama,' he went on, 'I regret nothing of what I have accomplished during this act, the longest, the most laborious and also the most painful in the entire play. The action will change. When you wake up tomorrow, a world of events will have occurred in the wings... In a few words, since time is short, I have no further need to weigh upon your poor heart. You can no longer oppose me, Suzanne; no one can do anything more; what use would a hostage be to me? Find an opportunity to be alone with Lady Frances, and you shall have a great joy, with a great pain.'

"He left us.

"I'm finishing this letter at the inn at Versailles where we are staying. I'll address it to your mother. I pray to God that it will reach you, my beloved husband, and that I shall eventually have an answer from you!"

Sir Paulus MacAllan shook the ash from his cigar and turned the page. There was another letter, dated the following day, from the Chateau de Belcamp.

"A great joy, he was right to say—and, alas, a great pain! I learned today that you have been arrested, Richard, my poor Richard. Must our dearest hopes end in such misfortune, then? You are in prison! In solitary confinement, it's said! I am still writing to your mother, but your mother never replies. I sometimes think that my letters are being intercepted.

"In telling me of your arrest, Lady Frances said to me: 'Don't be afraid; Comte Henri will respond.' But how can Comte Henri respond now that he is a prisoner himself? And yet, my father kissed me this morning more affectionately than is customary. He has also kissed our child. I have not explained anything to him, but I think he knows everything; his eyes told me that, and it seemed to me that there was a tear in them as he kissed our little Richard.

"I talked to him about you. He turned away and did not reply, but I know him. His anger is past, long past, and it seems to me that I see a sadness in him that is like repentance.

"If he wished, Richard, the Regent has personal obligations to him, and he still has more influence in London than he thinks. If he wished..."

At this point, Gregory Temple's successor stopped reading abruptly and set the sheaf of papers down on the desk.

"Yes, indeed!" he said, pensively. "Personal obligations! His Royal Highness will be particularly flattered when he arrives at that passage, which I have strongly underlined. Mr. Temple has told his daughter that the Regent has obligations to him... and his daughter has written as much to Richard Thompson... in every letter, damn it! And if Richard Thompson recovers his liberty, he'll be permitted to broadcast it from here to Rome! Now, what kind of personal obligations—the word is there—can a Regent of England have contracted towards a Policeman? I certainly bear old Gregory no ill will, but I wouldn't sell that single line for ten guineas!"

He relit his cigar, which had gone out, and continued.

"If he wished... Richard, something in me tells me that he will, and I hope.

"But I mentioned a great joy... our cherished infant, our beloved little Richard—you saw him not long ago, I know, and I have sought your kisses on his lips. When I think that my husband has been so close to me and that I was not able to press him against my heart! You have often accused me of being cold, Richard, because anxiety and distress has suddenly thrown mourning-dress upon the youth of our love. It's perfectly true; I did not know how to smile in the midst of these terrors, and the weight that oppressed my soul prevented me from responding to your caresses. And yet, perhaps I am indeed cold, for my former gaiety appears to me as impossible as the folly of a dream. But I love you, Richard, and I wish that you could see my poor eyes wearied by tears. Why can't I die for you?

"It's him, our blond cherub, the charming loved one who consoled and deceived my maternal need—the one of whom I spoke in all my letters, saying: 'Ah, if ours were like him!' Comte Henri did not lie: a great joy after a mortal

pain. I adored our son in this dear infant, and God's bounty willed that all those misplaced caresses found their way to their true object. I always thought, while cradling little Edward Elphinstone on my knees and in my heart: 'Our little Richard is exactly the same age... and I accused myself of madness while I added secretly: It seems to me that he has his father's features...'

"His father being you, Richard, in my private thoughts...

"It's him. The dream was reality itself. I have your child in my arms, and I am astonished not to be able to love him more in calling him my son.

"A great joy! A great joy! I have been a mother for more than two years, and I knew nothing of maternity but tears! A great joy! A celestial and supreme joy! I have my son, my son knows me and calls me mother. He loves me better than that stranger whose name he previously bore.

"I have to talk to you about her. Lady Frances Elphinstone has told me that she was your friend. Who is this woman? God preserve me from humiliating my husband, but you are the son of Fanny Thompson and the former secretary of Gregory Temple. You cannot be on friendly terms with the great ladies of London. I have seen little of the world of the English nobility myself, to which my birth gave me no entitlement, but I have seen enough to declare that Lady Frances Elphinstone does not belong to it. She is elegant and grand, but not like our ladies; her distinction is not theirs; she is ignorant of certain things that we know well; her very grace, which is exquisite but does not resemble ours, makes her an outsider.

"Lady Frances, I would swear on oath, has never set foot in an aristocratic drawing-room in London. She is marvelously beautiful, but her beauty is not English.

"She is very good, miraculously spiritual; she has the boldness and gaiety of a Frenchwoman. She told me about your journey to Paris and your expedition to the Colisée; she has also told me how you wept when you returned to the woodcutter's hut. But she does not wish to tell me what tie attached you to Comte Henri, and she refuses to explain the motive that could have brought a Countess of the English peerage to play the role of mother to someone else's child..."

The brass button was still in the partition wall. Sir Paulus MacAllan touched it; the bell sounded outside and the hidden door opened, framing the jaundiced and immobile face of Mr. Forster.[171]

"An 1817 *Peerage*," Sir Paulus requested.

The door closed, to open again a little while later. Mr. Forster, without coming in, gave the voluminous almanac to his superior, who said: "Remarkably clear weather today, Mr. Foster!"

"Yes, sir, remarkably clear," the automaton replied.

Sir Paulus MacAllan riffled through the *Peerage*, eventually arriving at the Elphinstone article, which he scanned. He shrugged his shoulders.

"I was sure of it," he murmured. "A fake Countess–that's one in the eye for the French!"

He yawned, and skipped several pages of the manuscript, murmuring: "I declare that I'm saturated with conjugal and maternal love; let's find something else..."

"*...Comte Henri has now been imprisoned at Versailles for eight days. A trial has been ordered–on instructions from above, it's said, in spite of the Magistrate's opinion. My father let slip in front of me that it isn't a real trial; it's merely a pretext to keep the prisoner locked up.*

"*You know that Comte Henri, under another name, was once my father's friend and right arm. Beneath his unexpected relentlessness one might perhaps find the key to the puzzle...*

"*I have had to leave the Chateau de Belcamp, from which my father has been expelled after a violent argument with the Marquis. I'm staying with Lady Frances Elphinstone in the Chateau-Neuf. After having it out with the Marquis, my father has disappeared. Even Robert Surrisy, a young man with whom he has conversations that seem to be concerned with some mysterious enterprise, does not know where he went and supposes that he is in London. Pray to God that he is there for your sake, Richard! And pray to God also that he abandons his idea of staying in France and making war on Comte Henri de Belcamp! I don't know why that war frightens me more and more, not only for him but for ourselves, but I sense a fog around me that is becoming thicker and thicker. There is an abyss of mysteries on the road we are traveling, so large and profound that we might all fall into it...*

"*No one is against me, assuredly, but the whole world is for Comte Henri, who is my father's enemy. Everyone is taking his side, whether by virtue of professed affection or binding ties that it is impossible to define. Lady Frances is his slave, and insists that your devotion is no less than hers. The entire country is celebrating the outcome of the investigation in advance, there being no doubt about it, and anyone who mentions Gregory Temple thinks he is showing clemency in not accusing him of madness.*

"*Should I give you an example of the incredible prestige exercised by Comte Henri from the depths of his prison? There are two young women who love him, and who remain friends, as if he were the Sun, of whom no one can be jealous. That's nothing. These young women have abandoned their fiancés: two proud and brave young men. The fiancés, who are still in love, are Comte Henri's slaves!*

"*Now, I remember that I too have been his slave, and I ask myself whether he has a hand large enough to hold every one of them by a different chain... and I reply, having interrogated my own thoughts, that there is an even greater miracle, since I have not ceased to belong to him even though my chain is broken. I am still his slave. Why? Because I love you, Richard, and I have more confidence in the power and the will of this prisoner than in the intervention of my father, who is free. A voice cries out within me: Your husband will be saved by Comte Henri de Belcamp! And I pray for him, while pressing our little Rich-ard to my heart...*"

"What do you want, Forster?"

The jaundiced face had appeared in the frame of the little doorway. "To speak to the Chief Superintendent, sir," replied Forster, who was something of a clown deep down.

"Well, what is it, my boy?"

"Mr. Temple has just come into the courtyard. The porter's dog recognized him and is capering about all over the place... it's always tried to bite me!"

"Mr. Temple!" echoed Sir Paulus, stupefied. "What the Devil? You're dreaming on your feet, Forster!" While he was speaking, Suzanne's letters disappeared into his coat pocket.

"If the Superintendent wants to come and see," Forster said, amiably, "the window of my cubby-hole looks out on the courtyard."

Sir Paulus MacAllan got up. Forster's cubby-hole was a small space serving as an anteroom between the chief's office and the barracks of his underlings. Forster, who had been the chrysalis in this cocoon for many years, had found the means to stow himself away there with all his documents. Forster came to the threshold of the office 30 times a day without ever crossing over. He was an excellent clerk, a perfect movement, as one says of watches.

At the moment when Sir Paulus put his pince-nez to the bull's-eye that lit Forster's cubby-hole, Mr. Temple, having crossed the yard, was going into the vestibule; Sir Paulus saw him only from behind, but he recognized him and returned to his office in a bad temper.

In every country, you would be able to find much that is ridiculous in these old organizations, and a great deal of pettiness too. Although the splendor of the bureaucratic species, the odious and miserable fruit of our civilization—leguminous, meticulous, difficult, important, ignorant, trenchant, tiresome, useless, noxious; paid to be obstinate and revenging himself on the public who pays him for the humiliating tedium of his domestic circumstances; as malicious as he is unhappy, proud because he is disdainful, and intolerant of any kind of culture because his every pore exudes boredom—is French, and only attains the full extent of its cruel savoir in the immense administrative marshes where it is cultivated in France, you will encounter its produce in its humblest and simplest state in every latitude. It even exists in England, especially in the antique offices of the Metropolitan Police.

Still, in the depths of these limbos, somewhere under the ridiculousness and behind the pettiness, there is a heart. From compartment to compartment, I know not how, the news spread that Gregory Temple, the former Chief Superintendent, was inside Scotland Yard. Everyone remembered Gregory Temple very well. It cannot be pretended that curiosity made no contribution to the excitement that brought every recluse from his cavity within an instant, but there was more to it than curiosity.

"God bless you, Mr. Temple," said the doorman in the vestibule. "We'd like to see Your Honor here more often."

"I would like to speak to Sir Paulus MacAllan, my boy," the former Superintendent asked, with a sort of timidity–for he felt as an old mariner feels when he sees his vessel and the sea again for the first time after his retirement.

"I'll take Your Honor up."

"Don't disturb yourself, my boy..." Mr. Temple began–but several voices from the staircase interrupted him.

"God bless you, Gregory Temple!"

Half a dozen constables were there, caps respectfully in hand; the former Chief Superintendent was visibly embarrassed, and murmured: "I'm only here as a mere visitor, my lads..."

"Everyone at Scotland Yard remembers you, Your Honor," was the response. "You were a gentle and just chief."

Mr. Temple climbed the stairs as quickly as he could. In the main corridor other constables, sergeants and inspectors formed a hedge of doffed caps: "God bless Mr. Temple! Why did you leave us?"

Not one was missing. Tears came into old Gregory's eyes.

"My friends," he said, in a tremulous voice, "my good friends, thank you!"

He shook more than one hand as he passed by, but he went quickly and without turning round.

Inspector Hoary was the last. Mr. Temple embraced him and said in a low voice: "Don't raise a clamor for me, my old comrade... not unless I'm here in triumph. Go back in, my lads, I beg you... I order you!"

He turned the corner while all the brave man, moved to tears, went silently back to their stations. The door of the Superintendent's office was at the end of the corridor. Mr. Temple wiped his eyes before knocking on it, and took the time to compose his features. It was Walter, the valet, who came to open it.

In France, a valet is an item of domestic furniture. In England, he follows his master, with whom he makes up a single whole gentleman. In the times of Dunois,[172] such a one would have been called a man-at-arms: a combination of a knight, a horse, a groom and a valet. The poorest sub-lieutenant in the English army has his valet–who does not carry his lance, it is true, but who shaves his beard. The gentlemanry is a flower very like the knighthood.[173] Although our English allies were not always the first into battle in the Crimea, it is because they were busy in their tents. The English valet is invariably as gentle as he is tough, and as tough as he is humble. He would like to batter everyone who raises a hat to him.

Mr. Temple introduced himself timidly. Walter told him: "His Lordship can't be seen, my man."

"Would you let Sir Paulus MacAllan know my name," Mr. Temple insisted, softly, handing over his visiting card.

"What does your name matter?" Walter replied, raising his voice. "You could be the Prince Regent himself..."

"Animal!" cut in the voice of his master, who had come to peep through the inner door. "Don't you recognize Mr. Temple? Orders don't apply to men like him. Come in, my old and respectable master; I'm absolutely delighted to see you in good health."

He disappeared–and Mr. Temple, who had cast a furtive glance at the immobile insipidity of his features, crossed the threshold.

Sir Paulus wheeled him out an armchair, saying: "How are you, my dear chap? Lovely weather, today... don't you find it so?"

"Superb weather, sir," the old man replied, as he sat down. "I've come..."

"It must be six weeks, at least, since we've had such remarkable sunshine. You're enjoying it, now, my dear chap... while the rest of us remain in harness."

The former Superintendent's eyes made a tour of the office.

"Yes, yes," said his host, with a satisfied smile. "It's been renovated somewhat... indubitably, my dear chap... today's tastes, you know... What news is there of Miss Suzanne Temple, if you please?"

"She's well, thank you... but may I ask you for a favor?"

"Ten, sir, or even 15!" cried Sir Paulus. "You're at home here, sir, I assure you. Here are our files, and although it's certainly irregular to permit a stranger... your former position... and the great honorability of your character... there are, however, two, that with the best will in the world I could not let you have... the two files removed in your time..."

"Removed in my time!" Temple echoed, becoming pale. He was obviously making a desperate effort to maintain a calm, conciliatory and humble attitude, but his fever was behind that mask, and in spite of all his efforts his eyes were flashing, to say the least.

Sir Paulus MacAllan was sitting facing him in his easy-chair. He had the pitiless coolness of the neutral.[174] He was also experiencing a vague pleasure by virtue of being enthroned before his old superior. "Removed under your administration, my dear sir," he corrected himself, "to put it more grammatically. The file relating to the Browns, mother and son, and to the assassination of General O'Brien in Prague in 1813."

Gregory Temple's arms slumped.

"Those! Precisely!" he murmured. Then his gaze went straight to the two drawers, whose situation had not changed. He got up, as nimbly as a young man, and opened both of them with a practiced hand. They were both empty.

"Is the cigar-smoke bothering you?" Sir Paulus MacAllan asked.

"I don't remember ever having omitted to take away the key to this office," Temple thought aloud.

Sir Paulus touched the button on the partition wall.

"God bless Your Honor!" said Forster, from his frame. "I was the first to see you in the courtyard... and have you been well all this time?"

"You were the one who conducted the inventory," Sir Paulus put in. "Tell my respectable friend and master how the Brown and O'Brien files were missing on the day after his departure–which is to say, two days before I took up my post."

"That's the exact truth," Forster replied. His face disappeared at a gesture from his superior.

Sir Paulus continued: "I was advised to follow the matter up, but my opinion is that conducting oneself as a true gentleman comes before everything else. I recoiled from the thought of doing wrong to a man of your age and in your situation..."

"Did you suspect me, sir?"

"I didn't suspect you, my dear chap... it's purely and simply that you were responsible... but our new administration is strong, you know, very strong; it can show indulgence if the need arises. The O'Brien file related to a superfluous affair in which you involved our police on an amateur basis. I belong to a sterner school, and I confess that my interest in the O'Brien file was mediocre. As for the Brown file, I think I can tell you that it marred the archives slightly. I count on making a new one, whose first inclusion will be *The Book of the Adventures of John Devil the Quaker*, you know... and in the O'Brien box I shall enclose the most beautiful flower in my crown, dear master. Oh! I ought to confess: here, where you failed dismally, we have succeeded gloriously. And it's no small honor for me to have surpassed at the first stroke my illustrious master Gregory Temple. In the O'Brien drawer, I shall enclose the Bartolozzi file, as soon as Richard Thompson has paid his debt to justice."

Temple forced back a word that had already sprung to his lips. He shut the two drawers and returned to his seat. "My visit has a double purpose, sir," he said, ruddy with the effort of keeping his voice calm. "I also came to talk to you about the Bartolozzi affair."

"We are grateful in advance, dear master, for any useful information that you can provide."

"I have only one thing to offer, Sir Paulus. You are on the wrong track; Richard Thompson is innocent."

Sir Paulus MacAllan had expected these words, for he replied without emotion: "So much the better for him, my dear master, with all my heart–but there are terrible appearances against him. Since I have had him arrested..."

"You did not have him arrested, sir," Gregory Temple put in.

Sir Paulus looked up at him, his expression mingling slight astonishment and abundant compassion. "Would it have been you, by any chance, dear master?" he murmured.

"It was me, sir, may I be punished for it!" the former Superintendent replied, somberly. "All the ideas you thought you had were furnished by me. James Davy was my agent."

"A charming young man," said Sir Paulus, in a forced manner. "He's traveling abroad on our behalf, and through him we have had news of you from time to time."

The old bloodhound could not suppress a scornful smile.

Sir Paulus consulted his watch and called "Walter!" before adding: "My dear sir, I don't need to make my excuses to you. You know the duties of our cruel profession. I have a meeting at the Session House to familiarize myself with the Recorder responsible for this deplorable Thompson affair. If not for that, I would gladly have given up my entire day."

"It is necessary that I also see the Recorder, sir," Gregory Temple replied. "May I ask for a place in your carriage?"

"Most honored, of course, of course... Walter! My hat and gloves. If milady or Their Lordships come asking for me, you can tell them that I'll be dining at the Hanover Club with you know who. The carriage, Walter! My dear master, we are at your disposal."

At that time, the House of Sessions, or Central Criminal Court, was already part of the building complex at Newgate. It was between that edifice and the prison that the Press Yard was situated, where undisciplined prisoners received, long after the time of which we speak, the barbarous punishment of the birch.

Sir Paulus MacAllan's elegant carriage stopped in the Old Bailey, and the two Police Superintendents, the old and the new, went arm-in-arm into the somber house of criminal justice. I do not think that there is any monument in the world more lugubrious in appearance than Newgate. It is the incarnation of English melodrama–which is to say, the perfection of horror: of red-stained blackness, of that sinister mud in which one can discern streaks of blood.

The jurisdiction of the Central Criminal Court extends throughout the Counties of Middlesex, the City, Kent and Surrey. The Lord Mayor is the official Judge, but he never sits without the help of a Recorder or Common Sergeant, who is the real Examining Magistrate. The Recorder looks into documents, by contrast with the Coroner, who can only investigate the scene of a crime or a corpse.

Timothy Bennett, the Common Sergeant for the session, was a gentleman of good appearance, short and stout but well-built, who would not reach a definitively apoplectic state for two or three seasons yet. He was not much older than Sir Paulus MacAllan, his close friend, and–like him–could pass for a second-rate dandy. His office, which was as bright as a cellar for storing coffins, had a view of the Old Bailey through a robust iron grating. He was working, sitting at a table where there were the remains of a ham, coffee, rum cakes and a jug of sherry.

"Lovely weather, isn't it, my dear Bennett?" Sir Paulus said to him as he came in, winking to signify that he was not alone.

"Is the weather really lovely?" replied the Judge, good-humoredly. "The weather's always the same in here, damn it!"

"Take my word for it, Bennett, the weather's what I'd call remarkable! Here's my dear and respectable predecessor, who wishes to talk to you. Mr. Temple, Mr. Bennett; Mr. Bennett, Mr. Temple." He struck an appropriate pose to pronounce the sacramental formula of English introduction.

The two gentlemen bowed to one another, after which the Judge shook the Superintendent's hand vigorously.

Sir Paulus MacAllan shrugged his shoulders and made grimaces behind Temple's back. "Bennett, my dear," he said, taking the sheaf of Suzanne's letters from his pocket, "I've gone through this. It's less curious than I thought."

"It throws daylight..." the Judge replied.

"Of, course, of course, my dear. It throws daylight."

Bennett went on: "Obviously, it throws daylight..."

"Manifest daylight, my dear!" Sir Paulus cut in, again.

After which, the three gentlemen fell silent, looking at one another in slight embarrassment.

Sir Paulus' gestures and grimaces had put Timothy on guard; he did not know the steps of the dance. "Will Mr. Temple accept a glass of sherry, perhaps?" he began. "What do you think, MacAllan, my dear?"

"Mr. Temple belongs to the old school," Sir Paulus replied. "I'm sure that our manners astonish him. He must know, however, that His Royal Highness likes cheerful companions. Mr. Temple has taken the trouble to come here because he wants to tell you something, and we must get to work; time is precious."

"I am entirely at Mr. Temple's disposal," said Timothy. "Time is precious, indubitably."

"Sir," the former Police Superintendent began, slowly, because he was collecting himself, "I came to ask for your permission to see Richard Thompson, my former secretary at Scotland Yard headquarters." Behind him, Sir Paulus shook his head negatively.

"Impossible, sir," Timothy Bennett relied, briskly. "I would have wished with all my heart to be agreeable to a man like you, but the accused, Richard Thompson, is in solitary confinement. The Lord Chief Justice himself could not grant your request."

The dull and profound pallor of the former Superintendent's features was briefly marbled by red streaks. The terrible effort that he was making to contain himself was now so apparent that the Judge interrogated Sir Paulus with a glance. Sir Paulus touched his forehead in a significant fashion.

There was a mirror facing Temple, in which the long, fair-haired and lymphatic face of Sir Paulus was reflected. Temple saw the gesture. "No sir," he said, turning round, "I'm not mad; look at me carefully." His words were cold, but passion quivered beneath his calmness. His face was cold, but his eyes were burning.

Sir Paulus' attitude changed; he began to play with his pince-nez in the manner that reasonable people adopt in order not to respond to the importunities of children.

"Gentlemen," Gregory Temple continued, "it might not be prudent to push me to the limit, no matter how low I have fallen."

Timothy Bennett affected great astonishment. "Now then," he murmured, turning to his friend. "What's bitten this respectable gentleman, my dear?"

"My dear, Mr. Temple believes that Richard Thompson is innocent," Sir Paulus MacAllan replied.

Bennett burst out laughing.

"And you do not realize," Sir Paulus went on, in a coldly supercilious tone, "that Mr. Temple has considerable influence at court; His Royal Highness is indebted to him."

"That's right!" cried Timothy. "Personally indebted, on my honor!"

"Personally, as you say," repeated the new Superintendent. "We must bear that in mind."

Sweat was accumulating beneath Gregory's hairline. "It will be unfortunate for someone," he said, between clenched teeth, "if I have to go to the Regent."

"Don't make threats, Mr. Temple," said Bennett, calmly. "I have the honor of reminding you that I am here in my capacity as a Magistrate."

"I'm not making threats, sir; I know that I'm speaking to a Magistrate. I'm making a final effort to clear a conscience."

"I have the right to listen to you as a witness," Bennett said, in spite of his friend's gestures. "Your deposition will go before the Court."

Temple raised his right hand convulsively. "I swear before God to tell the truth," he cried, "the whole truth, and nothing but the truth: Richard Thompson is innocent!"

"He is your son-in-law," Sir Paulus observed, glacially.

Gregory started as if he had felt a serpent's bite. "Ah!" he said, clasping both hands to his breast. "I shall not be killed at a single stroke; I shall have time to light a torch in that darkness!"

"Calm down, sir," said Bennett, in a tone newly pregnant with interest. "No one wants to kill you, thank God! Do you know the guilty party?"

"Yes," the former Superintendent replied.

"Pray name him."

"It is James Davy."

"My God!" jeered Sir Paulus MacAllan.

"In fact, we know that perfectly well, Monsieur Temple," observed the Recorder. "Richard Thompson was arrested carrying Assistant Commissioner

James Davy's identification certificate; he had come into possession of it and was using it to mislead the investigation. In that sense, the guilty party is indeed named James Davy."

"You are still a young man," old Gregory said, painfully, "although you occupy a position that was reserved in my time for veterans of the magistrature. Honor and good faith still exist at your age. I swear to you, on the hope of my salvation, that James Davy himself gave his identification paper to Thompson, as Nessus gave his poisoned shirt."[175]

"That's a fable," Sir Paulus interrupted. "Definitely not!"

"Why would James Davy set a trap for Thompson?" the Recorder asked, more seriously.

"Because every hunted creature wants to put the hounds off the scent. James Davy knew that I had my hand upon him."

"You? What had he to fear from you, now that you are a mere private individual?"

"The release of Richard Thompson!" cried the old man, striking his breast. "For it is me, and me alone–deceived by James Davy–who caused Richard Thompson to be arrested!"

The new Superintendent of Police made a gesture with his shoulders that clearly signified: "What answer to you expect to such extravagant claims?"

"Don't you know, then," Mr. Temple went on, his impotent passion bringing tears to his eyes, "that your James Davy and the Comte de Belcamp, accused in France of a double murder, are one and the same person?"

"Yes, by God, I don't know that, my worthy sir!" cried Bennett, losing his seriousness. "Why not go tell your stories to the judges in France, who certainly deserve to listen to them, I swear on oath!"

"Don't you know, then," Gregory burst out, his tone and his gestures truly those of a madman, for the explosion of anger too long contained resembles dementia, "that your James Davy is Tom Brown?"

"Tom Brown as well!" groaned Bennett, writhing with laughter.

"And John Devil too, by God!" Sir Paulus threw in.

Gregory got up and put both hands on the Superintendent's shoulders. "And John Devil too," he howled, spraying the other's face with the foam from his lips. "John Devil, yes, John Devil as real as you are–you, blind from birth, incurably deaf and wretchedly stupid!"

Sir Paulus MacAllan recoiled, because he was afraid. Temple was terrifying to behold. When Sir Paulus' shoulders could no longer support the old man's clenched hands, Temple's arms fell. He remained in the middle of the room, quivering, his eyes lowered, his legs trembling, like a man stricken by a curse. "Oh, it's true!" he stammered, horrified and without knowing what he was saying. "It's true! I am the cause of all this... and I am mad!"

"My dear," said Sir Paulus, prudently taking up a position some distance away, on the other side of the table, "I believe it's necessary to call a Constable, not to arrest this poor fellow but to take him as far as the street. It's charity, my dear."

The Recorder rang, and added with sincere sadness as he drank a glass of sherry: "That's the poor human brain for you!"

A moment later, two cCnstables led Gregory Temple away; he let them lead him like a child. As they reached the Old Bailey, after passing under the arch, the Lord Chief Justice's carriage, drawn by his magnificent team, was climbing the hill at a rapid trot. His Lordship's gaze fell upon that man, supported under the armpit on either side, and he pronounced the name of Gregory Temple loudly, adding, mingling prophetic pride with banal compassion: "There's something I predicted a long time ago!"

Temple collapsed against the wall outside the place where the scaffold was being erected, and remained as motionless as a fallen meteor. The two constables, having accomplished their duty–which was to put a man into the street–went back into the Session House, just as Sir Paulus MacAllan, bowing deeply before the Lord Chief Justice, informed His Lordship that the weather was exceptionally clear today, and that one might certainly call it remarkable.

In London, as in Paris, there are people of a similar kind who form a circle around a man who has fallen down. In Paris, curiosity is almost invariably helpful, and every day of the week, you can see poor working men and women playing the role of Providence, clubbing together to meet the needs of a crying child or an old man felled by hunger. Paris smiles even upon the wretched, for those who have a heart.

In London, curiosity is too often ungenerous. Bad luck has determined that I have seen it disdainful and sarcastic more often than not. I have sometimes come away grieving for the insults the city has in its mouth. Everything is ugly in London, from the crushing weight of pitiless wealth to the inconceivable harshness with which the poor treat the poor.

There is a word, alas, which too often turns out to be the truth: intoxicated, meaning both drunk and poisoned. Poisoned by gin, needless to say; there are those who admit it: their drunkenness is a process of slow poisoning.

Around every prostrate body, if it is a man, the crowd says: "He's drunk!"–and if it is a woman, "She's drunk!"

Around Gregory Temple, there were a dozen cockneys who were laughing and saying: "He's drunk!" Two or three of them had charity enough to produce the variant: "He's mad!" None went away. After ten minutes, Temple asked for a drink of water. One man found it in himself to render this service with commendable urgency, and extended his devotion as far as to hold the cup while he drank. On opening his eyes gratefully, the former Chief Superintendent recognized a famous pickpocket, but did not have time to safeguard his purse.

After ten further minutes, a tilbury stopped abruptly before the group and everyone cried; "A physician! A physician!" In London, doctors do indeed bear that title, which has now been adopted by Bosco and Robert Houdin.[176]

The physician made his way through the circle, grabbed his instrument-case and rolled up his sleeves like a man glad to win the right to have a little article inserted in *The Times*, saying: "*We note with pleasure the following evidence of humanity: Today, at midday, in the Old Bailey, before a crowd which applauded his generous action, a young doctor, J. N. White of 17 High Holborn, a specialist in the illnesses of childhood, saved the life of a poor man struck down by apoplexy with the aid of a blood-letting device operated with all the skill for which the young practitioner is already well known. Doctor J. N. White refused any recompense.*" What is more, the insertion of these lines would cost him two guineas. What a heart! Take due note.

Temple had not got up to pursue the pickpocket, but at the sight of the helpful physician, a supreme effort brought him to his feet. The cockneys wanted to restrain him so that he might be forcibly bled–it would afford them a momentary distraction–but Gregory got through to the middle of the road and turned the corner of Green Arbour Court, famous throughout the three Kingdoms for the steep and narrow staircase that Jack Sheppard, pursued by an army of Constables, descended one day on horseback at the gallop. Everyone in London will tell about that magnificent feat, but very few would dream of showing you the little window by the staircase of the room where Oliver Goldsmith wrote *The Vicar of Wakefield.*

Temple had not shaken off any of his cockney persecutors when he moved into Green Arbour Court, but the famous staircase stopped some of them; at the top of the stair was one of those astonishing labyrinths that Londoners call passages or courts, which often form veritable interior villages, full of crossroads, where the Devil himself could not find his way. Temple, who knew the layout of the fantastic quarter like the back of his hand, thanks to his profession, ducked through two or three alleyways and was soon free of inconvenient followers. He came out into Cheapside,[177] and set himself to marching straight ahead at a rapid pace, without knowing which way he wanted to go.

The busy crowd that encumbers the City overflows considerably into Cheapside, but it is Fleet Street most of all that is the natural bed of that brutal current. The two distinct streams going up and down that great artery of London commerce has to be seen before any notion can be conceived of the grossness, lack of restraint and savage egotism that might become the way of being of an entire people. It is a place of business; time is money; one must hold one's course. Given these three axioms, woe betide trampled women or old men thrown under omnibuses. Time is money; it's a place of business; who wouldn't hold to one's course?

There is no room to slide a handkerchief between the flow that goes up with terrible violence and the tide that comes down no less impetuously. Business deals are done coming and going–respectable interests, as they say–orders for cotton thread crossing over with orders for cutlery: two trains of avidity at full steam, which grind and interact incessantly. Every elbow in a woman's ribs is worth 10,000 pounds sterling. What would women be doing there? It's a place of business. All the men look like bulldogs or boxers. What would children be doing there? Commerce is like war; it has its enduring necessities: time is money. Old men can stay at the fireside. Better to break an arm than lose a good commission!

What the Devil! Women, children and old men don't go to stand in front of the cannon at the firing-range! What use are women who don't have bank accounts, children who don't yet have checkbooks, old men who don't have them any longer? One might as well cripple them, pulverize them, massacre them, because they don't hold to their course; they still lose Fleet Street more than a million sterling every year. There is a time to be human. In the evening, the founders of iron, sugar and even cotton are family men. They get angry if anyone inadvertently elbows milady, and I don't blame them for that. But business is business. At midday, in Fleet Street, the cotton merchant would choke his own wife to get past. Go see for yourself, and hold to your course.

The current descending towards the Royal Exchange seized the former Police Superintendent and dragged him along, as strands of straw borne along by a rain-swollen steam are whirled along. There are swimmers so skillful that they no longer have to make an effort; old Londoners are so accustomed to these homicidal throngs that they let themselves float on the ebb and flow of the tide. As soon as they know how to swim, they no longer understand that others might drown them. They are calm within the protection of their elbows, buttressed like battering rams. Misfortunes will always happen to others; in consequence, there is nothing to fear.

Temple, in the midst of this turbulence, was also swimming, but in another sea. The prostration that had felled him a little while ago had given way to a vehement fever. Lucidity reasserted itself within his brain; he was conscious of having committed an act of folly; he was suffering–but all his fighting spirit had returned, more valiantly and tenaciously than ever.

The suddenness of his resurrection was not unconnected with the crowd itself, the agitation and the pressure–all of that emits a kind of fluid, that's certain. Poets have told me about the strange fecundity of the imagination in a crowd. Even more bizarre, calculators have boasted to me that a crowd is a propitious environment for resolving difficult problems. There is a reason for that, which is that there is no place on Earth where one is more absolutely alone than in a crowd. A crowd isolates in the same way that darkness limits the view; it isolates by the multiplicity of its distractions; it isolates yet again in the same way that excessively bright light can force one's eyes to close; it cradles thought like the sea; it puts attention on the defensive; it solicits effort; it overexcites the imagination.

Gregory Temple could not have been more introverted in the middle of a desert. He did not feel the pushing and the jostling; he was deep in thought.

I am not mad, he thought, *since I appreciate that my conduct has been that of an insane man. The blood rushed to my head; brutal passion was stronger than intelligent calculation. I was unable to vanquish the anger that the mere sight of that man stimulated in me. Why? Because he has taken my place. How miserable the human soul is!*

I am not mad; it's just that my head is weaker than it once was. I cannot help hating myself.

My science has killed Thompson, whom I love: Thompson, who is my daughter's husband and the father of my grandson. My science is not futile, though. A demonic influence led my calculations astray; and I know the demon. Thompson must be brought back to life.

I resolved the problem a long time ago. I saw the light on the day when my gaze fell upon the false postmark imprinted on James Davy's letter. From that point of departure, I retraced my steps, marching with a steady pace thereafter.

I encountered all Tom Brown's crimes like stopping-points along my route: la Bartolozzi at the center; O'Brien before that; Robinson and Turner thereafter; Noll Green and Lochaber Dick yesterday. Murders to hide murders... like crooked bookkeepers who make false entries to cover up their thefts. I know everything now—everything!

No, my science is not futile; no, I am not mad.

It is by means of my own science that Tom Brown has avoided me. I revealed the road of the impossible to him; he has preceded me along it, and perhaps I shall be able to catch up with him there!

He arrived at the corner of Lombard Street,[178] where the contrary currents formed that eternal backwash, bar and bore that business gets over by means of prodigious courage. Gregory Temple did not know where he was. His intelligence had been so completely absorbed by his obsession that he had been breathing the close air of his room in the Rue Dauphine in Paris, in the midst of his funereal dates and names: his implacable memento. He passed from one current to another without being aware of it, and drifted back into St. Paul's Square, bruised by new elbows, abused by other deliveries and other commands.

Is he stronger than me? he asked himself, extending his train of thought. *Has my formula become a wizard's wand in his hands? He's ahead of me, ahead of me! His supreme skill is to have no accomplices, and to make accomplices of everyone—blind accomplices who are ignorant. I arrived too late in France for Robinson and Turner. I arrived too late in England for la Bartolozzi. That's done. There stands before me a phantom evoked by myself: the impossible! And it is laughing, laughing while saying: 'Behold an old man who has lost his reason!'*

That was not all that was being said around him. There was also: "There's an unfortunate who hasn't sniffed the coal down below or has fluff to deliver up above." A few petty clerks, having no more heart than a balance-pan, shouted to him: "Hold to your course, old man!" Omnibus conductors called out to him: "Climb aboard! Pimlico! Chelsea! Paddington! St. Pancras!"

On the pavement, another crowd—this one of carriages—unwound without too many accidents, thanks to the miraculous coolness of English coachmen.

Gregory Temple saw nothing, and heard nothing.

I shall fight! he continued, following his obstinate reverie. *Until I draw my last breath, I shall fight! Let them laugh! The time will come when the truth will explode like the gunpowder in a mine. Ah, wretch! wretch! I have made myself small in order to become invisible. I have thrown away my armies in order to run faster. I said to myself: if I can only find, discover, know. I have found; I have discovered; I know—and I am still powerless! The light is in me, but I cannot make it shine forth! Superintendent Gregory Temple would have spoken so loudly that it would have been impossible not to hear him, but I have become nothing—nothing! I have no proof; I have no weapon. The impossible is around me like a net that will garrote me! My daughter will be a widow, my grandson an orphan–thanks to me! All thanks to me! Oh, I shall fight. I shall testify before the jury; I shall defend Thompson; I shall go to see the Regent! And if nothing can be done within the law, I–who have sworn to uphold the law–will set myself against the law. I shall get into the prison; I shall save Richard by active force!*

"Hey, bourgeois!" someone shouted into his ear in French. A man wearing the costume of a peasant from the environs of Paris put a hand upon his shoulder unceremoniously. "Are you sleepwalking, bourgeois?" he went on. "I've been talking to you for half a hour without any response."

Temple did indeed seem to be coming out of a profound sleep. He stared at the peasant dully.

"Pierre Louchet," said the other, laughing. "Messenger at the French Hotel in Leicester Square, whom you sent out this morning to deliver two bottles of liquor to the woman in Rosemary Lane. And there's a hussy who needs a shave!"

The former Police Superintendent passed his hand across his forehead. The peasant had dragged him out of the current, to the shelter of a corner at the gate of St. Paul's.

"I'm in full possession of my reason," Gregory Temple told him, with the hesitancy of a man who is not at all sure that he has not felt his reason totter. "You spoke to me about Robert Surrisy, and I promised to do something for you."

"You told me that if I told you the story of the child, with the name of the woman that was written on my door three weeks ago, you'd give me a tip... but it couldn't be worked out... so I took the two bottles of Hollands to Rosemary Lane. I asked for Mrs. Molly. I was shown up right away–there's no ceremony in that place. Mrs. Molly was sitting at the foot of her bed in a blouse and petticoat. She was crying out for a swig to drink, and seemed to me as if she'd already had more than a few! I came in with my two bottles, one in each hand. She laughed, putting her big black hand over her mouth. 'Is that for me, my pretty boy?' she asked. I was a handsome man once, in my time, even in my regiment... I answered as ordered: 'It's two samples of liquor sent to you by an old acquaintance who sells them, for you to taste; he wants to know what you think...'

"I don't know if she understood, but she opened one and took a draught that would have laid me low... but these Englishwomen are like sponges that drink and stay cold sober. Afterwards, she offered me the bottle politely, but an old soldier understands propriety, you know. I thanked her without any semblance of disgust, so as not to humiliate anyone, and I went back to the hotel. That's my report."

Temple had listened to him distractedly. His face visibly changed; his forehead cleared and a light gleamed in his eyes.

"Do you still want to return to France, Pierre Louchet?" he asked.

"Always, bourgeois," the woodcutter replied. "The milord sent me here to see what was what; that's already done. It's only the funds that are lacking."

"Come to see me this evening at the hotel, my boy," said Temple, putting a five-shilling piece in his hand. "You're good at errands; I'll give you one for your own country." He dismissed him with a friendly wave, and went around the cathedral to go into Watling Street, which runs parallel to Fleet Street but is usually as quiet as its neighbor is noisy and busy. Temple now had a goal. He walked rapidly with a firm step. His face no longer showed any trace of moral unease; his head was held high and his eyes were clear.

He followed Watling Street as far as Trinity Square,[179] which he crossed in order to get into Rosemary Lane. He went to Gentleman Ned's Hotel. It was no palace, but it did not resemble our low-class hotels. The dilapidated but clean doorway, which one reached via three stone steps worn away by erosion, gave access to a bridge crossing the small ditch that let daylight into the subterranean kitchens. The hall carpet was faded and worn but carefully patched. The stairway also had a carpet, as had the landing and all the rooms. No broken window or loose, worm-eaten floorboards can be as bad as a tattered carpet; it is like the rags of a black coat such as we have already mentioned. Since England is no longer very rich or very new, she has a cold appearance.

To the right of the entrance, a parlor with a vast fireplace whose grate was at breast-height displayed its blackened paneling, oozing the cold moisture of the last fog. As one passed the door one could smell gin, as one can smell tobacco, beer or coffee mixed with brandy on the pavements on to which our disreputable bars exhale their repulsive breath. Travelers of mediocre means were gathered around the table, enshrouded like the paneling. The parlor is always the nicest room in a hotel.

Gentleman Ned and his wife, pretty Molly, were lodged on the second floor, in a large enough room, provided with lamps and a carpet like all the rest. As pretty Molly had been already staying in the room for 24 hours, however, it was a untidy and dirty. The proprietor conducted Temple halfway up the stairs, and said: "I don't have a house in Grosvenor Square, sir, or even in Piccadilly, but I'll be damned if I often have guests of that sort! It'd take a cask of gin to satisfy that lady, on my honor! The room facing the staircase, Number 16. Go up!"

Temple knocked on the door of Number 16, through which a raucous and lugubrious song could be heard. There was no response, and the song never paused. Temple knocked a second time; the sinister song continued, and there was no response. Temple opened the door and went in. He had made sure in advance that Gentleman Ned had not yet returned.

The curtains were closed, plunging the room into semi-darkness. A single ray of sunlight came through the crack between the two pieces of threadbare serge, striking Molly's bony cheek obliquely. She was sitting at a table in the middle of the apartment, swinging her legs slowly back and forth. The bed was unmade; the red silk dress hung down, trailing on the floor; the hat was on top of the clock. There was no wretchedness there, strictly speaking, but it all exuded a horrible, heart-rending loathsomeness.

Lit thus, from behind, Molly appeared to have gigantic stature. Her muscular frame showed under her blouse; her cheek was a sickly green in the sunlight; her moist mouth seemed to have been struck in mid-convulsion by rigor mortis; her eyeballs had retreated into the depths of their orbits.

She was singing with her lips half-open and motionless.

The words of a language define a people. That is sadly true; drunkenness, over there, is not drunkenness; it is the death-agony produced by a toxin. It is fair to add that the terrible property of definitive English intoxication could not ever have resulted in anything more frightful than the face of that creature, whose innate strength, though enervated and prostrated, was still battling against a dose of poison capable of killing three young and healthy young men.

There were indeed, three stone bottles on the table, two of which were completely empty and the third reduced by two thirds. Molly had quaffed all that since Pierre Louchet's visit. Temple's envoy had not brought enough for her; a third bottle had been required—and the day was not yet half-over!

And Molly was still sitting up, balanced against the table. She was singing!

As he came into the room, Temple said: "Good day, Molly, my bonny girl."

She turned slowly towards him, and her body slumped to the left.

"Oh! Oh!" she groaned, laughing. "I'll fall over if I don't have a swig. That isn't you yet, my man Ned?"

She put the bottleneck to her lips; it clicked against her front teeth.

"I've come about this morning's gin," Temple replied, his spirits lifting.

"Gin, Master Knob? It's a long time since I've had real gin to drink. Do you know that gin's watered down nowadays?"

"Then you don't want more bottles, Molly?"

"More bottles, boss? You can't taste it and it burns your throat. I've seen the time when there was gin to drink in England!" She moved her head up and down gravely.

The dose was too strong, Temple thought. *She's incapable of answering me.*

But the former coal-heaver suddenly raised her voice. "I'm a lady now, and I'm not afraid of policemen!" she screeched. She let out an enervated laugh, which failed to precipitate her head first upon the floor.

"The gin's good, Molly," said Temple, "since it makes you as merry as that. I came to ask you if you needed any more."

"My man Ned has all the money," the big woman replied. "There's none left in the house."

"You can get it on credit, Molly."

"Who'll give you credit, then?"

"The seller, of course."

And what's the seller's name?" demanded Molly, for whom the thought of more bottles was as clarifying as the light of reason.

"What! So you don't know?" said Temple, whose sharp eyes tried to meet Molly's in order to judge the effect of his words. "It's Noll Green of Southwark."

The giantess' legs stopped swinging. Her eyelids fluttered. She turned her eyes towards Gregory Temple's hands as he came closer to the table. "Noll Green," she murmured. "You aren't Noll Green. You have five fingers on your right hand."

"Not me, Molly, not me! I'm a lot older than Noll. I'm only here on his behalf."

She pointed with her foot at a broken pipe lying on the carpet. "That's his," she muttered. Then, she drew herself upright. "I'm like a stone when I want to be. They won't make me talk."

"About him?" Temple asked, softly.

"And lots of other things, in truth," said Molly, thinking aloud. "But who can brag about making me talk?"

"About Noll the boxer, no?" Gregory Temple put in. "He can have the best, now that he sells liquor to rich men."

Ned's wife laughed silently. "It's not him, Your Honor," she said, suddenly adopting a respectful tone. "I know how to talk to Sheriffs. Do you think this is my first interrogation?"

"Molly, my bonny girl," Temple replied, doing his best to laugh, "I've come about the gin, and I'm no Sheriff."

"Then, be on your way, man. Random callers have no right to come into the room of a gentleman's wife. If Noll's been resurrected, I don't know anything about it. What does it matter to me?"

"It's Noll and Dick, Molly!"

"Yes, yes... with them, you always got a swig. They were friends... and they never quit one another, even on that night..."

"What night, Molly, my beauty? Would you like to come and see them both?"

She shivered from head to toe. A light gleamed in her dark head. "Who are you, man?" she asked, in a curt, dry tone.

The former Superintendent half-opened his greatcoat, and displayed a flask of French brandy that he had bought in Tower Square. "I sell this," he answered, "on account or on credit, according to the individual."

She extended her hand, as if in spite of herself.

"It's good stuff," Temple went on. "You must have treated yourself to some in Paris."

"I'm like a stone," muttered the big woman, rubbing her eyebrow. "I defy you to make me talk!" She was still stretching out her hand. Gregory uncorked the bottle noisily.

"Taste that for me, little mother!" he said, invitingly.

Molly put the bottleneck between her teeth, as a traveler lost in the desert might, who had not seen water for three days. She released a huge sigh after having drunk, and clicked her tongue.

"That's good," she said, "but I like gin better... real gin." Then, supporting her hands on the table as she was overtaken by dizziness, she added: "Was it you who was talking to me about Noll Green and Lochaber Dick?"

"Who are they?" asked the former Superintendent, affronted. "Are you dreaming standing up, bonny lass?"

The drunkard's dead eyes rolled in their cavernous sockets. "Someone was talking to me about Dick and Noll," she stammered, awkwardly, "but he wasn't dressed like you. He wanted to know..."

"That was some Sergeant in disguise, Molly. You must be on your guard."

"Oh, they can disguise themselves, young man! I'm like a stone when I want to be. Dick couldn't drink as much gin as me, no, though he could drink a bucket of beer... and I'm not afraid of Noll's fist. I've carried Ned, my man, for four leagues, coming from Boulogne to Paris. He only weighs half as much as a basket of sea-coal, gentleman as he may be!"

Temple brought a footstool to the table and sat down. "Get your pipe out," she said, "if you're a good companion."

Temple was a good companion–or, at least, a companion too skillful not to be armed with all the accessories of his role. He took a sailor's pipe from his pocket, which you would not have found in the tunnel at Vauxhall Bridge. Molly thumped his shoulder to signal her satisfaction–a blow that jolted his bones. She stuffed the pipe with sensuous glee.

The hour was getting late, though, and the work had not advanced a single step. The former Superintendent often pricked up his ears as noises sounded on the stairway. Gentleman Ned might return at any moment. He took a small handful of tobacco and kneaded in his hand to make a quid. Molly's dull eyes were upon him. "In Paris," she said, "I wouldn't have let you get me such a big mouthful, friend."

"In Paris, you didn't have a new hat and a nice silk dress, my child. Master Knob told me that you didn't have enough bread over there."

"Bread!" echoed the big woman, with ineffable scorn. "One always has enough bread! But until his flint struck the stone with a firm enough shock I'd been without a swig for a day and a night!" She pronounced the last words in a solemn tone, and her face expressed genuine horror.

"That didn't last long, happily," suggested old Gregory.

"It lasted until the evening when my man bumped into milord." She planted her two huge feet on Temple's knees in a familiar manner, and started smoking her pipe with pleasure. Temple had sweat all over his body. He had a strong suspicion that all the subtleties ordinarily employed in interrogations would be blunted against this milestone. It would take Moses' rod to make the spring gush forth. And yet, he was perfectly certain that Molly could revive his lost cause with a single word, and furnish him with the weapon he lacked. He was like a fox prowling around a hen house without doors.

Molly had fallen silent again.

"Ned Knob is rich now," Temple went on. "I can let you have five bottles on credit, if you want."

"Of gin?" said Molly, whose eyes had a livid gleam.

"Of gin or brandy. Now that he works for milord, one can have confidence, that's certain."

Molly drank a mouthful of brandy, and said with a vague intention of being equally clever: "That's certain, old man. How can you lose with men such as us? You could give us 60 bottles and bring them tomorrow, without any risk."

"Tomorrow it is! Sixty bottles."

He saw a hint of red in the big woman's cheeks. She had a confused notion that she should not let her pleasure show—but 60 bottles! She could not resist. She got to her feet with a violent effort and crossed the room in two or three long strides. She was scarcely tottering. As she came back, she moved her muscular arms, trying to dance. Her song, intoned in a masculine voice, burst forth like thunder.

She shut up abruptly and stopped in front of Temple, whose chin she caressed.

"God damn me!" she cried, for movement had modified the nature of her drunkenness and excitement had taken hold of her. "God damn me, and you too, gentleman! And the entire Earth! I've heard it said in churches that there's no gin in Heaven! My man Ned is very small, you see, but he still has more spirit than me. He told me: 'Be like a stone if anyone tries to make you talk!' Have I talked? Answer me? Never! When it's a matter of a swig... oh well, listen to this! My man Ned followed milord all the way from Blackfriars Bridge to the Palais-Royal in Paris, and from the Palais-Royal to..."

She hesitated.

Temple restrained himself with all his strength, brusquely saying: "Leave me in peace, good woman! Do I need to listen to your stories?"

The reckless anger of drunkenness made Molly's eyes bloodshot. "And what if I want to chat, old broker of stolen liquor?" she cried, adding a string of blasphemies. "It takes at least three bottles of gin to loosen my tongue, you know! And then I'm worth more than an advocate. I have my account. Be hanged if you won't agree that my man Ned has the spirit of four men!"

"Stolen gin isn't worth as much as the other stuff," muttered the former Police Superintendent, seizing the notion by the hair.

"Old rogue," Molly went on, fondly. "Yes, yes, I definitely remember seeing you somewhere–at Sharper's or St. Anthony's. My man Ned came to wake me up, in our hole, with a swig, and made me pick up a pickaxe and a spade. It was about midnight, and I walked quickly to keep warm. Master Knob was panting behind me. There was a ball thereabouts, and by all the Devils, Master Knob took me there the following day. I danced at Tivoli, and everybody looked at my red dress. The young French gentlemen brought me little glasses of brandy... you can drink as much from a thimble, can't you? I said to them: 'Damn you all, youngsters, do I look like a sparrow, to drink from a toy cup?' And I poured 30 of their glasses into Ned's hat. He cried: 'Gentleman, that's my treasure!' They didn't know what we'd done the previous night, on the other side of the wall... and no one knows, old man, because I'm like a stone!"

"Let's talk about our business instead, woman!" said Temple, churlishly, a soon as he saw her pause. "All this is nothing to me."

"Burn in the eternal fire, you!" howled Molly, seizing him by the neck. "I'll strangle you like a chicken if you don't want to join in my fantasy!"

She let him go and sat down on his knees. "They were both in the tavern of the other side of the road," she continued, complaisantly. "I mean the road that borders the garden where the ball was... and I'd eaten there at that tavern... my man Ned wanted to eat in the room... but he didn't eat anything because he was thinking about the two corpses we'd buried... that was why I'd brought the pickaxe and the shovel. No, he scarcely ate anything–he's still very young,... but me, I drank. Noll and Dick were friends, but we'll die too, isn't that true? It's a pity for them that they didn't drink all that they could! Pass the bottle, man–not the brandy, the gin!"

Old Gregory was becoming weak under the enormous weight of the giant-ess; his poor knees were giving way. He passed the bottle, and Molly stuck the neck in her mouth delightedly.

"Ha ha ha!" she went on, her laughter heavy. "You don't want to listen to me! The tavern had a French name, something like the *Gourmand de jour*. The French are gluttons, who like eating better than drinking. Master Knob had fol-lowed milord there from the Palais-Royal. Noll and Dick were waiting for mi-lord... Master Knob slipped into the fields and climbed up to the window to see what would happen. Milord hadn't come into the room, because he'd been lis-tening at the door, for sure. Master Knob had time to see that Dick and Noll had their daggers under their shirts. They were counting on putting an end to milord.

"Milord went in. He was bringing money. Noll and Dick had been work-ing for him, I don't know what at but it must have been some job, for he put 600 pounds sterling in banknotes on the tablecloth. They'd do anything for 600 pounds. Everyone knows very well that milord pays like a King, and it's a good job for a young man of Master Knob's age.

"The money was counted. Dick and Noll were half-drunk; they daren't attack milord, though, who was unarmed. They looked like a couple of bulls next to him, elegant as a woman–but it takes courage to go up against John Devil, when there's only two of you. They made signs to one another every time milord turned his head... about who would begin... Ned saw them clearly; perhaps milord saw them clearly too, for he sees everything.

"He was calm between the two of then, his elbows on the table. He sent for a punch of Madeira, rum and mint, to make a strong burn. He made himself comfortable. That was the opportunity: Dick and Noll were waiting, thinking that the liquor would give them heart.

"When the bowl was empty, they were completely drunk, but they still didn't dare.

"Milord got up, and suddenly said to Noll: 'It isn't good to steal from a comrade!' And while the boxer looked at him open-mouthed, milord said to Dick: 'Noll has stolen 300 guineas from you.'

"Dick rummaged in his pocket, which was empty. The 600 pounds was in Noll's waistcoat pocket.

"My man Ned, who was sitting on the windowsill, had been watching very carefully. If you asked him how the trick was worked, he couldn't tell you; John Devil is a sorcerer.

"Noll and Dick got up in their turn, shaky on their legs and their eyes bloodshot. Satan only knows what milord had put in the bowl. They were furiously drunk. Dick threw himself on Noll like a mad dog.

"Milord separated them, saying: 'Go out and box like Englishmen on the grass or the bare ground. I'll be the referee, and if one of you is killed, the other won't have any cause to worry.'

"They went out into the field. Milord was the referee. Noll was too strong for Dick, but before he was knocked senseless Dick had taken out his dagger and cut Noll's wrist. He went to lie down under a bush.

"Master Knob saw the whole thing, hidden behind an embankment. He saw milord go to Dick first. Dick was breathing like an ox. Milord lifted his head on to one knee and put a hand to his throat: Dick wasn't breathing any more. Noll was panting. Milord put one hand under his hair and the other to his throat, as he had with Dick. Noll stopped panting. Milord went away. And when we came with the pickaxe and the shovel, Noll and Dick were both quite dead. They were dressed, merciful God, like princes. While looking to see whether Noll had any rings, I saw that he had a finger missing, and that's how I recognized him. We got a good packet of clothes. While I was digging a hole, Master Knob uprooted thistles to replant over it, in the freshly turned earth. He's the brains, and I never contradict him–but the thistles were a bad idea, for they were bound to dry out... and if I had to find the bodies again, I'd go straight to the dead thistles, out there on the flat ground outside Tivoli..."

Temple's agonized legs gave way. Molly fell, as if a trapdoor had opened beneath her. Instead of trying to get up, she stretched herself out on the carpet. Lying thus, she laughed exhaustedly, terminally drunk. Then, becoming serious, she said, in a hoarse and sleepy voice: "I've said nothing about all that. They've never got a word out of me, for I'm like a stone. I feel weak, man. It's too long since I had a swig..."

An hour later, Gregory Temple was neck-deep in a bath, having given orders to the valet at his Leicester Square hotel to steam-clean the clothes that he had been wearing for two days. There were souvenirs of Sharper's in them, and perfumes imprinted by Gentleman Ned's domicile.

Temple retained these terrible effluvia in the depths of his nasal cavities. He wanted to turn himself inside out like a glove to bathe the interior of his body in hot water. The best thing to do in such cases is to breathe energetically in a gymnastic fashion, but it is never completely effective; as with all great pains, there is but one remedy: time. The odor of pretty Molly and Gentleman Ned was at least as tenacious as it was penetrating. An association of pharmacists, artists and scholars would make its fortune by inventing a cosmetic essence that exhibited similarly obstinate properties–but evil alone seems to be durable in the underworld, and the most gracious aromas become noxious after a few minutes of contact with the most beautiful bodies.

God has made the air pure; the Devil has obtained permission to attach a miasma to every vice: these are the two extremes. Between God and the Devil, woman have slipped eau-de-Cologne, that perfumery legion that bears a thousand names and always stinks. Pardon the word, but the verb to smell bad appears to me to be neither French enough nor forceful enough to describe the torture inflicted upon the nostrils by all the fine odors of these women. The divine Plato was very young, since he proscribed poets without even thinking of perfumers!

Gregory Temple got out of the bath and dried himself off with a towel. He had his hair cut and his beard shaved; his fingernails were filed and his teeth brushed. That sufficed for third parties, but seemed little to him. When a pestilential emanation has entered into one, it clings to one's mucus with prodigious stubbornness. The sense of horror can persist for a week, renewing itself with every one of the pulmonary aspirations that are life itself. One carries the evil with one like Horace's *atra cura;*[180] you may certainly flee, but the thorn is within your flesh and its poison travels with you.

Gregory Temple did not complain. Does the victorious soldier ever think of cursing his wounds? Gregory Temple was victorious once more, after having been so humiliatingly checked in the morning–and, according to the inclination of his nature, he felt triumphant, utterly and unreservedly. He fell quickly, but he got up again with equal swiftness. One should never be disdainful of adversaries who are made thus; it is the strength of the Hydra, which always lives in one of its seven heads, and Olympus needed Heracles to vanquish that reptile. As soon as he had got up again, Temple recovered his high spirits, as the English say; he recovered the summit of his self-confidence immediately, with a single bound, only remembering his defeat in order to aspire more passionately to the definitive triumph.

He had won his weapon. His notebook, which was close by, was already marked with hastily scribbled notes. He was running towards a new battle, whose strategy was being worked out in advance by his indefatigable need to work. His calculations, as we have been allowed to see, had completely changed their aim. We have seen him previously, shut up in his fantastic laboratory, pursuing with alchemical desperation the solution that evaded him. The problem was now fully resolved; the calculator had disengaged the unknown from his equation; the algebraic method that had led him astray had been definitely proven; he knew the answer. He could say to himself and cry out to others: "This is the man who is Constance Bartolozzi's assassin."

He had, therefore, progressed definitely, quickly and considerably–but the one he was pursuing had run ahead. The distance between the two remained the same, if it had not actually increased.

Following the example of those indomitable siege-victims who raise new ramparts behind their demolished walls, the citadel assailed by Gregory Temple remained intact. The enemy had abandoned his exterior earthworks, it is true, but he was still standing, solid and unwounded, behind the bank of a new fortress. From that he had attacked in his turn, and with his first strike he had filled the household of his adversary with mourning.

Temple knew the truth. His certainty was mathematical–but he was the only one who knew, and he was not the judge. The problem now was to communicate his conviction to those whose mission it was to judge.

Now, it was there that his adversary, whatever name he should henceforth be given–Tom Brown or Comte Henri de Belcamp, James Davy or John Devil–had forestalled him, cutting the terrain with trenches and obstacles, multiplying his defenses with that indefatigable activity and superior intelligence that nearly always forces victory.

From the very beginning, he had introduced himself near to Temple, without mistrust, and it was within the very walls of Scotland Yard police headquarters that he had prepared at his leisure his first engines of war. This very day, Temple had discovered a startling and entirely new proof of that. James Davy had remained alone in his office after his departure on the evening when he had given in his resignation as Chief Superintendent, and two files had disappeared: the Brown file and the O'Brien file.

Now that Temple had a key to explain the enigmas of the past, he found the same mysterious agent of his errors and misfortunes everywhere. It was James Davy who, while pretending to protect that quiet and loyal child, Richard Thompson, had directed suspicion upon him. James Davy who had been the witness of the secret marriage. Who knew whether he might not have been the original author of that romance? As one sows love, it grows. Suzanne and Thompson, both ignorant of life, must have yielded to some foreign influence.

Neither of them would have dared to conceive of an act of such gravity independently. Even more significantly, Suzanne–a spoiled child–had no real reason to fear her father; Richard, always treated favorably, was in a similar situation. Why had they not come to him hand-in-hand, and why had they not said: "Father, we are in love, complete our happiness."

Gregory Temple would not have responded with a refusal, that was certain. On his honor!

Once, it is true, an imprudent and prideful word had escaped his lips. He had said, speaking of the daughter of a lord in that playful mood so common in England: "One does not marry the son of an actress!" Could that have been sufficient, though, if the importance of the whimsical remark had not been magnified by some evil influence?

Now, there was no need to search for the influence: James Davy had been there when he had said it.

To make Richard into Gregory Temple's son-in-law, then to put Gregory Temple on Richard's track after a false accusation of murder: those were the premises of the syllogism-in-action, subsequently shaped into a thousand facets, that John Devil posed for his adversary. For the former Police Superintendent, a skilled, proven and self-confident detective, would find the traces, even on a false path. John Devil had done the rest by sprinkling seed upon the soil. The former Superintendent must always march behind, as if he were spirit-led, gathering an arsenal of proofs, dispensing the treasures of his skill in rendering those proofs probable, and finally plumbing the depths of one of those fine and difficult instructions that had made his name famous.

He had scarcely had time to polish his work when his son-in-law was ruined! And the ruination of Richard Thompson was the victory of John Devil.

Until now, John Devil's calculations had worked out precisely and terribly. Gregory Temple's work, carried out conscientiously and passionately, had such solidity that Gregory Temple himself could not destroy it. The history of judiciary errors is a long and frightful book. Societies, to serve the needs of legitimate defense, consign certain men to certain intellectual gymnastics, whose aim is to make them into exactly the kind of bloodhounds needed to hunt malefactors–but man, it must be confessed, does not have the sure instincts of the animal. The dog chases the wolf; when it does not find the wolf, it never falls upon a wandering sheep under the pretext that the sheep looks like a wolf–but man, who is above the dog in reason and idiosyncrasy, takes his wolf wherever he finds him, and when the wolf turns out to be a rabbit, well, what does it matter?

Errare humanum est! [181] cries the desolate axiom of the philosophers. And there has to be a wolf.

The real wolf, however, is in the woods, where he calmly continues his business.

Gregory Temple had caught a wolf. The wolf was a masterpiece, all the more so because John Devil had had a hand in it. Gregory Temple had now proclaimed that "this wolf is a ewe," but they had laughed derisively at him. His work was more powerful than he, as Pygmalion had succumbed to Galatea.

During the entire first phase of the battle, while he had been losing his reputation, his reason and his life–piece by piece, much as compulsive gamblers lose their honor along with their money–it was the unknown that had stood up before him. Now the phantom had a body. At the moment when the triumphant Gregory had launched himself forward to seize him, the phantom, holding all the pieces, had stopped him with a challenge and a threat: a serious challenge and a redoubtable threat, which would henceforth be the surrounding circumstances within which Gregory Temple, everywhere and always, would have to work. The second phase of the conflict would be even more terrible than the first. He who had previously retreated was now attacking. From the depths of his prison, he embraced his enemy with supernatural arms; he attacked both his head and his heart; he crushed him with contemptuous raillery and enshrouded him in mourning. He was determined, in consequence of some implacable experience, to demonstrate to the inventor the true range of his method; he was determined to demonstrate to the dialectician the power of his own argument; he was saying to the infant Archimedes: "Here is your lever!"

And the bewildered inventor saw his ideas in the new depths opened in front of him. Imagine the monk of Freiburg the day after the one when chance had caused a little sulphur and saltpeter to detonate in his hands. Imagine Berthold Schwartz [182] confronted with a mine charged with 10,000 kilograms of gunpowder, cleaving a mountain by its explosion! Imagine Salomon de Caus [183] leaving the boiler that had whispered in his ear the first secret of steam, suddenly seeing a viaduct bearing that demon with entrails of fire that is changing the face of today's world, drawing thousands of men in its rapid flight as if it were a whirlwind!

Gregory Temple had only caught a glimpse of the impossible. John Devil, his pupil, had received the principle from him and drawn out its consequences.

The fortress in which John Devil had enclosed himself was called the Impossible. He was within it, as Ariosto had placed the enchanter Atlantes [184] in his magic castle with walls of polished steel. In reality as in fairy tales, however, there is always a magic word to destroy the strongest enchanted castle. The impossible has its key too, because–as John Devil had said himself–human impossibility can never be more than the improbable extended to a certain extreme.

This is an idea for which we would have difficulty finding a wealth of examples, but the redskins of North America have a way of making war that is exactly similar to the duel engaged between Gregory Temple and John Devil. They never attack from the front, and their supreme skill is always dedicated to the sole aim of contriving a surprise. War, for them, is a matter of hunting men. Imagine, however, the most skillful among them–one of those brought to life by the inimitable brush of Fenimore Cooper. However great his skill and subtlety might be, he always leaves one final trace, because erasing the imprint of one step always requires a further step. The word that breaks the enchantment is that final trace: the key to the impossible is that ultimate footprint that can never be erased.

John Devil had not been able to escape that law. His final footprint–which is to say, his final crime, with the aid of which he had perhaps erased all his other crimes–must still exist somewhere. Today, Gregory Temple had taken the giantess Molly on his knees, in order to find out where to look for that final footprint.

Temple had opened his avid hand in this manner many times already, thinking he might seize a weapon. Indeed, John Devil, like some great painters, sketched certain details with incredible negligence–for example, that which led him to entrust Suzanne's child to Pierre Louchet. But in this case, as in others, there had been a reason for John Devil's negligence. He was marching very rapidly towards his ultimate goal, very rapidly and dead straight, despite the multiplicity of apparent detours. Each step taken, as we shall see, was a position taken. No one knew the secret of his endeavor, and his conquests were not always apparent. Far from it: some might resemble losses or checks; but they were conquests.

Now, the taking of the position rendered all the preparations necessary for its conquest redundant. The level altered; it was no longer possible to attack the new platform from below. John Devil, it could be said with all due rigor, gauged the solidity of each resort by the duration of its utility. Suzanne's child–and, in consequence, all that might be reported regarding that lever–had no further role to play after the double arrest at the Chateau de Belcamp. Once that was contrived, John Devil had no further need to concern himself with it. He left behind a happy young mother, and retained–as an explanation of his conduct should the need arise–the fact that Suzanne's secret was not his to reveal. Thompson's wife had chosen to retain the name Miss Temple; Miss Temple had not publicly recognized her child. How could he be reproached for rendering a service to a woman?

And so it was with all the rest. In his scheme, every tie that was no longer useful could be severed or released, but every vital attachment was a cable.

Today, however, Temple had a weapon: an authentic weapon. Why? Because an unforeseen circumstance had confused John Devil's calculations. On the evening of the performance of *Joconde* at the Opéra-Comique, Gentleman Ned had slipped into the coach stationed in the Rue Saint Lazare, and Gentleman Ned had a wife. An iron bar that should bear a house may thus contain a straw, and break under an infant's weight.

Temple had a weapon. Speculative minds remain young in spite of age, because age does not extinguish their passion. When he got out of his bath, the former Police Superintendent felt as strong as he had ever been. He girded his loins for the battle, and his excitement was already triumphant.

At 5 p.m., he dressed himself with great care, and climbed into a carriage that took him to Mivart's Hotel.

The fame of London's Mivart's Hotel far surpasses that of the Hotel Meurice in Paris.[185] Guests make a hotel's reputation, and all illustrious Europe had stayed at Mivart's. The magnificent caravanserail that has recently been erected facing the Louvre would have merited first place among all the hostelries in the universe if it were not already reputed to have a slightly mixed clientele. Kings do not like to reside, even for a day, in a palace whose attics have so many little rooms for hire.

At Mivart's Hotel, Temple asked for Count Friedrich Boehm. He was told to climb a lateral staircase whose steps and walls were decorated with Persian carpets, in the fashion of English luxury. On the landing, clad like the staircase, a silent-footed valet, dressed in ultra-ministerial black, discreetly asked his name and showed him into a vast antechamber, entirely lined in moquette. Temple handed over his card. Shortly thereafter, an Austrian Abbé with his great frock-coat and gendarme's boots, came to meet him at the drawing-room door.

The drawing-room, another box lined with somber woolen fabric, heart-rendingly depressing, contained four people sitting at a considerable distance from one another, around the grate where a log fire was burning. In addition to the priest, there was a doctor of theology, a doctor of medicine and a doctor of law. In Germany, people who are not doctors are at a premium.

The medical man was Dr. Weber, the lawyer Dr. Spiegel, the priest Dr. Arnheim. The first was responsible for the health, the second the business affairs and the third the conscience of the young Count Friedrich Boehm, who was no less a doctor than they, having submitted three theses to the University of Prague.

Dr. Weber, Dr. Spiegel and Dr. Arnheim had, indeed, the appearance of three perfectly respectable doctors. They had three honest German faces, pleasant and a trifle large, whose coloring gave an impression of kinship. Their three wigs were fair-haired; their six cheeks had a clear and pallid complexion; their 12 eyelids had the same tendency to come together periodically, beating the retreat of somnolence.

On entering that vast room, Gregory Temple lost the aftertaste of pretty Molly's tobacco, because the pipes of the three doctors and that of the young Count filled the air with a pure and vehement perfume of Levantine tobacco, delightful to connoisseurs. The doctors had porcelain pipes; the young Count had an admirable Turkish pipe with an amber stem. This was the eternal fire of Vesta; it was never extinguished.

Count Friedrich Boehm was a grandiose young man of sickly appearance, as handsome as a remarkably beautiful woman. His magnificent black hair, heavy and silky, extended numerous curls from the rim of an Illyrian cap in gold-embroidered velvet. He was wearing a velvet dressing-gown reminiscent of a Dalmatic,[186] hemmed by a silk torsade threaded with gold. Beneath his dressing-gown, he was booted and spurred.

If character can be judged by physiognomy, Friedrich Boehm must have been as brave as a lion and more timid than a child. There were strange harmonies–sad, even–in the curves of his noble but largely shadowed forehead. His tender gaze floated beneath the delicate line of his eyebrows, and his feminine coloring was concentrated in the strange melancholy of his smile.

He rose to his feet like anyone else in the world to greet Gregory Temple, and took a few steps towards him to welcome him, cordially but gravely.

"Thank you for coming, sir," he said.

"Count," replied the former Police Superintendent, "if you had not come to find me in England, I would have made the journey to Germany."

"To see me, sir?" asked Count Friedrich Boehm, lowering his eyes.

"To see you, Count... I need you even more than you need me."

The three doctors were standing up. They remained silent. Temple needed no more than a glance to judge a man–that was his profession–but in facing these three men, it was as if he had turned three pages of a book written in an unknown language.

Friedrich Boehm himself rolled out an armchair and offered it courteously to the former Superintendent.

"Count," Temple said to him, "it's necessary that we should be alone."

The doctors chose that precise moment to sit down, all three at the same time, and their three long pipes launched fresh clouds of smoke.

"I am His Excellency's lawyer," said Spiegel.

"I am his doctor," continued Weber.

"And I am his confessor," added Arnheim.

And all three went on in chorus: "By day, we do not leave His Excellency's side; by night, we sleep in his room, around his bed."

Gregory Temple refused the seat that had been offered to him.

"Count," he said, "our interview has ended before it has begun."

A hint of pink showed beneath Friedrich Boehm's pallor. He did not turn to look at the three doctors, who seemed perfectly determined to maintain their posts.

"What right have these gentlemen to tell you what to do?" Temple asked, frankly.

The young Count hesitated, and answered: "They are my friends."

"No more than that?"

"I am a minor," Friedrich added, lowering his voice, "and I have dispensed a million florins in the last four months."

"Are they your guardians?"

"No," murmured the young Count.

"We are better than that," Dr. Spiegel said, eventually, without turning his head. And the two others repeated, with a certain emphasis: "We are better than that."

All three of them were seated facing the fire. The former Superintendent's sharp eyes interrogated their oblique profiles.

In a tone so low that it was hardly audible, Friedrich Boehm said: "I have the honor to be the kinsman and ward of His Imperial and Royal Majesty Francis of Austria, and the Arch-Duchess Marie-Louise, wife of Bonaparte, is my godmother."

"Excellency," said Dr. Spiegel, severely, "you are touching on a State secret!" Arnheim and Weber turned with him like automata.

"Have you the will to act freely, young man?" Temple asked, holding his head high as his resolute eyes surveyed the three doctors.

"My friends," murmured Friedrich Boehm, whose pale temples were moist with sweat, "I give you my word of honor that no question will be raised between Mr. Temple and myself relating to the Empress Marie-Louise or her son, the little Duke of Reichstadt... I beg you to withdraw."

"And if the gentlemen wish to stay," added the former Superintendent, "my carriage is downstairs. In England, medical men take pulses, advocates plead cases and priests officiate at mass, and that is all–even when they have other missions to undertake for His Imperial and Royal Majesty, who is only master in his own land."

The three doctors got up without manifesting the least irritation. The triumvirate's spokesman was Spiegel. He went to Count Boehm and bowed respectfully, saying: "Excellency, we have done our duty; we shall make our report."

It was a simple affirmation, devoid of any threat. The others bowed and all three of them left with their pipes. As soon as they had gone, Temple took the young man's hand and said: "I know your history quite well, perhaps better than yourself; I pity you with all my heart and I am ready to serve you."

Friedrich Boehm's timidity seemed to change into astonishment. His great languid eyes fixed themselves upon his interlocutor; then his eyelids fluttered, as if a tear had been behind his eyelashes. "You know my history!" he repeated. "I have not told it to anyone, sir."

"Those three spies..."

"I cannot permit you to speak thus," Friedrich interrupted, excitedly, "about three men who were my father's devoted friends. They are trying to preserve me from the fate of my elder brothers; they will be defeated, for nothing can resist destiny, but they are loyal and worthy servants."

"Count, you are only 20 years old!" Temple murmured, unable to suppress a smile of superiority.

"That's young to die, it's true," replied the young man, "but I've already suffered a great deal."

There was such a proud seriousness in his tone, and a light of such high intelligence had suddenly appeared in his eye, that Temple's response died on his lips. "I am too forward," he said, after a pause. "Perhaps there have been other misfortunes, in addition those about which I know."

"What do you know? Or, rather–permit me to use the formula, since things that happen in your country are sometimes dressed in deceptive appearances–what do you think you know?"

"Count," exclaimed the stupefied former Superintendent, "your words make me doubt myself. I need to ask you straight away whether you have not come to London to learn the truth about the murder of General Maurice O'Brien, your cousin by marriage."

"And friend of my father, Major-General Boehm... indeed, sir."

"I don't know every last detail," Temple said, with a certain bitterness. "I will tell you what I know–or what I think I know, to use your own expression. General Maurice O'Brien was assassinated on the night before the appointed day of his marriage to a Frenchwoman, who had borne him a son. It is impossible for me to give you the exact dates because the papers relating to the affair have been purloined from police headquarters at Scotland Yard..."

"Ah!" said the young man, his eye brightening. "Purloined!"

The former Superintendent's perspicacity, usually so subtle, could not interpret the light that shone for an instant from beneath the Count's eyelids. Was it surprise, pain or pleasure?

"General O'Brien's assassin," Temple continued, "was, according to my personal conviction, a notorious English criminal, Tom Brown, nicknamed John Devil, who was in Austria at that time with his mother, Helen Brown, using the alias George Palmer. I would have been able to give the Tribunal of Prague the means to convict the audacious malefactor at the time, but two young men belonging to one of the most noble families in Germany were compromised. The affair was hushed up. Does all of that come under the heading of facts known to you, Count?"

"Similar calumnies have been spread against Counts Albrecht and Reiner Boehm, my beloved brothers," Friedrich replied, with glacial coldness. "I am not unfamiliar with them. Please go on."

"As you wish. Count Albrecht, the elder, had control of your family's immense fortune, augmented by the wealth of Maurice O'Brien–to which, permit me to tell you, your family had no entitlement, since the General had a daughter, born within wedlock..."

Friedrich Boehm raised his hand, then let it fall back. He was so pale that Temple paused to ask him: "Do you feel ill, Count? Should I call your doctor?"

Instead of answering, the young Count supported his head in his hands. "I shall speak after you," he murmured, making an effort. "It's for General O'Brien's daughter that I have come to London. Pray continue, sir."

"Count Albrecht must have believed that he was rid of the assassin–you understand that this is still my version of events, and I would be very happy to see it rectified–when he had paid the agreed sum of 200,000 Austrian florins, according to a witness that I shall confront you with in Paris. Count Albrecht had, indeed, no worries on that score for several years. The assassin was in the hands of English justice, in New South Wales–but he escaped, and returned to Europe. Count Albrecht had then to yield to further demands. On the day when he tried to resist them, a public insult was addressed to him at the theater in Vienna. A duel ensued, and Count Reiner became the administrator of the Boehm fortune in his dead brother's place. Is that right?"

"No, sir," Friedrich replied, "but nearly... I am listening."

"It was the same with Count Reiner, except that a dagger-blow replaced the sword-thrust. You have succeeded Count Reiner; you have, like him and your older brother, largely acceded to certain demands; like them you have become weary; you are afraid of being assassinated, like them."

"Never afraid, sir," the young man said, slowly, as an intrepid smile brightened his face. "But the assassin will have to hurry to kill me; if he does not, for the first time in a long while, a Count Boehm will die in his bed." He passed the back of his hand over his forehead and seemed to collect himself for a while. Then he looked the former Superintendent in the face. "This conversation must be confidential on both sides, sir," he said. "I shall not repeat any of it without your permission; can I count on the same discretion on your part?"

"I am a private citizen now," Temple replied. "I can commit myself to keeping a secret."

"I take that as a promise, sir, and I speak to you with an open heart. General O'Brien was assassinated; that is my sincere belief, even though the medical experts declared his death natural. My two brothers were assassinated. A terrible war in being waged in Germany between two organizations of *Vehmgerichte*,[187] one of which seeks to sustain the monarchy while the other serves the interests of the people. The Rosicrucians killed O'Brien, their implacable enemy, in the name of the people... The Sword Bearers have murdered the two Counts Boehm, who were conspiring against the Holy Alliance, in the name of the monarchy."

"Were they conspirators?" murmured Temple. "Does this inquisition of secret tribunals exist? I've already lived for a long time; I've used up more than half it in surprising the secrets of things and men. I've seen these mysterious associations swear on poison or the dagger–and almost always, profiting from the noise of their oath, a genuine malefactor has been behind them, serving his own cupidity or his own vengeance. We are no longer in the age of *Vehmgerichte*, but crime–which is everlasting–profits from such comedies... Have you heard talk of the murder of Constance Bartolozzi?"

"I was present at her condemnation, sir," Friedrich Boehm replied, calmly.

Temple flinched, as if he had been struck in the face. Then his two shaking hands touched his forehead–a gesture that betrayed his tottering reason. "Was there a man, then" he stammered, "who bore the name of Prince Alexis Orloff?"

"Myself, sir," the young Count replied, "during my first journey to England."

"And that journey took place at what time?" cried Temple. His hoarse voice made a strange contrast with that of his interlocutor–who replied: "In the months of January and February in the preceding year."

Gregory Temple fell silent, dumbfounded. His calculations, his theory, his science, his life's passion: was it all reduced to nothing? Was there only one truth: the madness roiling in his brain?

"My noble brothers were conspirators," Fredrick Boehm continued, his voice tranquil and grave. "The Sword Bearers exist and their oath is no game. The *Vehmgerichte* are of every era. The Emperor of Austria wept over the death of Albrecht Boehm, for whom he had a paternal affection; on the death of his godchild, Count Reiner, he made the journey to Buda,[188] where the crime had been committed, to preside in person over the Royal Bench of Hungary. The Sovereign's presence did not bring forth any light in that darkness. Unlike you, sir, I am very young and have seen little. I speak of that which I have seen: Germany. In that dark and supreme contest, Kings are no more the masters of those who fight for them than the people can direct their own champions. It is a duel to the death between two giants, which they have named Principles, Interests or Hatreds. You spoke of time and the things it kills. There is one thing that is dead, and that is obedience, Nothing any longer separates the vizier and the tribune, and Seïd is a Gracchus [189] who served the King, his master, in the manner in which the sons of Cornelius served the people, their slave.

"I have not come to you, Mr. Temple, to find out what happened to Maurice O'Brien in Prague, to Albrecht Boehm in Vienna and Count Reiner in Pest. My letter was a pretext. I have no need of information regarding the solicitor Wood, to whom my brothers dispatched millions, nor the firm of Balcomb & Co., which will astonish the world twice over with steam and something even greater. You have a Europe-wide reputation; to your name is attached the word detective, or one might say discoverer. I have lost a treasure beyond price; in order to recover it, I would give the last drop of blood remaining in my veins. I am the richest man in all Germany after the Prince of Liechtenstein, who has an income of 20 million florins. You have passions and duties that have impoverished you, save for the appeasement of your passion and the accomplishment of your duty. I have come to buy your aid."

Temple was making every effort to listen, but the precise meaning of the spoken words evaded him, because a bizarre idea had suddenly crossed his mind, heaping up the confusion in his brain. John Devil was in this! Whether it was the cry of his mania, which saw John Devil everywhere, or whether it was the voice of truth itself, that cry or voice evoked a phantom. Why did he not hold sway over this youth of 20 years who had need of him? Whence came this mirage that had already deceived his sight once before? Should he believe in Prince Alexis Orloff, now that this person was before his eyes, saying "Here I am." Was this the man who had left the homicidal wound on the throat of Constance Bartolozzi?

He looked at the young Count Boehm with fearful and troubled eyes, because the idea of the supernatural that had attempted to assert itself within him several times over was knocking twice as hard at the threshold of his skull.

He was a man of calculation; he had spent his life boasting of the rigor of his positivism, but these fanatics of deduction, these algebraists of the moral cipher, these ready-reckoners who add up and ponder columns of probabilities are always and intrinsically close to a dream-state. Their instrument possesses real power, since their achievements are prodigious, but you only have to deflect the needle at the point of its departure, or thicken one hair, and you may see them plunge into the most fantastic errors.

Gregory Temple stared at young Count Boehm, because he was asking himself whether he was not some diabolical illusion. Where did the audacity of John Devil end? Or his power? Had he, Gregory Temple, not been surrounded for three months by impossibilities and sorceries? Was he not the plaything of a prodigious conjuror, whose skill deceived not merely his intelligence, but his senses too?

He stared at Friedrich Boehm because he was saying to himself: Perhaps this is John Devil!

But what about that long black silky hair, whose ringlets curled over a woman's forehead? What about those large languid eyes, that pallor–so beautiful but mortal–which no artifice could produce?

No, this was not James Davy, and the bolts of Versailles prison were closed on Henri de Belcamp.

But there was someone who owed allegiance to John Devil, and was a sort of second incarnation of him, whom legend called his mistress: the beautiful Irishwoman. The brilliant silkiness of that black hair, the feminine curves of that face. There are disguises which are almost miraculous...

Gregory Temple looked hard. This could no more be Sarah O'Neil than John Devil himself. This tall figure emaciated by suffering did not belong to a woman. This was really a young man of 20 years, possessed of the ideal beauty to which certain romantic souls sing lullabies.

"I'm waiting for your answer, sir," said Count Friedrich, in the cool and quiet tone that had not deserted him for an instant since the commencement of the interview.

"How can it be," said the former Superintendent, lost in doubts and suspicions, "that you have come to reveal the secrets of the Knights of the Deliverance–to me!"

"You no longer have your responsibilities, sir, and the only Knight of the Deliverance in England, at the present moment, is me."

"Am I to understand," said Temple, in a low voice, "that I have Madame Bartolozzi's murderer before my eyes?"

The young Count's smile was melancholy and proud.

"I am a gentleman, sir," he replied, in a singularly sad tone. "I am a Christian, and the doctors say that I shall not reach my 22nd year... Sometimes, I cannot prevent the flow of blood, but I have never shed it."

Dusk was falling. The twilight shed its grey light through the curtains at the large windows and the coals shone more brightly in the reddened grate. The fire illuminated the former Police Superintendent, whose face was a study in scarlet, while a shaft of light from outside, falling upon the young Count's cheek, made it paler and more hollow.

They were alone, seated close together. Friedrich was speaking, while Temple listened with extreme attention.

"...The Empress of France, who was then the Archduchess Marie-Louise of Austria," Count Boehm was saying, continuing a story, "was only six years old when she held me over the baptismal font. I was brought up with her, in the Imperial Palace of Vienna, under the wing of Maria-Theresa of the Two Sicilies, the wife of Emperor Francis I, my master. Reiner, my second brother, was, as I have told you, the Emperor's godson. Albrecht and he were living with our father, who had a command in the Illyrian provinces, where we owned vast estates. My brothers were affiliates of the Istrian offshoot of the good cousins of Venice, thanks to their Governor, who was a Milanese gentleman. They were two noble hearts, and the University of Prague could not remember ever having seen two more valiant swords.

"The earliest thing I can remember is seeing myself, at the age of four, in the arms of the ten-year-old girl that I called my little mother. That was Marie-Louise, who was to have the great glory and the great misfortune to be the wife of Napoleon. There was no lack of people who detested politics in the House of Austria, but everyone rendered homage to the patriarchal virtue of Francis I and his family. The people of Vienna loved him like a father. Those first years of my existence left an impression in me of repose and respect. The city, with its Babylonian gates and its terraces overlooking the gardens of the People and the Court like promenades above a storm; the great lawns of Lachsenburg and the green slope of the flowerbeds of Schoenbrunn, climbing to the castle between two hedges, the tallest in the world, to the hill that looked out on one side upon the tranquil Viennese countryside though which the Danube runs, and on the other to the shaven head of Mount Leitha on the horizon, which announces and promises the Tyrolean peaks... all that remains in my memory, as pleasant as the gentle sleep of childhood from which youth is the awakening.

"I was still a child when Marie-Louise, my godmother, left Vienna for Paris, half-fearful and half-enthusiastic, dreaming of uniting two races of heroes, like Cornelia.[190] She wanted to take me with her. I left with her, and I was there when the marriage contract, copied from that of Louis XVI and Marie-Antoinette, was read.

"I did not have as much reason to love the Emperor Napoleon as Francis I, and the French Court was by no means similar to that of Austria. Everyone affected to regard me as a doll, brought into the country by a girl who had become a woman too soon. I was treated benevolently there, though, and one day, when he was in a gallant mood, the Emperor gave Marie-Louise permission to give me the rank of page. I refused, saying that I was named Boehm, and that I had the rank of Lieutenant-Colonel in the Austrian army. The Emperor touched my cheek with his white, slender finger. 'And what if the son of your godmother, as Emperor, were to make war on Austria?'

"I blushed, because I sensed that it was the wrong thing to say, but I replied: 'I love nothing as much as my godmother.'

"A few days after that, Marie-Louise gave the world a son, the King of Rome. She said to me in German: 'If he needs you, Friedrich, you shall be for him what I have been for you.'

"At the end of 1812, I left France for my years at University. My brothers were in Prague and had a summer residence in Reichstadt, a former family estate that had become an imperial possession by negotiation. In the Schloss of Reichstadt itself, the Emperor had installed a guardian for six young noblewomen. Among them was my young cousin O'Brien, aged 15 years, who had been placed there after her mother's death. I saw her, and I fell in love with her..."

Count Friedrich lowered his voice as he pronounced these last words, and his handsome head, whose pallor was now disappearing into darkness, was inclined over his breast. This story was very distant from the thoughts that held the former Superintendent's attention captive, but his intention remained violently excited nevertheless. He would not have been able to define the connection between this depiction of a noble and happy infancy and the terrible and mysterious events that clustered around him like a palisade of dire enigmas, but he sensed that there was a connection and a vivid sentiment of sympathy for the narrator awoke in his heart involuntarily.

"Not in the way that I love her today," the other went on, his voice suddenly tremulous in his constricted throat, "for a charming and blessed smile cannot resemble the convulsions of the death-agony. I loved her as one breathes in a perfume or contemplates the roseate horizon where the Sun is about to rise. I was 16 years old: I had fled France because my godmother had not realized that I was more than a child and that I was fearful of her caresses.

"I was grown up. I was said to be very handsome. I did not know the meaning of the word suffering. I was happy, joyful, full of magnificent hopes that made my future the most beautiful of poems...

"I loved as one loves in happiness, when one has the whole of a long life in which to make love. My love was so gentle and beautiful that, in contemplating my soul in mourning, I cannot help repeating my name, saying: 'Am I the same man?'

"For I love in tears now, and in suffering. I love with a heart that bleeds. I love with my poor soul in mourning. I have a great deal of anguish and very little hope. Every hour that passes bears away a little of my confidence; every day that passes removes a shred of my faith. I conserve the little breath the remains in my breast. I force myself to live, although I can sense myself dying, in order to have the time to find her again and perhaps to hear her say to me: 'I love you!'

"It seems to me that she must love me. It seems to me that it is my destiny to yield my last sigh within her arms, for I love her a hundred times more, now that I suffer–oh, a thousand times more! And if I were to be loved, if only for an hour, I would put that ultimate hour, during which I would live the whole of a felicitous life, above the hope of my eternal salvation!"

Count Friedrich paused again, because his exhausted breath was stranded within his breast.

Temple took his hand and squeezed it between his own, saying to him with feeling: "I was mistaken about you: I beg your pardon, Count." For the Englishman and the German are similar and sympathetic, in that they are both exceedingly fond of reveling sensuously in mourning and dead love affairs.

But it was not a cold passion, as constructed by the funereal poets of the German lyre, that interrupted the breath of this child. It was the kind of grand passion that resuscitates or kills, a virile but wholly young love as flexible and strong as a steel chain.

"They always went out together," he continued, as if his memory were drawing him along in spite of himself, "the guardian's six young women, escorted by two noble governesses, followed at a distance by two equerries in the Emperor's livery. Instinct guided me to whichever part of that immense park, full of marvelous solitudes, my path might cross with theirs. How many times have I seen her running madly about, frightening the wild deer in the glades? She did not resemble her companions. In the midst of those blonde girls whose plaits fell upon their shoulders, her bold and joyful face stood out beneath her crown of black curls. She was beautiful, happy, full of laughter...

"I often remained hidden in the woods, more timid than the deer that fled, even though I defended my post in peril of my life. I saw her through leaves swayed by the wind blowing from the mountains. Sometimes she was pensive, and I said to myself: 'She is dreaming about me!'

"She smiled at me, one morning when the sunlight played upon the dew. That moment remains vivid for me. I can see the shafts of light penetrating the shade of the wood, I can hear the distant fountain, I can breathe the odor of moist foliage. She is passing by, her arm around the neck of her best friend among her companions, half-turning to favor me with that rapid glance and that golden smile...

"But this is not a love story. I came to Prague to pursue my studies at the university. I did not see her any more. General O'Brien gave parties, and I received several invitations. My older brothers forbade me to go there. They were good to me, and we loved one another tenderly.

"One Sunday evening, at the Cathedral, by the light of the 24 gold and silver lamps that illuminate the monument of Saint John of Nepomuk,[191] I saw the graceful form of a young girl kneeling beside the white uniform of the General. My heart beat faster; I had recognized that black crown of fine and abundant hair where all the kisses of my dreams came to rest. It was the Commemoration; after the mass the faithful made their way to the Wenceslas Chapel, whose walls were made of precious stones, for Prague is one of the richest and most magnificent cities in the universe. Everyone knelt before the saint's tomb, on which are set his helmet and coat of arms; everyone touched the iron ring that his dying hand clasped when his brother struck him down from behind; everyone made the sign of the cross in front of the tableau by Lucas Cranach representing that fratricidal tragedy. I had taken a place close to the basin of holy water, fixed between two unpolished amethysts worth as much as the treasures of a crown, and I waited to present the holy water to the Emperor's ward. A man set himself before me and prevented me from so doing. She smiled at him. I could not see his face, but jealousy mounted within me, greater in proportion and more heroic than that of a King in some chivalric romance.

"He went out with O'Brien and his daughter. All three of them got into the same carriage, to descend from Hradschin to Kleinseite, where the General had his summer residence. I followed easily enough, for horses cannot travel at speed in the Spornergasse because of the steep slope. I can't tell you what I was thinking, but, for the first time, I felt in my breast and my heart the profound anguish that now accompanies my every breath.

"She had only come for one day.

"In the vacation, I returned to Reichstadt. She had grown. I could still distinguish her bursts of joyful laughter amid the tranquil chatter of her companions, but she was more often pensive. I searched for her smile in vain. She recognized me, however, for her eyes avoided mine, whose mute sadness she dreaded as a reproach.

"There was a lodge not far away for her guardian's castle, where I lived. One night, I was woken up by howling dogs. I jumped out of bed; hoofbeats and cries for help could be heard outside. One of His Imperial Majesty's wards had been abducted. I felt my lips become moist, and I lifted my hand to them, which came away stained with blood. No one had told me the name of the kidnapped ward, but I already knew by the shooting pains in my heart that it was Sarah O'Brien..."

"Sarah!" echoed the former Superintendent, shivering.

"The following morning," Count Friedrich continued, "Reichstadt learned about the General's murder. It was indeed Sarah who had been abducted. The search was utterly futile; her abductors could not be found.

"I had only the vaguest notion of the double judiciary investigation that followed the kidnapping and the General's assassination. Fever confined me to my bed. I had a long and painful illness; the doctors gave me up. Death has granted me a surcease, but I have never appealed against the doctors' sentence. I have never recovered the strength of my age and constitution. My wound is in the heart; my hours are numbered.

"When my health permitted me to return to Prague to resume my course at the University, I found the conduct of my brothers greatly changed. They had broken with their old pleasure-seeking habits. They were serious young men now, assiduously devoted to their studies. That assiduity presumably hid other preoccupations; my brothers were at the head of the Rosicrucian Brotherhood. The O'Brien affair was already unmentionable."

"Permit me to ask one question," the former Superintendent put in. "In the small amount that you were able to discover concerning that tragic event, was the name John Devil ever mentioned?"

"*Hans Teufel*," Friedrich replied, in German. "The common people attributed the death of the General to a mysterious and undiscoverable bandit of that name or nickname."

"And was there not," Temple then asked, "during your first sojourn at the university–I mean before the murder–a young man named Henry Brown among your brother's student friends?"

"No," replied Count Boehm, without hesitation.

"Nor a certain James Davy?"

"No."

"Was there, at least, some English student at the University of Prague?"

"There was George Palmer," Friedrich replied.

The former Superintendent smiled, and asked: "Do you know this George Palmer under another name?"

"Under several other names."

"Quite so!" Temple exclaimed, with an ironic gesture. Then, he went on: "I do not even have to ask you whether this George Palmer had disappeared from Prague when you returned after the murder."

"Mr. Temple," said the young Count, excitedly, "I beg you to take careful notice of the fact that you are speaking of my best friend, perhaps my only friend–the most noble heart and the highest intelligence that I have ever encountered in my life. After George Palmer received his doctorate, he and his mother returned to England."

"His mother!" repeated the former Superintendent, raising an eyebrow. "Do you know who his mother is?"

"Your present standpoint, Mr. Temple," Friedrich said, "is that of a man in possession of a deep-seated conviction that he has no wish to change. I warn you that you cannot judge Comte Henri de Belcamp. You are enemies, and your contest has taken place on a battleground other than the one on which we now find ourselves. His role has been to fight you, and to get the better of you on several occasions. I know that he has done so; you are not impartial with respect to him."

"Who are you, then?" cried Gregory Temple, whose hot blood always overcame prudence. "Who are you to speak coolly of such things and such men?"

"I am the last of an illustrious family on the brink of extinction," Friedrich replied, calmly. "I know what you do not. With my hand on my heart, if God took me at this very moment, I would die a Christian!"

"If you know what I do not, what good is there in coming so far to question me?"

"Because you might know something that I do not."

"Then continue, Count," said the former Superintendent, his brows furrowed. "You are very young to reject the experience of an old man–but after what I have deduced, we should not go our separate ways as yet, and I can swear an oath that you will be enlightened in spite of yourself."

"I refused to affiliate myself to the Rosicrucians," Friedrich continued, "until 1814, the year when my godmother, the Empress Marie-Louise, left France after Napoleon's abdication, and was confined at the Schoenbrunn residence with her son, the King of Rome. Before leaving Prague to go to her, I swore an oath on the rose and the cross. I was more dedicated to the daughter of Francis I than to Francis I himself, and the Rosicrucians, who had sworn mortal hatred to Napoleon the Emperor, were the natural allies of Napoleon the prisoner of Elba. There are bizarre games, in which the trumps often change color, as in whist.

"At Schoenbrunn, with the agreement of His Imperial and Royal Majesty, Marie-Louise chose me for her equerry. I heard no more talk of Sarah O'Brien. My love was not extinct, for I am one of those who never forget, but it was asleep and my life was entirely given over to my duties. A deputation of Rosicrucians, which included my two brothers, was now in Vienna. A dispatch service was established between ourselves and France. In Paris, Marie-Louise had once asked me to render to her son that which she had done for me; I began to pay my debt..."

"Is it permissible for me to ask, Count," Temple interrupted again, not without manifest sarcastic intent, "whether you had any news of your friend Percy Balcomb at this time?"

"Certainly, sir," Friedrich replied, gravely. "I was about to mention him. English justice commits strange errors–some of which, it's said, are willful. If you look into your heart and take the trouble to recall the events of this very day, you will not contradict me."

Temple looked at him, stupefied.

"At that time," Count Boehm continued, "English justice, confusing Percy Balcomb with the vilest of criminals, sent him to Australia, from which he returned–for the ways of Providence are profound–with the idea that he could crush England and change the face of the world. I shall say no more, Mr. Temple, because it is possible that at this moment you are still against us... but human patience has its limits, whereas brutal insolence has none, when it is sure of its impunity. Who knows whether you will be with us tomorrow?"

The former Police Superintendent remained silent.

"In 1815," Friedrich Boehm went on, "towards the end of March, we received–almost simultaneously–the news of the disembarkation at Cannes and the order to make all preparations for the release of the King of Rome and the Empress. Marie-Louise then bore the official title of Princess of Parma, of whose sovereignty Francis I was assured, but she had protested and called herself Duchess of Colorno. Her ladies-in-waiting, Mesdames de Menneval, de Brignoles, de Beausset and de Karaksai, crowned her that evening, giving her the title Empress.

"The Duke of Wellington was in Vienna. Under the pretext of his impending departure and for the pretended service of following him, my brothers and I retained all the post-horses for 25 leagues around Vienna; once the first relay station had been reached, it would have been impossible to pursue the illustrious fugitives. Night fell. Apart from Marie-Louise's faithful followers, there were 150 Rosicrucians, armed to the teeth, in the woods on the other side of the Gloriette.[192] At 10 p.m., I came to announce that the carriages were ready at the far end of the hedges, and I took the little King of Rome in my arms.

"As the women were going down the stone steps on the edge of the park, and as Marie-Louise appeared at the door on the arm of her senior equerry, military commands rang out from the groves situated to the right and the left of the hill that climbed to the Gloriette. In a trice, the lawn was white with uniforms.

"Black men, coming out of the castle itself by the lateral doors, surrounded us. Onslow, the subdirector of the Imperial Police, with his hat in his hand, invited the Princess of Parma to go back to her apartments. We had been betrayed.

"Marie-Louise left Schoenbrunn that same evening, never to return. The Chancellery in Vienna was assigned to her as a residence, and she was separated henceforth from her son. For my part, I remained with the young Prince, and when the Emperor had him made Duke of Reichstadt this year, with the rank of Colonel in the Austrian army, I received my Lieutenant-Colonel's brevet.

"I love Emperor Francis of Austria; for the Emperor Napoleon, I have nothing but the respect due to glory and misfortune. You are English, Mr. Temple, but you will nevertheless admit that the true sentiment pushing forward a whole army of young and generous hearts is the horror inspired by the egoism and treason of England...

"At the end of 1816, Count Albrecht Boehm was killed in a duel by Captain Baumgarten of the Imperial and Royal Artillery. Two months later, as he left for the city Ofen, to which he had been ordered by the Viceroy of Hungary, Count Reiner was stabbed on the boat-bridge between Buda and Pest by a jealous magyar who took him for his wife's lover. It is known to me that the magyar

Kerolvi and Captain Baumgarten are affiliates of the Sword Bearers. Reiner was in Pest to organize a league or offshoot of the Rosicrucians.

"I arrived the morning after the 'accident' to hear his last words. He told me his secrets and died in my arms.

"Those who knew all three of us would never have believed that I would be the last one living. My brothers were as strong and bold as two lions; I have only my family's courage.

"Reiner was supposed to come to London in January of the present year, 1817; I came in his place, and to accomplish one of his last wishes. Comte Henri de Belcamp was waiting for me under London Bridge when I arrived on the packet-boat. On disembarking, without taking the time to change my clothes, I got into a carriage that took me to Regent Street, to Constance Bartolozzi's house, where the Council of the Deliverance was assembled. I was received as a companion on the introduction of Comte Henri de Belcamp, and I took the oath. My name within the brotherhood was Pierre-Alexis Orloff, in order to put the surveillance of Austrian agents off the track.

"What was decided in Constance Bartolozzi's home, at that session and others, cannot be revealed to you. Outside the meetings, la Bartolozzi hosted social receptions and card games. One evening, I found myself there in the presence of Sarah O'Brien, and was informed that she was her paid companion. I often spend long hours asking myself whether Sarah recognized me. Her gaze fixed itself upon me several times. I went towards her, but my voice caught in my throat. I was carried out in a faint.

"A poor history, is it not, sir? Prolonged childhood and puerile timidity, which would doubtless merit a change of name...

"I do not know what happened to me. I thought I was dying. My love was so much stronger than my heart's capacity at that moment that it made my voice tremble and moistened my brow like an exhausting effort. Sarah seemed to me to be a thousand times more beautiful than before. She was a woman, and yet her eyes swam in that diamantine water that marriage, it's said, dries up. She had the wild pride and smiling capriciousness of a girl.

"Sarah was nothing but a girl, with her queenly bearing and her dazzling diadem of beauty.

"I wanted to know, I wanted to speak, I wanted to kneel at her feet in allegiance; I dared not. Happiness, dread and hope clasped my poor sick heart at the same time. I was paralyzed; I sometimes wish that I had died.

"What combination of circumstances had brought her down to that condition? She had been 15 years old when she left Prague, and could not have been ignorant of her birthright. The mystery remains unsolved; none of my questions has been answered; the lost opportunity could not be recovered.

"Sarah O'Brien had another name now, which was also Irish. In Madame Bartolozzi's house, she called herself Sarah O'Neil."

"I could have told you that, Count," Temple murmured.

"So much the better if you have known it long enough to satisfy me," said Friedrich, whose fatigue was now visible. "If only I can learn from you all that I have such a great need to know! But let me continue. A few months more and I shall have finished.

"On February 1, I was summoned to a meeting by the usual formula–not to Madame Bartolozzi's house, which surprised me, but to the very drawing room that I occupy here, at Mivart's Hotel. I had not left my room since I had seen Sarah; I had not given any authorization. I went.

"At 11 p.m., seven members were present. One of them accused Signora Bartolozzi of treason and offered proof that was only too clear, in the form of two letters from that unfortunate woman addressed to you, sir, which had been intercepted in your own office. Seven voices unanimously condemned her to death, and the execution was fixed for the following night.

"The following day, I withdrew a considerable sum from my bank and I hired a post-chaise. I intended to remove Madame Bartolozzi and take her to Dover, where I would embark on the ferry to Calais. I would have persuaded her to obey me rather than use force. I intended to explain myself to Sarah and offer her my hand. In the event of her refusal, I wanted to give her the whole of her mother's fortune.

"There is no need to tell you that; in London, more than anywhere else, money is master. Nothing resists money. Before my talisman, the doors of Madame Bartolozzi's house opened and the servants deserted their posts. At 2 a.m., I was alone in that abandoned residence–even more alone than I thought, alas, since one of the two women of whom I had come in search was absent, and the other was dead–killed in her bed, doubtless while sleeping, in the same manner that O'Brien had died, according to my brothers' accounts; dead with her arms quite relaxed, her mouth tranquil, her eyes closed, her jewels beside her.

"I left London the next morning, partly to flee the theater of that tragedy, partly in obedience to an order of recall from Prince Metternich. In Vienna where I resumed my service with the King of Rome, the firm of Balcomb & Co., by the order of the former solicitor Mr. Wood..."

"One of the most dangerous rogues in the three Kingdoms," observed Temple.

"I know that, sir; it is the misfortune of those who work in the shadows not always to have a choice in the matter of their agents. In Vienna, as I said, the firm of Balcomb & Co. sent me three demands for money. I had to pay; I paid."

"You had to?" Temple repeated, looking at him inquisitorially in spite of the near-complete obscurity.

"Not in the way you think, sir," the young Count replied. "If you had listened to me with the same good faith with which I am speaking... but I did have to; I had promised, in full awareness of the cause."

"In the letter that Your Lordship did me the honor of writing to me," the former Police Superintendent objected, "I found a copy of a missive addressed to Mr. Wood, containing a statement of sums paid to the firm of Balcomb & Co. since the first of January. That missive told an entirely different story from the one you are telling me now, Your Lordship."

"That missive had an objective that you will know soon enough. My intention is to hide nothing from you. I honored those first three demands for money, and my banker in Vienna denounced me to the Emperor. Francis ordered me to Hofburg. On his desk, he had a letter to the Governor of the fortress at Spandau. 'You are the last of an illustrious and loyal family,' he said to me. 'Your father was my friend. In the hands of a child like you, wealth like yours is endangered. You are mixed up in certain schemes; I forgive you, because I love my daughter, the Archduchess of Parma. My Council wishes to make you a State prisoner, but you shall not go to Spandau if you will consent freely to guardianship.' I agreed without hesitation and, taking advantage of the threat of imminent death written all too clearly in my features, I obtained His Majesty's permission to travel in Italy, France and England. In giving me leave, the Emperor, speaking in a low voice with concern in his face, made a brief allusion to my brothers' fate and recommended that I be prudent.

"My three traveling-companions were selected by the Council from among the family servants who could offer the most guarantees to the Court. We departed; a Prince's allowance had been allocated to me. I knew, in addition, that in Paris as in London, I would find bold speculators perfectly ready to overlook my minority in return for a fat commission. Scarcely had I arrived in France when I received a demand for 380,000 florins, which I was able to meet immediately..."

"Close to a million!" Temple murmured.

"I intended to press on to London immediately, but an incident held me up. On the morning of my arrival, I wanted to visit the garden of the Colisée. I was in the crowd, wondering at the fashionability of the bizarre diversion named the Russian Mountains, when I saw Sarah's beauty glide in front of me like a dream, carried down the slope at a hectic pace. I threw myself forward, but the crowd held me back, and when I reached the place where the travelers got out of the sleighs, Sarah and her escort had disappeared.

"She was in Paris. I remained for several weeks, moving Heaven and Earth to find her. All my efforts were in vain. At the beginning of June, only a few days ago, I was coming back from a horseback ride in the woods when I saw a well-dressed woman getting into a carriage at the end of the road, having just left my hotel. I was struck by her figure. The carriage passed me shortly afterwards, and I recognized Sarah O'Brien through the window of the carriage-door. I was on horseback, and I dug in my spurs: she would not escape me this time!

"After 50 yards, police sergeants barred my way. It is forbidden to gallop in the streets of Paris. The discussion only lasted for a few seconds, but when it was over, Sarah's carriage was out of sight.

"At my hotel, I found a fifth demand for money. The sum requested was in excess of a million. I had to pay, and would have done so this time as before, but I learned that the letter had been delivered by a young woman, elegant and charming, whose description exactly matched Sarah's. My mind, ceaselessly applied to the task of finding Sarah again, set to work. I had heard talk of you, and Mr. Wood had been indicated to me as the agent with whom I should communicate should the need arise. I wrote the two letters to Mr. Wood and to you–that is the explanation I promised you a little while ago. My refusal was nothing but a stratagem. It seemed certain to me that by means of this maneuver, whether through you or through Mr. Wood, I would be sure to find Sarah. That is all that I have to say."

The young Count Boehm stopped speaking.

Temple reflected for a moment. "Your principal aim, then," he murmured, without bothering to conceal his disdainful bitterness, "or, rather, your only aim, is to find this woman?"

"I love her," Friedrich whispered.

"And in consequence, apparently, you will not willingly listen to anything said against her?"

"I love her," the young Count repeated, with concentrated force. "I must live in happiness or die of joy!"

"Pain also kills," Temple could not help saying. Then, after a pause, he recovered the precise and firm voice that is familiar to us from the time when he was enthroned in his office at Scotland Yard. "You are 20 years old, Count," he said. "At that age, illusions are tenacious. While I was listening to you, a world of ideas occurred to me, some of which are extravagant–when dealing with a man like John Devil, it is sometimes necessary to seek wisdom in extravagance. It is I who has shaped him... please don't interrupt; I shall be clear and concise... It is I who has shaped him, I repeat, without wishing to and without knowing it: I know the roads that his mind travels. People like him always display to people like you, in the more-or-less hazy distance, some immense edifice under construction, saying: 'Here is my work; I am a great architect!' Crush England and change the face of the world, you said. That's all very well, it seems to me–but what rock is heavy enough, no matter what high summit it might be detached, to crush England, against which your Napoleon was broken? England lives and grows while her enemy is dying, pecked by the vultures of his impotent anger. And the world goes on its way, ignoring the role that charlatans make him play in their waking dreams!

"Enough of all that. I'm neither young enough nor poet enough to dispute the political theories of Punch or John Devil. You have put the question at the very top of some fantastic scale, but for me it is the very bottom; we do not understand one another. What is real are the millions that have been extorted from you. I would support that point if you were anyone else, but what good would it do with you? It's only a single drop in the vast reservoir of your wealth. I could

give you definite information about the man himself, but I would undoubtedly
be too late today. You have been forewarned, and if I were to tell you that your
Comte Henri was a dishonest employee of my Police, you would doubtless still
reply to me: 'I knew that.' "

"It is true; I knew that," Friedrich replied.

"All the better! Then, you don't have to search for the name of the man
who intercepted the unfortunate Constance Bartolozzi's letters–nor even, perhaps, the key to that funereal enigma. But I want to stick to one single order of
notions and confine myself to one single fact. I understand obsessions; I have
mine as you have yours. I know where Sarah O'Brien is, and I shall tell you."

"The price of such a service..." said the young Count, seizing his hands.

Temple withdrew from the gesture, which remained incomplete. "Count,"
he said, in a proud and sad tone, "I used to be rich... not like you, but enough to
live through a tranquil old age and to give independence to my only child. I am
now a beggar, for I have eaten up everything, including my daughter's bread. I
shall accept payment, and it will be an exacting one, but the money is not for
me, nor will it be for my beloved daughter. It will be for my justice–mine, for I
too am henceforth a Fehmic Judge. It will be for my vengeance!"

"You may name your own sum, sir."

"I have finished, save for one last word. In every market, it is necessary to
know what one is buying. It was John Devil–or George Palmer, or Comte Henri
de Belcamp, or, if you like it better, the proprietor of the firm of Balcomb &
Co.–who abducted Sarah O'Brien from the schloss of her guardian at Reichstadt. Comte Henri de Belcamp has been playing with you while he has been
plundering you. The mistresses of bandits are almost as famous as their heroes.
Sarah O'Neil is the Irish Beauty, the mistress of John Devil the Quaker."

"Do you have proof of that, sir?" said the young German, in a voice that
was scarcely intelligible.

"I will provide it, I promise you that, if you wish to follow me to Paris."

Friedrich Boehm rang for a servant and ordered torches to be brought in.
The light arrived, illuminating the mortal pallor of his handsome features and his
large eyes, to which slow fever lent a sinister gleam. "Have someone fetch Herr
Spiegel, Herr Arnheim and Herr Weber," he ordered. Then, turning to Temple,
he asked: "Would it suit you if we left for Paris [193] tonight?"

"First, I would like to know exactly who these gentlemen are?" the former
Superintendent asked.

"Three conspirators like me," the young Count replied.

The three doctors came back in with their pipes and their solid German
faces, resplendent with health.

"We leave for Paris in an hour," Friedrich told them. "Mr. Temple is
coming with us."

"Who will be accompanying mein herr?" asked Dr. Spiegel, who had to
make the preparations.

"Just one man," Temple said. "A Frenchman named Pierre Louchet." He got up in order to go and fetch his luggage.

Count Boehm, leaning on his arm, accompanied Temple as far as the door. As they arrived there, he took his white handkerchief–which was stained with blood–away from his mouth, and said in a glacial voice: "I'll be waiting for you, sir. If Sarah O'Brien is the mistress of Henri de Belcamp, I swear to you that I shall kill him!"

VIII. Versailles

The Russians build fairy palaces with the ice of the Neva, decorated with statues formed from blocks of rime. They give parties within–which, it is said, are splendid. My jaws are locked and I feel a frisson filling my veins at the mere thought of such Hyperborean fantasies. In a December dream, I saw quadrilles of semi-naked women, frozen solid, with diamond necklaces and flowers in their hair: everything frozen–beauty, love, light! The sounds of the orchestra froze in the vibrationless air, and I can still see the terrible broadening of those immobile smiles.

We have something similar here: Versailles, too, has fallen into icy splendor, frozen and dazzling. It is like another world, inhabited by marble statues, bored by the sight of monstrous yew-trees clipped into pyramids. There is nothing living there, save for those greenish waters whose every drop is worth as much as a glass of wine. That chateau freezes the Sun's rays! Those flowerbeds in mourning only lack mausolea. When the breeze stirs the foliage of those trees, one hears the noise of crumpling paper.

At the time when the German poet [194] saw the great fantastic parade on the Champs-Elysées, under the light of a livid Moon, flattened against a sky of blue porphyry, another grand procession had slowly and silently to descend the Giants' stairway to reach the Swiss fountain, around which the King's coaches were waiting. Bourdaloue [195] has preached; debased Molière has fled with Tartuffe in his pocket; Ninon [196] is conspiring on the Devil's behalf; Lent is everywhere triumphant. The King comes down, weighed down by the burden that he has been carrying for 62 regnal years: ennui–the great ennui, the patron of measured festivals, regulated diversions, ordered tableaux, fabricated parks and windowed palaces. The King comes down, closing his ears to the last strains of the music played for him, and no longer wishing to see the mute flattery of all those statues: the King, indifferent to the pale verdure of those trees that were sickly when they were brought to him; the King, detesting the waters that have come so far to parody the murmur of streams in his ear; the King, enemy of the nature he wanted to surpass, and simultaneously weary of all impotent imitations; the King, discouraged; the King, dying of etiquette; the King, choked between a ball and a sermon; the King, exhausted, sad, miserable; the King, Louis XIV, the great King, King of Colbert, Condé, Vauban, Bossuet, Le Sueur and La Fontaine! Behind him is his Court, heart-broken by the same malady, the most brilliant Court in the world: Saint-Simon, Sévigné, Bussy, Racine, Lully, Lavallière and so many other stars, bathed in the light of that Sun!

They are coming down and passing by, the adorable women, the divine poets, the great men. The master is yawning; Racine is yawning, as is his enemy Sévigné; and Lully, who warmed up Quinault; and everyone else. The horses make their way around the water at a funereal pace. They arrive at the point of departure. The King yawns. All the giants climbing back up their stairway are yawning. The entire party was a yawn.

And what tact they had in that Augustan century! Is not Versailles the best place for yawning in the entire universe!

Scarcely anyone yawns nowadays. Those coagulated magnificences become bored all on their own, and it is only two or three times a year, "when the fountains are playing," that the Faubourgs of Paris deign to come and picnic on the grass.

Since the time of Louis XIV, however, Versailles has had one moment of life, a few good days, during which its slumber, tormented by the noises of barrack-rooms, had a brilliant and cheerful respite. That was in 1817, in the month of June–and it was Miremont that woke Versailles up! There were a few significant differences, we concede, between Miremontese society and the Court of the son of Anne of Austria, but these differences were not all to Miremont's disadvantage.

The Siamese Ambassador certainly could not have seemed funnier next to the naiads of Neptune's bowl or the goddesses of the grand pavement than the Bondon de la Perrière trio: one grey tartan between two brown frock-coats, promenading their idyll of conjugal happiness along the hedges. Madame Célestin, grazing her two sheep in the shady paths leading to the Trianons, peppered her conversation with useful information; when she let go of their arms, they collected round pebbles or a few wild flowers, which they composed into a bouquet. She was a serious woman, so pure of mind that she once asked Monsieur Potel, the more learned of the two Deputies, what the word "bigamy" meant.

The other Deputy's wife, Madame Morin du Reposoir, also came frequently, in the company of Madame Besnard or with Madame Touchard, who sometimes had private conversations with the prisoner that made her companions jealous. The Chaumerons and Mademoiselle were now a sort of Versaillaise family. The Marquis willingly supplied dinner to those who came to see his son, holding a table open at the Hotel de France. The Chaumerons loved the Hotel de France, and were always taking away a few souvenirs.

The Marquis was living at the Hotel de France, with almost all his household. Madame Etienne, save for the chagrin of eating food cooked by others, was plumped up like a fighting-cock. She had been to a hotel once before, with her former mistress, when the floorboards had been taken up in the house, but that was to the Hotel de Pontoise! Julot and Anille came and went in harness; Pierre made himself useful: it was a party.

For company, the Marquis usually had his two lovely darlings, as he called Jeanne and Germaine. They both had their own rooms in the hotel. Lady Frances Elphinstone and Suzanne came to visit Monsieur de Belcamp several times a week. Suzanne was the only one of them who was sad; we know the cause of her sadness, but we also know what consolation she had at the bottom of her heart. The Marquis was not at all hard on her. No one ever mentioned old Temple, who was naturally considered to be a madman.

One evening, in the Hotel de France, the Marquis was holding a reception. Well-placed townspeople had solicited the honor of being introduced to him and the old gentleman put a certain ostentation into displaying the perfect liberty of his spirit. It was there, while the Comte was held captive, that a development occurred that will certainly astonish our readers, but which is too close to the heart of our story for us to pass over in silence. We are referring to the betrothal of our lovely Jeanne, which took place under the united auspices of her aunt, Madame Touchard, and the Marquis de Belcamp.

The husband-to-be was not Comte Henri.

The clairvoyants of Miremont had noticed some symptoms of reciprocal inclination between Jeanne and Comte Henri during the latter's brief sojourn at the chateau, but since his imprisonment, appearances had changed. There was nothing on either side but a frank and fraternal amity–the proof of which was that Jeanne permitted, with apparent enthusiasm, another suitor to make his approaches.

This other suitor was not Robert Surrisy.

Most surprisingly of all, Robert Surrisy, sad but calm, seemed to greet this definitive permission with resignation.

Jeanne's fiancé–for things had reached the stage where we might give him that title–was a young Englishman whom we already know, although he has not yet been introduced to the reader. It was Comte Henri's friend, Percy Balcomb, the hero of the Australian adventure and the present director of the great London firm of Balcomb & Co. Comte Henri had announced his visit previously; as chance would have it, he had arrived the day after the imprisonment.

The singular resemblance of which the young Comte had spoken struck everyone at first glance. They were the same height and had the same bearing; the cut of their features was the same too, to the extent that from behind, one would have thought them the same man. Nevertheless, there was no need of a lilac, rose or blue ribbon to differentiate between the two friends. Percy Balcomb's hair and eyebrows were much darker and his eyelids more shadowy. He wore a moustache, in defiance of English custom, and when he spoke, his deep and serious voice was in complete contrast to Henri's–all of which rendered any mistake impossible.

He was in France on business, and often spent his days in Paris. He was well-connected, for he had obtained permission to see Henri in prison at an hour when the gates were firmly closed against all whose entry permits were personal, and the Marquis himself could not accompany him on these visits.

Percy Balcomb professed a chivalrous amity for Henri; this, together with his other pleasant qualities, had immediately won him the friendship of the little company. The Marquis, one might have said, loved his son in him.

It was easy to see, from the very first, that he and Jeanne liked one another. Balcomb might be a Knight, but this Knight was head of a business concern: things were managed briskly and commercially. Henri, in his prison, put the question to Madame Touchard in the presence of the Marquis. The reciprocal advantages were stipulated, and as Jeanne, on her emancipation, would come into possession of the Turner inheritance, the dowry was fixed at two millions, payable on signature of the contract. All inherited wealth comes back into the community.

That day, the Marquis said to Henri: "Son, if you had taken the lead, I know that she would have fallen in love with you."

Percy Balcomb, a slave to his business, had gone back to London. After several days of waiting, the contract was ready.

There was much celebration–the word is not too strong. Everyone was thinking about the wedding, whose pleasures were contemplated by all as if nothing had happened. It was a celebration for everyone; the people who had interested themselves in the Comte de Belcamp had not the shadow of any anxiety, and the sour party of Miremontese society still maintained some hope of a row. Both were content.

As for public opinion, it was not even divided. The Tribunal was roundly accused of absurdity for having judged that there was a case to answer. The double alibi leapt so forcefully to the eye of every strong mind in the place that those who had an opinion to express declared in advance that the Examining Magistrate would spend the rest of his life in the petty sessions. The magistrature itself, it must be said, had been inclined to suspend proceedings, not because its conviction had been overturned but because more time was required, in its view, to solve the mystery.

It was whispered–irrespective of its probability–that the Examining Magistrate had given way to a superior influence.

Prudent persons suspended judgment, saying that the key to these judiciary enigmas tend to emerge suddenly at the least expected moment.

In sum, there were two murders...

Three murders, the old Marquis said, for that infernal machination of the two passports taken out in his son's name was evidently an attempt at murder.

Henri had arrived at the Chateau de Belcamp incognito; he had come from the other side of the world, he had seen no one in Paris. The cruel and cowardly enemy who had set the trap doubtless believed that he was still in a foreign country, where Henri might have had great difficulty establishing his presence at the time of the murder. But Providence had determined that things would be different. An entire community, with its Mayor at its head, would testify at the Assize Court. The Marquis had thought it his duty to address a signed letter to the Examining Magistrate to thank him for his decision. It was necessary that the question should be investigated at the highest level!

But it was in the prison itself that one could see the point at which the Administrators, at every level, regarded his conviction as impossible. It was not favors that were accorded to him; they were recognized as a kind of rights. In addition to his place of confinement,[197] two large and commodious workrooms had been arranged for him, which formed a veritable apartment. One of them served as his drawing-room. There, he received, in the full force of the term, a good and numerous company. Counselor Boisruel, of the Court of Paris, who had excused himself from presiding over the Assizes by virtue of his kinship, often came to see him, and did not hide the fact that he regarded him as one of the superior men of his epoch. Important individuals had wanted to be introduced to him, and the four Dukes—who would perhaps have left him in peace at the chateau—came to visit him in prison with their four Duchesses. The Faubourg Saint-Germain was now asserting its rights.

The newspapers, whose circulation was admittedly small in those days, but which printed nearly everything that passed through their editors' heads, attributed very diverse and exceedingly contradictory biographies to him. All of them were interesting; all of them were devoured by a public avid for sensation. For a long time, nothing outside of war and politics had excited similar attention; the general curiosity became feverish, and the trial promised to be a cause célèbre of the highest degree.

Outside of politics, we said—and the comment is well-judged. However, in those epochs of sharply-divided opinions, so close to revolutions,[198] who and what could be completely devoid of political significance? The biographies of Comte Henri de Belcamp—a labor of Penelope that was continually done and undone; a thousand-chapter novel into which every day imported its contingent of dramatic and marvelous facts [199]—could be divided into two distinct classes: the Royalist biographies and the Bonapartist biographies. No one can say whence the authors of these epics drew forth their contrary data, but it is certain that there were a good number of facts to be found in the midst of a great quantity of fables. Comte Henri's entire life was in there, in pieces, but it would have needed a historian to get to the bottom of it all. Some of them concentrated on his status as the son of an émigré and put forward the fact that he had brought back from abroad all his University achievements: doctorates from Edinburgh, Cambridge, Prague, Jena, etc. But he had not wanted to come back across the French border until true principles had triumphed. The others took advantage of his voyage to Australia, suitably amended and transfigured, in order to recount his visit to the Emperor. All of them, however, spoke vaguely of grand ideas and an immense future. What lay beneath these reticences could be interpreted according to the passion of each individual, for everyone thought what he wished, and nothing more. Contemporary history always has two versions, one white and one black, which are printed concurrently, and which simultaneously accuse one another of lying.

Comte Henri smiled at the renown of this romantic hero with a calm disdain at which others marveled. He put no affectation into the display of his profound indifference to the subject of all the noise that was being made around him. He did not even indicate whether he ever opened a newspaper.

His father read them for him; his father listened with indefatigable ecstasy to all the voices that talked about his beloved son. He was avid for fame, and literally intoxicated himself with the echoes of the concert. The visit of the Dukes, his kinsmen, had made him proud—he, who was so sincerely worthy; he, whose soul had such a serene hauteur. His adoration for Henri made him feminine; he had a heart as feeble and great as a mother. And who knows where his ambitions ventured now? Did he regret the loss of Jeanne, or was he still thinking of Germaine for his son, who was now a hero? Was he even dreaming of Lady Frances Elphinstone? What Princess was too highly-placed for Henri? His triumphant attitude was sometimes so naive and so complete that Miremontese society—impatient, jealous, weary of admiration—thought about ostracism, although it had read little of Athenian history. There were times when the heroic Comte Henri would have been condemned to death—simply in order to enrage the Mayor—had Miremont been the jury.

It was a warm and stormy summer day. Midday had sounded on the clock in the palace, whose rectangular profile was cut out in mat white against a leaden sky. Not a breath of wind stirred the water in the bowls where the bronze groups, disfigured by their useless pipes, were sleeping like "resting" actors, who could now only don their spear-carriers' spangles at long intervals.

A few provincials looked at the facade, as celebrated as the Opera's famous bow-stroke [200] and delivered historical dissertations, abundantly sprinkled with anachronisms. The palace no longer contained all the glories of France, as if serving as signboard and libretto at the same time, but travelers loved to see the yew-trees. Along the ramps, maidservants and soldiers were neglecting their children; under the first trees of the Avenue du Tapis-Vert, a dozen old ladies and a seller of bread-rolls were dozing.

On the *tapis vert* itself, a livelier spectacle offered itself to six gawkers scattered about the path. I challenge you to go to Versailles without seeing something similar; in the depths of all grief, there is always a tiny grain of gaiety. All the gaiety of Versailles is in that long square of scurvy grass, bordered by handsome trees and statues, which extends from Leto's flowerbed to Apollo's fountain. For hundreds of years, the gods and goddesses of myth, backed by hedges, have had no other recreation. There were three of them: two fat men and one thin woman. The two fat men, wearing blindfolds like Cupids, were groping their way around the square, trying not to step off the grass; the thin woman was knitting a stocking while watching them. The Bondon garniture! Simple souls, such were their pleasures. The twins had been coming here every day at the same time since the event. They each bet a five *sou* coin against their lady; they always lost, and were astonished that they made no progress.

This sojourn in the capital of Seine-et-Oise was not entirely without danger for the bachelor Florian, the fires of whose passionate nature had not been completely extinguished by an excessively stormy youth. He very often looked with a dishonorably-intentioned eye at some strong Norman wench who had designs on a soldier–but Madame Célestin would drag him away by the lilac armband and Florian would guiltily conceal the licentiousness of his thought beneath an obedient smile. Célestin was made of marble, like *Achilles Beneath the Cloak of Pyrrha* hewn by the chisel of Vigier.[201]

These two symmetrical vegetations were becoming familiar in the town of Versailles. In the hotels, foreigners were advised to look out for these curiosities, as temporary additions to those of the park. When families stopped to look at them, they let themselves be viewed complacently; the English were given permission to touch them.

The park's pathways were even more deserted than usual today, because of the threatening weather. Silence reigned beneath all the noble arches of the lateral avenues and the entire population of mythological figures flexing their muscles of stone as they posed in the bushes were showing off in vain. Around the groups, whose youth had heard so many noises and seen so many smiles, there was only the aging wood, defended by worm-eaten trellises, damp and sad retreats where bold satyrs no longer pursued authentic nymphs.

Not far from the grove of the colonnade, around the admirable garden that had been designed the preceding year to remind Louis XVIII of his flourishing Hartwell lawns,[202] the labyrinth extended its ultimate hedges. Two young people were there, walking slowly beneath the immobile foliage. The elegant and charming young woman was not leaning on her cavalier's arm. Her hands were clasped on the light fabric of her dress, and her veiled face was sadly inclined. They were not talking. They were walking some distance apart. They had been talking, though, for the young man was watching two tears rolling down his companion's veiled cheeks with melancholy tenderness.

It was Robert Surrisy with Lady Frances Elphinstone. They had indeed been talking, and their conversation had already lasted a long time. Lady Elphinstone was the first to halt, in front of a marble bench where the shade of hornbeams protected beads of dew.

"I'm tired," she murmured, in a husky voice, "Tired and feeble."

"Let's sit down, my sister," Robert replied.

She shuddered at that word and turned away, as if she wanted to hide a sudden rush of emotion.

Robert sat next to her on the bench.

"For me, Frances," he said, after a silence, "the moment when I learned that I was your brother was one of the most beautiful moments of my life. I loved you already; now that I see in you the daughter of my brave and unfortunate father, my affection is increased, and I have set you in my heart next to my mother."

Sarah offered him her hand; it was cold. There were no more tears in the corners of her weary eyelids.

"Aren't you happy too, Frances?" Surrisy murmured.

"Yes, Robert, very happy," she whispered. Then, collecting herself, in a voice that was tearful again, she said: "Oh, of course, of course I'm happy. The first time I heard your name, my heart beat faster, as if some cherished memory had awakened in me. The first time I saw you, my entire being was drawn towards you. Among all those young men on the packet-boat, my eyes followed you as if you were... my brother, indeed, Robert... and when you said, as you lifted your glass, 'my name wants to say smile, I am Robert Surrisy,' I don't know what childish enthusiasm lifted my heart..."

"Childish, my dear Frances, it's true," Robert said, with some confusion. "That pedantic refrain came to me at school..."

"The mere hazard could have been a premonition, Robert," Sarah sighed, "that your life would be full of good fortune!"

Surrisy sighed in his turn, and his masculine cheek had a hint of pallor. "I trust so," he thought, aloud. "I'm a soldier; my fortune is at the point of my sword." Since the first time we encountered him at the Croix Moraine, however, his face had changed. One would search in vain for the valiant traces of the joyous insouciance of youth. There were dark circles around his eyes.

"You are suffering too," murmured his companion. "You too have a broken love in your heart?"

Robert turned anxious eyes towards her. "Me too?" he repeated.

Frances blushed from the collar of her dress to her beautiful black hair, while her agitated breath suddenly made her bosom heave.

"I'm happy," she said, tremulously, "very happy to call you my brother."

The young soldier lowered his eyes. Lady Frances continued, in a former tone. "I'm telling the truth, Robert; we Irishwomen, it's said, have the hearts of children. Why should I not tell you that? I didn't expect to find a brother in you, and yet I loved you. I was attracted towards you by an affection that it was impossible for me to define. I had hope for you, I counted on you, I searched for you as one hunts the cure for one's suffering. Now that I know our collective and melancholy history, now that I can carry light into the depths of my soul, all that was obscure in me is bright... I went towards you as one pleading for refuge..."

"A refuge, Frances? From what?"

"From myself," the young woman replied, in a whisper.

"You're in love, then, my sister?" Robert asked, while his clouded features cleared.

"I don't know what to say," the young woman murmured, hesitantly. "My heart has already deceived me twice."

"You're in love, Frances!" Surrisy exclaimed, joyfully. "I know it—you're in love!"

Sarah went pale, and lowered her eyes. "I'm afraid of love," she said, in a low voice. "Every time that a barrier is raised up between me and the dreams that I forge as I please, every time that the roads where my thoughts flee are suddenly closed, I see that my destiny is there... and I am afraid of love."

"Is it *him*?" Robert asked, in a strange tone, in which there might have been affection or hatred, although no one could have said which.

"No," Sarah replied. "He too was, for me, a deceptive hope. I told you that I was in search of a refuge... there was a time when I hoped that I might love him."

"Did he ever love you?"

"I don't know. My own affection was not even that which one has for a brother. I admired him and I respected him..."

"So young, so handsome...!" murmured Surrisy, whose tone was dubious.

"But so great!" Sarah said, emphatically.

There was a silence that was not even troubled by exterior noises. Nothing echoed in the pathways: no breath of wind stirred the leaves; no drop of water fell from any of the marble lips in the dead fountains, whose pools were immobile mirrors reflecting immobility

"Frances," Surrisy went on, hesitantly, "was that other love from which you wished to flee so very redoubtable?"

"Was it love?" said Sarah, pensively.

"You were a child when you left Prague."

"Yes, I was a child; I was 15."

"It seems that you're reluctant to open your heart to me," Robert said, reproachfully.

"My brother," the young woman said, her voice recovering its firmness, "there is nothing on my conscience, and I cannot make a confession, because I don't know... if that's love... if that's destiny... I think that I'm dying of it, my brother, for fate has set blood between him and me!"

"In the name of Heaven, speak!" cried Surrisy.

"I shall speak," Sarah replied, throwing back her veil to display her beautiful face, pale but calm. "It is, indeed, necessary that you should listen to my story, in order to know my whole life as I know yours, so generous, so devoted, so beautiful...!

"It was the year before my mother died. We left the Trieste countryside to come to Prague, where General O'Brien, our father, had a military command. My mother was ill and sad; our father had a good heart, but he was an Irishman of light character, who avoided everything that wasn't cheerful. Perhaps I'm made the same way, for my mother often reproached me with a strange bitterness for having nothing German in me; she called me the Irishwoman... In contrast, I had nothing from the General but hugs and kisses. Do I need to tell you that I loved my poor mother anyway, with all my heart? Many times, in spite of my age, I undertook to inspire in my father the need for a wiser life. He listened to me, smiled at me, embraced me–and he ran away to look outside for the joy that was absent from the house, whose sad atmosphere was stifling him.

"My mother loved him passionately. She had no idea what to do to retain her unsteady husband on the threshold of the conjugal home. She wept and she pleaded. Perhaps she had a heart more elevated and more profound than our father's. She knew that she was dying.

"Our father loved her and feared for her. He fled after dinner, like a child throwing himself into the playground.

"As regards me, my mother was absolutely right. Although born in Austria, and in spite of the Austrian blood that ran in my veins, I was a little Irish girl, cheerful, foolish, talkative, incapable of understanding the unhappiness of my stay-at-home mother. In her place, I told myself, I would have known how to shake off sadness. I had said that to myself already, but when I once said it to her, she chased me away indignantly.

"Everything Irish delighted me, and I was disdainful of Germany. Our father, slave to my fantasy, had sent for a Connaught peasant's costume. I went out into the fields with my striped skirt and my red mantle. My mother was very annoyed, as if it were a serious fault. She sometimes tried to tell me the doleful and mysterious legends of German poetry. I shivered or I jeered. I had an innate dislike for that fastidious nonsense, full of rattling bones, tombs that opened and the walking dead. German ballads all come out of the cemetery; they're the gossip of grave-diggers. Give me the lovely stories that our father's Irish nurse, old Ellen, told me! Giants battling in the fog, the loves of the daughters of the sea, the faeries of Fingal's Cave who went a hundred leagues under the sea, the isle of pearls and the legend of Finbar, the saint with white hair... I could have spent my life listening to the naive and dear imaginings of the child-people. I was Irish, not German, since–to cap it all–I loved France and the French.

"When my poor mother died, following a long illness, I was not yet 14. Our father was then one of the generals most in favor at the Court. The Emperor sent him a warrant that placed me among the wards of the Imperial and Royal Schloss at Reichstadt, an honor solely reserved for orphans of the greatest houses of Bohemia. I left the General reluctantly, carrying away the conviction that he was already thinking of remarrying. I did not know all his secrets, though; when I asked him about it, he began to treat me as he had treated my poor mother: he laughed, he joked, he sang. The catastrophe that put an end to his life overtook him before he could tell me anything. It was only from my mother, who was jealous of the memory, that I knew of the existence of another woman and a son born in England. It was you who told me, a little while ago, that at the moment of his death my father was on the point of doing justice to Madeleine Surrisy, your mother.

"He was an honorable man; was there something of the memory of former affection in his coldness towards my mother? He was an honorable man, although the story of his marriage seems to me to be a grave stain on a man's life. Ireland is a fallen nation; our great ancestors would not have wished that honor...

"You know as well as I do the name that the Marquis of Belcamp's son adopted in Germany. I had already been in tutelage for some months when I met George Palmer for the first time, while I was visiting my father. Young girls always have a profound regard for the first person who does not treat them as children. I had that regard for George Palmer, who was my father's friend and dining-companion... you're redoubling your attention, Robert. I don't know whether my story will satisfy your desire to know, but I can assure you, at least, that after having heard me out, you will know all that I know.

"There were three young men at the University of Prague, cousins of my mother, the Counts Boehm. Their father, Major-General Boehm, sometimes visited us in Istria when I was very small. The sons, dissolute wastrels, had already received several notices of clemency from the Emperor, their protector, who was even the godfather of one of them. The Counts Boehm affected to be scornful of our father and said publicly that in marrying an old woman like their cousin, he had stolen their inheritance.

"The oldest, Albrecht, was the best swordsman in the university. Reiner, the second, was the king of the beer-garden [203] and the terror of the Philistines. We knew all that up at the house, because my father took great pleasure in stories of student eccentricity. I humbly admit to sharing that weakness. I liked the epics of *renards d'or and maisons moussues* [204] almost as much as my old Irish legends.

"The third Count Boehm was named Friedrich. He was almost as young as me. It was said that he would be a bad lot, like his brothers. He had come back from France, where he had been part of Marie-Louise's retinue.

"The three Counts Boehm were remarkable type–specimens of the superb race of Czech mountain-dwellers who were the masters of Bohemia. Friedrich, most of all, was the most handsome young man I had ever encountered in my life. He lived in the little town of Reichstadt during the university vacations.

"One evening, in Prague, Count Albrecht–who was drunk–insulted me as I came out of the theater. The following day, Comte Henri fought with him in the square and wounded him with his sword. I ought to add, however, that Comte Henri–who was then using the name Palmer and was known as 'the Englishman' among the students of the University–was a constant companion of the Counts Boehm, if not their friend.

"These Counts Boehm inspired a veritable terror in me, and I sometimes said to myself, while looking at Friedrich, who had the head of an archangel: if some poor girl were to fall in love with him...!"

At this point Lady Frances Elphinstone could not help smiling, because Robert was interrogating her with a smile of his own.

"Very well! Yes!" she cried, tapping her charming foot on the sandy path. "My lifelong dread has been to fall in love with him!"

"Be on your guard, then, little sister," Robert said.

Sarah became serious. "There is my father's memory between us," she whispered.

"He has proved to you, then, that the Counts Boehm assassinated Maurice O'Brien?"

Sarah did not answer immediately. She passed her fingers over her face.

"Proved?" she echoed. "What does one fact surrounded by profound darkness indicate? Frederick was 16 years old, and on the evening of the fatal day, I met him at Reichstadt, 12 miles away from Prague. But the fact is that they profited from the murder... and that he, now the sole heir, is in possession of my heritage, with the fortune that should be yours."

"If he was only 16, perhaps he didn't know...?"

"It's said that he's very ill," Sarah put in, dully. "If he dies, I shall pray for him."

Robert interrogated her expression with a furtive glance. Her brow was furrowed, but her eyes were moist.

"It was Comte Henri," she said, "who saved me from their clutches after the murder. He knew their plans; I was destined for the same fate as our father. You know Comte Henri well enough now that I don't have to tell you that no human obstacle can stop him in his tracks. He got into the castle and carried me away. He has never deceived me, except that one time; he told me that my father, accused of high treason and making ready to flee, was waiting for me. As soon as we were in the post-chaise, though, the whole truth was made known to me. I wept, in safety at least, for the death of my father. Henri had had the delicate generosity to bring my mother's former chambermaid with him. Throughout the journey, she served as our chaperone.

"In London–for it was to London we went, after crossing the whole of France–I was placed with a respectable family...

"If you had asked me then what my feelings were in regard to Henri, I would have replied: Imagine the worship of a devotee of a divine Savior. He was 20 years old; if Friedrich had had the beauty of an angel, he had the beauty of a knight. Of his projects, he let me see just enough to dazzle a child's heart. I thought, not that I loved him, but that I adored him. I said to him then, and I have said it a hundred times since: Every breath in my body is yours.

"My brother, you need have no fear. That man has a great heart. God knows that there are a thousand layers veiling his life, and God will judge him! For myself, I shall serve him!

"Comte Henri took nothing from me but my virginal affection. Sometimes, he rocked the cradle of my dreams in making me hope that I might be his wife. He was sincere. He saw that I was so beautiful and happy beneath his fraternal caresses that he thought he loved me. Comte Henri de Belcamp's kisses were as good and pure as my father's.

"Three things remain for me to tell you: Henri's journey to Australia; his conduct regarding the Counts Boehm; and the events that followed his return to Europe–and that will complete my own history.

"First, there is a mystery that will seem inexplicable to you. Henri's mother was in London, but it was not to her care that he entrusted me."

"The Marquise de Belcamp?" Robert asked her, at this point.

"I must forbid you to ask questions, my brother, because it is not permitted for me to answer any of them. All that it is possible for me to say, I shall say, and I assure you that the remainder would not modify your opinion about anything concerning me.

"Comte Henri left for New South Wales two months after my arrival in London. I was to make the journey in my turn once certain conditions had been met. Indeed, a solicitor by the name of Wood sent me a considerable sum of money in banknotes, and a letter containing Henri's instructions. The money came from Germany, from Albrecht, the eldest of the Counts Boehm; I was to carry forward the thread of a great enterprise. Rome was built thus, by the endeavor of a few bandits led by a demigod."

"Had he dreamed of the conquest of Australia?" Robert asked, smiling.

"He was only 20 years old," Sarah answered, seriously and pensively. "There was some sort of innate hatred in him, as strong as a passion. Until his dying breath, he will search out the heart of England in order to tear it out. It was in India that he wanted to found Rome, which always finishes by destroying Carthage. He was the demigod: he went to Australia to reap his harvest of bandits.

"He was only 20 years old. You will be beaten if you wait to do battle; he knows that giants must be attacked. It is in the bowels of the Earth that one buries the powder that blows up citadels. He did there what he is doing here. It takes a long time to excavate a mine, and one must have soldiers behind the breach one cuts.

"He excavated his mine, he enrolled his soldiers. In the depths of Sydney's Hell, he found a man who, multiplying Fulton's notion by itself, might change the basis of naval warfare and give to anyone who desires it the kind of superiority enjoyed by the first cannon unleashed against valiant lances in the Middle Ages. He was a convict there, as he is a conspirator in your country; he would be a brahmin in Delhi and a mandarin in China: that is his mission. He is the instrument required to gather and muster in a single sheaf–an innumerable and irresistible army–all the hatred that England has sewn across the surface of the globe.

"He was only 20 years old, but with a single word I shall make you admire and fear him. In his mind, he had resuscitated the Stuart family. Living enemies were not enough for him. It was a Stuart emerging from the Vatican who first brandished the flag of liberty; he raised up three worlds with a single thrust: hatred, love and faith. Once he was under way, though, events cut out a larger standard for him, signifying a universal war rather than the civil war that Stuart wanted to fight. It was no longer a matter of shifting the dust of a tomb. Napoleon came to land on the isle of St. Helena.

"When he learned that, we were in the utmost depths of that terrible Australian desert they call the bush, without bread or water, feverish, broken, dying. An escaped convict fleeing the implacable pursuit of the black police, as we were, told us about the celebrations held in Sydney on the occasion of the Emperor's fall. The last State vessel transporting its cargo of condemned men had put in at St. Helena and had seen the imprisoned giant. That day, Henri—with his mother in her final agony on one side and me, who had lain down to die, on the other—created in a single cast the plan that brought you all to your feet.

"Six months later, he was on St. Helena, accomplishing the impossible task of getting into the Emperor's prison. You know that part of his history, Robert, and you are helping him, even though he has broken your heart."

"Jeanne said to me once," Robert murmured, stifling a sigh, " 'Be his friend; I shall be your sister.' "

"Jeanne!" Sarah repeated. Then she added, softly: "She's a dear child. May God make her very happy!

"As soon as we returned to London, Henri's life became a network of mysteries. For my own part, I lost the thread in the labyrinth and I had to give up following it. Four men had escaped with us: Perkins the engineer, Noll Green, Lochaber Dick and a youth named Tom Brown."

"Gregory Temple," Robert put in, "often calls Henri de Belcamp by the name of Tom Brown. That name and that of George Palmer were in the notes that he sent me on the subject of General O'Brien's assassination by Hans Teufel or John Devil."

"Gregory Temple is a clever detective," Sarah replied. "His misfortune is to be confronted with an enigma whose keyword is not within the vocabulary of the Police. Gregory Temple is trying to prove that Henri de Belcamp, that being the name he has given him, is an assassin. As that task is impossible, he has gone mad.

"Henri, who always has his hands full of money, separated from me and set me up in a house in London. I took the name Françoise O'Meara there, according to a plan concocted with the Emperor's own surgeon, in order to facilitate correspondence between London and Longwood. That correspondence became more and more difficult and irregular. England wanted to choke off every least sigh coming from St. Helena. She was afraid that Europe might hear it.

"Perkins, however, had begun the construction of his machine, which would equip a warship with the speed of a horse. Henri recruited his army and entered into correspondence with Germany and Italy. There was a lodge of the Companions of the Deliverance in London, which met in la Bartolozzi's house. Suspicions were raised against that woman; I did not expect that I would subsequently meet and come to love her two children. It was a matter of the lives of all the conspirators; I was placed in the singer's house to keep watch on her. She hid herself from me and I saw nothing, but she was betrayed; someone more skillful intercepted her correspondence. She was condemned to death.

"In her house, I saw Friedrich Boehm again, still handsome and now the sole heir of that immense fortune, bought for the price of a crime. The hand of God seemed to weigh upon him. I was afraid, as I had been before, and more so, for I could not tell whether the emotion that stirred my heart at the sight of him was hatred or love. Oh, how I wish I loved someone else! Life, for me, wanted to say smile, like your name, Robert... but perhaps neither you nor I shall ever smile again...!

"For the first time since I had been following Henri, the Bartolozzi affair gave me occasion to doubt. I had always seen him marching boldly along those impracticable paths, and every time that he had said to me 'Do this!' I had only to be audacious–but there was some petty and low intrigue here. It was the cause, whether for vengeance against Gregory Temple or for some other motive, of Thompson and Suzanne's misfortune.

"Strangely enough, that petty intrigue suddenly seemed to take up an enormous space in his life. The man who dreamed of immensity held himself back for weeks in a duel with a policeman who was no longer even his employer. It seemed for a while that his sole objective in life was to send an innocent man to the scaffold.

"At that moment, I doubted him–why should I hide it? I doubted even more when, during his sojourn at the Chateau de Belcamp, everything was reduced to the level of bourgeois comedy–a comedy in which he seemed to be deceiving everyone. It only needed one night to convene the Supreme Council. Why was the Grand Master of the Knights of the Deliverance wasting two weeks playing that frivolous vaudeville?

"I was woken up by his arrest. This must be the nub of the matter. There was undoubtedly a great mystery behind that bizarre event, and I waited for the veil to be lifted, by him or by the law, which he seemed to confront from the height of an impregnable position..."

She fell silent, her hands crossed on her knees, while her large black eyes strayed into the void.

"Frances," Surrisy said to her, "I've listened to you carefully, and I still don't know what you think of the man who has been your entire family for four years. Nothing emerges from your words, so far as I can tell, but a strange coldness and a great deal of discouragement. I understand why you remained a slave while the glamour lasted, but the glamour had already disappeared when you adopted this new identity of Lady Frances Elphinstone..."

Sarah did not move, but said: "That which one has promised, one must do."

"I need more precise answers, my sister," Robert insisted, not in order to judge you, but in order to quit the path on which I am marching, if it is not the right path."

"Henri has never been beaten," the young woman murmured. "It is not a political cause that he serves, it is his own; it isn't for Napoleon that he's working, but for himself. He is strong; he will overcome the obstacle: profit and pass on!"

"Should I abandon Gregory Temple completely?"

"He's an unfortunate, blindfolded and lost in a place where a thousand roads meet. You can't save him, but you might be lost with him..."

"Are you sure that Comte Henri wasn't mixed up in our father's murder?"

"I'm sure," Sarah replied, this time without hesitation.

"Are you certain that he was neither the author of nor an accomplice in the murder of Jeanne's mother?"

"I'm certain of it."

"You have no fear for Jeanne?"

"None. He loves her."

"Then you believe him to be completely innocent?"

"I don't know. If he doesn't fulfill the promise he has made to Suzanne Temple–if he allows Thompson to be condemned to death by the Court of Sessions–he will have committed at least one murder in his life..."

Footsteps were heard, and joyous voices were raised at the other end of the alley: "Here they are! Here they are!"

Germaine and Jeanne came towards them, smiling and holding hands. Suzanne came behind them, carrying—as always–the little child in her arms.

"Six witnesses have come out of the inferno, over there in London," Sarah continued, in a low and rapid voice. "Six impostors! Pray God that Henri is not in there for nothing! Richard Thompson is condemned to death. Suzanne knows nothing... silence!"

"Well, milady," cried Germaine, "have you forgotten the time of our audience? The Marquis is waiting for you; we only have ten minutes to get to the prison."

Lady Frances got up; pale as she was, she gave little Richard a kiss.

There was a calm and profound happiness in Jeanne's lovely blue eyes. She was still a girl, but with something of the woman in her. You might have taken her for one of those child brides in whom the wedding ceremony has displaced the promises of virginal dreams. She offered her hand to Robert. "We've been talking about you," she said. "We're counting on you, and we both love you."

Robert felt tears in the corners of his eyes. Already she was saying *we*!

She went on: "I've told him that you're noble and good. He knows that our secret is safe in your hands."

They had a secret! They, Comte Henri and Jeanne–and Robert Surrisy was their confidant! Do you remember how he had thanked Henri on the bridge by the mill when Henri had saved Jeanne, his fiancée? What horoscope had sent that poor gentleman tumbling into a peasant's hut? What a cruel lie his name was, which wanted to say smile!

Robert's hands pressed against his wounded breast.

The young women went away; Jeanne alone turned round to bid him a gracious farewell from a distance. Robert was left alone. He sat down again on the bench, his head overhanging his breast. He held that position for a long time. When he roused himself, shivering as the sound of approaching footsteps became audible again, dark lines ringed his eyes, which were red with tears.

I've never loved her so much, he thought. *When I can see all this clearly, and say to myself: he is worthy of her and will make her happy, I shall take my sword to some part of the world where a soldier's death can be won. He had a good and generous heart, for he added: I shall fight for him, if necessary... and may I die protecting the man that Jeanne loves!*

The noise of footsteps sounded loud and clear, like those of a platoon marching in step. At the same time, though not on a drum, someone was beating out the rhythm of double time.

"By the left," commanded Férandeau's voice, "turn!" His mischievous profile and student's costume came into view at the end of the alley. He was followed by Laurent Herbet, whose face displayed the kind of ill-humored expression overlaid by a smile that the face of a peevish child acquires when revived by the promise of a toy or a slice of cake.

"Left! Right! Left! Right!" said the pupil of David, beating out his accelerated pace on his sample-folder with the aid of two little sticks of dry wood.

"What the Devil's got into you?" Laurent cried. "Let's take a serious matter seriously."

"The arts don't," Férandeau. "Models are posing as usurers, rents are increasing, the school of David is falling into the rococo... It's the moment of death for the fatherland... Hey there, Robert! Let's talk prudently, for fear of indiscreet ears. I've come to offer my intelligence, my courage and my arms to the cause of misfortune!" He stopped in front of Robert and added: "Halt! Attention! Face right!"

"You shan't snarl at me any more, old chap," Laurent said, sitting down beside his friend. "I've made up my mind. Germaine has promised me..."

"For my part, at least," Férandeau proclaimed, "I remain on a higher plane than these frivolous motives. I wasn't able to sell my last exhibition-piece. An insolent second-hand dealer said: 'Rub it out and I'll buy the canvas.' To arms!"

"What has Germaine promised you?" Robert asked Laurent.

"That she will love me," the other murmured, lowering his eyes, "if I follow Comte Henri freely and bravely."

"They're all in the conspiracy!" the pupil of David put in. "It's an Opéra-Comique affair. We'll find the Police waiting halfway along the road to the battlefield. Let's go!"

Robert kept silent and remained pensive.

"You won't congratulate me then?" said Laurent.

"Are the ranks complete?" asked Férandeau. "I offer myself in a supernumerary capacity, like a caterer or the official historian of the expedition. I'll limp like Tyrteus [205] if necessary, marching to the music and reciting victories and conquests in verse. I can play the flageolet, and I can easily learn the trombone. If you have enough combatants, give me a post in the fortifications, or I can buy horses from the chandlers of Normandy. What the Hell! One doesn't leave a comrade in the lurch. An idea! I'll bring my sketch-book and I'll stick myself in a corner. When the campaign's over, I'll publish 24 engravings representing your principal battles. Is it settled? I'll be hailed as a painter of everyday things, and I'll go down in posterity!"

Robert slowly lifted his head.

"You'll both be in my company," he said, coldly.

"That's right!" Laurent cried. "Are we talking Greek? You're as warm as a block of ice, old chap!"

"Perhaps there's a band on the bill," Férandeau suggested.

"In three days we can all be embarked," the former Sub-Lieutenant replied.

"And sailing the galley!"[206] said the pupil of David, sketching an *entrechat* in which one could already see the germ of that dance of character invented some years later, which placed our youth so high in the esteem of foreign travelers.

Robert put his hand on Laurent's shoulder. "You are determined?" he said.

"Yes–to the Devil with school. You see, everything that has happened here has turned my head and my heart. I give you my word of honor that I don't envy Jeanne her millions... but that double inheritance... the marriage to the Englishman... without Germaine and you, I would already have gone mad."

They got up together and walked arm-in-arm.

"I know the story of the inheritance," Robert said. "It has been related to me. That tormented me, too, but it's very simple at bottom. There's an English bandit, Tom Brown–or John Devil, as they call him–who found that he was the legal heir of Turner and Robinson. Both of them, even though they were getting on in years, conceived the idea of marrying. The idea came to them both at the same time because, without being aware of it, they had the same mistress, who died in London. Tom Brown, seeing that he would be disinherited by these two marriages, and ignorant of the existence of the wills deposited with Monsieur Daws, plied his trade as an assassin."

"That's very simple, indeed, as regards the bandit Tom Brown," Laurent replied, in a low voice, "but why were the two wills made out in favor of my mother's daughter?" His cheeks and forehead were red.

"Through circumstances," the former Sub-Lieutenant murmured, "that the future will doubtless explain."

"Thanks, old chap." said Laurent, shaking his hand, "but while I'm waiting for the explanation of these circumstances, I have to go to a place where the fighting will be long and hard."

"Psst!" hissed the pupil of David, who was walking behind them and already adopting a military bearing.

They turned round, and Férandeau pointed through the foliage at the gate of the Colonnade, over which a man was nimbly climbing.

"Bricole!" murmured the astonished Surrisy.

They approached stealthily. Briquet had crept as far as the pedestal in the middle of the peristyle bearing *The Abduction of Proserpine*. It was not the first time he had been here, because three gigantic letters, B.R.I., were already cut into marble of the pedestal. As he sharpened his knife in order to complete his work, Férandeau shouted in a terrible tone: "Trompe-d'Eustache! Bad boy!"

Briquet put his knife back in his pocket and came back over the gate.

"I was sent to look for you," he said. "They want Monsieur Robert at the prison."

"Who wants me?"

"The Comte, damn it! Since, you are, as they say, his briquet. Well, time's getting on and we haven't got all day."

The three young men immediately took the path to the jail.

There was a full house in Comte Henri's drawing-room. Madame Célestin was knitting between the two Bondons, still very warm after losing their bet against the lawn of the *Tapis Vert*. Monsieur, Madame and Mademoiselle Chaumeron were telling Many-Apologies, the Deputy's wife, the horrific story of 50 chickens snapped up in a single batch on Miremontese territory by a Parisian shark. The young women surrounded the Comte, who was sitting beside his father on the sofa. The room was vast and well ventilated, and looked out over the gardens. The furniture was simple but stylish. The table still displayed the remains of a comfortable meal. Many people in Versailles, and Paris too, would have envied Comte Henri de Belcamp his martyrdom.

"I say," cried Papa Chaumeron, in his capacity as a plain speaker, "that if the Government permits the capital to starve the surrounding regions, there'll be a catastrophe. You could take me to the King if you wanted to; I wouldn't mince my words in telling him the truth. Fifty chickens...! Trump!"

"How seriously our little Jeanne looks at you," murmured the Marquis, his hand clasping Henri's.

Jeanne blushed–and Germaine too, resonantly.

Henri looked at Jeanne with a gentle smile on his lips. "I have news from London," he said.

At that moment the door opened, giving passage to Robert Surrisy, followed by Laurent and Férandeau.

Henri interrupted himself, and left his place to go shake Robert's hand. "If you hadn't come," he whispered, "it would have been very unfortunate. It's set for this evening."

"So you two have secrets, then?" the Marquis asked, from a distance.

"Secrets that scarcely concern you," Henri replied, lightly. To Surrisy, he added. "My horse will go like the wind from here to Beaumont, but I'll need six relays to Saint-Valery-sur-Somme, the horses ready and waiting for me along the route. Can I count on you?"

"You can count on me," Robert replied.

"Then you must leave as soon as you get out of here."

"And the five other runners will leave at the same time as me."

"I'll mount my horse at midnight."

"We have eight or ten hours in hand; the relays will be waiting for you along the route."

"Thank you, Commander Surrisy."

They shook hands again, and the young Comte resumed his place beside his father, perfectly calm. "As I was saying," he continued, while Jeanne caressed the little child in Suzanne's arms to hide the emotion in her face, "we've had news from London."

"I call a spade a spade, myself," cried Chaumeron. "When's the wedding?"

Comte Henri took a letter postmarked London out of his portfolio. Studying Jeanne's anxiety with mischievous malice, he held up the sealed letter between his fingers for a long time so that everyone could see the English postmark. Only Gregory Temple, had he been present, would have been able to observe that the imprint was slightly blurred, like the postmarks of the letters written some time before by James Davy.

Comte Henri finally split open the envelope. The letter was from Percy Balcomb, a true tradesman, busier than a minister–a soldier of industry whose motto was time is money. Always under pressure, always galloping along the railways, this Percy Balcomb counted every minute. He announced his arrival at Versailles this very evening, at six o'clock. The contract would be signed thereafter, after which that perpetual motion machine Percy Balcomb would fly back like an arrow and make for the Royal Exchange, where he had a meeting the day after tomorrow.

"In truth," said Mademoiselle, "I wouldn't want a husband like that." Her lips were moist.

"One would need a dozen!" added Madame Célestin, whose two supports never absented themselves.

"Might there be occasion for a little ceremony?" asked Chaumeron, avidly.

Miremont vaguely scented a celebration.

"My children," said the Marquis, "someone has to volunteer to go to the hotel and order dinner."

"What a pity!" murmured the Deputy's wife. "I've got a stomach upset. I'd better confine myself to light things."

It was like one of those valiant regiments where every man replies present! when one asks after a lost child. Miremont got up as one to go order dinner.

"I shall think of you at my solitary table," said Comte Henri, in a melancholy tone.

Lady Frances Elphinstone lowered her eyes because Robert was trying to meet them with his own. Robert was red in the face.

The old Marquis clasped Henri in his arms.

Henri's eyes, firm and sad, were fixed upon Robert. His gaze seemed to be saying: You shall bear witness one day that I have lowered my pride to the extent of lying. "Father," he went on, returning Monsieur de Belcamp's caresses, "take my place next to Percy. We're his family now. He will scarcely be able to come to the prison this evening, for he will be entirely devoted to our lovely Jeanne, but ask him to hold back his departure for one day, and tomorrow I shall see you all united around me."

"Do you believe that?" cried the Marquis. "I'd give ten *louis* to see you standing side-by-side together."

"Would you like to know," said Chaumeron, "that I wasn't born yesterday and I know that if they were standing next to one another, they wouldn't look alike at all! Too right!"

At the moment of departure, one usually says: "until tomorrow!"–but while Jeanne offered her pale face to Henri's kiss, pretty Germaine, who was always alert and was waiting her turn, thought that she heard someone murmur: "until tonight!"

Comte Henri de Belcamp remained still and pensive for a little while in the middle of his solitary room. Then, he went back to the sofa and sat down, supporting his head with his hand. You might have thought him a marble statue, so impassive did meditation render the handsome contours of his face. After a few minutes, he sat up straight again, and a proud smile came to his lips.

"The hour has come," he said, "and the die is cast. I have played them all one against another, and set out the cards in this great game at the appropriate time. The probabilities are in my favor. My star is at its zenith. I have made all my enemies into instruments, and when the charge is sounded for the last time–for the true battle–it will be the sword of a knight without fear and beyond reproach that I shall brandish in my hand!"

He rang the bell. A junior prison warder, who seemed more like a servant–and did indeed serve him–immediately appeared in the doorway.

"I want to see Monsieur Roblot at once, Monet," Comte Henri said.

"The Assistant Governor has dinner at this time," the warder protested.

"Go and tell him that I'm asking for him urgently."

Monet went out. A few minutes later, Monsieur Roblot came in with a sullen expression. He had a packet of letters in his hand, still sealed, of which several seemed to be official. He was a man of about 50–an old soldier, if his impressive moustache could be believed, and a man whose temper was short and surly, to judge by his canine physiognomy and the expression in his eyes.

"You might let me have dinner in peace one night a week, damn it, Monsieur le Comte!" he exclaimed, as he opened the door noisily. "I need my job, God knows, but if I had two inmates like you, I'd hand in my resignation. What do you require?"

"Could you send me one of those little cases that serve as overnight bags, my good Monsieur Roblot?" the young Comte replied, smiling.

"You got me up for that!" the other growled, looking at him furiously.

"For that and another thing, my good Monsieur Roblot. We have to rearrange some details this evening..."

"Before my dinner?"

"If you would allow it."

"This is becoming a tyranny, Monsieur."

"Do you think I'm on a bed of roses?–as Guatemotzin [207] said to his minister. I assure you, Monsieur Roblot, that I'm at least as tired as you... but when the wine is tapped, it must be drunk. Buy one of those little cases for me, I beg you, if you do not have one of your own."

"May I ask why, Monsieur?"

"Certainly. There's no mystery in it. It's for a journey."

"A journey!" exclaimed the old soldier, throwing up his arms.

"A short journey," the prisoner concluded, amiably, "which might last five or six days at the most."

Monsieur Roblot's arms fell back. "Devil take me!" he said, forcibly. "You've gone mad!"

"You told me that, my dear Governor," the prisoner riposted, emotionlessly, "in those exact words–I remember it well–the first time I asked you for permission to take a little stroll around the town every evening before going to bed."

The Assistant Director's bushy eyebrows came down, hiding his lowered eyes.

"For my part," the young Comte went on, "and my memory is very precise in this regard, I placed my hand on your shoulder and I whispered in your ear: *For the best!*"

"What the Devil...?" Roblot began, angrily.

"It's a way of wishing one another goodnight, employed by neighbors and friends," the smiling prisoner went on. "But between the two of us, former soldiers of the Empire..."

"Enough, Monsieur. I'm only holding on here by a thread, and I have a family to feed."

Henri adopted a more serious tone. "Firstly, Captain Roblot, you must not be anxious about your family; that's the least of your worries. If you lose your position, I promise you in the Emperor's name..."

"Let's talk sensibly, I beg you, Monsieur le Comte," the other interrupted, calmly. "I'm an old soldier, it's true, but not much of one. It's ten years since I retired here, where I'm quite happy. My vocation was to be an Administrator. If anyone offered me a Colonel's epaulettes, I'd say much obliged. One evening, over in Paris, to which I go once a year, friends came up, Roblot this, Roblot that, the tricolor, the eagles, good stories of the German campaign... and punch in the Murat style,[208] a thousand bombs! There was three times more than it needed to turn the head of a family man who wasn't used to getting drunk. There you go–I've taken the oath... but, you see, if I'd believed that you were guilty, I'd have been cut into a thousand pieces rather than let you go out."

"I know that you are honor itself, Captain. I have an appointment–do you mind if I start to get ready?"

"You can start and finish getting as ready as you wish, damn it, but you'll have to run me through if you want to make your six-day journey! You're innocent, that's obvious 36,000 times over, and the Inspector said to me only yesterday that the Judge is carrying on like an old fool... but why the Devil can't you wait till you're acquitted to go gallivanting about?"

Henri, taking advantage of the permission granted to him, began shaving in front of a mirror suspended from the window. "No, my dear Monsieur Roblot, no," he replied, teasingly, between two strokes of the razor, "I don't want to wait until after my acquittal."

"In that case, Monsieur le Comte–your servant–open your window when everyone's asleep and jump out into the courtyard."

"It's too late, Captain. I've a dinner appointment outside the prison this evening. Pray take the trouble to sit down."

"That's all, damn it! Enough of this madness–my soup's getting cold."

The prisoner turned to look him in the face. "My good Monsieur Roblot," he said seriously, "it wouldn't suit me at all to play the role of practical joker with respect to a man of your age and character. Make no mistake about that. I have told you how things stand; it's necessary."

"Necessary! Necessary!" repeated the other, scarlet with rage. "It's also necessary, then, that for six days, you must strike the prison warders blind! And that your room should not be full of people! It's necessary that, for six days, all your visitors should go to the Devil! I assure you that it's impossible... and I won't do it, damn you!" The addition of the last phrase [209] is an indulgence that we shall excuse, with the strictest delicacy. Must an honest man be gagged?

Roblot plunged both hands wrist-deep into his trouser pockets, and began pacing rapidly around the room.

Henri passed the razor over his second cheek. He remained silent for a few moments, entirely absorbed in this task. "It's necessary," he repeated, eventually, while brushing his chin. "I acknowledge that your objections are perfectly fair and reasonable. I anticipated them, and have taken measures in advance. No one will come to see me for six days. For six days, at least with respect to me, all the employees in Versailles will be blind. Will that satisfy you?"

"Do you think you're talking to a child, Monsieur?" muttered the other, who stopped in front of him and removed his hands from his pockets in order to put his arms behind his back.

The threat implicit in this posture did not seem to have any effect on Henri, who carefully put his razors back in their box, saying: "Be so kind, I beg you, to open your letters."

Roblot thought he had misheard. Henri repeated it, and Roblot said: "Will my letters from the Minister inform me about your six-day journey?"

"Exactly," replied the young Comte, who placed a pretty rosewood box under his arm and went into the neighboring dressing-room. "Read them."

The Deputy Governor sat down at the table, on which he placed his packet of letters. He took his silver-framed spectacles out of their case and wiped them, after having breathed on them.

"You can talk yourself up endlessly," he muttered, through clenched teeth, "Comte you may be, and a charming fellow... well brought-up... but a demon deep down. If your discharge from prison is in here, by thunder, I'll reward myself with a glass of Madeira after my soup."

He placed his spectacles on his plump and ruddy nose.

"Ministry of Justice," he read, taking up the first letter that came to hand. 'Monsieur le Directeur...' Very good! 'I have the honor...' Ah! ah! It's the order of business for the next session. You come sixth. The jury will deliver their verdict, that's all... innocent... you are innocent. That's perfectly obvious."

Henri put his head out of the dressing-room. He now sported a new-born beard and moustache. Roblot, who glanced at him, seemed not to be at all surprised by that.

"What date, approximately?" Henri asked.

"From July 25 to 30. Good riddance for both of us, wouldn't you say, Monsieur le Comte?"

"Read the others," Henri said, disappearing back into the dressing-room.

"The second one... Ministry of the Interior... that's new! Hang on! Hang on! Incommunicado! You! Why the Devil's that, I wonder?"

Henri's head appeared again. The line of his eyebrows now cut forcefully across his forehead, and his physiognomy was already profoundly modified–to which Roblot paid no particular attention. He was repeating, in stupefaction: "Incommunicado! Why the Devil should you be held incommunicado?"

"You haven't guessed?" Henri asked, smiling.

"I'm damned if I have."

"My dear Governor," the young Comte put in, lightly, "it's so that no one will come to see me for six days."

Roblot looked at him, flabbergasted. "Is your arm that long?" he murmured.

"Just long enough, my old friend."

"Then why not get a key to this place?"

"Because I'm here for a reason."

"There's no political significance in your case, for God's sake!"

"Absolutely none."

"If there's no politics involved, what purpose can be served by your presence in Versailles jail? What the Devil? I might not be as sharp as Talleyrand, but I know the Moon isn't made of green cheese."

"My dear Governor," Henri said, emerging from his dressing-room yet again, "I assure you that Talleyrand, sharp as you might think him, wouldn't understand this any more clearly than you do. Finish reading your letters."

Roblot opened a third letter. "Detailed instructions from the Interior..." he said, scanning it.

"Read it!" Henri called, from the depths of his dressing-room. "It's the details that are important."

"I can't see anything important in them myself... the number of your new room... the name of the guard who'll be specially assigned to it..."

Comte Henri came out in his shirtsleeves, with brown hair whose brilliant curls put a new gleam into his eyes.

"All the same," murmured the old soldier, not without a certain residual suspicion, "there's no one like you for disguises. Without having seen under the makeup, even I could have passed you on the street in broad daylight without recognizing you. There's the voice, though–you have the Devil of a voice, worth half a dozen descriptions. One can't change one's voice."

"That's true," said Henri whose smile took on a singular quality. "One can't change one's voice. So, my guard will be Mestivier?"

"Did I tell you that?" Roblot exclaimed.

"I don't believe so, my old friend. And I'll be in cell Number 2?"

"That's right. How did you know?"

"How did I know that you'd jump to the ceiling simply because someone tickled the palm of your hand and said: *For the best, good cousin?*"

"Yes, yes," muttered Roblot. "There's a lot of the old leavening left in France, that's sure. But the Devil may take me if I've any desire to see a Revolution myself, Monsieur le Comte."

"There are horses which draw and those who let themselves be drawn, my dear Governor. Do you know why no one has ever been put into cell Number 2?"

"My God! I never asked myself that question."

"Do you know, at least, why one never puts water in a cracked jug?"

"Bah!" said Roblot, who left his mouth open.

"My brave friend," Comte Henri said, softly. "Lock me up in cell Number 2 and seal the bolt, and I'll be in the Armory half an hour later. Those who are writing to you don't know that you will save me the trouble of picking the lock and moving back the bolt. Either one of those exercises spoils one's outfit, and I intend to look my best this evening. You understand that I must keep these little secrets from everyone. Your colleagues and superiors know nothing about you; you shall know nothing about your colleagues and superiors, for the signatories of these letters are acting in their administrative capacities, and are nothing but machines for transmitting orders. The absence of your Governor was not ensured in isolation; the cell was chosen according to plan, just as the selection of Mestivier as guard has been planned. Believe me, you won't regret being on this side of the fence. We're strong!"

While he spoke in this familiar manner, striking by virtue of its very simplicity, old Roblot lowered his head. He was no longer thinking about his soup getting cold.

Henri continued dressing as dusk fell.

It is difficult to express the precise difference that exists between the get-up of the English true gentleman and our own conventional dress. The clothes are the same and yet it is always easy, even for casual observers, to distinguish the English black jacket from the French black jacket. There is a difference in style, or a distinction of cachet, as an experienced tailor would put it. The proof is that a Frenchman dressed by a London tailor immediately takes on the appearance of an Englishman. Why, though, does an Englishman dressed by a French tailor never become a Frenchman?

Henri, having finished dressing, was an admirable and perfect Englishman.

"Have we decided?" he asked old Roblot, whose bushy eyebrows were as fleecy as storm clouds. The old fellow's silence did not trouble Henri's serenity in the least. "My removal," he continued, "will have to take place tonight. It's as simple as saying hello. You don't have to account to anyone, and Mestivier knows his own part. No one but Mestivier will have the authority to go into my empty cell, to which he will bring my meals at the appointed hours. As far as the prison staff and visitors from outside are concerned, you have protested against your orders, which are real, official, unassailable..."

"And if the Governor returns?" Roblot asked, in a low voice.

"I give you my word of honor that he will not return."

The old soldier was still silent.

"Well?" said Henri, his tone becoming imperious.

"Well!" cried Roblot, getting to his feet, his face turning purple. "All that won't budge me, Monsieur le Comte. There it is! May the thunder strike me down if you get out of here! I'm a jailer, by all the devils in Hell! And the good cousins won't stop me! I don't believe in phantasmagorias. I shall write to the Minister to find out who the sorcerer is in all this! We'll see if the Devil's black, damn it! After all, some rogue might have forged these letters and signatures. I'm a companion like you, but I refuse to march without a master's orders. And don't you move, since I've thrown caution to the winds, or I'll put you in irons in a bottle that can't be broken, name of a name of a name of a name!" He ground his teeth, I swear, and his eyes, mottled with blood, stared his prisoner in the face.

Henri was just putting his gloves on; he took one off. He picked up a little box bound in red leather from the table, and opened it. The contents of the box were red. "You have a wife and children," he said, slowly. He took a step towards Roblot—who tried to meet his eyes, in spite of being dazzled by the lightning that was brewing in the depths of Henri's pupils. "Do you know," Henri went on, "the punishment reserved for a forsworn companion who bars his Master's way to the fountain?"

"His Master's?" Roblot repeated. Henri's hand touched his and he recoiled.

"Has your Circle been told," the young Comte went on, "as it should have been, that a man is in France—not *a* Master but *the* Master, thus named by the very will of him who is in exile?"

"The Emperor?" stammered the old soldier, in a tremulous voice.

"Has it been told," Henri asked again, taking the red object from the box in his hand, "that the same will has made this man, at a single stroke, a Knight, an Officer, a Commander, a Senior Officer, a Great Eagle of the Legion of Honor?"

The red object, a large silk ribbon, was unrolled, and Henri set it about his neck. "Good cousin," he finished, "By faith, hope and charity, I order to you open my way to the fountain."

Roblot bowed his head and replied: "I am ready to obey you, Master."

The Sun had set, but the twilight still lingered. Three men, one of whom was wearing a light cloak over his elegant black costume, were standing in front of the door of cell Number 2. The other two were Deputy Governor Roblot and the guard Mestivier, who had an enormous bundle of keys in his hand. "The prisoner will be safe in there," he said, in a mocking tone, as he gave a final, turn to the massive lock.

"You answer to him," Roblot said, loudly.

"Yes, yes," muttered Mestivier. "By God, yes... see you later!"

He drew away. The man in the cloak linked arms with Roblot and went with him along the long corridors of the jail. Neither one of them said a word. When they arrived in the courtyard, the sentries presented arms, and they passed through.

At the exterior gate, Roblot called the turnkey.

"The Comte de Belcamp is incommunicado," he said.

"The permits are revoked, then!" the turnkey replied, joyfully. "All the visits are finished with!"

Our two companions passed through again; they were outside. Roblot did not stop until they reached the end of the Avenue de Paris. "Monsieur le Comte," he said, sadly. "I have done my duty to one side; I have betrayed the other. I need my place among those who are supported, or else I shall be taking yours."

The prisoner, who did not seem to be showing any of the emotions normally associated with the achievement of liberty, answered seriously and firmly: "In six days, at 7 p.m., I shall be at the door of cell No. 2. I swear it on my honor." At the same time, he took a piece of paper from his pocket and put it in the old soldier's hand. "One can answer to anything," he went on, "except for the will of God. I shall be running a great danger. If I am not at the rendezvous at the appointed hour, it will be because I am dead. Then, my old friend, don't wait for an hour or hesitate for a minute; leave with your wife and children, not forgetting Mestivier. Go to London; take this paper to the address written on it; you will be a rich and tranquil man for the rest of your days. Thank you, till we meet again!"

He shook the older man's hand, and went away at a rapid pace.

In the Marquis de Belcamp's drawing-room at the Hotel de France, everything had the appearance of a simple and happy family gathering. Dinner had been finished about an hour before, but various Miremontese stomachs were still in the process of digestion, assisted by small comestible items pillaged during dessert.

The cynosure of all eyes was, of course, Mr. Percy Balcomb, sitting on the sofa beside the Marquis, in exactly the same position that Comte Henri had occupied a few hours earlier during their visit to the prison, between his father and the young women.

"One has to search hard for resemblances," Madame Célestin said, having resumed her knitting, "to discover the portrait of Comte Henri in that Englishman!"

The right-hand Bondon and the left-hand Bondon immediately made the same gesture of approval.

"Of course," Mademoiselle riposted, feeling slightly queasy because of the atmosphere of betrothal, "what we have here isn't a matter of two living phenomena to show off in a fairground..."

"Too right!" Chaumeron exclaimed. "She'll be a plain speaker!"

"They're all inclined that way," added the mother. "All the Chaumerons, that is."

While counting stitches under her breath, Madame Célestin said; "Fourteen, sixteen, eighteen... it'll be their husbands who won't be."

"I shan't need a pair of them, Madame," the eldest daughter riposted.

"Too right!" said Chaumeron. "Trump!"

"Quite nice, for a maid," observed Many-Apologies, perfidiously.

"Madame Bondon knows well enough that one may laugh in society," Madame Chaumeron put in, in a conciliatory tone, "but to return to the topic. I think that if it weren't for the beard..."

"And the color of his hair," added the Deputy's wife.

"And the cast of his eyes," supplied Madame Célestin, mockingly.

"And the voice..." Chaumeron began.

"Oh, as for the voice," they all said, in chorus, "It's a matter of black and white."

"That's everything," Madame Célestin concluded, placing one of her knitting needles in her hair. "Personally, I don't haggle as if I were at the market. I keep to the rank where Providence placed me. Those who want to play with clever words are only wasting them. I don't say that for Mademoiselle Chaumeron, who is a well-brought-up person who's old enough to know what she's doing, since she can walk without a harness... I take no pride in the astonishing resemblance exemplified in my family, and the Messieurs Bondon have enough money not to have to show themselves off in a fairground, not including my dowry–for I had a dowry! No one's taking offense. I just say this: except for the beard, the features and the rest, the Comte and Mr. Balcomb are as similar as two drops of water. That's my opinion, and it wasn't worth the trouble of insulting two decent men for so little a thing."

She went back to her knitting. The Deputy's wife was envious of the speech. Madame whispered to Mademoiselle: "You'll never be anything but a fool!"

And Chaumeron added, speaking frankly, with a parent's authority: "You'll get your reckoning–you've made me look bad too. If you stir again, you'll be sent to bed. So there!"

If it is necessary now to offer our own personal opinion on the question of the resemblance, we should say that it existed, but only in the measure reported by Comte Henri in his Australian anecdote. There were very striking similarities in height and build, the contours of the face and the cut of the features, but their bearing was not at all the same and there was an essential difference in the way they stood. Apart from the beard, the eyebrows, the hair, the cast of the eyes and the pitch of the voice, there were indefinable qualities of some kind that rendered any confusion impossible.

One was an Englishman, through and through, maintaining–not ridiculously, but at least perceptibly–an English accent. In addition to everything else, his chesty voice–serious, profound and baritone–had the guttural intonations of British oratory to distinguish it from Henri's vibrant tenor. Bear in mind, though, that I defy you to recognize the voice of your own brother when it pronounces an English sentence correctly for the first time. The English language, afflicted by chronic bronchitis, contrives an instantaneous ventriloquism, and that effect is even more appreciable when an Englishman speaks French. Chaumeron's opinion that if they were placed next to one another, Percy and Henri would not resemble one another at all, was quite plausible. Separated, they had a family resemblance that leapt to the eyes on first sight. That was all, because the details gave the lie to that first impression, and their resemblance went no further than causing a start of surprise such as we have all felt at some point in our lives.

Miremontese society was too sincerely devoted to the game of backbiting, in which everyone in turn receives one or more nips, for scars to take long to form. Mademoiselle sulked for three minutes and that was all. Pray to Heaven that the misfortune of celibacy might be so easily healed!

They were waiting for the Notary and the widow Touchard, who was growing into the figure of a very important person. Madame Besnard said that she must be counting out the dowry this very evening. Now, you would not believe how desirous they were of seeing those two millions. The source of these millions was mysterious; one might even add that it was sinister. The only person who felt it very forcefully was perhaps our lovely Jeanne herself. The others saw nothing beyond the millions–the millions were the Sun! Miremont felt nothing for millions but a tender and respectful affection. At bottom, what was it all about? Two dead relatives–however distant they might be–previously unknown. Who, in Miremont or anywhere else, would refuse that magical lottery-ticket?

The business with Comte Henri, far from doing any injury to the millions, had familiarized everyone with the idea of the two murders. They had become used to the idea, which cast no more doubt on the millions than it did on Comte Henri. The millions were as innocent as Comte Henri himself–whose sole accuser, Temple the madman, had become invisible, as if the ground had opened up to swallow him along with his accusation.

There was much talk of the dowry; there was also talk of the wedding-dress; the English were not as well known on the continent as they are today, but they had a universal reputation for magnificence. A wedding-dress provided by an English millionaire who was marrying millions would have to be splendid!

A few voices had noted the absence of the three idlers–as they called Robert, Laurent and Férandeau–but no one was astonished. Férandeau was of no account; Miremont had always despised the arts. Laurent must be jealous because he had inherited nothing. Robert was a suitor who had been shown the door. They did well to hide.

Why had Laurent not inherited anything, though? Why everything to the sister and nothing to the brother? That, certainly, was a Miremontese question of primary importance–but one must at least concede millions the capricious right to favor pretty girls. Laurent had nothing, and that was fine, since it was the millions' whim. And besides, that was as much as the Chaumerons had got.

Germaine, Suzanne, Frances and Jeanne were chatting together, while the old Marquis conversed warmly with Percy Balcomb. There was something genuinely touching in the emotion that the sight of Jeanne awoke in that serious young man, apparently so cool, whom the burden of business affairs had so strangely transformed since the time when he had gone adventuring with Comte Henri in the Australian forest. He had not had time for love in his life, which had first devolved into misfortune and conflict and then had been given over entirely to the other battle–victorious, this one–that had made his fortune. Superior in every other respect to those of his own age, he was new to love; he sometimes approached his dream with the rigor of a methodical operation, sometimes lingering in naive idylls and childish timidities.

He was sincerely and profoundly in love; that was obvious. Jeanne shared that love, but there had been no sign of the precious fever of initial attraction between them. They had cut into their romance at a middle page. It was as if they had found one another again after a time apart. Miremont explained that by saying: "Mr. Balcomb is so busy!" In general, however, it must be confessed that the business of love is to forget business. To that, Miremont said: "The English are so original!"

That is true; you will not find an Englishman in the whole of vaudeville who is not an original.

"You'll make her very happy for me, won't you, Percy?" the Marquis said, caressing Jeanne's gentle profile with his eyes.

"I shall do my best, dear sir," Balcomb replied. "I feel that I love her more every day."

It was observable every time he contributed to the conversation that he spoke French without difficulty, but with that forced sobriety peculiar to a foreigner who is not familiar with the ordinary usage of a language.

"I don't know," the Marquis de Belcamp went on, "why the thought of my Henri is incessantly between the two of us. One often says more to a friend than a father, especially when the friendship is forged in the midst of great peril. I gather that you know his great secret, Percy?"

It was in his smile more than anything else that Balcomb resembled the young Comte de Belcamp. He smiled very rarely, although his character was far from being somber. He smiled this time, and made no reply.

"Mind you, I'm not interrogating you, Percy," the old man said, swiftly. "It would distress me to hear my son's secret from anyone but himself." He paused, but soon continued, carried away by the idea that preyed upon him incessantly: "Nothing will prevent me from thinking that this bizarre affair has been cooked up by the enemies he faces on the political battlefield... he almost admitted it to me... and the duel between the two principals is to the death now... There are times when I am afraid."

Percy's eyes met Jeanne's.

"You're not listening to me," Monsieur de Belcamp went on. "How can I speak of anything but love? But it's because I too was once in love, Percy. My Henri is everything I have left in the world. I have loved! Pray God that you will never know where the terrible and sublime madness can lead! Oh well! When I interrogate my heart's memories, it bleeds all over again, for there are wounds that never heal. When I try to compare my tenderness as a lover with my passion as a father, it seems to me that I have given Henri an even greater part of my soul."

Percy's two gloved hands took the old man's and squeezed them tenderly. "You're a good man, Balcomb," the Marquis murmured, with tears in his eyes. "Yes, you're a good man, and my Jeanne will be happy."

"Monsieur Berthelot!" announced Pierre, who was wearing his ceremonial livery. On the formal instruction of the ministerial officer, he added: "The Royal Notary!"

Monsieur Berthelot, a Notary of two eras, made his entrance like a dancer, his step gracious and solemn at the same time. He was bald, and combed the hairs from his nape over the top of his head, where they remained fixed by means of a substance that is the particular property of a dozen Notaries and a few rare physicians. He carried his red box very well, and his gold-rimmed spectacles went very well with it. We do not concede the pretension affected by the Notaries of Paris of being the only handsome Notaries; there are plenty of them in Versailles. Monsieur Berthelot was clad in dancing-shoes, and his toes were no more than half-afflicted by gout. He could easily have carried Madame

Célestin in the folds of his black vast black coat. He panted as he talked, and every time he exhaled he smiled benevolently all around, at the ladies most of all.

The widow Touchard came in behind him, in full dress. All Miremont glanced sharply at her, to see if she had the dowry, but her hands were empty and the pockets of her silk dress did not seem at all puffed out.

"Monsieur le Marquis," said Master Berthelot, breathing out and smiling at the ladies, "Monsieur Balcomb... Mesdames... Mesdemoiselles... I have the honor to be your servant." He wiped his forehead with a cambric handkerchief, taking care not to interfere with the substance sticking down his hair, and went on: "Mortified to have perhaps kept you waiting... a long way to Versailles... several unions... the contract of Mademoiselle Bruno and Monsieur le Duc de Cernay, outside the gates... the Duc somewhat ruined, but still... a Duc!"

We cannot do justice to the eloquence of the Notary's "but still."

He sat down, smiled at the ladies, breathed out, mopped his brow and opened his box, with the aid of a little silver key that dangled flirtatiously from his watch-chain.

Miremont listened more attentively than to a sermon. Monsieur Berthelot, having secured his spectacles with a little movement of his finger, and felt his chair to see whether any of its four feet were in danger of slipping, coughed contentedly and began to read the contract.

"In the presence of Monsieur Fortuné Berthelot and his colleague, *etcetera*, are represented Percy Balcomb esquire, head of the firm of Balcomb & Co., domiciled in London, England, Sloane Street, Brompton, stipulating in his own name, and Demoiselle Jeanne Constance Herbet..."

"Many apologies," the Deputy's wife put in at this point, perhaps with good intentions, "but mine made mention of fathers and mothers... my contract, that is..."

Too right! thought Chaumeron–who added aloud, however: "That's out of order!"

Madame Touchard, with cool disdain, said: "The notary has no need of shopkeepers to tell him his job."

"Trump!" Chaumeron concluded.

Monsieur Berthelot smiled at everyone, and continued in the clear tone that is the charm of an authentic lecture: "Demoiselle Jeanne Constance Herbet, emancipated minor, domiciled in the place called the Priory, commune of Miremont, canton of l'Isle-Adam, department of Seine-et-Oise..."

The two Bondons had the same idea, which was to applaud, as this passage seemed to them to be clear and well-phrased. Madame Célestin gave them each a lump of sugar that she had kept back from her coffee, and they thought better of it.

We shall not parade the Royal Notary's complete work before the reader's eyes; suffice it to say that the thing was done in a very good style, even accommodating a few of those flourishes that embellish literary studies, without ever abandoning the straight path of formality. In listening to it, Mademoiselle felt her heart beat faster more than once, and our pretty Germaine was very pale.

It was a rich contract; the Deputy's wife herself could not say anything contrary. The reciprocal advantages of the spouses were balanced with a breadth that softened the voice of the Notary. I do not know why death, anticipated in every line of these expansive poems, does not worry anyone. It is there, a stipulant party; it promises before the Notary to come at its appointed hour; one bows when it talks; it is quite simply a black rose among so many fresh flowers. I have heard promissory notes of thousands of francs exacted for the widow's mourning. The Notary is philosophical! The husband is there. Would you like him to name the price of the tears that will be spilled on his tomb? He is in love—for, bizarre as it may seen, love survives these prodigious barbarisms. He thinks, perhaps sadly, poor darling, I am afraid to bury her! And the romance of marriage proceeds amid the perfumes of funeral pomp. Why not simply wear the widow's mourning-clothes beneath the wedding-dress?

When Monsieur Fortuné Berthelot arrived at the paragraph relating to the dowry, attention was redoubled. The dowry consisted of all the movable and immovable property that had come and would come to Mademoiselle Jeanne Constance Herbert. A brief indented line stipulated that two million francs were payable on signature of the contract.

There was a long-drawn-out murmur in the Hotel de France's drawing-room. Bear in mind that until that moment, they had talked about millions without entirely believing in them.

In 1862, a million is still a very tidy sum as pocket-money, but you greet 20 people a day in the street who have one or more millions. The title, moral value and exchange rate of a million has decreased considerably. The voice of the Notary, sensitive to the poetry of wealth, no longer quivers as it pronounces the word million. The marriage contract is blasé regarding the music, once so rare, of the two syllables. One sometimes even hears it said of a man that "He's only got a million."

In 1817, a million was as vast and resplendent as an Egyptian pyramid whose four faces have been encrusted with gold. Dreams stopped there. It was a fortune, and it was absolute.

The Miremontese murmur was initially composed of two words: Two millions; two millions; two millions!

Madame Célestin stopped knitting.

"Trump!" muttered Chaumeron. "By damn!"

The Deputy's wife sighed from the utmost depths of her envious chagrin. "Many apologies! I'm only a woman... but it seems to me a trifle steep to hand over such a sum on signature of the contract."

"As steep goes, it's steep," said Madame Chaumeron.

Mademoiselle, swallowing the spite from her lips, whispered in the learned Potel's ear: "That's called buying a husband for cash!"

The two Bondons asked their lady if she had any more sugar.

The widow Touchard was privately of the same opinion as these whisperers. To shelter herself from any responsibility, she said. "My niece is emancipated; she exacted that herself."

"And the clause is in Jeanne's interest," added the Marquis. "Mr. Balcomb will immediately invest the sum in his own house of business."

"You don't say!" muttered Chaumeron. "It's no shanty, then! Sly dog! Immediate investment, by damn!"

Percy remained still, his eyes half-closed, perhaps lost in some elevated calculation. One would have thought that these discussions did not concern him in the least.

Jeanne's hand made a slight imperious gesture and Monsieur Berthelot continued his reading, after having smiled at the ladies.

When the article arrived in which the two spouses made a mutual donation of their entire wealth in the event of death, Percy finally broke his silence.

"I beg the notary," he said, his English accent giving more precision and more bite to his words, "to modify that disposition. Should I die without issue, my family is rich; it pleases me that my wife will inherit the fortune due to me. If God reserves for me the terrible misfortune of losing my wife, Laurent Herbet, my brother and my friend, and Madame Touchard, who has been a mother to the two orphans, are the natural heirs."

Jeanne offered him her hand, and made no protest. She only said: "May everything be done as you desire, Percy; I have no other will than yours. But if God ever makes me a widow, I would not need so many riches to weep and to die."

Germaine threw her arms around Jeanne's neck, with tears in her eyes.

"Very sweet," said the Deputy's wife.

"Affectation!" grated Mademoiselle.

"Me, I don't want for anything!" exclaimed Chaumeron. "I owe nothing to anyone. I say that it's pleasant to see such things! So much the worse for those who aren't content! So there!"

Madame Touchard rubbed her moist eyes, and the Bondons both grimaced like children about to cry.

There was one moment more solemn still. That was the one in which Madame Touchard, after the signature, took the dowry out of an old portfolio she had brought. Miremont did not have eyes enough to look at the two millions. No one knows exactly what form Miremont's imagination could give to a dowry of two millions. The simplest was a gold cup as big as a hayrick, but that could hardly be carried in a portfolio.

When the two millions appeared in the form of a banker's draft, made out by Rothschild of Paris in favor of Rothschild of London, there was a ripple of disappointment. But, in the end, it was no less marvelous. Everyone wanted to see the precious piece of paper and touch it, like a holy relic. It was passed from hand to hand; the Bondons sniffed it.

"Ah," said Many-Apologies, sadly, as she handed it on to Mademoiselle, "you'd be set up for life with the fiftieth part of that, my poor chick!"

"A fortune doesn't create happiness," Mademoiselle replied.

"But it helps to marry one," Madame Célestin put in.

"My God, Madame!" Madame Chaumeron riposted, "Eat your dinner twice if you're rich enough!"

And Papa Chaumeron, caressing the paper with a gesture and a gaze that were equally untranslatable, said: "I only say this. There's a trump!"

The bill of exchange passed into Percy Balcomb's portfolio. Notary Berthelot closed his box, drank a finger of sugared water, smiled at the ladies, and left.

The right-hand Bondon and the left-hand Bondon leaned impetuously towards Madame Célestin, in such a manner that one would have been able to put the three heads of the Bondon garniture in the same hat. They asked, with one voice: "Will there be something to eat now?"

There was of course, something to eat. Pierre and Madame Etienne came in with plates, the sight of which warmed the Chaumerons' hearts. Madame Etienne went directly to Percy Balcomb and made a speech in which the memory of her former mistress was eloquently mingled with all sorts of sincere felicitations. Then the plundering of the plates began. How limited an animal man is! At least monkeys have four hands for grabbing. With two hands, however–two simple hands–the Chaumerons did marvelously. It needed less than three slabs of *paté*, to suppress Mademoiselle's chagrin. The Bondons, always alone in the middle of the crowd, made a picnic at one corner of the table; Madame Célestin made sure that the food was equally divided between her two husbands.

The compliments were offered with hands and mouths full. The Marquis, lost in meditation because he was thinking about his Henri, had given the first kiss to the bride-to-be.

Chaumeron cried: "No standing on ceremony! Love one another, my children! That's it!"

"Good luck! All the good luck you deserve, Jeanne!" wished Germaine, in a tremulous voice but from the bottom of her poor little heart.

"And may Monsieur le Comte be present at the wedding-feast!" added Lady Frances, with a peculiar smile. The Marquis kissed her hand.

"As for that," the Deputy's wife continued, curtsying to Jeanne, "you have known poverty, my little darling..."

"What! Poverty!" protested Aunt Touchard.

"Many apologies... I mean that she never got the white meat of the chicken at dinner in your house, my neighbor."

"Your chambermaids will be better dressed than you ever were," added Madame Célestin.

"Ah, we would certainly never have believed that you would fulfill this dream," Mademoiselle let slip. "You're lucky!"

Suzanne came to embrace Jeanne without saying anything. The two Messieurs Bondon offered her their cheeks.

The old Marquis drew his Miremont around the table, and the engaged couple remained alone on the sofa, watched over nevertheless by the pointed glances of Mademoiselle, Madame Célestin and the Deputy's wife. They could be seen hand in hand, both wearing expressions of calm and profound happiness, occasionally exchanging a smile with a few sparse words.

"Monsieur Morin du Reposoir," observed the Deputy's wife, "conducted himself in a different manner in his time."

"It's none too warm," Chaumeron observed. "The English are never ardent wooers, for fear of hurting themselves. If it won't offend Monsieur le Marquis, I'll offer the company a drop of champagne, to buck things up a bit. All round, Papa Chaumeron!"

The Marquis immediately ordered the champagne, and Miremont bucked up, no longer thinking of anything but feasting.

At midnight, Balcomb got up and kissed Jeanne's hand. "Love me as I love you," she said, "and we shall have Heaven on Earth."

"Are you going already?" came the cry from every side.

"It's necessary that my wife's dowry be in London tomorrow," Percy replied.

"And my poor Henri will not have seen you this time," murmured Monsieur de Belcamp.

Percy never lingered long over good-byes. He was seen exchanging a few whispered words with Lady Frances, and moving towards the door after shaking the Marquis' hand cordially. "Miss Temple," he said, quite simply, as he passed Suzanne, "I shall be glad to act on your behalf in London."

Suzanne looked at him in astonishment. He moved closer to her, and murmured rapidly: "No matter what you are told, have no fear; I have sworn to save him."

No response came soon enough to Suzanne's trembling lips. She wanted to speak, but he was already bowing with cool politeness before turning and leaving the room.

Nights at Versailles are silent and deserted, but the solitude of its streets is superabundantly guarded by an army of sentinels sheltering behind every corner, whether it belongs to a barracks, a hospital or a palace. Thanks to these wise precautions, the statues in the royal courtyard have still not been purloined by persons of evil intent. The houses in Versailles that are neither palaces nor hospitals nor barracks, belong to bourgeois individuals who do not like to let their womenfolk go out at night for fear of the sentinels. Many go as far as dying celibate, and the greater number have no cooks–all for fear and hatred of sentinels.

In the larger thoroughfares, bordered by sad trees, one encounters patrols rather than passers-by. These patrols arrested the last stray dog more than 50 years ago. For 20 years, they have not found as much as a rat. They get bored looking at the large and beautiful houses on both sides of their route, whose widows display no lights and whose gardens, from the largest to the smallest, all attempt to resemble the great king's park just a little.

The sentinels and the patrols do not like Versailles any more, because Versailles does not like the sentinels and the patrols.

A man was going along the Rue des Réservoirs at a tranquil pace. The night was calm; the Moon hid behind white clouds. From time to time, a sentinel called, "Who goes there?" and the man patiently answered: "Friend." He turned into the Rue de Maurepas in order to reach the boulevard and went out by the Porte Saint-Antoine, where he answered "Friend" for the last time as someone said, "Who goes there?"

The high road to Marly was in front of him. He took it, gradually increasing his pace until it soon became a run. An eighth of a league from the Porte Saint-Antoine, a peasant was standing in the middle of the road holding a magnificent saddled horse by the bridle. The coachman-gardener at the Chateau de Belcamp would have recognized it immediately, in spite of the darkness, as Comte Henri's English mare.

The man's pace relented as he drew closer to the peasant, and he said in a stage whisper: "*For the best!*"

"What do you seek, good cousin?" said the peasant, who handed him the bridle.

"I seek the fountain."

With one bound, our man was in the saddle. "Are there wolves in the forest?" he asked.

"Two gendarmes on horseback passed by ten minutes ago, going towards Marly," the peasant replied. Our man put a *louis* in his hand and spurred his horse, while the other cried: "*Bon voyage!*"

Our man was already distant; a minute later, the horse's shoes could no longer be heard.

In 1817, passports were rigorously checked on every road. Our man seemed not at all anxious about that, for he galloped freely in the direction followed by the two gendarmes. In ten minutes, he had reached Chenay, where everyone was asleep, and began to move along the great wall of Marly. Two tall shadows soon showed themselves along the road; they were the two mounted gendarmes.

Far from pausing, he urged his mount on. The two gendarmes came to a halt and turned their horses. "Hey, my brave fellows!" he cried. "How long will it take me to get to Marly-la-Ville, breaking the back of a bonny beast?"

"Ten minutes, the way you're going. Is that where you're from?"

"From Chenay, by God! And my wife's in labor..."

"Ah, the doctor!" said the good brigadier, who added: "Make way, Thomassin."

"Many thanks," said the horseman, slipping between the two like an arrow. "Provided that I can find him..."

"A pretty mare, Brigadier!" Thomassin risked.

The Brigadier replied, authoritatively: "How do you expect to get your promotion and further your career if you still don't know, at your age, how to distinguish a horse of one sex from the other!"

"Wasn't it a mare, Brigadier?"

"Get on, and keep your eyes open! Evildoers and enemies of the State would have a fine time if there wasn't a Brigadier here with the simple gendarme!"

Our man was already passing like a whirlwind alongside the aqueduct, whose massive arches were silhouetted against the grey sky. He climbed the hill to Marly at the gallop and came down again the same way towards the Seine. The mare went willingly, with no need for spur or voice to urge her on. The Saint-Germain rise was climbed and the town passed through without a moment's pause. The gendarme and the Brigadier were still discussing the sex of the beast whose rapid hoofbeats were already clattering on the Pont de Poissy.

At Triel, horse and rider left the highway to take a by-road leading to the north, without having stopped for anything other than taking the time to light a squat candle and consult a road-map of the Seine-et-Oise department. It was 2 a.m. when they reached Pontoise; as 4 a.m. sounded, our man saw the silhouette of Beaumont church against the nascent dawn, after covering 15 or 16 leagues because of the detour he had made in order not to pass through Paris.

A few hundred paces from the town, a man was standing in the middle of the road, holding a saddled horse by the bridle, like the peasant on the road to Marly. He was whistling a tune and stamping his feet, because the morning breeze was fresh. "Hey!" he cried, from the greatest distance that his voice could carry. "Is that you, Monsieur le Comte?"

"It's that fool Férandeau," murmured our traveler. He signaled with his hand to silence the other, but the pupil of David had a flask on a bandolier around his neck; it had been carried forth full but was empty now.

"Tut, tut!" he replied. "Do you think that I can sing 'Silence! Prudence!' like the Neapolitans of the *Muette de Portici*? [210] Say 'For the best!' to me and I'll answer 'What do you seek, good cousin?' It's stupid! All the wolves are abed, and I'm going to do likewise. Good day, Monsieur de Belcamp, how's it going? And at home? I've been gulping away here for two long hours, without reproach. When you're the top man in the Tuileries, you'll give me a worthy commission, won't you? I've made sketches for the decoration of the Pantheon... or something else, it's all the same to me. A square if you wish... or an annuity."

Our traveler had dismounted. It was indeed Comte Henri de Belcamp. "I recommend my horse to you, Monsieur," he said.

"Is she warm, poor Cocotte? [211] I'll take her very gently to the inn so she doesn't catch cold. When shall we be enthroned in Paris, Monsieur le Comte?"

"I've seen men found behind bushes with bullets in their heads, Monsieur Férandeau," Henri said, coldly, "who conducted themselves more prudently than you."

"Mute as a sacred ibis with the ungodly!" said Férandeau, making a grand academic gesture. "Faith, Hope and Charity, what! I know who I'm talking to. If I'd known I'd be thanked like that, damned if I wouldn't have been playing pool in the Rue Dauphine. Gratefulness exiled from the Earth flies back to Heaven—an allegorical subject!"

Henri put his hand on the other's shoulder and looked him in the face. "You're an honest chap," he murmured, slowly. "It would be a pity..."

"What would be a pity?" asked the artist, fearfully.

Henri withdrew his arm.

"No practical jokes!" said Férandeau.

"Go to bed," said Henri, buckling his little case on to the fresh horse. "Absolute silence, and carry out Monsieur Surrisy's orders to the letter. If not, comrade, you'll die young, I promise you, and your sketches will never be paintings!"

He spurred his horse.

Férandeau remained still. When Comte Henri had disappeared around the first bend in the road, he blew into his cheeks forcefully. "We're pariahs, then!" he exclaimed. "I refuse to decorate the Pantheon; I'll become an engraver in copper-plate; I'll knit down below like Madame Célestin...[212] Gee up, Cocotte—that's liberty for you!" He removed his old overcoat and put it on the back of the shivering mare. "Gee up, then, Englishwoman! The stern Surrisy will give me a lecture into the bargain—no chance! I'll see about handing in my resignation. Come to bed, Cocotte!"

Comte Henri was burning up the road to Beauvais. The further the way advanced, the less dangerous his journey became. For anyone who questioned him, Henri was henceforth a peaceful denizen of whatever town he was passing through, riding out for a few leagues in order to see how fast his horse could go.

Beyond Beauvais, in the village of Fouquenies, he found Laurent waiting for him with a fresh mount: a beautiful Picard horse full of fire.

"Monsieur Herbet," Henri said to him, "I know that you are awkwardly prejudiced against me, and that your present conduct is no more than that of a man of honor. You are in love with a dear child whose heart still does not know its own direction but who is worthy of you and will love none but you."

"How do you know that, Monsieur le Comte?" Laurent, whose attitude was still hostile.

Henri offered his hand. "I am still very young, Monsieur Herbet," he murmured, looking at him frankly and firmly, "but, believe me, I can speak as a father; I am at the head of an enterprise that would turn anyone's hair white. I know because she has told me."

Laurent blushed and smiled. An instant later, he had tears in his eyes. He embraced Henri and said, forcefully: "Monsieur le Comte, I shall die for you, now, if necessary."

"It won't be on account of Germaine," Henri replied, cheerfully. "It's not a matter of dying, Laurent my friend; in four days you'll take up your position here for a second time, and you'll be waiting for me again."

"What!" the stupefied medical student exclaimed. "Now you've got away, you aren't going to stay over there?"

"I have to be tried, Laurent, and I've given my word. Farewell!"

And they parted again. There are good Norman horses in the Oise and also in the Somme, but no one can find anything available for hire but the poorest hacks, even for silver or gold. At Beaumont, it was Surrisy who had chosen the horse; at Fouquenies, it was Laurent; all went well. At the following relay station, Comte Henri found an unknown and a Bucephalus of lesser virtue, which stumbled for six leagues between his legs; at the next station, there was another unknown and something like an overgrown goat. It was after noon when he came in sight of Hallencourt, his last station before Abbeville. With his fine mare, he would already have finished his journey.

This time, there was a vigorous animal whose bridle was held by a handsome Picard in a blue blouse, embroidered in red at the collar. The Picard did not respond to the name of good cousin and did not seem to know the way to the fountain, but his horse still had his nose in the oats when Comte Henri dismounted from his sorry steed to get astride this new charger.

Fortunately, this one picked up its four feet, which struck sparks, and departed like a flash of light.

"The bourgeois is waiting for you on the far side of Epagne," cried the Picard, waving his hat. "Leave Morin at Moreau's inn–I'm his son-in-law–and we'll all be fine."

Morin went faster than a hare, thank God. Provided that the father-in-law, Moreau, had one like him, nothing would be lost, No more than an hour was required for Comte Henri to catch sight of the little bell-tower of Epagne and Abbeville. Henri, whose eyes were already searching for "the bourgeois," saw that precedent had been broken. Instead of a man standing beside a horse, there was a rider in the saddle following the same route as he, holding another mount by the bridle.

Two fine beasts!

At the noise of the gallop, the horseman turned, displaying the candid features of Robert Surrisy–who immediately stopped, raised his hat, and dismounted at the same time as the Comte.

A peasant lad who was walking along the roadside came forward. "Fiot," Robert said to him, "tell Papa Moreau to keep Morin for us. He'll be paid for four days stabling as if he were on the road."

Henri and he shook hands. "Would Monsieur le Comte like to give me permission to set him on his way?" Robert asked.

"With all my heart, Monsieur Surrisy, but at a gallop. I've lost two hours, by my calculations, and now it will be daylight when I arrive in London tomorrow morning."

"Tomorrow morning?" Robert repeated, incredulously. "Don't you feel the air on your left cheek? Look which way the dust is blowing. The wind's west-north-west, strong enough to take the horns off a billy-goat. It'll be necessary to go as far north as Holland to catch it. From here, tacking, you'll not touch Dover in 24 hours, I can assure you!"

"You seem to understand that," said the young Comte, smiling.

"I'm a little rusty, but I can still trim a sail when the need arises, jib, mizzen or brigantine," said the former Sub-Lieutenant. "I was a *pilotin*–a ship's boy,[213] as they say over there in England, before becoming a soldier of France."

"And you think that a ship–a sailing ship, I mean–would take 24 hours to cross the Channel today?"

"I'd rather bet on 36."

"It's time to gallop, Surrisy! I'm not going to Dover. I'll catch a better wind than that! I'll double the Isle of Thanet a long way out, go into the Thames, and 12 hours after leaving the mouth of the Somme, I'll be disembarking under London Bridge!"

"You'll need the devil as a guide," said Robert, "but that's your lookout, Monsieur le Comte." [214]

They galloped in silence for two minutes.

"How far will you go with me like this, Surrisy?" the young Comte asked, abruptly.

Robert hesitated momentarily, then he answered, with feeling: "Monsieur de Belcamp, I don't know where the game will end. This isn't the first time we've rode beside one another... that day when you saved her life, it's absolutely certain that neither Laurent nor I would have arrived in time to prevent her being crushed or burnt... Well, she was all the hope and happiness in my poor life. I thought that she loved me; as for me, it was adoration that I had for her. You've taken her from me... you're my misfortune. There's an oath that binds me to you, it's very true, but every man has his passion which, when a certain hour sounds, might be stronger than his faith... that much is certain. I have felt it, I assure you. Without the memory of what happened at the bridge by the mill, who knows whether I might not be trying at this very moment to break your head on this road, where the dust is like a fog and where no one is visible at present, as far as the eye can see?"

"Given that you have a pistol, Monsieur Surrisy, "and that every officer in the French army is the raw material of an assassin, it's the easiest thing in the world, for I have no weapon."

"Actions change their name according to circumstance, Monsieur le Comte," said Robert, whose voice had become duller. "A French officer who avenges the murder of his father cannot be confused with the majority of assassins."

Henri turned towards him, pale but calm.

"I repeat, Monsieur, that I am unarmed," he said, slowly. "Yesterday, I signed my marriage contract with the one you love, and I am carrying on my person two millions that are from her."

"Millions!" murmured Robert, bitterly. "She had no millions when I loved her!"

"And I, who love her, Monsieur Surrisy, would not have married her without the millions she possesses."

"Dare you admit that, Monsieur le Comte?"

Henri put his hand upon his heart, and retorted: "Those who live on when I am dead will say: He gave everything to his work, even his love!"

Robert fell silent.

The horses galloped on in a cloud of dust, for the wind was increasing by degrees as they drew closer to the sea.

"Monsieur le Comte," Surrisy began again, "there are words that it is futile to speak. I don't believe that you are a criminal. If I believed that you were a criminal, nothing in the world would prevent me from coming between Jeanne and you, sword in hand. I know one part of your life from Lady Frances Elphinstone. You're surrounded by mysteries; the task that you have undertaken explains the veil with which you have enveloped yourself. I have made my sacrifice. If I hate, my hatred is driven back to the very depths of my heart. Instead of fighting you, I serve you. Will you permit me to ask a few questions about subjects with which I am very personally and very directly concerned?"

"To noble and loyal companions like you, Robert," Henri replied, his tone affectionate and soft, "I allow all questions, and I answer them from the heart when my duty allows."

"Yes," murmured the former Sub-Lieutenant. "There always remains a shelter where your silence may take refuge. First, I want to ask you if you knew me when we met one another at the Croix Moraine on the day you arrived at the chateau?"

"Yes," Henri replied. "I had seen you at Police Headquarters in Scotland Yard, with Mr. Temple."

"Is it true that you were employed there as a Police agent?"

"That's true... for the cause that we both serve, Monsieur, I have done more distressing things, even more glorious than that!"

"Did you know then that I had accepted a mission from Gregory Temple?"

"Yes–but I did not know the object of that mission."

"So you didn't know the name of my father then?"

"No, I only learned that yesterday, from your sister."

"Have you thought about the unhappiness that might result for her?"

"It has made me shiver!" the young Comte retorted, in a tone so sharp and full of candor that Surrisy looked at him. "There is a story as strange as mine, whose primary concern is my conduct towards your sister, a dear and generous creature who shall have her recompense in this world if God does not shatter my projects in my hand. Sarah has not been able to tell you the whole of that story, for its thread is broken several times over so far as she is concerned. It touches a great secret that must die with me or burst forth on the day of our victory... but what she has been able to tell you has sufficed, I don't doubt, to give a mind as honest and righteous as yours so strong a presumption in my favor that it is almost equivalent to certainty. I can add one small thing.

"The most grandiose edifice is not composed solely of massive stones the height of its facade; it includes a thousand light and cheap materials that the poor make and fashion in their humble wretchedness. For the edifice that I am constructing, I am at one and the same time the architect, the stonemason, the carpenter and the assistant who grinds straw in his mortar. I make everything: that is my pride! With speculations whose grandeur might perhaps crush you, I mix–as is necessary–microscopic intrigues. Here, the tiny has the same importance as the vast, and you know well enough that in our marvelous human machine, a nerve as thin as a hair, if suddenly injured, can leave your whole arm hanging inert at your side, struck by paralysis. I have been a Police agent in London; at the Chateau de Belcamp, I made your sister play the role of coquette... I've done worse, or at least smaller still... and the sum of my actions would raise the Tower of Babel."

Henri's spurs touched the flanks of his horse, which leapt forward in the dust. Robert followed him with difficulty. He could not help admiring from behind that noble figure and head so proud, around which blond curls were fluttering in the wind.

Abbeville was a long way behind them, and our travelers had already glimpsed the swollen Somme several times between gaps in the hills. Its waters seemed leaden beneath the squall.

"How far do you count on accompanying me, Monsieur Surrisy?" Henri asked, for the second time, at the moment when the sea suddenly appeared as a great line of vague blue on the horizon.

"If I were your friend, Monsieur le Comte," said Robert, whose heart seemed swollen and full of trouble, "you know that it would be for good and all."

Henri slackened his pace to offer his hand. "You are already my friend without knowing it and without wanting to be," he said, "but you are trying to find words to express a desire that seems to you puerile and scarcely worthy."

"No, on my honor!" Robert exclaimed, blushing in response to his companion's smile. "There's no idle curiosity or childishness in me. As regards the army in which you are the general and I am a soldier, I am perfectly prepared to wear a blindfold over my eyes, as my oath requires me to do... but as to that which concerns me and mine..."

"And what can you see here, Robert, if not the very ark to which your oath binds you? I am on the road to the fountain, to employ our symbolic language..."

"If I were sure of that...!" Surrisy began, with his eyes lowered.

"Have you the right to demand that certainty from your Master?"

"If I were sure of that...!" Robert repeated, as if he had not heard. Then, he continued, in a tone which mixed supplication and threat: "Listen, Belcamp, the darkness in which I am marching weighs upon me. The thought of Jeanne fallen prey to an unknown tortures me. I have a sister now; I love her, and the sight of her has revived the memory of my father. Is that enough motives? Is there one among them that is puerile and scarcely worthy? Is it necessary to mention all the accusations hanging over you? Is it necessary to add that if you are a criminal–as so many voices proclaim, one of which is the voice of my mother–then I will be your accomplice: me, the son of your victim?

"If I were sure of it, I said, if I could see, even from a distance, this mysterious monument whose sole architect you are... not finished, but merely showing its foundations above the ground! Saint Thomas wanted to touch the Savior's wounds, and I'm no saint! Remember that so far as you are concerned, I only have motives for hatred. Be just, and do not deny your debt, you who have ruined my happiness; be sincere with regard to one who is frank. Bend the rule, if the rule is iniquitous. Offer proof, since there is beside you a faithful heart that asks for proof. We're the same age, Belcamp; I am brave, I swear to you, and you can see that I am strong. Hatred, when it yields, sometimes becomes inexhaustible affection. If I were sure of your work, I would be sure of you, and I would say to you: 'Go forward without taking care to look behind you. Your back is guarded; your shadow has a sword; I am there–me, your brother!' ''

They were about to climb a steep hill, from the summit of which they could see Saint-Valery-sur-Somme, which they had already by-passed. Beyond Saint-Valery, on the right, was the Somme, broad as a sea, littered with boats battered by the squall. In front of them was the cape and the little port of Hourdel, huddled in its bay. On the left, the ocean stretched away.

Comte Henri had listened to Robert's speech with a benevolent smile. "There have been times in my life," he murmured, "more than one, when the affection of a brother has hindered me strangely. There were times when I would have marched over my shadow!"

"Is that a refusal?" Surrisy asked, his brow furrowing.

The Sun was sinking towards the horizon. Henri consulted his watch.

"Four thirty," he said. "Five o'clock by the time we get down there. The diligence takes 30 hours and the mail-coach 24. We've gained little–but once at sea, we'll make up for lost time. Gee up, Saint Thomas! You have no faith in anything; we shall give it to you, in everything."

The two horses, launched into the descent, crossed the valley at full tilt. Their riders kept silent in the meantime. Henri was thoughtful; solemn patience was visible in Robert's face.

After 20 minutes, they had reached the tip of the cape, from which they could see the sea stretch from horizon to horizon. A young herdsman kept watch there on his sheep, which were grazing meager and salty grass. Comte Henri withdrew a telescope from his case and scanned the open sea. It was not exactly a tempest but the sea breeze had freshened and fishing boats were coming back under full sail. By contrast, a few coastal trading vessels trying to go out with the ebb tide were having great difficulty picking up wind in spite of the current that was pushing them. Further out, there were two brigs running the same course, trying to catch the wind to make headway along the coast. They were two fine sailing vessels, both tacking ever more sharply together as they valiantly resisted being driven back. Nevertheless, when they turned to come about, they both seemed to have lost considerable headway.

"Monsieur le Comte," said Robert, "there's no need to be a mariner to see that the port is closed for today. I doubt that a naval sloop could reach the Isle of Wight with the wind head on!"

"Little boy!" called Comte Henri.

The shepherd came towards them.

"Are you from Hourdel?"

"The master's is near there."

"Here's an *écu*. Lead the two horses to your master, who will take them to Soleil d'Or, at Saint-Valery. There will be two *écus* for him."

The boy threw his hat in the air and whistled like a blackbird. Shortly afterwards, his flock, his dog and he–holding the two horses by the bridle–were going down the steep slope.

"Did you see what you were looking for?" Surrisy asked.

"They're coming," Henri answered.

"I could only see the two brigs," he said. "Good boats–but they'll finish up coming back to harbor, you'll see. Ships are like beautiful girls: they can't give any more than they have!"

"Man of little faith!" murmured the young Comte, whose lips maintained their stubborn smile. As he said it, he extended an arm towards the southeast, in the direction of the little port of Carjeux, which was hidden by the convolutions of the coast.

"Yes, yes," said Robert. "If we had to go down to Le Havre, it would be a different matter. That's obvious." As he finished, he saw a fleecy cloud of smoke that made a narrow border festooning the coast as it unwound in the wind. The pointed tips of two little masts soon appeared in an indentation in the cliffs, then the black orifice of a chimney that was vomiting vapor.

"A steamboat!" Robert cried. He added, in a scornful tone: "An odd plaything!"

At that time, everyone who went to sea, for short or long voyages, affected the most profound contempt for the application of steam to navigation.

The chimney and the two masts, however, made headway against the wind and the tide.

"You know about that, Surrisy?" asked the young Comte.

"I saw Monsieur Jouffroy's experiments on the Seine last year; it's ingenious, but it can't put out to sea."

"We shall, however, put out to sea in it today."

"The Devil you say!" exclaimed the former Sub-Lieutenant. "Cross the Channel against the wind in this weather, with a ship that has two broomsticks for masts and whose mainsail is too small to serve as a handkerchief! You might as well put a horse on a bundle of sticks!"

"You're free to stay here or come along, Surrisy."

The wind was blowing from the sea; the little steamboat's paddlewheels were now distinctly audible. As she advanced her progress against the wind and the tide, a fringe of curiosity-seekers could be seen on the crest of the cliffs.

She soon emerged from behind the last point that hid her from the gaze of our two companions and came into full view, one wheel out of the water and spinning like a top, the other deeply entrenched under the waves. There were about 20 men on the bridge, all of whom took off their hats and waved them in the air as they raised a hurrah. Comte Henri similarly took off his own hat and saluted three times.

"They'll drop anchor and send out their launch," Surrisy said. "Let's go, by God! No one in the world can boast of having left me behind!"

He was the first to throw himself on to the winding path that led to the little harbor situated within the point. He would obviously have been happier going up than going down, to mount an assault on this very rock defended by a Prussian regiment. Courage is a relative virtue, and everyone chooses his own danger. Robert went into this one as a man resigned to the ultimate peril.

The steamboat had indeed dropped anchor. Her two wheels were motionless. She turned in the wind to display her stern, on which her name was inscribed in letters of gold: *Deliverance*.

She was a ship of about 2,000 tons, narrow-hulled and admirably fashioned. She was rigged as a schooner; an experienced eye would have noticed six sealed gunports above her waterline.

Robert stopped halfway to the beach to see all this. On reading the schooner's name, he took his own hat off and saluted silently. His expression, as he looked at Henri, expressed a measure of repentance.

The launch had left the *Deliverance* and was being rowed towards the shore. There were six oarsmen and an officer in it.

"I'm losing more than one prejudice today, Monsieur le Comte," said Robert, as they arrived at the bottom of the slope. "But one is not reformed in a minute, you know. I admit to you that I have more confidence in that brave launch than in your puffing devil with its two millwheels!"

Surrisy had never been more than a midshipman. From Aspirant to Admiral, naval officers possessed an extremely opulent vocabulary of insults where steamboats were concerned. As for able seamen, they had employed the ultimate invective from the very first in declaring that these tubs were only fit for marine soldiers.

You can call a man an escaped convict in our Western ports; convicts are men of the world and escaping requires one to have hands at the ends of one's arms; but if the words "marine soldier" are mentioned by chance, there will be a slashed belly.

The officer commanding the launch gave two orders in English. At the first, the oars became still; at the second, they were hastily shifted to the vertical, as if to salute a superior officer.

"Everything going well, Perkins?" said Comte Henri, touching his cap.

"All right!" Perkins replied, in English. He was a solid fellow with good sea legs, which allowed him to keep his balance in the surf, like a bear walking backwards on its hind legs. Then, in French, he added: "*Très bien.* Very well, milord, except that I've put the key under the door back home, and that the machine is to be sold at the Auction Mart." [215]

"We're going to remedy that, Perkins. Let's get a move on, I beg you."

The launch was beached in relatively quiet water, thanks to the shelter provided by the point, a rickety shelf that stuck out like a breakwater. Two sailors jumped overboard to serve as points of support.

"We were expecting you to be alone, milord," said Perkins, in a significant tone.

"You shall welcome two of us, comrade."

"May I ask who this gentleman is?"

"Lieutenant Robert Surrisy."

"Of the Navy?"

"Of the Imperial Guard."

The sailors shifted, looking at Surrisy with sympathetic smiles. He had never seen sailors with such white faces and so orderly in their appearance–but one must expect anything aboard a steamboat.

Henri set foot on the gunwale and leapt from bench to bench. Robert did likewise, but his campaigns in Russia and France had accustomed him to more solid ground. He staggered and fell into the arms of one of the sailors, who gave him two big kisses on his cheeks.

"Captain Gauthier!"[216] Surrisy cried, rendering the accolade on the wing.

"And me?" said the next.

"Lieutenant Renault!"

His eyes were moist and dazzled, but he was already looking for others.

"That's all for now, boy," said Captain Gauthier, a cheerful fellow whose moustache was already going grey, but to whom an entire regiment would probably have come running at the first sound of the violin.

"I know more than 20 myself," added Renault. "It's only a matter of starting the dance."

"The others belong to the Military Academy, the Navy, *etcetera*," Gauthier continued, displaying his companions to Surrisy with a gesture that served as a summary introduction. "We make such a crew as has scarcely been seen... but when we're aboard, around a punch-bowl, I'll make a formal presentation."

"Lower your oars!" shouted Perkins, imperiously. "Pull!"

The Captain, the Lieutenant and the rest immediately set to work. The launch slid alongside the flat rock, the ten oars striking the water at regular intervals. The launch–assisted, this time, by the tide–flew like an arrow towards the *Deliverance*. The crew of officers rowed miraculously.

On board, everyone was on the bridge. The *Deliverance* had a crew of 30 men, of whom ten were genuine sailors, stokers and so on; the remainder were French officers, several of whom had held superior ranks in the Imperial Army. There was one Colonel of artillery. It was the latter, most of all, who welcomed Comte Henri with a deference close to respect.

The captain commanding the *Deliverance* was an Englishman, Edmund Abercrombie, who had occupied the post of Second Officer on the first American steamboat.

Robert had serious enthusiasm in his heart, and a kind of concentrated repentance. He would have believed in Henri if a single French officer had been included in a crew of pirates and escapees from Newgate–for where conspiracies are concerned, contingencies often leave little room for choice. The sight of the men gathered around him increased Henri's stature in Robert's eyes; he now seemed to be set upon a pedestal. Robert asked himself, contritely, how he could ever have doubted Henri.

An English command was muttered on the quarterdeck and was conveyed, repeated by the clear voice of a midshipman, to the depths to the engine-room. The piston set to work as soon as the valve had whistled; the beam swung and the giant's cough, slow at first, soon became a fit. A cloud of smoke sprang forth from the chimney; the wheels hesitated, then turned; and the schooner, nose to the swell and to the wind, set itself to stride unceremoniously over the liquid mountains, just as the two discouraged brigs came piteously back to shore with their topsails furled.

It would require several more years for that illustrious body, the Ministry of Marine Affairs, to take an interest in the force that defied the wind and laughed at the violence of currents. It is true that the Academy expressed, at about the same time, the opinion that a velocity of ten leagues an hour in a railway train would suppress human respiration and kill all the unfortunates mad enough to devote themselves to such foolish pastimes. There is no point in blaming the Ministry or the Academy. All progress constrains some vested interest or bruises some pride. If in doubt, don't do it, said ancient wisdom; modern wisdom responds: if you don't know, prevent it! Will there ever be a count of the men and ideas put to death in the name of the phantom idiot that wise men call *Improbability*?

According to Horace, the first man who braved the wrath of the waves on a frail plank must have had a heart triply encased in bronze. That is admirably true. We should add that the wise men of every era endure a crushing burden of cruel insults. But, in every era, the sages having lain down across the high road on which humanity marches, humanity passes on. The improbable, that grotesque scarecrow, withdraws its fogs in the face of light. Miracles, declared impossible, are contentedly paraded in our streets–and all goes well. Look! This was not much more than 40 years ago. If you look hard, you will certainly still find, alive and nibbling away at the scraps of his budget, one of those Spartans whose trembling hand tried to stop the advance of steam.

Do you understand? They are not all dead! They travel by rail like Jouffroy's sons, from whom they have stolen Fulton's glory! And when another marvel comes into view, they crack their faces with their final smiles while blaspheming: That cannot be!

This was only 40 years ago, and the universe has been transformed. Peace and war are changed; the extremities of the Earth have come together; capitals shake hands; Lafayette only needs ten days to embrace Washington.[217] It is in pronouncing the word impossible that it is nowadays necessary to have a heart enwrapped, not by a triple layer of bronze but a tenfold layer of donkey-skin.

That nimble craft–first-born of French invention, son of the magnificent genius whose splendor is borrowed by every nation, fruit of the tree that France herself, insouciant and ingrate, always neglects to water, but whose least shoots became giants abroad–went forth, giving her bow to the wave and bouncing like a cork tossed by a make-believe storm in a basin.

On the way to Folkestone, as the last rays of the setting Sun displayed the cliffs of Boulogne in the east, it passed a navy corvette. The corvette wanted to see this mechanical doll at close range: a very easy matter, with good sailors, a good ship and the wind! Perkins took the helm and the smoke emerged a little more thickly from the chimney. The mechanical doll responded to the tiller; you know in advance that the corvette saw nothing of her but smoke.

The promised punch bowl was served on the bridge. Meanwhile, in the cabin, the general staff held council, presided over by Comte Henri. Here, Comte Henri was known to everyone as Commodore Davy, or *milord*. Robert was surrounded by old comrades and new friends, nearly all–like him–members of the old Imperial Army who had served the Emperor on land and sea. They were mostly young, like him, and some were already known for heroic actions. He experienced a kind of moral intoxication. The dominant atmosphere was, moreover, one of enthusiasm. They talked of revolution as if it had already happened, and of Commodore Davy as a demigod possessed of supernatural power. The hour of combat was ardently awaited.

Here was the advance guard of the movement: the holy battalion, each of whose soldiers had deserved to march in the first rank–but the army existed, entirely ready despite its dissemination. In a few days, the empty cadres [218] could be full.

The *Deliverance* had already made the voyage to France several times, and her engine, entirely new, had not been idle since her first departure, embellished with foliage and flowers, from the workshops of Balcomb & Co. Perkins had built five others, including the great 800-horsepower engine, still an impossible thing that–even in London, the city in which the inquiries of genius are most freely permitted–had excited universal mistrust.

Captain Abercrombie's papers were in order, and the navy was his property; he had been able to continue his operations freely since the Balcomb Company had suspended its payments. The *Deliverance* was well known in the Royal Exchange and the Bourse, where capitalists were already dreaming of utilizing her speed in their operations between Paris and London. She was a purely commercial vessel, and her services would belong to the highest bidder. While waiting for her to become a shuttle, in due course, this commercial vessel had already delivered to London Bridge a few dozen young and old moustaches to whom the air of France was valueless.

Night had completely fallen, and the corvette was out of sight, when the general staff emerged from the council chamber. Every face was radiant. The former Colonel ordered that the glasses be filled, and proposed a toast to the health of the Emperor, which everyone drank standing up, with their heads bare.

"We shall see the flag again," said the Colonel, "and it is to Commodore Davy, after God, to whom we shall owe the victory."

All the extended glasses were clinked again, and the Commodore's name resounded in the midst of acclamations.

Perkins had left the helm. He went down to the council chamber, where he shut himself in with Henri.

"Well?" the young Comte said.

"Well, milord, if your pockets are full, perhaps we'll arrive in time."

"Perhaps!" Henri repeated, frowning. "Mr. Wood's letter informed me that the sale was tomorrow."

"Yes, yes, I believe it's tomorrow... but it only required a few hundred thousand francs to pay our creditors, and we'll have to count in millions at a public sale. How much are you carrying?"

"Two millions."

"Perhaps it will be enough."

"Perhaps!" Henri said, once more.

"There is 10,000 pounds' worth of steel, copper, etc, milord, and half as much in workmanship. That's nothing... but it's a Perkins machine... by the same Perkins who demonstrated the *Deliverance* in front of 400,000 cockneys, lined up on the banks, boats and bridges from Rotherhithe to Vauxhall Bridge... The Perkins of whom every constructor in London is jealous. Milk and Blunt [219] will bid 30,000 pounds, Powells will offer 40, Samuel Brand will go to 50..."

"And what will he do with it?"

"He'll destroy it."

The young Comte remained silent and pensive. Perkins went on: "Don't worry–I'll make you another one even stronger, more beautiful, lighter. I'm growing taller; they'll never be able to fight against me."

"For that," Henri said, "we'd need more time."

Perkins shrugged his shoulders. "What would you gain by fetching that man from his rock?" he murmured. "With my machines, I'll fill the house of Balcomb from its cellars to its roofs with gold. In ten years, the seven seas will be smoking. There's no longer anything but dead wood in Milk and Blunt's shipyards. Powells will go bankrupt and that old rogue Samuel Brand will hang himself in rage."

Henri was not listening to this optimistic prophecy. "You've received nothing, then, from Prague or Vienna?" he asked, abruptly.

"That's right," Perkins replied. "I've received a letter addressed to that old rogue Wood, which stopped the payments. The young man said in the letter that he'd had enough, and that he wanted to make restitution if, in fact, his brothers had caused harm to anyone. I've never seen to the bottom of that business, you know... I'm only concerned with the engines, thank God! We didn't get the payment of the 30th, after having demanded settlement of that of the 15th. Milk and Blunt, Powells and Samuel Brand were watching us... They bought the credit notes and got an order to seize our effects; then they fell on us like three lead weights... and the boiler's burst. Just like that!"

"I believe that Friedrich Boehm intended to come to London?" Henri said.

"I forgot!" Perkins exclaimed, laughing. "He came to consult old Temple, who knows everything... except what he doesn't. Our friend Wood was afraid, already feeling the rope around his neck. He cooked up a devil of a scheme with that scorched cat, Ned Knob. Young Count Boehm and the former Chief Superintendent were arrested as soon as they set out for Paris."

"On what pretext?"

"As accomplices in the assassination of la Bartolozzi. By the way, did you know that Thompson has been hanged, poor chap?"

Comte Henri became so pale that Perkins took his hands to hold him up. "You've a good heart, all the same," he murmured. "When I say that he's been hanged, that only means that it was set for today–I wasn't present at the ceremony, you understand. He was a very nice young man, and everyone liked him, even though he was old Temple's son-in-law, as everyone learned during the investigation. That one did him a bad turn... and brought half a dozen witnesses for the prosecution out of the ground, who threw him in the water with a stone around his neck."

Henri poured water into a glass and lifted it to his lips.

"Are you absolutely sure of what you're saying?" he asked, in a changed voice.

"About the witnesses?"

"No, about the date of the execution."

Perkins counted on his fingers. "Indeed, milord!" he exclaimed, after having thought twice, "since we've been at sea, I've lost track of the days of the month. Perhaps it was today; perhaps it's tomorrow. What's certain is that it's said that Count Boehm and Gregory Temple will be sent to the next Sessions as accomplices in the murder, as well as Fanny Thompson, who hasn't appeared in Court... As for the matter of old Temple, that gave the whole world a good laugh."

The Greenwich clock was chiming 4 a.m. when the *Deliverance*, under full steam, passed the magnificent hospital in which England shelters its seamen in their old age. At 5 a.m., the ship set Comte Henri and Robert Surrisy down at the London Customs.

London extends a kind of hospitality unique to it. At the moment when your foot touches the soil of the great Babylon, no one takes the trouble to inquire whether you are a malefactor or an honest man. Your morality is set aside, while your baggage is intensely scrutinized; the London Customs are famous throughout the universe.

Henri and Robert were conducted to the Custom House, where two gentlemen were keen to interrogate them, sniff them, weigh them and pat them–after which they were put outside.

Henri offered his hand to Robert. "We go our separate ways here, Surrisy," he said. "You've seen what you wanted to see. The meeting place is the Spencer Hotel, Oxford Street. I shall not be in London for more than 30 hours, and perhaps I shall not be here as long as that. At the hotel, you'll be kept informed, and you'll be able to meet up with me there. Till we meet again!"

He leapt into a cab in front of the monument to the Great Fire of London, and instructed the coachman to take him to the Old Bailey. All along the way, he shivered feverishly. His coachman could certainly tell him what he wanted to know, for nothing is as popular in London as matters of criminal justice. Cold, businesslike, sad London is as avid for judiciary melodramas as our gay Paris. Their character, it seems, is irrelevant; the performances of rope and blade have equally large followings. But Comte Henri dared not interrogate his coachman. As I said, he was shivering feverishly.

He came to a stop at exactly the same spot where Temple had collapsed against the wall as he came out of the Session House. He paid his fare, and the carriage went back along the road.

Comte Henri was alone in the middle of a deserted street, whose two ends were obscured by a thickening grey fog. A ray of sunlight reddened the rooftops, but the lower parts of the houses seemed black. Henri's eyes were fixed on the very place where the former Police Superintendent had endured the insulting curiosity of the cockneys. He too felt faint, and the cockneys would have taken him for a drunkard as well. He took a whole minute before raising his eyes to that sinister stage from which the scaffold projected, like a bridge suspended between captivity and death.

As he finally interrogated that black facade–which certainly could not re-ply, for no trace remained of the play that had been performed, and the com-pleted drama brought mourning-dress to its decor–a bell rang, accompanied by the sound of wheels audible through the fog in the depths of the Old Bailey. Comte Henri turned; a high-sided cart formed of thin planks emerged from the fog. The planks were plastered with yellow paper, softened twice over by the dampness of the printing press and the fog. On the yellow paper there were gi-gantic letters, which trembled with the movement of the cart: *Latest News*! *Ex-tra*! [220]

What an apparition! It was, if it is permissible to treat such a subject lightly, the playbill of the next spectacle and the program of the funereal panto-mime, produced for enthusiasts. All this latest news emerged fresh from the presses of Ave-Maria Lane.

A deep breath inflated Comte Henri's chest. He knew his London like the back of his hand. A single glance was sufficient to determine what it was about. One no longer sells programs after the curtain has fallen. He had arrived in time!

"Hey, gentle sir," the conductor of the chariot called out to him, laughing, "are you already booking your place for tomorrow morning? If you want to be the first to buy you'll have, for the price of a penny, 16 printed pages in brand-new type, on paper of superior quality, published by Martins, the leading house in Paternoster Street and Europe! The life and death of Richard Thompson, nicknamed John Devil, son-in-law of Gregory Temple and assassin of la Bar-tolozzi: his adventures, his transformations, his famous escape from Sydney, his loves and a great deal else... the ink still wet!"

"Friend," Henri said to him, putting a crown in his hand, "you have ren-dered me a great service without knowing it. Drink to my health!"

"But don't you want the book, milord?" cried the dealer from the house of Martins. "You're wrong. There's entertainment for men, women, and children. I thank Your Lordship. This morning, I have to go to Pentonville, Islington, Kingsland, Hackney and Hoxton. I'll come back via Bethnal Green, won't I? And I'll sell my thousand, if it please God... It won't do any harm to the poor devil who'll be hanged..."

Henri was already going away from the Old Bailey. The dark cloud that had earlier been cast upon his features had vanished. The proud and calm face that has been present throughout our story had returned. He took Holborn, then Chancery Lane, and went into the inextricable labyrinth of back streets separating Lincoln's Inn Fields from the back of Covent Garden.[221] The longest, narrowest and most famous of all these cut-throat alleys was Low Lane, where Sharper's flourished.

It was about 10 a.m. Robert Surrisy had used breakfast as a pretext for looking around the Spencer Hotel in Oxford Street, hoping to see something of his friends the conspirators. He found cold roast beef under metal covers shaped like bells, plenty of ham, tea, white coffee and ruddy gentlemen who mixed their thick stout with aqueous ale, but no conspirators. There was not a single man there from the crew of the *Deliverance*.

Robert had no one to see in the whole of London. He became war-weary after making his meal, and went out for a walk in Hyde Park. He was deep in thought, sparing no more than a distracted glance for the King's sheep mowing the velvet lawns, the King's ducks paddling in the Serpentine, or the King's turkeys clucking in the shanties of Kensington. Unfortunately, the statue of Achilles–as the bronze of the Duke of Wellington is called in London, without laughing–had not yet been erected; otherwise, he would have been able to kill five minutes in measuring exactly how far the infatuation of a people and the bad taste of an era might extend.

He was lost in thought. The problems posed by recent events had been partly resolved. He had wanted to see; he had seen. That crossing would remain in his memory. Whatever the mystery was that enveloped the life of Comte Henri de Belcamp, there must be an explanation as vast and complex as the mystery itself. What Robert had seen gave Comte Henri the right to don any mask and adopt any disguise. He could, perhaps have wished that the demonstration had been less striking, for his love for Jeanne lived on in the depths of his heart, and the man who had forced his admiration was his rival–his fortunate rival. But his was the soul of a soldier. The enthusiasm of devotion to a cause could silence the voice of passion within him. So, at least, he believed; and several times already, words had come to his lips, saying: "As long as she is happy, I shall be what she wants me to be: her brother."

He caught the distant whiff of gunpowder, and that helped him.

"You're French, Monsieur," said a familiar voice behind him, startling him. "I'm a French peasant and former soldier of the Emperor, and I have no bread."

"Pierre Louchet!" Robert cried, before he even turned round.

The woodcutter jumped for joy and snatched his hat from his head, holding it humbly in his hand. "The Lieutenant!" he said, with tears in his eyes as he threw himself upon Robert's hands. "In the name of all that's holy, God is good!"

"Are you still here then, my poor Pierre!" said Surrisy, astonished. "How can you have been abandoned after carrying a message like the one with which you were charged?"

"Are you mixed up in that, Lieutenant?" the woodcutter exclaimed, excitedly. "It's a Forest of Bondy,[222] believe me. The Devil couldn't find his way through it. You talk about my message? I hampered the English there... or the French... does anyone know the country these people belong to? I lost the letter on the road, that's true–the letter that he gave me–but I remembered the address and the name, because it wasn't difficult. I've been to Mr. Wood in the Strand. I said to him: '*For the best*!' He answered, 'As you please,' and I'm still running. Lieutenant, do you know an old man named Mr. Temple?"

"Certainly."

"That one's on the way to becoming as mad as a March Hare, but he seems to me to be a brave and honest man at bottom, though. Listen! All the scheming isn't finished yet, and I get dizzy when I look down to the bottom of that hole... So I became an errand boy in Leicester Square, which is the French quarter, and whenever I saw someone there who had the look about him, you know, I said to him quietly: '*For the best*!' But guess what? Barbarous bankrupts or commercial travelers, not so much as the pigtail of a good cousin!"

"Let's go in here, Pierre," said Surrisy, stopping at the door of a pretty tavern near the park gate in Piccadilly. "You can tell me your story while you eat."

"Can't say no to that, Lieutenant."

Surrisy installed them in a comfortable enclosure and the eternal roast beef arrived beneath its fake silver bell. Robert lifted the cover and Louchet looked fondly at the superb beef joint placed at his disposal. "To eat good food," he murmured, "this is the place–but people are dying like flies in the street, for lack of it. Excuse me if I get a move on–it's urgent." He put a thick slice on his plate, and attacked it with relish.

"Eat, eat, my friend," Surrisy said. "We have time."

The woodcutter put down his fork. "Will you leave me in London?" he asked.

"I promise that I'll take you back to Paris."

"My eating won't make me ill, then. May you be rewarded. Where was I? The father of the boy who's going to be hanged, wasn't it?"

"You've told me nothing about that."

"Good, good... We're up to Monsieur Temple, who sent me to carry two bottles of gin to a great she-devil, over on the other side of the Tower. Well, it turns out that he knows my Englishman and my Englishwoman. The Englishman isn't the father and the Englishwoman isn't the mother, as I'd suspected myself, since she only kissed him the once–the little one, I mean... a lovely child! It's another Englishman who's the father... and he, old Temple, turns out to be the grandfather... Go on!"

He thumped the fork on the table and drank a mouthful of ale. "To cut a long story short," he went on, "needless to say, Monsieur Temple should have taken me to Paris then to dig up the two dead bodies in the field beside Tivoli..."

"The two dead bodies!" Robert put in.

"And it would have been easy to find the spot," Pierre Louchet went on, "because of the dried-up thistles, and one of the dead men should only have four fingers on his right hand."

"What are you talking about, old man?" said Surrisy, shaking his arm. "Are you dreaming?"

"You don't know, then, that the Englishman is in prison in Paris?" asked the woodcutter, astonished. "In prison for having killed a man in Lyon and a man in Brussels at the same time?"

Surrisy's mouth remained wide open.

"Yes, yes," Pierre continued, "it seems funny at first glance; it's no short distance from Lyon to Brussels, and save for traveling on a broomstick like the witches of old... but see here: the two dead bodies at Tivoli struck the blows while they were alive, and the Englishman laid them to rest afterwards, under the grass, to make sure they didn't talk... not stupid, eh, Lieutenant?"

Surrisy was pale. His brow was convulsively furrowed.

"Ah," Pierre went on, "there's a lot more. He's John Devil, that one, you know–and under that name, he'll strangle an innocent tomorrow, like the brutes these English are, from first to last, in this country. Anyway, we left that evening, in a nice little mail-coach, me on the bench with a jabbering coachman, who knows how to mutter *right*! *left*! and then go flat out... It's just as easy to say *hue*! and *dia*! to the poor beasts. There were five of them inside: the consumptive, the three Germans with their pipes, and Monsieur Temple..."

"You haven't yet mentioned either the consumptive or the three Germans," Robert pointed out.

"No doubt, Lieutenant," Pierre replied, "since it's the first time I saw them. The consumptive was a handsome chap all the same... grander than you, and as soft as a schoolboy... The three Germans called one another doctor... I never saw such lovely pipes! Anyway, we arrived at the first relay station, five leagues from London, on the Dover road. It was a little inn to the left of the road. There was a light there, and I passed the time looking in. I saw that Mr. Wood who'd shown me the door; he was with a sort of monkey dressed as a gentleman. The monkey went to wake some poor wretches who were sleeping on the table; they came to surround the carriage while the horses were being changed, and one of them lifted an old stick, saying–I remember the words–'In the King's name!'[223] and something afterwards that meant 'I arrest you.' I shouted through the carriage door: 'Give me something to hit them with and I'll take care of them, by myself, quick as shaking salt!' Old Temple was of the same opinion, and the consumptive too, but the three doctors put themselves into the gendarmes' hands. They weren't what we call gendarmes, you know, but they were still policemen. Then one called the consumptive 'Prince' with a Russian name: Alexis Off... off... Mr. Wood and his monkey weren't there any longer. Monsieur Temple said to me: 'Go back to London and wait for me; this can't last.' I ask you! See how long it's lasted already, and that's how many days it is since I last ate!"

He pointed at the roast beef, already half-consumed.

"And what's the outcome of all this?" Surrisy asked.

"I can't even read French," Pierre Louchet, "And there's only English newspapers here. It's a pity, for they say that they put everything into them... I went to the Court of Sessions, because I heard in Leicester Square that Monsieur Temple and Monsieur Orloff–Prince Alexis Orloff, that was it!–were due to be questioned. I had to fight to get in, but didn't see or hear anything. They're out on bail, but I don't know where, and Monsieur Temple hasn't been back to his hotel."

"In your presence," Surrisy inquired, "have you ever heard the one you call the Englishman referred to by the name Comte Henri de Belcamp?"

"Belcamp!" repeated the woodcutter, stupefied in his turn. "It's the son of Monsieur le Marquis who calls himself the Comte de Belcamp!"

"It's the son of the Marquis," said the former Sub-Lieutenant, "who is in prison at Versailles, accused of having committed a murder in Lyon and a murder in Brussels on the same evening."

Pierre Louchet pushed his plate away.

"The son of Monsieur le Marquis can't be John Devil, though!" he stammered, dumbfounded.

Robert put a hand on his shoulder and said, slowly: "March straight ahead, comrade. Remember that the Police of more than one Kingdom would stop at nothing to crush us. I believe that Mr. Temple is an honest man, but he's fighting against us–who knows if his retreat, his arrest and everything else might not be scenes in the same comedy? I've sacrificed more than you to the cause we both serve, although I haven't gone without bread. Do as I do: wait and be ready. The man who has planned these moves is your leader and mine–and of all those who will draw the sword for the Emperor's cause."

"In that case," Pierre Louchet said, "we must find Monsieur Temple, bind his hands and legs and cut out his tongue–because I don't know everything myself, Lieutenant, but I know enough to be sure that Monsieur Temple will kill him!"

Between the Stock Exchange and the Bank of England, not far from the center of the kingdom of jargon of which the Stock Exchange is the capital, there is a vast and handsome building situated at the corner of Lothbury and Throckmorton Street, which fulfills the same, or nearly the same, function as our Hôtel des Commissaires-Priseurs in Paris: it is the Auction Mart, where public auctions are held. This kind of sale is commonplace in England, where it is often practiced in the absence of the extreme circumstances that are associated with it here. The Auction Mart, an arena of intense speculation, is often the scene of forced sales, when voluminous heaps of merchandise and other objects are accumulated there in considerable quantity. A particular language is spoken there, which seems to be a dialect of the picturesque idiom of the Stock Exchange. Englishmen of every estate take great delight in slang. Doubtless by way of punishment, as the English language crosses the Channel it becomes a genuine and stupid argot in the mouths of social lions, as a fashion, and sportsmen, as a joke.

Today, there was a numerous and noisy crowd in front of the Ionic-on-Doric facade, beneath the white fronton. It was not yet 2 p.m. Consequently, the Stock Exchange clock had not announced the overture to the mercantile dealings. They were all idling around, discussing the day's news.

The day's news was the sale of the great Perkins engine, put up for auction by virtue of Balcomb & Co.'s suspension of payments.

The engine was under the portico: an admirable mass of polished iron and scintillant copper. Experts were examining its gears, movements and valves with magnifying glasses; learned men were discussing friction and the means of transmission; laymen were measuring the enormous diameter of the boiler.

"It's a glutton," said Samuel Brand, a stout Jew with a hooked nose, round eyes, and jaundiced skin as taut as a drum. "It'll eat up more good oil than Perkins reckons. Don't they say, gentlemen, that he once undertook–for pleasure or some other reason–a voyage to Port Jackson?"

"They say a lot of things like that," replied a little man as sharp as a penknife, Mr. Milk of Milk and Blunt. "Don't they say that young Lord Peyton owes you 500 pounds sterling, Mr. Brand, because you advanced him 100 guineas?"

"There's a law against slander, Mr. Milk," Brand riposted.

"That makes two laws, with the one against usury, Mr. Brand."

"Devil take me if that will ever work!" cried Mr. Powells, another bigwig in the Port of London. "He's tried to simplify Watt and add Cowley and Vivian into the mix.[224] On my honor, he's an impertinent clown, and his machine is a crock!"

"You'd have to be a bull to buy that!" said Blunt scornfully.

"A lame duck, or God may punish me!" Samuel Brand added turning his back.

Others were coming up, examining, measuring and touching. The employees of the auction house gravely offered their opinion. A few women made a tour of the engine: shop-owners talking about their business or ladies hotly debating some nugget of gossip or item of clothing. There were, needless to say, more than enough cockneys.

Exchanges of this sort could be heard:

"I tell you, Mrs. Cake, with all that copper and iron, not to mention the steel, a locksmith wouldn't have to go to market for five years."

"And don't you think, Mrs. Bloomfield, that it would make an awful lot of knives."

"And a lot of cooking-pots, in the Lord's name."

"Sir Arthur is carrying on something shocking, you'll see, my dear!"

"Lady Elizabeth's flounces were no less than seven inches wide, I swear... and I can tell you in all seriousness that the dress came from Paris by the last packet-boat. Ah, there's Sir Lionel!"

"On my honor, I set myself at your feet, miladies... did you know that they're stuffing horses into these vats now... eight hundred horses, I've been told... it's a complete mystery to me!"

"You have an adorable pince-nez, my dear lord!"

"Brought from Paris by the last mail-coach, I can certify in good faith, Mesdames."

"Gentlemen, it's forbidden to tap it with hammers." This from an employee.

"Is it made of glass, my friend? I've always thought that rather fragile."

Two modest figures, one belonging to the Royal Mathematical Society, the other to the Royal Philotechnic Society:

"What I call a pretty law, sir, is one that increases symmetrically by squares or roots, directly or by inverse reasoning, like the law relating to bodies falling through a vacuum. Every geometric progression has a particular charm."

"Of course, of course... I will go so far as to say indubitably... but that unity they call an atmosphere seems to me as variable as a barometer, sir. I don't like poetry, you see... their cavalry of steam will burst that iron like an eggshell!"

A cockney:

"And yet there's a schooner on the Thames that works on clockwork. I've seen it!"

"We have not been introduced to one another, sir, and I have not answered you... an isolated fact proves little. Is there water vapor in your watch? It goes, though, I suppose. We need a jury... and I shall appeal against its decision in advance, if it is favorable. My opinion is as solid as a rock!"

The serious buyers gathered in a corner.

"Are you bidding for that, Bradley?" said Samuel Brand.

"Why, if you please? There's metal and men in the company. When I want to, I'll do better."

"Does anyone know what the Devil Balcomb intended to use that Leviathan for?" said Powells.

"To go bankrupt," quipped Samuel Brand.

"I'm permitted to say," insinuated a bull, "that Black and Storm of Greenwich mean to buy it to establish a tugboat on the Thames."

"You aren't serious!" put in a lame duck. "The Walter Company intends to construct a monstrous packet-boat to start a service between London and New York... it'll carry 1,200 passengers."

Everyone burst out laughing.

"And Perkins himself," added a third, "isn't as finished as they say. There's a masterpiece under construction at Munro's, and they're already talking of cutting the crossing to Bengal by two thirds."

They laughed again, but certain cunning glances interrogated the range of faces. After five minutes dickering, Powells, Milk and Blunt knew as well as Samuel Brand that there would be a hard-fought contest over this engine, which had been declared useless and impractical by all the serious men in the market.

The bell rang and the great door opened, displaying the three beautiful interior galleries. A platform had been erected not far from the door, especially for the sale of the Perkins engine, and the auctioneer was already at his post with his little ivory hammer and his collection of candle-ends.

Save for certain insignificant details of form, the conduct of sales by auction is the same in France as in America, Germany and England, so we shall not linger on any minute description. The ceremony began in the middle of a perfectly sufficient number of serious enthusiasts, inflated tenfold by idlers of every sort. The commissioner or auctioneer, having given his preliminary lecture, put up the Perkins engine for an opening bid of 10,000 pounds sterling–250,000 francs.

Among our readers, those who have special knowledge of the matter must either set their appreciation aside or take the circumstances into account in making their calculations. The Perkins engine could only have the value of a fantasy. It was a monster whose price could not be based on any existing standard. Present-day values are of no relevance whatsoever to the historical facts we are relating. One could say that, according to the wind, the humor or the whim of the auction, the Perkins engine might be worth nothing today, or millions. For its time, it was an admirable thing, and in the final analysis no one, among those in the know, had any hesitation in regarding it as a masterpiece. Without any other point of comparison, however, and no experience having been laid down, opposed interests silenced the hymn of praise. The price thrown out by the auctioneer raised a long murmur.

"Is it jeweled like a chronometer?" Samuel Brand shouted, churlishly.

"Does one joke with serious tradesman?" added Milk, disdainfully.

"I might have taken it as a repayment of a percentage of my debt," said Mr. Powells, "if it had been a matter of a thousand guineas."

"Your servant, Messieurs," concluded the sharp little Milk, who stuck his hat on his head and went towards the door."

Behind the auctioneer, the strong face of Perkins could now be seen; he stood quite still, pale, his brow furrowed.

In London, three auctioneers in consultation can–with the consent of the interested parties–lower the level of the reserve price. The auctioneer, seeing everyone resolutely turn their backs, sought the opinion of the creditors and Perkins himself–in the absence of Mr. Balcomb, the proprietor of the bankrupt company–and went away to consult two of his colleagues.

On every side were heard the words: "Wasting time, wasting time!" But something happened that killed the few minutes that followed. A plain brougham, drawn by a handsome horse, drew up outside the portico in front of the machine. A young man, dressed in black with the strict elegance, got down and came up the steps.

The name of Percy Balcomb immediately ran from group to group, and there was a stir of general curiosity, in which not the slightest trace of benevolence was mingled.

"Let's see! Let's see!" was heard on every side. "That's a rare bird!"

"I've asked 20 times for him to be pointed out to me in the Stock Exchange, but he's too great a lord to take care of his own business."

"Milord has been traveling..."

"Milord will soon be sleeping in the Fleet."

The hope of seeing milord in the debtor's prison gave birth to numerous smiles. Two hedges formed on either side of the door. Few people in that respectable gathering, in truth, knew Percy Balcomb. His pleasant appearance and the exquisite distinction of his clothing made a favorable impression on all those who were tradesmen. The mere curiosity-seekers saw him as a handsome dandy who had played fast and loose with the guineas in his chest, and that was all. He took his place behind the auctioneer just as that individual, rapping the table with his ivory hammer, announced to the audience that the consultation had been concluded.

"At 5,000 pounds, the Perkins engine!" he cried. "Five thousand pounds!"

The choir of tradesmen replied: "It's too much...! Half that would still be too much...! Put it up at 2,000 and we'll see!"

A few new faces became visible in the crowd: faces unknown to the regulars at the Auction Mart. More fortunate here than at the Hotel Spencer, Surrisy would not have had any trouble finding several faces that he knew around the table. A substantial fraction of the crew of the *Deliverance* was here, its Captain at their head.

The auctioneer was already hesitating in the face of this general disfavor when Percy Balcomb's eyes met those of Captain Abercrombie.

The Captain blushed, as he had never done before a line of cannons, and said in a timid voice: "Five thousand pounds, sir!"

Perkins lifted up his head, and his coarse face brightened. Once the first bid was in, interested parties had the right to bid higher. Perkins stared provocatively at those who had sought to humiliate him cruelly and whistle at him–him, the author of a great work! He said, in a high voice: "I'll bet 100 *louis*, cash down, that neither Samuel Brand, nor Milk and Blunt, nor Powells will let it go now for less than 20,000 guineas!"

"Nonsense! Stupidity! Pride!" the groups muttered.

"I'll bet 200 *louis* against 40,000!" cried Perkins.

" A million! Let's go, then! At least, it can be put on display for a shilling admission, like all machines that don't work!"

"Is it any good for steering balloons?" asked Mr. Milk, shrugging his shoulders.

"Five thousand guineas?" the auctioneer repeated.

"Five thousand two hundred," said a bull, who wanted to break it up and sell it by the pound.

"Three hundred," the Captain replied.

"It's a gambling game..." Samuel Brand began–but he was interrupted by the vibrant and calm voice of Percy Balcomb, which pronounced distinctly: "Ten thousand guineas!"

There was a stir of excitement in the crowd. The bigwigs exchanged glances.

"It wasn't worth the trouble of lowering the asking price," murmured the innocents.

"Eleven thousand!" Powells threw in. And he added, in a stage whisper: "To give a piece to Black and Storm, who are somewhere down there."

"Oh, that's what you want!" growled Blunt. He touched Milk's arm; Milk made a gesture of assent and put in; "Twelve thousand!"

"Fifteen thousand!" Samuel Brand bid, proudly.

"Twenty thousand!" said Balcomb.

"My hundred *louis* are won," cried the radiant Perkins. "Two hundred against 40,000–20 to one!"

There was silence around the table. Eyes lit up and foreheads were furrowed. The impassive auctioneer sang out: "At 20,000 pounds, the Perkins engine!" He was reaching out towards the candle when the Captain put in: "Twenty thousand and a hundred."

"Twenty thousand two hundred, by God!" said a hoarse voice behind him.

The tallest members of the crowd could see a pale and grimacing figure at shoulder-height to the Captain. Gentleman Ned was there.

"God damn me!" growled Powells. "The dressed-up monkey must be an agent for Walter. Twenty-one thousand!"

"Twenty two!" Milk immediately bid.

"Twenty-five!" said Brand.

"Thirty thousand," Balcomb put in, removing his gloves and making himself comfortable.

"Let's go, gentlemen!" cried Perkins laughing. "Two hundred against ten for 40."

"Thirty thousand guineas, the Perkins engine!" chanted the auctioneer

"If Black and Storm establish a tug," said Blunt, "they'll have the whole of London!"

"Thirty thousand five hundred!" croaked Milk.

"Forty thousand!" Powells riposted.

"Fifty thousand!" howled Samuel Brand, whose closed fist thumped the table furiously.

"Sixty thousand!" Percy Balcomb continued the sequence, cool as a statue. There was a long-drawn-out murmur. Milk and Blunt lowered their eyes. Samuel Brand wiped droplets of sweat from his forehead.

Powells put his hands in his pockets. "I'm too rich for such foolishness," he said. "Paying 1.5 million francs for a silly thing that'll have to be broken up or sold for 1,000 pounds is idiotic. I'm handing in my resignation."

Perkins had crossed his arms in front of his chest, and was posing triumphantly.

There was a tumult of chatter on every side.

"At 60,000 pounds, the Perkins engine!" proclaimed the auctioneer—and when no one responded he added: "The candles!"

A little flame sprang up on the desk. An observer endowed with a piercing gaze might have noticed a slight tremor at Percy Balcomb's temples, but from ten paces his face was made of marble and the expression of his features displayed imperturbable certainty.

Many eyes were fixed on him at that moment.

"Once!" said the auctioneer when the second candle caught alight.

"They must be keen to hold on, to bid 60,000 pounds," Blunt said.

"It's probably their final effort," observed Milk. "Let's find out! Sixty thousand one hundred!"

"Sixty thousand two hundred!" snarled Brand. "I'll follow you to the Devil if necessary!"

"Eighty thousand pounds!" said Percy Balcomb, in a voice he might have used for saying good day to a friend in the street.

"Bravo!" cried Gentleman Ned. "There's a lord!"

"Two millions!" murmured the crowd.

That one will go as far as ten millions, the bulls thought, unanimously—as did the bears and the lame ducks.

No one but the auctioneer could hear Balcomb's heart beating. On his features and in his gaze there was absolute calm.

Milk, Blunt and Samuel Brand did as Powells had done; they stuck their hands in their pockets. "It's a good result for the creditors," Blunt said.

"If he has the money in his pocket," Brand replied, "Black and Storm will finish up in Bedlam."

"Eighty thousand pounds, the Perkins engine!" the auctioneer said, slowly.

And the first candle was lit.

The bigwigs exchanged a few muttered curses that emanated from the depths of heir hearts, but none dared overbid. There was a good reason for that. The debts of the Balcomb bankruptcy did not amount to two million francs; in consequence, all this could be no more than a maneuver to push the auction beyond reasonable limits. One shilling more and Balcomb would probably stop, triumphant with the success of his ruse, and abandon the engine to the imprudent purchaser. A public sale is a game in which everyone must also work out his adversary's strategy.

The first candle went out and the second was lit.

The auctioneer heard Percy Balcomb breathe more easily. The unknown faces in the crowd could hardly contain the enthusiastic expression of their joy.

It was settled. The Perkins engine, whatever its real value, would revert to its original owner, at a price of two million francs.

The third candle was lit.

A profound silence now reigned in the hall, where everyone was still and mute.

"Three times!" said the auctioneer, as the last candle flickered. And he added, as his duty demanded: "At 80,000 pounds, the Perkins engine!"

A frail voice–the voice of an old man–broke the silence and set the entire assembly a-tremble, like a solitary traveler who hears a vague noise in the night.

The voice said: "Eighty thousand and five pounds."

Was it a madman?

It had to be a madman.

It was a madman–for he could be seen, with a white head and ardent eyes, sliding his meager feverishly quivering body between Blunt and Samuel Brand. He stopped between the table and the platform. His eyes were fixed on Percy Balcomb.

Percy Balcomb's blood flooded his face. His eyes fluttered, then he became as pale as a corpse.

The old man–it was an old man–nodded his head in a familiar fashion, and smiled.

That smile cut like a blade.

The bulls, the bears and the lame ducks watched with their mouths agape. Even the bigwigs were intensely intrigued, and asked themselves: What's that about?

Balcomb returned the greeting gravely. After changing color twice, his face had resumed its statuesque impassivity, but he had two large drops of sweat on his temples. Everyone expected that he would casually cover the overbid of five pounds, given that he had earlier been making increases of ten thousand *louis*. He remained silent.

"Eighty thousand and five pounds!" said the auctioneer, addressing himself to Balcomb alone. "Is it necessary to light up, sir?"

Balcomb nodded to signal his assent.

A murmur ran around the room similar to the one that his last valiant overbid had excited, when he had leapt from 60,000 to 80,000; it lasted while the three candles burned out.

"Your name, sir?" the auctioneer asked the old man, as the third candle burned low.

The old man climbed the platform steps and answered the question.

The ivory hammer came down. The last candle was smoking.

"All seen, all heard, no one having spoken," the auctioneer announced, solemnly, "the Perkins engine is sold for the price of 80,000 and five pounds to Mr. Gregory Temple esquire, former Chief Superintendent of the Metropolitan Police."

The crowd dispersed, chattering and laughing. A skillful hand appropriated Sir Arthur's pince-nez, without making any bid; we cannot answer at this point for Gentleman Ned.

A few moments later, Percy Balcomb left, surrounded by Perkins, Edmund Abercrombie and the crew of the *Deliverance*. They looked like a funeral cortege.

Instead of replying to the discouraged questions of his friends, Balcomb came to a sudden halt and said: "Messieurs, I leave for Paris tomorrow. A quarter of the day and an entire night remain to me. Captain Abercrombie, I order you to have the three-master *Eagle*,[225] which is anchored at Greenwich, brought upriver. That vessel will have the honor of transporting to the coast of Guinea those you know and our friend Perkins' engine. It must be loaded at Saint-Savior's dock today at ten o'clock in the evening. Perkins, you must retain the dock's largest crane for the whole night. Messieurs, we must either greet tomorrow while doubling the isle of Thanet with the engine, or break our swords and mourn our hopes. I'm going to play my last hand, and I have no need of you: until tomorrow!"

XIII. In Extremis

It had the form of a gaming die that had been hollowed out: it was a hole in a block of stone, a perfect cube, whose smooth walls were painted with yellowing distemper. There was a window, cleft horizontally like a lipless mouth, protected by a single iron bar. The English had already been writing and speaking the language of benevolent reform for a long time, with fluid prolixity, but Portland stone has its own language, less loquacious but more eloquent, and Newgate is still standing.

The dungeons of the Middle Ages were hideous in a different way; perhaps, all things considered, they were more so–we have seen nothing of them but ruins. Newgate carries itself well, and health is always beautiful. Newgate is hideous among all things hideous, and the Mazas [226] jail, the stone bogeyman that grimaces in the *in-pace* [227] in the midst of our civilization's smiles, is a palace of gaiety next to Newgate.

It was possible to breathe in the cell. The number of square feet required to sustain human life is scientifically determined; the ventilation hole was of sufficient dimension to ensure that asphyxia did not occur. It was furnished with a massive wooden chair attached to the wall by a chain and a wooden frame covered by a woolen mattress. An even greater luxury, a tallow candle, burned at ground level in a leaden tray.

This luxury was expensive. In a parliamentary debate on the prison regime that took place several years later, after the accession of George IV, there was talk of candles that sold for a guinea.

The dungeons of the Middle Ages were damp and dark; they had strange vaults, frightful shackles, iron collars sealed into the granite, as one can easily see at the Porte-Saint-Martin Theater.[228] These souvenirs, however they might be exaggerated by painters and poets, are terrible, lugubrious and shameful. The stone box in which English humanity encloses its captive would not be so effective in the theater; it is incomparably less picturesque. It is more akin to the peace of a coffin. The sinister has no flourishes here; the ugliness is sober, the horror puritan.

It was nearly midnight. The wild beast imprisoned in this cage was not asleep. By the vacillating light of the candle that lit it from below, you would have recognized Richard Thompson at first glance, in spite of his thinness and the mortal transformation that had worked upon his physiognomy. He was sitting in the chair, with his head and neck bare. He had no clothes but trousers and a shirt. His hands, crossed on his knees, were held by that special kind of handcuffs the English call manacles. His legs stuck out straight in front of him; his head was slumped forward.

His hollow cheeks were so pale, and the immobility of his depression was so complete, that one could easily have believed him dead if it had not been so difficult for a corpse to maintain that pose on a narrow chair.

Next to him, a crumpled piece of paper lay on the stone floor.

The clock of Saint James's Church chimed. The prisoner hunched his shoulders like a man who feels cold, but he did not get up to get his overcoat, which was thrown across the foot of the bed. He brought up his knees to touch his head, and adopted the pose that painters routinely attribute to unfortunates afflicted by idiocy.

He was not an idiot, though. After a minute or two, his lowered eyelids lifted slightly; his poor eyes, swollen and hot, stared straight ahead, fixed on the wall.

The light struck the wall vividly. There was a kind of crude sketch on the plaster, traced in charcoal by a childish novice hand. That sketch had drawn the tears from his eyes. It represented–God knows how, but in a fashion that left no room for misapprehension–a woman kneeling next to a sleeping child. Underneath it, two names had been inscribed: Suzanne, Richard.

Once, a turnkey had tried to erase it while cleaning the cell. Thompson had gone down on his knees to kiss his feet. The man had shrugged his shoulders; he was not spiteful. The sketch remained on the wall. Thompson spent his hours looking at it.

His imagination and his heart, less impotent than his poor garroted hands, gave the color of life to that vague outline. His dream animated the shaky lines of the design, and that cold wall had often smiled via the moist eyes of his wife and the half-open lips of the little child, who stammered his father's name.

"Sixty-eight days!" he murmured, his eyes fixed on the sketch. "Suzanne loves me very much. Does she know that I shall die?" His eyelids fell again, while his pale lips moved as if they were murmuring a prayer.

We have seen the handsome actress' son, doubtless brought up in an atmosphere of gaiety and pleasure, when he retained a certain joyous insouciance in his character; we have seen him already stricken, but still retaining the savor of his son's kisses on his lips. Lady Frances had only criticized one thing in this brave and good youth: his weakness.

Well, there are weaknesses that are nothing but noble kindness. Richard was not weak in the face of death. When he wept, it was that two cherished persons might visit him in his solitude; the only thing that softened his heart now was the thought of Suzanne and little Richard.

He suffered a great deal. He suffered too much, and had none of those motives to support him by means of which exalted souls withstand torture. He had neither political faith nor religious belief to confess. He had not fallen on a battlefield. It was an obscure and miserable death that was in prospect, which approached upon his youth like the level of a homicidal tide coming to drown an unfortunate whose feet are stuck in quicksand. God had removed his joys one by one before riveting him with the immobility of that slow death-agony.

He had been loved; he had taken into his arms the idol of his heart; she who adored him had given him a son; he could have counted the hours of that felicity as soon as they had fled. A wall had emerged from the ground, a wall of mourning, separating him from all his joys and imprisoning him in despair.

He had never seen Suzanne again in all that time, and Suzanne had not written to him once.

Oh, love finds a means of scaling the walls of a prison and piercing its thick oaken doors! There is no dungeon so dark that it cannot be penetrated by a ray of love! One letter, one line, Suzanne's name under the three words: I love you! But nothing. Where was she? Did she know?

He did not doubt Suzanne. He suffered. He sometimes thought about the future of the sad child who would grow up under his mother's wing. He heard them talking about the one who was no longer alive. The child asked for the story of his father. But what story would the widow's tears tell? This was the hand of iron that clutched his heart. What story...?

He said to God: *The world has condemned me, as thy will be done... but for her, oh, for her, let the radiance of your light fall upon my innocence! May she not have that pain and that shame; let there be honor in her mourning!*

He said also: *I have suffered three times over. Render my tortures to them as joy. They are my heirs, Lord, who had no heritage of my own. May my death be a patrimony! I shall bless your hand that strikes me, if it amasses for them the treasures of your mercy!*

No, he was not weak. Blessed are those who have no hatred. He doubted James Davy now, and he regarded Gregory Temple as his executioner, but neither James Davy nor Gregory Temple had once been cursed by his lips.

It was all over. The preliminaries of the investigation, sent from Paris by the former Chief Superintendent of Police, had that terrible solidity typical of all his works. English justice, directed on to that path and impatient to be finished with an affair that had reflected so unfavorably on the Police and held them up to such ridicule, had moved forward rapidly. As always happens once the tied hands of the bold malefactor are no longer to be feared, witnesses had surged forth from all sides.

At Sharper's, in Jenny Paddock's room, we saw the first rehearsal of a comedy that played for several days to an audience, with a marvelous cast and with complete success. The sequential depositions of the maiden chickens administered the final blow to Richard Thompson, and succeeded in convincing the jury. The verdict was then affirmative on all counts, and the Court pronounced the sentence of death.

The crumpled paper that lay on the floor at the prisoner's feet was a copy notifying him of the decision of the Judges of the Appeal Court, rejecting his petition.

A few minutes after midnight, the warder in charge of Thompson opened the door of his cell and came in. His manner was churlish. It was the same one who had spared the sketch on the wall. He had a scarlet face and troubled eyes. Scarcely had he entered when his eyelids fluttered and his thick eyebrows frowned.

"Have you some more bad news to tell me, Clarke, my friend?" Richard asked, quietly.

"Aren't you going to bed today?" stammered the man, whose tongue was thick. "Devil take me! My compassion will cost me my job!"

"I'll go to bed if you say so, Clarke," the prisoner replied, "but I'm not sleepy."

"Sleepy!" echoed Clarke, turning abruptly on his unsteady legs. His gaze fell upon the sketch, and a curse stuck in his throat as he looked hastily away. "May I be hanged myself if I don't dream about all this!" he muttered. Then, in a hoarse voice, he added: "I've had a drink to give me heart, Mr. Thompson. Would you like a drink too? It bucks you up!"

At that moment, the sound of a carpenter's mallet was heard, knocking mightily on wood.

The prisoner raised his head, and a sentiment of anguish was readable in his expression. He looked around questioningly, as if in search of a means of flight.

"Do you want a drink?" Clarke repeated, turning his eyes away from him.

"Why drink?" said Thompson, his voice catching in his throat.

The man made no reply. The mallet struck the wood again, waking resonant and sinister echoes in the long corridors of the prison.

"Suzanne! My poor Suzanne!" murmured Thompson, putting his hands together.

"Yes, yes," muttered Clarke, putting his sleeve to his moist eyes. "And the little child, right? My God, yes! May I burn in Hell! You didn't have to kill the actress, lad!"

"I swear on my hope of salvation that I'm innocent!" Richard cried.

"My God, yes! It's all the same to me, lad. It's the thought of the one who's there on the wall, you see... I've got a wife and kid too. Oh, I've had a drink. Do you want a drink?"

He opened his jacket and displayed a bottle. One of the men erecting the scaffold outside began to sing. Clarke set the bottle on the floor and clenched his fists. Then, as he saw that Thompson was shivering, he went to get the overcoat from the foot of the bed, and put it over the prisoner's shoulders.

"It's not fear!" the young man said, trying to smile.

"It's Lewis who sings like that," growled Clarke. "I'll go see to him. Have a swig, lad."

"It's the cold, you see," said Thompson, who was calm again. "Thank you, my friend, but I don't need a drink. It's for tomorrow isn't it?"

Clarke grabbed the bottle and stuck the neck in his mouth.

"At four o'clock in the morning," he answered. "I've told the wife about that thing on the wall... she said that you wouldn't want anything to eat or drink..."

"Aren't they sending me a priest, my friend?" the prisoner put in.

"I knew I'd forgotten something! It's Lewis and his wretched song. The minister's outside with his Bible."

"Please tell him that I'm ready."

Clarke took a step towards the door, then he stopped and came back. "The wife said that you'd have something to send," he murmured. "You know... for them on the wall... it can be whatever you want."

"Thank you, my friend," Thompson replied, in a tearful voice. "I have a locket around my neck. If you would like to do me a great service, you might remove the lock of hair from within it and place it on my heart, when I am taken to be buried. If you could cut a lock of my own hair, and place it in the locket, I'll tell you tomorrow morning to who it should be sent, my good friend."

The turnkey withdrew the hand that Thompson had taken, and hurried out of the cell.

Thompson remained alone. The blows of the mallet no longer made him shiver. He opened his shirt and took out the locket dangling from his neck. He looked at it for a long time and pressed it against his lips, murmuring: "Adieu, my dear Suzanne! Adieu, my little Richard!"

Then he became still, absorbed within himself.

After a few minutes, Clarke's voice was audible again in the corridor.

"It's our job to take precautions, Reverend," he was saying. "The Dean had said that he would come himself... but since you have the letter, signed by him, to say that you're replacing him, that's all right..."

Then, doubtless in reply to a question posed by the Reverend, he said: "They're all innocent, you know, but this one... me, I've never seen the like in the 15 years I've been eating the King's bread. The actress was strangled, that's for sure... afterwards, some time from now, some rogue will probably say to us, as he climbs on to the platform out there: 'It was me who strangled the actress...' Around here, it's not as rare as cows with three horns. Go in. When you want to come out, knock hard on the door and ask for Joseph Clarke."

The door opened, and was then locked and barred.

Thompson saw a minister of the Anglican Church in front of him, whose face was bare and who carried a voluminous Bible in his hand. Thompson looked at him, searching his memory for the familiar face that the unknown visage–austere and gentle at the same time beneath its black hair–resembled.

He stood up politely.

The Anglican minister placed his Bible on the bed and lifted up his large hat and his black hair at the same time, displaying the graceful blond curls beneath which the young and bold face of James Davy was smiling.

Thompson moved back, stupefied. An exclamation rose from his breast, but the Reverend's hand was already upon his mouth.

"Better late than never, Thompson," he whispered.

"Something told me that you'd come, James," Thompson murmured, with tears in his eyes.

"I've lost track of all my names, Richard," said the Reverend, smiling. "Call me Henri. That's my real name: Henri de Belcamp. My friends will know me by that name henceforth."

"Henceforth!" Thompson repeated. "I can't tell you what that word means to me now."

"It means the future, Richard: youth, happiness... do you think that I've come here to prepare you for death?"

"How did you do it?" the condemned man asked. Joy produces trivial questions.

"I promised Suzanne that I would save you, Richard."

This time, it was not the last word that Thompson repeated. Even the idea of salvation disappeared before the thought of Suzanne.

"Suzanne!" he cried. "Oh, tell me about Suzanne! Tell me about my little Richard..."

"I'll tell you everything you wish, Thompson—but while we work, if you please; I haven't brought you the wings of Icarus... and Icarus couldn't get through that abominable slit they call a window... You've got black trousers; that's one thing already. Throw off your overcoat, and be quick, for another visitor is coming and I must be alone to receive him!"

Comte Henri was busy while he spoke. His handkerchief was quickly suspended over the keyhole, to block out indiscreet peeping; the overcoat was thrown on the bed and the big Bible was opened.

The huge Bible was the principal contents of that precious case that Comte Henri de Belcamp had brought from Versailles. It was a box of theatrical make-up.

We know that Comte Henri was a skillful transformer of faces. In the blink of an eye, Thompson, half-willingly and half-reluctantly, was painted from the tip of his chin to the roots of his hair: an artwork by a veritable master, which reproduced unmistakably the face of the Reverend James Davy.

"Will you explain...?" Thompson began.

"Of course," Henri interrupted. "Firstly, Suzanne has but one malady, and that is sadness. She still loves you with all her dear little heart..."

"Oh, thank you, thank you...!" Thompson murmured.

"That's not all. In the second place, little Richard is beloved by two mothers: Suzanne and Sarah. He's the happiest and most beautiful child in the world. If you cry, damn it, you'll spoil my painting. You don't need to think, poor friend, that I'm performing some act of heroism; I'm purely and simply doing my duty, and I still remain indebted to you for all that you've suffered. I hope one day to be fully acquitted of that other debt."

"Generous friend!" Richard exclaimed. "Don't you remember everything you've done for me?"

"Hold still while I position the wig. To you, and to many others, I have lent little; I have borrowed more, but this is not the time to settle our account. The very honorable Peter Trump, Dean of St James's, wouldn't be able to set you right like this, no! But Mr. Temple has taught us many other things!" He laughed as he continued: "Imagine that the good Dean, Peter Trump, is held prisoner at this moment by four beautiful women–of whom two are Countesses, no less–who know not what they do! Next year, if you wish, you'll be the lion of the season, after such an escape."

"I shall get away, then?" Richard said, letting himself be turned back and forth like an infant.

"Are you beginning to doubt yourself, Thompson? On my word, if I were not perfectly sure that in a quarter of and hour you'd be free and clear, the noise they're making out there would certainly stop me laughing." He stopped for a moment to listen to the carpenters who were hammering with all their might.

"It's a long way from here to liberty!" Thompson sighed.

"Two hundred paces and five minutes of effrontery, friend. I got in easily enough; why should you not get out? Hold out your arms, please, so that I can pass you my quilted coat... and pay close attention to this. The Reverend speaks very quietly; he has lost his voice."

"So that's why I couldn't hear you in the corridor!"

"Precisely. I've taken precautions, because I can't change your voice as I can your face. Peter Trump's replacement must walk at a discreet and tranquil pace, without affectation. Try, I beg you... more dignity... I should say, more vanity... you've come to perform a great deed, and your name will be in tomorrow's *Times*... now, the hat. If anyone happens to ask, you're John Gravesend, Assistant to the Vicar of Saint James's. Repeat the name."

"John Gravesend."

"Lower... whisper it effortfully... have you forgotten that you've lost your voice?"

"John Gravesend," Richard repeated for the second time, "Assistant to the Vicar of Saint James's."

"Perfect. You'll follow Clarke very meekly, your Bible under your arm. If he says nothing, you say nothing. If he questions you, answer from the depths of your poorly throat: 'Oh, the unfortunate boy! Oh, the poor young man...' "

"And you?" Thompson asked.

"Don't worry about me. When I pass through the walls, I have to be on the road to Paris in a few hours time–that's promised. Are you ready?"

"I'm ready to risk a thousand deaths to see my wife and child," Richard replied.

"You aren't risking anything at all... as long as you keep cool and don't hurry. Now, be sure to remember this: on arrival at the vault, you say to the turnkeys: 'My friends, pray for the poor unfortunate who is going to die...' You turn right, as if to go back to Saint James's, and you go quietly past the church. There, you take the first side street you come to, and you go down towards Smithfield as fast as your legs can carry you. You reach the Thames, go over the bridge, and throw the quilted coat into the river. You'll still have the frock-coat and the Scottish cap that's in the right-hand pocket. You stroll around Bermondsey until 4 a.m., and at that moment you go into the Nelson's Sword Inn, at the corner of the St Laurence Dock. I'll be there. Is that clear?"

"It's clear, but let me ask you...?"

"You know everything you need to know, and I've no time to lose. Here's your Bible."

He pushed the admirably disguised Thompson towards the door. "Are we there?" he asked.

"Let's go," said Richard, taking his courage in both hands.

Henri gave three loud raps of the door with his fist and cried in a strangled voice: "Clarke! Joseph Clarke!"

Footsteps sounded in the corridor almost immediately.

Henri withdrew quickly, sat on the chair next to the bed, and supported his head on the bedcover. He was already wrapped in Richard's overcoat. Only the back of his bare head was visible, and the prisoner also had blond hair.

The door opened. Clarke had continued to give himself heart; he was already three-quarters drunk.

"Well, Reverend?" he said to Richard, who moved to leave.

"Oh, the unfortunate boy!" whispered Richard, from the depths of his throat.

"Yes, yes, for sure. And have you seen what's on the wall?"

They went out together into the corridor. Henri, however, could hear Richard reply "Oh, the poor young man!" and Clarke's continuation, in a pompous tone: "When you have a bad cold like that, Reverend, you have to prime a quarter-pint of gin with cinnamon, pepper and pimento..."

There were doubtless other ingredients in that medicine for a bad cold, but the turnkey's voice was lost in the distance.

The door was closed again. Henri consulted his watch, which showed half past midnight. Thompson's transformation had not taken ten minutes. He stretched himself out comfortably on the bed and closed his eyes against the noise of the mallets that were hammering bolts into the scaffold.

It was probably not in order to sleep that Comte Henri de Belcamp had closed his eyes–but he had, as sportsmen say, done a 50-league stretch on horseback in his belly, and two nights without sleep weighed his eyelids down. He dozed, whether he intended to or not, lulled by the hammers of the mortuary carpenters.

People who have taken a great many risks in their lives–the adventurous pioneers of the new world, the heroes of those solitary epics where the prospector for gold and the savage spin out their implacable battle in the boundless arenas of virgin forests and prairies; our European soldiers when they have been fighting as partisans for a long time–all know how to sleep with one eye open, resting like a bird on a branch. Comte Henri was a soldier, an adventurous pioneer, a savage, a man whose existence consisted of continually wagering his all, hour after hour. He could close his eyes on the rim of a precipice, because he was perfectly self-possessed. There was an instinct in him that remained awake, standing sentinel.

Sleep, for him, was no complete loss of consciousness, but merely a brief truce given to effort and calculation.

Tonight, while he slept, he was waiting.

He was on the pallet, his face turned to the wall. The light, still set on the flagstones in its leaden tray, illuminated his back, enveloped by the overcoat and a few sparse curls of his blond hair; nothing reached his face but reflections from the ceiling or the bleak wall.

After half an hour or so, there was an indistinct noise in the corridor. It sounded like footsteps that someone was trying unsuccessfully to muffle. Henri did not move. Voices whispered on the other side of the door.

"I'm risking a lot," murmured Clarke, "whose thick tongue was articulating with difficulty. "You must know that. You've been in the thick of it. And how can the poor young man be made to tell you this or that, since no one's said a word to put his hand on the gate?"

"I've passed through the gate myself," said another voice.

"And that must have cost you dear, is my answer to that! Me, I'll get out of the way, because I haven't the heart to see the poor devil tonight. He's as gentle as a lamb, isn't he? And he's daubed the Devil of a thing on his wall..."

"What thing?"

"A woman he did with a piece of charcoal... and a child..."

Henri shifted on the pallet. His head lifted slightly. His gaze interrogated the wall. He saw the sketch, smiled, consulted his watch again, and returned his head to the pillow.

"Clarke, my friend," said the stranger's voice–an old man's voice, hoarse and feeble–"you know that I still have a long arm, in spite of everything. I won't be with the young man for more than half an hour, and you'll be 20 guineas better off."

"My wife really needs a new mantle..." Clarke muttered.

"Twenty guineas without any risk. It's one o'clock. No one will come before three to get him dressed..."

"Four o'clock, it's fixed... and the Constables with the Sheriff ten minutes beforehand."

"So we have four times as much time as we need."

The key clicked against the lock, as if an unsteady hand were searching for the hole.

"Well," said Clarke, "it's not for the 20 guineas–may God punish me if I tell a lie! It's because I'm sick at heart tonight, and I can see that poor thing on the wall dancing all around me. If someone took my wife and my little kid like that...!"

The latch slid from its bed, creaking; the wheel-bolt whirred; there was a little clink of gold.

"To get out," Clarke said again, "knock hard on the inside and call me by name. Hell's Devils! I think my head's spinning!"

The door opened, then closed on Gregory Temple.

The former Police Superintendent remained at the threshold for a moment. The light, striking him from below, hollowed out his wrinkles profoundly and put shadows under his eyes, which gleamed vaguely nevertheless. He was wearing the costume of a Newgate warder; he had evidently got here by means of comedy reinforced by money.

Comedy, thus reinforced, always gets results. One can invent new tricks, but the old ones are good.

The collar of his jacket came halfway up his cheeks, and the heads of a bunch of keys were sticking out of his pocket. He had a Scottish cap pulled down to his eyebrows. His troubled gaze had a feverish intensity as it scanned the stone box. He shivered slightly. When his eyes reached the crude sketch on the wall, they turned away from it.

"Richard!" he murmured.

The sound of calm and steady respiration came from the bed.

"Is that courage?" the old man thought aloud. "Or is it the brutality of a man who doesn't care about himself? Does the soul die before the body in those who no longer hope?" He shivered again, more strongly. "I couldn't sleep," he went on, "with that noise of mallets." For a second time, he called: "Richard!" And when there was still no reply, he went closer to the pallet and repeated, impatiently: "Richard! Richard Thompson!"

"I'm not deaf," growled the sleeper. "I can hear you quite well!"

Temple certainly had no suspicion of what had occurred. In the unlikely event that he had had any suspicion, those words would have made him faint, for the tone, accent and voice were identical to poor Richard's. Henri had imbibed the science of imitation that completes great actors.

"Don't you recognize me, Thompson?" Gregory asked, his tone betraying his feverish agitation.

"Indeed," was the rude response. "You're the rope that will hang me."

"I'm the father of your wife, Richard! I've made a mistake; I've come to repair my error."

"If you repent, be pardoned," said the pretended Thompson. "I've talked to the priest, and I want to die a Christian... but I want to die as a man, too. You've brought memories that might break me: go away!"

"But it's liberty that I'm bringing you, my son, my poor boy!" exclaimed the old man, seizing his arm. "I know that I've done you a great deal of harm; I don't ask you for affection or recognition... but listen to me, in the name of your wife and your son!"

Richard's head dug into the hard pillow. "I'm listening," he said, in a gloomy tone.

"That's not courage," murmured Temple, with a bitter smile. "That's the despondency of the death-agony." He got up and paced around the room. His hand pressed his forehead several times over.

"Richard!" he cried, suddenly and violently, "You're my son, I want you to be my son! I shall die mad, do you hear? And you must avenge me!"

He stopped beside the bed. The prisoner remained still and silent.

"You must avenge yourself!" the old man went on, supporting himself on the meager mattress with both hands. "You must avenge your wife's tears. Oh, my head is lucid now. I see as clearly as I did at 20. I shall tell you shortly how you can escape from here... before that, it's necessary that I explain your duty... for if I remain prisoner in your place, my son, you must act in mine!"

The pretended Thompson breathed noisily. Sometimes that is the vigorous response of the constricted chest that wishes to break free, but it can also express disdainful and discouraged incredulity.

Temple let himself fall into the chair. He put his clenched hands to his forehead, which was sweating profusely.

"Be certain, Thompson," he went on, changing his tone, "that the things I have to tell you are exact, precise, authentic. My fever might be killing me as I speak, but I swear to you that I'm in full possession of my faculties. That man is fleeing. That man believes he is saved... the one who has made your life pure Hell... the one who changed my joyous Suzanne into a pale statue... the one who has set my head to boil and who is nailing the boards of your scaffold at this very moment."

"James Davy," murmured the prisoner.

"Ah!" cried Gregory Temple, clasping his shaking hands, "You're listening to me at last! God will prove stronger than the demon! Yes, James Davy! What do his other names matter now! James Davy, the triple, the tenfold assassin. James Davy is in London. He is doubtless triumphant... but he is lost! His flight will kill him, if you are still a man and if you can follow my instructions successfully. Richard, Richard, to save you I am probably risking more than my life! In God's name, tell me that you will obey me, for there is a fire in my skull, and a voice calling me to my destiny!"

"You have not yet commanded me to do anything," Thompson said, coldly, moving nonchalantly on his bed. "I have no trust in you, save that resulting from the fact that no man any longer has the power to hurt me. Explain, if you wish, what I must understand."

The old man's breast yielded up a groan. "That's how it should be!" he murmured. "He's an unfortunate child. Why has the thought of my daughter grown so within me, since I thought of dying?" His disheveled grey hair hung down over his haggard forehead and there was a sinister gleam of frenzy in his eyes. "I'll explain myself, Richard," he went on, although his tone was submissive. "I understand your mistrust, but hope that you might leave it here. What good would it do me to deceive you, poor child? The rope is around your neck. The ruination of that man, believe me, will not merely avenge me against him, but all the wretches who have humiliated me. I abhor them even more than him now. MacAllan, my successor... the Lord Chief Justice... and the Regent! The Regent, who said to me once, like a Sultan in the *Thousand-and-One Nights*: 'Ask anything you wish of me...' The Regent, ingrate debtor, obligatory insolvent, who laughed at me in front of all his servants in his court clothes and said: 'I do indeed owe this old man one thing... lodgings in Bedlam!' "

He ground his teeth and his hair shifted on his skull. "Oh, oh!" he said, in a voice that was like a dull croak, "I want to take the severed head of that man by the hair and smash it into all their faces. The noble brutes! The sovereign caricatures! I would like to hurl fistfuls of mud and blood in their faces! Do you know what I was, young man, before this demon took my composure, my intelligence and my memory? I was Gregory Temple, and how many princes of the blood trembled before me! I knew everything; I saw everything! The King, if there had been a King, would not have dared to speak to me as to his Ministers. To know everything! Can you comprehend the prodigious figure of that force? To know everything, in a world where everyone, even its master, has something to hide! I had that power... and I have fallen so low that the thieves of Saint Giles's look at me and laugh when they meet me in the street!"

"And you are full of hatred?" said the prisoner, with a calmness that made the old man leap from his seat.

"Yes!" he croaked, his cry strangled by mad rage. "Enough hatred to throw you as prey to the executioner, sad and feeble child whom fear has already changed into a cadaver!" He stopped, biting his fists. "But no, no... don't listen to me... you're right... I haven't yet explained myself... what you have to do is so easy! Don't you love the father of your wife just a little, Richard?"

To that question, which arrived so unexpectedly, the prisoner replied with one evasive word: "Once..."

"That's just! That's just!" Temple murmured, with sudden emotion. "You've suffered a great deal... for a long time. If I can convince you that he is the cause, the only cause of all that..."

"Tell me what I must do," Thompson interrupted, in a more forceful tone.

"Good, my friend! You're right again. That's the main thing... if he is convicted over there by default that will be enough for me. What does his death matter if I can hang his corpse in effigy at the Regent's palace gate and shout to all those who insulted me in the thousand voices of the press: Shame! Shame! Shame! Oh well, I have in Paris a treasure of proofs, and the final one, for which I came in search–for I divined its existence by means of the calculations that they all mocked–is in Paris, hidden under a few feet of soil, in a place that I shall describe to you."

"Describe!" said Thompson, who seemed interested, and even impatient.

Temple looked at him, lost as he was in the shadow of the bed. Then his eyes looked back at the candle-flame, as if he were tempted to lift it up to get a better view. But his thoughts were deflected by the wind of his passion and his madness.

"You know what an alibi is, Richard," he went on trying to establish a simple and concise demonstration. "The French judges find themselves confronted with such an alibi as has never been seen before. Imagine a triangle, A B C. Two crimes have been committed simultaneously, one at point B and one at point C. A man is accused of both crimes, and the man has clear proof that, on the day in question, he never left A. You know that my system of detection now rests on a geometrical base, since I arrived at the conclusion that every malefactor tries to drive his judge back into the realm of the absurd. For me, the actual inventor of the instrument, all this work projects no shadow of mystery. Here is the hand of an adept: every letter is signed by it. James Davy, in posing this problem, is crying out to me: It is I who am the assassin, but the Magistrates of France do not know it; they are working from old axioms, with old methods. The triple impossibility that stands before them like an unassailable palisade will stop them permanently–unless someone can put the recipe for the trick into their hands.

"James Davy is accused in France under the name of Comte Henri de Belcamp. In this case there were, at a given moment, three Henri de Belcamps: one at point A, who was himself; one at point B, who was Noll Green the boxer; and one at point C, who was Lochaber Dick. It's quite simple, isn't it? Well, here is a paper that will give you the exact topography of a field situated in Paris, behind Tivoli, where the corpses of Noll and Dick can be found, both assassins having returned from points B and C on the eve of the day when James Davy was arrested at point A. You will notice that on that day, at the Opéra-Comique theater, ten witnesses–listed in the same paper–saw blood on Comte Henri's cuff and shirt front. Take this piece of paper and the key to the room that I occupied in Paris, at Number 19 Rue Dauphine; I entrust them to you."

The hand of the false Richard Thompson must undoubtedly have been itching, but he did not yet know all that he needed to learn, and his arm remained still. "Mr. Temple," he said, finally pronouncing the master word of the role that he was playing, "throughout my trial here, the Judges and Advocates were speaking of you as a man who had lost his mind. I can't say that I believed it, because I know that you're capable of assuming any disguise, but I must confess to having had some doubts. I have a hope of salvation other than you... what means of escape are you offering me?"

"The simplest, and the most dangerous for me," the former detective replied, without hesitation. "You take my clothes, and I remain in your place."

"The difference in our ages..."

"I have everything I need to transform you into an old man."

"And once transformed into an old man...?"

"May God have pity on us, my son-in-law! At your age, and in your situation, I would not have asked so much! Once transformed into an old man, you go out with Clarke, who is drunk, and who will take you as far as the western corridor, which gives out into the courtyard of the Press. You pay Clarke five pounds, and he puts you into the hands of one of his colleagues who is more expensive; that one has already received 15 pounds, you will give him 15 more, and he will lead you to the North Gate, where you are expected to deliver 30 pounds and a blow of the fist to the old master porter, who is an old acquaintance. Once in the street, is it necessary to tell you to put one foot in front of the other, alternately, to get away on foot?"

The prisoner's hand opened to take the key and the paper. Then, while starting to turn over, he said: "That's exactly what I needed to know, Mr. Temple."

The former detective shivered at the sound of that voice, which seemed to him to have changed completely–but there was no time for the doubt to deepen before the shock of certainty arrived. Indeed, the prisoner simply turned around, and placed his face in the full glare of the light: the serene, firm and intrepid face of Comte Henri de Belcamp.

The set of the old man's face decomposed. He tried to speak or cry out, but his voice stuck in his throat. Henri, still stretched out on the bed but now propped up on his elbow, with his head upright, looked at him.

For a minute, it was obvious that madness was in search of Gregory Temple. His eyes, which had been burning bright, became dull, as if stunned. He stepped back several paces, not stopping until he reached the wall. Then a shiver took hold of his entire body, shaking his legs, his arms and his jaw, while his face took on a livid pallor from chin to forehead.

Throughout the time that this crisis lasted, Comte Henri studied him silently, in a cool and indifferent manner.

After a minute, the blood flow returned to the old man's cheeks, and his half-closed eyes glimmered. At the same time, his right hand plunged convulsively into his waistcoat, and he took a step forward.

The young Comte smiled and said: "One forgotten detail: your old acquaintance, the porter, took your pistols away, and must return them to me as I go out, to complete my impersonation."

"Wretch!" cried Temple, who had foam on his lips. "To get out of here, you'll have to go over my dead body!"

"If it's absolutely necessary, master," Henri replied, his smile disappearing, "I'll go over your dead body." He added, with a seriousness in which there was both a terrible threat and a strange mildness: "And I don't need a weapon to make a cadaver of you."

Gregory Temple's eyelids were infused with blood. He was afraid of dying, crushed by the anguish of his impotence. A vision came to him that put ice in his veins. He saw himself lying on the flagstones, too weak to get up; the other was bending over him, the right hand at his throat, the left at the nape of his neck...

And he had that sensation of strangulation in which one tries in vain to draw breath.

He made a desperate effort. His lungs gulped air avidly, and he opened his mouth to let out a cry that might penetrate the walls.

"Wait for the carpenters to declare a truce," said Comte Henri, letting his head fall back on to his pillow. "No one will hear you."

All those working on the scaffold were, indeed, hammering at the same time, producing a deafening row.

Henri added: "I have saved Richard Thompson, your daughter's husband, but his destiny is still tied to mine."

The old man's eyes had a savage gleam as he croaked: "May my daughter be a widow!"

There was no hint of surprise in the young Comte's expression, but rather a cold pity.

"What's a bandit?" he thought, aloud. "Here's a veteran of the army of the law!" Then he added, slowly: "Gregory Temple, I'm compassionate towards those whose hearts have been carried away by madness. Don't be indignant at the use of the word–it has not the same significance here as in the mouths of your insulters. Perhaps, like you, I have my obsession: an idol to which I shall sacrifice everything I love. It's not me who has declared war on you; I warned you that I had certain weapons, and that the war would be fatal for you. I have no hatred or rancor against you; I love those you ought to love, and are forever ready to throw on to the gaming table like a last bet in your desperate game. Don't cry out, Gregory Temple; you're weak, here as everywhere, compared to me. There's nothing on the other side of that door but a drunken man who is undoubtedly asleep. To wake him up would require, not your broken voice, but mine–which sounds like the call of a clarion. I've told you: I must get out of here, even if I have to trample upon your dead body. Don't cry out; my hand is a powerful gag–and, on my conscience, if you remain quiet, I have no need or intention of hurting you."

While the Comte was speaking, Gregory Temple had lowered his eyes. He, too, was an indomitable man. He was aware of his weakness, but he was not beaten, since his enemy disdained the use of force. He who settles owes nothing, says the philosophy of money-men–and in those prodigious duels described in Homeric epics, it is often the overwhelmed who kill...

Gregory Temple used the time that he had been given to search for a weapon. He studied the narrow battlefield slyly; he turned his gaze inwards, and the sweat that ran down his leaden temples testified to the effort he was making to control the violence of his fever.

There was a complete and truly profound contrast between the two men, even apart from the triumphant power of the one and the exhausted impotence of the other. In this unarmed combat, comparable to that which takes place between the judge and the accused, the former Magistrate resembled the guilty party, and the other–the outlaw, the escapee from every prison–had the calm and the authority of the man of law on his bench.

"Mr. Temple," Henri went on, after a brief pause, "it has been given to you to exercise a considerable influence on my life. I shall not go as far as to say that the influence has been beneficial, but at least I shall refrain from affirming that it has been unfortunate. Thanks to you, it is true, I have suffered a great deal for a long time, but suffering tempers the soul and it might be that a part of my strength has come to me from you. Mr. Temple, you have been the lover of Madame la Marquise de Belcamp, my mother."

"Helen Brown!" said the former detective, drawing himself up to his full height in bitter disdain. "Me!"

"Not Helen Brown in her shame, sir–not the girl as beautiful as a saint whom the men and women of your aristocracy soiled and ruined; not the angel already fallen and tottering on the edge of the abyss, whom a soldier of the days of chivalry, the last gentleman, my father, the Marquis de Belcamp, covered with the stainless mantle of his honor; not even the woman carried away by victorious passion who threw away the nuptial robe and trampled her salvation underfoot in a fit of vertigo as cold and terrible as London itself, and who plunged willingly into the darkness of a bottomless gulf with the cry of an exile returned to his motherland; not Helen Brown the filthy legend–but a model of seductive decency and noble spirit: a woman who appeared and disappeared like a charming meteor on your misty horizon... a creole... are you beginning to understand? ...an enchantress..."

The Chief Superintendent interrupted, rudely. "You're lying!" A nervous tic agitated his body and his lips.

"Lady Caroline Dudley," Henri continued, calmly.

"You're lying!" Gregory repeated.

"The mother of the bandit Tom Brown," the young Comte finished, fixing him with his implacable stare. "The Tom Brown who is my brother and your son."

"You're lying!" Temple repeated, for the third time–but he collapsed on the chair and covered his face with both hands.

Also for the third time since he had been in the prison, Comte Henri consulted his watch, calculatingly. "I have the time," he murmured, talking to himself. Then he went on: "Mr. Temple, the time and the place may seem strangely appointed for the long and solemn explanation that needs to take place between us, but it may be years before we find ourselves face to face with one another again. You will be a prisoner; I shall be free–and when you are free, the mission to which I have devoted my life will have put an ocean between us..."

"Before anything else," cried the former detective, "prove what you say!"

"The proof is in your conscience and your hatred, sir."

"You have no other?"

"Yes, indeed. You wore, and perhaps still wear, around your neck a locket containing a drop of dried blood: a bizarre relic of a night of intoxication. In the gold of that locket, Caroline Dudley drew a heart with the needle that had pricked her vein, and traced the letters intended to say..."

"*Heart's blood*," whispered Gregory Temple. "An H and a B."

"An H and a B," Comte Henri repeated. "Helen Brown."

Temple opened his shirt with a convulsive gesture. He tore away the locket, a souvenir of long ago, and ground it beneath his heel, saying: "When in doubt, one washes one's hands!"

A spark lit up in Henri's eye. "That's a spiteful heart!" he murmured. That was all. He resumed, calmly: "I warn you, sir, that I shall rely neither on your heart nor on your memory. I am not here as a supplicant but as a master, and the explanation that I mentioned a short time ago has not yet begun."

"Are you in a position to show me this Tom Brown?" demanded Gregory, whose distress seemed to increase more he reflected.

"At the desired hour, perhaps."

"And will this Helen Brown, who is said to be dead, re-emerge from the ground?"

"Perhaps, if it is necessary."

There was silence, which Henri broke first.

"Mr. Temple," he said, "you were dying at the time when Helen Brown was judged, sentenced and sent to Australia with your son, Tom. She had always kept his secret as a last resort. She was counting on you, but at the vital moment, your illness rendered her secret useless. You were born to strike, not to help: everyone has his destiny! I departed for New South Wales a free man, and I returned a free man: we shall soon talk about the double motive that took me so far away from Europe, where I had the prospect of an easy and happy life.

"When I returned to Europe, I had accomplished a duty and solidified my grand plans. I do not forbid you to smile, sir, but I must count the seconds henceforth, and I don't want any interruption. I was introduced to you by Lord Payne, who was acquainted with your close relationship with the Secretary of the Admiralty. I only spoke to you about the Admiralty.

"It is a remarkable thing: the Police, surrounded by such loathing, inspires an extraordinary devotion in its adepts. I pleased you under the name James Davy, and I don't have to remind you of all the little ruses, all the delicate attentions, all the skillful flirtations you undertook in order to make me a proselyte. I allowed myself to pray for a long time after having been converted, because your theory seduced the romantic side of my intelligence, and I was not slow to realize that I could advance my mission in your offices even better than at the Admiralty. You have taken me for a thief and an assassin, Mr. Temple..."

"And you were a conspirator, weren't you?" the detective jeered. "We know that story like the back of our hand!"

"And in a few months," Henri continued, taking no notice of the interruption, "I shall be the first Minister of a powerful empire... and Europe turned upside down will inform you of the wretchedness of your obstinacy along with the annihilation of your scepticism!"

"If that's so" cried Gregory, shrugging his shoulders, "you can tell me your secrets!"

"I have not yet told you one of my secrets," the young Comte replied. "That will come. There was a time when my strength was knowing what you did not, because you were still fighting. Now, you can no longer fight; you are more completely defeated than you suspect. I can enlighten you with one word–hang on! Your present impotence will extend into the future. The chain that chokes you here will follow you outside. If it were not held by me, you would be free, and I would say to you: go ahead, accuse, strike! I have nailed you to the ground, I have paralyzed your arm, I have condemned your tongue to mutism."

"Open that door, then," the detective challenged, "and we'll see the effect of your witchcraft!"

"That door will be opened, sir," Henri answered, seriously, "but you do not know enough yet; I want to offer further proof. Listen... at the office in Scotland Yard to which I was attached, I once came upon two letters from Signora Bartolozzi, each of which was a betrayal. I think you know that, since you have seen Friedrich Boehm?"

Gregory Temple nodded affirmatively. Everything regarding the affair of the actress immediately captivated his attention.

"That was your great misfortune," Henri went on, "and the point of departure of your ruination. Knowing, as I did, all the workings of your detective machine, I did not doubt for a single instant that your suspicions would sooner or later settle on me, who was with you under a false name and had suppressed the letters. I took precautions; I directed you on to a false path, and drew a veil over your eyes. At that point, I only wanted to gain time until the moment when my grand plan, set in motion in England, would permit me to go on to France... everything would then have been concluded between us."

"Am I permitted to ask whom you accuse of the murder of Constance Bartolozzi?" Temple put in, with a sort of calm.

"Your son, Tom Brown," Henri replied, without hesitation. He went on: "In France, the fatality that pursued you throughout this affair confronted me three times over: I met your daughter again; I recognized Robert Surrisy, with whom you had investigated the murder of his father, General O'Brien, and who had become your agent in addition; and, finally, there was the daughter of Constance Bartolozzi, with whom I fell in love..."

"And that was certainly not for the millions that should have bought her your business enterprise!" Temple jeered.

"Without those millions, sir," Henri replied, "You would have been saved. I beg you to note in passing that all my actions were directed, not against you personally, but against your theory, which would inevitably lead you to me... because your theory, following probabilities blindly as water runs down a drainpipe, would encounter my love for Turner and Robinson's heiress, even if Robert Surrisy, Suzanne, old Madeleine and others had not been there to serve as a guiding thread..."

"In passing," the detective interrupted, "was it this Tom Brown who killed General O'Brien?"

"Yes, the assassin of General O'Brien was your son, Tom Brown, just as your son Tom Brown, who was Turner and Robinson's natural heir by virtue of his mother, was the assassin of Robinson and Turner. I'll pass over the details of my conduct towards Thompson and your daughter–they have both forgiven me and they love me, since I am their benefactor–and get to the Versailles business, in which, unfortunately, I found you confronting me yet again.

"It is inconceivable that you have not noticed one rather curious fact. While you moved Heaven and Earth to prevent the order being issued that there was no case to answer, you found me an assistant rather than an obstacle. I refused to proffer certain explanations... I left gaps..."

"But how do you account for the two passports in the name of Comte Henri?" said Temple. "Isn't it obvious that you were making use of my algebra there, and that you were contriving an argument of absurdity?"

"I shall take care, master," Henri replied, affectedly, "to draw an entirely different sap from your savant lessons, if ever I should put them into practice. I answer you again with one word: your son, Tom Brown, the natural heir, was overtaken by me, the legal heir, the only child of Helen Brown born within wedlock. I was in his way, even supposing that he knew nothing of the wills in favor of Jeanne Herbet or my intention to marry that young woman. Here, doubtless without your knowing it, your son Tom Brown has been your accomplice: he wished to strike three blows with a single stone. Incidentally, I have the honor to inform you of my marriage to this same Jeanne Herbet…"

"In your position!" Temple exclaimed. "You dared to give that terrible weapon to the prosecution!"

"No, I confess that I drew back from that. Innocence herself would limit her confidence in human justice. I was obliged to stage a comedy. I married Mademoiselle Herbet under the name that I wore a little while ago at the Auction Mart: Percy Balcomb. The name belongs to me–I earned it."

"And you dare to make such a revelation to me!"

"Once again, Mr. Temple," Henri said, emphasizing his words carefully. "I'm making this confession to a dead man."

The former detective shivered, and looked at him suspiciously.

"Morally dead," the young Comte went on, smiling. "That's all that I meant. But, by way of compensation, should you be dead in the more extreme sense, then I shall resurrect you before quitting this place for much more important things. Until then, I shall briefly resume the subject under consideration. I defended myself against you as best I could; I had the right to trade blow for blow, for I was not the aggressor; I do myself the justice of saying that I did not strike excessively hard. Now, the conclusion: you will understand shortly that with the high position that awaits me in the near future, I cannot be content with half-measures. Caesar's Minister, even more than his wife, must be above suspicion. I am a jurist; I cut to the quick, always in anticipation of your attacks, for I had no enemy but you in all the world. I leave nothing behind me: in Prague, I have the decision of the Royal Tribunal regarding the O'Brien affair; in London, I have the jury's verdict against Thompson. *Non bis in idem.*[229] In France, I shall have a judgment. As for your son Tom Brown–who, continuing the course of his exploits, appears to have decided to unravel my life with the patience of Penelope–I have the corpses of Noll and Dick, his murdered accomplices, in the field by Tivoli to use against him. Here ends my first discourse."

Was there an atom of truth in this story of Tom Brown? The division might explain many seemingly inexplicable things, but perhaps not all. And the crushed locket certainly rested on the floor, reflecting the light of the candle, whose wick was now grazing the rim of its leaden holder. Who had revealed to Henri the mystery of that drop of blood and the two initials that were both an exclamation of love and an infamous signature?

"Let us sing, as Virgil said, of slightly greater things,"[230] the young Comte went on, too quickly for the liking of his listener, who wanted time to think. "You have heard it said at the Chateau de Belcamp, master, that I am a doctor five times over; it is true. I remember telling you myself that a man in that situation, according to the simplest axioms of probability, could do better than choosing a criminal trade. I add that, in my particular case, I am the only son of a gentleman, heir to an honest fortune, and adore the father I love: all of that seems to me to add to the moralizing effects of study.

"You have seen my life at close range for more than a year. I am a man of the great world, and I have neither depraved tastes nor insatiable vices. Without making any effort at all, I am rich; and I could live in idleness with my arms crossed. Would you like to tell me what human motive could have precipitated the young Comte de Belcamp, at the end of his brilliant studies, into the most ignominious depths of London? For it was from the utmost depths of that mire, you understand, that the verdict of the Court of Sessions uprooted Tom Brown to send him to Australia.

"And if you will admit that, during that period, given the authenticity of my attendance at the German Universities, I could not have been a criminal in London at the same time, in consequence of which it is highly probable that the convict Tom Brown was not your humble servant, can you tell me what possible motive could have sent me to the Australian territory that is the terrible sewer of our civilization?

"My mother? You have hit upon it, sir. I had never ceased to love my mother. But was that sufficient? No. My obsession was born...

"Oh, you're clever, I'm not one of those who deny it, but you had a theory, and a theory is a cannon with a hole at either end. You have not considered this: probability is impotent with respect to those whose vocation is to exceed the probable.

"You may still smile and pour disdain upon me as you do your vulgar enemies–the conspirator who escaped you while you were chasing a criminal. There's that gleam in your eye, master, as in the days when we were following a trail. Don't rejoice. The trail is good, but it leads to an impregnable fortress.

"I was ambitious. I loved liberty. I had read and devoured the epic history of the American War of Independence. My father had been one of the heroes of that struggle; I too wanted to strike a blow at England. I went to Australia to preach my crusade. Child, do you say? It's true; I was a child, as Australia was. A desert does not rebel. But I have become a man, and Australia too will attain puberty. Patience!

"There is a rock between Australia and England called St. Helena. You shiver, this time, Mr. Temple! We detest the same men. The Regent of England and his instruments insulted you cruelly yesterday; tomorrow, they will castigate you. Do you want your revenge?"

The old man had indeed shivered, but he looked up calmly and frankly as he said: "Sir, one does not seek to avenge oneself against a nation. God save the Regent! I am an Englishman."

"And a gentleman too, Gregory Temple!" the young man said, slowly. "I am sorry to be your enemy." He listened. All the noise had ceased. The scaffold's last bolt was in place. "Time is pressing now," he said. "I shall force you to respect me if you continue to hate me. You are an Englishman: I shall not insult England. Besides, it is a great nation for having spread hatred and terror of its name throughout the entire surface of the world, despite the fact that the world liberty–cherished by all–is inscribed on its feudal escutcheon and its invader's flag.

"That was my first task: to run a glance over the map of the world and search out those who, like me, detested England. From my own standpoint, I looked first towards the West, Africa and America, across the confused archipelagos of Oceania that still knew no other oppressor than the English. From the coast of Africa, I heard two voices: the raucous choir of English slave-traders and the song of the liberating canticle that includes this stanza: 'Destroy impious slavery, in order to ruin at one blow the French colonies and the Yankee plantations!' The hidden motive was of little importance to me. I said: 'Daughter though you are of two deadly sins, hatred and avarice, the suppression of the slave trade will be one of the great achievements of the century, and England's most honorable.'

"From the coast of America, I heard the distant hymn of deliverance sung from the Mexican border to those of the two Canadas. That poetry was in English too: 'We are free, but we wish to perpetuate slavery!' Facing Africa, I saw France–not the France of Europe, but that distant fatherland which has the flag for its protection: the colonies that call the fatherland their mother, and the one named the Ile-de-France.[231] The French flag was lying on the ground; the flag of England was fluttering in the wind, bearing its folds like a finger pointed towards that other isle, an imperceptible point lost in space, where England was fortifying a prison and hollowing out a tomb. That was still France, though.

"To the north, I saw those enchanted lands which, as the crow flies, stood between me and Europe: another French patrimony, India, the treasure of the world. The shadow of Dupleix [232] appeared to me, amid the immense territories bathed by the Indus and the Ganges, a domain derisory in its scantiness.

"My gaze crossed those dazzling countries, passed over threatened Persia, and was arrested by the incommensurable extent of that other empire, Russia, the geographical and natural enemy of England. I was in Europe and I searched for England. I saw the German states, where–despite the temporary alliance forged to crush France–the name of England is abhorrent. I saw Italy, educated by the enslavement of the Archipelago, Spain dishonored by Gibraltar, Portugal paying tribute, Holland annihilated, France mocked by the two islets made by its sand, Jersey and Guernsey, and conquered Paris, full of redcoats, reducing the history of France to the battle of Crèche [233] and the treason of Waterloo...!

"*Further away, and separated from the rest of the world*, as the Latin poet says,[234] I finally saw the home of the English: a little tract of land divided into three parts, of which one oppresses the others. Enemies everywhere, even in its own house! Wounded enemies, trampled underfoot, but implacable: the highlanders in the north, the Irish in the west.

"I studied this tableau throughout the hours of a long night, and my tired eyes saw nothing but an eagle perched on the rock of St. Helena, which was gazing at the empire of the Indies over the continent of Africa...

"In the Eagle's eye, I read this thought: 'England's heart is in India, and India is 80 million of the vanquished beneath the whip of a few thousand oppressors.' And on that point of land that separated the Eagle's eyrie from the paradise of its conquest, on the extreme tip of Africa, on the Cape, there were these words: Good Hope."

"It is also called the Cape of Storms," murmured Temple, who was now containing his profound emotion within himself.

Comte Henri got to his feet. "I accept the augury," he said, his head held high and his eyes shining. "If the storm comes, so much the better. I want every thunderbolt for my ally!"

"If you have no other soldiers but the lightning..." said the former detective in a provocative tone.

Henri peeled off Richard Thompson's overcoat. Instead of replying, he said: "You are sure of your box?"

Temple had said as much himself. Some time before, when he believed he was talking to Thompson, he had pronounced these words: "I have everything I need to transform you into an old man." The London Police were then famous throughout Europe for the incredible perfection of their disguises.

Temple hesitated... but he wanted to know–and what did a disguise matter while the closed door remained between Comte Henri and liberty? "I am weak and you are strong," he murmured. "What good would it do me to resist you?" While saying this, he gave him a bound copy of his famous book entitled *The Art of Discovering Malefactors.*[235] The book was hollow, like the pretended Anglican minister's Bible; it contained colors, brushes, pomades and mirrors.

"God desires, master, that you should remain wise to the end, for we shall have to get through a difficult moment, and your head is hot. Will you extend your submission so far as to hold the mirror for me?"

"No," Temple replied.

Henry took up the candlestick and put it on the bed, next to the box, and knelt in front of it.

"I have soldiers," he went on, while calmly beginning to make himself up, "and you could have been more obliging without fear of betraying the curiosity that you have; I have no desire to hide anything from you. The more you know, the less fearful you will be. I have 200 soldiers in Africa, armed as is necessary, believe me... I have 400 more in a certain American port. In France and England, the difficulty will be transport, for if I have a great fleet, I must have a great army... but we will be more than 2,000 strong when we leave St. Helena. In India, 30,000 Afghans await us with 10,000 Sepoys. Will that be enough, do you think, to build an army of 100,000 men a month after our arrival?"

The brush was gliding over his cheeks and around his eyes.

There is no intelligent Englishman who does not regard India as a perennially-charged powder-keg, to which the least spark might set fire.

Was all this a phantasmagoria or a reality?

In reality, no expedition of adventurers has assumed such redoubtable proportions since the great wars of the Testudo.[236]

The old man's blood was boiling in his veins. Keeping his voice down, he said: "And the Eagle will only have his wings to carry him over the African continent?"

Henri drew back to assess the effects of his painting. "Today," he said, "you have struck a blow in the dark that failed to kill us."

"At the Auction Mart?"

"Precisely. English patriotism is a grand sentiment, and all grand sentiments have their inspirations. You acted as if you knew that the Perkins engine was a petard destined to blow England up."

"An infernal machine!"[237]

"Were you already at Scotland Yard when the one exploded against the First Consul was dispatched from England?" Henri asked. "I have put your face on my head, Mr. Temple, do you see?" He turned abruptly and lifted up the candlestick.

The old detective's wrinkles shifted. "It seems as if I'm looking into a mirror, Monsieur le Comte," he stammered.

"This infernal machine," Henri continued, calmly, "does not resemble the other. It is made for combat, not for murder. The frigate of war pierced with 80 gunports that will receive it in its belly is already constructed, waiting for it."

"Constructed?" said Temple.

"And armed," the young Comte added.

"In France?"

"Much closer to St. Helena than that... and within reach of brigs of war, also steamships, which will sail under its flag."

"It is to this that Providence has brought me!" murmured the former Superintendent. He wiped the sweat from his forehead.

"You know how to take a hint, Mr. Temple," Henri replied, continuing to make himself up with minute care. "Either steam is a utopia, or it is the greatest invention of modern times; in the former instance we shall run aground and will have to begin again... in the second, we shall laugh at your ponderous fleets."

"They will believe me this time!" cried Temple, putting his trembling hands together. "They will be compelled to believe me, when I bring them this gigantic testimony!"

Henri added the last touches to his wrinkles.

"With that engine," he continued, "if Napoleon consents to be liberated, he will be at Pondicherry three weeks before the news of his escape from St. Helena." His bright eyes suddenly dazzled Gregory's gaze as he added: "The French Empire of India, Mr. Temple! Have you the strength to calculate the infinite... and was I right to tell you that I shall change the face of the world?"

"And it is I who have prevented that? May God protect my fatherland!" cried Temple, with tears in his eyes.

"I only had two millions," the young Comte said, "and I knew that Count Friedrich Boehm was behind you, with his immense fortune. What good would it have done to fight? My two millions will serve another purpose, and while we are speaking, Mr. Temple, the engine is going down the Thames on a fine sailing ship."

The former Police Superintendent made a rapid movement, as if he wanted to hurl himself towards the door. Henri barred the way, and Temple cried: "Fool that I am! Don't I have the receipt from the Staunton warehouse, where the engine is stored?"

"In your portfolio, I think?"

"Doubtless."

"And your portfolio is on the lid of your writing desk, in your room at Mivart's Hotel, in Count Friedrich Boehm's apartment, free on bail as you both are. Friedrich Boehm was your ally yesterday; he gave you 80,000 pounds sterling. Tonight, he will take them back from you because, for the price of a smile from Sarah O'Brien–or the price of the hope of a smile, I should have said–I have bought the body and soul of Count Friedrich Boehm."

Temple was still thunderstruck.

Henri de Belcamp closed the box again. The transformation was complete. On his young and supple torso he carried the old head of the detective, topped with a grey wig. "Now, master," he said, the calmness of his tone taking on an imperious quality, "I need your jacket and hat."

The old man shivered from head to toe. His alert, piercing eyes arrested for a moment on his adversary's face, then they became bleak. Their pupils seemed to be abruptly extinguished behind his half-lowered eyelids. Yet again he darted the glance of a caged beast towards the door.

Comte Henri tapped his foot.

Temple fixed his dull stare upon his adversary; he frowned, and every wrinkle on his face deepened. He burst out laughing, so suddenly and unexpectedly that Henri was stupefied.

"Your jacket and your cap, sir!" Henri ordered, for the second time.

Gregory Temple immediately took them off. "You'll have to kill me if all that's true!" he said, stridently. And he laughed again.

Henri already had the cap on his head; the jacket was still in his hand. He was so strong and so tall, while the other was so puny and frail, that the idea of murder could only make him feel disgust. "If you get in my way now, Mr. Temple," he said, however, "and if I have no other means of reducing you to silence, that is perfectly true. I shall kill you, for it would require the hand of God himself to stop me on the road along which I am marching. Far from barring my way, though, you will serve me, as you have served me throughout your life: your indefatigable hatred has been my incessant salvation. Without you, how could I get out of here, leaving an empty cell? You shall take my place, as I took Thompson's. You have given me a map of the field where Noll and Dick are buried. You have given me the key to your arsenal of proofs... and tomorrow, if any suspicion is aroused behind me, I leave you here with the mission to stifle it."

"As loudly as my voice will permit," grated the former Police Superintendent, who had resisted too long the fit in which his condensed fury could not help bursting forth, terribly, "I shall shout out all that you have told me, assassin or conspirator! I shall unveil you. I shall unmask you. Here, in France, everywhere! Wretched madman, if you have dreamed of setting fire to the world, you should have kept your secret! You shall not kill me without resistance, and during the struggle, my voice will penetrate that door. You will be found half-dead. If you spare me, I shall speak out! What you are to me, you have made! You have given yourself away in your blind pride! I am like an earthworm next to you, but I am your conqueror."

Henri had an implacable smile on his lips.

"You will end as I wish, master," he said, as he made ready to put on the warder's jacket. "We two do not fight like other men, and if I put you to death in the end, it will be by means of an unexpected blow struck by an unknown weapon. Speak out, by God! Raise your voice! Cry out! When you are found here in place of the escaped Thompson, affirm that you have been dueling with John Devil within these four walls. Say that John Devil is Comte Henri de Belcamp and that Comte Henri de Belcamp, shut up in Versailles prison, told you his life-story tonight, in Newgate! Write to Paris that Percy Balcomb and Comte Henri are the same man, even though Henri's father and Percy's wife say the opposite. Send men to Tivoli to dig up ground that will be empty. Have the Police open your room in the Rue Dauphine, from which your papers will be gone. Add to that story a fleet of steamships and 60,000 soldiers armed for the conquest of India... did I tell you about my 110 cannons? I have a 110 cannons, do you hear, with ammunition. Have I told you about my 10,000 rifles? I have 10,000 rifles with bayonets and cartridges. My fleet is ready. Don't forget anything, master, for God's sake! Don't forget anything! I need you to say all this, to amalgamate all these fables, to accumulate all these impossibilities.

"Do you see what I'm doing? Do you recognize your theory? I'm treating the Government of England as your bandits treat a detective. I'm throwing in its eyes, by the handful, through you, the powder of absurdity that you have invented. I'm thickening between it and me, thanks to you, the fog of improbability... and through that fog my engine slips, my artillery rolls, my men march. The giant of iron and copper that will defy your vessels must be approaching Gravesend as we speak... the tide is in its favor and the wind is blowing from the north. The engine will double Ramsgate, enter the Channel, reach the ocean. As I live and breathe, your theory is great, sovereign, marvelous: it is the Archimedean instrument with a simple lever... for, to set it in motion, it is sufficient to confide its secret to an honest man previously accused of madness!"

The detective's throat let loose a profound groan.

"Madness, if you say that someone other than Thompson was shut in this cell!" Henri went on, no longer moderating the savage glee of his triumph. "Madness, if you speak of John Devil, except to give that name to Thompson himself. Madness, if you make the prisoner of Versailles travel on a moonbeam like a sorcerer! Madness again if you confuse Balcomb and Belcamp in the presence of people who know them both. The cadavers of Tivoli–dreams! The papers in the Rue Dauphine–illusions! And the fleet–oh, the fleet and its cannons! Madness! Madness! The three Kingdoms will laugh. Furious madness, such as there never was in Bedlam!"

There was bloody foam on Gregory Temple's mouth–because all this was true. He could already hear it: the cry of incurable prejudice, in the face of the improbability of his denunciations: Madness! Madness! Madness!

The impotence of his rage had become agonizing.

He wanted to speak, but he could not. His voice choked in his throat. His eyes displayed their whites; the corners of his lips subsided. He clenched his fists, and took a step towards the door. He made a supreme effort to stand up straight, and collapsed heavily on the floor.

Henri put a hand on his heart and waited for a minute in silence. His features had changed; they expressed profound commiseration. When the minute had passed, he lifted Temple and carried him carefully to the bed. He threw Thompson's overcoat over him, after turning his head towards the wall.

"Hey! Clarke! Joseph Clarke!" he called, knocking loudly on the door. His eyes, however, were watching Temple, who did not shiver in response to the shout.

The key grated in the lock.

"I was asleep!" said the warder. "Do you know that it's almost time?"

"Let's get going, Clarke," Comte Henri ordered, pushing him out of the door. "We're late. You'll have to come back to see the prisoner, who's been taken ill. Here's your five guineas."

"Thanks, Mr. Temple... it's for the wife and the kid."

As they arrived at the end of the corridor, the pretended Temple spoke to the other rapidly: "Clarke, if any misfortune overcomes you, go to Mr. Wood's house in the Strand... there's a contract providing you with an income of 60 guineas a year. See to the prisoner!"

Clarke was dumbfounded. Through the corridor window, he heard the gate of the exterior door open, then close again, and the rapid footsteps of a man in the street.

XV. The Eagle

A foggy and miserable dawn broke on one of those scenes that it is necessary to have seen in order to have any notion of them: the festival of the Old Bailey, whose youthful glory had already eclipsed the splendors of Tyburn. There is no accounting for the appetite of London curiosity-seekers for the dramas of the gibbet–except, alas, for the hideous fashionability that makes part of the Parisian population avid for scaffold nights.

Who makes up this audience, then? The key to the mystery is a horrid one; the learned claim that the audience is exactly the same as that in our theaters. Those whom certain people like to call the lower classes are not always in the majority. One sees good middle class folk there, wrapped up warm against the quinsy–animated cigars of whom a few are certainly Havanas–women (I am not speaking of ladies, you understand) who hide names beneath their veils. That is the claim. I have heard something more incredible said: at the windows of miserable rooms that can be hired in order to obtain a better view–the obscene boxes of that infamous performance–the faces of young girls can be seen. In Paris, the flower and pearl among cities, beloved of the world, I have heard talk of beautiful children taken there by their fathers and mothers! Do they promise to bring them again if they are very good? In Paris, heart of the world!

The somber frame jutted out from the windows, suspended over a crowd as heaped-up, molded and compacted as herrings in a barrel: one of those crowds that drown and kill. The mob emitted a continuous breathless murmur in which no one could distinguish the rattling throats of asphyxiated women. The windows of the neighboring houses were mouths full of heads, presenting strange mosaics formed of juxtaposed faces with avid eyes aflame. Another crowd was on the rooftops. Eccentrics had hooked cords over the cornices and were suspended by the waist or the armpits, facing the beam from which a man would be suspended by the neck.

The man who was to be suspended by the neck had, however, carried out his savior's instructions to the letter; he had cast off his clerical garb as he passed over London Bridge and–now dressed like everyone else–he had killed the hours of night as best he could. While the curious crowds were waiting for him, also killing time by crushing dogs and children, Richard Thompson, dead on time, was going into the Nelson's Sword Inn on Saint Savior's Dock, facing the large crane. He had only been there for a few minutes when a young man with a frank and smiling face came straight up to him, saying: "*For the best!*"

Richard did not feel safe while his feet were still on English soil. Now that he had been given the hope of embracing Suzanne and his child, life was doubly dear to him. He offered his hand unhesitatingly and answered: "What do you seek, good cousin?"

"My master's Bible," answered the stranger.

"And who is your master?"

"Reverend John Gravesend, Assistant to the Vicar of Saint James's."

Richard opened his frock-coat and displayed the Bible.

"Get up, then, good cousin, and follow me," said the stranger. "I shall lead you to the fountain."

At the end of the quay, there was a little boat with two oarsmen. It was daylight now, but the fog was thickening. Richard and the stranger got into the boat.

"Lieutenant," said a voice that made Thompson shiver, "a launch full of men just passed by... I say men, but they had the look of true fellows... I couldn't see them very well, on account of the fog, but one called out: Good day, Corporal!"

Richard threw himself towards the oarsman. "Pierre Louchet!" he cried, seizing him by the hands. He could say no more than that, and was trembling thereafter.

The woodcutter's face expressed joyful surprise. "My luck's in!" he said, winking at the Lieutenant. "It's all familiar faces this morning. This one's the Englishman who kissed and wept–Ton...son, you know? The two *écus*... the one who wasn't the mite's father, and who had the little portrait..."

"Do you know my wife and child, then?" Richard stammered, turning towards his guide.

"Mr. Thompson, I'm the brother of your friend Sarah, and the friend of your dear wife, who is staying in my sister's house. Lean to port, Pierre, wretched sailor!"

"It's not a trade, Lieutenant. I only learned for exercise."

"I've dandled Little Richard on my knees," the Lieutenant went on. "I'm Robert Surrisy."

"Ah!" said Thompson. "And you're Sarah's brother!"

"The madwoman told you the story of the notebook? And the name that wants to say smile? The novel has concluded like that... and another has begun whose denouement might, God willing, bring her happiness. But we'll talk about that once we're aboard, Mr. Thompson–because, in spite of my name, I can only talk about the happiness of others." He moved the tiller to avoid the cable of a barge and added, as he stifled a sigh: "Press on, boys! Press on!"

A few minutes afterwards, between Deptford and the Isle of Dogs, the boat came alongside the *Deliverance*'s launch, full of Pierre Louchet's "true fellows." The *Deliverance* herself was warming up in front of the bridge over Deptford Creek.

This time, Pierre Louchet recognized the faces and became mad with excitement. "Captain Gauthier! Major Lointier! Lieutenant Renault! And the Colonel too, by God! Who'd have thought it?" In mid-rhapsody, his gaze encountered a tall calm figure in the steamboat's bridge. He shook Robert's arm.

"The other Englishman!" he murmured. "The one who wrote the mother's name on my door. Mr. Temple says that he's an assassin!"

"Silence!" Surrisy answered. "That's the General!"

At that moment, an immense clamor, full of complaints, groans, imprecations and blasphemies, emerged from the Old Bailey, the theater of the scaffold, and rose up into the fog that was happily defending the sky. The spectacle had been cancelled; a strip had been pasted over the playbill. It was not the condemned man who had emerged from the open window, nor even the executioner and his assistants. Worse than that, it was not even the Sheriff arriving like an embarrassed stage-manager to announce the indisposition or absence of a principal player. It was the carpenters, come to dismantle the scaffold.

Yes, the London cockney is law-abiding; yes, London enraged flees before a Commissioner reading the Riot Act under the protection of four Constables armed with staves; yes, London is meek and timid, like those fearful children whose bad temper evaporates at the first sight of a bundle of birch-rods—but, by all the devils in Hell, one ought not to rob it of its hangings!

An assembly gathered for some frivolous purpose—political, for example, or religious—can easily be dissipated by reading the Act to the mob, but a meeting gathered to see a hanging is a different matter! Even the strongest governments must stop short of certain excesses. Promising a hanging and not delivering is slipshod! These 15,000 citizens excited in vain had their livings to earn. When would the hanging be, pray tell? Would the lost opportunity be recovered? They could have it another time.

Windows were broken. There was a commotion beneath the windows of Mansion House. The Constables courageously arrested a stray Frenchman who was asking for directions, a blind Irish crone and the president of a temperance society who had drunk a little too much brandy and was trying to hold up the tottering walls of the Tower. Without this firmness on the part of the Constables, who knows what might have happened?

The *Deliverance*, trailing her long standard of smoke behind her, was already gliding towards Gravesend, passing in its rapid course all the fine sailing-ships of the English Navy, which were then unrivalled in the entire world. There was no one on the bridge except the officer on watch and the men required to steer her. All those who had the right to take part in the council were gathered in the wardroom.

At the conclusion of the council-meeting, Comte Henri took Friedrich Boehm's hand and put it in Robert Surrisy's. "This is the man your sister has loved since infancy," he said to Surrisy, "in spite of events and despite herself. He was 16 years old when your father died. He will be your brother. He wants to restore the General's property to you. Now that Counts Albrecht and Reiner are no more, I alone in all the world can explain certain mysteries to you: light will be cast, if God grants me the time, and you, Monsieur Surrisy, will bear the name of O'Brien, which belongs to you as to your sister. My life has been toilsome, as you now know, and that is my excuse. For years, I cannot remember having wasted an hour. It may be, Surrisy—for each of us looks at things from his own viewpoint—that you carry a grudge against Count Friedrich, who is innocent of the misfortunes that have befallen your family. Remember that he is your superior in our hierarchy, and that when we bid our imminent and final farewell to Europe to fight our great battle, it is he who has furnished our best flag; thanks to Friedrich Boehm, the King of Rome and the Empress Marie-Louise will be on board with us."

"I bear no grudge," Robert said, his eyes fixed on Count Boehm's noble face. "If he wishes, I can indeed be his brother, for you have told the truth, Belcamp; Sarah has already told me about him."

A hint of pink showed in Friedrich Boehm's pale cheeks. "To die beloved and to die in combat!" he murmured, with a smile that proclaimed his ecstasy.

But there was another heart in search of Surrisy. When the ships became sparser in the broadening Thames, all three of them—Surrisy, Friedrich and Richard—came together on one of the benches on the rim of the large hatchway. Richard and Friedrich tried to speak at once, one of Sarah and the other Suzanne; they poured their hopes and their happiness into that poor soul of a soldier, who no longer had either hope or happiness—but who, however, was also murmuring a name that no voice echoed: Jeanne! Jeanne!

To die beloved! he thought, while answering the avidly egotistical questions of the two lovers. *To die in combat!* Then, he silently added, in the valor of his heart: *For myself, I am betrothed to my sword, and I shall find my true happiness in dying.*

Aloud, to his joyous companions, he said: "Sarah is as beautiful as a flower decked with dew; Sarah will love you; Sarah loves you... Suzanne has wept a great deal; during her morning prayers, God had to whisper in her ear: 'Your happiness is coming...' Will your first kiss be for her or little Richard?" They did not hear the sigh that was stifled in the depths of his breast.

Thanet was rounded; Ramsgate was already fleeing to starboard. London was still foggy, but here there was bright sunlight. On the channel's horizon, there was at present only one large ship running southwards under full sail.

Henri mounted the quarterdeck and ordered everyone to the bridge. When they answered the call, all the old soldiers wore their uniforms; Henri was wearing the broad sash of the Legion of Honor over his clothing. They caught up with the ship, whose stern was newly inscribed with the name *Eagle*. As they arrived alongside, Henri ordered that the gangplank be lowered.

The tricolor fluttered from the *Deliverance*'s mizzenmast, and the same colors were displayed at the *Eagle*'s stern. It was only for an instant, but tears ran down all those bronzed faces. Between the *Eagle*'s mainmast and mizzenmast, the deck had been visibly caved in for a length of several meters. Through that opening the shining back of the Perkins engine could be seen, its copper and iron rippling in the sunlight. Fifty French officers were ranged around the engine.

Henri removed his hat and put his hand to his breast. A single great cry passed from one ship to the other: "Long live the Emperor!" Then the two tricolors were lowered. The *Eagle* set a course for the southwest, and the *Deliverance* continued on its way to the French coast.

Five days had gone by since the preliminaries of the marriage of Jeanne and Percy Balcomb had taken place at the Hotel de France in Versailles. We are in Miremont, in the widow Touchard's house.

The day was coming to an end. Germaine and Jeanne were sitting under a little harbor hung with honeysuckle, from which they could look out on the charming countryside that has been described several times in these pages, though not the vast panorama of the plain extending halfway to the Croix Moraine, nor the complete horizon that was visible from the chateau. The Priory, situated halfway up a slope, looked out on the Belcamp park, bordered by the curve of the Oise. The eye was arrested on one side by the hills that extended towards l'Isle Adam, and on the other by the verdant jumble over which rose the old windmill with its antique arch.

Madame Touchard was entertaining the Curé. They were sitting together on a wooden bench, set against the wall of the house between the drawing-room windows, framed by rosebushes. The aunt had set down her work, on the amicable advice of the priest, who had said: "My dear lady, you're missing the view." They were chatting together, while a servant was lighting the lamps in the room behind them.

Jeanne and Germaine were chatting too, but with lowered voices. The Curé had tried in vain two or three times to hear a little of what they were saying through the flowery partition. Germaine was very pink; Jeanne, calm and gentle, had her beautiful pallor. Germaine was scarcely listening to the aunt's conversation with the priest but Jeanne caught a few words, which increased her distraction.

"But in the end," Germaine said, "you loved him. I remember it well."

"I love him still, as I loved him," Jeanne replied. "He is a brother to me."

"One does not marry one's brother, and you would certainly have allowed yourself to marry him."

"I knew that he was as candid and noble as gold. His wife will be happy."

"There you are!" exclaimed Germaine, angrily tapping the sandy ground with her foot. "Me, I was inconstant, unfaithful, capricious, and everything one might wish, the day when I danced with Comte Henri de Belcamp... and you, because you always had good reasons at your service, you set aside poor Robert, with no one saying a word... not even him!"

There was a pause, during which the aunt said to the Curé; "Men who have no family, you understand... that can certainly lay them open to slander, but one sees similar wills every day... My late sister had the tone and manner of a decent person, in spite of what she became... Monsieur Robinson and Monsieur Turner were both cousins and had the same heir: a thoroughgoing villain, it's said... and that was doubtless a motive to disinherit him..."

"It's still an astonishing story!" murmured the Curé.

"Robert is the best of men," Jeanne thought aloud. Then she added, with a smile: "Hasn't my poor Laurent reason to be afraid? You came close to falling in love with Comte Henri, Germaine!"

"Me!" Deputy Potel's daughter cried, indignantly. "I'm not in love with anyone!"

"Except Laurent, I hope?"

"Since you've become as rich as a well," Germaine said, with concentrated spite, "you're not the same any more!"

"I'm not the only one who's rich," Jeanne said, pensively.

"That only makes it funnier!" Germaine replied, dryly.

"Like you," said the aunt, "I thought things would have dragged out longer, and that we would have been involved in all sorts of complications but it has all happened as if by magic. Jeanne was already a free agent, you know?"

"And who put the idea of making her a free agent into your head?"

"Comte Henri de Belcamp."

"On what occasion?"

"From the very first. My sister Constance had lawyers in London. One was Mr. Daws, with whom the two wills were deposited; the other was Mr. Wood... something like a solicitor. It's Mr. Wood that has taken care of it all. In less than two months, everything has been concluded, and Jeanne will now be able to lay her hands on all of it, if she wishes."

"It's you, in fact," Germaine continued. "It's you who was on the point of falling in love with Comte Henri. For my part, he frightened me, that's all... I found him too handsome, and that whole story of Georgelle in Australia was for you. How lovely it was when he told it! But then, he had saved your life. Come on, Jeanne, I'm not jealous. If he'd fallen in love with anyone here, it was you."

"Jealous?" Jeanne repeated, smiling.

Germaine blushed to the whites her eyes–but it was already getting dark, and the two drawing-room windows were brightly lit, displaying cherrywood furniture upholstered in yellow fabric in the Empire style. Germaine thought that no one could see her blush. "All that to marry Percy Balcomb!" she went on, in a pert tone. "You'll explain that mystery to us some day, won't you?" She looked at Jeanne, who was lost in thought, and threw her arms around her neck, murmuring: "I don't know why I always talk like this. You're the best person in the world, as you're the most beautiful. It's just that I thought that there was no one in the whole world for you but Henri and no one for Henri but you. Growl at me if you want to, but I had to say something... oh well, yes, if Henri had chanced to fall in love with me, I would have gone mad. If I were a man, I'd have wanted to serve him like a slave... and I told your brother that I'd marry him if he devoted himself to Henri!"

She stopped, shivering.

Jeanne gave her a long kiss on the forehead, and murmured: "Don't tell that to anyone but me, Germaine..."

The voice of the old priest was raised, but Germaine was paying less heed than ever to that direction; Jeanne was the only one who heard.

"From the first day!" said the Curé, astonished. "He spoke to you about the two legacies on the first day!"

"As two more-or-less distant eventualities," the aunt replied.

"And he asked you for the birth certificates?"

"You know, we were in dire straits in the household. Since their mother's death, the two children had been a heavy burden on me... there were complaints... there was gossip... I said that I did not know what to do... I spoke of showing the two children the door..."

"It was in that first conversation that he advised you to make Jeanne a free agent?"

"That day or the next..."

"This is serious," said the Curé.

"Why is it serious, since he often visited my sister in London and knew about her business affairs?"

The old priest rapped loudly on the lid of his snuff-box. "Madame," he exclaimed, as if involuntarily, "your sister had already been assassinated!"

The aunt moved back on the bench.

"What's the matter, Jeanne?" Germaine asked. "Your hands are getting cold."

"Someone's come for Mademoiselle Germaine," announced a maidservant at the drawing-room door.

The Curé got up. "An unhappy story, my good lady," he concluded. "God preserve me from suspecting the son of our worthy Mayor. But... but..."

"But what?" demanded the aunt, with a certain combativeness.

"Germaine, my child," the old priest called out, "is the boat ready?"

"Yes, Monsieur le Curé."

"Goodbye then, my good lady," the other said, in some haste. "My rheumatism is coming on, and I won't be sorry to avoid the detour by the mill bridge, which would take me a quarter of a league out of my way. Peace be with you!"

The aunt stayed behind, irritated and thoughtful. The Curé kissed Jeanne silently, while Germaine tied the ribbons of her straw hat, and they went off together, going directly to the riverbank where Deputy Potel's gardener was waiting with a punt.

Scarcely had they passed the corner of the path when Briquet came in sight at the other end of the garden. Jeanne hurried to meet him. She did not say anything, however, and it was the aunt who asked: "Have you better news this evening?"

"That Madame Etiennne's an old fool," replied Briquet. "I'll get my own back on her come the Day of Judgment. It's become monotonous, her always calling me Trompe-d'Eustache. A mere cook has no right! As for the news, Monsieur le Marquis is still the same. The Pontoise doctors don't understand it at all–you can only get good medicine in Paris. The pharmacist opposite our place in the Rue Dauphine would eat up that fever with two dozen pills!"

"Has he had a bad day?" the young woman asked him, with concern.

"Who can tell, in that house? It's like a great mortuary. Pierre and Mademoiselle Fanchette are always sighing. Anille and Julot have gone into the park to woo one another with their claws. This place is full of bumpkins! Madame Etienne looks at you like a gravedigger and talks about the funeral of her former mistress. The doctor's installed in the drawing-room, where he drinks coffee all the blessed day long. Pierre says that he might be a little bit better..."

"Ah," said Jeanne. "Did you ask him if he wanted to see me?"

"No one goes into his room except Madeleine, Robert's mother... another one whose pleasure it is to brush hair on heads that have long since been bald."

"No one's said anything about Comte Henri?" asked the aunt.

"Not a whisper. The cook's making a fuss about a wretched bar in the gate that I brightened up by engraving my name with file... which was discovered to be mine because I'd also put my name on the handle. What's there to make a fuss about?"

"And the post?"

"Nothing official," replied Briquet. "I still make my little Parisian jokes, as if they could be understood in the depths of the country! Nothing at all! It's funny to have three masters by day and not to see hide nor hair of them... not even Monsieur Férandeau. Such is life! I could gladly have a bite to eat after my journey."

He was taken in to supper. On reaching the kitchen he rubbed his hands together energetically, saying: "All the same, I'll put it on the letter-box some day."

He meant his name, Briquet; his was a strange and powerful passion, like that which heaps up scraps of paper bearing autographs. I once knew of a maker of music-boxes who collected buttons. He was comfortably off and whipped his lackeys in the pits of theaters.

"I'm not worried about Monsieur Balcomb," said the aunt. "The London mail won't arrive until tomorrow evening. But your brother... and the Messieurs."

"Three scatterbrains," murmured Jeanne, as if to avoid the necessity of replying.

"Of course, of course," said Madame Touchard, "And sometimes very awkward... but all the same, the house seems sad and too large."

Jeanne took up a candle.

"Already!" exclaimed the aunt, astonished.

"I'm tired," the young woman replied.

"I wanted to talk business, my child; that money you have in your writing-desk..."

"Tomorrow, aunt. I'm tired." She offered her forehead for Madame Touchard to kiss and went upstairs to her room.

Her room was still as simple and meager as it had been when she was in her aunt's care. There was a little bed with white calico curtains, a hickory-wood chest of drawers, an old writing desk and four chairs with straw seats. For ornamentation there was an infant Jesus on the chest and a Virgin on the wall by the bed. She had millions, and was engaged to be married to a millionaire. Title-deeds worth 200,000 francs a year had been shut up in the little old writing-desk with the shaky lid that very day.

Jeanne deposited her candle on the chest and opened her window. The window had he same view as the garden, but broader and clearer. The Priory, as its name indicated, was an old dwelling; Jeanne's room had a turreted balcony with an iron balustrade. Jeanne put a chair on the balcony and sat down.

Night had completely fallen. A red Moon was rising behind the tree-fringed hills. A few white clouds moving slowly across the sky imparted profound tints thereto because the Moon, as large and dull as a huge bronze disc, was giving forth little light as yet.

Jeanne crossed her hands on her knees. She was still dressed in mourning. Her face was sad and sighs rose from her breast. I do not know why she was even more beautiful like this. In the clear night, lit by the vague reflections of the candlelight and the gleam on the horizon, there was an angelic nimbus around her pure and melancholy young head. Poets have seen similar faces in ecstatic visions, and painters too—who are poets with coarser instruments. I recognized it one day during a song by Beethoven; on another occasion, I perceived her black hair floating amid the sober and divine chords of a sonata by Mozart. She possessed the beauty that is everyone's dream, the unique and sovereign beauty of clay modeled by God, fired to transparency and displayed by the radiance of the soul.

Her stare lost itself in the night.

There were two lights amid the shadows, one close by and the other distant. The first was in Madeleine Surrisy's little cottage, the second in the Chateau de Belcamp.

As Jeanne looked at these two lights a sigh rose to her lips. She sent a kiss towards the chateau, murmuring: "My father!" Then she turned her eyes to the other light that came from the cottage.

All exterior noises were dying away. From within the house, the voices of the servants could still be heard, and the heavy footsteps of her aunt, occupied with her household duties. The invisible bell-tower—lost, like the village, in the shadow of the mount—sounded nine o'clock. The mill-wheel fell silent, and the sound of the river's flow became audible.

Jeanne was as motionless as a somber and delightful statue. "Another four hours," she murmured, when the bells had finished chiming.

She got up and went to kneel beside her bed. She prayed for a long time, her eyes fixed on the image of the Virgin.

When she went to sit on the balcony again the two lights were still shining, isolated in a countryside enveloped by darkness.

The evening breeze rippled the silvery white ribbon that wound around the foot of the hill. The Moon was higher now; the sky became paler, veiling the diamantine light of the stars. The noises in the house ceased, magnifying the other vague sounds that emerged from the darkness, whose murmurous chord is called silence.

Ten o'clock sounded, then eleven. Midnight tolled its twelve chimes while the Moon, at its zenith slid like a mute and splendid ship through the foam of clouds. Jeanne remained on the balcony, and the two lights still shone.

"Madeleine's awake," Jeanne said, shivering at the sound of her own voice broke the silence. "My father is suffering..."

At a quarter to one, she went back in and took a wad of papers from her writing desk, which she clasped to her bosom; her features displayed an expression of grave melancholy, devoid of agitation or dread.

She opened her door without hesitation and went downstairs, taking precautions against anyone hearing her but with a firm tread. She went out. The fat guard-dog came to yap at her feet. Outside, once she had shut the garden gate, a feeling of solitude took hold of her, perhaps at the same time as the cold. She hesitated and stood shivering, two paces from the gate, but only for an instant, and was soon on her way towards the towpath. Once she was at the water's edge she resolutely set forth along the leveled path that led to the mill.

To her right, the white facade of the Chateau-Neuf glistened like a marble palace.

As she arrived at the mill bridge–whose weak superstructure, poised on massive supports, was reverberating in response to the outflow–she stopped and leaned against the worm-eaten balustrade. She was as easily visible there as in daylight. Her eye followed the watercourse as far as the landing planted with willows, where her eyes had opened to catch sight of Comte Henri for the first time.

Then she resumed walking, albeit with a tear in her eye. She was now going in the direction of the old chateau.

Two hundred paces from the mill, she turned left to go into the big meadow where Madeleine Surrisy had seen two shadows on the evening when she carried the Marquis' letter to the post-box at Saint Leu–the letter that brought Gregory Temple to the chateau. She crossed the meadow and reached the avenue that came down from the esplanade to the Oise, opposite Madeleine's house. There, she stopped and sat on the trunk of the old uprooted tree. Her hands were held against her heart.

She waited. The rendezvous had been arranged for the same place where they had exchanged the first words of love: sweet things whose echo, reawakened in the silence, made her heart beat even faster. On the evening of the marriage contract, at Versailles, Henri had said to her: "In five days, at one o'clock in the morning, I will be there."

Every place has its savor and its language a well as its appearance. Come back to a place after a long absence and it is the particular perfume of the air that first grips your heart, even before the caresses of the landscape. Then, there will be some familiar sound: the chime of a clock whose carillon makes up a chord that nothing else resembles; the plaint of a waterfall; the striking of a hammer, clutched perhaps in a hand that has grown weaker with time! Once, in a garden where I experienced the happy dream of adolescence, I wept; two thick branches were brushing against one another in the crown of a linden tree, and I recognized the monotonous and mysterious instrument that had accompanied the song of my first dream...

The night was as quiet and calm as that of the other rendezvous. Jeanne listened to the same breeze in the same foliage, and the tranquil Oise murmuring the same caress upon its banks. She let her head fall into her hands. Anguish fettered her soul. Why?

In the distance, in the direction of l'Isle-Adam, there was a noise–but it was so distant that the ear could scarcely make out its nature. Perhaps it was the sly scuttling of a game-animal in the undergrowth–but the wind was blowing from the northeast. No, it did not sound like the tiny hooves of a roe deer; it was the iron shoe of a horse on the sandy road. The pace of its gallop was already distinguishable. Here came a rapid shadow gliding along the towpath.

The planks of the old bridge resounded, and the miller's dog howled.

"Henri!"

"My beloved Jeanne!"

There was a long silent kiss. Then, as on the other occasion, they sat down next to one another, while the valiant horse–whose sweating flanks had Henri's cloak as a blanket–cropped the grass without the need of any tether.

"Jeanne, my beloved wife," said Henri, whose face testified to his weariness but radiated enthusiasm at the same time, "our days of trial are coming to an end. While they pursue the shadow of a criminal here, the soldier will fight and carry off his obscure victories, prelude to an immense triumph. God has conspired with us. Everything is gathered: our men are embarked, the Perkins engine is sailing for the coast of Guinea... and I have come back to submit to my final test before placing myself, free and strong, at the head of my army!"

Jeanne offered her beautiful face to his kisses, but remained silent.

"Free," she murmured, eventually, with a profound sigh. "You are free today, Henri, but tomorrow..."

"Today, I am enchained by my promise and my duty, Jeanne; tomorrow that chain will be broken..."

"Listen to me," the young woman said, insistently. "I have my entire fortune with me–the fortune whose source was mourning and torment. Take it and flee."

She half-opened her cloak and offered Henri the papers she had taken from her writing desk.

"Flee!" Henri repeated. He recoiled as if a brutal hand had wounded him in knocking him back. A mortal pallor covered his face. "You didn't even say, let us flee!" he added.

"If that is what it takes to persuade you, Henri," Jeanne murmured, "let us flee! Let's flee very quickly. I'm ready."

He came closer again, and put Jeanne's cold hand to his burning lips. "But you know everything now," he said, in the vibrant voice that clung like a rope, wound around like a restraint, and whose tone descended so profoundly into the heart. "To you alone on Earth I have given my entire secret... and it is you, Jeanne, who advises me to flee!"

"I implore it on bended knee, Henri, because I love you and I am afraid."

"Whoever does not trust me does not love me, Jeanne!" murmured the young Comte, whose head hung down.

Jeanne's hands clasped her heart. "My God!" she cried while two great shining tears rolled down her cheeks. "My God! Can one give more than her conscience to the one she loves?" Then she turned towards Henri and said, with the coldness of grand passion: "My fortune is nothing; I detest it. My life is little, for I should like to die. My honor... I am mad... I suffer... The words of my prayer burn my mouth and my heart... I love you... I hate the day when I saw you... I am so unhappy that I sometimes hope for the world's compassion... and I am so happy that I fear the jealousy of Heaven! I will go with you to the heights or into the depths; there is a chain around my heart; I belong to you; you conceal my religion, you are my conscience. If there is more to give, name it! I will give you anything!"

She supported her head on Henri's bosom, where his heart was beating violently. By means of a stern effort, however, he steadied his trembling voice and said with austere sadness: "Jeanne! That is not the fashion in which I want to be loved."

A sob made the young woman's breast heave. "My God! My God!" she repeated, from the depths of her anguish.

He went on slowly: "I do not want my wife to weep; I do not want my wife to suffer; I do not want a single anxiety or doubt to be mixed, this evening, in my wife's prayer. I do not want her to say or to think: I no longer know what honor is. I do not want to come between her and her religion, and I have chosen her conscience to be my own."

Jeanne covered her face with her hands. "When you are here," she murmured, "I believe..."

"I want my wife to have no need of the sound of my voice or the persuasion of my voice to believe, because I can no longer be here and cannot do the work of ceaselessly supporting a wavering trust. The door of my cell might wall me in; I might die... and if I am a prisoner or dead, I want my wife to do my will, free and active outside my prison or beyond the tomb. Because I am in love I want the love between you and me, Jeanne, to become something greater than love itself, and that is faith."

She threw her shivering arms around his neck. "Forgive me!" she stammered through her tears. "Forgive me and pity me! I am not worthy to love you!"

"One says that when one is no longer in love, Jeanne," replied Henri, whose tone was increasingly painful and bitter.

Then she slid to her knees, and cried out between the sobs that burst forth: "You are lost, Henri! I tell you that you must flee! Not alone... both of us... oh yes, both of us, for I want to lose myself with you!"

Comte Henri leaned over Jeanne's forehead and kissed it. All emotion had disappeared from his voice when he replied.

"Are you only talking about some new danger, Jeanne? I have admitted from the outset that my life is danger itself, and that there is nothing in my life that is not danger–danger of shame, defeat and death! I admitted that, quite simply and sincerely, as worldly-wise spouses always discuss fortunes and positions before sealing their contract. I admitted that to you so that you would be able to make a decision in full awareness of the circumstances–but I must not delude myself; these faithful precautions were not sufficient. One cannot instill the terrible idea of permanent, habitual and ceaseless danger–ever-renewed and ever-ready to submerge one like a sea in which one swims–in a dear child like you at a single attempt. The thought of exaggeration arises spontaneously, and one imagines involuntarily that one is adrift in a full-blow poetic fiction. If I had known that some peril would alarm you, I would have been more severe. One tends to be gentle in giving a docile pupil her first lesson.

"Get up, my beloved Jeanne, and remember that since the day I ceased to be a child, I have breathed peril as you have breathed the air that sustains your life. I don't know the cause of your fright, but I guarantee in advance that it cannot prevail against my confidence. As I said a little while ago, it is the sea in which I swim. What does one more storm matter when the heart and arm are strong, exercised, indefatigable? Sit down here beside me and speak, so that I may know everything, that I may leave you happy and consoled, and that I may carry away with me for the hour of my last trial the revivifying warmth of your sweetest kiss and the balm of your adorable smile."

He was smiling, so calm, so valiant, so proud that Jeanne's tears dried up as she listened. She obeyed like a child, as valiant as he within her frail envelope, and perhaps as strong.

She sat down, her hands in his, but her poor heart was beating rapidly and as she spoke she could not match him smile for smile. "Henri," she said, having collected herself, "it is indeed necessary that you should know everything: so many things have happened since you left! You are no longer accused of two impossible murders carried out at the same moment in two different places; you are accused of having killed two men at the *Gourmand du jour* restaurant on the night of May 15 and 16, on the eve of your father's birthday."

Jeanne could not help fixing her eyes on the young Comte's. The Moon, at its zenith, had eaten up the clouds; its light was bright and clear. The least detail of Henri's physiognomy was as distinct as in daylight. If he had remained impassive this time, perhaps suspicion would have taken root in Jeanne's mind, for surprise is a natural thing and its suppression requires an effort–but Henri did not hide his surprise. It was, however, free from disquiet.

"Ah," he murmured. "Then I must have one more enemy."

"Gregory Temple..."

"No, Gregory Temple is in London, reduced to the most deplorable state. The doctors will declare his madness incurable now."

"Gregory Temple," Jeanne continued, "left an active and implacable agent in Paris: Robert Surrisy's mother, Madeleine."

"That's right," said the young Comte.

That was all. Jeanne went on: "Whether Madeleine received instructions from Mr. Temple, or whether she acted on her own behalf, an excavation was made in the vicinity of Tivoli, and two bodies were discovered in a shallow grave that had been patched with turf. They knew where to dig–the instructions they were given mentioned thistles replanted above the hole, whose dryness had doubtless prevented them from taking root... the grave was hollowed out at the first attempt beneath a clump of desiccated thistles..."

"These details are familiar to me," Henri interrupted, coolly. "Tom Brown has done his work: go on."

"Tom Brown!" Jeanne repeated, shivering.

"Have you heard the name pronounced before?" the young Comte asked.

"Yes," Jeanne replied. "Many times, in the last three days... your case is on everyone's lips and fills all the newspapers..."

"In what connection was Tom Brown mentioned?"

"I shall tell you shortly. First, I should finish the matter of the two men killed at Tivoli. We have all been questioned as witnesses..."

"You!" cried Henri, stupefied this time.

"Everyone who was in the box at the Feydeau Theater."

"That's right," said the young Comte again, with a bitter smile. "Lady Frances, Germaine, Monsieur Potel and Suzanne... and you certainly could not have said anything other that there were two bloodstains on me?"

Jeanne bowed her head.

"You said that, and you have done well, Jeanne," the young Comte pronounced, gravely. "It is only by a lie that I can be lost."

A sigh lifted Jeanne's breast. "On my salvation, Henri," she cried, "I don't believe that you're guilty!"

"Do you, indeed, do me that kindness?"

"Oh, don't mock me, and don't debate words I let slip. You love me... have pity on me!"

He drew her to his heart and murmured: "All the happiness I shall give you in future, thousand-times-beloved child, would not compensate for those tears. I shall have to fight a duel!"

"I would have loved you in spite of you," she said, kissing him. Then, drawing back, she continued: "Take note that I am not the only one who believes you to be innocent. Germaine, that dear creature, Lady Frances, Suzanne and my aunt are defending you... and your father, your admirable father: love, trust, generosity and loyalty made flesh. I have only seen him once since your departure, and he certainly doesn't know that I'm even closer to you than he is. It's adoration that he has for you, Henri, and I shall worship with him for the rest of my life."

"My beloved father," murmured the young Comte. "With you, Jeanne, he is the better part of my heart... but why have you only seen him once since my departure?"

"I'll leave that question until the end, and the answer will be sad, Henri... let me follow the thread of my revelations. You were asking me about the name Tom Brown–this is what happened on the day after your departure for Paris at No. 19 Rue Dauphine, where Mr. Temple's lodgings were."

The young Comte started, and did not take the trouble to hide a marked increase in his attention.

"A lame boy," Jeanne continued, "the son of the concierge at that house, No. 19, came on that morning to see the local Commissioner of Police, and declared that a pestilential odor was coming through the chinks of the door in the lodging-house where his father worked. The door was that of a room let to an Englishman, who had been away for more than a week, taking his key with him. The Police Commissioner went to the place; the concierge, his wife and daughter offered such accounts of the mysterious behavior of this Englishman–who was Mr. Temple–that the Magistrate believed that a crime must have been committed, and did not hesitate to force the lock.

"Everyone expected that they would find themselves confronting a corpse, so fetid was the odor emerging from the cracks and the keyhole, but there was no corpse. The odor came from a plate of meat abandoned on the table, whose decomposition had filled the narrow room with a miasma. But the law officer suddenly found himself in the presence of discoveries relating to a bloody crime, even more important than material proof. It was bringing the documents assembled in the room into the daylight, together with the exhumation at Tivoli, that gave your trial this new and dangerous aspect."

"What was in the room, then?" Henri asked, unostentatiously but without fear.

"There was what you have mentioned: the trace of a strange and implacable madness. A kind of motto repeated everywhere, made up of a word, a name and a date: *Memento – Constance Bartolozzi – February 3, 1817*. It covered the wall-paneling, the hangings, the ceiling, the floor, the furniture, the curtains, everything... Henri, that man is our enemy, but he is my mother's avenger!"

She stopped, because a spasm constricted her breast.

"Jeanne," Comte Henri de Belcamp replied, "That man is a great mind, a Magistrate of integrity, a loyal and courageous soul. I am not his enemy. When I am no longer here, in two days, you shall see a great joy; that man's daughter will have recovered her husband and will be able to name her son, the foreign child that she was accused of always carrying in her arms. Ask them then what I have risked for their happiness. Against the injustice of men there is much that I can do, but against the hand of God there is nothing anyone can do. It is God who determines madness."

"That word, that name, that date," Jeanne went on. "*Memento – Constance Bartolozzi – February 3, 1817*, written thousands of times in large or microscopic letters, were found at the head of a multitude of papers filled with calculations, traced in numbers, in letters known or unknown. All of it related to you, or at least to a person that justice now takes to be you: Tom Brown."

"The man who killed your mother," Comte Henri said, slowly.

Jeanne shivered from head to toe. Her gaze fixed itself momentarily on the young Comte, whose face expressed a gentle and merciful sadness. "Oh, that's true!" she cried. "Those who accuse you are mad. Could I possibly adore my mother's murderer?"

"In any case, could an assassin smile at his victim's daughter?" Henri murmured, whose serenity was as profound and measureless as the calm of the splendid night itself.

Their hands came together. Jeanne went on. "Among all these items, in the midst of a voluminous correspondence, two in particular attracted the attention of the law officer. The first was a huge blackboard standing in front of the window and covered in writing, much of it figures. This board represented the sum of the calculations of probability by means of which Mr. Temple had discovered Constance Bartolozzi's assassin. The law officer recognized that Mr. Temple had a theory of his own that was as learned as it was ingenious, which he characterized himself under the title *the impossible*. I don't know how to explain it. What I can tell you is that in a corner of the board these various named were bracketed together:

"Henry Brown (London)

"James Davy (London/Paris)

"Henri de Belcamp (Paris)

"Richard Thompson (London/Paris)

"George Palmer (Prague)

"Tom Brown (London/Australia)

"The sum of these names, united by the bracket, was *JOHN DEVIL THE QUAKER*.

"The board has been preserved.

"The second item is a complete biography of this Tom Brown, or John Devil, from his earliest years, carrying as a superscription: 'This is dedicated to the author of *The Book of the Amazing Adventures of John Devil the Quaker*, published in London in March 1817.'

"It is a terrible chaplet of crimes, each one supported by justificatory notes: a history combining the exploits of Tom Brown and his mother Helen. That frightful poem ends with the most odious of all these despicable actions:

Tom Brown is represented as abandoning his dying mother in the middle of the Australian desert...”

Jeanne’s eyes were still on Henri; at that moment she saw his face change–but a dark cloud covered the Moon, and the entire landscape was veiled in shadow along with Comte Henri’s features.

The cloud passed; the Moon shone. Henri’s face was noble and serene again before Jeanne’s gaze.

“If they could only see you,” she murmured, “they would know perfectly well that you are incapable of a despicable act! Everything that I’ve told you, Henri, I know thanks to your cousin, Monsieur Boisruel the Counselor, who came to the chateau yesterday, and whom your father refused to see.”

“And what does our cousin think?” Henri asked, unhurriedly and indifferently.

“He doesn’t know... he’s afraid for you... he’s sad.”

“I’m grateful to him for the keen interest that he’s taking in me. And why did my father refuse to see him?”

“In answering that question,” Jeanne said, lowering her voice in spite of herself, “I come to the explanation of why I have only seen the Marquis de Belcamp once since the signature of the marriage contract. Henri, your father is very ill...”

“My father!” cried the young Comte, all of whose coolness vanished as if by magic. “Very ill! In danger, perhaps?”

“Perhaps,” Jeanne murmured, sadly. “The doctor is uncertain.”

Henri had got up by virtue of an involuntary movement, as if his immediate impulse had been to hurl himself towards the chateau–but he sat down again and crossed his hands over his knees, thinking aloud. “That cannot be. You alone know my secret, Jeanne... only you and those who have sworn the pact of the *Deliverance*. I am no longer free. In God’s name, speak quickly! All the rest is nothing–but that which concerns my father touches the very bottom of my heart, as if it concerned you.”

“You are right to love him, Henri,” replied the young woman, pensively, “for I have never seen love like that which he has for you. I did not know my mother; it seemed to me that mothers alone could love with that boundless affection. Your name was incessantly upon his lips, and he found a thousand ingenious detours to return the conversation to you–always to you. To doubt you seemed to him a blasphemy. He sought out Germaine and me because we always wanted to talk about you. The idea that you are guilty, not of murder but of anything at all, was inconceivable to him. In the depths of your prison, you were his best hope and his dearest pride. When he thought of you, he was ashamed of himself for being so little. You had transcended everything, and your family’s noble past seems to him like a shadow next to your light...”

She stopped.

"You used the past tense," murmured Henri, deeply moved. "Can it be that the exhumation at Tivoli and the Rue Dauphine business have made an impression on that upright mind?"

"I don't know if he knows either or both those facts," the young woman replied.

"What, then?"

"There is something else, Henri..." She paused. "But as to this, I have seen nothing myself, and what I tell you is hearsay. On the very night of your departure, or rather the morning, at about 3 a.m., someone knocked on the door of the Hotel de France in Versailles, where your father was staying. A carriage was there, containing a woman whose face could not be seen–it was covered by a thick black veil. She asked, in a feeble voice that could hardly be heard, for the Marquis de Belcamp. The Marquis was woken up, and came down himself. The veiled woman uncovered her face to him alone. She said nothing. The Marquis fell to the ground, where he remained unconscious.

"When he recovered his senses, instead of going back into the hotel, he climbed into the carriage, which was a cab from Paris, and on his instruction the coachman set out for the Chateau de Belcamp.

"That was the very same day that I saw him. He came back to Versailles on horseback, at about the time when we were usually admitted to the prison. He was so changed that I could scarcely recognize him. His cheeks were the color of Earth; his eyes gleamed in the depths of their hollowed orbits, as if he had risen from his bed after a long fever. His voice was feeble and he hardly seemed to understand what was said to him.

"It was particularly difficult to explain to him than an order had come from the Ministry consigning you to solitary confinement, and that the prison door would henceforth be closed to him. When he finally understood, he fell unconscious for a second time, which lasted longer than the first.

"When we woke, he said to me: 'I shall not come back to Versailles again.' Then he tried to mount his horse again, but we put him in the *berline* and I accompanied him. He remained silent the entire way. I tried to talk to him about you, but he gestured with his hand to tell me to be quiet. He refused to let me come into the chateau. Since then, the door has been closed to me."

"And this woman?" Henri asked, his voice much changed.

"I have told you everything I know about the woman."

"How? The servants..."

"The servants have not seen her again since her arrival at the chateau de Belcamp."

"The doctor..."

"The doctor has slept at Belcamp these last four nights. Save for one occasion, he has not seen the woman."

"Has she gone?"

"No one knows."

“Is she dying?”

“No one has seen a coffin.”

There was a long silence, during which Henri was plunged into a profound and toilsome meditation. Then Jeanne went on. “There is one person who does not sleep at the chateau, but who is nevertheless even closer to your father than the doctor.”

“Who is this person?”

“Madeleine Surrisy.”

“Madeleine!” the young Comte repeated, dismally. “They will kill me in my father’s heart!”

“What have you done to Madeleine, Henri?” Jeanne murmured.

“I loved her husband. Thanks to me, she will see her son rich before dying... and will perhaps hear him called by his father’s name.”

Three o’clock sounded from the little church of Miremont. Henri kissed Jeanne’s hands more tenderly; she knew that he would soon have to go. “What I’ve told you has made no difference to you?” she sighed.

“I knew in advance what our enemies were capable of, Jeanne,” the young Comte replied, with a melancholy smile.

“And you’re going to put yourself in their hands!” This was said in a tremulous and prayerful voice.

Henri put Jeanne’s hands against his heart. “Only the guilty flee,” he said, without concealing the melancholy weariness that underlay his firmness. “I am the son of the Marquis de Belcamp, I am your husband, and I am the leader of a noble army. My father, my wife and my soldiers must assist in the triumph of an innocent or the death of a martyr.”

“Henri, Henri!” Jeanne pleaded, putting her beautiful hair in his bosom. “That should not be for me! Flee, flee! I ask you on my knees.”

He sat up straight. “Jeanne,” he said, pronouncing the word in a strange tone, “do you love me better than your honor, then?”

The young woman did not reply immediately. Henri felt her hands grow cold and shiver in his. Then, slowly and with a kind of solemnity, she withdrew them in order to put her arms tightly around his neck. Her eyes–her beautiful eyes, as clear as virginity–shone with a profound and dolorous passion. It was she who offered her pale lips, appealing for her husband’s first kiss. And amid the silence of these chaste first fruits, she said: “I don’t know how much I love you. I know that I love you enough to give you more than my life. Henri, my adored Henri, do as your conscience and your genius bid. May I never be an obstacle in your path. You have chosen me as a confidante; you have opened to me, with your heart, the vast horizons of your imagination. I have understood, I have admired, I am kneeling. If you wish to prove your innocence to someone, I say to those who need proofs, to your father, to your friends, to the world: go and follow your destiny. But I repeat that it should not be for me; I have no need of proof. Whatever you do, whatever is done to you, vanquisher or vanquished, you are my love and my honor; the entire universe might give you the name of criminal and I would keep you in my heart as one keeps a persecuted faith. I am to you what the priest is to God, and my soul will follow you to the scaffold and beyond!"

They got up together and walked towards the meadow, where the horse was waiting patiently.

"God owes me happiness because of you," Henri murmured. "Those who are attacking me are strong, but they have allowed me to grow up and I shall prevail." He stopped as he put his foot into the stirrup. "I shall prevail, Jeanne," he repeated–and his voice had such a quality that the young woman's heart quivered with the pace of its beating.

He looked at her rapturously for a moment; then his saddened eyes were lowered. "But if God is not willing," he continued, in a murmur, "then the kiss your lips gave me was a final farewell."

Anguish stifled Jeanne's reply.

Henri went on, in a serious and firm tone. "Jeanne, there is a man who loves you, chivalrously. If I die, be his sister or his wife." He was obliged to support the young woman, who was fainting in his arms. "I took you from him," the Comte de Belcamp continued. "I bequeath you to him. Why weep? Does he who makes a will bring forward the final hour? I am full of life, my beloved Jeanne, and among those who will defend me in the hour of peril, that good, loyal and valiant young man Robert Surrisy will be placed in the first rank. In case of misfortune, it will be him that I shall appoint, with you, as executor of my will. Are you listening to me?"

"I'm listening to you, Henri," the young woman murmured.

"I am proud," he said. "I believe that my enterprise is myself. If I die, the vast association whose leader I am will be a body without a soul. A flag will be my shroud, and it will not be exhumed in future to flutter above the world without long preparations. If, like Moses, I die within sight of my promised land, there will remain one ultimate duty to complete–one alone! Will you complete it?"

"What must be done, I will accomplish."

"A man is waiting, a long way away, to whom I have said: 'Before the year 1817 has run its course, destiny will have spoken. Interrogate the sea, sire, from the heights of your isle; the sea will answer you. One day, you will see a little ship with neither sails nor oars, which will be propelled by a cloud. If she carries the English flag, that is liberty: prepare yourself. If she carries the tricolor, God has not been willing; and if a black flag flutters at its peak, adieu, sire–I shall be lying beneath the marble of a tomb...'

"If I die, Jeanne, you and Robert must take my schooner–which is called, alas, *Deliverance*–and go to the isle of St. Helena. Raise the standard in view of the isle, two hours after sunrise: first a tricolor, then the black flag. Will you do that?"

"I swear that I will do it."

Thank you, then, and au revoir, my dear Jeanne. Now I say to you, as before: there is a voice within me that cries to me: we shall prevail!"

He lifted her up in his arms. She was bathed in tears. Their lips came together once more. Then Comte Henri leapt into the saddle and galloped away. Jeanne's arms were extended towards him. As he crossed the bridge, she saw him blow her a kiss. An instant later, he disappeared into the shadow of the mill.

Jeanne went slowly back to the Priory. She spent the rest of the night on her knees, but the words of her prayer did not get as far as her lips.

Henri was burning up the road on the way to Versailles.

Monsieur Roblot, Deputy Governor of Versailles prison, got up that morning red, bloated, congested and ill. He cursed his children, who came to say hello to him, and picked a quarrel with his wife. His eyes were hot and haggard; the furrows in his forehead were deeply engraved; his toes were tortured by gout; his head was as heavy as lead.

He went into his office in his dressing-gown and slippers. Instead of the white coffee he was normally served he demanded a knuckle of ham and a bottle of Thorins.[238] There had been long and forceful quarrels in the Roblot household over less than that, but this morning the Deputy Governor challenged his wife with an expression so savage that she dared not do battle with him, in spite of her intrepid character.

On the table in the office, there was an open letter and two sealed letters. It was the open letter, received the previous evening, that had put the Deputy Governor in this sorry state. The other two letters were his morning post, and he had no knowledge of their contents as yet.

He immediately slumped down into his armchair and growled: "Imbecile! How did he get to be Governor? A mystery! Nephew of the dressmaker of the mistress of the husband of the niece of the confessor of the Minister's aunt! Nepotism is a revolting thing. I'm no one's protégé, by thunder! I'm the son of my endeavors!"

He took up the letter, adding: "And what a fine son they had, those endeavors! Hurled at a recalcitrant door like a cannonball... and look what's happening! You'll drink at the fountain, you dumb ox! That'll teach you to surround yourself with liberals!"

He unfolded the letter and gazed at it sadly. "He's the Governor!" he cried. "His word is his command! 'I shall return tomorrow morning...' He goes his own way, that one. Damn it! If I can fire one volley at him, before leaving..." He continued, in a melancholy fashion: "Because I'll have to go, old girl; it's the order of the day. You were like a fish in water here, and you amused yourself by making mischief... Go drink at the fountain!"

He crumpled the letter in his hand. "But why, in God's name, does he have to come back today instead of tomorrow? Monsieur le Comte has given his word that he'll be here this evening. I was safe. Out of sight, out of mind. That's what they call destiny, that is: fatality, bad luck, misfortune!"

Mechanically, he took up one of the sealed letters and held it for a moment between his thumb and forefinger.

"I'll bet a franc that this is something nasty," he said. "Misfortunes never come alone... 'Court of Assizes of Versailles...' These Judges weren't born with a silver spoon! I don't know why they scorn the Administration that values them highly... especially when it's an old soldier... Let's see what the Court of Assizes at Versailles has to say..."

He broke the seal, and leapt out of the armchair.

"An interrogation!" he cried, in a strangled voice. "An interrogation, to-day!" His arms fell and his scarlet cheek turned ashen.

"That's wonderful," he said, dejectedly. "What am I going to tell the Examining Magistrate? My prisoner is invisible." He reddened again in a paroxysm of rage. "That's the last straw, damn it! You've got yourself into this mess yourself! Go see if there's bread to dip in the fountain for the children! So the square-bonnets want an interrogation now! That'll amuse them. It'll make trouble. I'll bet 20 *sous* that the last letter will bring it further forward. That'll please me, on my word!"

He opened the third missive convulsively. It was from the Minister of the Interior, sent by express. It read as follows:

A message has reached us from London via Boulogne, transmitted by telegraph. Scotland Yard headquarters has received information that the pretended Comte de Belcamp is in London. Concealed behind that name is the famous bandit John Devil. An Inspector will call today on the personal instructions of the Minister.

Roblot got up and walked around his office, arms extended, in the fashion that the romances of the Round Table attribute to good King Arthur when his helmet had been cleft by violent blows.

"C'mon, c'mon, c'mon," he repeated three times over. "Isn't there anything more? What a pity there isn't a fourth tile [239] to make up a little square. The Governor, the Inspector and the Examining Magistrate. Bravo! Face the audience! Stop the music! I'll start by blowing myself up."

He opened a drawer that contained a pair of heavy pistols.

"There's a gentleman who wants to talk to you," said a servant, opening the door slightly.

"Is it the Governor, the Examining Magistrate or the Inspector?" Roblot asked, suffering a sudden attack of madness. "Send them to the fountain to play *lanlaire* [240] to the subscriber of their choice!"

"There must be wine or liquor hidden under the bed, that's for sure," said the old woman. "He's already drunk!"

Roblot pointed the barrels of his pistols at her. She fled in alarm. Roblot followed her.

"Felicity!" he howled into the corridor. "I won't kill you. I know you're innocent. My only intention is to put an end to my days. Where's the gentleman? Perhaps it's the one who saw Caesar on the eve of the battle when he swallowed his biscayen.[241] Or Pompey. I've come unstuck, creature! Unstuck! Unstuck! Tell the fellow to come in... At least, it's not the Prefect, more's the pity! And bring the ham, coffee, wine, brandy... I'll kill myself afterwards!"

He went back in, fell into his armchair and put his head on the table.

"I'm ahead of time, my good Monsieur Roblot," said a voice behind him that made him quiver, as if one of his two fat pistols had just exploded in his ear. He turned round and saw an unfamiliar face.

"It doesn't add up!" he moaned. "I'm dreaming standing up. The Devil may carry me away if I don't know that voice!"

The stranger, an old man with a mild and modest face, smiled behind his wrinkles. As Roblot looked at him more closely, he straightened his arched back and lifted up his wig of white hair.

"Monsieur le Comte!" cried Roblot, dumbfounded. Tears came into his eyes. He got up unsteadily, drunk without having touched a drop, and threw himself down at Henri's knees.

"Good Lord," he said, sobbing, "that's a nice touch... a touch that does you honor! My word, rogues have some good in them! And I know more than one well-set-up man who, once the key of the door was in his pocket... C'mon, c'mon, my heart almost stopped in my chest, but everything's all right now; I'll clap you in irons, by God! And I'll be burned alive before I let you out of my sight now!"

"It will be compensation for my promptness," said the Comte, smiling.

"It'll be anything you want! I've got you, and I'm not letting go again...and I won't give you the cell with the sawn-off bolt, either. Hell's thunder! You never told me you were John Devil!"

"John Devil!" Henri repeated. "I've heard it said that he's escaped from prison many a time, but never that he came back of his own accord."

"Very well!" cried Roblot, heartily. "Once more–anything you want. You see, the Governor could arrive any minute, the Magistrate too, and the Inspector as well. I've got work to do... the wife and children don't live on air. I've been worried for three days, because your case has taken a turn for the worse. It's said, with good reason, that it wasn't brought for nothing. For myself, I would have put my hand in the fire to swear that you were innocent, in the beginning– and see what's come along. The Tivoli story, the Rue Dauphine business–there's the key to a half-solved puzzle... and when I saw those three machines tumbling on my head... but you don't know what I'm talking about...?"

"I do indeed," Henri put in.

"That's fine... Carry on being the one who knows everything. We'll skip that. I promise you that you'll be fashionably parceled up: I'm too scared! I said as much, when I realized that I was going to lose my job..."

"Have you forgotten what I told you do in case of misfortune?"

"Go on!" Roblot replied. "John Devil's said many others things–that he'd give annual incomes to all the jailers that he's struck down! Excuse me! My head was almost on fire. See!" He displayed the two pistols, laughing dully. "But what I do want to know is why you've come back."

"Because I learned that the interrogation was set for today," the young Comte replied.

Roblot stared at him, his stupefaction redoubled. "Well, you're not lacking in virtue, that's for sure," he muttered. "Or else, all this must be hiding some infernal ruse. Besides, I thought to myself: for an ordinary Comte, he makes himself up rather well! He can give himself any face he wants... That's not a good sign. Ah well, who knows. It's all over now: the fountains, the Knights of the Deliverance, the great Eagles of the Legion of Honor, with their faith, hope and charity. I'm laughing at it now that I have my head out of the water, my word! During those three days, I honestly thought such things. I told myself ten times over, and more, that I was an imbecile. Let's go, Monsieur le Comte–we have to go back into our egg like a good little chicken."

"I'm ready, my dear Monsieur Roblot," Henri said.

The old soldier was not overcome by joy. In most men, joy produces generosity, indulgence and mercy; in others, it is egotism that exalts naively. The latter walk by without noticing you, their triumphs carelessly crushing you; their expansiveness comes with brutal and pitiless insolence. For the most part, they are not at all what one would normally call mean fellows; it is their way of being happy.

Without knowing it, and without having any consciousness of his ingratitude, Roblot avenged the atrocious fright he had had.

"My God!" he went on. "You're ready! I believe you are! No more deceptions to carry out! I'm doing my duty and my job, by God! When one has been almost ready to blow one's skull apart, one can jeer a little at the swords of the Knights of the Deliverance. They've only to turn up here! I've got buckshot waiting to greet them... bang! I tell you these things politely, Monsieur de Belcamp. If you try to involve me in another farce, I'll put a bullet in your brain–it's my duty."

"My good Monsieur Roblot," the young Comte replied, "I am entirely at your disposal, whenever you wish."

"Yes, yes, by God!" the Deputy Governor exclaimed, emphatically. "That's the very word. At my disposal, entirely!" Seized by a vague remorse, he went on: "But we've time in hand... and after all, you've got me out of trouble. Would you like a glass of Thorins, my prisoner. I like to do things politely. To the French soldier!"

"A thousand thanks, Monsieur Roblot, but I'm very tired and my only desire is to lie down."

"I understand... You have to collect yourself for the interrogation."

"You're mistaken, Monsieur. I have nothing to say but the truth."

Roblot burst out laughing. Then, he became serious, while he stared at the young Comte. "My sacred word!" he muttered. "They'll give you up to God's goodness without confession... but a warm cat dreads cold water, and I know my physiognomy. Hell's thunder! I'll be able to tell the children, one day, that I've been face-to-face with John Devil in my own office... How extraordinary! It's true that I have a pair of pistols, but..."

He picked up his pistols and stuck them into the braces holding his trousers up, while he searched a monumental bunch for a particular key.

"It won't be me," he said, "who'll leave those toys on the table." When he turned round, though, key in hand, he let loose a cry of terror. Comte Henri was playing with two superb pistols whose damascened barrels threw two rays of reflected sunlight into his face. He let the key fall and immediately reached for his own brace, but the two gleams were already threatening; he saw the open mouths of cannon at the height of his eyes and heard the batteries open fore. He almost felt the shock of two bullets hitting his forehead at the same time. All old soldiers are not obliged to be heroes.

As he was dying of these terrible wounds, Comte Henri's soft voice said: "I have no further need of these, which I took for my journey. Permit me to offer them to you, my dear Monsieur Roblot."

The Deputy Governor's eyes cleared; he saw that the pistols were being offered to him butts first. "You do well," he stammered, "to surrender your arms." Then, perhaps seeing the absurdity of his pose, he added: "I can't accept them, Monsieur. The clerk should have them."

He recovered the key and drew back the bolt of a door that let out into one of the prison corridors. Henri went through first, at his invitation.

A few moments later, Henri was installed in an admirably secure cell, as he had been assured by Monsieur Roblot. Monsieur Roblot also promised him that he would no longer be served by Mestivier, his usual warder, to whom he had promised a promotion. The door was locked, and Henri soon heard the footsteps of a sentinel walking back and forth outside his door.

As for Roblot, he had changed his mind; he asked for the ham and the bottle of Thorins to be taken into the dining-room. His wife and children were invited to the feast, and the servant received an order to make strong black coffee, because Monsieur had to work with his head.

"Refrain from judging your master, my girl," he said. "He's a man far out of your reach." Then he addressed his family: "You're eating my bread; that's very good... far be it from me to think of criticizing you... but do you know how much it costs me? Have you, perhaps, realized that it takes the gravest circumstances–the most terrible, I might add–to trouble the serenity of an old soldier? Be happy and tranquil; never know the need or the gnawing worries. May all this weariness, all these dangers, be on my head, as my sex and my duty requires! Always present at roll-call. Devotion, fidelity, vigilance, coolness in the face of danger–engrave that motto on my tomb."

He ate the ham.

The Governor arrived; the Examining Magistrate conducted the interrogation; the Inspector made his call; Monsieur Roblot received their felicitations.

Days passed then, while the investigation was pursued with extraordinary vigor. Comte Henri was kept incommunicado with the utmost rigor. Roblot said, figuratively, to his superiors, that he was lying down across their doorway.

Roblot did not know everything, however, for letters from Percy Balcomb arrived at Miremont, with London postmarks.

It must be said that Miremont was not much interested in news of Percy Balcomb, nor in the delay imposed on Jeanne's marriage. There were other feelings in the air, thank God! Since the uncertain era of its foundation, Miremont had never experienced such a fever. That locality, previously obscure, now attracted the attention of the whole of France, and even Europe; it sensed this, and became proud. It subscribed to newspapers in order to see its name written therein.

We ought to add that Miremontese opinion had been completely overturned yet again by the new complexion imposed upon the young Comte's case. The secrets of an examination always leak out. Miremont knew, vaguely, the story of the law's recent discoveries. The legend of John Devil was a prodigious success in *society*. The little Chaumerons played at burying one another in the fields of Tivoli.

The Marquis' situation did inspire a certain pity. Pity is a compound sentiment, into which enters a sufficient *quantum* [242] of vengeance: Miremont proves the point. Think of all the respect that had been lavished on that man! Had he not forced society to kneel before his son, a brigand? He was very unfortunate, to be sure, but he had a *berline* and an income of 18,000 a year. No one dreamed of accusing him of complicity in these tenebrous horrors of course–but after all, one had only known him for three years, and there were many mysteries surrounding him.

That woman who had sought him out in Versailles, in the middle of the night... the veiled woman whom he had taken to the chateau and whom no one had seen since...

"Trump!" said Chaumeron. "It's laughable. Oh, damn it!"

There were continual comings and goings between Miremont and l'Isle-Adam, where Godinot, the Police Commissioner, had an office full of mysteries.

Many-Apologies hoped to be Mayoress, and Madame Chaumeron thought that the position of Second Deputy would revert by rights to her husband. She counted without Madame Célestin, who had dreamed of elevating her two Bondons to that important position.

Every day, according to a rota, Don Juan Besnard, Mademoiselle or someone else was dispatched to Versailles by express. They returned with gossip by the basketful. There was then a meeting at the home of Madame Morin du Reposoir, chaired by the Deputy's wife, and Assizes were held. Miremont lived twice or three times over, one might say; Miremont amused itself. For them, this was a memorable era.

Take note, too, that there were other things than Belcamp gossip. The Chateau-Neuf also presented a whole series of puzzles to be solved, and the Priory contributed its contingent of charades. The three idlers had returned. Where from? It would have required a clever man to tell them. Robert Surrisy was always on the road to Paris; Lady Frances was traveling; Suzanne... believe it if you can, that blonde, timid and sad Englishwoman was walking in the Chateau-Neuf's park with a handsome young man–also English–and they took turns to embrace little Richard, who called them "Mama" and "Papa."

"Married!" said Chaumeron. "Beat the tambourine! Tricky!"

Suzanne seemed happy, even though she had learned that her father, having been released on bail in London, was in a madhouse.

Lady Frances Elphinstone, although she was no longer little Richard's mother, had a story no less bizarre. At the Hotel Meurice in Paris, according to Godinot's report, there was an Austrian Count, as handsome as a star but dying of consumption. Lady Frances Elphinstone spent her nights by his bedside. Count Friedrich Boehm, as he was called, had also come from London. He was not only visited by Frances but also by Robert Surrisy and Suzanne's Englishman. In spite of the state of his health, he had moved Heaven and Earth to see Comte Henri in prison at Versailles.

Was Many-Apologies not right to say that all of this had the reek of John Devil about it?

Robert Surrisy was often to be seen with Jeanne, as if nothing had happened between them. Laurent had never been more at ease with the lovely Germaine. Férandeau was turning into a serious man. One day, when Mademoiselle came back from Versailles, she related that she had seen a crowd gather outside a print-seller's in the Rue de la Paroisse, where all Miremont was exposed. This Férandeau, traitor to hospitality, had sold his album to an editor before becoming a man of politics. He had delivered Miremont for the price of a meal at the *Veau-qui-tette*, his dream. The whole of society was there: Don Juan Besnard, avaricious, brutal and idiotic; Chaumeron, mounted on a cockerel's legs and followed by his brood; Morin du Reposoir, Deputy, fine quality; Many-Apologies, humble but poisonous; Madame Célestin, finally, knitting in hand, needle in her hair, grazing her two Siamese lambs...

A faithful pupil of Louis David, Férandeau had not attached any great importance to these frivolities. He was in the process of becoming famous in spite of himself. Such is the history of all caricaturists. The vocation of our greatest comic artists initially leads them astray towards tragedy.

No one greeted Férandeau any longer on the roads in the vicinity of Miremont.

All this was mysterious, but the mystery did not stop there. Madeleine Surrisy, the peasant who conducted herself like a nun, was mixed up in something. She alone was admitted to the chateau, and Madame Etienne confessed that her former mistress had received similar visits from a bird of ill-omen not long before her death.

One night, Blondeau the local Constable was poaching ducks along the Oise when he heard voices in Madeleine's cottage. Robert and his mother were arguing. The mother said: "He's an assassin!"

Always and everywhere that word: *assassin!*

What would the denouement of this drama be? Chaumeron did not mince his words in expressing his opinion; he said: "If I were Judge, the wheel, too right!" The two Bondons had never seen the guillotine in action and lived in hope of it coming to Versailles on "Comte Henri's day." Many-Apologies was counting down the days to the execution, and was mending a puce silk dress for the occasion. Mother Chaumeron had told eight or ten little girls that, if they were good, they could have a picnic on the grass in the groves of the Trianon...

But the other camp appeared to have an equal and opposite confidence. That goblin Germaine mocked everyone and predicted that Miremont would be bowing and scraping to Monsieur le Comte again. She went laughing and singing to the Priory or the Chateau-Neuf, where Comte Henri's adherents met, and there was not a shadow of doubt as to the fortunate outcome of the trial. Theirs was a devotion that went as far as enthusiasm, for sure. Suzanne taught her child the name Henri, and could not speak of him without tears in her eyes. Her husband, since she was married, professed a kind of worship for the young Comte. Jeanne, Germaine, Robert, Laurent and Férandeau himself were like devotees around the Holy Sepulchre.

The two parties were equally balanced in numerical terms. If the faction commanded by Many-Apologies and Madame Célestin had possessed as much courage as venom, civil war might have covered Miremont in blood.

While these passions seethed, the chateau—formerly so joyful, whose doors had opened so widely and hospitably—was neutral, mute, immobile. You might have thought it deserted; the doors and windows were closed; no more crowds thronged the footpaths in the park, upon which the grass was already encroaching. A sad thing that could serve as a measure of the abandonment was that the great table of the birthday dinner remained standing in the middle of the lawn, and the garlands of foliage still hung, desiccated, from their supports of iron thread.

What was inside this chateau in mourning? Immense love deceived; great sorrow; boundless discouragement. The walls gave passage to neither sobs nor tears. There was a funereal silence, a bleak despair.

And there was one profound mystery among so many that the curious eye could not penetrate at all: a woman had gone into that house and had not left it. What was behind those thickly-curtained windows? A prisoner? Another victim?

The Marquis de Belcamp had only left his home once, shaking like a moribund, paler than a phantom, but upright and with his head held high. He had gone to hear mass and to kneel before the altar.

What was going on there? Under the proud panache of the great oaks, somber and slowly stirred by the breeze, the old manor displayed its melancholy silhouette. Something was enveloping it that was neither a veil nor a mist—it was not the eye that perceived it but the heart—something that could not be put into words: a vast and sinister impression, similar to the solemn anguish of the hour that precedes a storm; a mortal and profound frisson, from which emerged the idea of the eternal justice of God.

On the sixth day of the session, at 5 a.m., a numerous crowd had already gathered around the tribunal. They were waiting for the door to be opened on the disputation of the case of Comte Henri de Belcamp. A thousand contradictory rumors were running through that mob, composed of peasants and members of the lower middle class. It was said, among other things, that the accused had refused an advocate and would conduct his own defense.

Hundreds of stories were related, including this one: Monsieur Roblot, the Deputy Governor, an old soldier, had risked his own skin several times over in confronting the accused, a terrible man who could obtain weapons at will. Even though Monsieur Roblot might be taken for a brave soldier, etc. etc.

The half of the crowd that knew nothing of John Devil sought instruction from the other half.

As 7 a.m. approached, Monsieur Huchon, the clerk of the Court, went into his office and made the well-known gesture of Robinson Crusoe discovering Friday's footprint in the sand. The lid of his desk, which he had left black and intact, now carried seven letters engraved with a knife and perfectly legible; the sum of the seven letters formed the name Briquet. The clerk summoned the office boys. Intelligence having been gathered, it turned out that a thin and unprepossessing youth with hair the color of road dust–the favorite shade of Paris street-urchins–had arrived the previous evening with a letter to the Minister requesting three seats for the day's session.

At eight o'clock, Chaumeron the plain speaker was heard in the corridor. He wanted eleven seats, on account of the fact that he was a neighbor of the father of the accused.

"Young man," said Madame Morin du Reposoir to the clerk of the Court, "I am the First Deputy's wife in the same locality."

"Here's a Commander of the National Guard and a Municipal Counselor," Madame Célestin added, proudly, using both hands to point to the right-hand Bondon and the left-hand Bondon.

"Monsieur le President's seats!" commanded a senior lackey.

"The General's seats!" demanded another.

"Now, now, children! The Prefecture!"

"Let me pass–I'm from the Bishop!"

"The Minister's, if you please!"

"The Receiver of Taxes!"

"For Mademoiselle Léocadie of the Opéra..."

"Monsieur Huchon, your wife promised me–I'm the greengrocer, you know..."

"Hey, Huchon! Your friends!"

"Is there a little something for the concierge and her daughter?"

"Monsieur Huchon!–My dear Monsieur Huchon!–Are you making a
fuss?–Blackguard!–I bought you a drink yesterday!–Lord Huchon, you'll be
destitute!–Oh, he's a fine chap, this Huchonneau!–Subaltern!–There! You're a
love!–I'll catch you later, good-for-nothing!–A thousand thanks!–Go to the
Devil!"–all of this at the same time. Half of Huchon was dressed with bunting,
the other half was on the Gemonies.[243]

At 9 a.m., the session commenced. In the seats reserved for the Bishop,
the Tax-Collector, the Prefecture, etc. it was discovered that the Presiding Judge
was a rather small man. The Public Prosecutor excited a certain curiosity.
Mademoiselle Léocadie coughed a great deal behind her fan to attract the attention of the Advocates. The concierge and her daughter chewed Marseille cara-
mels. Everyone was as cheerful as a chaffinch. The Court of Assizes is one of
the most joyful places in this universe!

When the accused appeared, there was a profound silence. The concierge
had expected to see a man with blue hair and horns; she was mortified. Mademoiselle Léocadie smiled at the Advocates.

At 3 p.m., the session was adjourned. The charges had been read, the accused interrogated, the witnessed depositions received, the indictment heard. We
leave these things in shadow by design. We place justice, so to speak, upon a
pedestal around which the curious crowd circulates, and we occupy ourselves
with the crowd. The profound respect that we profess for justice did not extend
to the audience.

The crowd needed this interval; it threw itself outside delightedly.

"Ah, it's lovely so far! There's a man with light fingers!"

"That idea of the two passports!"

"My dear, he has eyes like a woman's. Do you know the story of Lesurques?" [244]

"Nine millions at a stroke!"

"Has Monsieur Huchon found you a seat?"

"The gendarmes blocked my view–it was worse than being behind a pillar!"

"But what did he do, then, when he put his left hand under the head and
his thumb under the throat?"

"He's as guilty as Cain!"

"Innocence radiates from his eyes! You won't find a jury who'll convict
that one!

"Monsieur," Mademoiselle asked a robed Advocate, very proud to be thus
approached, "what if the jury can't make up its mind?"

"They'll be put in Sainte-Pelagie," [245] Briquet replied, as he passed by.

"Well," said Chaumeron, elbowing through the crowd to rejoin Many-
Apologies, "was I nicely placed,[246] or what? My daughter had a stool. It's just a
matter of not keeping her tongue in her pocket. Carried away!"

"The monster," wailed Mademoiselle. "Killing two men who were on the point of getting married!"

"Hey, Monsieur Potel, what do you say about it? The pot's boiling..."

"I haven't formed an opinion, Monsieur."

"Time will put that right... should we have a snack?"

All these common, insignificant and wretched things were said with extraordinary passion. A crowd is a monster that howls nonsense.

Henri, meanwhile, left the session hall and was escorted by gendarmes to the room reserved for accused persons to rest. His solitary confinement, rigorous as it had been, necessarily concluded with the hearing. Since that morning, Henri had been surrounded by all those who loved him. Within the crowd–avid for banal emotion, dressed in finery and rags, worn calico and velvet, mottled with sordid stains, jewels, decorations and embroideries, sweating wretchedness or reeking with perfume, a disparate and crowded flowerbed, more terrible and more attentive than at any theater–Henri had recognized several cherished faces.

Jeanne was in the first row, a beautiful madonna in mourning, hiding her emotion under her veil, contriving an occasional smile and holding back her tears. Not far from her, Suzanne and Richard Thompson were sitting next to Lady Frances Elphinstone. The pale and handsome face of Friedrich Boehm was displayed behind the insubordinate features of Germaine, angry, agitated, enthusiastic, sometimes triumphant and sometimes discouraged, not knowing how to hide their fever. Scattered here and there in the audience were serious faces, marked for the most part by a military appearance, with fine moustaches or grey beards. Robert Surrisy, Laurent and Férandeau were standing up, as close as was possible to the door of the clerk's office.

But Henri's gaze had sought in vain, scanning the hall many times over, for his father's white hair. The Marquis de Belcamp was not there! A father's presence next to the fatal bench carries great authority. A jury is not the exact letter of the law; it is a conscience, which may be enlightened, misled and moved by every human means. The absence of the Marquis de Belcamp deprived Henri of one of his best weapons.

It was not for this reason that Henri scanned the room from time to time with an anxious and sad expression. He had no need of weapons. In the depths of his heart, there was but one voice and one speech. It was not for himself that it complained when it said: "My father! My poor, beloved father!"

He hoped during the reading of the charges, during the debates–which were curt and heated–and during the indictment addressed to the jury eloquently and skillfully. As he withdrew, he was still hopeful, for his eyes were still slowly surveying the assembly. In the doorway, several hands were extended to shake his own warmly. Count Friedrich Boehm's hand held on longer than the others. Henri and he exchanged a rapid signal.

There were two sorts of people in the audience who took Henri's side without knowing why: good lower-class folk and great ladies. All the young women were also on his side, but they knew why, for there was a heart in their eyes. Many people in the assembly detested him because he was a Comte, others because he was handsome, young, rich and who knows what else? Some hated him because a woman had blushed while looking at him, or paled, or smiled...

These words are not spoken with bitterness. The source of our impressions, abruptly uncovered, often makes us ashamed when it does no make us laugh. But those who took up their various dispositions after the thunderous indictment of the eminent Magistrate who occupied the Public Prosecutor's chair, all thought that Henri would be convicted.

When he had left the hall, those who had shaken his hand went out.

Robert went over to Jeanne.

"Your mother has killed him!" murmured the young woman.

"I shall save him!" Robert replied. Then he added: "My mother is a noble woman, who is doing her duty as we shall do ours."

A tear came to Jeanne's eye as she offered him her hand. "Forgive me," she murmured. "I am unjust because I am suffering."

"Oh," cried Germaine, "that man who spoke against him! If I could ply a sword...!"

"Has he consented?" asked Lady Frances, in a whisper.

"My sister," Robert replied, "since he is in the hands of the law, we have no authority over us but that of Friedrich Boehm, who is master."

"God be praised!" said Frances, blushing. She seized her brother's hand as he moved away, and forced him to bring his ear very close to her lips. "May Friedrich save him, and I shall be his!" she murmured.

A little while later, several groups of two, three or four people left the Rue Saint-Pierre, which was crowded in front of the Palais de Justice, and went into the Rue de Jouvencel, which was deserted. These groups did not come together again, and those comprising them continued walking to and fro.

Among all the people surrounding the Palais, these were certainly the calmest and coolest. They were not arguing; they made no attempt to guess the probable verdict of the jury; they did not give the accused the benefit of their noisy sympathy, any more than they pursued him with their curses. They were, for the most part, the men of military bearing of whom we have already spoken.

There were Englishmen among them, for the names of Perkins and Abercrombie were pronounced. These names were advanced like a key, and if you had examined these rough and austere faces at close range you would have recognized Captain Gauthier, Lieutenant Renault, Pierre Louchet the woodcutter, and a part of the valiant crew of the *Deliverance*.

In the middle of the main group, composed of Abercrombie, Perkins, Robert Surrisy and Laurent, stood Count Friedrich Boehm, whose face was the palest of all. "Messieurs," he said, "God alone knows how this contest will turn out; as it is not possible for us to weight the balance, we must be ready for any eventuality. Abercrombie and Perkins will depart immediately for Dieppe, so that the ship can raise anchor the moment milord sets foot on the bridge."

"We are here on milord's orders," objected Perkins, reluctantly.

"Milord knows what he's doing," Abercrombie added. "All these puppets have roles in his comedy. I'll wager a hundred pounds against ten shillings that he'll come out of it as white as snow."

"As our leader," Robert replied, "Comte Henri de Belcamp undoubtedly has the right to have his secrets; but each of us also has the right to see that which might have escaped his view from the depths of his prison. Events have moved on; the wind has shifted. If it's a comedy he's playing, to borrow your expression, to some end of which we know nothing, the boards of his theater are now situated over a powder-keg. Our rules are sound when they say that a captive Master is no longer any more than an Honorary Commander. We are all under the orders of Count Friedrich Boehm here... at least until a member of the Supreme Council makes himself known."

A short stout man with bold and intelligent features touched Friedrich's shoulder just as he was about to speak. "Admiral!" murmured the young Count, recognizing him.

"I have the authority you demand," he said, curtly. "I am a member of the Supreme Council. Other titles are of little importance." He fixed the two Englishmen with his imperious gaze. "Messieurs," he added, "leave now, and don't stop until you're aboard. The blows that are striking your Grandmaster are coming from on high and from a distance. Go, or be guilty of treason!"

Perkins and Abercrombie withdrew silently, followed by two Frenchmen charged with facilitating their departure.

The man who had been addressed as Admiral continued: "Is everything else in hand, Messieurs?"

"All our men are in place, Master," Surrisy replied, "And all our weapons. We'll attack the escort in the Avenue de Paris as it makes its way from the Palais de Justice to the prison. The horses are ready, the relays waiting along the route..."

He was interrupted by a restrained voice saying: "*For the best*!"

The groups were dispersing towards the end of the street. Robert fell silent. The stranger pulled his hat over his eyes and said in English: "All is well!" Then he disappeared rapidly around the corner of the Ecole Normale.

A woman dressed in black came up the Rue Jouvencel, where there was not a soul to be seen save for conspirators. It was the approach of this woman that had caused the alert to be sounded. She marched straight up to Robert Surrisy, who frowned and took a step towards her.

"What do you want, Mother?" he asked.

The peasant woman took him by the arms and drew him aside.

"There's a spy in your midst," she said. "You're risking your life, child, on treacherous cards. Take care!"

She went on.

When Robert went back to his companions, he said to Count Boehm: "Do you know that man?"

"It's Admiral M***"

"No, by God!" cried one of the crewmen of the *Deliverance*. "I was assigned to Admiral M***' ship. I pledge my head that it isn't him!"

"Where did you meet that man?" Robert's interrogation continued, while every face went pale.

"In London, at la Bartolozzi's house," Frederick replied.

"In the presence of Comte Henri de Belcamp?"

"No," Frederick replied, having consulted his memory. "I never saw him in Comte Henri's presence."

"Messieurs," Robert said, in a firm voice, "The Comte de Belcamp, from the depths of his prison, has eyes more penetrating than ours. To all our offers he replied: I do not want that. I'm countermanding the order regarding the interception in the Avenue de Paris. Before the hearing ends, you'll know the new dispositions determined by the Master, Friedrich Boehm..."

The session was about to reopen, and the Rue Saint-Pierre was crossed henceforth only by latecomers and the troubled souls who had not been able to obtain places inside. The class of curiosity-seekers who await news outside is neither less impressionable nor less interested.

At the other end of the Rue Saint-Pierre, in the Avenue de Paris, not far from the Town Hall, a man was sitting all alone on a bench. The sentinels who had been replaced at the municipal gate had been able to see him there since morning, bent double with his hands crossed on the head of his cane. He was a grand old man with disorderly white hair crowning a thin face, pale and painted with suffering. His eyes were bleak and staring, although a fever was darkly illuminated there on occasion. His hands often trembled on his cane, as if a sustained frisson had overtaken his entire body.

We have described him because, in the state he was in, you would have passed him by without recognizing the Marquis de Belcamp.

Monsieur de Belcamp was absent from the audience, but he was not far away. What he was doing there, he would certainly not have been able to tell you himself. He was the victim of a profound and crushing lassitude; there had been the numbness of despair in those sudden shivers that agitated his weakened body at the least noise from the courtroom.

His back was turned to the opening of the Rue Saint-Pierre. He was not hiding, but the glances of the passers-by embarrassed him and brought a fugitive flush to his face.

When the hour sounded, he listened. It seemed that an idea occurred to him, and then died away. Once or twice, tears had rolled down his cheeks.

Another person, very different in appearance, whose agitation was of an entirely different kind, was walking up and down the avenue. This one, dressed in black from head to toe and wearing a white cravat, was a civilian employee of the Palais, and his distinguished dress said that he did not belong to the lower ranks of the judiciary. His head was bare, because his head was on fire. From time to time, he moped the sweat from his temples with a handkerchief.

One would have been able to take him as a comparative exemplar to set alongside the Marquis de Belcamp, he representing anxious preoccupation, while the latter personified great sorrow. "After all," he said, talking to himself with curt and rapid gestures, "there's not a single eyewitness. It's only a mass of circumstance costumed in probabilities... and yet the life of that young man isn't pure, that's obvious! Nor clear, assuredly! It contains a mystery... ten mysteries! The more one penetrates that darkness the less one sees there..."

He turned back towards the Town Hall after taking a hundred paces away from it. "A noble visage!" he continued. "The proudest and most intelligent head I've encountered in my whole life! The distinction of a prince, my word! And dignity! The least of the words he speaks are cast in bronze like those of Tacitus! For myself, I don't believe him guilty... which is to say... Devil take it all! It's an indecipherable puzzle, No! On my honor! I don't believe it! I don't believe it!"

He was speaking so loudly as he passed the bench where Monsieur de Belcamp was sitting that the old man looked up in spite of himself. Their eyes met. Counselor de Boisruel, for it was he, stared at him open-mounted. Then his face, of a man who has seen everything, put everything to the test and plunged to the very depths, expressed the grave and sympathetic commiseration of an honest heart.

"My good, my excellent cousin!" he said, going towards him excitedly with open arms.

Monsieur de Belcamp's hands remained immobile, crossed on his cane. One could see, however, that his rigid, seemingly frozen face was making an effort to smile. That alone would have rent your heart.

His lips parted slightly, and in a voice that had changed as profoundly as his features he said: "Good day, Boisruel. You're not ashamed of me, then?"

The Counselor drew back. His physiognomy, which was very fluid, changed from white to black as an evil thought struck him.

"Have you abandoned him already, then?" he murmured.

Monsieur de Belcamp's breast yielded a profound sigh, distressing to the ear. "Oh, Boisruel, my cousin," he quavered, by virtue of the effort he was making to suppress his sobs, "I am a man who has had the greatest pride in his heart. Does God intend anyone to love like that—even his only son, even an ultimate hope!" He did not move, but something was visibly tearing him up inside, and two tears forming in the corners of his eyes were turning into liquid fire.

Boisruel sat down beside him on the bench, seized by the contagion of that terrible anguish.

"You've come out of the hearing?" he asked, for the sake of saying something–for if they have good hearts, the most expert and least susceptible of men may be disconcerted to the extent that they become childish, in the face of heartbreaking misery.

The Marquis returned his stare to empty space, and made no reply.

"Now then," cried Boisruel, rousing himself, "you mustn't believe that all will be lost, my worthy cousin! I, who am speaking to you, in my soul and in my conscience, am very far from being convinced."

A pale gleam lit up in the old man's eye. He made a effort to part his lips, but only to give passage to a sigh.

"I don't condemn him," the Counselor went on. "I tell you frankly: your son is wrong not to say anything; I'll wager that he's protecting someone. Who? That's the question... and it's serious, certainly, because no one is entitled to protection when it's a matter of honor. But he's young... perhaps he has an exaggerated sense of obligation... if that's the case, I won't condemn him. Juries, you might say... I understand perfectly; they're not always the pick of the bunch, and Our Lord has forgotten to grant some of them the piercing sight of an eagle... but remember that this affair is as confusing to the clear-sighted as to the near-sighted. Nothing's certain–nothing! And in the end, everyone in the world, even the people making up juries, knows the maxim: if in doubt, abstain."

"Doubt," murmured the Marquis, like an echo.

"I understand perfectly, by God! Caesar's wife must be above suspicion. The Marquis de Belcamp's son... that's obvious! But Caesar's wife can be anything but! I've seen Caesars' wives suspected who stuck to it and carried themselves off very well. What we have here is a well-made case, you see, one might say very well made or admirably made, from the viewpoint of what these young Magistrates regard as their duty... The Judge who reads out the indictment isn't looking for the whole truth; he's looking for a guilty party, at any price... that can be corrected several times in the course of the proceedings. True justice doesn't have these fixed ideas: it looks as hard for innocent as for guilt... but youth has to have its fling... I say, therefore, that although, from the viewpoint of that bizarre calculation, sustained by a few cuttings of Laubardement,[247] the investigation is miraculously worked out... you can take it for granted that public opinion, in spite of its short sight, will take account of that. The man who emerges victorious from a contest in which his adversary is fully armed, even with weapons whose use is prohibited, comes out clear and thoroughly washed. He's waterproof."[248]

"He'll have to be fireproof," said the Marquis, bleakly.

The Counselor looked at him attentively. "If you know more than I do, cousin..."

Monsieur de Belcamp seemed about to fall off the bench; when Boisruel put out his arms to hold him up, the old man pushed his away coldly. "I shan't fall until I die," he whispered.

"My God!" said Boisruel. "No doubt, no doubt... you're a family of Knights... but Knights sustain one another, and I don't understand why you should break your lance before the end of the tournament. There are fantastic things in there, I'll grant you–things with which a court hasn't concerned itself since the adventures of Don Quixote... The Prague business regarding the solemn rogues of the Rosy Cross, like the London business pertaining to Irish home rule or the Companions of the Deliverance. There's one witness, of the fiery kind, that Madeleine Surrisy, who chills me to the bone... with half a dozen madwomen of that sort you could have convicted Louis XVIII of the murder of Robespierre! [249] To recognize someone's voice, after years, is simply extravagant. One would be hard-pressed to recognize a Stradivarius violin... but a man, whose vocal chords are ceaselessly breaking and changing, is purely extravagant! Apart from that there's the assassinated couples, and that's certainly enough, by Jesus! The two brewers first, the two bandits afterwards. That part of the investigation, above all, is marvelously constructed; the rest's just padding. We don't have John Devil to judge, or any other British *Fra Diavolo*,[250] but only Comte Henri de Belcamp. Well, on my soul and on my conscience, nothing's proven. Even the identity of the two English malefactors..."

"Two English malefactors?" murmured the old man, as motionless as a statue on the bench where he was sitting.

"Yes... the two corpses at Tivoli..."

"Ah!" the Marquis said again. "Two corpses..."

Monsieur de Boisruel continued, with a certain impatience. "The witness, the famous witness who should have brought proof of the double murder, Gregory Temple, has not come. God has paid him a visit: he's locked up in Bedlam! And the first time I saw my young cousin, I believe I remember that he and Gregory Temple were walking arm in arm... All in all, it's not important. Arguments with the force of the two blank letters can't cut off a man's head!"

"Two blank letters!" the Marquis repeated, slowly

"The two letters postmarked Paris and Saint-Denis found in the portfolios of the two false Comtes de Belcamp..."

"Ah!" said the Marquis, whose face was animated like a waxwork mask coming to life.

"Don't you know about that, for God's sake? The two letters that are supposed to have served as the signal to fix the time of the double murder, in Lyon and Brussels."

"No," the Marquis replied. "I don't know."

"In that case, then, you know nothing?" cried Monsieur de Boisruel, indignantly.

"Nothing..." replied the gloomy echo

Once more Monsieur de Boisruel studied him attentively. On reflection, he thought: *His illness... his intellectual faculties are enfeebled...*

"Well, my excellent cousin," he resumed, now intent on retreat, "As I said, as much as possible has been made of the blank letters... and the fact that the Saint-Denis office where one of them was posted is on the road from Belcamp to Paris; but nothing can come from nothing... There's an opaque, impenetrable darkness overlaying these four assassinations. Only God and time can cast light therein."

"Yes...God..." said he Marquis, giving no other sign of life than the mechanical movement of his lips.

Monsieur de Boisruel got up. "Now," he went on, to cover the leave that he had to take, "there are the famous drops of blood at the Feydeau Theater–but the help rendered to a child in the street is a proven thing... and, in conscience, that's not a hanging matter... Cousin, I'm going to look in on the hearing. Should I bring news back to you?"

"No," said the Marquis.

The Counselor bowed, and withdrew.

The old Marquis de Belcamp, alone again, maintained his strange immobility. If it had been snowing one would have taken him for one of those unfortunate victims of the cold who have only frozen blood in their veins. After a few minutes, however, his lips moved and he whispered: "Blank letters! I remember a blank letter..."

As night was falling, a loud noise was heard from the direction of the Rue Saint-Pierre. A crowd similar to those that swarm out of theaters erupted into the Avenue de Paris, laughing, gossiping and calling out. The old man was seized throughout his body by one of those long *frissons* of which we have spoken, but he maintained his petrified stance. These words fell from his mouth: "Will it be a matter of the justice of men?"

The sound of familiar voices gradually shook him out of his immobility. Footsteps were drawing near.

"It's simply effrontery!" said the humble but barbed voice of Madame Morin du Reposoir.

"Trump!" murmured Chaumeron. "No mincing!"

"Everyone knows full well that he speaks as he wishes," added Madame Célestin. "Stay beside me, brother-in-law!"

"Men are such deceivers!" Mademoiselle went on.

Miremont had halted ten paces from the Marquis to form a group.

"Did you see how that little Germaine compromised herself?" Mademoiselle went on. "It's repulsive."

"And the lovely Jeanne too! Milady Balcomb! And there's one, that Balcomb, who doesn't often send news since he carried away the wedding-present!"

"Too right!" said Chaumeron. "Go see if he's coming!"

And Miremont laughed wholeheartedly.

"Lady Frances and that Suzanne with the mad father don't conduct themselves much better," observed Many-Apologies. "But did you see the three idlers? It's said that as for them... who knows? Idleness can lead a long way; it's the mother of all vices."

"It won't be long before the precious Henri settles his account," Chaumeron decided. "I speak my mind, me! An example must be made... will he serve?"

"Yes, yes, yes," said the three ladies. "We need one–and we'll have one!"

Madame Célestin was more peevish than usual, because she did not have her knitting. She understood from a few inarticulate moans that her Bondons were demanding to be fed. "Can't you wait...?" she began, sharply.

Papa Chaumeron interrupted her, however. "Not stupid, the idea of soup!" he exclaimed. "The whisper is that the jury's split. There's a silly idea! Losing sight of their objectives, those fellows! If they're split, they'll probably be squabbling in their room till midnight. Me, I don't mess about. I vote for soup and boiled beef. Whack!"

"It's dear in Versailles, eating... this trial will cost all of us a pretty penny!"

Miremont sighed.

"Yes," said Mademoiselle, "but at least it's in a good cause."

"These children," said Chaumeron, pointing his finger at her, "are as honest as the old Romans of the Augustan Empire. As for the high price of food, that depends where you go; I know a little place in the Avenue de Sceaux where the prices are rather nice. One, two, three... whoever loves me, follow me!"

The deliberations of a jury are secret, but at every Session you can always find some obliging and well-informed individuals in the hall of the not-yet-lost or the open air outside the Palais who will tell you exactly what is happening in the sanctuary where the jury is convened. These people cannot know, but they know.

A jury, as everyone knows, is composed of 36 citizens fulfilling certain conditions of social status and honorability; eventually, the objections of the prosecution and the defense whittle this number down to the 12 names forming the definitive Areopagus.[251] The oral debate is primarily directed to the end of convincing the jury, which has nothing to do with the administration of the law and is restricted to the analysis of matters of fact. The most irreconcilable enemies of this institution can deny neither its grandeur nor its benefits; its most enthusiastic advocates admit that it is not without its faults and is seriously inconvenient in more than one respect.

The principal inconvenience lies in the deliberation itself. When the jury, returned to its bench, comes to pronounce before God and before men its terrible yes or its merciful no, it is not the opinion of 12 citizens that constitutes the verdict. It is the opinion–very often, at least–of one dominant spirit, agitated, impassioned and energetic; of one speech, inspiring and facile; of one superiority; in a word, of one will, which happens to be found among that dozen complacent, timid and profoundly indifferent consciences, extracted against their will from the beloved pursuit of profit or duty.

Perhaps the future will invent a cellular jury.[252]

Our 12 jurors of Versailles were all supremely honest men of the world–tradesmen, for the most part. Their number included an advocate, a doctor and a professor. The opinion of the majority was that it did not know. The defense, presented in the greater part by the accused himself and completed by an officially-chosen member of the Versailles bar, had been clear, curt and striking. The scaffolding cleverly erected by the Public Prosecutor threatened ruin. In the previous chapter, Counselor Boisruel summarized for us the argument that a specialist might follow, but the jury was rather confused: it did not know. The advocate, the doctor and the professor were the only ones who had formed convictions.

The doctor said yes; the professor said no; the advocate, gladly accepting the responsibility of mediation, fervently argued yes and concluded no. Three-quarters of the way through his discourse, the jurors had lost all fixity. An attempted count of votes revealed ten affirmative and two negative. No weakness there!

The professor spoke, and garnered six votes at a stroke, neither more nor less. Comte Henri was acquitted on the spot. But the doctor spoke too, restating the indictment in the happy style of a man used to making toasts at scientific banquets. Six votes were won back and the scaffold loomed!

It was time for the advocate to resume the debate. He pleaded no, but carefully this time, and concluded with a thunderous yes.

There were six votes against six.

Blood rushed to the jury's head. The discussion lasted nearly another hour. Miremont had had time to dine at Escalot's in the Avenue de Sceaux, detestable but not dear. The rush of blood to the head is yet another of the hazards of the institution. The doctor and the professor had already exchanged distressing words. The advocate was sick to death of crying: "But it's so obvious! My God! It's as clear as daylight." The nine jurors who were not talking and who had a migraine rebelled in unison and demanded their turn to argue. It was obvious that there were no two opinions alike. That which convinced one caused another to doubt. A fact that said crime to some cried innocence to others. Six against six! Six white, six black. The contest was ardent, to the point that the blacks became whites, but the whites became blacks.

Six against six, still!

"Messieurs," said the professor, "a man's life is at stake."

They knew that perfectly well, the unfortunates, since there was cold sweat on their temples. There was no stupid jester there, nor evil spirit, capable of turning these ominous matters into jokes.

"Let's acquit him, on the off chance," risked one voice.

"Messieurs," cried the doctor, "there's a threat to society to be considered!"

"Let's convict him, then," suggested another voice.

The advocate immediately seized upon these two formulas to compose a compartmentalized tirade on the obligatory theme: let us acquit if our consciences allow it; let us convict if our consciences demand it.

That tirade usually lasted 20 minutes, watch in hand, and finished thus: "Let us consider the question in the calm and dignity of our function. If, on the one hand, we believe that the interpretation of the rights of society is mistaken, if the charges accumulated against the accused appear to us more specious than serious, if the piercing eye of God has granted us a glimpse of innocence through these cleverly thickened mists, let us not hesitate, let us be without dread, let us acquit! If, on the other hand, the efforts of the defense have been powerless to convince us, if, in spite of all the talent, etc, etc, etc, let us hesitate no further, let us beware of yielding to the counsel of weakness, let us convict!"

There are family men who forget themselves and come to blows with well-intentioned individuals capable of similar harangues. But among the martyrs there is always someone to throw in the ultimate groan; "If, however, we don't know..."

"Then enlighten yourself. Let's debate it!" And the advocate pitilessly reopens his box of eloquence, more terrible than a machine of torture. He confronts the fors with the againsts, he mixes them up, entangles them; the last ray of light disappears behind the dust that he stirs up. Acquit or convict! It isn't difficult, though. The amazing thing is that he is quite sincere. He holds a torch in his hand, which someone has simply forgotten to light.

Six against six. Two hours had passed since then. The doctor asked for another vote: nine against three, convicted.

The professor went straight to his adversary and shook his hand. The doctor shivered. A few words were exchanged, but as the advocate was speaking again, speaking still, speaking more and more, no one heard these words whispered in the doctor's ear: "*For the best!*"

A few minutes later, the jury came back in to the hall, which was packed as tightly as an egg and quivering with impatience. The proud and gentle face of the advocate seemed to say: "I have finally managed to make them listen to reason." In the midst of a profound silence, the doctor, who was the foreman of the jury, pronounced the verdict: "By unanimous decision, no, the accused is not guilty!"

There was great applause, with an undercurrent of a few protests and a few expressions of surprise. Jeanne fell into the arms of Germaine, who was laughing and crying.

"Trump!" cried Chaumeron, from the depths of the hall. "I always said that there wasn't enough to whip a cat. Of course!"

When Comte Henri came in, calm and dignified, to hear the decree, everyone discovered that he certainly had the face of an innocent man. The auditorium of an Assize Court does not detest convictions, but let us justly acknowledge that it adores acquittals. The ladies waved their handkerchiefs at the handsome and noble young man who had suffered so much, despite the heroic attitude that he had always maintained; the men had an ardent desire to shake his hand. Everyone was joyful, and cries of enthusiasm greeted the words of the presiding judge declaring that the accused was free to go.

Henri's friends surrounded him, and bore him in quiet triumph from the Palais de Justice. Miremont came in a body to congratulate him.

"Many apologies," said the Deputy's wife, "Monsieur le Comte knows how devoted I am to the Mayor's family. Here's a day that has filled us with so many emotions!"

"These two Messieurs haven't a dry thread on them," added Madame Célestin.

"Ah," sighed Mademoiselle, "When one takes such an interest in people one knows..."

"Too right!" cried Chaumeron, offering his large and hairy paw. "Ah, the King's Prosecutor has had his bill! So much the better! Well done! Neat trick! All done! Bang!"

"There we go, my God!" murmured Roblot in Henri's other ear. "I came in person to see you acquitted. I had my duty to do, didn't I? But that doesn't get in the way of feelings. Despite appearances, what, you have the friendship of the old soldier! And he has only this to say to you: Frank as gold! He is good through and through!"

Meanwhile, Madame Etienne was shouting "Victory! Victory!" as she crossed the Avenue to Paris as far as her stout legs could carry her, heading for the bench where Julot, Anille, Pierre and the gardener-coachman were surrounding the Marquis de Belcamp. "They arrived first, an account of their youth, but it's me who is the most content. I would have kissed them all, the jurors and presidents, except for the Prosecutor's lot.[253] Oh, my good master! Victory! Victory!"

They had all come from the chateau as best they could, and their interest was sincere.

Night was falling. The street lamps along the Avenue de Paris were being lit. The old man had not changed his posture; his hands were still crossed on the pommel of his cane. He listened dejectedly to what was said around him, and did not seem to understand any of it.

Madeleine Surrisy suddenly appeared in the midst of the servants.

"The Comte de Belcamp has been acquitted," she said.

"Ah!" said the Marquis, whose lips were trembling. "Acquitted... and free?"

"And free," Madeleine replied.

The old Marquis made an effort to get up. She helped him. It was she who ordered that the *berline* should be brought.

"Aren't you waiting for Monsieur le Comte?" asked Madame Etienne.

There was no response to this question.

The coachman came back with the carriage. Monsieur de Belcamp got in first, with considerable difficulty; the peasant woman followed him.

"Free..." she repeated, when the door was shut. "But not for long. They are betrayed!"

Silence reigned in the *berline* then, as it took the road to the chateau.

At that moment, Chaumeron was carrying Miremontese society along with words to this effect: "Whoever loves me follow me! I have a presentiment that the kitchen will be warm tonight at the Mayor's place, and that we'll be enjoying a midnight feast. We'll have a good result. Light up!"

Others were already making haste along the road to l'Isle-Adam, Henri and his companions on horseback, Jeanne in Lady Elphinstone's coach. By eleven o'clock, the Chateau-Neuf was full. Jeanne, Germaine, Lady Frances and Suzanne Temple were gathered around the tea table while groups formed here and there, chatting animatedly. Comte Henri, standing up at the mantelpiece, was writing.

"I have offered you my hand loyally and with all my heart," Robert Surrisy was saying to Friedrich Boehm. "I don't know whether you owe me a fortune, but I have no need of it and I release you from the obligation. Let us be brothers, since my sister loves you; you will have paid me in full if you make her happy.”

Friedrich had a portfolio in his hand, which he gave to Frances. “Sarah,” he murmured, more timid than a child, “I don’t want to wait until my will, for good fortune has already given me life. This is your brother Robert’s fortune; he shall receive it from you.”

Jeanne joined the hands to Laurent and Germaine, and put her lips to the burning jaw of her friend, murmuring: “At least, as I depart, I shall leave you happy.”

Billy, the little groom built like an athlete, came in and said: “I went half-way back to Versailles, milord. Your Lordship has been deceived; there are neither soldiers nor gendarmes on the road.”

Henri thanked him with a nod of the head without pausing in his writing. “Richard!” he called, as he added the bold flourish of his signature to the bottom of the piece of paper.

Thompson came towards him.

“You have suffered for me,” Henri said to him, “and without wishing to, I have done considerable harm to your wife’s father. Take this; you are poor and far from home, while I have no need of my French possessions.”

Suzanne overheard, and came to him with tears in her eyes.

“To business, Messieurs!” Henri ordered, as she opened her mouth to offer thanks.

Everyone immediately gathered around him.

“Don’t take the word treason too seriously, Messieurs,” the young Comte said, almost cheerfully. “No secret association has ever been without its traitors. When Judas has performed his function, it is only a matter of going a little faster and striking a little harder. Until now, everything has smiled on us and Providence herself seems to have been our accomplice. The most difficult part is over, believe me, and those who want to close the doors of a prison on your leader now reckon without their guest. He who gets in my way henceforth will have to take my last breath with my last drop of blood. Now, we have powerful friends and our real enemies are not in France. I see around me here heartfelt joy on every face; you are too cheerful, and I am conscious of having contributed towards that happiness There is only you, Robert Surrisy, my dearest friend, to whom I cannot pay my debt. You said to me this evening, with your noble smile that still covers sadness: ‘For my part, I am betrothed to my sword!’ May the sword that is your replacement for a lost treasure at least be glorious; you are the first after me, Surrisy: I name you my Lieutenant.”

He extended his hand to him, and drew him to his breast to kiss him on both cheeks.

“Friedrich Boehm,” he continued, “it would be beyond my power to find you a further recompense. I have given you my dear, sweet sister Sarah O’Brien, the companion of my youth, the auxiliary of my first dark and mortal combats. I know you now, and I know that you are worthy to possess this heroic diamond. You have forgiven my earlier suspicions and the watchmen with whom I surrounded you–Spiegel, Arnheim and Weber–are now your friends. Leave with them for Vienna, immediately. Get the Empress and the King of Rome to Genoa ten days from now, or I shall come in search of them myself."

Count Boehm lifted Frances' hand to his lips and shook Henri's, saying: "God be with us! I shall carry out your order or die!"

"Laurent," Henri went on, "also my brother by the alliance that has fulfilled my life's dream, you have no need of me to win the heart of that dear child who has devoted such generous affection to my trial. As our Germaine chooses, I shall leave you in France or make you my aide-de-camp."

"May he be with you!" cried Germaine. "I will wait for him, or I shall go to join him. Since I am Jeanne's sister, I will be the wife of a soldier, as she is."

"Is there any need of a historical painter?" asked Férandeau, querulously.

"Later," Henri relied, smiling. "At our first battle you shall choose between the iron and the brush, Messieurs, we shall be on the road to Dieppe in an hour; before we go, I want to say farewell to my father. Once that is done, I am all yours."

"Your father!" said Jeanne. "Henri... Madeleine is with him. Take care!"

"He loves me, and he is a Knight," Henri replied, his handsome face radiant with confidence. "If there is a cloud, I shall dissipate it with a word and a kiss..."

The night was dark and moonless. Henri left the Chateau-Neuf alone and headed for the old manor at a rapid pace, following the path along the Oise. As he crossed the mill bridge, the little village clock chimed midnight. He was going along the winding path that went up to the esplanade when he heard a galloping horse in the distance. The noise was coming from the direction of the Croix Moraine. He stopped. Now that he was no longer in the midst of all those devoted hearts, a sad presentiment had slipped into his soul. The horseman, meanwhile, was coming down the opposite slope; he came out in front of the mill, dismounted, and picked up a big stone with which to hammer at the door.

"Hey!" he shouted. "Wake up! I'm a gentleman and I'll reward you! Will you show me the way to the Chateau de Belcamp?"

Henri immediately recognized the voice and accent of Ned Knob. He put his fingers in his mouth and whistled. Gentleman Ned threw away his stone, took his horse by the bridle and crossed the bridge.

"Just tell me where you are, friend," he muttered, "for I've already come close to breaking my neck 20 times over."

Henri emerged from the shadow of an oak.

"Milord!" cried Gentleman Ned. "You were thought to be in prison over there! I've come to ask around the neighborhood to find a way of getting news to you."

"Tell me your news," the young Comte ordered.

"There's something sad first," replied the little clerk, pulling himself together. "At least, I think it's sad for a gentleman to lose his legitimate companion. My pretty Molly had been a widow for some time, milord. I don't like to do things by halves, you know. We were married at Saint Anthony's by One-Eyed Gillie, who was a Reverend before going to Sydney... and I bought a drink for everybody to prove my generous character. Molly, my wife, set herself alight, poor dear, while trying to light her pipe. I don't know what happened, but we saw her surrounded by blue flames as if the blood in her veins were rum. She asked for another swig... I had her plunged in the well, your lordship, for I'm not lacking in intelligence, but they held her under the water too long and you'd have to be a sorcerer to say exactly whether she was burned or drowned. What a wedding-night! She'd chosen me while I was in a wretched state, milord, and I'll have trouble finding another woman with a figure like hers."

He wiped away a sincere tear.

"I thank your lordship for having let me tell him that at such length," he went on. "Now, here's the news. In London, the Minister's out, the Lord Chief Justice has been replaced, and Sir Paulus MacAllan's been shown the door. The new Superintendent of Police has already seen Gregory Temple twice in the madhouse, and Mr. Wood sent me to Paris to tell you that the English Government will be able to demand your extradition–I think that's the word. No one in the world's like my pretty Molly, who was a stone when she wanted to be. Perkins' workmen have been talking since the forge went out. The sea air will be good for you, to all appearances."

"Is that all?" the young Comte asked.

"No," Ned replied. "Mr. Wood told me to tell you this in his own words: '*Helen Brown has arrived in London.*' "

Comte Henri started so violently that Ned stopped. He went on in response to a mute but peremptory order; "She was very ill, very poor, and Mr. Wood has given her money to retire to the country."

"Is that all?" Henri asked, for a second time–but his voice had altered.

"That's all regarding London, milord, for I suppose you've received your correspondence. There was a letter from Africa... no one knows the contents, of course... as for what's going on in Paris, on the road over by Saint-Denis, I met a whole flock of crows... a little way behind there were gendarmes. They questioned me and I told them that I was a young lord, personal secretary to the English ambassador. It's good to be a well-set-up fellow, you see. The crows and the gendarmes were heading the same way as me; I suppose you won't be sorry to know that."

The young Comte reflected for a moment, then his extended finger pointed to the Chateau-Neuf lit up on the other side of the river.

"Tell everyone there to mount up immediately!" he said. "Every one of them knows the road he must take. Robert Surrisy must wait for me in the forest alone, at the Bueil crossroads. Remember that carefully, and go relay my orders."

He turned his back and continued along the path to the esplanade.

At the very end of the path, a black shadow went past. He recognized the tall figure and dark costume of Madeleine Surrisy.

He felt a great weight upon his heart.

The manor gate was wide open in spite of the late hour. Pierre was standing in the courtyard, where the dog was prowling anxiously, sniffing the wind and emitting the occasional muffled howl.

"Monsieur le Marquis is waiting for Monsieur le Comte," Pierre said.

There was no lighted window in the entire chateau save for that of the master bedroom.

Henri, as we know full well, was a man used to danger; his entire life had been an eternal contest of intrepidity against peril. We might add that his courage was not the banal species that expresses itself with closed fists, sword or musket. It was valor unarmed: a calm and almost superhuman coolness, passing through mortal risks in the sweat of combat, without the brutal intoxication of the fight. It should be said that this is the valor of modern times that will henceforth make great men and great kings–for the universe will not shudder much longer at the odor of gunpowder, and the last bouquet of the flowers of war will fade away in the tavern. This valor contains the others, be assured, because he who can do the greater thing can do the lesser, except that this valor regards violence as an argument of the lowest order and the worst kind. It takes its path, modest in its pride; wine does not increase it, which is something that cannot be said of the other; its activity is thoughtful; it dies calculating. I would represent it, were I a painter, in the form of a beautiful Minerva with neither shield nor lance, smiling and pensive above a volcano.

Comte Henri was thus, no matter what the mystery enveloping his life might be, and despite the doubt that would soar above his death. That night, as he went through the long galleries of his father's house, listening to the sound of his own footsteps on the tiles–whose echo came back to him from the depths of shadow–he was astonished to experience an impression resembling fear. His tight chest experienced an unfamiliar anguish; a mourning-veil passed before his eyes...

Pierre opened the door to the Marquis' room and bowed, announcing in a sonorous voice: "Monsieur le Comte!"

Henri went in, and the heavy door closed behind him.

It was perfectly simple, no doubt, and things had never gone differently during his sojourn in the chateau; even so, the noise of that door closing gave him a kind of shock. He had a vague idea that it would never open again–not to his youthful, lithe and indefatigable step, which laughed at distance.

Madness! Every one of us has our moments of weakness. In Comte Henri, such anxieties hardly had the time to be born, and vanished instantly before the bold breath of his will. He arrived thus, his pride even more indignant than his audacity; he escaped this vague weakness that his soul's presentiment inflicted on his body as malaise and stood up straight, invincible again.

His strength was gentleness. He presented to his father a smiling and tranquil face, although distress clutched his heart again at the sight of his father; the Marquis de Belcamp looked like a man about to die.

We have all seen the great changes that can overtake people nowadays, especially in old men to whom age has previously spared its injuries. They suddenly fall apart, to use the popular expression. It is indeed a fall. Their feet, so steady yesterday, have stumbled over the rim of the well called death.

The Marquis de Belcamp was sitting in the middle of his bedroom, at a table on which a lamp was set. His room, very large and furnished in an antique manner, remained dim in the inadequate rays of the lamp. The white alcove with its muslin-draped bed would normally have introduced a cheerful note, but the alcove could not be seen today. Two tall and ancient Savonnerie [254] tapestries were closed over it on their iron rods, as stiff and opaque as a bulkhead.

There were no books or papers in front of the old man, who maintained almost the same pose that we have seen on the stone bench in the Avenue de Paris at Versailles. His blanched hands were crossed on his knees, and his dull eyes were staring into the void. At the opposite side of the table, as far away from him as possible, lay two letters. They were still unopened.

The light of the lamp struck the wrinkles deeply hollowed out in his face at right angles. There was less torpor, but also more suffering, in his hollow eyes and his ravaged features. His eyelids had taken on the same ardent hue that heated the pallor of his cheeks.

Henri's first steps had brought him rapidly towards his father, but he stopped, separated from him by the entire width of the table.

"Do you still trust me, father?" he asked, quietly, in a sadly respectful tone.

"Why would I have lost my trust in you, Monsieur?" the old man asked, his intelligence suddenly flaring in his eyes. His voice was much firmer than one would have thought possible, seeing the agony imprinted on his face and the mortal trembling of his limbs. But his tone also contained a kind of dark sarcasm that was not in his nature, so tender and so good.

"Father, my beloved father," Henri murmured, "While I could not defend myself, someone has been slandering me to you."

The rigid muscles of that face could no longer smile; there was no way of telling how the immobile features of the Marquis could express bitter and terrible irony.

"Slandering!" he repeated. Then, as his voice became bleak and his gaze uncertain, he added: "They have acquitted you, I know... but there is another justice than that of men."

Comte Henri crossed the margin that separated them and knelt before him.

The old man experienced a kind of shock. His hands quit his knees and reached out involuntarily. One could see in that moment, and in that single gesture, more clearly than in any explanation or history, all the tortures that had been required to desiccate his heart.

Passion revived, as an electric impulse can impart movement to a dead man.

Oh, that man had loved! And as one makes a corpse by letting blood flow from open wounds, he had been killed by the draining of the affection that had run through his veins. His son! His soul! The recompense that God had given him in his old age for such long sadness and such patient resignation: the son of the wife, guilty and horribly lost in the depths of the inferno, into which depths he had wanted to bear his merciful love like Orpheus; Henri, the living portrait of Helen; Henri, who had her adorable features and her voice, more penetrating than a caress; Henri, valor, science, mind, beauty, nobility, affection, alas! Henri, Henri, who had paid in a few days the debt of joy accumulated throughout a long life!

His shaking hands supported themselves on the young man's shoulders. Two huge tears ran down his cheeks.

Henri thought that his cause was won again, and tried to put his arms around the old man–but Monsieur de Belcamp's hands were snatched back, and his eyes, opening very wide, were painted with sudden horror.

"Assassin!" he stammered, between grated teeth. And while indignation brought Henri to his feet like a spring, he added more distinctly: "Don't try to plead your defense or lie your way out of it. I've seen Helen Brown, your mother."

The young Comte's cheeks became almost as livid as his father's, but he kept his voice calm and his gaze steady as he replied: "I am punished for the only lie I have told in my life."

"Coward!" murmured the old man. "Miserable play-actor!" All the blood that was left in him was around his eyes. "You have put a benign face on all the odious things you have done; you have sewn your infamy into a mantle of heroism. Helen has told me her entire life-story, from that night in Prague to another night when you abandoned a dying woman, who was your mother, in the Australian sands."

"I told a lie," the young Comte said, slowly, "to console my father's heart and to draw a shroud, as one performs a funereal duty, over the memory of my mother. My lie has struck me down; that is justice. Monsieur de Belcamp, I did indeed fall, deprived of sensation one terrible night beside the dying Helen Brown. I awoke in a cell, where I was told: 'Your mother is dead.' That is not the lie, but I betrayed the truth when I told you that Helen Brown had repented in her final hour. Helen Brown's final hour, like all the hours of her existence, struck terror into my agony. Helen Brown had died–for I believed her dead–cursing and blaspheming."

The old man had but one word: "Slanderer!"

Henri said: "Helen Brown is here, I know that, for a woman came in with you who has not gone out. I offer her a challenge: let Helen Brown show herself and give the lie to my words!"

The old man was upright now on his stiff legs. His tall figure was drawn up to the full extent of its height. Wrath had brought him back to life. His brows were knitted above his darkly-illuminated eyes.

"Why did you come here?" he asked, rudely, instead of replying.

"To take my leave of you, Monsieur," Henri replied, "for I am setting forth on a long and perilous voyage."

"Is there some distant woman you have to strangle in her bed?" said Monsieur de Belcamp, with cutting sarcasm. As he said it, he put his hand to his heart. With life, suffering had come again. Beneath his white hair, his face shuddered. At one moment, his eyes were dull; at another they hurled forth a savage gleam. "Go!" he went on "Your punishment awaits you outside..."

Henri knelt down again.

The Marquis repeated, heatedly; "Go!"

As Henri made as if to obey, with all the respectful pity that his mouth could not express written on his face, the old man held out his once-firm hand towards him and repeated: "Cowardly play-actor!"

This had no impact on Henri, whose noble visage retained its dolorous gravity. If he was an actor, he was a sublime actor!

He took a step towards the door. His father's voice stopped him. "Aren't you going to open your correspondence before you go?" he said.

He pointed at the two sealed letters on the other side of the table. The veins in his temples were swollen. He could walk and gesticulate freely. He took several steps into the room, as if to test that unexpected strength that had revived him miraculously.

Henri took up the two letters and examined the postmarks. A vivid red replaced the pallor of his cheeks.

"Is there a blank letter in there, Monsieur?" asked the old man, in a provocative tone. "A letter without writing, whose perfidious silence wants to say choke, poison or stab!"

Henri broke the first seal.

The old man continued, for his fever put words into his mouth like drunkenness. "I received for you, on the day of my birthday party, one of these blank letters..."

"It was from Helen Brown, Monsieur," Henri interrupted him. "If you had given it to me, I would have told you in advance about all these misfortunes that have befallen our house. I have sinned by lying once, and once by omission; I did not want to talk about Helen's other son, Tom Brown. If the judge had laid his hands on the blank letter that they addressed to me, precisely in order that it might be found on me or among my papers–for that trap was the complement of all their other ambushes–I would have been condemned to death.”

Monsieur de Belcamp took several more steps, then he sat down next to the window; his hand pressed his burning temples; he listened. The effort he was making now was to suppress a doubt. Henri's last words had struck him hard; perhaps he was already waiting for the defense plea that he had refused to hear a little while ago.”

But Henri's gaze fell involuntarily upon the letter he had opened first. He said nothing. A terrible anguish distressed his features.

The letter was from San Salvador in the Congo, dated six weeks earlier. Its brought news that natives of the borders of Zaire had burned a partly-constructed frigate on its slipway, pierced with 48 gunports and fitted out to receive an 800-horse-power steam-engine.

Henri was thunderstruck; the letter shook in his hand.

“Have you received important news?” asked the Marquis, whose vacillating thought had turned with the wind of his fever. “Or have you heard the sound of hoofbeats? For myself, I heard them some time ago. The gendarmes are in the park.”

“The gendarmes,” murmured the young Comte, with the smile of one whose hope is lost. His gaze, where there was a reproach and a threat, was raised towards Heaven. He tore open the second envelope convulsively. It was from Wood. It had arrived the previous day. It said:

I learned in the Stock Exchange that the three-master Eagle *has foundered under sail, and went down with all hands and cargo while passing through the Azores.*

“They're coming!” said Monsieur de Belcamp, pricking up his ears. “Madeleine didn't lie to me.”

Henri slumped down and put his head between his hands. “God did not want a stain on his blade!” he murmured.

He heard his father get up and walk. The window was opened, then shut. But what did that matter to him? The catastrophic wreck of his thoughts made him dizzy.

He saw the splendor of his dream more clearly at that moment than before. A mirage, as rapid as thought itself, showed him with wondrous clarity the Giant of St. Helena founding an Asiatic France in the paradise of India. Nothing is as radiant as the wealth one has lost; India with all its marvels fled before a diamantine cloud.

His father took the lamp from the table.

Calcutta conquered, a fleet departed: the first fleet of steamships; fortresses charged with cannon, which could run against the wind with the speed of an Arab stallion; it was France again, France the sovereign of the seas; it was Napoleon amplifying the epics of Alexander the Great, Caesar and Genghis

Khan–Napoleon, who touched England with his lightning as he passed by, and who was coming to make sacred Paris the capital of the universe...

The curtains of the alcove slid and grated on their rods.

Outside, from the distance of his dream, Henri heard the echo of his name, which was audible even above the vast chorus of the Emperor's name!

"Look!" the old man instructed him, standing at the entrance to the alcove, whose depths were illuminated by the lamp.

"My mother!" cried Henri, waking from his dream with a great start.

There was a dead woman on the bed.

"Your mother, who has a crucifix on her breast," said the Marquis, his eyes wandering. "Your mother, whom you came to slander!"

She was still beautiful in that ultimate sleep, although the passions that had degraded her life had left their forceful marks upon her face.

Henri put his hands together, and tried to approach. The old man barred his way.

"She is purified now!" he said, emphatically. "She has told me that your true name is John Devil! I have spent my nights and my days by her side. Look at me! I never loved her as much! Agony wins, do you hear? I shall die of having adored both of you!"

The young Comte tried to interrupt him, for he could see that a kind of transport was taking possession of his brain. "Father, my dear father...!"

"Shut up!" the old man commanded. "I am calm. Your voice cuts into my heart like a serpent's tooth. You have the same voice. I shall no longer hear it... Gregory Temple was right... John Devil... Helen Brown... and I am the Marquis de Belcamp!"

The breath caught in his breast, and his throat yielded nothing more than a few strangled sounds.

Someone was ringing loudly at the gate.

Father and son met one another's eyes.

The father said, coldly. "It's for you... but this time, I shall be obliged to testify against you... I don't want to... They acquitted you in their tribunal. At the chateau de Belcamp, your father is a judge too. For my part, I convict you, and here is my sentence!"

With a rapid and violent gesture, utterly unexpected in one so weak, he took a pistol from the inside of his coat and cocked it.

In the distance, the gate was opened, and closed again.

But in the time it took to raise the weapon, Henri, with all the power and supple strength of his youth, had pounced as silently and smoothly as an enormous tiger! He seized the old man's frail wrist in his hand. The old man subsided, crushed, without even pressing the trigger.

Henri had grabbed the pistol. He caught his father, whose livid lips were flecked with blood and who had a rattle in his throat.

"Coward!" cried Monsieur de Belcamp, with a final effort. "Curse you! Damn you to Hell, parricide!"

Henri deposited him in an armchair at the foot of the bed, and knelt in front of him.

"Bless you, father," he said, with the beautiful smile that the old man had seen in his dreams at another time. "Bless you, my beloved father, poor tortured soul, bless you! Bless you, martyr to honor and affection! I can no longer tell you what I am; the future will absolve me; others will tell you what my task in this life was–a task worthy of our knightly ancestors. My father, it is not men who have vanquished me; the hand of God has weighted the balance. If the great battle were not lost without resources, I would defend myself, even against your feebleness and I would appeal against your arrest. My life is my own, here as everywhere, and I have braved many other perils... but the contest is ended, for I can no longer advance upon my enemy. England can now forge armies similar to mine, and the weapons being equal, I would be no more than a madman fighting alone against an entire nation... I wanted Jeanne to share in my happiness and my glory; I want my fall to be mine alone. May my beloved Jeanne be happy with one who is brave and gentle, with my friend of a few days, my brother by the sword and by the heart, Robert Surrisy... Tell them that I united them with my final thought..."

He paused, standing up tranquil and proud. "Father," he said, "the Belcamps who were judges here were not executioners. My blood will remain on your hands; I want you to be able to live. You have passed sentence; let it be obeyed; I shall carry it out."

He put the barrel of the pistol against his temple and pressed the trigger just as the spurred boots of the gendarmes sounded in the tiled corridor.

And he fell, as young, beautiful and grandiose as his dream.

The blast of the pistol had scarcely deranged the curls of his fair hair. He fell, giving to death that valiant smile with which he had earlier greeted hope, liberty and life.

He fell, repeating: "Bless you, father...!"

Jeanne dressed in widow's mourning. The Marquis de Belcamp called her his daughter, but she did not have to care for him for very long, because he never recovered from the terrible blows he had received on that fatal night. He died a few weeks later with the name of Henri on his lips and in the following circumstances.

It was the end of the month of September. Jeanne was guiding the steps of the tottering old man along one of the footpaths in the park. At a turn in the path, they found themselves face to face with a man who stood before the Marquis, bareheaded. They looked at one another silently for a long time; you would not have been able to say which of them looked more like a phantom.

Eventually, the old man said: "I recognize you, Gregory Temple. What do you want with me?"

"I want to tell you, Armand de Belcamp," the former Chief Superintendent of the Metropolitan Police replied, "that our pride is nothing but humiliation, our wisdom folly, our light darkness. A man was condemned to death last Friday by the Session Judges. He was hanged on Wednesday. He called himself Tom Brown. On the scaffold, he declared himself guilty of the murder of Maurice O'Brien in Prague, and the murder of Constance Bartolozzi in London. This man was the son of Helen Brown."

The Marquis collapsed into Jeanne's arms. She raised her weeping eyes to Heaven.

"Oh, Madeleine, Madeleine!" the old man murmured, in a final sob.

A groan answered him. The peasant woman was prostrate behind him, her face hidden beneath her black hood, kissing the Earth at his feet.

The Marquis de Belcamp was carried to his bed, where he languished for three more days.

Tom Brown's death cleared up a part of the mystery. The son of Helen and Gregory Temple claimed for himself the murders of the General and the actress.

But what about the other murders charged to the account of John Devil?

It is not for us to add anything to the strict letter of this bizarre legend of the 19th century, which began in darkness and finished in mystery. We merely observe that Helen Brown and, through her, her son Tom, were the heirs of the two brewers, Turner and Robinson. Henri de Belcamp alone stood between them and a fortune of nine millions; they had an obvious interest in his destruction. As for the double crime perpetrated in Paris, Noll Green and Lochaber Dick knew but one master: Tom Brown.

In the region where the events that we have related occurred, no doubt remains, and the memory of Comte Henri de Belcamp is the object of a cult for all those dazzled by his rapid passage through life.

It was at the end of the same year, 1817, that the English Admiralty commissioned the building of the first steam-powered warship.

In mid-October that same year, four young men dressed in black and four beautiful young women in mourning, one of whom was carrying a child in her arms, met on the quay in the little port of Saint-Valery-sur-Homme. At high tide, they boarded a lugger, which left port on the ebb tide and headed for the open sea.

The sea was calm and the wind was blowing upstream.

Three or four leagues out to sea, a steam-driven schooner flying the American flag was idling. When the lugger had come through the navigation channels and doubled the Hourdel, the schooner came around and steered towards her. The two ships came together off Bayeux and the lugger's passengers went aboard the schooner. The latter vessel no longer had the name *Deliverance* on her stern. It merely carried two white initials on a black background: *J.D.*

The lugger tacked towards the land; the schooner got up steam and, like a racehorse shown the whip, she surged westwards with the Channel current. The many crewmen on the bridge were grave; the schooner too seemed to be in mourning.

The passengers formed four couples, three of whom were united by the ties of marriage; these were Suzanne Temple and Richard Thompson, Germaine and Laurent, and Sarah O'Brien and Friedrich Boehm. The young woman and the young man who were not married bore the names Jeanne Balcomb and Robert Surrisy.

The next morning saw the schooner outside the Channel, steering south-southwest to follow the coast of Spain and take the great road to India.

On the far side of the equator, in the immense desolation of the Atlantic Ocean, a rock emerged from the shadows at the first rays of the morning Sun–a Sun that was sad by virtue of its splendor, whose glare burned the Earth as the kiss of Jupiter set fire to his lovers. It was now November; three weeks had passed since our travelers had quit the French coast.

A few houses were aligned on the island, their roofs low and square, carrying the British flag. There were warships in the harbor, which carried the same colors on their poop decks. Here and there, amid the grey stones, or above the parapets at ground level, you would have been able to see a musket gleam in the arms of a sentinel in a red uniform. But even from the highest point of a three-master's mainmast, you would not have been able to perceive the cage of Longwood, where the imprisoned lion languished.

A man came out of the melancholy house by the little gate that gave out on to the "pleasure ground." [255] This man had the appearance of a gardener. The sentry presented arms; it was the Emperor. He had been granted permission to have no sentinels in the enclosure but outside, at every exit, English hospitality was on watch.

The Emperor had a book in his hand and his telescope under his arm. He sat in the meager shadow of a clump of arborescent ferns, in order to have no English uniform within his view. He opened his book and tried to read—but he was dreaming.

After an hour, joyful cries roused him from his meditation. All the children of the little French colony were passing by the enclosure, laughing and playing. A little girl with beautiful golden curls saw the Emperor and left her companions, coming to put her blonde head in his lap. It was the Emperor's favorite, the daughter of loyal General B****.

They chatted. The child asked: "Why are you sadder than usual today, sire?"

The Emperor smiled, and answered: "The wind is blowing from France."

Then, bathing his delicate hands—still finely-formed, in spite of their plumpness—in the child's curly hair, he asked in his turn: "Do you know your prayers, little girl?"

The brave General B**** was not a very fervent Christian. The little one laughed, and countered: "What use is that?" Then, with the boldness of childhood, she added: "And you—do you know yours?"

General Montholon approached, with a letter of permission to walk on the heights—for it required a license signed by Hudson Lowe to cross the bounds of the little property of Longwood.

Alone, the Emperor slowly climbed the path that led to the summits of the chain of hills, from which he loved to gaze contemplatively out to sea.

The melancholy mist of which the *Mémorial*[256] speaks so often was dissipating in the Sun's rays; the ocean sparkled in the distance. There was not a single ship in sight in the entire extent of the sea save for the English vessels anchored in the harbor.

The Emperor sat down, shading his sad face beneath the broad rim of his straw hat, and he let his gaze wander across the horizon.

Behind that terrible wall of distance, there was not only the spectre of glory and power, not only the call of liberty, not only the smile of the fatherland, but also the two greatest loves the human heart can contain: a young woman; a dear child...

It had not been within the power of Napoleon himself, free and seated once again upon a throne, to augment his military glory; his testament affirms that he had renounced all political aspiration—but his wife, his son, France...!

Was there, meanwhile, a cloud appearing out there between the double azure of the sky and the sea? Or was it, rather, that miracle of human genius, that prodigious work of the century of invention, the first steamship: the *Deliverance*, doubtless preceding a heavier flotilla, coming to say to the captive: Be ready?

Ah! It was indeed a ship, for the telescope distinguished a black dot in the middle of the cloud. The heart of the vanquished giant must have leapt within his heart. What dream did his genius entertain at that moment? In spite of the promises made in hours of resignation, what battle-plans suddenly gushed forth in the shock of that hope? What vast movements of armies? What upsets of the map of the world?

As the ship came nearer, its two sail-less masts became visible, separated by that somber chimney from which the tresses of smoke emerged. It came as rapidly as a wish; it grew larger; its white wake was already visible!

It came too close. Why that futile bravado? The ships in the harbor had signaled its presence. The sound of a cannon-shot sent forth from the fort echoed repeatedly, but it was still coming closer. Two English frigates and two brigs put on sail, crowned with white waves, and the harbor artillery signaled to the batteries at the fort.

The ship did not alter course; it came on. Was it an illusion of the vertiginous sky? The tricolor was displayed at the top of its mast: the dazzling flag of so many victories! And cannon, too–French cannon–saluted the Imperial flag with a salvo.

Was it, then, an official courier arriving, with face uncovered, to announce a second French Revolution, or perhaps a first European Revolution?

The English squadron was already maneuvering to put the schooner between two fires.

The schooner finally stopped its approach. She was so close that the Emperor could see the uniforms of her watch on the bridge.

At a particular moment, all the heads were bared; the crew, hands on hearts, let out a cry whose echo did not reach as far as the island.

The tricolor flag was slowly lowered. A black flag was raised.

Then, the schooner turned about and sped away, enlarging in a matter of minutes the distance that separated her from the English vessels.

The last will of Comte Henri de Belcamp had been carried out to the letter.

When the cloud vanished over the horizon, the Emperor looked up and contemplated the sky.

He went back down to Longwood. The blonde girl came to offer him her cheek.

"Child," he said to her, "you asked me what use prayer serves. For a dear one like you, it is the servant of life. For a condemned man like me, it is the servant of death."

THE END

Afterword

I. Who was John Devil the Quaker?

John Devil the Quaker was Comte Henri de Belcamp, *alias* Tom Brown. He was the man who murdered General O'Brien and Constance Bartolozzi, who hired Noll Green and Lochaber Dick to murder William Robinson and Frank Turner, and who then murdered his hired assassins.

Readers may imagine that they have been told a different story–that all these murders were committed by another Tom Brown, who was not Henri de Belcamp but was, in fact, the illegitimate son of Gregory Temple and Helen Brown. They cannot, and should not, believe that, however. The principal source of that information is Henri, who has every reason to lie about it, and the subsidiary sources are equally unreliable.

Apart from a couple of casual lies told by Henri in Part One–the more important of which is the statement that Tom Brown, generally thought to be his mother's son, was merely someone who happened to have the same surname–the first mention of Tom Brown as a distinct individual is in the story told to Robert Surrisy by Sarah O'Brien. She, too, alleges no more than that a person of that name, who is not Henri, does exist–and she does it in the context of a conversation in which she admits that she is under Henri's orders. In retrospect, it is easy to see why Henri might have ordered her to make that claim; he is desperate to retain Robert's services, and that requires him to counter the evidence of Madeleine Surrisy that he is the murderer of General O'Brien and the despoiler of the Surrisy family fortune. Indeed, the surprising thing about Robert's conversations with Sarah and Henri is that he is so easily deterred from reaching that conclusion, given what his mother must have told him. Like Sarah herself, he appears to be blinded by Henri's charisma, desperately eager to set his entirely natural and perfectly logical doubts aside.

Sarah's support for Henri's earlier allegation that there really is another Tom Brown also prepares the way for Henri's Newgate tirade, when we are given a much more detailed account of his identity–whose effect on Gregory Temple is sufficiently shocking to render the detective literally speechless (conveniently, given that there are all kinds of objections he could have raised had he only had sufficient presence of mind to think of them). Given that Henri is a proven and prolific liar whose motives in spouting off to Temple are–to say the least–dubious, there seems to be no reason at all for the reader to believe what he says. After all, we know perfectly well that he did commission the murders of Robinson and Turner, that he did kill the two assassins, and that he went to extraordinary lengths not merely to frame Richard Thompson for Constance Bartolozzi's murder, but also to ensure that he was convicted.

The third account of the separate Tom Brown is more interesting, in its narrative context, than its predecessors, in that it *seems* to imply that both Gregory Temple and the narrative voice have accepted Henri's preposterous story. *Seems* is, however, the operative word. The account in question is offered to the Marquis de Belcamp by Gregory Temple, who actually says very little–and what he does not say is probably far more significant than what he does. It is entirely possible that none of what Temple says is true, the whole scene being devised in order to offer a little comfort to a dying man. Even if it is true, though, what does it actually amount to?

A person named–or, to use the excessively literal translation preferred in the text, "*calling himself*"–Tom Brown, under sentence of death, has claimed the credit for two prestigious murders? So what? Is he to be believed, without any further evidence? Surely Gregory Temple, of all people, could not be content with that. But the only comment Temple adds, so far as the narrative voice is prepared to tell us, is that: "*This man was the son of Helen Brown.*" (Not, it should be noted, "*my son.*") How does Temple know this? What possible evidence could there be to persuade him of it? He does not tell the Marquis, or the reader–and the reader, if not the Marquis, must be prepared to suspect that he is simply lying. In the absence of any supportive argument, there is not the slightest reason to believe that what he says is true, and some very good reasons for believing otherwise.

The narrative voice, pleading uncertainty, adds an oblique observation of its own to Temple's statement: "*Noll Green and Lochaber Dick knew but one master: Tom Brown.*" They certainly did, but the man they knew by that name was definitely and incontrovertibly Henri de Belcamp. If what Sarah had said to Robert Surrisy had been true, and if what Gregory Temple had said to the Marquis de Belcamp had been true, then Noll and Dick would have known two Tom Browns, as would Mr. Wood the solicitor; they clearly did not. What this statement by the narrative voice tells us, therefore, is the opposite of what it pretends to be telling us: it is not telling us that Henri was not the Tom Brown who was John Devil the Quaker; it is reminding us that he was.

The story told by *John Devil* is not without unsolved mysteries and vexatious puzzles, but the identity of John Devil the Quaker, serial murderer, is not one of them. The real mystery of the text is not whether Henri is guilty or not, but why the narrative voice should refuse to say that he is, having set out such firm evidence to that effect–and why it reports brazen lies while making only feeble and seemingly hypocritical attempts to withhold its endorsement therefrom.

Given that the narrative voice becomes so unreliable in the later chapters of *John Devil*, it may be as well to remember what it shows us with crystal clarity in the earlier ones. It shows us that the man who instructed Noll Green and Lochaber Dick to go to Brussels and Lyon, then got into a carriage with Richard Thompson, who knew him as James Davy. It also shows us Comte Henri de

Belcamp, in his father's castle, sealing and posting the two blank letters that gave the signal for the assassinations. Although it does not show us the murders of Noll and Dick–leaving that story to be told at third-hand by pretty Molly–it does show us Henri making his way to the scene of the murder and making his way back again (observed all the while by Ned Knob). There is no narrative space, however thin, during which a substitution could have taken place, even if one could imagine a motive for anyone else to intervene in the sequence of events or concoct an alternative explanation of Henri's expedition. No matter what he says about the matter subsequently, Henri is definitely responsible for those four deaths.

Although we are not shown the murder of Constance Bartolozzi, we are shown in considerable detail the mass of false evidence accumulated to throw suspicion on Richard Thompson and to ensure his conviction. No one but Henri could have put together that mass of evidence; no one but he had any reason to put it together, and even he makes no attempt to deny that he did it. Given that the basic components of the frame–the initialed handkerchief and the stolen IOU–must have been planned before the murder and could not have been set in place by anyone but the murderer, it would be absurd to think that the murderer could possibly be anyone other than Henri.

The murder of General O'Brien is similarly reported second-hand, at a much greater distance. In addition to Madeleine Surrisy's belated ear-witness evidence, however, there are several items of circumstantial evidence strongly suggesting that Henri is responsible. Given that he is certainly guilty of the other murders, the fact that this one involves an exactly similar method becomes much more significant, but the most significant item of all is that it is Henri, not any-one else, who blackmails the Counts Boehm thereafter. He could not do that if he did not have first-hand evidence of their procurement of the murder and the stolen marriage contract, and he could not have either of those things unless he is the murderer.

The alibi he offers to Gregory Temple–that he could hardly have been a bandit in London and a student in Germany at one and the same time–is patently silly, but if it had any weight at all, it would make it more difficult to account for the presence of the London bandit in Prague than that of the German student in London. Nor is it plausible that the London bandit or the Counts Boehm had any substantial motive for abducting Sarah O'Brien, as Henri claims in trying to ex-plain why he certainly did abduct her.

Given all this evidence, the procrastinations and prevarications of the nar-rative voice go far beyond mere teasing and become manifestly perverse. If all this is the case, as it clearly is, why not simply say so? It is one thing to report all Henri's lies, quite another to abrogate the responsibility of offering any sub-stantial correction.

Unlike the mystery of John Devil's identity, the mystery of the narrative voice's treachery is not readily soluble. It is possible that Féval simply lost control of his own plot–that he had forgotten what the narrative voice had shown us in earlier chapters when he came to write the later ones, and tangled himself up in hasty improvisations and flagrant self-contradictions. There is, however, an abundance of textual evidence that this was not the case, and that something more complicated was going on.

On two separate occasions, Féval's text refers to the stratagem used by Odysseus' wife Penelope in Homer's epic *The Odyssey* to keep her suitors at bay while she awaits her husband's return. (Without that device, of course, the *Odyssey* would be a "pure" story with the barest minimum of plot; it is Penelope's plight that lends a measure of urgency to Odysseus' wanderings, setting a deadline for him to return home–a deadline which, in the great tradition of narrative melodrama–he meets in the very nick of time.) What Penelope does is to tell the suitors that she cannot choose between them until she has finished weaving a symbolic shroud for her husband. She works on it every day, then secretly unpicks the work she has done by night, thus making no net progress.

The first time Féval refers to this incident is in Chapter VIII of Part Two, in a passage whose explicit reference is to *"the biographies of Comte Henri de Belcamp"* published in the newspapers, which add up to *"a thousand-chapter novel"* full of contradictions. The narrative voice sums up this commentary with the observation that: *"Contemporary history always has two versions, one white and one black, which are printed concurrently, and which simultaneously accuse one another of lying."* This is the prelude to the conversation between Sarah O'Brien and Robert Surrisy in which Sarah adds the first narrative support to Henri's claims that he is not the Tom Brown who is generally thought to be Helen Brown's only son.

There seems little doubt that Féval is conscious here that he is unpicking work that he has painstakingly done, for the purpose of procrastination. Why? Perhaps the decision was his own–but Penelope was working under external pressure, and the likelihood is that Féval was experiencing pressure too: pressure from readers who were following the serial and pressure from the editor who was publishing it. The editor may only have wanted it spinning out, in which case the new complication may simply be a stretching device, but it seems probable that there was more to it than that.

The most plausible hypothesis regarding the source of the external pressure operating on Féval is that the readers and the editors had become fond of Comte Henri de Belcamp. They liked him–and because they liked him, they did not want him to be guilty of the crimes with which he was charged. Ordinarily, readers do not have the power to make such determinations, although editors routinely do, even when they are dealing with books. In the context of a daily newspaper serial, however, readers certainly did have the opportunity to make their feelings known and felt.

The second time Féval refers to Penelope, he does not do so in the capacity of narrative voice. While Henri de Belcamp is lecturing Gregory Temple in

Newgate, accusing Temple of having fathered the Tom Brown that actually committed all his crimes, he observes that Tom Brown "appears to have decided to unravel my life with the patience of Penelope." Penelope was, of course, unpicking her own work, and so was Tom Brown–for Tom Brown is, of course, the architect of Henri de Belcamp's life, the dark foundation on which all his dreams of glory are built.

Féval had been writing newspaper serials for 20 years when he penned *John Devil*; he must often have felt like Penelope, spinning out stories for the sake of spinning them out, in order to keep his readers in a state of suspense. As a pioneering writer of popular fiction–the *roman feuilleton* was the first fiction to reach a mass audience, and the first to make pandering to that audience's multitudinous whims its top priority–he must have been very acutely aware of the uneasy amalgam of adoration and menace comprised in the relationship between a bestselling writer and his readers, and the analogy with Penelope's suitors must have struck him quite forcefully. Unlike Penelope, though, he always had to provide his own *deus ex machina*; the only hero who could ever save him was one of his own improvisation.

In the end, the only savior who could come to the aid of Comte Henri and his beleaguered creator was a chimera: a scapegoat on to which Henri's crimes could be loaded, thus giving him the possibility of being misinterpreted as a tragic hero and his creator the chance to imply that his ending was far kinder to Napoleonic ambition that it had initially set out to be.

At the end of the day, though, Henri did do it. He really was John Devil.

The effect of external pressure to relieve Comte Henri de Belcamp of his darker side by separating him from his evil twin is the most probable explanation for the fact that the narrative voice of *John Devil* changes its character in Part Two of the novel, becoming far less sure of itself. When it asks, as Comte Henri de Belcamp delivers his "explanation" to Gregory Temple in Newgate, "*Was there an atom of truth in this story of Tom Brown?*" it is offering the reader an opportunity to rejoice, and to say: "Yes! Yes! I knew that nice Henri de Belcamp–such a handsome and softly spoken chap!–had to be a hero, not a villain. I like him far too much to believe that he was guilty of so many murders and so much treachery. Yes, I want him to be innocent, and now you have given me the opportunity to believe it. Thank you!"

Some readers, of course, might have taken a different view, and offered a response along the lines of: "What are you asking me for? You're the narrative voice–you're supposed to be informing me." They would, however, have been a tiny minority. Few newspaper readers, in 1862, would have given a great deal of thought to the responsibility and reliability of narrative voices, even though some contemporary writers–notably Gustave Flaubert–had recently become deeply concerned about matters of narrative authority. Those readers would not yet have encountered the "third person limited" viewpoint that has now been standardized as a method of narration, locating a story's point of view inside the consciousness of one character at a time, thus facilitating the identification of the reader with the character by placing the reader in the character's shoes. They would have been used to first person narratives in which a character told them his own story, and they would have been used to third person narratives whose viewpoints were located outside the characters, as active narrators or "fly-on-the-wall" observers, but they would not have thought very much about the different effects, limitations and utilities of these various kinds of viewpoints.

Paul Féval, on the other hand, would have been well aware of the problems of managing then-conventional viewpoints, and he would inevitably have discovered, even if he had not anticipated, the particular difficulties thrown up by a story like *John Devil*. The kind of "omniscient narrator" which seemed natural in those days as a storytelling mode–and is, indeed, perfectly natural as a means of story*telling*–is not well suited to the narration of mysteries, simply because it is omniscient. How can an omniscient narrative viewpoint maintain a mystery for its readers, except by deliberately withholding information? Many readers may, of course, be tolerant of such a strategy, and many might not even notice it, but that does not eliminate the essential dishonesty of the pose.

Féval's awareness of this problem is clearly manifest in the way he tries to manage the narrative viewpoint of *John Devil*. He tries hard to make his narrative viewpoint a fly-on-the-wall observer, which can report on what occurs when

it is permitted to be present, but knows nothing of events on which it is not
privileged to eavesdrop. It is for this reason that the characters in the story spend
an unconscionable amount of time emoting like silent movie actors, forever
lowering and raising their eyes, blushing and going pale, shivering, quivering
and visibly fighting back tears. All of that is to emphasize that the narrative
viewpoint only has the power to infer thought and emotion, without having any
privileged access to the characters' motivations or any conclusive ability to
judge whether or not they are lying. It cheats, of course–it often forgets itself
sufficiently simply to tell us what characters are thinking and feeling, and it occasionally throws all caution to the winds and subjects the reader to a rapid in-
formation-dump–as, for instance in Chapter IV of Part One, when the account
Henri gives his father of his adventures is summarily interrupted so that Helen
Brown's back-story can be filled in. For the most part, however, Féval tries hard
to follow the rule that would ultimately be enshrined as the first principle of
popular fiction: show, don't tell.

From the viewpoint of the modern reader, the most annoying aspect of
Féval's narrative voice is not its occasional diversions into omniscience but its
habit of stepping back from the story to deliver little homilies on the invidious-
ness of the English, the exotic national character of the Irish, the popular
amusements of Paris, the pollution of the streets of London, the sad state of Versailles and so on. Such "metanarrative moves" have been all-but-banished from
modern popular fiction, which considers commentary not merely unnecessary
but outrageously intrusive. Flaubert, who did not think that authors had any right
to pass moral judgment on their characters, would have approved wholeheartedly, although the motive for the elimination was not so high-minded; modern
editors strike out such intrusions because they "get in the way of the story." The
editor of *Le Siècle* did not, because he believed–probably with good reason–that
his readers liked little homilies of this kind, provided that the arguments set out
therein flattered their preconceptions.

As *John Devil* evolves, its narrative voice becomes far more conscientious
about not telling the reader what is really going on, and it also becomes much
more selective about what it shows. The viewpoint becomes gradually more rigorous in its pose as a fly-on-the-wall, but it also steers clear of certain scenes
that might help the reader understand what is happening. It does not, for instance, allow us to know what Helen Brown actually said to the Marquis of Belcamp before she died in the castle. Nor does it allow us to know what Gregory
Temple wrote on his blackboard after his fateful confrontation with Henri in
Newgate, or how he was able to revise his conclusions as a result of the new information he had received.

The nature of the metanarrative commentary also changes, not so much in
becoming thinner as in becoming more oblique. It persists in inserting little es-
says–like the discourse on the jury system that precedes the synoptic account of
the manner in which Henri obtains his not guilty verdict, and the observations on

"modern valor" that accompany Henri's final journey to meet his father–but its purpose in doing so is not so obvious as that of earlier tirades against the English and various corruptions of popular taste. Some items of this commentary, in fact, demand to be deciphered–the passage containing the first reference to Penelope is an obvious example.

The narrative voice of *John Devil* becomes more selective in order to create space enabling the reader to reach and hold on to a false conclusion. Its running commentary becomes more oblique partly in order to sustain and support that space, but also to apologize for it. It is in the commentary that Féval continues to drop hints concerning his own dereliction of authorial duty, and the reasons for it. It was not the first time he had done that, and it would not be the last; indeed, by 1862 he had become so accustomed to the necessity that he was beginning to write stories making fun of it.

Being forced to change horses in mid-stream was routine business for writers of *romans feuilletons*, and Féval was used to it–but we may be perfectly certain that he never got to like it, and that he continued to push the envelope, continually attempting to put things into his serials that he would almost certainly be instructed to remove. His motives for doing this were undoubtedly complex, but one of them was surely his determination to carry forward the cause of popular fiction, to make it more ambitious, more adventurous and more versatile than its readers and publishers wanted it to be. *John Devil* is, in consequence, not merely a fine example of authorial ambition, adventurousness and versatility, but also–alas!–a fine example of the manner in which such ambition, adventurousness and versatility can easily be stifled by the dead hand of editorial control responding meekly to established reader demand.

The only logical conclusion the careful and courageous reader of *John Devil* can come to is that Henri and Tom Brown were the same person, and that Henri really was a multiple murderer. No matter how angry this makes us with the narrative voice for having colluded in giving the opposite impression, it is the truth of the matter. There is, however, one way to interpret the later phases of the plot that reconciles some of its apparent inconsistencies. Since the narrative voice tells us so little, we are surely free to speculate as to what might actually be happening. Perhaps, therefore, we should be prepared to consider the possibility that Henri does not know that he is lying: that he has actually come to believe in Tom Brown's separate existence.

The reader will recall that during the iconic scene when the fictional detective story is first displayed to us in all his glory, Gregory Temple indulges in a little tirade of his own, addressed to the absent Lord Chief Justice. In the course of that tirade, he raises the possibility that, in forcing criminals to become cleverer, his method of analyzing crimes by motive and opportunity might also lead them to back towards the moral light, on the grounds that education is good for the soul.

When Henri is lecturing Temple in Tyburn, he too touches on this point, offering his own education as evidence of his moral enlightenment, and hence of the impossibility of his being the murderous Tom Brown. Perhaps he is right; perhaps the intellectual refinement that Temple's book has forced upon him has shown him the error of his earlier ways and led him to repentance. Perhaps he has, in consequence, dissociated himself from that aspect of his personality, separating out his "higher" Napoleonic ambitions and creating narrative space for him to think of himself as an out-and-out hero.

If this is so, and Henri has become a split personality, then perhaps there really is a powerful metaphorical sense in which his evil twin is the "son" of Gregory Temple. Perhaps reading *The Art of Discovering the Guilty* allowed him to discover the guilt in himself and to begin its exorcism. In this respect, of course, Temple's influence would not have been working in isolation for long, for Henri has not merely been enlightened intellectually–he has also fallen in love.

When he first pulls Jeanne Herbet out of the water, thus saving her from drowning after already having saved her from being crushed or burned, there is a moment when he almost becomes Tom Brown again, putting his thumb to her throat–but he immediately recognizes the inconsistency in what he is doing. He is her savior, not her killer. He cannot treat her as a mere obstacle in his path because he is not that kind of man any longer; he is Henri de Belcamp now, having left Tom Brown under London Bridge. He is model of chivalry now, and there is only one thing that a model of chivalry can do in his present position: he must fall in love. So he does–and having done so, the possibility that he will ever be Tom Brown again, or that he ever was Tom Brown, becomes simply unthinkable. The exact extent of that unthinkability is carefully measured out in the two impassioned speeches he makes to Jeanne, first when he claims her love, and secondly when he reaffirms it on his way back to his trial-by-ordeal.

This is, of course, all pure fancy. But if it were so, it might help to clear up a few of the enduring mysteries of the plot–not least the question of why Henri frames himself in France while simultaneously framing Richard Thompson in England, by giving his hired assassins false passports in his own name. His ostensible motive for doing that is supposedly to have himself acquitted of the crime on the grounds of impossibility, but that makes no sense at all. For one thing, it is completely unnecessary–if Noll and Dick had carried out the assassinations independently, without using the false passports, no one would have the least reason for suspecting Comte Henri de Belcamp; even if Noll and/or Dick were caught, they could only point the finger at Tom Brown, alias John Devil the Quaker; whatever may or may not have happened in Australia, the scene on the bank of the Thames establishes that they had never heard the name Comte Henri de Belcamp until Henri gave them documents bearing it. For another, the alibi it provides is far from invulnerable, as the actual course of events readily demonstrates; all that is necessary is for proof to be produced that Henri hired the two assassins–proof that becomes attainable once he has provided them with false passports in his name.

Suppose, however, that when Henri tells Jeanne that he must be tried for the murder of Robinson and Turner, he is not talking about the necessity of protecting himself from double jeopardy. Perhaps, whether he is consciously aware of it or not, he really does mean that he must be tried and found innocent in order that he may believe himself innocent–that it is part and parcel of his symbolic repudiation of what he refers to more than once as his "shadow." If so, that might help to explain his curious attitude to his father, and the apparent desperation with which he wants his father to believe the account he has given himself. Perhaps that is why he can sway, in the course of his final confrontation with the Marquis that he had only ever told one lie, when an ordinary count reveals far more. Perhaps Gregory Temple eventually realizes that Henri really did believe what he said in the course of his Newgate rant, and thus feels free to support the lie in offering the Marquis de Belcamp a little final solace. Perhaps, after hearing what Henri has told the Marquis that is why Helen Brown betrays Henri by telling his father that he really is the scapegrace assassin Tom Brown–he is, after all, repudiating the part of himself that is an echo of her.

If this were the case, it would not be without literary precedent, in such works as Edgar Allan Poe's "*William Wilson*" (1840) and–perhaps more pertinently–E.T.A. Hoffmann's *Die Elixiere des Teufels* (1816) and James Hogg's *Confessions of a Justified Sinner* (1824). Both of the latter examples carefully maintain their ambiguity as to whether there are, in fact, two individuals rather than one, and in both instances the authors invoke the possibility that the evil *doppelgänger* is, in fact, a device produced by the Devil. If Féval had models like this in mind at any stage in the planning and composition of his novel, John Devil's name may be more revealing than it seems, and the examples provided by those models might help to explain the frustrating question of why, if Henri and Tom were the same person, the narrative voice does not simply say so.

It is entirely possible, given the circumstances under which the serial was composed, that its ultimate confusion is an accident of circumstance rather than something deliberately contrived, but we should at least be prepared to take the possibility seriously that what Féval did was deliberate, and that the ambiguity of the conclusion was both planned and managed, as self-conscious as any contemporary exercise in postmodern metafictionality.

If this were so, we could not prove it, but it is certainly worth noting that *John Devil* was not the only novel Féval wrote that ends with a similarly deep and seemingly self-contradictory ambiguity. To do that once, twice or far more often might be the result of continual carelessness or routine editorial interference, but when one looks at other examples in which Féval did exactly the same thing, the possibility that the ambiguity and self-contradiction is intended comes to seem much more likely. All three of my other translations of Féval's works, *The Vampire Countess*, *Knightshade* and *Vampire City*, which are otherwise very various in length and manner, have similarly self-denying endings.

The Vampire Countess is a version of *La Vampire*, which is often cited in lists of Féval's work as a later item than *John Devil*, although it is almost certainly earlier. The catalogue of the Bibliothèque Nationale lists a book edition of a two-novel omnibus in which it is featured, *Les Drames de la Mort* (*The Dramas of Death*), in 1856, but Jean-Pierre Galvan does not mention this in his bibliography, apparently assuming that the date is a misprint for 1865–for which date another edition is recorded, albeit from a different publisher. (Galvan was unable to identify a serial publication of either novel in the omnibus, although they certainly read like serials.) Whether its original date of publication was in 1856 or 1865, however, *The Vampire Countess* certainly has interesting affinities with *John Devil*. It features a conspiracy of individuals with personal grudges against Napoleon, which is taken over by a Hungarian Countess who is gathering a vast fortune by courting a series of rich husbands and disposing of them as soon as she collects opulent marriage-settlements.

As the title implies, the central character of *The Vampire Countess* poses as a vampire, and also as her own sister, in which guise she has black hair rather than blonde–just as Henri adopts dark hair when posing as Percy Balcomb and Tom Brown. The Countess might, in fact, really be a vampire; the novel's narrative voice carefully refuses to make a final decision on this point, leaving one of the four scenes of vampiric manifestation to be reported second-hand, two to be reported as experiences of characters who are very probably hallucinating, and the last to be represented as a newly-fledged folk tale. The concluding chapters take this ambivalence at least to the brink of self-contradiction, if not beyond.

In addition to the *doppelgänger*-strewn plots and the use of marriage-settlements as a plot lever–plus casual references to Achille de Jouffroy's dual role as a steamboat pioneer and popularizer of vampires–it is worth noting that the quasi-symbolic use of the legendary John Devil in that eponymous novel is very similar to the deployment of the vampire in *The Vampire Countess*. It is, however, the exaggerated hesitation between logically incompatible alternative explanations that forms the strongest point of comparison between the two novels. Exactly the same pattern can be seen in the novella translated as *Knightshade*, *Le Chevalier Ténèbre* (*Le Musée des Familles*, April-May 1860), whose shortness drastically reduces the probability that its ambiguities could be the accidental result of editorial pressure.

Knightshade is very obviously the work of a man fascinated by the craft of storytelling and the manipulation of audiences. It contains a series of tales-within-tales told by and featuring two masters of disguise, who might be brothers supernaturally empowered to return repeatedly from their graves to persecute the innocent, or who might instead be two ingenious English confidence tricksters. Jean Ténèbre and Ange Ténèbre–suggestively, if not pedantically, John Darkness and Angel Darkness–are both quasi-symbolic figures closely akin to John Devil. The narrative voice suggests at one point that the elder might be best regarded as a personification of the deadly sin of avarice, while the younger personifies lust.

This notion is carried forward into *John Devil*, as is the flagrant and self-conscious reliance of the storyteller-within-the-story on techniques of manipulative narration intended to have particular effects on his audience. Henri even offers two overlapping, and seemingly contradictory, versions of the same adventure in order to produce very different effects in his father and Jeanne. It is difficult to figure out what actually happens in *John Devil* not merely because so much of what the reader is told is relayed by witnesses whose honesty we have every reason to doubt, but because so many of the tales in question are manifestly contrived to be literally seductive.

If, as seems probable, Féval saw *John Devil* as a kind of melting-pot into which he might pour everything he had learned during his career as a writer, then it is not implausible that he might have intended from the very start to add in the fundamental ambiguity of *The Vampire Countess* and *Knightshade* as well as various other aspects of their symbolism and superstructure. The main narrative of the novella translated as *Vampire City, La Ville Vampire* (*Le Moniteur Universel*, September 25-October 25, 1874, book 1875)–which is also presented as a second-hand account–similarly proceeds with relentless seductiveness to a conclusion that cannot be logically reconciled with its beginning. Although the narrative voice does have a means of extracting itself from that impasse, there is little room for doubt that the impasse itself was deliberately and carefully contrived.

Given these further examples, it is obvious that, by 1860 at the latest, and probably by 1855, Féval had developed an abiding fascination with the seductiveness of narrative technique and with the manner in which audiences could be drawn into mazes of ambiguity and contradiction from which there was no easy escape. Seen in this context, it becomes much more plausible that that incoherence of *John Devil*'s concluding phases was calculated, and the unreliability of all its storytellers–including the author's own narrative voice–quite deliberate. If so, it also becomes more plausible that the question of whether Henri de Belcamp was or was not Tom Brown is supposed to be answered both yes and no, rather than one or the other.

If this is the case, then Féval was doing something in *John Devil* and some of its comparable works that was much more ambitious, and much more peculiar, than merely inventing the detective story. Why would he play such arcane and convoluted games with his readers? We do not know and cannot now find out. Perhaps, if he really was doing it deliberately, he did not know himself what exactly the mischievous side of his personality was up to. There are, however, some other clues in the pattern of his life and career that might cast further light on the question.

Paul-Henri-Corentin Féval was born in Rennes in Brittany, on September 29, 1816, four years after the battle of Waterloo had put an end to Napoleon's imperial ambitions and secured the Restoration of the Bourbon Monarchy. He was the son of Jean-Nicolas Féval, a *conseiller* (literally "counselor," although his responsibilities would have been much wider than present-day U.S. lawyers thus addressed) at the Cour Royale de Rennes.

Although Jean-Nicolas Féval was not a Breton by birth, Paul formed a strong affection for the region and always preferred to trace his ancestry back via the maternal line to the Bretonnian Barons de Létang–who became, in his mind, models of chivalry whose decline and eventual decadence was attributable to the submersion of Brittany within the French nation-state. Although he was born long after the Revolution of 1789, Féval's natural sympathies were with the Breton *Chouans* who had mounted a spirited armed resistance against the Revolutionary army before maintaining a distinct ideological distance from the subsequent Empire.

Jean-Nicolas Féval died in 1827, before Paul's eleventh birthday, leaving his family in somewhat straitened circumstances. Paul, however, obtained a scholarship to the Collège Royal de Rennes. He was not happy there; the majority of the students were, of course, far older than he. They were also rather various in their political sympathies; this became particularly apparent during the July Revolution of 1830, when Charles X was forced to abdicate and was replaced by Louis-Philippe. The 13-year-old Féval took the side of the *Légitimistes* in supporting Charles, requiring his removal for several months from the college to the home of his maternal uncle, Comte Foucher de Careil–to which he subsequently returned during vacations.

After completing his basic schooling in 1833, Féval followed family tradition by embarking on specialist studies in the Faculty of Law. He presented his thesis in 1836 and became a lawyer. An old friend of his father secured him his first case, in which Féval undertook the defense of a man name named Planchon, who was charged with stealing chickens. He made a plea for clemency, attempting to minimize the significance of the offense and citing various extenuating circumstances, only to have his aggrieved client launch into a diatribe in defense of his dignity and expertise as a professional chicken-thief. The court thought this hilarious–and Féval had to concede, in retrospect that it was–but he never exercised his rhetorical talent in court again. It is significant that Féval took the trouble to include a vitriolic and phantasmagorical transfiguration of this event in *John Devil*, in the digressionary account of the mock tribunal.

Jean-Pierre Galvan, who has done a heroic job in piecing together what evidence remains of Féval's life-story, doubts that Féval actually set off for

Paris the day after his court appearance, as one of his contemporaries alleged, but it nevertheless marked a crucial turning-point in his life.

What does seem certain is that the first job he obtained there when he did arrive in the capital, working for a cousin in the banking business, proved no more to his liking than the law. He quit after a matter of weeks, concluding that the world of finance was even more corrupt and wretched than the realm of law. Its crass materialism seemed to him to contrast strongly with the aristocratic ideals he was still trying to maintain–an impression enhanced by the rapidity with which he lost what little money he had to a borrower who never paid him back. Various other misfortunes overtook him as he tried to scrape a living on the fringes of the world of publishing. He had probably been writing for some time without publishing anything, but various items of hackwork, including encyclopedia articles, copy-editing jobs and vaudeville verses got him a start and letters of recommendation from a neighbor obtained him work from various Catholic periodicals.

In 1839, Féval began to publish fiction, much of which dealt with Breton folklore. His first real breakthrough came in 1841, when the prestigious *Revue de Paris* published "*Le Club des Phoques*" (*The Seal Club*) and "*Le Bourgeois de Vitré*" (*The Bourgeois from Vitré*), but the *Revue* was so well aware of its prestige that it did not pay new contributors and Féval could not afford to work on that basis. He joined the *Société des Gens de Lettres* (Society of Authors)–in whose affairs he was ultimately to play a leading role–in November 1842, and set out to make a business of his vocation.

It was a very good time to form such a determination, because the world of French fiction was in the process of being changed forever by the amazing success of Eugène Sue's *Les Mystères de Paris* (*The Mysteries of Paris*), which was then being serialized in direct competition with Alexandre Dumas' *Les Trois Mousquetaires* (*The Three Musketeers*). Both these serials ran on into 1843 and both were triumphantly followed up, *Les Mystères de Paris* by *Le Juif Errant* (*The Wandering Jew*) and *Les Trois Mousquetaires* by *Le Comte de Monte-Cristo* (*The Count of Monte-Cristo*), which ran from 1844 into 1845.

Magazines and newspapers had been publishing "literary supplements" since the turn of the century, often using space beneath a *feuilleton*–a line ruled across the page about three-quarters of the way down–to set copy early, thus reducing the space that had to be filled at shorter notice to take account of current events. Serial novels were not included in such spaces until 1829, but once their popularity had been demonstrated, Emile de Girardin made serial fiction central to the marketing strategy of *La Presse* in 1836. Armand Dutacq's *Le Siècle*–then the market leader–immediately followed suit. By 1842, *feuilleton* serials were an important weapon in circulation wars, and Sue's serial took that conflict to an entirely new level. *Les Mystères de Paris* was so popular that public readings were held for the benefit of citizens who were lagging slightly behind in the rapid spread of literacy.

Initially, Féval's work was published in periodicals of much smaller circulation than such popular dailies as *Le Constitutionnel*, whose circulation was said to have doubled–to something in excess of 40,000–while *Les Mystères de Paris* and *Le Juif Errant* were running there. Five of his early short stories and novellas set in Brittany were collected in *Le Capitaine Spartacus* (*Captain Spartacus*) in 1843, but he moved decisively into the popular arena when his first full-length novel, *Les Chevaliers du Firmament* (*The Knights of the Firmament*), set in 17th century Portugal, appeared in *La Législature* from March 14-June 28. The eponymous organization featured in the novel is a company of chivalrous knights forced by circumstance to operate in a clandestine manner against corrupt opponents; the chevaliers ultimately fail to hold back the anti-royalist historical tide.

The Brittany-set *Le Loup Blanc* (*The White Wolf*), which ran in *Le Courrier Français* from September 23-October 27, 1843, is similarly inclined but more exaggerated and less downbeat. Its dispossessed hero has to take over an organization of bandits, the *Loups*, in order to displace his usurper and claim his birthright–somewhat after the fashion of British legends of Robin Hood–but he does win his small victory in the end.

Variations of the pattern set in these two novels were to recur many times in Féval's work. Dumas and Sue had already discovered that the best way to maintain reader interest in a long-running serial was to establish a cast of sympathetic characters continually under threat from villainous conspiracies of whose existence and motives they are largely unaware. When they moved beyond the small-scale conspiracies of *Les Mystères de Paris* and *Le Comte de Monte-Cristo*, however, Sue and Dumas tended to use actual historical figures–the Jesuits are the villains of *Le Juif Errant*, while the associates of the famous schemer Cardinal Richelieu fill the adversarial role in *Les Trois Mousquetaires*.

Féval preferred to invent his own conspiracies, although he often associated them with real organizations, whose history he was thus compelled to re-invent. He was cast by this necessity into the shady realms of secret history, and he became a highly inventive elaborator of fanciful theories in which actual secret societies were bound into a much grander pattern, like the one that ultimately bound the *Habits Noirs* series together with four other novels.

This kind of activity recurs very frequently, and far more earnestly, in the kind of modern "conspiracy theory" whose most spectacular literary exemplars include Robert Shea and Robert Anton Wilson's *Illuminatus!* (three vols., 1975) and Umberto Eco's *Il Pendolo de Foucault* (1988; tr. as *Foucault's Pendulum*). Féval was ultimately to offer far more variations on the theme than his initial competitors, and to be far more even-handed in his treatment of clandestine conspirators. The virtuous organizations featured in his first two novels were soon supplanted by ambiguous ones, but the chivalrous aspirations of the *Chevaliers du Firmament* continued to echo in many other companies, and the theme of an ambitious hero taking over a criminal gang for his own supposedly-higher purposes was to undergo a striking process of evolution as Féval's secret organizations became more powerful and more sinister.

The editor of *Le Courrier Français*, Anténor Joly, was sufficiently impressed by *Le Loup Blanc* to commission Féval to make a blatant attempt to cash in on the success of *Les Mystères de Paris* by writing a calculatedly-sensational exposé of *Les Mystères de Londres* (*The Mysteries of London*). This alleged translation from the English of "Sir Francis Trolopp" (Frances Trollope, mother of Anthony, was then a moderately popular English novelist) ran from December 20, 1843, to September 12, 1844. It did not prove as popular as its model, partly because the audiences at public readings could not take the same delight in hearing about a foreign capital as they did in following adventures set in familiar streets, but it was sufficiently popular to boost Féval's fledgling career considerably—and to earn him a reputation as an opportunist hack that he could never entirely shake off. Although the tales collected in *Contes de Bretagne* (*Tales of Brittany*) (1844) and *Les Contes de nos Pères* (*Tales of Our Fathers*) (1845) were much more ambitiously-intended, it was the oft-reprinted *Les Mystères de Londres* that defined his public image as a parasitic follower of examples set by Sue and Dumas.

It is worth noting that none of the three major feuilletonists had a literary image that corresponded exactly with his personal political views. Although Dumas was a fervent Republican, his best-known works appeared in Royalist papers and mostly dealt with the exploits of aristocrats and patriotic fighting men in the glory years of the French Monarchy, when Louis XIV and Louis XV lived amid the pomp of Versailles. Sue occupied the space in Republican newspapers parallel to that which Dumas occupied in Royalist outlets, but he too was some way to the left of his editors; he was an ardent socialist. Dumas and Sue were both heavily influenced, in both political and literary terms, by Victor Hugo, whose *Notre-Dame de Paris* (1831; tr. as *The Hunchback of Notre-Dame*) had provided a powerful exemplar for the kind of historical fiction they produced. *Notre-Dame de Paris* became a kind of beacon illuminating their playing-field, not only establishing historical fiction as its primary genre but elevating the city of Paris to something more than a mere location, more akin to a central character whose present condition was an organic development of its colorful life-story.

Les Mystères de Londres extended the pattern established in Féval's first two romans feuilletons. Its hero is Fergus O'Breane, an Irishman who has sworn eternal enmity against England, the conquerors and oppressors of his native land, after being framed for murder and transported to Australia. After escaping from captivity, O'Breane has visited St. Helena and spent four hours with Napoleon—exactly as Henri claims to have done in *John Devil*—before eventually returning to England in 1830, shortly after which the story's main action takes place. The plot explains by degrees how O'Breane has infiltrated London society in the guise of the Marquis de Rio Santo, while secretly commanding an organization of criminals called the *Gentilhommes de la Nuit* (*Gentlemen of the Night*). Although ultimately defeated, by virtue of his unwise but typically chivalrous love for a young woman, O'Breane manages to wreak a good deal of vengeance on the villain who framed him. *John Devil* recovers many elements from this novel–which was published before *Le Comte de Monte-Cristo* and may well have given Dumas an idea or two.

Féval tried to make up for the difficulties created by the foreign setting of *Les Mystères de Londres* in his next serial for *Le Courrier Français*, *Les Amours de Paris* (*The Loves of Paris*) (January 23-June 8, 1845), but then reverted to his Breton homeland in *Fontaine aux Perles* (*Fountain of Pearls*) (*L'Esprit Public*, September 14-October 18, 1845). He returned to Ireland in *La Quittance de Minuit* (*The Midnight Reckoning*) (*Le Journal des Débats*, January 21-May 17, 1846), a more earnest contemporary novel which featured an actual secret society of rebellious terrorists, the Molly Maguires. He advanced resolutely into Dumas' literary territory in *Le Fils du Diable* (*The Devil's Son*) (*L'Epoque*, February 16-November 16, 1846), and also followed Dumas' example by adapting it for the stage, with assistance from two other writers, one of whom–Frédéric Soulié, a writer of some reputation who had also cashed in on the *feuilleton* boom–Féval always regarded as something of a mentor.

In *Le Fils du Diable*–which was translated into English as *The Three Red Knights*–three brothers honor-bound to exact vengeance on behalf of an old friend, whose legitimate heir is now endangered by the usurper, have to obtain a secret release from jail to fulfill their duty. They swear that they will return in time to save their jailer undue embarrassment, but while they are out and about they have to adopt disguises. They costume themselves as a legendary red knight: a masked and caped figure who is, in effect, the first ancestor of the caped crusaders prolifically featured in modern comic books; the fact that there are three of them enables them to give the impression that the mystery man can be in several places at once. The central motifs of this novel, like those of *Les Mystères de Londres*, are all recycled or transfigured in *John Devil*.

After *Le Mendiant Noir* (*The Black Mendicant*) (*Journal du Dimanche*, September 6-November 22, 1846), Féval gave up *feuilleton* fiction for some time, concentrating on the theater and novels of a more respectable variety, seemingly in preparation for his first bid for acceptance into the Académie Française. The move was a trifle premature, and the Academy was hardly likely to accept a writer of such recent provenance, but he must have thought the tactic vindicated when the economic and political upheavals following the Revolution of 1848 applied the brakes to the *feuilleton* boom.

Féval promptly embarked on other experiments, founding two journals of his own, *Le Bon Sens du Peuple* (*The People's Common Sense*) lasted only two months in 1848, folding before the Communist Uprising in May, but *L'Avenir National* (*National Future*), published from July to September in the wake of Louis Cavaignac's violent suppression of the workers, lasted through 63 issues.

Féval continued to publish novels set in Brittany and Paris, and sometimes both, but none achieved anything like the circulation of his most significant earlier works. One of his Breton novels did attract enough favorable attention to be established as his most reputable work to date, though–a reputation it has maintained to the present day, when it remains in print, in a Breton edition of 1987 as well as French. This was *La Fée des Grèves* (*The Fairy of the Sands*) (*La Gazette de France*, June 27-October 23, 1850), the first of a projected series of *romans du Mont Saint-Michel*. It was based on an actual historical incident and is therefore more disciplined than some of Féval's improvised stories–a remarkable fact, considering that it was serialized alongside *Bel Demonio* which ran in *Le Pays* from June 28 to August 16, and he was presumably writing episodes of both novels simultatneously. *Bel Demonio*, set in Italy, was another novel in which Féval returned to his favorite theme of belated vengeance assisted by leadership of an organization of outlaws; it became the book *Beau Démon* (*Handsome Devil*), which was subsequently gathered into the secret history of the *Habits Noirs*.

Louis-Napoleon's *coup d'état* of 1851 restored a measure of stability, but at a cost that compounded the problems of most writers. It ushered in an era of censorship that delivered popular fiction into a distinctly hostile climate, removing Dumas and Sue from Paris, although both continued to write. With opportunities for serial publication much scarcer than they had been five years earlier, Féval issued two large collections of novellas in book form in 1851-53. The first of them, *Les Tribunaux Secrets* (*The Secret Tribunals*), added up to a fictionalized history of secret societies through the ages; its prose style was so atypically dense that Galvan doubts its authorship, but it is possible that the awkwardness results from Féval having originally intended to produce a work of non-fiction that was converted into a story series when he could not find a buyer. The second collection, *Les Nuits de Paris* (*The Nights of Paris*), is a more orthodox series set in different periods of French history; it appears to be a political riposte to the early parts of Eugène Sue's last great work, *Les Mystères du Peuple* (1849-56), a polemical history of a proletarian family from prehistoric to modern times presented as a series of novellas.

Although he published three serial novels in the first half of 1852, Féval slowed down again thereafter and again began to concentrate on more upmarket outlets. He became rather depressed in this period, probably due to external circumstances rather than any organic problem; the medical fashions of the day represented his trouble as a "nervous disorder" and he sought help from a disciple of Samuel Hahnemann, whose homeopathic remedies did him no harm and whose recommendation that he take more exercise undoubtedly did him good. He became an enthusiast for physical culture and married the doctor's daughter, Marie Pénoyée, who was eventually to bear him eight children. Exercise and marriage helped reinvigorate his appetite for work, and he returned to the renascent but diplomatically-restrained *roman feuilleton* arena with a will in 1854, soon recovering his former pace of production.

Féval's new fiction became increasingly uninhibited in its use of action-adventure themes, often addressing them in a semi-comedic manner. Although he made conscientious use of all the devices of melodrama that had now become standardized as the basic repertoire of popular fiction, he did so in a knowing and slightly ironic way, frequently juxtaposing moments of high drama with bathetic descents into slapstick. He returned yet again to his favorite theme in *La Louve* (*The She-Wolf*) (*Le Pays*, December 26, 1855-March 5, 1856), adding an extra-twist by foregrounding a female hero. As the title suggests, the story is a sequel of sorts to *Le Loup Blanc*; the gang that the Breton rebel Valentine de Poulduc takes over is the same one that featured in the earlier novel. Although the constraints of Breton history had already forced him to shape several of his novels as pieces in the same jigsaw, this was Féval's first serious move in connecting up the secret history that he was embedding within it.

As with *La Fée des grèves* and *Bel Demonio*, Féval published *La Louve* alongside another Breton novel, *L'Homme de Fer* (*The Man of Iron*) (*Le Journal pour tous*, December 8, 1955-January 26, 1856), which was the second–and, as it turned out, last–of his *romans du Mont Saint-Michel*. A sequel to the early novel, it tells the story of a devil-worshipping German count whose evil plans are thwarted by a self-sacrificing heroine; although it remains similarly imprisoned by the actual course of Breton history, it expresses a powerful yearning for an alternative–a feature that recurs in *Jean Diable*, although Féval never dared to take the extra step into the realms of uchronian fiction.

Féval did, however, begin to take greater liberties with secret history with *Les Couteaux d'Or* (*The Golden Daggers*) (*Le Journal pour tous*, May 17-June 21, 1856), partly set in California. It is a robust adventure story spiced with such *bizarrerie* as an imported Pawnee Indian who goes on a scalping spree in Paris. Féval was well aware that this was something of a transformation, and there is probably an element of self-representation in one of the comments made in *John Devil* about the artist Férandeau: "*A faithful pupil of Louis David, Férandeau had not attached any great importance to these frivolities* (i.e., his caricatures of Miremontese society). *He was in the process of becoming famous in spite of himself. Such is the history of all caricaturists. The vocation of our greatest comic artists initially leads them astray towards tragedy.*" (Part Two: Chapter XVIII).

Having found his *métier* as somewhat of a literary caricaturist, Féval hoped and expected to remake his reputation with the massive *Madame Gil Blas* (*La Presse*, July 22, 1856-September 16, 1857), another action-adventure story featuring a female hero. It was, however, *Le Bossu* (*The Hunchback*) (*Le Siècle*, May 7-August 15, 1857) that restored him to the height of his celebrity in the following year, carrying forward a similar spirit of blithe irreverence into classic Dumas territory. Although *Le Bossu* is, in a sense, a caricaturish pastiche, its humor does not attempt to deride or diminish its model; it is an affectionate, celebratory kind of humor which admits the artificiality of all the dashing swordplay and conspicuous gallantry while still making enthusiastic use of their reader-pleasing capacity.

Like *Knightshade*, *Le Bossu* is clearly the work of a man who has become fascinated with the mechanics of fiction and the effects on readers of various kinds of narrative moves. That self-consciousness was something Féval began increasingly to share with his readers, sometimes overtly but often in a playful and teasing manner. He became increasingly fond of having characters tell stories of their own within his stories, routinely allowing them to concoct elaborate lies without any correction or warning on the part of the narrative voice. The later chapters of *Le Bossu* ran alongside the early chapters of *Les Compagnons du Silence* (*The Companions of Silence*) in *Le Journal pour tous* (June 6-September 19, 1857). The latter recycled the basic plot-structure of *Les Mystères de Londres* yet again, in a context which allowed it to be gathered, along with *Beau Démon*, into the secret history leading via *John Devil* to *Les Habits Noirs*.

Les Compagnons du Silence complicates the dual identity theme that was already one of Féval's favorites with a feature that he was to adopt on a more regular basis: the juxtaposition of power and decrepitude. The diabolical Johann Spurzheim is the Chief of Police in Naples, who terrorizes others with his Machiavellian schemes despite being so physically frail that he is permanently bed-ridden. Unlike the hero of *Le Bossu*, who was only pretending to be a hunch-back, Spurzheim really is debilitated–although he was once a very active char-acter on the other side of the law. Spurzheim anticipates aspects of the character of Gregory Temple, and also–more explictly and more importantly–the secret master of the *Habits Noirs*. His transition from bandit to police chief reflects the one allegedly made by one of Féval's key source-books, a curious document that served as a "taproot text" for early crime and detective fiction: François-Eugène Vidoq's *Mémoires* (1829).

Vidoq (1775-1857) was a notorious criminal whose career had extended far longer than most because he also served as a police agent, thus giving him an immunity similar to–but more enduring than–that enjoyed by Jonathan Wild in England. Although Vidoq's tales of his exploits before his alleged retirement in 1827 were probably wildly exaggerated, in the great French tradition of fake bi-ography instituted by Etienne-Léon Lamothe-Langon–whose account of *L'Espion de Police* (*The Police Spy*) (1826) was probably its immediate inspira-tion–it was widely regarded as non-fiction. Its 1840 translation into English was a significant influence upon, if not the inspiration for, Edgar Allan Poe's "*The Murders in the Rue Morgue*" (1841) and it undoubtedly encouraged Féval in his depiction of problematically divided characters.

Whether the editor of *Le Siècle* invited Féval back into its pages, or the author made the approach, we have no way of knowing. In either case, the impending dramatic version of *Le Bossu* probably tempted them both to forge a new alliance. There is, however, one other event that was probably of considerable significance. In the early months of 1862, before *Jean Diable* began serialization, the exiled Victor Hugo published his first novel for many years: *Les Misérables*.

Given that *Notre-Dame de Paris* had exerted such a powerful formative influence on *feuilleton* fiction, the new novel would have been eagerly investigated by editors and writers in any case, but their interest must have been sharpened by the fact that Hugo had very obviously taken back some of what the feuilletonists had borrowed for further development. The plot of *Les Misérables* left no doubt that Hugo had read the work of his fellow-radical Sue, and was not ashamed to appropriate Sue's discoveries in melodramatic effect. Despite the political differences between them, Hugo had probably read Féval too; when he published another novel in 1869 that carefully sophisticated the substance of serial melodrama, *L'Homme qui rit* (*The Man Who Laughs*), he set it in London and invented a truly remarkable criminal conspiracy in the Comprachicos.

The temptation to use *Les Misérables* as a model just as *Notre-Dame de Paris* had been used, must have been very powerful, but it must also have been tempered with extreme caution. Hugo was, after all, still in exile–he would not return to Paris until 1870–and the government that had sent him there had not entirely relaxed its cautious attitude to the press. Indeed, Hugo's return to the arena of fiction probably increased the watchfulness of its agents. Féval and his potential employers had to be keenly aware of the fact that both of his chief rivals as writers of romans feuilletons–Alexandre Dumas and Eugène Sue–had, like Hugo, been sent into exile in the wake of the 1851 *coup d'état*. Although Dumas had taken advantage of an amnesty to return to Paris, he had not been able pick up the interrupted thread of the abruptly-banned serial that he had begun in the wake of the revolution of 1848, which he had intended to be his literary masterpiece and the capstone of his career: *Isaac Laquedem* (the incomplete text was reprinted in book form in 1853).

Like Hugo, Dumas and Sue had been banished for their Republican affiliations, while Féval was a royalist, but he was a "*Legitimist*" Royalist who was potentially just as much at odds with an Imperial usurper as hardened Republicans were. He had to be diplomatic on his own behalf, and however diplomatic he was, he was likely to invite disapproval from a large sector of his audience. By 1862, his work had been written under this kind of pressure for more than ten years, and the prospect of borrowing anything from *Les Misérables* must have seemed troublesome both to him and to his potential employers. Even so, *Les Misérables* was enormously popular, and the temptation to try to cash in on its popularity, if that could be done without inviting reprisals, must have been enormous.

John Devil's debt to *Les Misérables* is muted, but it is unlikely to be coincidence that Féval's novel reproduces some of the key elements of Hugo's dramatic situation. The hero of *Les Misérables*, Jean Valjean, is pursued and harassed by an intransigent agent of the law, Javert. This basic scenario is echoed in the contest between Henri de Belcamp and Gregory Temple, although Féval adjusted the moral balance considerably. Henri is far less of a paragon of persecuted innocence than Jean Valjean–although he certainly represents himself as one when he makes his fervent pleas to Jeanne–and no matter how insanely obsessive he becomes, Temple is always working for the ends of abstract justice, in pursuit of a murderer. Indeed, it is possible that Féval's careful adjustment of the balance between his chief protagonists, calculated to avoid some of the discomfiting aspects of the Javert/Valjean conflict, is what led him to create the detective novel.

The other echoes of *Les Misérables* in *John Devil* are subsidiary, but worth mention nevertheless. One of the key dramatic moments in *Les Misérables* involves Valjean surrendering himself to the law and returning to prison in order to save a man wrongly locked up in his stead; although Féval's Newgate scene is carefully complicated in the interests of melodramatic excess, it seems likely that he always planned to give it pride of place in his climax. Certain respects of the relationship between Valjean and Cosette, the child he promises to protect, are also echoed in *John Devil*, in Henri's key relationships with Sarah and Jeanne, although his relationships with their respective fiancés never lead to any scene comparable to the melodramatic high-point of *Les Misérables*, in which Valjean carries Cosette's fiancé Marius through the Paris sewers.

No matter how carefully he muted the influence of *Les Misérables*, though, Féval and his editor can hardly have been unaware that *John Devil* ran a far greater risk of being seen as politically contentious than any of the other novels he had written during the Second Empire. His earlier conspiracy theory novels had mostly been set in earlier periods of history, but *John Devil*–like *Les Misérables*–is set in the latter years of Napoleon's life and its plot bears directly on the Emperor's fate. Whether intentional parallels were being drawn or not (and they almost certainly were), everything Féval said about the doom of the First Empire's fallen leader was bound to carry implications for the Second.

It is easy to see, in this context, how the gradual unfolding of *John Devil*'s plot–in which Henri's pseudo-Napoleonic character is deeply tainted by his apparent status as a master criminal and multiple murderer–might have set alarm bells ringing in the offices of *Le Siècle*. Although we have no way of knowing whether or not it was editorial pressure that persuaded Féval to change the denouement of his mystery in a way that rendered it superficially nonsensical, it would have been very surprising indeed if his editor had allowed him to proceed to the seemingly-inevitable conclusion, given the ideological implications that could have and would have been read into it. If Féval changed course of his own volition, especially if he had always planned to do it, it was probably an exaggerated awareness of what he could and could not get away with that made him do it.

Consciously or not, with or without premeditation, the narrative condition of *John Devil* mirrors its time: uncertain, ambiguous, repressed and exceedingly well aware of the checkered history that had produced it. For ten years, Féval had had to keep his own opinions carefully under wraps, flattering Napoleonic ambitions in order to deceive them; in such circumstances, would it have been surprising had he decided to deal in irreconcilable contradictions, stubborn refusals of clarification and blatant narrative hypocrisies? The cruelty of Féval's depiction of Miremont's fickle, greedy and hypocritical *société* has already been mentioned, but the symbolism of the novel does not stop there. Its fascination with doubles, multiple pseudonyms and transformations is remarkably extensive, persistently reinforcing the axiom that "*contemporary history always has two versions... which are printed concurrently, and which simultaneously accuse one another of lying.*"

We cannot know now exactly how Féval felt about becoming the number one feuilletonist because his two famous rivals had been exiled by Napoleon III. He was presumably grateful that he was not required to suffer the same fate, but he may well have been slightly discomfited by it. The fact that *John Devil* did not carry through with its initial prospectus is doubtless significant, but so is the prospectus itself. Unlike the conspirators in Théophile Gautier's 1848 novel *Les Deux Etoiles* (*The Twin Stars*; tr. as *The Quartette*), Henri de Belcamp does not intend to rescue Napoleon for Napoleon's benefit but for his own; the *Deliverance* is merely his instrument and he wants to rescue Napoleon in order to use him, to cash in on his name and reputation. His dreams of empire may be glorious, but they are founded on the exploits of John Devil, an archetypal personification of greed unconstrained by morality, who stops at nothing in order to obtain his ends. As Henri points out, once he had the means of blackmailing the Counts Boehm, he was rich as well as clever; he could have lived in respectable idleness thereafter–but he chose instead to risk everything in a quest for empire. He is clearly and manifestly Napoleonic, but his manifest model is Napoleon III, not Napoleon I.

Perhaps Féval started *John Devil* in these terms knowing that he would not be allowed to continue for long, fully aware of the fact that he would be told to tone it down. On the other hand, perhaps he always intended to wreck it himself, because he felt deeply and sincerely that what the readers of contemporary Paris needed was to be shown–even if they could not see it–how far they had gone into ambiguity and self-contradiction, unable to commit themselves either to monarchy or revolution, bizarrely intent on trying to have both. Perhaps his narrative voice is transformed in the later chapters because the voice of French history had similarly lost its authority and its ability to make any sense of things. Perhaps Féval thought that France, like the Marquis de Belcamp–who never could take sides between King and People and lost everything in consequence– deserved no more in the final analysis but a few casual lies cast as flattering illu-

eserved no more in the final analysis but a few casual lies cast as flattering illusions.

Ironically, we can see with the benefit of hindsight that the effect of *John Devil*'s eventual change of direction was to bring the story more closely in line with the more familiar formula of modern detective fiction: the "surprise end-ing" that reveals the true identity of the criminal only in the climax, having care-fully misled the reader throughout. By comparison with later novels written in accordance with that formula, in which such surprises were carefully planned in advance and their groundwork scrupulously laid down, *John Devil*'s ending is bound to seem ridiculously arbitrary, but it would probably be a mistake to re-gard that arbitrariness as mere incompetence.

However the reader chooses to interpret it, the result of *John Devil*'s be-lated shift from one formula-to-be to another is a mystery of a kind that has rarely, if ever, been replicated since–a mystery in which the reader, in order to make sense of what seems to have happened in the novel's conclusion, must read between the lines to see through a belatedly-raised smokescreen to all the stories that might, and perhaps should, have been told. Whether this adds value to the novel's mystery elements, or merely exposes its flaws, readers must de-cide for themselves, but it surely does not detract from the novel's interest and significance as a historical artifact.

In 1875, the year in which he published the book version of *La Bande Cadet* (*The Cadet Gang*)–which proved to be the seventh and final novel in the cycle of *Les Habits Noirs* and thus put an end to his pioneering experiment in series crime fiction–Paul Féval's career hit the rocks in spectacular fashion. He lost an enormous amount of money–millions, in today's reckoning–by unwise speculation on the financial fortunes of the Ottoman Empire, and was ruined.

Féval's response to this disaster was as abrupt and decisive as his reactions had always been. He decided that God must have intended to teach him a lesson, and recanted his allegedly profligate lifestyle in favor of a return to the true values of Catholicism. This was the moment when he decided that it was time to exorcise his own dark self and to set his cleansed soul firmly on the path to glory. He called this about-face his "conversion," although it was actually a return to the values his mother had tried to teach him when he was a boy and to a faith that he had never actually forsaken; he had always worked far too hard to be authentically profligate, and always thought of himself as a Catholic. Nevertheless, as is often the way with converts and the "born again," he became exceedingly zealous in the exercise of his regenerated faith; he played a very active part in the movement to finance the building of the Basilica of the Sacré-Coeur at Montmartre.

The effect on his writing was profound and–at least from the viewpoint of lovers of popular fiction–regrettable. He continued to publish new works in some quantity, in the hope of restoring his fortunes, but he concentrated on works of Catholic apologetics and fictions of a morally improving and somewhat pietistic streak. He also began to issue "revised and corrected" editions of his old works, removing any material therefrom that offended his new moral hypersensibility. The *Habits Noirs* series was abruptly abandoned, because its writing had come to seem to its author like trifling with the Devil; he described his revisions as "an act of contrition." He made no further contribution to crime fiction and never attempted to redeem any of his crime novels for inclusion in the series of his "corrected" works. (Fortunately, his former publishers were not about to let those works fall into oblivion.)

It seems, however, that his act of contrition did not appease the offended deity; Féval had just about recovered a viable economic position when he suffered a second disaster in 1882, when the person put in charge of his finances absconded with his money. He had to be rescued from destitution by a fund-raising committee assembled by the Academy that had never let him in, chaired by the author Edmond About. The subsequent death of his wife redoubled the misfortune, from which he never recovered. He retired to a monastery and wrote nothing more until he died in 1887.

Understandably, Féval left behind memories and impressions that were decidedly mixed, and a reputation that was deeply problematic. Not only did he fail to win the literary reputation he had tried three times to obtain, but he failed to retain the kind of popular following that Dumas–and, to a lesser extent, Sue–continued to command. Although a handful of his best-known works were continually reprinted, the greater part of his phenomenal output was forgotten. Féval's eldest son, who became a moderately prolific writer of popular fiction under the signature Paul Féval Fils, did carry forward several strands of his father's work, writing numerous sequels to *Le Bossu*, but, for whatever reason, he never attempted to continue the *Habits Noirs* series or to write anything in the complex vein of *John Devil*; his own crime novels are distinctly anemic by comparison.

Having tried so hard to explain so many of *John Devil*'s contradictions, it seems only appropriate to add a few notes about some of the puzzles that remain insoluble. The most significant of these is the puzzle of Gregory Temple's locket. This was obviously a hasty and belated improvisation, for if Féval had intended its inclusion from the beginning he would certainly have found an earlier opportunity to draw the reader's attention to it, by way of "pre-corroboration."

The enigma presented by the locket is basically twofold: when did Temple acquire the locket, and how does Henri know that he wears it? We are not told exactly how old Suzanne Temple is, but all the textual evidence indicates that the Tom Brown whose separate existence Henri is alleging must be older, so Temple's one-night-stand with "Lady Caroline Dudley" must have taken place while he was still married to Suzanne's mother. It seems implausible, therefore, that he started wearing the locket when it first was given to him, and it is not at all clear why he started wearing it at all.

Whether or not Lady Caroline Dudley was Helen Brown–and if she was, it is remarkable that Gregory Temple did not recognize Helen when he arrested her in 1805–she can hardly have been confident that he ever would, and had no obvious way of finding out that he had, so she is unlikely to have been the one who told Henri about it. Suzanne Temple would be a more likely source if she could have found out the story associated with the locket, but it is unlikely, given the circumstances, that Temple would ever have told her or Richard Thompson what *B* was supposed to stand for.

Perhaps, while Helen Brown and Henri/Tom were waiting to be transported in 1814, hopeful that Gregory Temple might save them, Helen Brown did tell him that she had more than one reason to hope that Temple might help them out if only he could be persuaded to see them (although it is surprising that she did not take the same opportunity in 1805)? Perhaps it was sheer optimism that led her to believe that Temple would actually be wearing a memento to his own adultery, or perhaps she had actually seen it around his neck in 1805? Either way, her telling Henri/Tom at this point might help to explain why Henri/Tom's animosity against Temple is so deeply personal–as it clearly is, despite Henri's assertion in Newgate that he only ever wanted to attack Temple's method. Once the exorcism of Tom was completed by the accusation that he was Temple's son, of course, that animosity vanished, leaving the newly-cleansed Henri to take a much more benevolent attitude towards his "uncle."

If it is true that Helen Brown once had a pseudonymous one-night-stand with Gregory Temple, on which she pinned her hopes of avoiding transportation, this might also help to explain the curious intensity of Henri's animosity against Richard Thompson, whose framing goes way beyond the bounds of mere convenience. This too seems intensely personal, although Thompson–like Robert Surrisy—seems blissfully blind to its viciousness. Perhaps Henri/Tom, realizing that he might, had "Lady Caroline Dudley" really fallen pregnant have had a brother or sister in common with Suzanne Temple, had conceived a hatred of her and her own child almost equal in intensity to his hatred of her father. If so, that hatred too would have evaporated when Tom was exorcised—and the rescue of Richard Thompson, like the confrontation with Gregory Temple that was its immediate consequence, might also need to be regarded as an aspect of that ritual.

The second puzzle left annoyingly unsolved by the text is what actually did happen in Australia. Henri's account of the liberation of Percy Balcomb is obviously pure fiction—as, in all probability is the first story he tells his father. Sarah's account of a mass escape including Tom Brown is also dubious in the extreme—it is difficult, in fact, to believe that Sarah was ever there at all. This may be one instance in which it is safer to trust "common knowledge" than any account offered for tactical reasons, and to conclude that Helen and Henri/Tom did escape from Norfolk Island in the company of Noll Green and Lochaber Dick. We cannot even hazard a guess as to the exact circumstances in which Helen was subsequently abandoned, but we may charitably assume that it was not an entirely callous act, and that if Helen thought it was—thus contributing to her urge to betray Henri to the Marquis—she was mistaken.

One minor puzzle is the matter of the blank letter that the Marquis de Belcamp received on Henri's behalf on the morning of his birthday party. Henri's explanation that it was sent by Helen and Tom Brown in order to implicate him in the murders is patent nonsense. How could his possession of pieces of blank paper, even if he bothered to retain them, count as evidence of his involvement? The greater likelihood, surely, is that they were not really blank at all, but had been inscribed in the kind of invisible ink demonstrated at the meeting of the Supreme Council, and that they contained information concerning the Deliverance or the secret dealings of Balcomb & Co.

Another minor puzzle is the question of when Henri first found out about Robinson's and Turner's wills. Henri tells his father that he met them at a beer festival in Munich and introduced himself to them as their nephew, in which capacity they were happy to see him, but the two brewers seem to be utterly unaware in the Prologue that Helen Brown has any son other than the notorious bandit Tom. Nor is it obvious why Henri should invent such a fiction, given that he could just as easily have found out about the wills when Robinson and Turner presented themselves at Scotland Yard after Constance Bartolozzi's murder.

That is surely the likelier contingency, since Henri has apparently made not the slightest effort to locate his rival heirs until he goes to the oyster-house to eavesdrop on the brewers. Perhaps he was in Munich for the beer festival, and perhaps he did meet his two cousins, and perhaps he eavesdropped on them there as well, but he surely did not introduce himself to them, nor did he find out that at that time that he was not the heir presumptive to their millions.

There are a few other puzzles, like Richard Thompson's disappearing manacles, but all of them are trivial and all of them are presumably the result of simple carelessness; two small inconsistencies in the time-scheme are pointed out in the *Chronology* appendix.

It ought to be emphasized that acknowledging Féval's crucial contribution to the early evolution of crime fiction does not detract from Emile Gaboriau's importance within that tradition. Gaboriau's principal innovation, which was absolutely crucial to the evolution of the genre, was an inversion of perspective. Féval had always been, and continued to be, far more interested in criminals than detectives; he always foregrounded the adversarial point of view. His reasons for doing this were undoubtedly complex, but one of them relates to his own skeptical attitude to the law, which is displayed with ferocious effect in *John Devil*'s accounts of the mock tribunal, Sir Paulus Allan's conduct as Scotland Yard supremo and the deliberations of jury appointed to consider Henri's guilt.

As a writer, Féval retained a powerful contempt for everything he had hated during his meteoric career as a lawyer; the force and endurance of that contempt are amply demonstrated by the fact that, nearly 30 years later, he took the trouble to incorporate a savagely sarcastic pantomime version of the dramatic conclusion of the career in question into his pioneering work of crime fiction. In consequence, he always approached the subject of crime, and criminal justice systems, from an angle that prevented him from reaching the position that was left to Gaboriau to develop: making the detective the taken-for-granted hero of the detective story.

This may seem a glaringly obvious move to us, looking back through the lens of subsequent history, but it was by no means obvious to Féval's and Gaboriau's contemporaries and successors. In taking a jaundiced view of the activities of policemen and criminal justice systems, Féval was very much in tune with his times. Most 19th century police forces still relied almost exclusively on clandestine informers, thus resembling the KGB or the Stasi far more closely than the modern Sureté or Metropolitan Police, and those judges not open to casual bribery usually had strong political prejudices; cynicism was inevitably widespread.

The cynicism of popular attitudes to the law in general and policemen in particular is reflected in the fact that French popular fiction is extraordinarily rich in central characters who are on the wrong side of the law. Féval's chief rival as a Second Empire feuilletonist was Pierre-Alexis Ponson du Terrail (1829-1871), the author of a long series of picaresque novels starring the lovable rogue *Rocambole*, whose name is preserved in the adjective *rocambolesque* (which implies extreme improbability as well as flamboyant irreverence). The most famous successors of *Rocambole* and *John Devil* were the masked master criminal *Fantômas*, the creation of Pierre Souvestre and Marcel Allain, who flourished between 1911 and 1948 and Maurice Leblanc's gentleman burglar *Arsène Lupin*, whose career extended from 1907 to 1939.

Although the most striking and surprising thing about Gregory Temple, from the viewpoint of modern aficionados of crime fiction, is that he is not the hero of *John Devil*, that refusal of automatic moral superiority is not particularly surprising in historical context. There is an important sense in which Temple (whose surname is as significant, in its way, as Devil) is one half of a complementary pair who complete one another by each providing the other with a definitive challenge. Unlike Sherlock Holmes confronted with Professor Moriarty, or Batman by the Joker, Temple is relegated to playing second fiddle, while John Devil is the leading partner in the dance–but it is, after all, criminal activity that necessitates, stimulates and shapes the evolution of criminal investigation and legal redress, not vice versa. Gaboriau's discovery that detective story plots function much better, in dramatic terms, if the reader's consciousness is not merely morally allied to but existentially united with that of the detective, was not a belated realization of the obvious; it was a clever inversion of the "natural" pattern of priority.

Like modern thriller writers who have revived interest in the workings of the criminal mind, Féval took it for granted that John Devil–seen as a symbolic representation of criminal deviance in its broadest sense–deserved pride of place over the detective whose art had been shaped to combat him. He also had literary tradition on his side; in early 19th century historical novels and plays, police agents of every rank were almost invariably schemers working to further the interests of their patrons, and Gregory Temple's devotion to the ideals of justice was a conspicuous exception rather than the rule.

Gaboriau's triumph–echoed throughout the tradition of subsequent crime fiction–was partly a matter of redefining public attitudes to the police, helping to rescue them from the opprobrium routinely attached to them. As a "convert" from the legal profession, Féval knew even better than the majority of his contemporaries how deeply flawed contemporary criminal justice systems were, and he was keenly aware of the fact that the actual distribution of virtue and villainy was far more problematic than formulaistic *policiers* were later to imply–but in terms of the tactics of popular fiction, Gaboriau's move was a very clever one.

In hailing *John Devil* as a foundation-stone of modern crime fiction, it is important not to forget that stories whose plots hinge on mysterious murders were by no means new in 1862; they had first become commonplace in the "Gothic" fiction produced in vast quantities in Germany, England and France in the last decades of the 18th century and the early decades of the 19th. Very few of those plots had involved any kind of methodical investigation, however, and the character of such investigations, where they do occur, seems very odd to the modern eye, because they are almost invariably based in the assumptions of an antiquated legal system.

All Gothic murder mysteries set in the past, and the vast majority of those set in the present, had to take place in contexts where the investigation of crimes was the sole responsibility of Examining Magistrates employing quasi-inquisitorial procedural systems. If there were no witnesses to a crime—or none prepared to give evidence—conviction under such systems only be obtained by means of a confession. Crime fiction of the Gothic era, like the legal systems it represents, is orientated almost exclusively towards the pressurizing of witnesses and the extraction of confessions.

In much earlier eras, when torture was still licensed, this had not been unduly difficult, although the results were by no means reliable. As physical torture was gradually circumscribed and ultimately proscribed, legal systems and their fictional representations relied ever-more-heavily on psychological pressure of various kinds, giving rise to countless Gothic mysteries in which murderers have to be tricked or surprised into giving themselves away—a kind of plot that still survives today, albeit in fugitive forms. As legal systems evolved, and the role of police forces changed, so did the scope offered to writers of fiction for the representation of criminal investigations. Nor was the role of fictional representations restricted to passive description; it had a prescriptive and propagandistic element too.

The significance of scrupulously objective and cleverly penetrating logical analysis in criminal investigation was first championed in fiction by Voltaire's *Zadig* (1756), and then by Edgar Allan Poe's three stories featuring C. Auguste Dupin (1841-45), the model for countless subsequent amateur detectives. Even Poe was far enough ahead of his time, however, that he enjoyed no contemporary success and very little contemporary influence. He made slightly more impact in France than in America, partly because his work was translated into French by Charles Baudelaire, but while the kind of logical analysis he had attempted to depict was not yet accommodated within legal procedure, let alone the operation of actual police investigations, the scope for its fictional development inevitably remained narrow.

No matter how obvious the moves may seem in long retrospect, therefore, it was by no means easy to bring all the foundation-stones of modern crime fiction together simultaneously. Paul Féval's creation of Gregory Temple is an imaginative masterstroke whose long neglect by genre historians is dreadfully unjust, but it is not surprising that scope still remained for Emile Gaboriau to complete the process of establishing the detective as a key folk-hero of modern times.

Chronology of the Plot and Historical Context

1757

The Marquis of Belcamp is born on May 16.

1762-67

Gregory Temple is born. (He is "50 or 55" in March 1817.)

1770

Helen Brown is born.

1777

Constance Bartolozzi *née* Herbet is born.

1786

Helen's father, Nicholas Brown, dies. Because his partners in the firm of Brown, Turner, Robinson & Co. cannot become her guardians under English law, her father's former solicitor, Mr. Wood, is appointed as her guardian. (Although he seems to be a party to her subsequent ruination, neither she nor her son seems to bear him any grudge.)

1788

Helen Brown is convicted of stealing some diamonds from the Duchess of Devonshire; her cousins, deeply ashamed, liquidate the family firm and leave England, Turner for Lyon and Robinson for Brussels. The Duchess, however, appeals for Helen to be pardoned and takes her in; Helen becomes a star of the social scene.

1789

The French Revolution begins. Louis XVI dismisses Jacques Necker on July 11; the Marquis de Belcamp is a Colonel in the first regiment to march on Paris thereafter, but he refuses to fire on his own countrymen and goes into exile. He meets Helen Brown as the Duchess of Devonshire begins to tire of supporting her.

1790

Gregory Temple first enters the office that becomes his lair. Madeleine Surrisy joins the Marquis de Belcamp's London household; it appears that the Marquis de Belcamp's marriage to Helen Brown follows soon after, although it might have taken place already.

1790-93

Henri de Belcamp is born. (The textual evidence is contradictory; he claims to have been 17 when he presented his doctoral thesis at Edinburgh in 1810, but also says that he was 15–although he looks no more than 12–when he turned up on his father's doorstep in 1805. Henri is born in the year following his parents' marriage, so 1791 may be the most plausible date, although Sarah O'Brien says that he was "only 20" when he went to Australia in 1814; she is probably speaking loosely.)

1793

The Marquis de Belcamp's French estate is sequestered and he loses his income; Helen returns to her life of crime in order to sustain her social life. When her secret is discovered, the Marquis falls ill; he recovers to find her and Henri gone; he subsequently becomes acquainted with Gregory Temple.

Madeleine Surrisy secretly marries Maurice O'Brien.

1794

Robert Surrisy is born. (He has recently learned to walk at the time of Napoleon's Italian campaign in 1796.)

1796

Maurice O'Brien marries Henrietta Boehm after Madeleine tears up her marriage certificate.

1797-99

Sarah O'Brien is born. (She is "18 or 20" in March 1817.)

1798

William Robinson meets Constance Bartolozzi.

1799

Frank Turner meets Constance Bartolozzi.

In November, Napoleon Bonaparte overthrows the Directory and establishes the Consulate.

1800

Jeanne Herbet is born.

1801-02

Ned Knob is born. (He is "15 or 16" in March 1817.)

1804

On December 2, Napoleon I is crowned as Emperor.

1805

Helen Brown, now a member of Thomas Paddock/John Devil's gang, is arrested by Gregory Temple. On the day that she is sent to prison, Henri turns up at the Marquis de Belcamp's house.

1806

The Holy Roman Empire is abolished; its last Emperor, Francis II, becomes Francis I, Emperor of Austria.

1808

Constance Bartolozzi promises to marry William Robinson.

1809

Constance Bartolozzi promises to marry Frank Turner.

1810

In February, Napoleon marries Marie-Louise of Austria. General Maurice O'Brien is condemned to death by the Rosicrucians.

Henri de Belcamp presents his doctoral thesis at Edinburgh University; soon afterwards, he is reunited with his mother and they leave the country, remaining together for a month.

1812

On March 16, General O'Brien seeks out Madeleine Surrisy. The Marquis de Belcamp begins to hear rumors of Henri's "double," Tom Brown, who is said to be the same age.

In June, Napoleon's army marches into Russia, entering Moscow in September, before being forced to begin his retreat therefrom on October 19.

1813

Henri claims to have met Robinson and Turner at a beer festival in Munich, learning that each of them has an illegitimate child, before returning to London.

Later that year, General O'Brien is murdered in Prague while Henri is at the University under the name George Palmer; Sarah O'Brien is abducted immediately afterwards (by Henri) from the schloss at Reichstadt.

On August 12, Austria declares war against Napoleon.

1814

After the allies enter Paris on March 31, Napoleon is forced to abdicate on April 11. The Marquis de Belcamp returns to Miremont.

In June, Helen and Tom Brown are arrested and transported, while Gregory Temple is incapacitated by "morbid cholera." Shortly thereafter, the Marquis de Belcamp receives a letter from his son saying that he too has sailed for New South Wales.

1815

On March 1, Napoleon lands in France, forcing Louis XVIII to flee. On March 20, the Emperor enters Paris and the "Hundred Days" begins. On June 18, Napoleon is defeated at Waterloo, abdicating again four days later. On August 17, Napoleon arrives in St. Helena.

1816

On September 29, Paul Féval is born in Rennes.

1817

In January, following Reiner Boehm's death, Friedrich travels to London; he encounters Henri de Belcamp and visits Constance Bartolozzi's house, where the Council of the Deliverance is awaiting him; he also sees Sarah O'Brien there.

On February 1, Constance Bartolozzi is condemned to death by a meeting of the Council at Mivart's Hotel after sending two letters to Scotland Yard that were intercepted by Henri, who is employed there under the name James Davy. On February 3, the sentence is carried out.

On March 14, Gregory Temple and James Davy interrogate Sarah O'Neil at Scotland Yard. The pamphlet describing the life of John Devil the Quaker is published and Temple resigns as soon as he sees a copy. Ned Knob reads the pamphlet at Sharper's before eavesdropping on the meeting between Noll

Green, Lochaber Dick and the Quaker, after which the Quaker gets into a cab with Richard Thompson, who addresses him as James Davy.

Subsequently, the Quaker calls in at Percy Balcomb & Co., where Perkins brings him up to date on the progress of their projects, and James Davy identifies himself as Comte Henri de Belcamp to the manager of the Buckingham Hotel, where Sarah O'Neil is registered as the Comtesse de Belcamp.

On May 8, Henri arrives at the Château de Belcamp. Richard Thompson and Sarah O'Neil go to *Le Colisée* in Paris, where they are seen by Gregory Temple.

On the night of May 9-10, the Knights of Deliverance meet in Madeleine Surrisy's cottage. (The novel's time-scheme apparently loses two days at this point, for the following night is subsequently identified as that of May 12-13, when Robinson and Turner are simultaneously assassinated in Brussels and Lyon.)

On May 15, Noll Green and Lochaber Dick are killed in Paris, while Henri is absent from the performance of *La Joconde* at the Opéra-Comique, having been tracked to the *Gourmand du jour* and back by Ned Knob.

On May 16, Henri is charged with both these crimes at the Marquis de Belcamp's birthday party.

In July (probably on the 17th or 18th), Gregory Temple meets Pretty Molly in Rosemary Lane, then Friedrich Boehm at Mivart's Hotel; they set out for Paris but are intercepted, arrested and freed on bail. Jeanne Herbet marries "Percy Balcomb," who departs thereafter for England, crossing the Channel with Robert Surrisy in the *Deliverance*.

On July 20 (probably), the Perkins Engine is auctioned to pay off the creditors of Balcomb & Co. At midnight thereafter, Henri changes places with Richard Thompson in Newgate, after which Gregory Temple arrives with the same intention. (Thompson has been in prison for 68 days, but the day of his arrest is slightly confused because of the two missing days in May.)

On July 30, Henri's trial begins in Versailles; following his acquittal, he goes to the Château de Belcamp for his final confrontation with his father.

Late in September, Gregory Temple visits the Marquis de Belcamp to tell him that someone calling himself Tom Brown has been hanged at Newgate after confessing to the murders of General O'Brien and Constance Bartolozzi.

In mid-October, the steamship *J.D.* leaves France for St. Helena; it arrives in early November to display a tricolor, followed by a black flag, to the anxious eyes of Napoleon Bonaparte. Shortly thereafter, England begins the manufacture of the first steam-powered warships.

1862

Jean Diable *is serialized in* Le Siècle *between August 1 and November 28.*

1863

Jean Diable *is reprinted in two volumes by E. Dentu; a second edition is issued in the same year.*

Dramatis Personae

Abercrombie, Edmund, Captain of the *Deliverance*.

Anille, assistant to Madame Etienne.

Arnheim, Doctor, Friedrich Boehm's traveling companion.

Balcomb, Percy, see Belcamp, Comte Henri de.

Bartolozzi, Constance, née Herbet, leading actress at the Princess Theater in London, mother of Jeanne and Laurent.

Belcamp, Comte Henri de, alias James Davy, George Palmer, Henry Brown, Percy Balcomb, John Devil the Quaker, John Gravesend and Tom Brown, a master criminal and polymath. Also poses briefly as Richard Thompson.

Belcamp, Marquis de, Henri's father and Mayor of Miremont.

Belcamp, Marquise de, see Brown, Helen.

Beleuil, a *patache*-conductor operating between Paris and l'Isle-Adam.

Bennett, Timothy, Recorder at Newgate.

Berthelot, Fortuné, Notary of Versailles.

Besnard, "Don Juan," Madame Besnard's son.

Besnard, Madame, a widow of Miremont.

Billy, Lady Elphinstone's groom.

Bird, Jeanie, "maiden chicken" (false witness hired out by Sawney).

Blondeau, the constable of Miremont.

Blunt, industrialist.

Boehm, Count Albrecht, elder brother of Friedrich, cousin of Henrietta and (once removed) of Sarah O'Brien.

Boehm, Count Friedrich, younger brother of Counts Albrecht and Reiner Boehm, cousin of Henrietta Boehm and (once removed) of Sarah O'Brien. Also known (briefly) as Prince Pierre-Alexis Orloff.

Boehm, Count Reiner, elder brother of Friedrich, cousin of Henrietta and (once removed) of Sarah O'Brien.

Boisruel, Vicomte de, Counselor of the Royal Court of Paris, the Marquis de Belcamp's cousin.

Bondon de la Perrière, Célestin and **Florian**, identical twins of the Miremont *société*; Célestin's wife is Madame Célestin.

Brand, industrialist.

Bricole, see Briquet.

Briquet, alias Bricole and Trompe-d'Eustache, a manservant shared by Robert Surrisy, Laurent and Férandeau.

Brown, Helen, cousin of William Robinson and Frank Turner, also the Marquise de Belcamp, alias Lady Rowley and (perhaps) Lady Caroline Dudley.

Brown, Henry, see Belcamp, Comte Henri de.

Brown, Tom, a possibly non-existent criminal probably not related to anyone significant, allegedly hanged at Newgate; see Belcamp, Comte Henri de.

Chaumeron, Cécile, one of the eleven daughters of Monsieur and Madame Chaumeron; another is just referred to as "Mademoiselle."

Chaumeron, Monsieur and **Madame**, members of the Miremont *société*.

Clarke, Joseph, warder in Newgate Prison.

Curé of Miremont, The, Parish priest of Miremont.

Daniel, member of Mr. Wood's domestic staff.

Davy, James, see Belcamp, Comte Henri de and Thompson, Richard.

"Devil, John," see Belcamp, Comte Henri de and Paddock, Thomas.

Dudley, Lady Caroline, see Brown, Helen.

Elphinstone, Edward, see Little Richard.

Elphinstone, Lady Frances, see O'Brien, Sarah.

Etienne, Madame, cook at the Château de Belcamp.

Fanchette, Suzanne Temple's maidservant.

Férandeau, an artist.

Féval, Paul, the provider of the narrative voice.

Forster, Constable, operative at Scotland Yard.

Fortunés, The, staff at No. 19 Rue Dauphine, including Monsieur Fortuné, the porter; Madame Fortuné, his wife, the cook; Coquinet, their son; Bijou, their daughter.

François, gardener-coachman at the Château de Belcamp.

Gauthier, ex-Captain of the Imperial Army, now a crewman of the *Deliverance*.

George III, King of England.

Godinot, Monsieur, Commissioner of Police for l'Isle-Adam, an old school-friend of the Marquis de Belcamp.

Grant, Alastair, proprietor of the Bank Corner oyster-house.

Gravesend, John, see Belcamp, Comte Henri de and Thompson, Richard.

Green, Noll, boxer, ex-convict and hired assassin.

Green, Solomon, see Temple, Gregory.

Herbet, Jeanne, daughter of Constance Bartolozzi and either Frank Turner or William Robinson.

Herbet, Laurent, Jeanne's older brother.

Hoary, Inspector, operative at Scotland Yard.

Huchon, Monsieur, clerk of the Court of Versailles.

John, "maiden chicken" (false witness hired out by Sawney).

Julot, assistant to Madame Etienne.

Kate, member of Mr. Wood's domestic staff.

Knob, Ned, former clerk to Mr. Wood.

Lisbeth, Lady Elphinstone's seamstress.

Little Richard, Richard Thompson and Suzanne Temple's son. Poses (unknowingly) as Edward Elphinstone.

Lochaber Dick, professional ale-drinker, ex-convict and hired assassin.

Lointier, ex-Major of the *Deliverance*.

Loo, member of Mr. Wood's domestic staff.

Louchet, Pierre, woodcutter and former corporal in the Imperial Army.

MacAllan, Sir Paulus, Gregory Temple's successor as Chief Superintendent of the Metropolitan Police.

Milk, industrialist.

Morin du Reposoir, Saturnin, Deputy Mayor of Miremont.

Morin, Madame, his wife, nicknamed "Many-Apologies."

Napoleon Bonaparte, French Emperor, exiled to St. Helena.

Numph, "maiden chicken" (false witness hired out by Sawney).

O'Brien, Maurice, General, husband of Madeleine Surrisy and Henrietta Boehm, murdered in Prague.

O'Brien, Sarah, daughter of General O'Brien and Henrietta Boehm, alias Sarah O'Neil, Lady Frances Elphinstone and Françoise O'Meara, nicknamed "the beautiful Irishwoman."

O'Meara, Françoise, see O'Brien, Sarah.

O'Neil, Sarah, see O'Brien, Sarah.

Orloff, Prince Pierre-Alexis, see Boehm, Count Friedrich.

Paddock, Jenny, widow of Thomas Paddock and proprietor of Sharper's.

Paddock, Thomas, nicknamed John Devil, the proprietor of Will Sharper's Spirit Shop.

Palmer, George, see Belcamp, Comte Henri de.

Perkins, ex-convict and inventor of a new kind of steam engine.

Pierre, manservant at the Château de Belcamp.

Potel, Germaine, Guillaume's daughter.

Potel, Guillaume, Deputy Mayor of Miremont.

Powells, industrialist.

"Pretty Molly," Ned Knob's mistress, a former coal-heaver.

Prince Regent, The, George III's son.

Princess Caroline, the Prince Regent's wife.

Prudence, Lady Elphinstone's chambermaid.

"Quaker, The," see Belcamp, Comte Henri de.

Renault, ex-Lieutenant of the Imperial Army, now a crewman of the *Deliverance*.

Robinson, William, brewer, one-time partner of Helen Brown's father, Nicholas, who moves to Lyon following Helen's disgrace.

Roblot, Monsieur, Deputy Governor of Versailles Prison.

Rowley, Lady, see Brown, Helen.

Sam, Lady Elphinstone's coachman.

Sam, "maiden chicken" (false witness hired out by Sawney).

Satan, the alleged father of John Devil the Quaker, according to a scurrilous pamphlet probably written by Comte Henri de Belcamp.

Saunder, Alastair Grant's employee.

Sawney, a broker of false witnesses and judge in the mock tribunal.

Schwartz, Dr., a possibly-imaginary former doctor operating a station in Australia.

Schwartz, Georgelle, his probably-imaginary daughter.

Spiegel, Doctor, Friedrich Boehm's traveling companion.

Sultan, a guard-dog at the Château de Belcamp.

Surrisy, Madeleine, one-time servant of the Marquis de Belcamp in London; first wife of Maurice O'Brien and mother of Robert.

Surrisy, Robert, the son of Madeleine Surrisy and General O'Brien, former Sub-Lieutenant in the Imperial Army

Temple, Gregory, detective; some-time Chief Superintendent of Scotland Yard and author of *The Art of Discovering the Guilty*. Poses briefly as Solomon Green.

Temple, Suzanne, Gregory's daughter and (secretly) wife of Richard Thompson; mother of Little Richard.

Thompson, Fanny, actress; Richard's mother.

Thompson, Richard, Gregory Temple's some-time secretary and (secretly) husband of Suzanne; father of Little Richard. Poses briefly as James Davy and as John Gravesend. Also see Belcamp, Comte Henri de.

Toby, "maiden chicken" (false witness hired out by Sawney).

Trompe-d'Eustache, see Briquet.

Turkey, Sir Alexander, Governor of Newcastle Penitentiary in Australia.

Turner, Frank, brewer, one-time partner of Helen Brown's father, Nicholas, who moves to Lyon following Helen's disgrace.

Walter, Sir Paulus MacAllan's valet.

Weber, Doctor, Friedrich Boehm's traveling companion.

White, J. N., a physician.

Will, "maiden chicken" (false witness hired out by Sawney).

Wood, J. H., one-time solicitor to Nicholas Brown; Helen Brown's guardian following her father's death; Ned Knob's some-time employer.

Notes

Foreword

[1] Féval is not the only claimant to this particular honor; there are a few English contenders similarly inspired by the successful institution of Scotland Yard. Chambers' *Journal* published an anonymous account of *The Recollections of a Police Officer* in 1849-52, although little detective work is featured therein, and Charles Dickens' *Bleak House* (1852-53) gives a very minor part to a professional detective named Bucket, whose role amounts to little more than passing on the results of enquiries made by a solicitor. Wilkie Collins' *The Moonstone*, featuring Sergeant Cuff, was not published until 1868 but Collins had earlier published a humorous short story, *"The Biter Bit"* (1858), whose central characters are Chief Inspector Theakstone and Sergeant Bulmer of the "Detective Police." They solve a robbery, although they do not use a logical method– interestingly, their amateur rival, Sharpin, attempts unsuccessfully to do so, and fails spectacularly. Féval does appear to have been the first writer to feature a professional detective using a method of logical analysis in a full-length novel, and this is surely the most important precedent.

[2] More information about *Les Habits Noirs* can be found in J.-M. & Randy Lofficier's book *Shadowmen* (ISBN 0-9740711-3-7), also available from Black Coat Press.

[3] Forthcoming from Black Coat Press in 2005.

[4] Emile Gaboriau (1832-1873) introduced the character of Monsieur Lecoq in *L'Affaire Lerouge* (*The Lerouge Affair*) in 1866. Interestingly, one of the leading members of the Black Coats is also named Lecoq.

[5] Forster, E. M., *Aspects of the Novel*. London: Edward Arnold, 1927. cf Chapters 2 and 5.

[6] *Knightshade* (ISBN 0-9740711-45), *Vampire City* (ISBN 0-9740711-6-1) and *The Vampire Countess* (ISBN 0-9740711-5-3), also available from Black Coat Press.

Prologue
Chapter I

[7] The Metropolitan Police, whose headquarters in 4 Whitehall Place had a door that let out into Great Scotland Yard, had not yet been founded in 1817; Robert Peel created the force in 1829. Later in the chapter, we discover that Temple has been at Scotland Yard for 27 years (since 1790), so Féval's alternative history is quite extensive, at least insofar as it pertains to English law-enforcement. Féval gives Temple's rank as *Intendant Supérieur*, which I have translated as "Chief Superintendent" as there was no such rank in the Metropolitan Police when it was first created, the senior official at the Whitehall Place headquarters being

the Police Commissioner, but the literal translation seems reasonable in view of the fact that we are dealing with an imaginary institution.

[8] The anatomist Franz Joseph Gall (1758-1828) was convinced that cerebral functions were localized, so that protrusions of the skull were indicative of pronounced mental faculties; his system, which he called *craniology*, was renamed *phrenology* by his followers.

[9] The parish of St. Giles's, whose name is preserved by a road to the south of what is now New Oxford Street, was long notorious for poverty and vice.

[10] George "Beau" Brummell (1778-1840)–Féval has "Brummel"–was the celebrated English dandy who pioneered various fashions of male dress adopted into common usage in the 19th century.

[11] A form of torture once applied to prisoners who refused to plead to a charge in an attempt to save their property from confiscation should they be found guilty. It involved placing the reluctant prisoner between two boards and piling heavy stones on the upper one. A graphic description can be found in Victor Hugo's historical novel *L'Homme qui rit* (1869; tr. as *The Man Who Laughs*), which appears to have been Hugo's response to the manner in which various feuilletonists had made free use of the substance of his early works. In a subsequent footnote, Féval claims (perhaps mistakenly) that the Press was still in use in Newgate and in the Fleet in 1820.

[12] The Marquis of Vauban (1633-1707) was a famous military engineer and Marshal of France, whose sieges were invariably successful and whose fortifications–arrayed along the northern frontier–were reputedly impregnable.

[13] The Chevalier de Saint-Georges (1745-1799), who was as famous a musician as he was a fencer, was a pillar of pre-Revolutionary high society.

[14] The reference is to *Exodus* 7:12, when the serpent made from Aaron's rod swallows those made from the wands of the Pharaoh's sorcerers.

[15] William Hogarth (1697-1764) was an English painter and engraver who satirized the follies of his age.

Chapter II

[16] The French word *brasseur* (*brewer*) is also used in a loose sense to mean "*businessman*," so *brasseurs fidèles* can also mean something like "*honest brokers*."

[17] "*Booths*" seems more likely, but as Féval takes the trouble to translate his *boîtes* as "*boxes*," I've taken his word for it.

[18] Féval has *kari*; there is no such word in French and the only meaning recorded by Webster's International Dictionary (an alternative spelling of *karri*, a kind of eucalyptus) seems irrelevant, so I have taken a guess that he is attempting a phonetic rendering of a then-esoteric import of the British East India Company.

[19] Wolfgang Amadeus Mozart's opera *Die Entführung aus dem Serail* (1782), which was also adapted as a ballet, is known in English as *The Abduction from*

the Seraglio and in French as *La Révolte au Sérail*. I have retained Féval's French title as the two brewers saw it performed in Lyon and Brussels. The opera tells the story of the capture of a beautiful Spanish maiden, Constanze, by a 16th century Turkish Pasha. It was considered rather scandalous at the time.

Chapter III

[20] Joseph Lancaster (1778-1838) was a famous educationalist; the "mutual" or monitorial system, which he developed in association with Andrew Bell and Jean-Baptiste Girard, involved the use of older and more proficient pupils to help in the tuition of their fellows. His first school was actually established south of the Thames, in Southwark, in 1798. At the height of his fame, there were 95 Lancastrian schools in operation, but he quarrelled with his trustees and emigrated to the USA in 1818.

[21] François-Joseph Talma (1763-1826) was Napoleon's favorite tragedian; he appeared in Shakespearean roles at Drury Lane, on the far side of Covent Garden from the rookery Féval describes.

[22] Since Féval claims to have seen this unlikely legend with his own eyes, I have retained it as written; he adds a note at this point to explain that it could be translated into French as Cabaret de Guillaume Filou, which I have omitted.

[23] Johannisberger and Lachryma Christi are fine wines, the former Rhenish and the latter Neapolitan.

[24] The double entendre implied by *doreur* (gilder) is less obvious than the one implied by the references to the prince regent's "night-cap," but imaginative readers will doubtless be able to make their own judgment as to what it was that Princess Caroline used to "make a frame" for John Devil.

[25] Canning was actually a Tory.

[26] Jack Sheppard (1702-1724) became the most famous thief in England, despite his manifest incompetence, because of his escapes from custody, including one from the theoretically inescapable depths of Newgate prison. He featured in several theatrical productions before the historical novelist W. Harrison Ainsworth cashed in on his legend in *Jack Sheppard* (1839). Unlike Sheppard, Robin Lewis and Jeremy Drummer are not mentioned in the Newgate Calendar or its sequel, so Féval probably invented them.

[27] *Bière cuite*, which I have translated as "warm beer," is susceptible of more sinister readings; *bière* also means coffin; *cuite* signifies cooked rather than warm.

Chapter IV

[28] Féval has "*une anguille sous roche*," a conventional phrase whose literal translation is "an eel under the rock."

[29] There is an actual Exmouth in Devon, whose name Féval presumably borrowed rather than trying to figure out where on the Thames a smuggler's vessel

might actually be lurking. The continental landing-places of the two "old hands" are also fictitious.

[30] The tilbury has presumably turned left into Sloane Street, the hospital to which Féval refers must be the Royal Hospital, which is beyond Cadogan Square to the south.

Part One: The Chateau de Belcamp
Chapter I

[31] The London sewers, one of the great achievements of Victorian engineering, were still in the future when Feval wrote *Jean Diable*, let alone in 1817; the ever-increasing amounts of raw sewage pumped into the upper Thames, much of which accumulated on its banks to either side of the city of London because of the tidal counterflow, was a major problem for the city's denizens and visitors throughout the early 19th century.

[32] The founder of French Classicism, Jacques Louis David (1748-1825) had, in fact, won the Grand Prix de Rome in 1775 after two unsuccessful attempts; he returned to Paris in 1780, after which he became court painter to Louis XVI before entering wholeheartedly into the spirit of the Revolution; he eventually became Napoleon's court painter.

[33] *Trompe-d'Eustache* is the Eustachian tube, which connects the middle ear with the nasopharynx, enabling the pressure on either side of the eardrum to be equalized. At the time when Féval was writing, a *briquet* was literally a tinder-box, although it was used colloquially to signify a loyal friend, much as "brick" was once used in English. A *bricole* was either a breast-strap or a ricochet, so this individual's nicknames offer a richly confused harvest of implications.

[34] The *ranz-des-vaches* is a Swiss pastoral melody.

[35] Henri IV, born in 1553, was King of France from 1589 until his assassination in 1610–a time whose turbulence was akin to that of two centuries later in that France was split by wars of religion.

Chapter II

[36] Bucephalus was Alexander the Great's favorite horse.

[37] Frenchmen are routinely named after the saint on whose day their birthday falls, although they usually have other forenames as well; we shall discover subsequently that the Marquis' familiar name is Armand. St. Honoré is far better known in France–and his name far more widely preserved–than elsewhere in Europe, and May 16 is still celebrated there by some bakers, whose patron saint he is.

[38] Mercury fulminate, discovered in 1779 and used thereafter as a primer for gunpowder, was renowned for its instability; it was not until 1865 that Alfred Nobel incorporated it into the first practical blasting-caps.

[39] This pun is just about translatable into English, which also adopted the term *pistole* for the Spanish coin of that name.

[40] The reference is to *The Rake's Progress*.

[41] The Marquis de Lafayette (1757-1834) was a famous French general and statesman who enlisted in the American Revolutionary Army as a volunteer in 1777. He was a Royalist member of the States General when the Revolution began and was commander-in-chief of the National Guard from 1789-91. He left France in 1792 because of his opposition to the Jacobins and did not return until 1800. Jacques Necker (1732-1804) was the French statesman who convened the States-General in 1789 and was dismissed on the indicated date; he was briefly recalled thereafter but resigned again in September 1790.

[42] The first Almack's was a famous gambling club established in Pall Mall by William Almack in 1763. The name was subsequently applied (as it is here) to the assembly rooms Almack opened in King Street, Saint James's, in 1765. "At the beginning of [the 19th] century," the Dictionary of National Biography claims "it was described as 'the seventh heaven of the fashionable world' "–a status it retained until 1840.

[43] It was not unknown at that time for children as young as Henri to be placed in the care of a university; it had happened to Féval following the death of his father–and it is possible that the text's confusion as to how old Henri is may be due to Féval's confusing the age at which Henri supposedly went to Edinburgh with the age at which he went to college in Rennes.

[44] Dugald Stewart (1753-1828) was a Scottish philosopher whose most noted work was a three-volume study of *Elements of the Philosophy of the Human Mind* (1792, 1814 and 1827). His first chair at Edinburgh was in mathematics (1775), to which he added the chair of moral philosophy in 1785, eventually retiring in 1810.

[45] Thomas Reid (1710-1796) was the principal founder of the school of Scottish philosophy to which Stewart belonged; he wrote several pioneering books on the philosophy of mind and the powers of the intellect.

[46] Claude-François, Marquis de Jouffroy d'Abbans (1751-1832) and his son Achille, Comte de Jouffroy d'Abbans (1785-1859) were men to whom Féval frequently referred in his novels. The younger of the two is mentioned in *The Vampire Countess* [Black Coat Press, 2003] because he was the original adapter of a three-act melodrama based on John Polidori's novella *The Vamypre*, which was produced at the Théâtre de la Porte-Martin in 1820, having been extensively rewritten in the interim by Charles Nodier and the theater's manager [collected in *Lord Ruthven the Vampire*, Black Coat Press, 2004]. The Marquis de Jouffroy's early experiments with steam engines were bedevilled by bankruptcies

and political troubles (including imprisonment and exile) but he built the first working model of a steamboat in 1778, then built a full-scale version, the *Pyroscaphe*, which was launched on the Saône near Lyon in 1783. When the American inventor Robert Fulton exhibited a steamboat on the Seine in 1803, he acknowledged his debt and credited Jouffroy with being the true inventor of the steamboat. The Comte de Jouffroy continued his father's work alongside a more successful career as a journalist. If the Marquis de Jouffroy had not experienced such violent financial and political upheavals, the history of steam locomotion might have been very different—an awareness that underlies the later phases of *John Devil*'s plot.

[47] Victor Cousin (1792-1867) would not have been well known in 1817, at which time he had not yet published any of his philosophical works, although he had begun teaching at the Sorbonne in 1815. Like the others named, however, he was readily describable as an "eclectic" by virtue of his intellectual versatility.

Chapter V

[48] When Louis IX went off crusading in 1249, he disembarked in Egypt at Damietta, on the coast of the Nile delta, to which he laid siege. Rossbach was the village in Saxony where a Prussian army led by Frederick the Great crushed a combined French and Imperialist army in 1757.

[49] Féval adds a footnote at this point reminding his readers that the whole of this report relates to conditions in Australia at the beginning of the century, when women were not yet routinely subject to transportation. By the time he wrote *John Devil* this had changed—not, in this respect, for the better.

[50] There was, in fact, only one sea-monster for whose benefit Andromeda was chained to a rock by her father Cepheus; Perseus killed the monster and married her.

[51] Paramatta, or Parramatta, was then a small town 14 miles northwest of Sydney, on the river of the same name; it has now been absorbed by the city.

[52] Tophet was situated at the southwestern extreme of the valley of Hinnon, also known as Gehenna; because idolatrous Jews sacrificed children to Moloch there (cf 2 Kings 23:10), the name became symbolic of a place of future torment (cf Isaiah 30:33) that formed a model for the Christian Hell.

[53] Féval has "Muhlleton." Lord Howe Island, about 500 miles from Sydney—mentioned later in the chapter—would have been a more likely stopping-point than Middleton, which is much further north; Norfolk Island is a further 500 miles away from either, and would have been extremely difficult to locate or reach in the kind of craft Henri describes.

Chapter VI

[54] Bobèche and Galimafré were two famous circus clowns of the period, still active and in vogue in 1817, having begun their careers in the 1790s. In literal

terms, a *bobêche* (Féval wrongly attributes a circumflex accent to the e in the clown's name) is the socket into which a candle is fitted or the drip-tray that collects the wax; a *galimafrée* is a gallimaufry (i.e., a hotchpotch) or the combination of holding one's breath and then letting it out; the words were adapted into names by the clowns because they were conventionally used as semi-affectionate terms of abuse.

[55] *Reposoir* means "resting-place"; it is used here in a parody of aristocratic nomenclature. The English equivalent might involve referring to a couple retired from a successful career in trade as "Lord and Lady Jones of Dunroamin."

[56] The first version of *The Menaechmes*, also known in French as *Les Jumeaux–The Twins*, in English–was a comedy by Plautus; it formed the basis of a similarly-titled piece by the leading French dramatist of his era, Jean-François Régnard (1665-1709) and was the principal source of Shakespeare's *Comedy of Errors*.

[57] As the word *garniture* does exist in English, and for want of a better one, I have retained Féval's term. It is used in French and English to refer to any assembly of "trimmings," including (as here) those that might be used to dress a mantelpiece.

[58] *Mons mirabilis* means "marvelous mountain"; the "mire" part of Miremont's name is highly unlikely to have been derived by Féval from the English word, and French readers would have been far more likely to associate it with the French *mire*, which refers to a gunsight (*mirer* means taking aim). Indeed, the Miremontese society introduced in this passage provides Féval with a means of taking satirical aim at conventional targets of contemporary disdain, at which he happily blasts away.

[59] Robert Lovelace is Clarissa Harlowe's despoiler and effective murderer in Samuel Richardson's novel *Clarissa* (1748-49). Richardson had a greater reputation in France than in his own country, and Féval often used "Lovelace" as a generic term for rakish rapists.

Chapter VIII

[60] Féval has *haute vie*, which he obligingly translates as "high life," before going on to explain that that is what the English call their aristocracy. As this is not true, it seems sensible to avoid the circumlocution and omit the explanation.

[61] Féval has "Iona" rather than Ierna, "Millet" rather than Miletus, and "Tyr" rather than Tyre. The names reflect a common confusion; the inhabitants of ancient Ireland, like the inhabitants of Miletus in Ionia, were described as "Milesians"–but they first acquired that name because they were supposedly descended from a legendary Spanish King named Milesius, not because they supposedly came from Miletus. Féval was by no means the first person to make this mistake, however. His subsequent account of the derivation of the names Neil, Brien, Connor and Diarmid similarly employs a good deal of poetic licence; he

may be mocking James Macpherson's fake Ossianic epics rather than imitating them, although it is possible that this was one of the few enthusiasms he and Napoleon had in common.

[62] Aspasia, born in Miletus, was a famous beauty of the 5th century B.C. In Athens, she became the mistress of Pericles, and her house became the center of Athenian literary and philosophical society.

[63] I cannot tell which of Connemara's many hills is indicated by this rather unlikely label.

[64] Féval appears to have forgotten that John Devil's beloved was described in the pamphlet as "*la belle Ecossaise*" (the beautiful Scotswoman), not "*la Belle Irlandaise*" (which I have translated as the Irish Beauty, on the assumption that the effect of the additional capital letter is to transform the adjective into a noun), as he writes here and at the head of the chapter. Sarah O'Neil had, of course, been described by the narrative voice as "la belle Irlandaise" (the beautiful Irishwoman). In a much later chapter, Gregory Temple will allege that Sarah O'Neil is "*la belle Irlandaise*" who is notorious as John Devil's mistress, but it is unclear how he reaches this conclusion.

[65] In order to assist me in resisting the strong temptation to censor this discomfiting comparison, I recalled the speech made by the young hero of Roddy Doyle's *The Commitments*, which proclaims in ringing tones—as the justification for the founding of a Dublin soul band—that the Irish are the blacks of Europe (and Dubliners the blacks of Ireland). The comment that follows in Féval's discourse is, of course, entirely untrue; all Americans love the Irish, especially on St. Patrick's Day.

[66] *Grisette* is usually employed in French fiction as a double entendre; its literal reference is to the smock of a female laborer, but in Bohemian Paris the label was attached to "kept women" one step removed from the status of streetwalkers.

[67] Surrisy's name is reminiscent of smiling because it resembles a derivative of *sourire*; the pun is untranslatable. I have chosen to translate Féval's "*veux dire*" as "trying to say" or "wishes to say" rather than the more conventional "means" because Surrisy does not actually mean "smile".

[68] A French reader would surely realize, although Lady Frances and Richard Thompson apparently do not, what Surrisy actually means. It is surprising, in view of the context in which she first heard his name, that Frances could possibly imagine that he had in mind a dance hall named after the Colosseum rather than the Roman original, where gladiatorial combats were staged.

Chapter X

[69] It was presumably Ambroise Hozier (1764-1830)—the last of an appropriately long line of famous genealogists—who was acquainted with the Marquis de Belcamp.

[70] Jean-François Régnard, as cited in Note 56 above.

[71] In addition to its other museums and art galleries, 19th-century Munich had its specialist glyptotheque (a collection of sculptures) and pinacotheque (a collection of paintings).

Chapter XI

[72] The reader will remember that the Chateau de Belcamp was introduced as having been built in the time of Henri IV, whose assassin was Ravaillac.

[73] Féval has the cook say that there is *"une anguille de Melun sous roche,"* thus adding the name of the Seine town of Melun to the phrase previously used in chapter IV of the Prologue; I have used what seems to me the most appropriate English equivalent in these circumstances.

[74] Wagram is a village northeast of Vienna where Napoleon's army defeated the Austrian army of Archduke Charles in 1809.

[75] The *Carbonari* (literally charcoal-burners) were a secret society formed in Naples during the reign of Murat (1808-15) by Republicans dissatisfied with French rule. Once the French had been expelled, the movement spread throughout Italy as a liberal opposition to the reactionary government. Carbonarism spread into France in 1820 and played a significant role in French politics until the Revolution of 1830.

[76] Sir Hudson Lowe (1769-1844) was a British General appointed Governor of St. Helena when Napoleon was exiled there in 1815.

[77] Barry Edward O'Meara (1786-1836) was Napoleon's physician on St. Helena; he published an account of Napoleon in Exile in 1822.

[78] Longwood was a farmhouse in the interior of St. Helena that was Napoleon's residence during his exile.

[79] The Comte de Las-Cases (1766-1842) was a French historian who followed Napoleon to St. Helena, where he began recording the Emperor's memoirs. He was expelled from the island in November 1816 and imprisoned in the Cape colony for attempting to forward a letter to Lucien Bonaparte without the Commandant's knowledge.

Chapter XII

[80] This meaning of the French *muscade* is difficult to translate. It refers to the trick in which a little ball is concealed under one of three "thimbles" or upturned cups, which are then shuffled; when a member of the audience is asked to identify the thimble under which the ball is hidden, it is never there. The most popular English version is, of course, the infamous "three-card monte" trick, but it would hardly be apt to compare the attempted rescue of Napoleon to a game of "find the lady."

Chapter XIII

[81] Lady Frances is sometimes descibed as a *victomesse* and sometimes as a *comtesse*. If Lady Frances really had been the wife of a viscount or an earl, her own title would have been Frances, Lady Elphinstone; she could only be Lady Frances Elphinstone if she were the daughter of a duke, Marquis or earl, which she is not even pretending to be. I have translated Féval's titles literally, even though they are mistaken.

[82] Louis XIV had a chateau at Marly-le-roi in Seine-et-Oise, not far from Versailles; Louis was, of course, nicknamed the Sun King.

[83] Presumably Jean-Jacques Rousseau (1712-78), who was one of the instrument's most notable advocates.

[84] Louis Dominique Cartouche (c.1693-1721) was a famous robber whose career–cut short when he was broken on the wheel–became the subject of several plays, like Jack Sheppard in England.

Chapter XIV

[85] *Le jeu de l'oie*–literally, "the goose game"–was a primitive board-game played with dice, akin to the modern Snakes and Ladders; although it is no longer played by children, it is fondly remembered by historians and can be played on-line.

[86] Lotto was the usual English name in the early 19th century of the game that eventually evolved into "housey-housey" or bingo.

[87] I have left this name as Féval has it because I cannot identify a likely equivalent on modern maps; there is a town called Rhodes in New South Wales, but it is not in the position indicated.

[88] Austerlitz, in 1805, was the crucial battle in Napoleon's Austrian campaign, after which the Peace of Pressburg was signed.

[89] There are, in fact, no monkeys in Australia, nor any marsupial equivalents; it is possible that Féval is thinking about koalas. Strictly speaking, there are no squirrels either, but the term is loose enough to be applicable to various local species.

Chapter XV

[90] Genesis 29.

[91] I cannot identify the game Féval refers to as *vingt-quatre*. It may be a three-player variant of *Tarot*, in which each of the players is dealt 24 cards.

[92] This is a convoluted joke; *été* and *poule*, in addition to their literal meanings (summer and chicken) are terms applied to particular maneuvers in a quadrille–which is of course, a "square dance" in which partners are regularly exchanged. These two are also known as the *main gauche* and the *main droite*, so there is a mild perversity in Madame Célestin's reserving the former to the right-hand Bondon and the latter to the left-hand one. The literal meaning of *pastourelle* is

shepherdess, while *chassé-croisé* is the French equivalent of "take your partners," thus achieving a similar inversion of expectation in the Bondons' scrupulously unconventional arrangement.

Chapter XVI

[93] Féval renders the final sentence into English.

[94] Goritz was then the capital of the tiny Austro-Hungarian crownland of Goritz
and Gradiska, which lay between Carniola and Italy, not far from Trieste.

Chapter XVII

[95] The first reference here is to the Roman general Marius, who was driven out
of Rome in 88 B.C. but found no solace in the ruins of Carthage and returned to
take his revenge a year later, while the second is presumably to Milton's *Paradise Lost*. The lead-up to the citation, however, might well have reminded
Féval's readers of Victor Hugo's *Les Misérables*, published a few months earlier
which also features a character called Marius. Hugo's Marius is the fiancé of
Cosette, the adopted daughter of Jean Valjean; Valjean saves Marius' life by
carrying him through the sewers of Paris in one of the novel's most famous
scenes.

[96] The reference is obviously to the Jacobite rising of 1745; the rebels who
joined forces with "Bonnie Prince Charlie," the Young Pretender, included
Macdonald of Glencoe, but his forename was not Bryan. The only Bryan Macdonald I can locate in the 18th century died in 1707, long before George II came
to the throne.

[97] Jacques Mallet du Pan (1749-1800) founded a political journal in Paris in
1783 and was forced to flee to England in 1792. The reference may, however, be
misspelled; if so, the intended referee is likely to be General Claude-François de
Malet (1754-1812), who plotted to take over the government in 1812 and was
shot.

[98] Georges Cadoudal (1771-1804) was a famous Chouan partisan; he features as
a character in *The Vampire Countess*.

[99] Jacques Clément (1565-1589) assassinated Henri III in 1589.

[100] Robert Damiens (1715-1757) was executed in an extremely brutal and messy
fashion after attempting to assassinate Louis XV.

[101] Louis Mandrin (1724-1755) was a bandit whose name was often coupled
with that of Cartouche.

[102] The bandit nicknamed Poulailler (the literal meaning of the word is "chicken-
farm") flourished at a later date than Cartouche and Mandrin, but achieved comparable celebrity a decade or so before the Revolution.

[103] The literal meaning of *patache*, in this context, is a public coach; in familiar usage, however–presumably for that very reason–the word always carries the implication of a run-down vehicle perpetually liable to break down.

[104] The Directory was the five-man body which formed the executive power of France from November 1795 until the *coup d'état* of 18 Brumaire 1799.

[105] Sannois is the local vintage in the area where the story is set; the reference to its quality is ironic–Suresnes wines had fallen into such notoriety by the 19th century that the first (1872) edition of Larousse described them forthrightly as "*très-laxatif et très-médiocre*".

[106] In stark contrast to his claim to be a plain speaker–by which he actually means that he is downright rude–Chaumeron's exclamations are exceptionally difficult to translate. *Tapé* can be rendered with reasonable equivalence as "too right" but *Attrape!* is rarely used in circumstances that would license its nearest equivalent ("Tricky!") and *Atout!*–here and elsewhere rendered as "Trump!"–is even more awkward. An *atout* is, indeed, what the French card-players call a trump, so I have adopted that meaning with the implication that Chaumeron employs it as a cry of triumph.

[107] This gross double entendre is slightly more subtle in French, where the phrase might just about be construed as a reference to the purchase of candles.

[108] Alcibiades was an Athenian general and statesman famed for his willful and capricious temperament.

[109] The reference to carnival is to its original meaning ("farewell to meat") in the context of the last day of feasting before the Lenten fast.

[110] Romulus, the legendary founder of Rome, fought against Tatius, the legendary King of the Sabines, whose women had been abducted by the Romans; their combat is represented in a famous painting by David, and would therefore have been a natural subject for one of his pupils. David painted an equally celebrated rendition of *The Oath of the Horatii*, whose battle with the three Curiaces is also mentioned here.

[111] The English equivalent would be "The Sucking Calf."

[112] Férandeau refers to the Opéra-Comique as the Théâtre Feydeau because it was located in the Passage Feydeau; the great farceur of that name was not born until much later.

Chapter XIX

[113] The literal translation of this establishment's name is "The Gourmand of the Day."

[114] A *roulade* is a kind of musical performance that one might indeed expect to hear from actresses playing princesses on the stage of the Opéra-Comique, but it has several other meanings capable of contributing nuances to this climactic double entendre; the nearest English equivalent might be "a roll in the hay."

Although the Palais-Royal was a mere pleasure-garden in 1817–and had been associated with the Orleans family rather than the Bourbons in former times–the suggestion of the previous paragraph that "the entire Palais-Royal" was a front for prostitution under the Restoration was the kind of cynical suggestion that Napoleon III's censors were more than happy to tolerate.

[115] Charles-Guillaume Etienne (1777-1845) was a popular dramatist of the day, who was involved in controversy when he was accused of plagiarizing the work that got him elected to the Academy, *Les Deux Gendres* (1810); the musical play *Joconde; ou, les coureurs d'aventures*–the title is the French name of the picture better known in English as the Mona Lisa–was first produced in 1814.

[116] Jean-Blaise Martin (1768-1837) was the Opéra-Comique's leading singer in this period, and did indeed top the bill in *Joconde*. François Elleviou (1769-1842), a singer from Féval's home town of Rennes, and Alexandrine-Marie-Agathe Gavaudan (1781-1850) are highly likely to have been on the same cast, although Mme. Gavaudan's more famous husband, Jean-Baptiste-Sauveur Gavaudan (1781-1850) would not.

[117] This passage is obviously allegorical; the explicit association of the star with the Legion d'honneur instituted in 1802 by Napoleon presumably explains its symbolism, while Féval–a Breton with a strong affection for his native region–would have maintained a profound regard for the Breton rose used as a emblem by the chouans who had fought against the revolutionaries. The fact that the champion of the rose is identified as a regular at the Café Valois (the Valois being the French royal family which preceded the Bourbons) reinforces the suggestion that it is here being employed as a symbol of royalty.

[118] Hop o'my Thumb is the usual English translation of *Petit Poucet*, the eponymous hero one of Perrault's classic fairy-tales.

[119] This character is mangling his diction because he is English, and his French is terrible. The subsequent items of dialogue given in italics are given in English by Féval, and reproduced without amendment except for the correction of one seeming typographical error (rogue for rogne) whose inclusion might have been a joke; "*me rogne*" is translatable as "clip me."

Chapter XX

[120] The River Meander–from which the word "meandering" derives–was in Asia Minor.

[121] Paphos was the old capital of Cyprus, but there are two sites routinely called by that name and a third set of ruins that is even older than Palea (i.e. Old) Paphos, which is thought to be the city's first incarnation. Palea Paphos housed a famous temple of Venus (or Astarte in pre-Roman times) while the more recent was a commercial center; the suggestion of the phrase in the text, unsurprisingly, is that the women cited were whores.

[122] A spencer–named after the second Earl Spencer (1758-1834)–was a short, close-fitting jacket initially worn by men but soon adopted by women and children. The term was also applied to a kind of wig.

[123] Rosine is the ward of Doctor Bartholo in Beaumarchais' comedy *Le Barbier de Séville* (1775), which became the basis for several operas, the second and most famous by Rossini (premièred in 1816 but not presented in Paris until 1819).

Chapter XXI

[124] Feval has "*agapes universelles*"; the religious sense of *agape* ("love-feast") refers to the celebration of communion with bread symbolizing the flesh of Christ; as previously mentioned, St. Honoré is the patron saint of bakers.

[125] Gamache's wedding–an expression used in France as a proverbial description of a lavish feast–refers to an episode in Cervantes' *Don Quixote*.

[126] Charles-Maurice de Talleyrand-Périgord (1754-1838) was one of the most famous–and most versatile and wily–French statesmen of the day. First elected to the States-General in 1789 he quarrelled with Napoleon and played a leading role in the Restoration.

[127] Féval has "*académico-bonnetière*," the second element of which refers specifically to the hosiery business.

[128] The French *fée*, literally "fairy," here translated by "a bit of witch," also features in the phrase "*vieille fée*," which is equivalent to the English "old hag."

[129] This is one of many manifestations of the conjoined-yet-divided nature of Miremontese society, which Féval goes to some lengths to symbolize and emphasize (although the Constable is presumably confused because he is drunk). First Consul was Napoleon's title before he declared himself Emperor; the "Imperial family" consisted in 1817 of Napoleon's second wife, Marie-Louise–the daughter of the Austrian Emperor Francis II–and her son, the so-called King of Rome, of whom we shall hear more later in the story.

[130] Féval has *éployée*, which–according to Larousse–can only be correctly used to refer to the extension of an eagle's wings. The sarcasm of applying it to the tail of a dindon (turkey-cock) is redoubled by the fact that the latter term is commonly used to mean "fool."

[131] The 300 Spartans who made their stand at Thermopylae (along with 700 Thespians) against Xerxes' invading army of Persians in 480 B.C. were all killed. Féval appears to have confused this event with the battle of Marathon ten years earlier, from which a runner was sent to Sparta to obtain support for the Athenians, who won the battle without them; legend has it that a runner (perhaps the same one) was then sent to Athens to report the victory but dropped dead on arrival.

[132] A rogatory commission is one established to interrogate witnesses.

[133] Themis was a Greek goddess who personified law, order and abstract justice.

[134] The French title of the second part, *Le procès criminel*, has slightly different implications from its most obvious translation, in that the French system gives judges greater powers and responsibilities of investigation. It could, therefore, be translated as *The Criminal Investigation*, or even as *The Legal Process*, and carries all the implications that would be thus signified.

[135] The first line of Féval's text obligingly includes a parenthetical translation of his *Juge Bamboche* as "puppet-justice." I have used it here even though "The Puppet Judge" might be a stricter translation. I have, however, used the latter within the text whenever the reference is clearly to the Judge as an individual.

[136] Féval has "fun tribunal."

[137] Vespasian (9-79 A.D.) was humbly born but enjoyed a distinguished military career before becoming Roman Emperor in 69 A.D., two years after he became Rome's commander-in-chief against a rebellion in Judea; he left his son Titus (40-91 A.D.) behind to continue the war, and it was he who razed the Temple in 70 A.D. as a punitive measure before eventually succeeding his father as Emperor. The saying rendered by Féval as *"L'argent n'a pas d'odeur"* is popularly credited to a biography by Suetonius, allegedly spoken when Titus objected to his imposition of a tax on public lavatories. What Suetonius actually wrote was that Vespasian responded to the objection by holding a coin under Titus' nose, asking him if it had an offensive smell, and when Titus denied it, Vespasian said: *"Atqui e lotio est"* ("But it is from piss.") It was also Suetonius who reported that Titus was popularly described as "the delight of humankind."

[138] Genevieve of Brabant was the heroine of a popular Medieval legend, who lived in a cave for six years after being falsely accused of adultery. The tale of Simple Jack is not, of course, a comparable English folk-tale but a grotesque transfiguration of Féval's sole endeavor in advocacy.

[139] Proserpine (Persephone in Greek) was the Queen of the Land of the Dead during the six months of every year that she was resident in "dark Tartarus"; as befit a symbol of the changing seasons, she spent the other half of every year in Olympus. "Mrs. Potiphar" (Féval has Madame Putiphar) was the wife of Joseph's master, who attempted unsuccessfully to seduce him and then charged him with the offense (Genesis 39).

[140] Paul Scarron (1610-1660) was a humorist and satirist, the first husband of Madame de Maintenon. His *Roman Comique* was published in 1651; Ragotin and Madame Bouvillon are characters therein.

[141] The full quote from Cicero is *Quousque tandem abutere, Catilina, patientia nostra?* ("How far at last will you abuse our patience, Catiline?")

[142] Gaius or Caius (110-c.180 A.D.) was a famous Roman jurist, whose *Institutiones* became a standard legal manual, an important forerunner of the Code of

the Byzantine emperor Justinian the Great (483-565). The Pandects, a key element of the Justinian Code, is a 50-volume summary of the opinions of jurists; the whole project is the foundation-stone of civil law.

[143] "Chancellor Stair" is Sir James Dalrymple, the first Viscount Stair (1619-95), whose *Institutions of the Law of Scotland* was a standard text; Sir William Blackstone (1723-80) was an English jurist whose *Commentaries on the Laws of England* (1765-68) similarly became the standard text; Edward Christian (?-1823) was a professor of law at Cambridge University who edited Blackstone's *Commentaries*; he was a very strange and violent character whose younger brother, Fletcher, led the mutineers of the Bounty. I have not been able to identify the author of the *Syntagma* cited by Féval; he renders the name Clamorgan, which is extremely unlikely, so I have substituted Glamorgan on the assumption that one of the earls thereof might have been a jurist.

[144] Johann Gottlieb Heineccius (1681-1741) was a famous German jurist.

[145] In Greek mythology, Philemon and Baucis were a married couple who offered hospitality to two peasants who turned out to be Zeus and Hermes in disguise; they became attendants of a temple and were changed into trees growing side-by-side when they died.

[146] Bertrand and Raton are featured in Jean de la Fontaine's fable *Le singe et le chat*; Bertrand the monkey restricts himself to cracking chestnuts that the cat Raton has to retrieve from the fire, thus becoming a type of specimen of those who profit by the labor of others. A political satire of the same title by Eugène Scribe, first produced for the stage in 1833, would also have been familiar to Féval's readers, though not to the characters in *John Devil*.

[147] Lycurgus of Sparta was credited by tradition with originating that city's laws; he probably lived in the 9th century B.C. The Decemvirate, or Commission of Ten, was established by Appius Claudius in 450 B.C. or thereabouts, to study Greek law and codify Roman law; it eventualy became a government but was overthrown by a popular insurrection.

[148] Féval has Silberradt but must mean Hans Silberrad (1707-1760), who was professor of law at Strasbourg. I cannot identify the Englishman cited as Loe under that name or Lowe. Robert Joseph Pothier (1699-1772) was a French jurist who published a translation of Justinian's Pandects; Claude de Ferrière (1639-1715) was one of his eminent predecessors.

[149] This is a pun, *gallinam* (a hen) being phonetically reminiscent of *Gallina* (a Gaulish woman). The remainder of the phrase means "If someone [does something to]..."

[150] I have exploited the multiple English meanings of "turkey" in order to produce a weak simulation of Féval's observation that *Dindons parle de l'Inde* (because the first syllable of *dindon* sounds like *d'Inde*).

[151] Féval renders the name Saunie, but Sawney is the usual spelling of a once-popular nickname for a Scotsman (derived from Alexander via Sandy). Féval might have in mind the legendary brigand and alleged cannibal Sawney Bean.

[152] A titus (named after the Roman emperor cited above) was a hairstyle in which the back was cut short.

Chapter II

[153] *infandum* means "not to be spoken of"–here used in a slightly stronger sense than the English "say no more."

[154] In Greek legend, the Danaides were the 50 daughters of Danaus, who killed their husbands on his instructions and were penalized in Hades by pouring water into sieves.

[155] Féval gives this term in English; a hundred was a division of a county, and a Hundred Court was a body of local landowners. The jurisdiction of Hundred Courts was abolished by the County Court act of 1867.

[156] The Court of Common Pleas was one of three superior courts of common law at Westminster, which had jurisdiction over civil suits between subjects. It was abolished and replaced in 1875.

[157] Féval offers this as a translation of his *poulets vierges*.

[158] Numph is presumably a familiar version of Humphrey.

[159] Féval has *Kaërbran*, which is presumably Breton orthography; since he is applying it to a Welshman, I have substituted a more orthodox spelling, but the consequent reference (to a place whose name would mean Bran's Fort or the Fort of the Crow) remains stubbornly mysterious.

[160] The Gloucester in *Richard III* (and *Henry VI Part 3*) is perhaps intended, rather than the one in *King Lear*.

[161] Féval has *Kaen*; I have corrected the apparent typo to clarify the reference to the famous actor Edward Kean (1787-1833), whose career was flourishing in Drury Lane at the time when *John Devil* is set, but it may be a deliberate hybridization of Kean and Cain.

Chapter III

[162] The term "burker" was current in English at the time, having been derived from the name of William Burke, the senior member of the infamous partnership of Burke and Hare.

[163] This list of criminal trades is slightly problematic because it includes a number of slang terms; "touts" is probably apt enough as a rendition of *raccoleurs* and I have used "smelters" for Féval's *fondeurs*, on the presumption that he is talking about people who melt down stolen objects made of gold or silver

[164] Féval attempts to render this name phonetically as Mohna-Mahrée.

[165] A pibroch is a tune played on the bagpipes; like the previous reference to "the King over the water" (the Old Pretender, called James III by the Jacobites) this

emphasizes the highlanders' alleged continuing loyalty to the deposed Stuart dynasty. In fact, Jacobitism had virtually died out by the accession of George III in 1760 and was certainly not rife in the army's Scottish regiments.

[166] This is a literal translation of Féval's *rosée-de-coeur*, which Larousse does not recognize. Webster's does acknowledge that "dew" was sometimes used as a synonym for spirituous liquor, but does not recognize heart's-dew as any particular type. A poem by Lord Byron refers to the "heart's dew of pain" and it is conceivable that Féval picked up the phrase there.

[167] Mivart's Hotel in Brook Street, opened in 1808, was one of the most fashionable of the Georgian era; it was purchased by William Claridge in 1855 and was expanded to become Claridge's, in which form it remains one of the finest in London.

[168] Féval gives the names of the Counts Boehm in their French forms, but I have substituted Friedrich for Frédéric, Reiner for Reynier and Albrecht for Albert, just as I have substituted Helen for Hélène in the name of the unfortunate Marquise de Belcamp.

Chapter IV

[169] Taking license from its representation as a proper name, I have left *Fadeur* in French because "the goddess Fadeur" sounds so much better than "the goddess Insipidity."

[170] Féval adds a note at this point suggesting that the Parisian equivalent of Portland Place would be the Rue de Paix; the point being made is that it is very far from being a "low quarter"–thus casting suspicion on Sir Paulus' beloved young Lords rather than honest criminals.

[171] Féval has Foster here, but I have altered it to correspond with the first chapter of the prologue.

[172] Jean, Comte de Dunois (1402-68) was a bastard son of the Duc d'Orleans famous for his military exploits and gallantry.

[173] I have translated Feval's *chevalerie* as knighthood because "chivalry" would sound wrong, although it loses an important aspect of the wordplay.

[174] The French *neutres* signifies "neutered" as well as "neutral."

[175] In Greek myth, Nessus was a centaur who abducted Heracles' wife, Dejanira. Heracles killed Nessus with a poisoned arrow but–acting on Nessus' deceptive instructions–Dejanira saved some of his toxin-impregnated blood and used it to impregnate one of the hero's shirts, which drove Heracles to immolate himself.

Chapter V

[176] Bartolomeo Bosco (1793-1850 and Robert Houdin (1805-71) were the great pioneers of modern stage magic; the latter was also a builder of automata. Bosco's surname was adopted by several subsequent magicians, while Houdin's was elaborated by the American stage magician Harry Houdini. Houdini also

revered Bosco, whose dilapidated grave he discovered and purchased, deeding it to the Society of American Magicians.

[177] One cannot get out into Cheapside from the Old Bailey now, although one can get into the extension of it that is Newgate Street. It seems more probable, however, given that Temple subsequently passes into Fleet Street, that he actually came out on to Ludgate Hill.

[178] There is no junction between Lombard Street and Fleet Street, and never was; nor can one easily drift from Lombard Street to St. Paul's; one could, however, easily get from Fleet Street to St. Paul's by going up Ludgate Hill.

[179] Watling Street–the beginning of the old Roman road that once led to Dover–leads eastwards from St. Paul's, nowadays reaching no further than the heart of the City. Rosemary Lane, which is now Royal Mint Street, is much further to the east, near Tower Hill. The only Trinity Church Square to be found on today's maps is south of the river.

Chapter VI

[180] The line from Horace is *Post equitem sedet atra Cura*: "At the rider's back sits dark Anxiety."

[181] "To err is human."

[182] Berthold Schwartz was a 14th-century alchemist born in Freiburg (hence the reference in the previous sentence) who was rumoured to have invented gunpowder.

[183] Salomon de Caus (1576-1626) was a French engineer credited with the discovery that steam could be used as a motive force.

[184] Atlantes, known in some tranlations as Atlas, is featured in Ludovico Ariosto's epic *Orlando Furioso*.

[185] The Hotel Meurice, overlooking the Tuileries, remains one of the best in Paris.

[186] A Dalmatic is the outermost ceremonial vestment worn by deacons and bishops.

[187] Féval has *franc-juges*. Although the term "free judges" does exist in English, it seems more reasonable to use the German term that Friedrich Boehm would undoubtedly have used, especiallly as *vehmgerichte* can also be found in English dictionaries. Such secret courts were a powerful institution in Germany from the 14th century to the 17th–although their origins may go back further, especially in Westphalia. Publicization of their activities provided a paradigm example of the typical attributes of secret societies. The organization that maintained the network of vigilante courts had an elaborate repertoire of secret signs and passwords, initiation ceremonies and ceremonial objects (notably daggers engraved with the mysterious legend SSGG, which stood for *Strick, Stein, Gras, Grun*–i.e., rope, stone, grass, green). The President of such a court was the *Freigraf*–hence the French *Franc-juge*. The suppression of the institution began in the 17th century, when it was restricted to its Westphalian base; it was abolished

there by Jerome Bonaparte, who had been given the throne of Westphalia by Napoleon in 1811.

The *Franc-juges* feature prominently in Féval's collection *Les Tribunaux secrets* (1851-52)–as they should, given the enormous influence their methods and affectations exerted on subsequent secret societies.

[188] Féval has Bade (Baden) but it is an obvious misprint for Bude (Buda).

[189] Seïd (whose name is Frenchified by Féval as Séide) was the slave and first convert of Mohammmed. Following its use by Voltaire, the French version of his name was used as a synonym for blind and fanatical devotion. Gracchus was the surname of an important Roman family; the two sons of Tiberius Sempronius Gracchus and his wife Cornelia both became famous in Rome in the 2nd century B.C. as tribunes and orators before being assassinated while attempting to restrain the greed of the aristocracy.

Chapter VII

[190] The wife of Tiberius Sempronius Gracchus, as mentioned in the previous note.

[191] St John of Nepomuk (c1345-93) was educated at the University of Prague, and became Vicar-General of the Bishop of Prague, who was engaged in a long and bitter conflict over eccelesiastial rights and property with Wenceslas IV of Bohemia. His body was placed in St. Vitus's Cathedral after he was deliberately drowned; it is still there.

[192] The Gloriette was planned a belvedere on Schönbrunn Hill as part of the original palace complex, but it was not built until 1775. It is a triumphal arch flanked by arcaded wings with a huge imperial eagle perched atop a globe on the roof.

[193] Féval has "Prague" but that is obviously an error.

Chapter VIII

[194] I do not know which "German poet" Féval is alluding to here.

[195] Louis Bourdaloue (1634-1704) was a Jesuit famed for his severe moralizing.

[196] Ninon de Lenclos (1620-1705) was one of the great beauties of her age; her salon was frequented by the most notable people in France.

[197] Féval uses the word *pistole*, which has no English equivalent in this meaning: it is, in effect, a comfortable kind of cell reserved for important persons.

[198] Féval's reference is to the fact that as having followed on the heels of the 1789 Revolution, the subsequent establishment of the Empire and the Restoration, the year 1817 was not far from the eve of the July Revolution of 1830.

[199] The direct reference here is to the strategy by which Penelope delayed her response to the suitors while awaiting the return of Odysseus from his wanderings. Given the immediate context, however, Féval seems to be reflecting on the difficulties of his own task, and this paragraph might offer some clues as to the

reasons for the story's subsequent retreat into obscurity and confusion. He might conceivably have been asked at this point to spin the story out and keep it going–inconveniently given that the whole scheme, save for the final summary of Henri's "secret," has by now been set out for the reader's consideration; if so, its subsequent twists and turns might be improvisations calculatedly unravelling certain aspects of a design that he had painstakingly assembled, without any real hope that they could be revised and replaced with equal effect.

[200] Féval has *coup d'archet*, presumably a reference to the moment when the orchestra first strikes up.

[201] According to one of two rival accounts of Achilles' youth, he was disguised as a girl–named Pyrrha–and hidden among the daughters of Lycomedes of Scyrus. Vigier was one of the sculptors credited with many of the statues of the Gardens of Versailles.

[202] While he was in exile, Louis XVIII lived at Hartwell House in Buckinghamshire, where he and his court created a miniature Versailles.

[203] Féval has *bier scandal*, which is neither French, nor English, nor German.

[204] A literal translation of *renards d'or and maisons moussues* would be "golden foxes and mossy houses," but they would not become more meaningful in the process. Both phrases are italicized by the author to emphasize their metaphorical quality; their import–referring to university life–is deducible from context.

[205] According to legend, Tyrteus was a lame Athenian schooolmaster in the 7th century B.C., lent to the Spartans–when the latter were instructed by an oracle to obtain an Athenian military leader for a campaign against the Messenians–because the Athenians did not want to help their old rivals. The war songs he composed spurred the Spartans to victory.

[206] This literal translation of *vogue la galère* ("let the boat sail on") cannot convey the additional suggestion of being popular (*en vogue*) in the gallery (*galerie*) which prompts Férandeau to demonstrate his *entrechat*.

Chapter IX

[207] Guatemotzin (c1497-1525), the nephew of Montezuma II, was the last Aztec King of Mexico; he defended Mexico City against Cortès' siege. He is alleged to have made this remark to an agonized companion while they were being tortured with boiling oil in the hope that they might reveal the location of hidden treasures.

[208] Joachim Murat (1771-1815) was a French Marshal who married Napoleon's sister and became King of Naples. He was executed in 1815 after trying to reclaim his throne, having sided with the allies against Napoleon following the Emperor's return from Elba.

[209] Féval renders the phrase in question as *sacrebleu*, which is slightly stronger in French than the *parbleus* and *morbleus* that I have long been translating,

when the occasion seemed appropriate, as "damn it," so in this instance, I have emphasized it in a slightly different fashion.

Chapter X

[210] *La Muette de Portici* is an opera by Daniel-François Auber, with words by Eugène Scribe and Germain Delavigne. Férandeau could not possibly have referred to it in 1817 because it was not written until 1828.

[211] *Cocotte* is a child's word for hen or duck–the equivalent of the English "chicky" or "ducky"–but for a horse (*coco*) or a mare (*cocotte*). *Cocotte* is also used as a euphemism for "whore." The reader will recall that Pierre Louchet's goat was also addressed as *Cocotte*, but Louchet probably did mean it in the childish sense.

[212] Férandeau presumably has other models than Madame Célestin in mind: the old women who knitted in the shadow of the guillotine.

[213] Féval's own translation of *pilotin* is "seaboy."

[214] This pun almost translates, although the first part of the sentence is difficult; remarquer–which I have rendered as "guide" because its literal derivation here is from remarque, meaning landmark or beacon–usually means "to notice," as "to remark" usually does in English, hence importing a double entendre into regarde, which I have rendered as "lookout."

[215] Féval gives the last phrase in English as "Auctions-Mart."

[216] The captain's name–presumably not by coincidence–would inevitably have reminded French readers of Théophile Gautier, whose novel *Les Deux Etoiles* (1848; tr. as *The Quartette*) had described a conspiracy to rescue Napoleon by means of a submarine.

Chapter XI

[217] Lafayette, as previously noted, was the French general who served in the American Revolutionary army; thus "Lafayette embracing Washington" becomes a florid way of talking about a journey from France to the USA.

[218] *Cadre* has a double meaning in French, the other–apart from the ranks of an army–being "frame."

[219] Féval has Milk and Blum here and elsewhere in this chapter, but changes it in the next chapter to Milk and Blunt; the latter seems to me to have the better ring to it.

[220] Féval has (in English) "*Just issuing! Dispatch!*"

[221] In terms of modern geography, Henri must have gone along Newgate Street to Holborn Viaduct, turned left off High Holborn and then turned right again.

[222] *Une forêt de Bondy*, in French common parlance, means a den of thieves; the reference is to a location on the Seine, near Saint-Denis, where the last Merovingian King, Childeric II, had been assassinated in the 8th century and Charles V's courtier Aubry de Montdidier had been murdered in the 14th century.

[223] Féval has Louchet offer a phonetic rendering of a phrase which he, as editor, translates as "by the King," although he then has Louchet paraphrase it in the more likely formulation of *Au nom du Roi*.

Chapter XII

[224] James Watt (1736-1819) invented the condenser that made steam engines practicable, patenting the device in 1769. Andrew Vivian was one of several less famous partners of Richard Trevithick, with whom he took out a patent on a high-pressure steam engine in 1802; it was never successful, but one of the experimental machines they built was a barge propelled by paddle-wheels. I cannot identify a pioneer of steam power named Cowley and strongly suspect that the name's inclusion here is a joke. Richard Cowley, Marquess of Wellesley (1760-1842), the older brother of the Duke of Wellington, played a key role in securing India for the British and extinguishing French influence there, so Henri is indeed trying to combine the legacies of Watt, Vivian and Cowley—but the speaker cannot know that.

[225] Féval, of course, gives the name of the ship as *L'Aigle*; I would not normally translate such names, but given the symbolic quality of the name, and its relationship to several other passages in which Napoleon is referred to as "the Eagle," it seems reasonable to do so—just as it seems reasonable to leave the acute accent off the second *e* in the name of the *Deliverance*.

Chapter XIII

[226] The reference is to the *Maison d'Arrêt Cellulaire* in the Boulevard Mazas in Paris, which was known as Mazas from 1850-58 until the family after whom the Boulevard was named objected.

[227] An *in-pace* is a recess in the wall of a nunnery in which nuns condemned to death were sealed. It is a contraction of *requiescat in pace*, the opening of the Latin version of the prayer for the dead intoned at funerals.

[228] The Porte-Saint-Martin Theater was showing Féval's dramatic version of *Le Bossu* when this line was first published, so this is a subtle ad, but the reference is to an earlier phase of the theater's history when it specialized in Gothic adaptations. The fad began in 1820 with an adaptation of John Polidori's *The Vampyre* by Féval's hero Achille de Jouffroy, in collaboration with Charles Nodier and the theater's director, Jean-Toussaint Merle. (This play is available from Black Coat Press in *Lord Ruthven the Vampire*, translated by Frank J. Morlock, ISBN 1-932983-10-4.) Merle followed up its great success with other productions in the same vein, including *Bertram, ou le Pirate* (1822) based on a tragedy by Charles Maturin, and *Le Monstre et le Magicien* (1826), adapted from Mary Shelley's *Frankenstein* (to be published by Black Coat Press in 2005).

[229] *Non bis in idem* means "not twice for the same thing," presumably referring to the legal principle of double jeopardy, whereby one cannot be tried a second time for the same offense having once been acquitted. Thompson's conviction would not, however, guarantee Henri immunity from being tried for Constance Bartolozzi's murder.

[230] This is not a direct quote from the Aeneid, although it clearly refers to the epic's first line, and perhaps its 207th, which urges the defeated Trojans to preserve themselves for better things.

[231] Mauritius.

[232] The Marquis de Dupleix (1697-1763) was the governor of the French possessions in India. He distinguished himself when war broke out between France and England, but he was politically isolated and it was all to no avail; he returned to France in 1754, where he could not recover the money he had spent in financing his endeavors.

[233] At the battle of Crécy in 1346, the French army led by Philippe de Valois was heavily defeated by one led by the English King Edward III.

[234] I have not been able to ascertain which Latin poet referred to Britain as "separated from the rest of the world."

[235] In earlier chapters, Féval gave the title of Temple's book as *L'Art de découvrir les coupables*; here the word *malfaiteurs* is substituted for *coupables*; I have adjusted my translation accordingly.

[236] Féval has *guerres de la Tortue*; I have used *Testudo* rather than *tortoise* or *turtle* because English usually retains the Latin name of the defensive formations adopted by the Roman legions, which is presumably what he means.

[237] The original "infernal machine" was a barrel of gunpowder wrapped around with iron shrapnel–what would nowadays be called a nail bomb–that was supposed to explode as Bonaparte's coach went past on the way to the Opéra. The bomb exploded a few seconds too late to kill Napoleon but 26 innocent bystanders were killed and a further 52 injured. The term was subsequently applied generically to all manner of nasty devices planted with murderous intent.

Chapter XVIII

[238] Presumably a reference to Romanèche-Thorins, nowadays the source of Beaujolais nouveau.

[239] The word *tuile* (tile) also carries the meaning of "catastrophe."

[240] *Lanlaire* was a traditional tune whose name only survived in a phrase used to dismiss beggars.

[241] *Biscayen* is the English form of *biscaïen*, a kind of musket so-called because of its origin in the vicinity of the Bay of Biscay; the same word is used for the bullet used in the gun. Although the reference to Pompey suggests that the

"César" to whom Roblot refers must be Julius Caesar, there must be a second meaning to account for the firearm; alas, I have no idea what it might be.

[242] Féval gives this in Latin as *quantum sufficit*; he was, of course, writing long before the advent of quantum theory, drawing his inspiration from the same original meaning as Max Planck.

Chapter XIX

[243] The Gemonies was a flight of steps on the Aventine Hill in Rome, down which the bodies of criminals were taken to be thrown into the Tiber; the first half of the comparison refers to the custom of dressing ships with little flags to celebrate their return to port.

[244] Joseph Lesurques (1763-1796) was convicted of the assassination of a courier and executed; he was subsequently proved to have been innocent.

[245] The convent of Sainte-Pelagie was converted into a prison during the Revolution, and was presumably still serving in that capacity in 1817.

[246] Chaumeron presumably means the phrase *crânement casé* to signify something of this sort, but the reader could easily take a more literal view of *crâne* (skull) and imagine a second *s* in *casé* to infer the second meaning "Am I a crackpot?"

[247] Jean Martin de Laubardement (1590-1653) was a Magistrate who served as Prosecutor in several famous trials, including those of Urbain Grandier (as featured in Aldous Huxley's *The Devils of Loudun*) and the Marquis de Cinq-Mars, a conspirator against Cardinal de Richelieu.

[248] Féval's *C'est l'épreuve de l'eau* does not mean waterproof in the modern sense, but rather in terms of surviving a trial by water, as on a ducking-stool. Given the Marquis' reply, however, the shorter form seems preferable.

[249] Louis XVIII (then the Comte de Provence) had left France in 1789 and did not return until 1814. Maximilien Robespierre, one of the leaders of the Revolution and architect of the Terror, was guillotined in 1794.

[250] *Fra Diavolo* (Brother Devil) was the nickname of Michele Pezza, Pezzo or Bozzo (1760-1806), whose reputation as an Italian bandit was partially redeemed in France by his claim to be a Bourbon partisan. Féval included an account of his career in *Les Tribunaux Secrets* (*The Secret Tribunals*) and built him into the secret history that bound *John Devil* into a sequence extending from *Beau Démon* to the *Black Coats* series, proposing that his hanging in Naples had been unsuccessful and that he survived for a long time thereafter, playing a key role in many other criminal conspiracies–including the *Black Coats*–as the godfather–like figure of Colonel Bozzo-Corona. He is, therefore, a kind of archetypal figure in Féval's work, of whom such quasi-allegorical figures as Jean Ténèbre and John Devil are reflections.

Chapter XX

[251] The Areopagus was the supreme tribunal of Athens before 462 B.C.

[252] Féval presumably means a jury driven by an electrical cell or storage battery.

[253] Madame Etienne here refers to the Public Prosecutor and his assistants as the *parquet* (referring to the well of the Court) thus invoking a double entendre the commonplace meaning of parquet being "floor."

[254] The Savonnerie was a tapestry factory that flourished from the 17th to the 19th century, so-called because it was initially established in the soap-works at Chaillot (a *savonnerie* is a soap factory).

Chapter XXII

[255] Féval gives this slightly unlikely phrase in English.

[256] *Mémorial de Saint-Helène* (1822-23) was the title of the Comte de Las-Cases' record of Napoleon's memoirs, cut short because of his banishment from the island.